The Second

The
SECOND

A Novel about Spirituality, Religion, and Politics

Alan J Cooper

Foreword by
Douglas H. Hopp

EXILE
editions
Fiction, Poetry, Translation, Drama and Nonfiction

Library and Archives Canada Cataloguing in Publication
Cooper, Alan John, 1950-, author
    The second : a novel about spirtuality, religion, and politics / Alan J Cooper ;
foreword by Douglas H. Hopp.
    I. Title.
PS8605.O6525S42 2013   C813'.6   C2013-905114-7

Design and Composition by Michael P.M. Callaghan
Typeset in Fairfield and Lucida fonts at the Moons of Jupiter Studios

Published by Exile Editions Ltd ~ www.ExileEditions.com
144483 Southgate Road 14 – GD, Holstein, Ontario, N0G 2A0, Canada
Printed and Bound in Canada by Friesens in 2013

Canadian Sales: The Canadian Manda Group, 165 Dufferin Street,
Toronto ON M6K 3H6   www.mandagroup.com   416 516 0911

North American and International Distribution, and U.S. Sales:
Independent Publishers Group, 814 North Franklin Street,
Chicago IL 60610   www.ipgbook.com   toll free: 1 800 888 4741

Dedicated to
my Chicago cousin,
the late Arthur Franklin Cooper III

FOREWORD

This story looks at how religious and spiritual thoughts affect deeds in today's society. Often we look at our world through technological devices, with our view tempered by the medium we use. "Things" become paramount, yet what is present or happening is governed by thoughts, themselves invisible, and by unseen actions, only the results of which may be apparent. The actual deeds, especially those outside our vision, are inferred in a process that is imprecise, potentially misleading and clouded further by any human giver of information creating his version of what has transpired.

Today, religion is often dismissed as having lost much of its relevance, yet religion or the interpretation thereof remains, especially in the United States of America, pivotal to the shaping of media communications, political policy and public sentiment. The real substance of any religion is the summation of thoughts and ideals. Whether those ideals emanate in earnest from an intrinsic spirituality, or instead grow into a dogma governing socially acceptable behavior while camouflaging materialism and the manipulation of power, remains an open question.

In *The Second*, we see a complex and highly intelligent young woman, Chantelle Fouriere, who is a trained physician and effuses a sensitivity and morality that is painfully absent in established religion. Chantelle thus feels compelled to share with anyone willing to listen her thoughts, interpretations and explanations of stories about biblical characters and events, along with the deeper implications for life and society.

The story of Chantelle is seen through the eyes of Arthur Franklin, a young Chicago architect who is the son an American Jewish mother and a Canadian Protestant father. Arthur serves as narrator and sometime romantic partner of Chantelle, and throughout the story, it is Arthur's diary that the reader is viewing. The diary is quite descriptive and provides a thorough if not unbiased window onto the proceedings of Chantelle's life, their effect on Arthur himself, and the role of a counterpart who goes by the name Terry Hardy. He also is a gifted public speaker and self-appointed preacher but has quite specific and, at the start, undisclosed motives that underlie his ministry.

Chantelle, while extremely well-educated in all manner of historical minutiae, is relatively naive, comparatively impecunious, and vulnerable to the machinations of organizer Hardy, with his warped but sweeping agenda. For financial, organizational and public-relations reasons (Chantelle is quite attractive), Hardy takes Chantelle under his wing, with her serving as a lecturer and facilitator for his organization. She circuits the continent, especially the U.S., speaking in public places and at academic institutions, sharing religious and moral views on varied topics, current and historical, all the way back to biblical times, while occasionally making reference to prehistorical and prehuman animal development.

During Chantelle's forays across North America, the dialogue on theological, political, military, and economic topics becomes central to Arthur's diary pages, and within it, a number of opinionated and strong-willed persons make appearances, sometimes fleetingly but on occasion resurfacing several times, contributing to an ongoing series of debates and diatribes. Addiction issues also surface, affecting at times two of the principal characters. Personalities, both good and bad, are intermittently revisited, in particular members of Chantelle's family, lending a stabilizing "closed loop" to an otherwise cross-country crusade, with nary a return to home.

As can be the case with outspoken individuals, particularly ones espousing a radically different approach to religion, interactions between Chantelle and forces of traditional dogma or zealots therein create horrendous challenges for her. Hardy becomes a major force in the fallout, and the imperfect system of jurisprudence plays a key role in the events that follow.

Douglas H. Hopp, DVM, DipCompMed, CD, MMW

With your web enabled mobile device scan the QR
for Mr. Cooper's five-minute talk/trailer about the book
or view at: www.tinyurl.com/TheSecond-AJC

Friday April 27 2007

Early on in my undergraduate years studying architecture in Chicago, a professor suggested that if I kept a diary, I could better know myself and so harness those skills I had. He was a reformed alcoholic and I guess he could see an insidious something, but I did not dismiss his idea as a bad one, since I had never been able to communicate with my mother in particular and had written, as a child, rebuttals I was never allowed to voice. As things then wound out, that journal became a place to vent thoughts that I had previously bottled up and perhaps was one reason why later, when pursuing my master's in Architecture, I began to win awards. Yet after I had been out in the actual profession for a while, nothing would come to dominate that diary more, for a thousand days, than the thoughts and acts of one other person.

I was alone on a Friday evening, as was my wont, trying to sketch out thoughts never given time during the work week. Three years had passed since I had graduated and the Chicago firm of Cork & Church had dazzled me with visions of carrying forward the architectural enlightenment of the city. But the job due Monday was reflective of the drivel by then landing on my desk. Architecture was becoming consumptive and the dreams of three years earlier were distant at best. I was feeling increasingly expressionless but nothing could have prepared me for what would happen that night to begin a change in me.

The green of spring was bringing new life to the 100,000 square miles around the Great Lakes, but underneath this spring's renewal there lurked a feeling that the continent's heartland was in trouble. Construction was still bustling but many of the contracts had been entered into in the years prior, and any optimism from a boom now gone was giving way to a new diffidence. The United States could smell debt, the worst ever, and across the Great Lakes, the cities of Detroit and Cleveland lay dead, Toronto lay in Canadian abeyance and Chicago, a city that sat at the hub of the continent and linked the waterways all the way from the Gulf of Mexico to the North Atlantic, sat sick.

1

As the hands of my watch ticked past 9:00 p.m., I took in a long breath and reared back to get a better view of what lay in front of me. As the breath then came out, I knew I had done enough for the day and so lifted away from my desk, got my beloved bush pilot jacket and toddled out of my office to charge across the firm's warehouse floor and escape outdoors.

Lake Michigan was breathing a free feeling into the eastern part of the city in what seemed like about 60 F, and for a moment I felt invigorated. I probably should have stayed outside for the short walk home but opted instead to head west, as was Friday's rite, to the Drake Hotel for a glass of California red.

Once inside the Drake, I did not savor the wine at week's end but instead quaffed a half-carafe, then went back outdoors to start the trek home down Michigan Avenue. I ambled past its designer stores and clutter shutting down for the evening, and within minutes, arrived at the steps of my old low-rise on Huron. Suddenly, though, I found myself stopping at the bottom and feeling a need for more outdoors, and so continued south.

As the time then reached 10:00 I was approaching the Chicago River where it flows into Lake Michigan, and I found the breeze bracing. I ventured across the river's bridge and proceeded southeast, in the direction of Grant Park.

Soon I was entering the park and found the blackness of night relieved from time to time by the treetops lit by lower lamps. Deeper into the park,

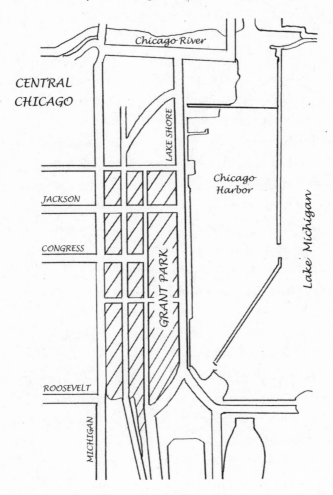

I came to see a floodlight, washing over a broad lawn that contained hundreds of people who looked to be concentrating on something of consequence.

I could make out a silhouette higher than the heads of the listeners, and the silhouette had the shape of a tall woman who was making gestures. As I kept up in my approach, I began to hear her soft alto voice. "One would have to have a low opinion of God to think God perfect. Perfect is a construct of our human minds and a fast-fix for certitude. But perfectionism can breed disappointment, and the people disappointed are often consoled by being told they are members of an elect few, gifted with hearts and minds of distinction.

"Yet among any peoples at any time, there can emerge a person whose gifts are so harmonized as to bring new life to those people. Jesus of Nazareth was one example and, as he professed in Aramaic, was a messiah or deliverer. 'Christ' would have been the rough translation into Greek but Jesus did not say he was the son of God – people spun that caption and when Jesus balked, they put the words into his mouth anyway."

My eyes lowered to the lawn and I felt I had heard enough. "Thank God I'm Jewish." I turned to walk away but my next step was halted by her following words: "An obscure rabbi, that is teacher, whose teachings were smeared. Jesus healed the blind by saying 'Open your eyes,' but soon after his death, his words were made literal and his parables spun to every end."

I looked back to eye the woman's silhouette as she continued, "An imperfect teacher such as Jesus can happen in many forms – Gandhi, Gorbachev, Canada's Tommy Douglas – all of them shared with us their principles.

"It was not the Jews who killed Jesus nor was it the Romans but instead it was the kind of self-righteousness that Jesus challenged. Yet the dogma he fought came to be resurrected before his body cooled and a political middling politician, rebranding himself Paul, concocted that Jesus had to be the son of God or his messages meant nothing. Paul's argument was that the teachings of Jesus had more spell if he were the actual son of God, so he had to be and therefore he was.

"So much for Greek logic. About 500 years earlier, Socrates's students had also tried pulling the immortal stunt on his soul, and Buddha's followers had attempted a similar deification, but Buddha would have none of it. Unfortunately for Jesus, he got himself killed and the poor bastard is probably still rolling over from the distortions.

"I should not say 'bastard' because Jesus was born with two married parents, and no one anywhere is illegitimate. Shakespeare showed us the fallacy of illegitimacy centuries ago. but in Jesus's case we nevertheless still try to trace Joseph's lineage back to King David, despite Joseph not being Jesus's biological father.

"Jesus-by-Joseph or *Yeshua-bar-Joshua* – the Greek *Christos* was not his last name – may have been a bit of a bastard around the dinner table, insulting his hosts *et al*, but hey, God's not perfect, so why should Jesus be? What's more, you might be angry too if you'd been rejected by your hometown for being, ahem, early, or as one local asked in the Greek New Testament, 'Is not this Jesus the, ahem, son of Mary?' Unheard of, you might say, for a nice Jewish girl to get pregnant ahead of time and true enough in Jerusalem, but Nazareth was kind of a Dodge City not far off the spice route and the Asiatic town had been run by Roman officers. Furthermore, Mary had been betrothed to someone before Joseph and being betrothed in those days meant a lot more than just being engaged.

"Hats off to Joseph for marrying Mary or she may have wound up a comfort girl like another Mary – Magdalene. Jesus held Mary Magdalene in high esteem and she was the first to witness his empty tomb after the body had been removed by another Joseph, who was not happy with the judgment on Jesus. Peter did not believe Mary's report of an empty tomb, because he was jealous of her, but he decided nonetheless to take a look. Then, after Peter's trip up the hill, he managed to milk the male dominance of the land and take credit for discovering the tomb empty.

"Jesus never left a norm for doctrine or organization and after he died, his apostles began preaching a kind of Jewish revivalism, oriented to Temple worship, with gentiles at the back of the synagogue until they accepted the Jewish law. The word 'christ' was not then in use but born-again Saul-turned-Paul saw its marketability outside Jerusalem, and so with Roman roads running anew through the Middle East, Paul was told by his doctor Luke that they could walk across *goyim* country and get non-believers to blend their brands of paganism into Paul's brew. He could, for example, establish Jesus's mother Mary as the big V – but I am past my permit time tonight.

"Truth and love are principles, not rules, and the stronger our consciences, the less we need rules."

The applause was polite, except for the wolf howls that Americans often make, and then the hundreds began to disperse. Why I stayed watching I don't know, but suddenly I found myself moving forward toward the podium. When I got within 10 feet of it, I caught sight of the young speaker's long legs and her bubble bum as she bent over to retrieve her little speaking stand.

I tried to be casual in my final approach but still sputtered in asking, "May I help you with this?" The striking young woman showed no surprise when turning, and she raised her face back to me. "Thank you, yes. It's wet on the bottom. I'm taking it over to my car. That old Volvo parked over there, just off the lake."

My eyes did not follow her pointing, since I was struck with my close-up look at her. She was tall, almost my six feet, and had long, dark hair. Her smile was wide, her lips generous and her eyes looked to radiate the kind of trust that sometimes comes from confidence.

A male voice then arose from a large shadow on my right, "Are you alright, Chantelle?" and she turned to face the voice with a calm response, "I think so, thank you." She swiveled back to me with that same broad smile. As I then continued to edge forward, my eyes stayed locked on hers and I saw them to be soft, round and brown, set upon an oval face that seemed to radiate good health from lots of sleep, fresh air and a touch of sun.

Before I took my next step, out of that shadow came the source of the male voice, and as the man pressed forward toward Chantelle, I sensed a threat. I kept up my pace and held eyes straight on her, as if to dismiss what was coming in on my right. To my heart's delight, Chantelle's smile held on me.

The other male nonetheless got there first and threw out a long arm to introduce himself, as would a military man to a stranger before negotiations. Chantelle twisted herself to shake hands but still kept her body turned to meet mine and in one more step, I too was close enough to offer my hand. When I did, I deliberately nodded and offered a humble-sounding "Arthur Franklin" in contrast to the other entrant's aggression.

Chantelle's handshake was firm, almost masculine, like that of a strong swimmer. Her eyebrows were dark and gave off a sense of mystery to an otherwise wholesome face. Chantelle was more fit than thin, and she reminded me of a black stallion from some film I had seen in childhood. Her hair was not the black that I had surmised from afar but was dark brown and fell straight down to her shoulders, gleaming against the park lights.

Chantelle was wearing blue jeans with no belt, and her thighs filled the jeans in suggestive sensuousness. Her stomach was athlete-flat but her Venus mound protruded and seemed to beg my hand to cup it. She was sporting brown cowboy boots running halfway up her shins, and an off-white Oxford-cloth shirt tucked in at the waist.

I tried to fix my eyes on Chantelle to make the other person appear an intruder and for a moment, he actually seemed taken aback. But then he introduced himself to me and did so with a slight smile and a European accent, "Terry Hardy." Any competition from that point on was moot, and it quickly became clear that he wanted only to present his credentials and underscore to Chantelle how far he had come to hear her.

The three of us then stood there stiffly, at a half-pace from one another, and I could not help noticing that we were all about the same height, given Chantelle's cowboy boots. We were also all trim, though Hardy looked decidedly harder, with his brush cut and emaciated face.

Some awkwardness could have settled in, but Terry Hardy abruptly excused himself and departed, leaving me alone with the beautiful woman just met. My eyes turned back to Chantelle's and I sensed again that earlier trust, as if I were an aspiring actor whose moves were being supported by a proven lead. "Forgive me, Chantelle, but I'm a hobby student of accents. You're from the upper Midwest?"

Her smile lessened a little, as if she needed to clarify, but her forehead also dipped as if in apology, and I found it charming that a woman so striking could feel the need to say sorry for anything. "Arthur, I'm not American."

Curiosity then seized me but along with it came a touch of presumptuousness as I tried to console. "You have a whisper of an accent, softened by time. You have lived stateside for at least 10 years."

She corrected, "I have been in the United States for six weeks, since early March," and when my face betrayed confusion, she added, "I'm French Canadian."

I came back fast with my index finger going up, "But your..." and she jumped in, "Not from Quebec," and I gave what I thought a knowing smile. "You're from straight north! Manitoba!" and Chantelle gently corrected again, "Northeast. A town two hours north of Toronto."

Suddenly, my inquisitiveness overran any sensitivity. "Where is your patois?" and Chantelle's smile disappeared, before her face turned to her old Volvo, parked past the grass. "I didn't have room for it in my car."

I lowered my head. "Sorry. Condescension is not my usual," and the gorgeous smile that came back heated the inside of my chest. Chantelle's teeth were resplendent and her eyes were so forgiving that they seemed to accept fool me who dared to keep looking at her. Here I was, drained from a piece of work that I did not like, wine inside me and suddenly in a city park at night, face to face with a woman just met – a woman of more beauty than I had ever beheld.

Maybe the alcohol fed a fantasy or gave me a sense that Chantelle too was sharing in the moment but in any case, I took another chance. "May I buy a non-Chicagoan a coffee? There's a delightful place up on Huron, a 10-minute walk north." Her smile lightened as she looked again at her Volvo. "Or a two-minute drive."

Chantelle squinted a bit, as if lost in a moment's thought and so I thought to add, "The street is safe for your car..." She smiled again less broadly. "I have an early morning, Arthur, though an herbal tea sounds lovely, thank you. If you're on foot, perhaps we can take my car and you can point the way. I don't know Chicago."

Buoyed by the surreal, I carried Chantelle's stand over to the old Volvo 544 and laid it into the back, before I sank myself into the passenger seat next to a stick shift. I then turned my head to the driver's side, to ensure that I would absorb the sight of Chantelle entering the car, and as she cradled herself down into the driver's seat, I saw again her long legs that stretched under the tight denim. She turned to smile at me and I noticed her nose had a little ski jump at its end, above a firm chin.

Chantelle's next words took me by surprise. "I love your green eyes, Arthur," but before I could register anything beyond glee, her face turned back to the dashboard and she started the car. Two minutes later, the old 544 was easing its way into a spot, down the street from my apartment, and off we went back along the block to the café.

Balzac's was a coffee-and-wine bar, a stairway down from the sidewalk, in the lower floor of an old row house, and in the front at the lower level was a patio with three white tables, all empty in the cool of late April. We opted to sit inside and as we entered, found the café to be dark and intimate, with a half-dozen rectangular tables of thick wood lit by large candles. Two other couples were near the rear, so we decided to sit down near the front to have space for talk.

What does one say to a 5'10" ravishing young woman who felt comfortable enough to slip away with me, a stranger at night in a Chicago park? I felt a little ill at ease but also, by then, very dry from the wine of an hour earlier.

I sought to quash the thought of coffee or herbal tea and said with a learned voice, "The house red here is full-bodied and it can warm up a tummy on a cool spring night." Chantelle hesitated but then said she would have a small glass. When I then went and returned with a full carafe and two large wine glasses, Chantelle gave a look of concern and she took to reminding me she was driving.

I was too caught up in myself and showed scant regard for her early morning. I quipped that I did not have to drive, since I lived down the street, and made things worse by not bothering to look for Chantelle's reaction. Instead, I looked to the wine and poured her half a glass, with myself a full one.

When Chantelle took a measured sip I finally put my eyes back on hers but did so in part to see how much I could get away with in one big swallow. When she then lowered her glass and gave me a polite smile, I took the look to be one of approval for the wine and I glowed back while keeping my glass tipped to my face.

When I finally lowered my glass back to the table its 10 ounces were gone, and as I picked up the carafe again to offer, as if scripted, Chantelle gave me a quick "No, thank you." I was already anticipating her answer, pouring myself another but this time without any gauge of her reaction.

With the new wine in me, I could afford my second gulp to be slower and I again checked Chantelle's eyes to ensure I was still getting some look of approval. The smile was still there but her face had an overlay of concern. When I then paused in response with my second glass half-lowered, Chantelle gave a quiet sigh, as if to dismiss my gulp as something necessary for a few people on a Friday evening or perhaps something to settle a fast night's pace.

At least that was my interpretation. Maybe the vagueness of the smile came from Chantelle's uncertainty as to what to do next. With the alcohol then in me, I chose to take the more accepting spin and added the notion that her smile reflected a kind of contentment with how things were going. In any event, with my nerves chemically pacified, I tried to express an interest in something she had talked about in the park. "Chantelle, isn't it rather radical for a Christian to suggest that Jesus was fathered by someone other than Joseph? And I don't mean God."

Chantelle's eyes lowered to the candle in the middle of the table before they came back up to me. "Arthur, I read somewhere that Benjamin Franklin had two role models, Plato and Jesus, and I think Ben Franklin was too discriminating to give much consideration to Jesus's social legitimacy, let alone his deity."

I loved the way things were going and felt I had to add, "As Shakespeare suggested, legitimacy shouldn't be an issue for us. Would that we had heeded Shakespeare!"

Suddenly, Chantelle dropped her smile and her face turned down toward the candle in the middle of the table. A silence fell over the moment and I was not sure, in the dark room, but sensed a tear forming in Chantelle's eyes.

I managed for a moment to rein in my self-centeredness and put my right hand forward with palm up as if to gesture help. Chantelle lifted her watering eyes to meet mine and her smile came back a little, as she placed her left hand on mine. Chantelle's next words showed again that trust but as she spoke, I sensed the trust coming not from any sense of libertarianism but from some esteem that should have appealed to my higher sense of values. "Arthur, my childhood town never accepted the fact that my birth father was someone other than the father who raised me. I am half Greek."

I got a chance to recover. "That explains your mysterious beauty," and Chantelle's smile widened as if to acknowledge my kind reply. She squeezed my hand and took a second sip of wine before her eyes went back to the candle flame. Chantelle then continued: "Twenty-five years ago in the spring of 1981, a Greek freighter came up the Saint Lawrence River and into the Great Lakes but did not stop in Toronto or Chicago or any other big city. Instead, once north of Detroit, the ship veered eastward onto Lake Huron's Canadian side and finally came to dock at the tiny Georgian Bay port of Midland.

"That giant freighter dwarfed the little city and awed its people. The Greeks were celebrities both in Midland and the surrounding area. Nearby was a smaller town named Penetanguishene, partly French Canadian, orphaned centuries ago in English Canada. 'Penetang' as the locals called it, had a kind of Gallic openness that captivated the Greek sailors, a third of a world from their homes. The freighter's captain was seduced by a woman named Camille and shortly thereafter, the Greeks were gone."

Chantelle's head lifted and her eyes came straight on mine. "Camille Fouriere became pregnant and all of Penetang rejoiced, with shouting coming loudest from Pantel Fouriere, heralded father of the child-to-be. Pantel and his wife Camille had produced no children but for one in their first year of marriage, and Roxanne was an only child of five years, in a town whose families numbered four, five or even twelve children.

"As that 1981 drew to a close, I was born and spent New Year's Eve with my mother in the tiny hospital in Penetang, with my five-year-old sister Roxanne sleeping alone in her unheated home. Her father Pantel was out-of-doors, drunk, but when he awoke at daylight Pantel did manage to wade through the snow and reach his cold home. When he then opened the unlocked front door, he found Roxanne wandering barefoot over the kitchen's cold linoleum and she burst into a cry, asking where her daddy had been. He quashed the question with the announcement of Roxanne's new sister."

I had a slow sip of wine but did not take my eyes off Chantelle and she continued: "For a long time, Pantel never fully understood how his wife had become pregnant, but he and Camille had been pressured to crank out more and as things stood, little Pantel had reasserted his manhood for all doubters to witness. I don't know when my sister Roxanne began to hate me but in a few years, she came to learn of her mother's affair with the Greek captain and Roxanne told the entire story to schoolmates. Soon the whole town knew but my mother said she had been forced to work as a short-order cook because she had married a drunk, and while supporting her family, had been raped by the captain of some Greek sailors.

"From the start, I was dark even by French Canadian standards, and judged to be mysterious. Soon I was also tall and so the bastard Chantelle stuck out in school or any other time walking in the village."

Chantelle lowered her eyes and took in a visible breath. There I was, with a beautiful young woman just met and she trusting me enough to share a point of personal pain. I did want to admit that, while Chantelle had spoken, my eyes had been falling to her thighs and I had been glancing at her long dark hair while fantasizing some suggestion from her illegitimacy. The moment called for kindness and so I lifted my wine to suggest that she do the same. Chantelle swirled hers in a sort of contemplation and then brought the wine to her lips.

Perhaps I should not have said what I said next and maybe I was lying to myself about wanting only to comfort a person in pain, that person being a stunning woman who had just revealed to me a storied past and was drinking with me in an intimate place, down the street from where I lived, only minutes after meeting me in a Chicago park. "Chantelle, would you like to come back to my place and talk for a while?"

Chantelle's eyelashes lifted and her eyes opened wide before she looked straight up at me. In an instant, I regretted any suggestion from my question, and I tried with a contrived smile and bowed head to communicate that I had only the best of intentions. But I surmised that Chantelle saw the act for what it was and perhaps was accustomed to such games, yet she gave a response in the most forgiving of tones, "Arthur, I must tell you..."

The evening's images were changing all too fast for a tired young man, full of wine. My next words made things worse. "STD?"

Chantelle snickered, "No," and I tried to appear the world-minded man. "You're spoken for? That guy in the park?" She gave a little laugh and shook her head. I got worse. "Your cult! You can't do this!" and Chantelle looked at me again with a directness that seemed to make my comment foolish. She then gave that same apologetic look, along with an answer I would not have thought possible: "Arthur, I am a virgin."

I dropped my eyes to the flame and for a second or so, sat in silence before Chantelle added, "Sex is something I have feared for years. I am 25 but still don't have the confidence."

The Friday evening had just taken another twist, yet Chantelle's sheer humility was so ingratiating that I tried again to sound helpful. But in so doing, I inadvertently suggested that virginity at age 25 was a flaw and compounded the error by saying that my being half-Jewish might be a handicap of like sort. Chantelle responded "Thank you, Arthur. I think you should know I am tall," and I tried to recover by asking if Chantelle's group contained Jews and she answered again with a gentle put-down, "Principles and free minds know no race."

I was not doing well and tried to steer the talk back to the romantic. "Free minds have imaginations. Are people allowed to have fantasies?" and Chantelle blushed but responded with a soft voice and slight smile, "I pray that you do, Arthur."

My eyes again fell straight to her thighs inside the tight jeans. She squeezed my hand. "Let me walk you home to your apartment, Arthur."

By that point, I was a little boy caught in a fantasy and I tried to hide it, while getting up from my chair in proper response. Yet as Chantelle's chair grated back on the wooden floor and she looked down to lift it more quietly, I dropped my decorum long enough to pour the last of the wine into my glass and gulp it down. I then took her hand and we began a slow walk down the street to the bottom of my apartment building steps.

When we arrived, I started up the steps with Chantelle behind me in hand, but when her arm then came to stretch out full with her standing firm on the sidewalk, I suddenly realized she had never meant to come in. I then eased down the one step and when my second foot touched the sidewalk, I looked deep into her eyes and raised both hands to the sides of her face. I put my lips forward as if to kiss her and Chantelle closed her eyes. When our lips touched, we pressed them together, before they came back and then met again, slightly apart. Our lips ran over each other ever so gently, and we each gave a sigh as we tasted each other's tenderness. Then our mouths opened more and our tongues touched.

As if on cue, we eased our bodies up the stairs, and once inside, plopped down on my living room loveseat. We locked in a hug, Chantelle put her head on my right shoulder and I sensed again the trust and the need for me not to betray it. My right arm moved to cradle her head, and I ran my other hand down over her hair. She nuzzled deeper into me and I kissed the top of her head.

I was on my home couch, with a beautiful young virgin just met and a bastard to boot, and my first thought was, Thank god for the wine. I lifted Chantelle's head until her lips touched mine and my tongue went between her lips and all over her tongue. She opened her mouth wider and pulled my tongue in more, and we explored each other again and again. A minute later, our lips retreated to a point inches apart and we looked deep into each other's eyes, trying to communicate. I then eased us into a question but in doing so, as only I can, sabotaged the moment. "Chantelle, how did you survive the label 'illegitimate' in a small town?"

Her head pulled back to see my face and when my eyebrows wrinkled to show my concern, she lowered her face to my chest as if the words she were about to speak were easier when done with no visible reaction from me. "I was fortunate. Penetang did not have a nursery school or kindergarten but I began as a toddler wandering up to our tiny library and the librarian sort of adopted me. Thérèse Roberge was as pretty as her name and she had arrived from Quebec City one summer. Soon, she began lending me children's books in French and English, and I pored over them, while mother was away at her job cooking and Dad was wherever after finishing his school-bus runs.

"One autumn day, neighboring Midland announced an area-wide literacy contest in both French and English, and our village of Penetang wanted someone from the eighth grade to put big Midland down. No one could be found and I was only in grade six but the librarian Thérèse had already filed my name, without the town of Penetang knowing. I was then lucky enough to win a scholarship for use at any Canadian university, and Penetang never dreamt I would later choose a non-Quebec one. I chose the University of Toronto.

"The big wheels in Penetang held me up as a symbol of how good its education system was and I was skipped a grade and then another, so that by the time I entered grade eight, I was a tall and awkward 10 years old. But the same big wheels fired Thérèse Roberge from her library job, saying she was a lesbian who messed around with illegitimate children. With that branding having already been pounded home to me by my mother and sister, I went into a kind of depression."

I looked into Chantelle's eyes and put both my hands on her shoulders. "Mothers can be wonderful…So you became a rebel outcast?"

Chantelle's face smiled and she looked up to the ceiling. "My dad rescued me. He went to the scholarship sponsors and worked it so that I could be transferred to a good high school in Toronto. I knew that I would miss my dad and he me, but it seemed the only way out. Dad was afraid to go to Toronto because, by then, the city could be a threat to his sobriety, and my mother and sister wouldn't visit, so I visited him. I started grade nine at North Toronto Collegiate."

My face and brows lit up. "At age 11! Where did you live?"

Chantelle brought her eyes back to mine. "A member of the scholarship committee and a kind psychiatrist, Doctor Fisher, secured for me a home with a loving family, and one of its members was a man named Regis Brandin, who was a retired professor. Both became mentors."

I had almost forgotten that Chantelle and I had started to become romantic. "So your evangelism started in North Toronto?" and Chantelle's eyes moved sideways and up toward the right side of her brain, as if to create a story. "I wanted to go into opera and drama but my mother said that I should not put my shame on display. I also wanted to learn other languages but my mother and sister said they were only for stuck-up Toronto intellectuals. I needed their acceptance, if not respect and at one point when I came to need glasses, my mother saw it as a trick to try to make me more sophisticated. I acquiesced to getting welfare frames in Midland. "

I lowered my hands down Chantelle's arms. "What about your Toronto school and mentors?" and she took my hands in hers, "The school channeled me away from vocal music, saying it was relegated to lesser students, and I was put into instrumental with the French horn. We did win an Ontario-wide competition and my Bach solo was fulfilling, but afterward when I was lent an expensive Alexander French horn and took it home one time to Penetang, it somehow got a big dent in it. As for my voice, it was never again to be."

I raised my brow as if Chantelle's point needed balance. "Except for public speaking," but she did not look in the mood to have her spirit lifted. "I wanted to become a priest and did pastoral help during the summer in Penetang's hospital for the criminally insane but I kept getting into trouble." Her eyes then went deep into mine. "I did not leave the church, Arthur, it left me."

I then took my turn squeezing our hands. "Hence your role now," and Chantelle clarified, "That came much later, after I finished school."

At that moment, I came again to realize I was dehydrated and so offered to fetch some more wine, but Chantelle declined and I had to do the job myself. Shortly thereafter, I decided we had talked enough and after downing another half-glass, I began caressing her right thigh, before lowering my head and mouth to a place above her right knee. I kissed Chantelle's inner thigh and she gave out a long, slow sigh of release.

Saturday April 28 2007

I awoke on the loveseat at 7:00 a.m. and looked around to try making sense of my surroundings but then remembered I had been with a beautiful young woman just met. For a second or so, I could not recall her name, but then it came to me. I called out "Chantelle" and there was no answer. I pulled myself up to saunter across the living room into the bedroom but suddenly realized I had to pee badly, so I veered left toward the washroom and noticed on my little hallway desk, her note:

> *Dear Arthur,*
>
> *I am sorry that I had to leave but my shift begins at 6:00. I stole some of your toothpaste, soap and hot water.*
>
> *Your gentleness helped me through a time I had feared for much of my life. Thank you.*
>
> *xo,*
>
> *Chantelle*
>
> *P.S. I would love to share that herbal tea we never had. I work at Northwestern Memorial Hospital.*

I had no memory of the evening, beyond being on the loveseat, and felt a little shame but then shrugged it off and said to myself that I must have done something right to make a young lady leave such a gracious note, as well as give me her address. Soon I felt stable enough to whip myself into my weekend regimen of showering and shaving, throwing on some brown safari slacks, cotton turtleneck, safari shirt and hiking boots, then downing a bowl of oats, blueberries and honey, along with grapefruit juice and a lot of coffee.

I spent that Saturday morning as I did all Saturdays, at work, arriving at 10:00 to greet the faux furniture at Cork & Church before I waded back to my rear office. My office was an oasis: generous in size – 15 feet from the front to a Palladian window at the back that overlooked Lake Michigan – and 12 feet wide; the ceiling was nine feet high and had two ceiling fans that I had erected in defiance of the central air conditioning; there was another window on the north wall and at the back half of the room, the window was six feet high and had eight rectangular panes, two abreast. I had replaced all of the glass with Scottish amber, and in the mornings, with the sun flowing in from the east off Lake Michigan, the whole office had the ambience of an autumn harvest.

The room's walls and ceiling were a light brown; in fact the whole office was a blend of multiple browns. The floor was oak in untreated strips and its openness made the room look larger, while still retaining a feeling of earthy warmth.

The office's front door lay open to the right and it was antique wood, with a frosted oval window. To the left of the doorway, at the northwest, stood a green Norfolk pine, six feet in height and offset by another of like size in the far southeast corner, next to the Palladian window. At the front right of the room and just past the swinging space of the open door was a desk of washed-out walnut, and above the desk hung a sprawling watercolor of an old tree, living out its life in Mississippi.

On the left side of the desk were three drawers, the top drawer holding a stack of computer paper, four tip pens, two green highlighters and a brown Magic Marker. The middle drawer held works-in-progress and the bottom contained an alphabetical list of clients, together with briefings considered necessary on client prejudices. The bottom drawer also had a file of 'thank-you' letters from people whose feedback I liked to ponder from time to time.

Set along the opposite wall on the north was a beech-wood table that stretched six feet from the pine at the front to a spot near the rectangular window at the rear, and the table had one thin drawer set under its top that held 20 or so sheets of draft paper. I loved the table's clean sweep with its light beech, and when I had first seen it at a conference in Uppsala, Sweden, I had bought it without thinking about how I could ship it back. Money had not figured into the consideration and I had been more interested in the effect that the table would have on my mind when drawing. Call it toilet training if you will, but I hated clutter and needed to have total tidiness before embarking on any project.

Above the table hung a huge corkboard, and on it were 20 green thumb-tacks rearranged from project to project to meet my mood. At the table was an old oak chair that matched another at the desk, and a third sat at the rear, with all three ready to be shuffled around to meet the needs of most meetings.

The air on all levels at Cork & Church smelled like an old vent but the Palladian window could be opened, as well as two of the rectangles in the north window, and with the ceiling fans on and the front door open, the office's air could actually change at seemingly every instant. Because of this freshness I would often catch myself swiveling my head to smell the pines or staring toward the rear to admire, through the Palladian window, Lake Michigan and beyond, for as far as the eye could see.

I had set myself the task that Saturday of designing a summer home for the chairperson of our biggest client but this time was trying the task without the list of client prejudices. I had only the mandate and my one attempt at paraphrasing it, the previous night, along with precious little time for carrying out the project. The home was to be a cottage in the Apostle Islands on Lake Superior, in an area of northern Wisconsin not unlike Finland.

I slid open the drawer under the worktable, pulled out a blank sheet of paper and laid it flat on the table top, then retrieved from the desk a brown Magic Marker and a fine-tipped pen. As the minutes drifted by, I found myself staring at the blank paper and looking up at the corkboard tacks, before reassembling them into a long rectangular shape under a slow sloping roof. I then looked to my right over the oak floor to view the Norfolk pine in the southeast and then back to the other pine on my left, remembering that these trees were native to New Zealand but wanting them to fuel thoughts of Finland.

Around minute seven, I jotted onto the top of the paper *Finnish Home on the Lake* and scribbled on the upper right-hand corner the notes *Integrate with nature* and *Counterpoint geometric with organic*. Then I started to draw.

Shortly, I scrapped draft one but ripped off the title and notes and set them on the upper right-hand side of the table, for eyeing with my peripheral vision. Then came scrap two. Each time I started to draw, I was feeling hindered by trying to second-guess what this client would buy, and scraps three to five were four more inches of drawing, before the minutes drifted into hours. Around noon, I took a break and stole a muffin from my boss's honor bar, and found an overripe banana and some apple juice before going back to my office.

Most times at the start of a project I tried to feel enthused, but this time I could not suppress my contempt for the client's obese chairman. At last around 2:00 p.m., a rush of frustration hit me and I did the house the way I thought it should be done. If my boss Willy Cork didn't like it, he would simply have to furnish me with a list of the fat man's wants and I could give him what he deserved. Cork and client would be happy and the only losers would be the Apostle Islands. Or so I thought then — I had too myopic a vision to appreciate what I was doing to myself and others.

Over the next two hours, I noted and sketched, until I finally rested my eyes on the floor, where lay scraps one to five. I then laid sketch six in the middle of the table before I put all stuff away to start the walk home, with the narrative having to wait until I got back to work on Sunday.

When I hit the warm air outside, the thought dawned on me that I was alone again at work on a Saturday, this time in the middle of spring, and I suddenly felt lonely. When I then reached my flat around 5:00 p.m., I caught sight again of Chantelle's letter and noticed more markedly this time the P.S. reference to Northwestern Memorial Hospital. It was not yet evening and I presumed Chantelle's nursing shift would soon be finishing. The thought that a ravishing young woman would be doing anything else on a Saturday did not enter my mind.

I telephoned Northwestern Memorial and was told in curt hospital-talk that the personal numbers of workers were just that. Then, like the quick-thinking actor I could sometimes be, I resolved to get her phone number by doing what a Scottish professor had once told me was called "Doing an Englishman": *schmoozing*, using half-truths and oral calisthenics.

I arrived by foot at the admitting desk just before 6:00 and tried pulling an Englishman on a veteran nurse but she was not to be duped. "Doctor Franklin, I can't give you Chantelle's number but can tell you she is still in Emerge." I did not clarify that I was not a doctor but let that part of the English trick work and charged down several corridors to hit the emergency unit. There stood Chantelle, tending to a patient, and at first she did not see

20

me but when she turned to tackle another person, I shot forward, "Don't nurses' shifts have ends?"

I caught sight again of that apologetic smile and with a turn of her head, she said, "Arthur! How lovely to see you. This is my Chicago home, and I eat and sleep here."

Suddenly, a man appeared and made a sound that I understood to be part of a doctor's training. "Hi, I'm Doctor Flem." He did not offer to shake hands but kept them sterile on his hips and I responded in kind, "How do you do, I'm Master Franklin."

Flem did not acknowledge my jab and continued, "Chantelle's work has been excellent but she should have a rest." The doctor then turned away, as if he had minded other people's business long enough, and he departed. I looked back at Chantelle and asked if she were busy that evening, and she replied that she had been asked out but had politely declined to remain on and work. I tried a genteel appeal. "Would a light dinner of eggs, spinach and tomatoes persuade you to stop?" and Chantelle smiled a gracious thank you. She excused herself to shower and change before she arrived back in belt-less jeans and cowboy boots, but this time with a denim shirt and a navy sweater over her shoulders. We left the hospital without body contact but once past the entrance, I turned and gave Chantelle a hug, and we embraced for so long that it was as if we were sharing a secret moment, one we both understood from some time long ago.

Once back in my apartment, I poured each of us a glass of red in my home's only glasses and we had that light dinner in my kitchenette. When we finished, I noticed Chantelle had barely touched her wine and so I shifted to do the dishes while she sat at the kitchenette, taking the opportunity to pour myself another glass and steal a sip of it. I then moved the two of us with glasses half-full over to the living room's loveseat and we set our wines down at each end on the floor. I took time to sneak another sip, in anticipation of being dry for a while.

I was not sure what had actually happened the previous night but did not want to get into it, for fear of focusing on my passing out, and so I tried talking about something that I thought would keep attention away from whatever I had done. "You work hard, Chantelle." She reached down for her wine, took a sip and then steadied her glass before she threw her hair away from her face. "I get a high from helping people, Arthur."

The next question I felt could lead to a moment of awkwardness, given the enigma of the previous evening, but the question I thought could also be posed with enough breadth to allow room for innocence. "Do you plan to work hard tomorrow?" and Chantelle put her glass back down on the floor and gently slapped her thighs. "I have done six straight days and have enjoyed the work but do need a day's rest."

The word "rest" teased me and I had by then twelve new ounces of wine in me, so I tried embracing the notion that Chantelle could stay for the night. "So I won't get a letter tomorrow?" and she turned her face straight to me and gave a matter-of-fact smile, "Not if you're up by 7:00."

I looked straight back at her, "Okay, smarty pants hard-driver, do you want to do something in the morning you've never done? You may lose your whole soul and reason for being but nothing beyond."

Chantelle bent down and took another sip of wine. "Arthur, you are all too fair. What do we do, rob an art gallery?" I then gave a big shrug with arms apart, "In effect. What I'd like you to see is a sketch that I did today and give me your view on it."

Her brow wrinkled. "You draw, Arthur?"

This woman had come to my apartment, slept over and had never asked me what I did for a living. I slowly lowered my head and softened my voice as if to make a point that I should have made much earlier, "I'm an architect, Chantelle." Her face shifted to a blank space in the room, "So that is what you meant when you verbally slapped Ross Flem with the term 'Master.'" Chantelle's face turned back to me. "Arthur, I am not an architect."

I put my right hand on her left arm. "You choose your colors well," and she turned away again, "Thank you. A lay opinion." I squeezed her arm, "A true one."

I fixed my eyes on Chantelle's face and let my right hand drift down her left arm to her left thigh. She looked into my eyes, and I slowly ran my hand up her thigh to a place within touching distance of her Venus mound, before I took my hand away to a harmless place behind her left shoulder. I smiled at her, then moved my left hand behind her right shoulder and pressed Chantelle forward to kiss her. When our lips met, we broke into a full French kiss and began slightly swiveling our heads, to underscore the meaning.

Suddenly, Chantelle was trembling and I caught a sense that whatever had happened the previous night, she was still a virgin. With both my hands on the back of her shoulders, I pulled our bodies closer still, until we fell into a long and comforting hug.

Seconds passed with the two of us in that embrace and my right hand stroking Chantelle's hair. Then I eased back and we stared into each other's eyes before, again, we tilted our heads to join our lips and mouths in a long and passionate kiss. My right hand again fell down to her left thigh and as we kissed, my hand shifted to the warm place where her two thighs met. I caressed her along the inside of her right thigh and when she responded with a light sigh and a deeper French kiss, her thighs opened a little and my right hand slowly made its way up. When I finally cupped her Venus mound, Chantelle gave out a long breath and we went into a deeper kiss.

My face then came back to catch her approval, and after I opened the front of her jeans, I eased my fingers down the front of her white panties until my hand felt a bit of resistance from the jeans themselves. Chantelle then slid them down to her knees and I pulled them off, along with her boots.

Her legs were fully in front of my eye and I saw again how perfectly sculpted they were. I guess she picked up my gaze, because she smiled the look that people give when they have bestowed some gift upon another.

I stood up, yanked off my hiking boots, shuffled out of my safari slacks and threw them over Chantelle's clothing on the hardwood floor. Then I slinked back onto the loveseat to take her in my arms and we gave each other a catch-up kiss. I unbuttoned her denim shirt and spread it apart to reveal her small firm breasts. When I then looked up into Chantelle's eyes and she smiled, I took her left breast in my mouth but this time, her sigh came with a feminine moan. When I sucked her breast some more, she sighed again and started stroking my hair. I slid my mouth across the middle of her chest to reach her right breast and I sucked again.

Minutes passed and Chantelle gently pushed me back and undid three of my buttons before she pushed her nipples against mine. We then pounced on each other's lips in a French kiss and this time it was my turn to sigh. I caressed her long dark hair and as if on cue, we both got up and made our way to the bedroom.

There we stood, near the side of the bed and embracing, before I shifted my hands and arms under her shirt to reach her back. I let my hands fall down her long back to rest atop her panties and bubble bum. Then I slid my fingers inside her panties and felt all around her bum's tightness, before my mouth went down again to her breasts and she helped me feed each one into my mouth. As I sucked, her legs spread apart and I started to pull down her panties.

Once nude, Chantelle revealed to me the heights that nature can reach. I slipped off my shirt, socks and underpants and the two of us fell onto the bed. We buried our faces into each other and when we entered into a long French kiss, I parted her legs with my right hand and she parted them more before she raised them up below her knees.

As I went into Chantelle, she let out a gasp as if I were hurting her but it seemed to last only for a moment, and her walls then closed on me such that my hard penis felt the liquid kiss of her tight vagina. It was delicious... In some long time thereafter, I came in Chantelle, before I fell asleep on her shoulder with my penis slowly going back to softness inside her.

In another hour or so when my eyes came back open, Chantelle was already wide awake or had never slept, and it soon became apparent she had not. Again, it was I alone who had drifted off, and so I quickly kissed her, to muffle any related discussion and signal all was well.

Chantelle excused herself to the bathroom and as she closed the bathroom door behind her, I bolted to the living room for my wine. By the time she came back out I was already back in the bedroom, lying nude on the bed, waiting to greet her with a smile. Once she was next to the bed, I took her with both hands and eased her down onto the bed before I looked into her eyes and gave her a light French kiss. I moved my head all the way down to her thighs and began kissing each thigh, while working my face up to her vagina. When my lips met her clitoris, I let my tongue caress it and

Chantelle gave out a low groan. I lowered my mouth down to her vagina and my tongue began to explore around the inside of its walls. Then I moved my face back to her clitoris and gently licked it again and again, before I started a slow rotation back and forth between her clitoris and vagina.

For 20 minutes we played that way and Chantelle's Venus mound moved up and down ever more in rhythm as her groans grew louder. She came to her first orgasm with me and it was Chantelle who then fell asleep.

I put my head down on the bed beside her but stayed awake and got up twice to go to the bathroom, as well as polish off Chantelle's portion of the wine, before I cleaned both glasses and put them away in the kitchen. Long hours thereafter, and with Chantelle having been asleep all the while, I managed to doze off.

Sunday April 29 2007

Shortly after 7:30 a.m., I awoke to the smell of garlic and coffee, and went to the kitchen to find Chantelle standing there nude but for one of my shirts. "Good morning, Arthur. I hope you don't mind my borrowing your Viyella to keep me warm. Its brown goes with the coffee."

I was nude too and gestured with arms full out, "Chantelle, escargots for breakfast?"

She turned to me with a smile, "Sorry, I haven't read the rule book."

By 9 a.m., we were in my office, my still wanting Chantelle's impression after having rushed through draft six. I also did not want to witness Willy Cork's temper on his dry Monday. I gave her two writing sheets and a marker pen from my top desk drawer and she shifted over to the drawing table to eye my work. Then, while standing, Chantelle looked at the work in relation to the Norfolk pine, before she turned to the right and peered down to the pine at the rear. She sat down and started jotting down her thoughts, with intermittent glances at my sketch. As for myself, I tried to behave, and sat down at the opposite desk to tackle a separate business pitch. But soon I found myself unable to stop peeking across the office and wondering what a layperson could possibly be writing about my work.

After what seemed like half an hour, Chantelle got up and handed me a short summary on a clean sheet, tossing the rough one into the wooden wastebasket under my desk. She then backed off to the long drawing table and leaned against it while I began reading.

Cottage in the Apostle Islands

First Impression

There is with the cottage timeless simplicity, sturdy functionalism and harmony with nature.

Symmetry

Against a broad canvas of floor-to-ceiling glass, framed by a wood roof, stone corners and front deck, there are lines traveling vertically and horizontally, all lending a sense of rectitude to the organic shapes within. Shapes such as the stone in the large fireplace are thus allowed due emphasis, and they complement a geometric rhythm that is further found in the solid rectangular eating table and large wood chairs. The organic shapes also give to the fireplace and total structure a sense of proportion and balance.

Compatibility with Nature

Variations on brown, as well as the wood and stone, harmonize with the outside forest as seen through the floor-to-ceiling glass, and lend a sense of life to the interior.

Sturdy Functionalism

The robustness of materials, quality of workmanship and simplicity of design assure a look of functionalism and durability. Furniture, flooring and walls all look ready to manage rambunctious children and the vagaries of changing humidity and temperature. The components' design is in a form that will not confine it to any specific period. The total interior feels practical but warm. It is free of ostentation but does not feel sterile.

Closing comment

27

A viewer is left with a sense that the home will care for its inhabitants for generations to come.

I read again Chantelle's words on line and its manifestations, of their dovetailing with nature, on the robustness of materials, the vagaries of climate and the home's enduring dignity. I then looked up at this young woman who had fallen into my life. "Chantelle Fouriere, interior designer?"

She was smiling, still standing, and her arms were folded in a job-done position. "Arthur, I studied photography in Midland under Budd Hudson but before studying, I borrowed a book from him on the principles of design. When writing now, I found myself trying to use some of the language that I understood."

I suddenly started. "Budd Hudson? His photography was featured here in Chicago at the YMCA on Wacker Drive."

I was deeply grateful to Chantelle and wanted to give her something in return, so before she could answer, I had a fast thought and leapt to my feet. "Well, photographer Chantelle, would you like to take a walk through Chicago?"

We exited Cork & Church hand-in-hand, to walk west past Michigan for several blocks to Washington Square Park, where we came across a street vendor. We bought two grapefruit juices and a bag of popcorn but I hogged most of it as we continued along, going corner-to-corner across the park.

We had talked while walking, mostly about buildings in Chicago, and I had done much of the talking out of a need I guess to hide my shyness or maybe to ensure this enigmatic woman would not suddenly disappear out of my life. She was too gorgeous to take for more than a glance, and her comfort with me still gave me a sense that it was all unreal, with the reality only being that she was, what some call, illegitimate.

I then thought a starting point for unraveling her mystery might be last Friday night's speech. "Chantelle, you spoke of rabbi Jesus of Nazareth but you don't believe he was the son of God?"

Chantelle smiled and looked up at the sky. "No, Arthur, nor do I believe did he" and I turned to her with raised brow. "Does your Bible not say Jesus performed miracles?"

She turned her smile to my face. "The Bible is not *my* bible, Arthur, but is one source among many for anyone seeking awareness. It is a collection of parables and sayings, distorted by years of oral stories passed down and the desires of people to have it written their way. The bible is a book whose New Testament was begun decades after Jesus's death and is a political and potentially lethal piece of poetry, given its distortions by powerful people. But for the same reasons, the bible is a work worth reading several times."

My face had the look of a puzzled child. "But what of Jesus's acts and words?" and Chantelle again looked upward as we walked along, "Much of what we have to go on, unless some future archaeologist helps us out, comes from what is called, yes, the 'Bible.' If one takes it at its best, that bible is a delayed and metaphorical description of some old photographs, with the New Testament's photographs often purportedly taken by Jesus's apostles, whose titles and roles confusedly overlap with his disciples'. How accurate those photographs are depends on the film used, the camera lens, the photographer and the developer."

By this time, I could not contain my enthusiasm. "Given what you are saying, what is your definition of God?" and Chantelle waved her hand. "I don't have one."

I looked downward and eased up in my walk. "...Then what is your understanding of God?" but Chantelle's stride held firm and she raised her left arm to the air. "I'm not sure, Arthur. I have for God a curiosity that does not sit still, and I believe God gave me a few brains and a great deal of freedom to possess such curiosity. My impression of God keeps shifting and is thoroughly repugnant to those whose minds must have their definitions fastened down."

I then sped up. "You doubt God, ever?" and her left arm went palm up. "Of course. God gave me the freedom to doubt but such doubt does not threaten my faith. Fear, I feel, is the enemy of faith, not doubt."

I opened up my free arm. "In what then, do you have faith?" and Chantelle kept her arm raised. "In the God within each of us and in some God outside of us. Each of us, Jesus, you, me, your gluttonous client, has within him goodness and the potential for not only grasping that goodness but also acting upon it. I have come to believe that helping others and contributing to general awareness are rewards for all affected. To those ends, I believe we should do all we can."

I pointed. "I suggest we work our way west, so I can show you Seward Park…Chantelle, what of religious rule makers who have tight definitions of God and everything that exists underneath Him?"

She shrugged. "Some gained power long enough to entrench a system that turned the seven deadly sins upside down and worked for that power base's purpose. It is a system founded on the four cornerstones of fear, greed, anger and guilt, and bricked to the roof with hypocrisy."

I bent forward, looked around and up at Chantelle, and again stretched out my arm as if to appeal. "But how can such a system sustain itself over a prolonged period of time and hold minds in prison?"

Chantelle's voice rose a little. "To begin with, I think one has to develop an appreciation for how strong each of the four cornerstones is. First, fear. If people of power and wealth furnish to vulnerable minds a list of do's and don'ts – those hungry people told they will be rewarded with a heaven after death – the power mongers have already blackmailed those poor minds with an appeal to their lower human traits of self-centeredness. The next concoction is a hell whose image goes beyond those poor people's restricted imaginations.

"By implication, those in power have sanctioned the worship of a god who manipulates human fear and self-centeredness to achieve the god's ends, shunting the follower's chance to attain any level of spiritual maturity. Compounding this disinformation further is the power brokers' tapping into the short-term greed of their underlings, the vast majority of whom are have-nots. They are told that if they follow a religious set of rules, good things will come their way, the visible proof of which is the power and material wealth flaunted by the ruling few.

"The next hot button pushed is anger. As the power-minded know from the start, the masses suffer from misdirected anger and such confusion allows the powerful the chance to channel that anger against a common enemy, be the enemy Copernicus, Galileo or the opponents in any war. The god that is thus worshiped is a hatemonger and war profiteer.

"Guilt sneaks its way in too but guilt as you know is a counterbalance, generated after the fact by a bad act or thought. Guilt does not inhabit the bigger realm of conscience, where a proactive presence of mind leads to acts of love and respect for all others. Guilt is thus a lower human trait, but when induced and capitalized upon by agents of a god who is a hate manipulator and greed-promoting tyrant, guilt can shake the have-not to such a degree that he will go to any length of histrionics to demonstrate subservience to that imperious god.

"When the poor, fearful, desperate, angry, guilt-ridden minds of the masses are thus enslaved, the power brokers know that the finishing touch has to be hypocrisy. The power brokers seem to know that contained within the human mind is a need for freedom of thought, that need springing from our genes' evolutionary opting for the better. But for that human mind to select, it has to think; for it to think, it must have freedom; for the mind to have freedom, it cannot have fear. Given, therefore, the need of the human mind for freedom, those powerful people know that their repression won't last beyond the short term, unless it is accompanied by the big lie. Hypocrisy accordingly becomes not only sanctioned by the god brought forth by those powerful people but is practiced by their concocted god in every expedient way.

"Only through hypocrisy and manipulation of those four cornerstones – fear, greed, anger and guilt – do the manipulated people not fuss over the fact that their so-called perfect god, himself a blackmailer, greed-spreader, hatemonger, guilt-inducer and liar, cannot possibly be a being of love. As for truth, the oppressed people never get to witness it and have no grasp of truth beyond the show business they have witnessed in that concocted god's the-ater. And so on such slavery of the mind goes for thousands of years, its being strongest where awareness is the least."

I grinned and turned to Chantelle, while slightly swinging away. "You do have a way of lightening up a Sunday in May, on a stroll through the streets of Chicago."

Chantelle fell silent and I tried to recover. "Chantelle, I think I hurt your feelings and if I did, I'm truly sorry. My own god and believe me, he's pretty shaky, has an infinite sense of humor."

I felt her hand squeeze mine but when she turned to me, I caught her worried face. "Thank you, Arthur. No, you did not hurt my feelings. I simply think I have done it again."

I stopped and turned to her with an inquisitive squint. "Done what, Chantelle?" and she was stiff in her reply. "My tongue has had me in trouble more than once." I held in my looking position. "Trouble?" and she visibly loosened up as we started walking more quickly again. "Arthur, we must be reaching the park. There is a vendor selling kielbasa."

I turned to look at the sausage vendor and then thrust out my free arm, quipping half-seriously, "You want us to eat pork sitting in the sun for hours? I heard hogs don't like heat. Probably didn't 4,000 years ago, either. Trichinosis is the kind of disease which, if its cause is not known, could work its way into a warm country's religion."

Chantelle was finally smiling again. "Non-Jews got trichinosis too...*Prosz´ polska kielbasa*. And to what can I treat you, Arthur?" I stopped and looked at her in surprise. "You speak Polish? You've been in Chicago only six weeks!"

Chantelle's smile grew wider. "There are Polish cottagers just south of Penetang near a French-Canadian village called Lafontaine. They go to the Roman church there on Sundays and I used to swim in the area." I then recalled her earlier question. "I'll have a sausage too, please, and in deference to you, a Canada Dry" but Chantelle took her turn quipping this time, "An American drink, Arthur. Canada has an America Dry. A tomato juice, please."

The vendor thanked Chantelle, "*To wszystko, dzi´kuj,*" and we walked into Seward Park. "Chantelle, the pictures I wanted you to see. There are a dozen trees and they hold for me spirits of lives older than Chicago. They're all oaks, over 100 years of age. This one, gnarled at its trunk, is 200 years old. A University of Chicago professor told me about it when I queried him on a sick tree in front of my flat. The gnarl makes me think of the happiness and pain that this old oak has seen. Lincoln said that after the age of 40, a man is responsible for his face, and this tree makes me think of Einstein's sad face. I wonder what this tree has seen."

Chantelle again said something that almost wiped away my diffidence around her mystery. "I love your mind, Arthur" and I turned to give her a hug.

We then took back to walking again and I felt on comfortable ground, "Perhaps we should name the trees. Don't you Christians christen boats?" and Chantelle gave a little shrug while squeezing my hand. "I don't, but sure."

I pointed to the gnarled tree. "Moses" and her arm again went out. "With its strength and imperfections. Jung" and I thought myself in a friendly joust; so, I grinned. "Okay, showoff, I'll anoint a fellow American, Fromm, and one who imputed secular values into scriptural ideals."

Chantelle seemed to be in her element. "*Peanuts*'s Schultz, American, and one who used humor to convey the spiritual" but I shot back, "Stanfield, Canadian. You in liberal Canada blew it on him for leader" and Chantelle stopped, looked at me with a blank face and pulled my hand back behind her. "You're right…How do you know about Robert Stanfield, Arthur?"

I smiled and kissed her on the forehead. "One of his family was with me in a group workshop in Boston. Marshall."

We started walking again. "As in Plan, Arthur? Tough act to follow. Richard the Third" but I was fast to come back: "Shakespeare didn't concur, yes-no?"

Chantelle slowed a bit and her face turned more sober. "The misread on the man Richard the Third may be evidence that even the most perceptive can still be propagandized. Unless Shakespeare was just playing politics to get his plays on stage."

We were reaching one of my favorite big oaks. "This one's arms reach everywhere. Bach" and Chantelle put her free arm on mine, "Yes, Bach. Servetus!" I paused in my walking. "Servetus?"

Chantelle smiled and her left arm jutted out. "A Spanish doctor" but when I winced "At the hospital?" she caught my concern. "Dead for centuries."

My brows went up in interest. "May I hear more?" but Chantelle lost her smile. "Please, later Arthur. I'm not ready to get killed just yet…Jesus."

I thought to lighten things up. "Now our forest has two token Jews. Okay, I'll flaunt my liberalism. Hitler favorite Wagner, whose excerpt triggered a storming out by a Jerusalem audience a few years ago. Banning Wagner is a bit like banning Shakespeare" and before Chantelle could respond, we had reached the bottom of the hill of oaks. "Chantelle, I know a place for a nutritious lunch."

She smiled again that memorable, apologetic smile. "I would love to, Arthur, but tomorrow I start three days of 12-hour shifts and I have to find time to sketch out what I'm going to say at Buckingham Fountain this Friday night."

At that moment, another name for an oak came to mind but I held it at bay.

Monday April 30 2007

I felt rested and was at my desk by 8:00 a.m., determined to hammer out the Apostle Cottage project before a 9:00 a.m. meeting, but both the sketch and Chantelle's one-pager were missing. Before I had time to panic, Cork barged into my office with sketch in hand, along with Chantelle's unsigned summary. "Franklin, he loves you."

I swiveled my head to greet the fat man standing. "I'm not sure he's my type, Bill" but he ignored the quip. "I didn't like it but he did. Your narrative was a touch airy fairy but he loved that too. You certainly outguessed me on this one, Franklin, and not even I can stop you from going to the top. As for Church, we'll always need his old money but you actually have talent."

I got through the Monday, finishing the pitch, and wanted to call Chantelle, letting her know about her narrative, but suddenly caught myself instead thinking of her needs – she had said she wanted to pull together her thoughts for a talk at Buckingham Fountain on Friday evening and I had learned she liked to put herself into a task, so I took my vintage TVR down to the University of Chicago and went swimming. I am told that ballet is better for fitness but I have never been able to squeeze in 60-hour workouts and someone said cross-country skiing was number three, which I will file in case I move to the Apostle Islands, or god forbid, the tundra of Canada but in the meantime, I will let swimming suffice.

The evening had a spring-like youth to it and after the swim, I decided it was time to phone Chantelle. But when I got home, I found she was out and wondered where she could be and with whom. I took to the kitchen and wedged a spoon of peanut butter down my gullet and washed it down with a glass of grapefruit juice. Then I took to the living room and turned on some classical music to soothe my mind but should have realized Mahler can often make things worse. I phoned the hospital again but she was still out.

I tried to lie down on the loveseat but then had a flash that Chantelle's doctor friend, Servetus, was not dead. I started turning over and over, trying to still my mind but finally got up around 10:00 p.m. and took the TVR out to clear the cobwebs. I buzzed around Chicago for a couple of hours and got home after midnight, tried to get to some sleep but tossed away.

On Tuesday, I awoke late and found myself short of the time needed to make Cork & Church's 9:00 a.m. strategy meeting before its 11:00 a.m. pitch. I shaved to World War I trench standards and showered too fast to rid myself of worry odor, then downed a banana and three coffees to drug myself awake before scrambling out and down the stairs to my TVR. The engine flooded.

I gave the car a kick. "English rheumatoid!" and then ran the block to Michigan and grabbed a cab to make the meeting. By then, I had a bladder about to burst and came to appreciate that I smelled like an octopus. Church began speaking, with a voice that sounded important and I think his words meant something but my mind was on my bladder.

When Church finished, I tried to make a dignified exit when Cork intervened. "Franklin, take your piss later. This is important." But I was at the door of the room. "Sorry, Willy, gotta go. Be right back."

At any urinal, I always seem short of time and have to push my pee out so hard that my anal canal widens, and I'd been told I could get hemorrhoids that way. This time I pushed so hard, a liquid poop hit my white underwear so, fearing a brown streamer on my beige slacks, I scurried over to the closest cubicle, tore off my trousers and flung them onto a hook, before I wiped myself with my dirty underwear and then popped out, half-naked, to stuff them into the towel bin. I then spun back to the cubicle to fetch my trousers but they had slipped off the door-hook and as I bent over to rescue them from the dirty floor, another liquid poop hit my thigh and I had to swivel down to the toilet and flush away, watching the summer-wool slacks crumpled on the floor out of reach in front of me.

It took six minutes to get back to the meeting room and Cork halted all talk long enough to give me a long glare, before his whore Trudi spoke. "I hope last night was worth it."

Chuckles emanated from around the room and then we all got down to work. At 11:00 a.m., we went on stage at the John Hancock Center and steered the client to the right of its thinking. Then I went home to re-shower, change my slacks and eat some raw vegetables before going back to work.

When I arrived, the entire place was empty until 2:00 p.m. and I took the time to race through the John Hancock follow-up, such that by 6:20 p.m., I was back at my building, going up the front stairs when suddenly someone on the sidewalk was calling out from behind me, "Mr. Franklin?"

I turned to see a middle-aged man. "I'm Doctor, sorry, Martin English. Chantelle asked me to deliver this rose to you. She is down at the public library again."

I was too stunned to shake the man's hand or, at first at least, graciously take the rose. "On Michigan?" and he put the rose forward. "Yes." As I accepted it, my head bent down toward the rose. "Thank you, Martin. For a doctor, you're a good person" and he turned to depart. "Thank you. So is she. Enjoy your rose."

The man had given me his first name but I had not given mine nor had I shaken his hand. I carried the long-stemmed rose into my flat and placed it into the only holder I had – a plastic cleaning bucket – then carried the bucket over to my bedroom dresser, where I knew I would see the rose before falling sleep. I then darted back out of the apartment, down the stairs past the TVR and over on foot to Michigan, where I speed-walked south to the Chicago Public Library.

There was Chantelle, head down on table 12 in the rear, plowed into a mess of paper. She didn't see me moving across the floor, but before reaching her I was halted by a large black guard who asked me to leave her be.

My face betrayed my surprise but I managed to rally. "She is concentrating that hard?" and the big black man was calm in response, "Sorry, but her looks were a little more than a few men could handle last night and she asked us to protect her rights to read unobstructed. Do you know her?"

I looked over and saw the top of her long dark hair, with her face down in her work. "I thought I did but she keeps growing so much, I'm not sure."

The library man grinned. "You've met our Chantelle. Please carry on."

I crept the last 20 feet to her table but as I closed in, her face lifted and I saw again her raw beauty. I managed a few words, "No one has ever given me a rose before and I wanted to thank you."

Chantelle's head leaned toward her right shoulder and she beamed a wide smile. "My pleasure, Arthur."

I tried to seize the moment. "Feel like a nine-minute tea break?" but Chantelle's smile went back to the apologetic one. "Thank you, but I can't. I'm having difficulty putting down what I want to share on Friday." I was not about to give up and put both palms forward to appeal. "May I walk you home after?" but the apologetic smile remained. "Bless you, Arthur, but someone from the hospital is picking me up at 10:00."

My mouth turned uncontrollably down. "Another doctor?" and Chantelle's smile lessened still. "Charles does not do surgery anymore but he still teaches. He is 82 years old and his hands don't do for him the work that he wants."

I lowered my brow and squinted. "Does he always chauffeur young ladies back to their abodes at night?" and Chantelle gave me the first scowl I had ever seen from her. "I tire at night, Arthur, and with Charles' help, I have enough time to get back to the hospital, swim, shower and crash before my 6:00 a.m. shift."

The squint lifted but my face went pale. I had done it again and so I tried to rescue, "You swim, too?" and Chantelle's smile came back. "I push hard with life, Arthur, and my body needs the water."

I smirked, "Do your goggles leak?" and her smile widened. "Always. I thought the leakage was caused by my buying the cheapest" and I grinned, "No, the high-priced ones leak too."

My eyebrows suddenly lifted and my mouth opened as if I'd made a great discovery. "That's it! Your sermon – God gave us swimming goggles to test our tolerance!"

Chantelle smirked, "Nice of her."

"Her?"

"He, Her, Who, Does, Big Bang."

Okay, I could play. "The Big G," and she gestured back with her hand and a softer smile, "Giving" but when I probed, "Why not Giver?" she kept her ground. "Not for me a noun."

I was about to ask "How about The Big G gerund?" but I picked up on Chantelle's restlessness. "Sorry, I'll go now."

Chantelle folded her hands forward on the long desk and lifted her soft eyes up to me. "How about a date, handsome?" and I squinted again, "But you said you were being driven..." She cut me off. "Shall we say, Friday night at 9:00 beside the Buckingham Fountain?"

As I walked away, the black library man who had halted me gave a look of approval and I found myself recalling the name that I should have given one oak back in the park, "Sitting Bull." I looked back to smile at Chantelle but she was already buried in her work.

I got home at 8:00 p.m. and after some thought, gave a ring to an old girlfriend, Cathy McCutcheon. Cathy was a bad architect of good breeding and one soon to become a senior at my alma mater. "Cathy? Arthur. I know we had talked about seeing each other this week but Cork & Church has landed...Cathy, I have met someone and feel wrong about our seeing each other."

I had been seeing pretty Cathy for months, since I had spoken one evening at the university, and now it had all terminated with one short call. I fell back into my two-seater and picked up a copy of Ayn Rand's *Fountainhead* that I had borrowed from the Cork & Church library but was too tired to read and television was not an option.

I decided to go to a movie I hoped was still playing on Ohio, just east of the close-by McClung Court Center. The film was Bergmann's *Fanny and Alexander* and the story talked of Christian hypocrisy in a way that I thought would be engaging for Chantelle. After the show, I went home to sleep.

The next three days were cranked up with Cork & Church executing the pitch it had won at the John Hancock Center and I got a swim in each night. Come Friday, I left work a touch early, and Cork's Trudi would normally have ratted on me, but short-man Cork had already departed with a new recruit, Kasia, to give her the firm's price of entry.

At home I ate, cleaned and changed, and then walked down Michigan, over the river to Wacker and down Lake Shore, making it to Buckingham Fountain exactly at 7:00 p.m. I found myself among 100 others as Chantelle took to her little speaking stand.

Friday May 4 2007

"About 15 billion years ago, our universe came into being and around five billion years ago, planet Earth emerged. Over the long period to follow, an atmosphere came to be as the ocean released oxygen, and about two-and-a-half billion years ago, that oxygen ultimately led to life.

"The probability of life happening on Earth was one in a billion but there are 100 billion galaxies known to us and our own galaxy has millions of planets, so the chances of life on Earth were pretty good, given the possible number of tries. It is also likely from those probabilities that other forms of intelligence also exist in our universe right now. As for other universes outside our own, they remain for the moment beyond our capacity to see, since astronomers can view only so far as the horizon of our own universe – 42 billion light years away – that is, the distance that light has managed to travel since our own universe's beginning.

"Astronomers have recently found a planet with a livable climate for much of the year, and it is only 120 trillion miles away. Its solar system is similar to our own and there are many other such planets circling the stars. For that matter, our own Milky Way contains billions of planet patterns similar to our solar system.

"In any event, here on Earth, things evolved to ever more complex adaptive systems and our own genetic schemata emerged recently, about 50,000 years ago.

"Nature and God are not perfect but are good parents, opting where they can for the better way. They don't always get it right and the only thing that always changes for the better is an organism operating purely within its own environment. But when that organism comes to mix with others, the combination is a compromise and the less-than-perfect product pressing ahead does so in a long process of trial and error, with evolution eventually occurring.

"About 350 million years ago, evolution gave fish the power to hoist their scaly selves out of the water onto dry ground, and last year the 380-million-year-old skeleton of a creature, intermediate between fish and land animal, was found in the Canadian Arctic. We human beings have inherited a great deal from our ancestral fish and it was fish that first had heads with wiring in the skull and a mouth with teeth. Fish were also first to wear their senses such as sight in sets and have a body plan, with paired appendages, a backbone and vertebrated family tree. And fish were, yes, first to develop complex social systems, with principles to govern co-operation, reciprocity, policing and political supplications.

"Nature does not reinvent the wheel if the wheel works and the construction of the human heart is the same as that of an insect, and the human eye like that of a frog. But the long process of trial and error also means that nature makes mistakes – snakes occasionally grow legs when embryos, and whales can have bones that look like hind limbs. And if a purpose may be assigned to everything, I need help in understanding the role of Canada's mosquito.

"Around 250 million years ago, after a major die-off of most species on planet Earth, dinosaurs came to develop and flourish – to be joined 25 million years later by the first true mammals. Then 65 million years ago, an asteroid hit near the Yucatan Peninsula, eradicating all remaining dinosaurs, but it is only in the last six million years that the human and ape branches of the family tree have evolved from a common ancestor in Africa.

"A six-million-year-old ape body frame has been found in Chad, a five-million-year-old one in Kenya and a female ape named Ardi lived in Ethiopia, four-and-a-half million years ago. Ardi is a good view of the early evolution of human beings but many of Ardi's traits don't appear in living apes or human beings and as Darwin came to appreciate, the evolution of the ape and human lineages have been going on independently for some time.

"A million years after Ardi came Lucy, and a million years later again, or two-and-a-half million years ago, lived another African child who was one of the last ape-persons before the arrival of the person-ape but still long before the creation of labor-saving devices such as stone tools and a half-million years before the domestication of fire. Other ancestors have been found in Chad, Tanzania and South Africa but we still don't know whether they are candidate ancestors or, like Lucy, are parts of an evolutionary branch that withered and died. One thing that is clear, however, is that in the long progression of hominids over the last six million years, it is only in the last 200,000 that we *Homo sapiens* have emerged.

"Among us *Homo sapiens* there began, in the last 100,000 years, a spread of human beings out of Africa and a big split came between eastern and southern Africa. The easterners evolved to become agriculturalists and traders but their southern cousins remained hunters and gatherers, with virtually no exposure to farming or trade until a few hundred years ago, when invaded by European imperialists.

"An environmental crisis nearly extinguished *Homo sapiens* about 80,000 years ago, along with a big drought 60 - 70,000 years ago, speeding up the exodus from Africa. The Australian Aborigines were the first to venture beyond, making their way along the southern edge of Asia. Then people spread to Asia 60,000 years ago, Europe 40,000 and America 15,000 years ago.

"In Europe's case, Neanderthals had lived in areas such as Southern France for several hundred thousand years but when invaded by waves of *Homo sapiens*, the latter outnumbered the Neanderthals 10 to one and had more sophisticated technology and behavioral systems. A woman's statue, 40,000 years old, has been discovered in Germany, replacing the previous oldest of 25,000 years, found in Austria a century ago, and in a cave in France, there have been found multiple drawings done by human beings 32,000 years ago. The European Neanderthals soon came to be displaced to marginal areas and were doomed to a slow extinction.

"Not, however, before the Neanderthals left a key mark – a bit of hanky-panky between those ancestors and archaic humans helped build the immune systems that many of us enjoy today. That crossbreeding with Neanderthals likely occurred soon after modern humans left Africa, providing resistance to diseases present outside the Dark Continent. The earlier-arriving Neanderthals already had enough time to adapt to new viruses and it is notable that some of the gene variants widely distributed around the globe today are absent from most of Africa.

. "But our work is still at best extrapolation – we have recently found further evidence that some migrating *Homo sapiens* may have interbred with Neanderthals, leaving complete *Homo sapiens* only of African descent –

remnants in both Siberia and Indonesia have been found of not-quite-human species from a time 30 - 50,000 years ago. These recent findings illustrate again how fragmentary and ill-understood human history still is. But if we assume some accuracy in our educated guesses, then around the time of the second exodus from Africa some 60,000 years ago, we human beings also apparently reached a watershed in our brain development, though there is evidence that our brain has evolved more quickly during the last 37,000 and especially the last 5 - 15,000 years.

"About 12,000 years ago, before the start of agriculture, with human beings still living in small nomadic bands and foraging for plants and hunting wild animals, the world's oldest known temple was built in southeastern Turkey. Known as *Gobekli Tepe*, or "Potbelly Hill," it was a religious sanctuary but it had no villages or drinking water nearby, and could have been a mini-center for early pilgrimages.

"When agriculture started, with wild sheep and goats being the first livestock to be tamed about 11,000 years ago, and pigs and cattle in the next several thousand years, agriculture then made a giant leap forward, 8,000 years ago, with the invention of the plough. Although wild grain patches had earlier been protected by foragers, they were hard to harvest and true agriculture would not begin until human beings planted large new areas of mutated plants that did not shatter upon ripening, making a stationary plant source with an attendant population. Nomadic leaders became replaced by agricultural leaders and instead of going hunting, farmers stayed home to guard the wheat. With a food supply thus assured through agriculture, farmers' markets appeared and within a few thousand years, civilizations and cities sprang up, with societies becoming interlocked and jobs having specialties, roads being built and a monetary system being created.

"The agricultural revolution led to something else – we human beings started to live not naked with nature but instead in an envelope constructed out of that nature, and perhaps the human impulse to gather for sacred rituals arose as human beings shifted from seeing themselves as part of the natural world to their seeking mastery over it. Though earlier tribal societies had been making gods out of nature, and primitive religions included burial of the dead and visual art over tens of thousands of years, when tiny villages began to separate human beings from the animal world, that schism led to a change in consciousness, allowing human beings to imagine different gods and begin accordant pilgrimages.

"When the first farmer planted wheat, he also became slave to the concept of fertility, and the bible's Old Testament is riddled with the expression, 'be fruitful and multiply.' Organized religion then increased, as a constant celestial order was judged necessary to bind these new, fragile groups of humankind together. Those who rose to power were accordingly seen as having a special connection with the gods. The human sense of the sacred and love of a good spectacle also gave rise to civilization as did agriculture, but as for whether organized religion preceded farming or farming preceded organized religion, perhaps no single path led to civilization and it is rather a product of the complex human mind.

"About 3,000 years ago, a leader named Moses gave his followers 10 rules to live by, with enough width to afford a reasonable degree of freedom. But what we are left with today is a set of rules whose perversions have kept in power a band of tyrants."

Just then a woman lunged forward, and before any of us could stop her, she struck Chantelle's face with a hammer. Chantelle fell quickly before her attacker tore off toward Lake Michigan and left us all jaw-dropped at a fallen Chantelle. She was not moving.

Saturday May 5 2007

Chantelle lay asleep in Northwestern Hospital, after her cheekbone had been set back in place. I slept beside her in a chair, but at 6:00 a.m. she awoke and her first words were slurred. "Arthur, I need to phone my dad and tell him I'm fine and that I love him."

I left the room to allow Chantelle time to talk with her family and when I returned, she had propped herself up and was managing a faint smile. But then her face suddenly went serious. "Arthur, I have a confession to make."

I sat down and squeezed Chantelle's left hand before I looked into her eyes to signal my listening. She took a long breath. "When I was a young girl, I used to pray to a god who I was told was a He and was connected to a far-off pillared city called Rome. My mother was a thing of her place and time, my Dad was a drunk and my sister despised me, and I needed someone with whom to communicate. And so I chose that god. For much of my childhood, I fantasized that he was responding but I came to realize he was not even listening.

"For a time, I tried to communicate with the animals around the rocks of Lake Huron's Georgian Bay, but one day I frightened a rattlesnake and she bit me. I started the walk home but fell. An hour later, my drunken dad found me, saw the bite and lifted me onto his back to carry me the mile to the hospital. But Daddy also fell and passed out.

"There we were, both on the ground for another hour but when Daddy awoke, he again put me onto his back and staggered the rest of the mile to the hospital. My drunken daddy saved my life and has not drunk a drop since that day.

"In the years that followed, I talked with my dad and found a kind and wise person. Arthur, I can't tell you how much I love my father."

Chantelle then drifted back to sleep but around 7:00 a.m., she started to pour forth as if she were back on her speaking stand. "Each of us, when born, is totally dependent and sees the risk in breaking away, but also built into us is a wish to be free. Then, some time thereafter, life gives us two broad options and many of us get steered to more dependency, within a system whose authorities entice us with security at great cost to our curiosity, with lives run by the dictates of others. The children who come to result cannot appreciably see what is real, and their love becomes a response to a guise by tyrannical mothers. As for any love of God...Am I brain injured, Arthur?"

I bent forward and put both my hands on her shoulders. "I don't think so, Chantelle." Her hand gripped my arm above my wrist. "Their love of God flows out of that guise and..."

My face stayed close to hers on the bed and I peered into her eyes. "Your mother?" and Chantelle's head turned away. "If we don't break loose from our attachment to our mothers, we will never mature in our love of God."

I bent forward more toward her. "Do you feel the same can be said of a father?" and Chantelle turned back and looked right at me, "I can't say, Arthur."

My head reared back. "You can't?" and her eyes opened wide. "Jesus said we need to leave behind our mothers and fathers, for us to source our faith, but my mind is prejudiced, since I never thought a person could love another person as much as I love my dad."

My eyes dropped to a space beside the bed and I pondered how I too loved my father and of course my mother but I had never known the closeness of which Chantelle spoke. She must have picked up on my pause and perhaps sensed some hurt of my own, since she then said, "I like to keep learning and feel I can learn worlds from you, Arthur."

My eyes turned back to hers. "A hack architect?" and Chantelle's right hand grabbed my wrist. "You are creative, Arthur, and have a need to fulfill that drive within you. That need is healthy and I need to be close to people like you. I have spent considerable time with others who suffer for suffering's sake, and when I am near healthier minds of any sort, I try to glean from them to help me grow. When I am with you, Arthur, I sense your glow from helping others. Have you always known this part of yourself?"

I shrugged and looked up at the hospital room ceiling. "I have felt it but thought it was some sort of eradication for guilt."

Chantelle still had hold of my wrist. "Arthur, guilt is that suspect sentiment that we talked about, and redemption is a sinner's invention. When you, Arthur, feel guilty for doing the work of your paymaster's devil, your only error is shortsightedness. You deserve freedom, not just from the prostitution you describe but from that restricted view of yourself."

I wasn't sure I was ready to handle this wisdom from a head-injured patient lying in a hospital on a Saturday morning, but I also thought Chantelle was sounding better and, in any event, we were then rescued by a nurse with two breakfasts. "I hope I'm not disturbing, Doctor Fouriere.. Marty ordered your breakfast and our station put together a second for Mr. Franklin."

Chantelle smiled. "That's kind of you, Brenda, thank you." The nurse left but my eyebrows shot up and I gave Chantelle a long, puzzled look. "That nurse called you Doctor Fouriere" and she smiled back her apologetic smile. "I'm a medical doctor, Arthur, but for the moment in Chicago, I'm a nurse."

Chantelle sampled the hospital breakfast before she asked me to remove her tray, smiled at me a thank you and turned over to drift back to sleep. I toyed with my food for a bit but soon put Chantelle's and my trays in the hallway and then sat down next to the bed. I began sketching in my mind how to redo the windowpanes in a natural-colored wood and put a mural along the ceiling.

Near 9:00 a.m., Chantelle again awoke. "Arthur? I believe I'm missing work," but Nurse Brenda heard her and rushed into the room. "Not this weekend, Doctor Fouriere."

"Brenda, please call me Chantelle. May I go outside?" and the nurse gave her a gratifying smile. "Thank you, Chantelle, yes you may but I have been instructed to stay in view of you, all weekend."

I took my cue. "In that case, why don't the three of us take a taxi over to my place, freshen up, have some brunch and then do a slow Chicago?"

Brenda and Chantelle showered in my apartment while I started breakfast and then Brenda took over while I cleaned up. Around 11:00, we all sauntered over to Lake Michigan for a walk south to Milton Lee Olive Park to watch the sailboats and shortly thereafter, we enjoyed an hour in the Art Institute before we managed to secure three tickets for the Chicago Symphony at 2:00 p.m...That gave us time to have a swordfish plate at a Portuguese place that I knew off Huron, and with Chantelle off alcohol for the weekend, I did my duty and was forced to consume her share of the wine.

Around 7:00, we all got back to my apartment and Brenda, whose eyes had never left Chantelle, suggested she go to bed. Brenda sat down next to the bed with some hospital magazines and I wedged myself into the living-room loveseat to try *The Fountainhead* again.

Sunday was much the same but for the first weekend in three years since I'd started work, I did not go to the office. Chantelle and Brenda both commented on my being uptight across the day.

Monday May 7 2007

At 8:00 a.m., Brenda and Chantelle left my apartment and I charged to work but upon arrival, found all staff in the board room. Cork's whore spoke first. "So, we all now know Franklin doesn't do the hours he advertises. We tried to reach you on Saturday after you snuck out Friday, and the rest of us worked all weekend."

Cork intervened, perhaps to get me onside. "Arthur, it will take us 12 hours to wrap up the Hancock job. Trudi can order in sandwiches and maybe pizza for supper. We'll use your office, since you have an uncluttered table and mine is covered with invoices."

I worked the 12 hours, including four after lunch when Cork and Trudi disappeared and those four were the most productive ones spent. The other eight were spent listening to people's voices or staring at my trees and thinking how Chicago's summer of 2007 was going to be sticky. I had no feeling for the autumn to follow or for the winter of 2008.

For the next two weeks, I gave myself to Cork & Church, while Chantelle helped the hurt in Northwestern Hospital. She was to try speaking again at Buckingham Fountain on the Friday of the second week and I found myself hitting the gathering exactly at 7:00 p.m. and sitting down on the lawn to listen. But before Chantelle actually started, I noticed more to the front that same guy Hardy who had aggressively introduced himself to Chantelle when she was first meeting me. I recalled he had then sharply departed and I had not seen him since.

Friday May 18 2007

"*Reasoning Greeks thought the question* of first cause not worth much consideration and regarded the Garden of Eden as a Peter-Pan place of eternal childhood – the god of that garden was an omnipotent leader for all to follow and was thus a foil for people's fear of freedom. Freedom carried with it a sense of responsibility and was too heavy a burden to bear, so people could be drawn back into a parent-infant servility as projected by a creator-created duality. The authority thus conceived was almighty and could explain truth, wipe away sins and assure security.

"The Canaanites and Hebrews started their histories with the same god but the townspeople Canaanites moved to multiple gods with less than universal qualities, while the Hebrews brewed one god with infinite power. Those Hebrew forbears to Christianity became willing servants to a god created in their own chosen image, and the marketing priests were all too quick to deliver. At first, the god was officially forbidden to be thought of but he was really *el-Shaddai*, an old Semitic name, meaning 'He of the mountain.' The early Hebrews had looked down from a hill onto the lush land of Canaan and had called the high hill a mountain.

"The chosen god then reciprocated by making the choosers the chosen few and insisted on godly respect for one another within that chosen group. The concocted god-almighty said to its fabled leader Abraham, 'I have made a perfect man and now I need a perfect people. Other nations will vanish but Israel will survive and I, god, will determine all matters of war and peace, striking those who oppose. Take none of the evil women from the non-chosen but only the daughters of Israel, and if you fail, I will punish you with boils, plagues and leprosy. These things I do, not in hate for all other tribes but in my love for you, my chosen few. In the end, you will be better off because you will have stayed closer to your god.'

"Any time those god-followers were too stiff-necked or disobeyed him as judged by them, they were overrun by lesser tribes of say, Assyrians. At other times, the god-creating people had their priests hurl children under the age of three into fire pits, to the frenzy of drums and cheers from the crowd.

"The invented god was also territorial and did not want Adam having any breadth in his spiritual knowledge. Thus, when a curious Adam defied the people's chosen god, that god proved himself a sexual neurotic and made Adam and Eve feel unclean about their natural drive for sex. That god also came to portray a life of agricultural fulfillment as part of a painful punishment for breaking the rules, in a decadent heaven called Eden. The concocted god also paved the way for a spin on the consequences of sin, punishment, redemption and salvation to retrieve Eden, and the concept of sin itself presupposed a natural law and moral order, with little recognition of the 'high' given by the natural necessity of benevolence.

"Human beings can be lonely and need to be part of society, but if that society creates rules based on the concepts of guilt and punishment, those human beings are denied the will to self-responsibility. Done away with also is the freedom to explore, examine and reflect, with followers destined to be slaves to a savior who restricts instincts and curiosities, under the guise of forgiving and rescuing.

"Despite, however, the pounding in of tribal rules, some spiritual principles did emerge, and as our Jewish ancestors matured, so too did the god created in their image. The tyrant god of a flooded Earth, plagues and holocausts for questioning children gave way to a suffering servant by the time of the bible's Second Isaiah.

"Faith embraces self-assessment, risk and adventure, not tautologically expressed certainties and the freedom for such faith should be of the same primary concern as eating, drinking, shelter and sexual fulfillment."

Saturday May 19 2007

On the following day in the early evening, Chantelle and I had fallen into blissful love-making and afterward I was stretched out nude along the loveseat, with my feet draped over the end. I was sipping cognac and stroking her hair.

Chantelle was also nude, sitting on the hardwood floor, propped up against the loveseat. Neither of us was saying a word and the silence lasted for about half an hour, giving me time to pour myself another cognac. When I resettled, Chantelle looked up at me with a dark face. "Arthur, it's odd for a Jew to drink as you do."

I tipped my drink in a mock toast. "Back 5,000 years ago, we Jews couldn't handle it, any time we wandered off around the spice route, and the rabbis got upset and told us that alcohol was a *goyim* poison we should not drink. Later, Russian tsars caught onto the ploy and used alcohol to placate the masses as did the Leninists. English landowners gave their serfs gin as did the robber barons, when serfs new to the city got their first cash and rarely made it home past the gin stalls. Sunday was negotiated as a day of rest to let the factory workers dry out, before they went back to slave labor on Monday, and the churches saw a dry Sunday as a boon to business. Gorbachev's downfall was in great part due to his effectively closing many of Russia's alcohol factories."

Chantelle stayed silent on the floor and was looking ahead but finally uttered something that should have disturbed me more, were it not for the cognac in me. "Arthur, I think it is time for me to go back to my job." I had no idea that she meant Canada and blurted out, "If you feel your patients…"

I did not see Chantelle the day after on the Sunday and got caught up on work. But on Monday, I was devastated to learn she had resigned from Northwestern Hospital and was scheduled to address her fellow workers on the following day.

Tuesday May 22 2007

"More than any other animal, we human beings have brains that acquire knowledge by exercising intellect rather than instinct, and inside that intellect, the most complex process is creative thinking. It seems we need a contradiction between an established way and a perceived need for much creative thinking, and a novel idea requires not only a broadness of understanding but also a negative insight.

"A few dedicated people, this year in 2007, are trying to chart out a book of life, the objective being not to produce human hybrids but to help us see how our bodies take shape. From that chart, we will someday be able to appreciate how a single-cell organism develops into what Darwin described as endless forms, all beautiful and wonderful.

"We are now at a time when we may develop a unified theory of all particles and forces in nature, and the solution to the universe may flow out of determining how those particles work. But we need to keep in mind that we are calculating only probabilities, with most mutations being not by need but chance. Probabilities and not certainties are all that quantum mechanics allows us, and even our going-in assumptions are not always constant. One schema superseding another constitutes only our moving to a new school of thinking and we still can find earlier schema useful in some circumstances – many an architect falls back on Newtonian principles for making preliminary calculations.

"As our world rushes forward, we can lust for a moment's still shot of regularities in order to compress them into theories, and we find tempting the thought of supplying missing pieces. But we must maintain an intellectual integrity that allows us to acknowledge that our theories are always falsifiable. We also must recognize that what we see at first glance is at best a coarse graining and our inner eye is prejudicially selective of details. What we thus see is not to be confused with anything beyond a superficial understanding of it, and if at any time we lose that intellectual integrity, we can deny real regularities and impose false ones, producing a contrived order that gives us only a cathartic comfort of illusion. An up-front lie can be woven into a complex system of sequelae that are all fraudulent, and they come to

53

embrace a whole hierarchy of mini-beliefs, ever reinforced by social directives. Myths then come to evolve as models and we string the whole hierarchy of beliefs and social directives together with ritual. We thus become vulnerable to theatrics, and in our exhausting time-short world, can be easily
taken by histrionics.

"Spiritual development involving truth, love and confidence precedes
physical and intellectual development, and if our spirituality is structured
upon false premises, we cannot glean the means to gauge truths. Ultimately,
we spiritually perish and our intellectual and physical integrity fall not far
behind.

"It is depressing how soon we shelve the fact that we were fooled four
years ago with talk of Iraq's weapons of mass destruction and are now being
told another demonization story on Iran. Almost a generation ago, Ronald
Reagan had the honeyed delivery of well-aged scotch, and we became intox-
icated with his talk of small government while he cut taxes, raised defense
spending, borrowed heavily and sent the world into the greatest economic
recession since the 1930s. Now there is talk in 2007 of its repeat in the year
to come.

"Science is not a threat to spirituality but science can have its purpose
perverted and its goal can become a source of power for abuse. The first loss
is truth and the second is moral imagination and without the one, there cannot be the other.

"Libraries in ancient Egypt and Sumer, that is Iraq, may have documented 5,000 years ago the progress of human beings for the previous
40,000. Much is lost but there remains hard data to support the probability
that a modern world civilization flourished more than 5,000 years earlier or
before 10,500 BC.

"The number 72 relates to an astronomical phenomenon called the precession of the equinoxes, and it is found in the dimensions of ancient structures around the world. Precession refers to the slow, cyclical wobble of the
Earth's axis and the visible position of all stars in the sky. The precessional
cycle is one degree every 72 years and precession is a process that has been
the physical reality governing many myths coming down to us from remote
antiquity.

"Ancient megaliths still existing around the world today share engineering techniques that could have been carried out only with the help of advanced astronomy. A full 40 of the Giza Pyramids duplicate a constellation of 10,500 BC, when the shape of the Nile corresponded to that of the Milky Way. Either they were built around 10,500 BC or during the thousands of years thereafter, with the knowledge and precision instruments of astronomy. The astronomical dating of the Sphinx, thought to have been erected in 2,500 BC, is that same 10,500 BC, as it is for the monumental edifices in Cambodia, erected just 1,000 years ago. This astronomical process is also repeated in Mexico, the Andes, the Pacific's Easter Islands and Japan.

"Ancient Bolivian ruins have blocks weighing hundreds of tons but were transported to almost three miles above sea level, and even if thousands of slaves were used, they could not have achieved such a feat. Instead, it would have required a high level of mechanical sophistication. Ancient Bolivian clamps, moreover, made use of an alloy that was part nickel but there is no nickel in Bolivia. In other parts of South America, there are drawings of animals that were already extinct before that pivotal period of 10,500 BC.

"There is a solid possibility that these giant structures from ancient civilizations all refer back to a common source that was a highly mechanical iron age, with fabled white-skinned men existing more than 12,000 years ago or before 10,500 BC. In 1992, in the state of Washington, was discovered a 9,000-year-old skull that was Caucasian.

"It seems possible that these Sphinx-like clues were part of a grand scheme trying to communicate over thousands of years to bring about the rebirth of a world that had been washed away in a flood. In our current era's 17th century and the English Renaissance, pioneer Francis Bacon was trying to complete a book, New Atlantis, before he died, and he spoke of a college of wise men who knew of a formerly advanced society with airplanes and submarines, and were endeavoring to carry forward an enlightenment of the world after the flood. And it just may be that the Pyramids were not tributes to the megalomania of egotistical pharaohs but gestures of spiritual immortality for all people via enlightenment. When the Giza Pyramids were opened up in the ninth century AD, no pharaohs were found.

"Our planet Earth's last ice age lasted 100,000 years and when it receded 11,000 years ago, or 9,000 BC, there were huge floods, triggered by an almost 400-foot rise in the earth's oceans. It is intriguing that so many of our world's ancient civilizations have myths built upon ancient floods. The legendary founder of India was counseled pre-flood to build a giant survival ship and load it with two of every living species, along with the seeds of every plant, and then board the boat himself. His ship was to be an ark that would have to undergo torment for many days and nights until it came to rest on the slopes of a high mountain.

"Ancient texts often interpret a symbolic rebirth and renewal behind a cosmic cycle. In the texts of ancient Egypt, whose first time is again that 10,500 BC, we see the sources of some of our own Judeo-Christian stories. Egypt's prime god was 'Atum' and Egypt was judged as god's chosen land, on which the gods deigned to sojourn. As for Egypt's 42 negative confessions, upon which each person was to be evaluated on judgment day, number four was 'I have not stolen,' number five 'I have not slain man or woman,' 19 'I have not defiled the wife of a man' and 38 was 'I have not cursed God.'

"Perhaps the seven universal deadly sins – anger, greed, envy, jealousy, lust, sloth and the number one pride – pre-date the commonality between Egypt's 42 negative confessions and Israel's later Ten Commandments. It is worth pondering that the seven deadly sins may originate in a pre-flood world civilization dating back over 12,000 years to at least 10,500 BC. If such universal values govern all of planet Earth today, maybe they will do so again after climate change causes the Arctic to melt and our oceans to flood."

On Wednesday May 23, Chantelle was back in her old Toronto job, specializing in problem newborns. It would be more than a year before she spoke again south of the border.

Friday June 22 2007

There must have been a dozen apostles who slipped into Chicago that June. Several drew audiences of 100 or more but Terry Hardy was the name most often mentioned among the followers. People felt comfortable with what he said and his European accent lent a sense of mystery as if he were privy to a worldly knowledge he would kindly share. But something about the way he had intruded, when I'd first met Chantelle, said Hardy had an agenda that I wanted to expose, and one Saturday afternoon in late June, I broke off work early to hear what he was going to say in Grant Park.

I discovered that Chantelle's portable stand had been replaced by a stage and a microphone, and as things got underway there was a bit of jostling going on at center stage, but Hardy was standing off to the side and had that same stone face that I remembered from first meeting him. For several minutes, it did not seem certain who was in fact to be the speaker but then a competitor was whisked off stage and several of his supporters were escorted away from the front of the audience.

Such heavy-handedness was witnessed by some in the audience, and a rumor started circulating that secret service people had permeated the gathering. Some people were thus uneasy about what was to follow but a steady Terry Hardy then came forward toward the microphone, and all eyes looked to the one taking over.

Soon any rumor murmuring was lulled by Hardy's reassurances to his listeners. He came off as a learned internationalist speaking to us as adults, making all the apostles of earlier evenings look adolescent. Terry Hardy spoke for an easy-to-grasp 12 minutes and I soon found myself nodding to the thrust of what he was saying. When he finished, the applause was responsive and I darted back to my apartment to relay the good news to Chantelle.

There was no answer, not even a machine and so I composed an e-mail in praise of Terry Hardy, trying as best I could to glean the essence of his talk.

Spiritual reality in this 21st century appears a mess. The scarecrows we created to keep evil spirits away now scare us themselves, and a full century after Einstein's discovery, our minds stay uncomfortable with randomness or infinity...

Chaos may be the reality but we need for the sake of manageability to choose from the information bombarding us and shape that chaos into some semblance of order. Observations have to stand still long enough for us to create premises and comprehensible phenomena...

It is a Himalayan challenge for us to face truth without panic and not despair from earlier disillusionment, while trying to derive meaning from where we are. Perhaps we need the growing pain of forlornness before we reconcile with freedom, and in that growing pain come to appreciate that disillusionment must come before wisdom...

Organized religion is a marketplace of social pressures, and adherence to a creed for social reasons gives us a suspect orientation. Organized religion with ecclesiastical bureaucracies restricts freedom and attracts people with authoritarian characters, offering a security at the expense of integrity. People who have not emerged from the dependency of childhood identify with that authority and can choose slavery in a system of quick fixes for psyches wanting answers to effortless questions...

The spiritually restricted people crave miracles and thus confuse cause and effect. If ritual disappeared, those restricted people would have to reinvent it. People also worn out by worry and injustice want a god to fall down to, in a begging for quick relief, with the people declaring, 'Make us your slaves but feed our needs.' But that god is a lie and if we follow him, we lose self-respect and respect for others, and we see no point in telling the truth.

Rather than blindly abide by creeds and handed-down ethics, we need to graduate from such dependency and see those codes as merely part of the input for a lifelong search into spirituality. We need to look to our consciences and see the god within each of us, ready to help. God gave us those consciences as part of our searching minds, and it is imprisoned thinking to condemn such realization as an act of pride. Quite the contrary – it takes humility to free us from childhood dreams of both omniscience and omnipotence, and it requires further humility to cast aside our fear-founded prejudices and develop an open respect for facts, in our ongoing quest for meaning.

The greatest leap forward can come from some harmony achieved between conscious religious states and unconscious religious influences. Let us therefore assess our institution's religion – does it purge childish wishes or oppress them – and in concert with our lifelong process of rebirth and reawakening, let those institutions themselves undergo the same kind of self-reassessment.

Spirituality is at the core of our struggle for wholeness, and the earnestness with which we assess our spiritual progress is an indicator of its strength – what feels bad within us will heal from our very recognition of it. Faith does not spring from the miracle but a miracle can come from faith in that god inside us all.

I sent the e-mail and felt so good about having done so that I went back to work to finish a project I had been working on. But when I reached the office, I found recruit Kasia rustling through some papers on her desk and after a moment's hello, left her desk to go back to my office. Two hours later as the time reached 9:00 p.m., I was preparing to leave and discovered Kasia still there. The nubile, young architect looked at me with a wry smile and popped me a half-question, "Arthur Franklin, alone again on a Chicago Saturday night? I thought *I* was boring."

I offered a shrug. "I'm into my work these weeks, Kasia, and my friend went back to Canada."

Kasia gave a coy smile. "Just a friend?" and I clarified, "A dear, close friend," but Kasia would not be assuaged. "Well, so that neither of us gets too dull or lonely, why don't we have a nightcap down at the Drake?"

The sip of California red made my cheeks pucker and as I swallowed more, Kasia must have seen my face brighten. "Do you plan to work away the entire summer, Arthur?"

Again I clarified. "The firm is a pressure cooker right now, Kasia, and my role is to whip through the small projects to keep the cash flow going, while Cork & Church ride out the coming recession. Church himself is trying to schmooze through some big project in Seattle but nothing has yet materialized, so for the short term, it looks like I'm going to be beating the heat, working seven days a week in our air-conditioned office."

Kasia's blouse was casually unbuttoned near the top and her skirt had visibly risen, with her sitting erect on the padded bar stool. "And your friend? Do you plan any vacation, this summer?" I tried again to be clear. "I may, sometime in the fall, or around Hanukkah and Christmas. She too is plowed into her work but we take time each week to touch base."

Kasia's skirt rose even higher as we finished glass three and she rested her hand on my thigh. "Arthur, can anyone help you to feel less lonely? It is going to be a long, hot summer."

I had that knack for sabotaging such opportunities but maybe my next words were meant to maintain my loyalty to Chantelle. "And I with an un-air-conditioned apartment."

I held myself in check that night but confess that, one Sunday near the end of summer and again in the air-conditioned office alone with Kasia, I did not.

For the most part, though, I was a bore through the summer of 2007. I worked, swam and read, and though I never again attended a gathering of the apostles, I heard stories of their plans for expansion into America's northeast and northwest. I heard also of the death of one apostle, caused by some followers of Terry Hardy. But I chose not to tell Chantelle, out of sensitivity for her.

The American real estate bubble did pop and there was a staggering mortgage crisis that broke across the entire United States. Building contracts ground to a halt but Cork & Church did manage to land the Seattle project and I spent all September and half of October working on it there. Seattle I found somehow Canadian – I liked the micro-brews and the chats in British pubs, and I almost did not want to come back to Chicago for the end of October.

Wednesday October 31 2007

Dear Arthur,

I would love it if you could come to my 26th birthday party on December 31. I want to see my dad and he does not go to Toronto. Dad is planning a quiet celebration for me in Penetanguishene.

Love,

Chantelle

The thought of seeing Chantelle in a crisp, cold, sunny Canada over the Christmas break gave me a lift that I had suppressed since she'd left. Suddenly I felt again I was embarking on a voyage of self-awakening.

Saturday December 22 2007

Before dawn, the vintage TVR managed to crank up in the cold and I departed a Chicago free of snow. Months earlier Kasia had given me a CD of what she'd determined was Canadian, and it was *A Country Collection* by Anne Murray. Classical music was more to my liking but in it went to psych me up during the dawn hours on the way to Detroit and the Canadian border. I listened to the CD four times, and after the first run-through, found myself singing back to the disc,

> *Out of a sky of silver, snowflakes begin to fall...*
> *oh, that sad old wintry feeling,*
> *I don't really seem to mind,*
> *that sad but sweet old wintry feeling,*
> *it seems to suit me fine.*

After crossing from Detroit into Canada, I sped northeast 250 miles to the edge of Toronto, then cut north and northwest for 100 miles, finally coming to a stop on Lake Huron's Georgian Bay in Chantelle's town of Penetanguishene. Her mother was first to come out and she eyeballed me from head to toe, the way my mother used to do when passing judgment on me as a child. Then Chantelle's mother yelled to her husband Pantel, while daughter Roxanne held fixed in the living room, watching, I could hear, a rerun of *Dallas*.

Suddenly Chantelle surprised me by arriving behind from the bus station and as I turned to greet her with open arms, Pantel reached the front porch and Chantelle's face beamed. She set down her laptop on which he had been working on the bus, ran to the little man and I have never seen a parent and child give each other such a long and loving hug. I then got my turn before I shook a happy father's greeting hand.

Pantel carried my small bag into the house but before he could introduce me to mother Camille, she shot a question about the sleeping plans and the question yanked Roxanne away from the TV long enough for her to come and gawk at me. Like her mother, Roxanne was buxom and she had a weathered look going well beyond the five years separating her and Chantelle. Roxanne was also overweight and I surmised resigned at age 31 to living in her parents' home, watching TV reruns.

Pantel must have sensed the tension and suggested he and I could take the two singles that Chantelle and her sister used to sleep on, and Roxanne could crash with her mother. Chantelle liked to wander the woods at night with her camera, anyway; so, she could use a sleeping bag in the living room.

I never did get introduced to Roxanne and after she went back to her TV, Chantelle, her dad and I moved to the kitchen and some chairs around a small table for some local apple juice. Camille took up a stance, a few paces away with her body against the fridge and arms folded in a defiant position. The tension came back but then Pantel gave me an endearing smile. "Arthur, I started off for Chicago once in 1966. I was 18 and even more of a fool than I am now. I'd read about a couple of famous Indians and wanted to be like them."

I suddenly felt more welcome. "And, when you reached Chicago, Pantel?" He waved his hand. "Didn't. When I reached Toronto, my friend's old Dodge died, we sold it for scrap and then drank the proceeds. A couple of days later, some Toronto policemen suggested that my drinking buddy and I head back north, and I haven't been that far south of Penetang for 40 years. Chantelle tells me about it in her visits home."

Sunday December 23 2007

Pantel cooked the next day's breakfast while mother Camille slept in, on her day off work. "You'll have to excuse my ignorance, Arthur. Is peameal bacon a problem for you?" and I looked askance. "Peameal?"

Pantel half-turned from the gas stove. "Sorry, I think you call it Canadian bacon, like calling rye 'Canadian' on 'Detroyit' hockey broadcasts."

I chuckled. "Thank you, Pantel. I love that kind of bacon," but gave a further look. "Detroyit?" and Chantelle caught my chuckle. "Arthur, you've gotta learn our lingo – Detroit has three syllables."

I tried to counter-punch by showing off my Canadiana: "Hoser English, where every tenth word is 'eh'?" but Chantelle retorted, "Not sure we can graduate you that far, since you don't have a tuque, lumberjack jacket, moth-eaten shirt, wool underwear, 'worky' socks and unlaced construction boots."

I grinned and waved my hand to the kitchen ceiling. "I know, tuque, not wool hat, and you put window cleaner on your French fries," but Chantelle pointed, "Vinegar on our chips."

I smiled and raised both brows. "Then what do you call those things in a bag?" and Chantelle's hand gave the wave of a wand. "One also calls them 'chips,' short for potato chips."

I caught Pantel's smile and turned to face him as I asked Chantelle, "How then can you, sorry, one, tell the difference, or is this one of the mysteries?" and Chantelle went back to pointing, "No, Arthur 'this' is a pronominal adjective."

I smirked and turned my head toward Chantelle. "Yes, yes, and it's 'really quickly' not 'real fast,'" but Chantelle came back, "Not quite – 'it' is a pronoun and you are not to be pissed at my corrections but pissed off, because 'pissed' in the true north means drunk."

At that moment, I had my face on Pantel but shot back at Chantelle, "Great White North, I heard. And I don't have my hoser case of two-four," but Camille then interjected, "White North! We have colored people up here. They come up from Jamaica to pick our apples before they raise hell in the bars. Worse than the Indians."

The room went silent and without thinking, I turned to Camille to let her explain herself but Chantelle intervened, "We still have Chelsea buns and peanut butter and jam, and we don't award political points for dropping the 'g' from gerunds."

I sat back in my kitchen chair and grinned. "I know, and it's 'university' not 'college' and schedule, pronounced *shedule,* does not mean you're drunk."

Chantelle looked to be at home with her dad. "We don't have bums except to sit on and an ass is someone who makes a fool of herself. And please don't swap your hands when using a knife and fork, and you didn't win the War of 1812 or there would be no Canada."

Pantel grinned. "But thank you for burning Toronto," and Chantelle kept jabbing, "Bell invented the phone here, not Boston, and we invented insulin, the in-field blood unit, a way of creating stem cells and the world guidelines for stem-cell research."

I tried to stay mindful that I was a guest but could not resist: "Not to mention the donut, snowmobile and bloody Caesar" and Chantelle held on, "Okay, two points, but only if you spell the word *doughnut.* True, we've absorbed more American culture since the 1969 movie *Easy Rider* when Dennis Hopper gave the finger to a redneck. We used to use the thumb for 'fuck off' but now have come to use the finger for 'fuck you.'"

Pantel suddenly lost his smile. "Chantelle, how much sleep did you get last night?" but her response was unexpected. "I hope to go out with Budd Hudson's old Leica tonight, Dad. Arthur, this morning I would like to take you over to a resurrected hamlet established by the French in the early 1600s."

An hour later, at the shrine of Sainte-Marie among the Hurons, I came to feel life as lived among Canadian Indians and French monks, 400 years earlier, but as Chantelle and I began to leave, my eyes looked up and I saw afar atop a big hill a huge white building that looked like Neuschwanstein, the mad castle of Bavaria. "What on earth is that, Chantelle?"

Chantelle halted and put her hands on her hips. "The Roman cathedral whose rulers kicked me out for trying to become a priest. People pay pilgrim- ages to it from as far away as Buffalo." She pointed. "You have to climb those huge rows of steps to get up to it, with your eyes always forced to look up, in presumed awe at the temple, halfway to heaven. Pope John Paul visited it."

I turned my head to the young woman I had grown to love. "Chantelle, are you ever afraid of there being a price on your head?" and she smiled as we began walking off. "Swimming helps as does helping others. After that, I am usually too sleepy."

Monday December 24 2007

The day before Christmas, church bells began to ring around suppertime and they penetrated every home in the village. Mother Camille and Roxanne went to church and Chantelle went out for some more nature, abandoning us again with her camera. Pantel made a fire and he and I took to staring at it while doing nothing.

After a time, Pantel suddenly broke the silence. "Arthur, I didn't know what to give you for Christmas. We have only one Jew in the area, up in Midland, and he didn't know either...Merry Christmas, Arthur."

Little Pantel stuck out his right hand and shook mine. In his left was a small bowl of German shaving cream that he'd had gift-wrapped in the Midland Jew's drugstore.

I took the gift and bowed my head, then looked back up at this father of Chantelle. "Pantel, thank you and Merry Christmas." I gave the little man a hug.

Tuesday December 25 2007

Cruising north from Midland to Parry Sound alongside the tall pines and round rocks of Georgian Bay is one of life's mini-vacations, even with a Roxanne. She had wanted a ride to the small city of North Bay to visit a man she'd met, and Chantelle had wanted me to see Temagami, and so on Christmas Day, the three of us wedged into the tiny TVR, with Roxanne and Chantelle taking shifts between the passenger seat and a tight space up the middle. We had all bathed.

After a short while, plus-sized Roxanne squeezed into the middle gave out a snarl, "Any music in this pillbox?" and I replied, "I don't have a radio but the CD has one Anne Murray."

Chantelle, who was pressed to edge of the passenger seat to give more room, managed to perk up. "Roxanne sings, Arthur! She sang for years in that cathedral we saw" but Roxanne snorted back, "Five, to be exact."

I veered my head back and asked in a moderating voice, "Did you study music, Roxanne?" and she huffed back, "No, I sang as backup behind Chantelle. She was lead singer in a Penetang choir, after taking piano from the town lesbo," and Chantelle again tried to placate. "Roxanne went on to make beautiful sounds in the cathedral," but Roxanne would have none of it. "While Chantelle dissected frogs in Toronto."

I thought it was time to referee. "I don't think my car has room for a cat-fight. Do you still sing, Roxanne?" and her voice suddenly softened. "I haven't, Arthur, for several years."

I held my eyes on the road but my ears caught the softening. "You have a captive audience. Go for it!" and she sharpened again a little, "…Verdi, Chicago boy?" and I smiled a wide grin. "Verdi, Canadian lady."

From her squeezed position through the middle of the tiny TVR, Roxanne spread her arms, entire width of the sports car, and began, *"Liber scriptus proferetur, In quo totum continetur."* She then burst into a round sound, almost too much for the little car to contain, *"Unde mundus judicetur…"*

After an hour cruising north along Georgian Bay, we turned right and wound northeast for 50 miles toward the village of Sundridge. The rolling hills and winding road were fun in the road-sucking TVR.

We arrived at Sundridge, sitting on the 1,000-mile-long Highway 11 yet still 40 miles south of North Bay, and so we decided not to impose on Roxanne's friend at suppertime and stopped instead at Sundridge's Caswell Hotel. Roxanne and I embarked on three hours of drinking Canadian beer, with Chantelle remaining in the room, watching some public-television program on stained-glass windows.

The Caswell Hotel had a long, maple-tree bar, and Roxanne and I took stools instead of a table as if to avoid eye contact. For a long while, we did not say much but the silence got easier to take as the beer went down. Around hour three, a bloated Roxanne staggered out and up the three flights to the hotel room.

As the time then drifted past 11:00 p.m., I swung sideways on my barstool to check out the people left in the pub and noticed a few Canadian hosers playing pool, along with one bearded man sitting off in an unlit corner beside a small round drinking table. A woman with him had long gone and the man was alone. He looked in the dim light to be dressed in a soiled beige parka and appeared to be in his 60s, with a face looking from a distance to betray decades of alcohol. At any rate, with the amount of swill in me, I decided that he looked interesting and ambled over with my beer to introduce myself.

The man went by the name of Lighthouse and Lighthouse had completed a master's degree in marine transportation at the University of British Columbia in 1969, after which he had spent a year traveling through the Hawaiian out-islands to New Zealand, before going all across Australia in an old Volkswagen camper. A year later he had re-entered school but his doctorate had been cut short by his participation in the Vancouver hippiedom of the early '70s.

Later, Lighthouse had been for a time in charge of all marine logistics along the British Columbia coast but had lost the job and had then begun a downward progression of social mobility, first with a job from 1970 to 1976 as captain of a cruise boat between Seattle and Canada's Victoria, then as crew member before being demoted to more junior jobs on the same ship. Finally, Lighthouse had been terminated and he had spent most of the last five years doing his best to keep the Caswell pub afloat with his intake of

Canadian suds. I did not ask him if the name "Lighthouse" had its roots in his years as seadog or in the red glow radiating from his nose.

We came to talk a lot about god knows what, and the last time I recall turning around to check the front door and think about Chantelle was around midnight – I was more comfortable looking through the dim light and past Lighthouse's nose to a window overlooking Lake Bernard beyond. At some point I tried to start up a subject that I judged dear to the heart of Canadians but Lighthouse waved me off. "No, Arthur, I don't follow hockey anymore, ever since a great player sold out to Hollywood and the Stanley Cup became directed by show business and the hope of a holy grail from an American TV network."

I dared to probe. "You don't like us Americans, Lighthouse?" and he looked off balance in his answer. "Sorry, it's just…are you Jewish, Arthur?"

Chantelle suddenly walked into the pub, over to me in the corner but it was too dark for me to see the sadness in her face. She did not sit down. "Arthur, one of the reasons for the unjust resentment of Jewish people has been their wisdom in dealing early on with the demon, alcohol."

I was not ready to be impressed. "Voltaire said one needs to push life to its extremes," but she would not have it. "Alcohol builds, Arthur, insidiously and cunningly. Setting aside those poor people born chemical alcoholics, others I have seen drink to wash over a problem, before they come to a point where the drinking takes over and shifts from symptom to the primary illness."

To my surprise, Lighthouse jumped in with a gravelly voice, "You're right, my dear, and for some of us, that's the way we want life to stay. In 10 years, I'll be dead but for those precious 10, I believe life is better drunk than sober. I don't want to see life except through French impressionistic eyes – I've seen enough of reality and want each night to spill out of this spot with enough stuff left to stumble over the snow, home. The front door is unlocked, so I don't have to worry about a key, and then I pass out."

Lighthouse got up and started toward the door, and Chantelle and I followed, with her watching Lighthouse as he ambled up the village street. As for me, I struck out for the third floor and collapsed onto the first bed inside the door beside a snoring Roxanne.

The next day, the three of us cruised north on Highway 11 past South River, over Trout Creek and into the little city of North Bay, where we had all assumed Roxanne's drop-off would be prompt. But suddenly, we had to endure the hospitality of a pasty-faced host in an overheated apartment. His boom-box was overrunning all talk and while the TV was soundless, it was locked on a weather channel that dominated all visuals in the apartment. Finally, at mid-morning, the four of us, sitting in over-soft furniture, began taking in gobs of lasagna but 12 noon did eventually come and a circumspect Chantelle rose to thank the host.

Chantelle and I then began a cruise up into a hilly coniferous land, north of Southern Ontario. We were headed for Temagami, land of eastern North America's only virgin forest.

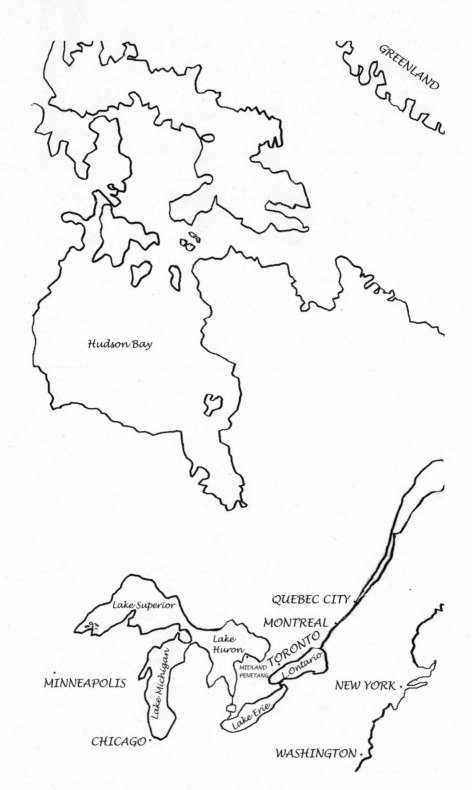

GREENLAND

Hudson Bay

Lake Superior

QUEBEC CITY

MONTREAL

Lake
Huron

TORONTO

MINNEAPOLIS

Lake Michigan

MIDLAND
PENETANG

L. Ontario

NEW YORK

CHICAGO

Lake Erie

WASHINGTON

Wednesday December 26 2007

As Chantelle and I ventured north, we were going vertically up and as the deciduous trees began to fade away, the whole scene came to look like millions of Christmas trees, stippling the white hills all around. The road was clear but the snow high and white, white beyond a white I had ever seen. The sky was powder blue, the clouds were cumulous-of-fair-weather and were it not for trucks grinding down from somewhere north, I would have guessed Santa Claus to be just above the next hill.

Fifty miles north of North Bay, I had to ask. "Chantelle, I've seen the Canadian Rockies and they are magnificent…" I then turned my head to her. "Where are you taking us?" She smiled at the scene. "Temagami, Arthur. Yes, the Rockies are breathtaking but Temagami is a gentler kind of poetry."

A hundred miles north of North Bay, we reached a sign that pointed to Lake Temagami, 15 miles to the west and when we reached the lake, we were told the ice was strong enough to support our car. We drove across frozen water for almost two miles before we came to a stop at an island lodge. After checking in with a cheery-faced host, we spent the rest of the afternoon exploring the island before having a lovely supper of northern pike and vegetables and then making love in our one-room cabin.

Next morning, Chantelle took me by foot in the cold, clear air over another two miles of frozen lake until we reached Temagami Island and one of the old growth trails. "Arthur, there have been two times in my life when I feel I have almost touched God and both times have occurred with trees. Once was with the giant redwoods of Lady Bird Johnson Park, north of San Francisco, and the second happened right here on the snow, underneath these 300-foot trees, all 800 years old.

"God and Bach are what I felt. Bach, father of 20 children, father of so much. I sensed heaven in the trees, the lake, the ice-age rocks and the white snow, and the trees reached up as if in joy, singing to me of Bach,

> *Mache dich, mein Herze, rein, Ich will Jesum selbst begraben.*
> *Denn er soll nunmehr in mir. Für und Für. Seine süße Ruhe haben.*
> *Welt, geh aus, laß Jesum ein!*

Make my heart pure, I would Jesus bury.
For he shall find in me sweet repose his dwelling.
World, depart and let Jesus in.

"Tinges of that feeling have never left. God is my creator and catalyst, and gives me both the freedom and tools to make or break myself, while I take life as far as I can. Thereafter as I approach some limit, faith in God takes over and carries me on."

To sneak a peek at another old growth, we had to drive across Lake Temagami to an area named Red Squirrel Road where the trees were being logged, and my Illinois plates may have been enough reason for one logger to try driving us off the road. Only the dexterity of my TVR saved us from a frozen ditch and I could not hold my tongue: "Chantelle, your North certainly does have its share of rednecks!" and she came back fast with, "As does your Bible Belt, Arthur." For a moment, I was not sure how to respond but she then stretched her long arm around my shoulders. When I settled a bit, I turned to Chantelle and told her I loved her. She smiled the same smile that I remembered from the Chicago coffee house, the night I had met her.

I wanted more of northern Ontario and Chantelle, but had to drop her back at her childhood home on December 31, the Monday of her birthday. Then I shot down to Toronto and veered southwest for a fast four hours to Detroit and on to Chicago. Chantelle later went home at a gentler speed on the bus with her laptop, the 100 miles to Toronto.

When I got to Chicago, it was early New Year's Eve and I decided to wander over to the Loop. I had intended to phone Chantelle at midnight and wish her Happy New Year but after the eight-hour drive and subsequent bottle of wine, I sauntered back to my flat before midnight and collapsed.

The record winter of 2008 wore on, until the first day of spring coincided with Good Friday, and Chantelle was to chair a free seminar. On the Thursday night prior, I bolted out of Chicago and slept that night at a B&B in Windsor, Ontario, across the river from Detroit. Then I got up at 5:00 a.m. to a farmer's breakfast, before I bolted the 250 miles northeast to Toronto, arriving just after morning rush hour at 9:30.

Friday March 21 2008

Chantelle and I hugged for so long that had there been any diffidence felt from our being apart, it disappeared as I sensed again a tenderness I had almost forgotten possible. But the morning seminar meant we did not have time for any further intimacy and in short order were walking hand in hand, the one mile west to the University of Toronto's Knox College. As we crossed Queen's Park, Chantelle paused to hug an oak tree she said was a mentor

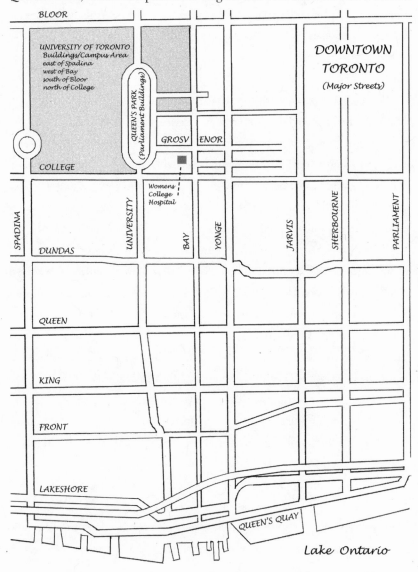

and then she started waxing about how the ancient Greeks had worshiped trees. At that moment, the thought crept into my mind that my beloved Chantelle could be ponderous but before I allowed any further fruition on that thought, I whisked us off to the campus.

Knox College was a castle of Scottish stone masonry, squared around a quadrangle, with a stone walkway running through the middle and dividing the quadrangle into two broad lawns of like size. The walkway was 12 feet high and had an arched ceiling of sculpted stone that draped down each side into eight cut-stone pillars, punctuated at disciplined intervals. Interspersed between the pillars were stone outlinings that could have held stain-glass windows but instead of there being windows, the frames were open to the air.

The walkway itself was of crushed stone and wide enough to allow for the thirty or so oak chairs set up that morning toward its eastern side, at the place where Chantelle was to facilitate the seminar. Participants were to have read some material beforehand but as with most gatherings involving topics of a non-credit nature, few would have done much in the way of preparation, and that reality left a few keeners to dominate the process. Chantelle made some opening remarks:

"In 1896, a manuscript of the Gospel of Mary Magdalene was found in a Cairo antique market but it was not for another 50 years until 1945, or two years before the Dead Sea Scrolls were found in 1947, that an Arab peasant in Egypt discovered an earthenware jar containing 13 papyrus books bound in leather. His mother burned by accident much of the papyrus but the rest found its way to Cairo's Coptic Museum, and there experts determined that what had been found was the essence of the Nag Hammadi transcripts, a canon of Christian scripture that had evolved by the year 200. After the 1945 discovery, the transcripts took a quarter of a century to reach the public domain in the 1970s, and in recent years, a great deal of sensationalist writing has been written on them.

"The Nag Hammadi transcripts record much of an early Christian belief in Gnosticism during the period after Jesus's death, but Gnosticism as a belief system was not unique to Christianity and had been around in the eastern Mediterranean for 500 years. A key trade route between the Eastern and Western cultures had been through the Middle East and Gnosticism had gleaned its philosophies from a variety of spiritual traditions.

"*Gnosis* is a Greek word connoting knowledge and the Gnostics believed that the secret of *gnosis* was to know oneself at the deepest level, thus simultaneously knowing God. Only when people came to discover who they were, could they experience enlightenment as a new life or as a resurrection. Whoever came to know this *gnosis* was ready to receive redemption through *apolytrosis*, literally meaning 'release.' Gnostics believed there was within everyone a divine power in latent form, and whoever achieved this insight and consequent release could communicate one on one with the divine."

A woman about 20 in age, sitting several rows back in the group, asked how such a resurrection could be compatible with the resurrection of Jesus but before Chantelle could respond, a woman slightly older and closer to Chantelle turned around in her seat and interjected in a leather-lunged voice, "Being resurrected back to life was an age-old tradition in many beliefs, and Jesus's time was one of hallucinations, visions and ghost stories.

"The Gospel of Mary Magdalene affirms she was first to witness the empty tomb but the Gospel also says the resurrection was only Mary's vision in an ecstatic trance. Another Gnostic Gospel says that the same vision is what Peter himself had after he saw the tomb empty. But by the second century, only certain resurrection appearances were judged to have conferred authority and those appearances were all attributed to the male successors of Peter. A similar scam later occurred on the virgin birth."

The younger woman sat drooped like a scolded sophomore and Chantelle sensed she should try soothing the situation with a bit of context. "The Gnostics did affirm that Jesus had died but said the divine spirit within Jesus could not die. Jesus for the Gnostics was thus not the Peter-Paul son of God but the servant-heir of humanity or *Anthropos*, the incomprehensible all, from which emanated not theology but anthropology.

"The Gnostics reminded us that Jesus had spoken not of sin and repentance but of illusion and enlightenment, and instead of coming to save us from sin, had come as guide to help us access our spiritual understanding. Jesus was a Socratic teacher, further along on a journey to heaven-on-earth but if his students were able to get his message, they could progress even further and create new routes.

"The Gnostics thus believed Jesus was not offering a set of answers but rather encouraging questions and engaging us in a process of searching to keep ourselves growing. Jesus was thus a christ or teacher of the people but so can we be. We can save ourselves and experience enlightenment in a resurrected life as did he by first knowing ourselves and recognizing the god within. In this new light, salvation as Jesus tried to communicate, was a state of transformed consciousness available to us all in the here and now."

A clean-cut young man, second from the front and off to the side, was sporting a crucifix atop his jacket and he shot back at the fiery woman. "Jesus died for our sins! Otherwise, as Paul says, what would have been the point of his dying? It certainly wasn't to help any Gnostic enlightenment," and when he said the word "Gnostic" he coughed it out as if he were making the sound "obnoxious."

The fiery woman lashed back, "Jesus died not for our sins any more than our tutor Chantelle here would die to clean our slates. The cleaning is our responsibility," but the young man shot again at the firebrand that the seminar was all about Christianity, not Hinduism and Chantelle opted to step in. "Levels of heaven are here now as Jesus tried to teach, if we open our eyes and ears to spiritual clarity.

"The Gnostics did question the orthodox institutions of the time but Gnostics regarded all doctrines, including their own, as only approaches to truth. Other theologies or anthropologies such as Hinduism and Buddhism's human spirit being 'in' a body thus worked their way into Christian Gnosticism as it tried to select the best from world learning. But given the influence of Hellenism on the Middle East, Gnosticism remained closest to the Greek philosophical traditions. It is perhaps expanding for us to understand that Quakers today believe that whoever recognizes that inner spirit can communicate directly with the divine."

The group went quiet as if the participants were awakening to something new. Chantelle continued: "Gnostics saw the interchange of ideas as pivotal to one's self-understanding, and evil for example was not viewed as a moral absolute but as an illness or *kakia* from which one could be freed. Gnostics believed that most people suffered from such an illness because those people lived unconsciously without foundation. Within such a void of awareness, Gnostics saw the susceptibility of people to the dogmatists, with their absolute answers, quick fixes and guarantees of salvation from a barren life on Earth."

The timid young woman then perked up as if she was finding Chantelle's clarification a boost to her confidence, "I understand Jesus had been rejected by his village of Nazareth because he was Mary's child," but suddenly the slightly older woman turned to Chantelle. "Was this the reason Jesus said, whoever does not hate his mother and father cannot be his disciple?" and Chantelle again treaded gently. "Among the 52 texts discovered at Nag Hammadi was the Gospel of Thomas by Jesus's twin brother, and Thomas tried to clarify that Jesus was differentiating the divine Mother and Father from those of ours on temporal Earth. What God worked in Jesus of Nazareth, God can work in us all – divinization allows every son and daughter to share in the learning relationship, balance the stance of our parents' words against our own discernment and carry forward the ensuing spirit. Jesus taught that any follower who learned of this freedom could develop a mind that would be the father and mother of his truth."

The mention of Jesus having a twin brother was more than the pious man could bear and he folded his arms against his chest in a defiant position before he let out a scoff. The raspy woman looked to sense a pending victory and shouted to the air that the Gnostics saw in God a father and a mother, and that in the period after Jesus, women were teachers, leaders in Christian groups, evangelists, even prophets. They sat, she said, together with men in the early church and by the year 200, Christian women were in business, social functions, cultural activities and athletics.

But the crucifix was not going to allow this to pass. "Gnostic women were tainted with pride and had no modesty. They were bold enough to speak in church, baptize people and even pretend to priestly office, all in violation of the Judeo-Christian tradition."

The heretofore timid young woman surprised all with an interjection of her own, "Those women refused to follow the Patrician rules that flowed out of the god of Israel, and in following equality between laity and clergy or between the sexes, the Gnostics were not unlike other Middle Eastern contemporaries." The timid woman's voice then grew louder. "Some of that Gnostic rivalry with Peter and the Patricians may have stemmed from Peter's attitude toward women."

The raspy woman may have sensed a recruit and she smiled wryly. "Peter had a hate-on for Mary Magdalene. In the Gnostic Gospel's *Pistis Sophia*, Peter complained that Mary of Magdala was dominating Jesus, and in the Gospel of Philip, Jesus's favoring of Mary Magdalene was shown to have caused such resentment among the disciples that Mary had to plead to Jesus that Peter made her hesitate and she was afraid of him because he hated the female race. As for Jesus himself violating Jewish convention by talking openly with women and including them among his companions, Peter and the pirates would have had him crucified."

Chantelle again attempted some balance. "Part of the turmoil stemmed from confused communications, and Gnostics appreciated the significance of language. They questioned as had Jesus the accuracy of secondhand interpretations, and words such as 'kingdom' had multiple connotations for them. The Gnostics argued that God is not a king, not even a benevolent one, but God is our Servant, Creator and Catalyst, ready to help us re-create, provided we ask in good faith and the help does not impair our God-given freedom."

Chantelle carried on to the muted group: "The Gnostic program had little hierarchy, and instead of offering an easy baptism, required the kind of self-discipline found in, say, higher forms of Buddhist learning. The Gnostics understood that the human conscience needed to be exercised, just as an arm or intellect does, but that such exercising could not be done in a rules-oriented environment, where people were given a spiritual paint-by-number set in their most formative years. Thus for the Gnostic, human conscience was greater than outside rules but the Gnostic had also to acknowledge that such a reality took insight and therefore effort, and that such seeking inevitably involved inner turmoil. "

Suddenly, to turning heads, an older gentleman dressed in a navy jacket with faded crest and sitting near the rear spoke up in a baritone voice,

"Because of their Roman military model, the Patricians seemed to have no notion of authority emanating from knowledge and had only a restricted definition of authority flowing only from power. They appeared to have no understanding of discipline connoting autonomy and not just punishment."

Heads held on the older voice as if he had just delivered a philosophical shock and he went on: "Needless to say, an awe of God not involving fear or humility, not meaning humiliation was beyond Patrician thinking. The Patricians taught that if people did not have fear and instead wanted their God-given freedom, they did not have enough humility and had too much of that pride mentioned earlier."

People continued to listen to the older man. "The Patricians condemned any Gnostic sourcing beyond scriptures as proof of such pride, claiming the only safe route was that of the scriptures as spun by the Patricians. The swallow-and-follow throng would thereby recognize the limits of human understanding and welcome a *que sera sera* acceptance of those limits. Gnostics on the other hand believed truth could be revealed in a number of ways but betrayed its illegitimacy if attempted to be shown through force."

The resonating voice of the older man, or maybe his tweed jacket, lent a tempering effect and in any event, he held his ground. "Many Gnostics saw Adam and Eve as the true benefactors of humankind, their trying to help us see the difference between light and darkness and become liberated from the dogma surrounding a king-and-lord *demiurgos* or demigod. The serpent moreover was not seen as a devil's agent but was more like the ancient Egyptian serpent that swallowed its tail and represented the recycling of life. As for the Patrician sacraments, the Gnostics saw them at best as instruments of discovery, not arks of salvation."

The raspy woman jumped back in. "Faith in the Patrician sacraments is thus magical thinking, enwrapped in Vegas paganism, with symbols becoming media vampires that overtake any meaning. The Patrician god is a product of an immature people, unable to grow past the fantasies of early childhood."

No one spoke and the raspy woman filled the gap: "The Gnostics said that those fools who endured an hour or more of suffering and death to get eternal salvation were buying into a fable of Christ's passion-laden death and a martyrdom follow-up. Peter and his crew thus coerced people to the executioner, with those people clinging to an illusory sacrifice before a cannibalistic god, buying eternal life through the suffering of one hour, rather than a lifetime of spiritual progress."

The sharp-tongued woman then pressed on and swept her arm back to where the older man was sitting. "And as this gentleman pointed out, the Gnostics hit at the core of Patrician Christian thinking, mocking a jealous god who claimed there was no other god beside him. The Gnostics said that a vengeful god was an immature one, full of human frailties and not an arbiter of truth. If there were no other god, then why and of whom should that insecure god be jealous? Aristotle had posed a similar question in his musing about a first cause, and had suggested that any censorship by a god was tantamount to proof of concealed evidence about another form prior.

"The Patrician god was a king-and-lord demigod designed by communications marketers who recognized the human flaws in followers and wanted a god to mirror those flaws. Those communications wizards established a dictatorship and ensured, over time, an authoritarian pope and imperial hierarchy to solidify strength and longevity. Hell became a place of eternal damnation and was thus a weapon of mass destruction for blackmailing the fear-fed throng into following the path prescribed by the Patricians."

The senior gentleman than added a chuckle as if to impart a sense of lightness into the group. "Lucky for us, a recent pope declared hell to be just a concept," but the raspy woman would not let up. "God knows when the carrot heaven will get such a pronouncement." She then went on: "The Patricians created a fear-and-blackmail manual for the masses and a Roman military form of organization. Protocol was developed around the sharing of food in the Eucharist, sex in marriage, birth in baptism, sickness in ointments and death in funerals, all of it working best against the most vulnerable."

Chantelle again tried to leaven with some empirical information. "What followed Jesus's death in 33 AD was a 150-year power struggle between the two main sides, with Peter and his Patricians on one side and the Gnostics on the other. The Nag Hammadi texts were denounced as heresy but not before picking up a following.

"Gnosticism appealed to a few people who wanted the freedom to be curious but that freedom, as touched on, did not fit well with fear. There is arguably nothing of greater suffering than what is caused by the freedom of conscience and people prefer peace, even death, to a freedom of choice in coming to understand good and evil.

"Gnostics were also perceived as ethereally Greek in a Mediterranean world by then increasingly under Roman subjugation. The language of the Gnostic was that of the philosopher, with *autopoiesis* or subjectivity needed to combat human inertia, *kenosis* or self-emptying needed to transform new life from the death of old and *perichoresis* or mutual indwelling with divine love needed to free the mind for spiritual refinement. By comparison, the thinking of Peter and the Patricians was the aqueduct thinking of the Latin civil engineer – concrete and easy to see. The Gnostics' consequent withdrawal from the masses only accentuated the Roman stereotype of them.

"Pressures were great and by the middle of the second century at the apex of the struggle, the increasingly powerful Patricians fell back on their bible's Paul, who had said women should be kept silent and subordinate to men, and priests should not marry

"The Patricians adopted the synagogue custom of separating women from men, and by the end of the second century, co-ed Christian public worship was gone and all feminine imagery was out of the Patrician canon. Women leaders were declared heretics and the Patricians said the Gnostics had seduced women by telling them to prophesy. Despite educated women in early Christianity having been in business, societies, culture and sports, they were excluded by the Patricians from both formal education and any social or political activity outside their families.

"By the year 200, the battle lines had been drawn and a Patrician canon of scriptures was wedged into place. People came to identify more with the concrete structures and ornaments of the Patrician orthodoxy than with the bodiless spirit of Gnosticism. It required spiritual maturity and self-discipline, and was thus a weak vehicle for mass marketing. Its program would never appeal to but a few. By comparison, the Patrician orthodoxy was simple and could be followed either blindly or in a trance created by special effects.

"The Gnostic churches lasted only a few centuries, while the power-winning Patricians began to write the history. The first Patrician canon was published around 140 and a bigger version was published 200 years later in 367. Books at odds with the Patrician canon were purged as heresy and by the latter half of the fourth century the Patrician Archbishop of Alexandria purged all books judged heretical. As for the Gnostic scriptures, they had already been buried and remained so for 1,600 years.

"Any religion tends to be a combination of intellectual theorizing among the elite and quick fixes among the fearful, and Patrician Christianity obliged the fearful by absorbing the doctrine and rites of each subterranean cult of the *Imperium Romanum*, weaving into Patrician rituals the local superstitions and primordial beliefs, wherever Patrician expansionary forces spread. Philologists tried to expose the Patrician canon, and Alexandrian philosophers said the Peter-Paul thinking was confounding the wisdom of the world, but Patrician Christianity bulldozed over the critics and robbed us of the ancient world's cultural harvest."

The seminar hour was reaching its end but the vocal members wanted to rant on and a few other keeners wanted to hear more. What followed was an impromptu discussion of what transpired after the Gnostics' decline and Chantelle started it off. "By the fourth century, the heathen Roman emperor Constantine saw religion as a trump card for rejuvenating Roman power, and while he himself remained heathen, he nonetheless decided that his empire should be Patrician-Christian, and he hijacked Christianity as a mind-controller to counteract Rome's military decline.

"It was Constantine, not Pope Sylvester, who convened 300 bishops at Nicea in 325 to fasten down the nature of their christ and the early results were a sham – the majority of Christians were followers of the Alexandrian Bishop Arius, who along with the many Christians of Jewish background, maintained that Jesus was not consubstantial with God but instead was a human being chosen by God, in other words a prophet. Not the slightest authentic basis could be found for Jesus being a son-of-God *mysteria*, and Jesus's god-son references were Aramaic allegories long used by other religions in the Middle East. It is interesting and perhaps ironic that such a prophet is the very Jesus of the Islamic Qur'an.

"As for the Greeks, they regarded the Latins as theological sophomores but the Greeks were divided, and lost to the organized Romans in the three-in-one issue of father, son and holy spirit. Then, after another 125 years, at the Council of Chalcedon in 450 or so, Rome eliminated all Christian literature that contradicted the concocted trinity."

The senior man gave Chantelle a broad smile and leaned forward in his chair. "Constantine also got Jerome to translate the organic poetry of the Bible's Greek into a geometric Latin, with expressions such as 'Son of God' bearing little relation to Jesus's teachings.

"Legalism had always been a Roman strong point, and with Constantine setting the theme, the new Latin-church clergy took over from imperial Rome in function as well as appearance. Constantine ravaged Byzantium and renamed it after himself, and Constantinople would stay that way until the Ottomans took it back 1,100 years later in about 1450."

Chantelle succumbed to a moment of pride and added that Turkey's Greek intelligentsia had in that 1450 fled to Florence, bypassing a Rome no longer intellectually dominated by Greeks, and had triggered the Italian Renaissance. The group went silent again but this time perhaps not out of earlier reverence for learnedness but out of polite dismissal of a teacher's flaw in relevance. Chantelle was rescued by the smiling senior. "One of the grandest manifestations of Roman church rigidity was Augustine. He closed the door to the humanism of the classical world and created the dominant outlook of Christian Europe for 1,000 years. Born to a pagan father and a Christian mother in 350, Augustine had lived a life of sexual decadence, before he began a life of denial as professor of rhetoric."

The crucifix wearer suddenly twisted to the older man as if to correct. "Is Saint Augustine not to be praised for seeing the ills of his earlier ways and repenting?" but before the elder could respond, the raspy woman came back on an attack, "Disgustin' Augustin' was an anti-intellectual and a hater of classical literature. He declared it the duty of the orthodox intellectual to identify heresy and stomp it out. Augustine used Paul's guilt and anti-flesh sentiments as a combo to revitalize the concept of original sin and accordant baptism. He was a mob orator and knew how to stoop low for vulgar appeal to exploit prejudices."

Before the crucifix-man could come back, the smiling senior perked up again. "Augustine taught that human suffering, whether deserved or not, was the result of an angry god, and Augustine did his best to suffocate the natural curiosity of children – when one child asked him where did light come from on the first day, Augustine replied that he would show the boy and slapped the child's cheek.

"Augustine taught that the Greek thinking of pursuing truth for its own sake was both an illusion and a sin of pride. He created an educational system focused on Roman Christianity and during the fifth and sixth centuries, the public system of education disappeared in the Western world, with the Roman Church capturing minds during their most formative years. Augustine was a theorist of persecution and was used as a model, 1,100 years later, by the Inquisition."

The raspy woman lifted in her chair and shot her finger to the roof of the walkway. "The Patrician Christian religion could satisfy desires and fulfill fantasies, and its Latin spin gave license to self-deceptions. That male religion adapted like a virus and mutated to meet local conditions. Virgin births were already in vogue in the mythologies of antiquity; because purity meant being free of diseases, it ensured tribal survival."

The senior man again smiled and softened the conversation. "And there was a Mediterranean tradition of a divine father and human mother, with Horus born of the virgin Isis. Not to mention the many legends in Ovid, where god impregnates a girl who has a son."

By then, the raspy-voiced woman looked pumped with the senior's support and she half-turned to him on the edge of her chair. "Mary became known in Rome as *Theotokos* or Mother of God and was posthumously accorded humility, piety, sainthood and virginity. The virginity spin was needed to allow Mary to have given birth to Jesus without the concocted stain of original sin, and Virgin Mary cults sprang up across Europe during the Middle Ages. Then, 150 years ago, the doctrine of Immaculate Conception codified that sinless tradition.

"For oppressed women in the Roman church, the virgin-Mary myth allowed them to think of themselves as a mother-of-god inside their confined homes, and so ensure that so-called patriarchal societies were in fact matriarchal ones, where the prime ruler of mind during any ruler's formative years was the house-running mother."

The time was noon and Chantelle tried to conclude: "We ever improve as we re-create. That's the way we evolve, and Darwin 150 years ago never suggested there was not a God, only that the idea of God itself must be rethought.

"Darwin, Einstein and others were awed by everything that is, from thoughts to rocks. Trying to know an outside god is a counterproductive exercise, and whoever claims he sees an omnipotent, outside god is, I respectfully suggest, lying to himself. If we come to think of God as a process, along with how hard it is for that God to help us while not impairing our freedom, we shall keep moving forward by trial and error in our spiritual growth."

Chantelle took me for lunch, a mile north up Philosopher's Walk and beyond the campus, past the old brownstones of Toronto's Annex area to an Avenue Road coffee shop. Along the way, I could not resist commenting, "Chantelle, your Toronto group seemed liberal," but she was quick to counter, "Canadians are not as liberal as they like to feel, Arthur. Canada has a fifth of the planet's fresh water but Canadians abuse it by buying bottled water at 1,000 times the price."

At that moment, I rather relished the jab at what I sensed were smug Canadians. "So it is true that there is nothing more conservative than a liberal-minded thinker?" and Chantelle came back with a smile, "I think we align morality with our lifestyles – we don't so much reason beforehand as rationalize our prejudices after the fact. Gorbachev saved perhaps as many lives as Stalin took, and agricultural scientist Norman Borlaug has been credited for saving hundreds of millions, but suffering-advocate Mother Theresa gets the nod for our last century's most benevolent person."

My eyelids closed as if I regretted having asked Chantelle the question, but she kept on sermonizing anyway. "All of us appear grounded, for survival reasons, in fairness and generosity, repulsion against harm, respect for those who know more and communal co-operation. Monkeys have been found to go hungry before harming comrades to get food, and porpoises perform favors for peers, in expectation of a favor returned. Darwin believed that natural selection embraced an authentic altruism, but how we prioritize fairness, repulsion against harm or respect for authority and sense of community vary according to our circumstances."

God, my beloved Chantelle could be ponderous.

We had talked that Easter of hiking along the Niagara Escarpment but Chantelle wanted more to see her father. The days that followed on Georgian Bay should have been a vacation but for me were not and I started knotting about work. Chantelle did not help by talking about the theologian John Wesley who had feared death when on a ship from Britain to America, but was humbled by the fearless faith of the Moravians on board. I was overdosed and wanted back to Chicago.

The demands of work meant that Chantelle and I would not see each other until the summer of 2008 and the weekend leading up to Canada's birthday on Tuesday July 1 and America's on Friday July 4.

Saturday June 28 2008

Just after sunup, I charged out of Chicago in a top-down TVR and reached Chantelle's Penetang home before the end of the afternoon. Her Volvo was missing and Pantel was slumped out on the front steps, with hands folded as if in prayer. He greeted me with a nod and then lowered his head, speaking to the ground, "She's gone, Arthur, I fear for good. I'd love to comfort her."

The screen door slammed open and there stood Camille. "You did it! She started going crazy as a kid and you finished the job!"

I looked at Pantel but his head was still bent to the ground. He started to speak but was shouted out by the alto voice of Roxanne, who suddenly appeared on the porch. "She's pregnant! I can't hold onto a boyfriend and my sister gets juiced by some Jew!" Chantelle's mother Camille waved her fat arm. "The whole religion stuff was just for show."

I was tired from the drive but held back my rage and the screen door slammed shut but I could still hear the shrieks indoors. As I stood and stared at nothing, I finally took notice of the little man sitting on the front steps. "Pantel?" and he lifted his face up to look at me. "Arthur, I need to walk to an AA meeting but I'm feeling a little wobbly. Could you please go with me?" I offered my car but Pantel said thanks, but he needed the air and some time, perhaps to talk.

In the midst of my sexual jealousy, I was being asked to help a kind, little man and found myself reaching down to help Pantel up. On the mile walk to the AA meeting, he began to talk. "I slept drunk on New Year's Eve when Chantelle was born and Roxanne was only five years old, alone at home. Roxanne never forgave me or Chantelle for that night.

Chantelle was almost 10 pounds at birth and at 10 months, over 20 pounds but started walking. Then, at 15 months, she began to talk. Chantelle loved looking at books and by the age of three, was reading French and English. By five, she was reading our French weekly and got copies of an English one, through our librarian, from that Jewish drug store up in Midland. The paper was called the *Guardian*. From England, I think."

I was finding the walk helpful too. "Chantelle told me about the librarian and the scholarship contest in Midland" and Pantel perked up with my knowing. "Jealousy built in Penetang, especially in Roxanne, and Camille saw Chantelle as the devil's punishment for her fling with a Greek sailor."

I came to a stop. My gaze went down to the roadway and then to a vague building housing the AA meeting ahead in the distance. The thought that Pantel knew Chantelle was not his biological daughter had never dawned on me. "You know about that, Pantel? I guess I'm now facing a similar..." but he interrupted as if the talk he had already started was more important. "It was not long before Roxanne fed the news to schoolmates that Chantelle was illegitimate and when the news reached our church, it put the screws on Chantelle to wash away her sin and become a nun. But around the same time, some new thinking was reaching the Catholic Church, and Chantelle started studying the Bible and any book she could get from the librarian on religion."

I slowed and turned to Pantel. "Was that enough for Chantelle to survive the onslaught?" and he picked up his pace. "She came to have a close friend. Chantelle was curious about the shape of things and loved to wander the forest, and a Midland photographer named Budd Hudson found her in the woods one day peeling the layers off a mushroom and studying it. As things turned out, Chantelle became an apprentice to Budd. Hell, the whole reason Leica was in Midland was because of Budd Hudson.

"Later on, Chantelle caused quite a stir when she took a photograph of a certain gravestone in a patch of land next to Penetang's hospital for the criminally insane. The patients who had died there with no loved ones had for 100 years been dumped into the ground with no marker. Finally, one went up. Chantelle submitted a photograph of the land and marker to the Midland newspaper, along with the caption, 'A whisper from the trees, far off, but down below, only the sound of nothingness.'"

In Memoriam

From 1904 to 1970, this cemetery was the burial place for many of the long-term patients who lived out the latter part of their lives at the psychiatric hospital on this site. Over 300 people are interred here.

The Volunteer Association and the Mental Health Centre Penetanguishene. May 2004

Pantel and I reached the large, unpainted frame house at the opposite end of Penetang and he invited me into the open AA meeting where non-alcoholics could attend, but I declined and marched back the mile to the car for the 100-mile race back to Toronto. Within an hour, I was south of farmland and whisking by some insipid suburbs before I soon took the ramp for Avenue Road, down the six miles to Queen's Park and Chantelle's Grosvenor Street apartment. There, I buzzed her number 105 and kept on buzzing, but finally had to accept that Chantelle was out. I began speculating she was with the person who had made her pregnant.

I went over to Fran's restaurant on College Street for a hamburger and an old-fashioned milkshake, and there telephoned my mother in Chicago to say I was okay but found out Camille had already phoned with a demand for money. "You've knocked up a *shiksa* and a Jew-hating Frog at that! You're no better than the Polacks in Gary. She's not welcome."

I was stunned but tried to reason. "Mother, you yourself married a gentile," and she snapped back, "Not the same. He's a WASP and Churchill helped us during the war."

I tried to clarify. "Dad is Scottish Canadian" but my mother yelled, "Same thing and not an anti-Semite like the Frogs!"

I wanted to think my mother and I had been close. I had taken her to architectural exhibits and the Chicago Symphony; I had arranged a 65th birthday party for her and her friends; she had bragged when I had won awards. As a child, I had written her massive letters in argument against her rigidity but never did appreciate how much I had been a threat to her. Now, she saw a soft spot in me. "I even heard your *shiksa* is an illegitimate Greek! The Greeks tried to overrun us but we didn't let them inside our bodies!"

As I made my way back to the apartment, I began to wonder who the real bastards were. I recalled something said by a childhood hero of mine, Maimonides, that no one people were at the center of the universe. But I did not allow myself any thinking beyond that to ease my jealousy, and resolved instead to sit at the front of Chantelle's old building until she arrived home.

After an hour or more in the summer heat, I fell asleep with my body sprawling across the concrete entrance, and other residents must have let me be, thinking me a city drunk protected by the outdoor warmth. On the following Sunday morning as daylight arrived, a bird was trying to sing me awake, when suddenly I felt the heat of another body next to mine. "Arthur?"

I gave a squint up at the face smiling down at me. "So you arrive home in the morning, when I'm not in your way?" and Chantelle's smiled lessened. "You're never in my way, Arthur," but I would not let up. "To be with him?" and she replied, "With my patients, Arthur."

It had not occurred to me to think that Chantelle could have been at work on a Saturday night, one block away at Women's College Hospital. She put her left hand down on my right shoulder. "Would you like to continue your sleep in my bed, Arthur? I'm tired too."

I sat up awake and looked up at her with scolding eyes. "Have you ever had sexual intercourse with another man?" and her smile disappeared. "No, Arthur."

God, I could be orthodox. "How about felt up?"

"Yes."

"A doctor?"

"A priest in Penetanguishene, once he heard I was a bastard. He tried to rape me but to no avail." Chantelle stretched out her arm. "I was a tall swimmer."

I tried to control the talk. "That's the only man?" and Chantelle took in a breath of air and then released it. "The only man, yes, but there were several boys who wanted a bit of fun with the village bastard, and one nun who believed I was doing it with the librarian."

Chantelle, like Pantel, was showing an acceptance rare for me to see, and I lowered my head back to the steps. "Chantelle, your childhood sounds like a hop over rocks on a dangerous river," and her apologetic smile came back. "I entered adulthood unresolved on the issue of sex and you rescued me, Arthur. I don't know why I went with you to your Chicago apartment, that night, but I'm thankful I did."

I hardened again. "Chantelle, who got you pregnant?" and her smile went away completely. "I'm not pregnant, Arthur. I was late with my menstrual cycle after you left at Easter and I mentioned it while visiting home. My mother fantasized the rest."

Chantelle then put her long arm down around me and I the fool tried to recover. "Did you know that if one sticks to the right on Avenue Road, one comes down into the city faster? Kind of like speed-walking – one can time the lights so that instead of arriving early by running or late from toddling along, one gets here just in time."

Chantelle smiled and put her second arm on my other shoulder. "Arthur, you could use some more sleep."

We made love on her bed, with the music of Bach all around us, and then we fell asleep.

Sunday June 29 2008

Chantelle and I were to have spent two weeks driving out to Western Canada but Toronto had a last-minute cancellation for a permit that had been requested months earlier, and she was to speak that afternoon in Queen's Park. Chantelle was thus unannounced, but by the time she started, hundreds of people were wandering about, and many paused to listen to her.

"There is within each of us a self of evolutionary energy and that self must come to grips with the ego to give it perspective and assure it security. But the ego in turn needs to recognize the role of parent in that self, for the mind to feel comfortable with a god of unconditional love.

"This interaction of the ego and the self is called individuation, and individuation is critical both to building individuality and creating a sound foundation from which to greet the world. To the ontologically healthy person, the world makes sense and is a safe place to be, and any attempt to smother individuation or not acknowledge it causes dismay and chronic tension.

"If a person's self is suppressed, he can fall into in a state of fantasy created by that ego, since egos tend to assimilate stimuli and personalize them, allowing the person to regard himself as a deity or form of perfection. There is a Greek myth in which Ixion represents that kind of ego, and Ixion attempts to appropriate supernatural powers, including the ability to communicate with a fantasy cloud named Hera. But once our egos give in to such a fantasy, we are destined to live within a chimera, where the promise of a future golden age governs our every move.

"An ego-driven person may also objectify his chosen foes, out of some fear of being objectified first, and a snowball effect comes into play where the person tries to preserve his own identity by nullifying the individuality of another. The irony is that the more he feels the need to do so, the more each subsequent denial of the other person's legitimacy breeds a decrease in his own security, and a threat to the person's Peter Pan world is then potentiated, and the ego-driven person feels the need to nix ever more the perceived threat.

"Religious tyranny is the most ruthless and morally distorted form of this suppression, because such tyranny by its very dogma suppresses our individuality and pigeonholes autonomy as pride. Yet it is not the autonomous or self-disciplined person who suffers from pride but rather the person with the suppressed self – that person's mind is subservient to his fantasyland, and religious people often flaunt their false humility with the utmost arrogance.

"One reason for religious tyranny is the Christian bible and that bible's confusion of humility with humiliation. Humbling oneself in an honor/shame society can be perceived as making one powerless to defend status, but true humility is what is needed to fulfill the God-given need for spiritual growth and concomitant autonomy. The kind of autonomy needed allows for a kind of self-discipline where the person freed up can begin to live a life of principles, with that person able to assess new issues, using those principles as a foundation, rather than others' rules founded on fear and enforced by punishment.

"True humility allows one to feel well about oneself but not at the expense of others, and such humility does not make one feel unworthy in the eyes of a god who has created that person. God does not produce junk and any one humiliated enough to judge himself unworthy, relative to his god, sees that god as a big shot.

"Faith as a concept can also be distorted and our bible can be off the mark in addressing it. Some Christians claim faith is the substance of all things hoped for and the evidence of things not seen but faith, first of all, is not all things hoped for. God is not a pork-barrel politician, and prayer, if sincere, does not involve a negotiating session, where the supplicant uses a praise-repent-thanks strategy to clean his slate, before he gets down to the wish list. Prayers should, I suggest, be to our servant God from the god within us, and those prayers should ask God to be a good coach, giving us clues for using our own God-given gifts to help ourselves.

"Faith, secondly, is not the answer to questions beyond the grasp of the human mind. That kind of blindness stifles curiosity and any added glorification, using the trick of mystery, enhances them with the magical quality of a god who is a hoarder of knowledge. Instead, people need to distinguish between what they believe and what they believe they believe, and the desire of a mystery-faith is not the proof of faith but a betrayal of the opposite.

"A magical-mystery faith in a covetous god predictably sees doubt as an enemy, but doubt is critical to a person's spiritual growth, and questions triggering more questions expand the mind. Faith, moreover, gives the security needed to be both skeptical and heuristic, and the opposite of such faith is not doubt but fear. Those of blind faith, following the dictates of others, are caught in that fear.

"Sex, like individuation, is another primal drive, and is god-given, not to be suppressed. Human beings have evolved as the only living creature that copulates face-to-face, and one of the best routes for intimacy is via one's eyes. Sex, therefore, is not an Augustinian sin, and if we believe sex is, we fall into a type of tabloid thinking, which misdirects our testosterone toward violence, while at the same time condemning that God-given sex.

"As for Augustinian morality in general, the story of a prosperous young man, after his testosterone settles down, becoming shocked into a loathing of his life and being converted by a divine vision, has been a Mid-Eastern myth since ancient times and is a stock item in a number of biographies of holy men. Unfortunately, however, some fundamentalist leaders of Christianity, Judaism and Islam know that sex is an easy moral target, while also knowing that attacks against despotism, corruption or torture can lead to destruction of those leaders' lives.

"Understanding the effect of religion on rates of crime has critical implications for public policy, because preferential tax treatment is given to religious organizations that often cry for more punishment as a deterrent. Yet punishment has repeatedly shown it does not deter – exile, hard labor and flogging deter no one and prison recidivism is on the increase. The ex-con returns to society with hate, and society continues its judgmentalism and punishment after he has served time. Right-wing leaders cry that one cannot stop religion because without it, we would all be wicked, with society falling into hedonism, but notwithstanding elastic consciences, criminal arrest rates in the United States are one third higher in areas with high religious participation, and the orthodox cannot dismiss this fact solely on more stringent attitudes toward punishment in those communities.

"Individuation will be an unpopular process, bound to threaten the established order, since in any society, culture will be a signifying system through which the social order is experienced. But without individuation, people lose their capacity to assess what is right or wrong, by the very structure that is set up in the first instance to embrace that assessment."

Monday June 30 2008

After Chantelle's speech, she got a call from her hospital and had to go in early on Monday morning and so I made the two of us a Sunday dinner and then Chantelle put herself to bed for a dawn rise. I resolved to accept the situation as it was and overdosed on the rest of the dinner's wine.

Monday was in effect a holiday for much of Canada, because many people had taken the day off and had combined it with the country's birthday of Tuesday July 1 to get a four-day weekend. I had heard Canada was a playground in the summer, and Toronto was crawling that day with American license plates, along with people asking me, a Chicagoan, for directions. For a while, I almost felt of use on an otherwise empty Monday but in the evening, Chantelle and I were disturbed again by a hospital call and she had to postpone again our planned two weeks together.

It's no fun living with a doctor. They work worse hours than architects. At least with architecture, the work is feast or famine and the all-nighters occur only four to five times per year. Doctors, on the other hand, are in constant demand and there seems no seasonality to babies getting sick or being premature.

Communications between me and Chantelle came to revolve around logistics, or talk before and after sex, and even then the issue of time was always present.

Tuesday July 1 2008

The following holiday morning, I tried to stay in bed and indulge in a bit of loneliness but finally gave up and hit the shower, before making a nude beeline to the kitchen. Then while passing the living room, I caught sight of Toronto's *Globe and Mail* newspaper, left inside the front door, and the *Globe* highlighted activities for Canada's birthday, in Queen's Park among other places. After I had some juice, a bowl of oats, blueberries and honey, I settled for my caffeine hit from Chantelle's beloved tea and then put on a tennis shirt, shorts and my beloved hiking boots, before wandering over to Queen's Park.

My usual uptightness with time soon showed itself and I began pondering how these people could possibly be taking so much time to dither over what to order from a fast-food portable, looking not even to care what time it was. To me, they were squandering time in a hot Toronto while north of the city, Ontario's 10,000 lakes were perhaps to them a mystery. Many people were Asian and, I surmised, not used to lakes and maybe didn't even know what lay north. In any event, it did not fully occur to me that they could be having a good time, since I wasn't.

I sauntered around Queen's Park for about an hour and came to realize these people were having fun. While the time was still early for hot dogs, they were free that day, and with mounds of relish and mustard, tasted not so bad in their cold buns. Afterward, I opted to talk with some of the Asian parents about life in Toronto and I found their immediate trust in a stranger remarkable and somewhat un-American in this cosmopolitan city.

By noon, when Canada's birthday cannons began going off, the summer heat had already built and I chose to amble back to the cool of Chantelle's basement apartment. Along the way, I stopped at the hospital long enough to say hello, but was advised she was in an operating room. When I reached the darkness of her apartment, I went to the kitchen to retrieve the *Globe and Mail* and carried it over to the dining-room office. I shifted Chantelle's laptop away from the table center and laid out the newspaper under the green desk lamp, before I sat down with my back to the kitchen.

My right side was open to the living room but my left and front faced Chantelle's bookracks containing dozens of worn works, to which I had never paid much attention, other than being impressed with their scope. After a few minutes, however, of trying to interest myself in the news, I suddenly found myself peering over Chantelle's bookracks in search of stimulation.

To my left at the top was a spattering of old literary works, including leather-bound collections of *Poetical Works* by Robert Burns and Robert Browning, hard copies of Scott's *Ivanhoe* and Joyce's *Ulysses* and one leather volume entitled *Shakespeare's Works,* next to a paperback entitled *Northrop Frye on Shakespeare.* At the bottom stood some heavy medical texts that seemed to form a kind of foundation for the softer topics above, but at eye level, the books looked to be huddled into sub-groupings.

I knew Chantelle never did anything without design and I began to extrapolate why she had done such groupings. The first included two books that I had read – *The Quark and the Jaguar,* with its attempt to show the growth of the universe from tiny particles to high forms of intelligence, and Jacob Bronowski's *The Ascent of Man.* The second cluster had a mangled Bible, *The Qur'an, A History of Christianity* and *A History of the Jews,* next to a work I did not recognize other than its looking decidedly Eastern – *The Rubaiyat of Omar Khayyam.* The third group held philosophical works including Plato, a book entitled *Hume,* Nietzsche's *Twilight of the Idols* and *The Antichrist,* Adam Smith's *Theory of Moral Sentiments,* a book called *Mature Religion* and another, *Dostoevsky, Kierkegaard, Nietzsche and Kafka: Four Prophets of Our Destiny.*

Across from me on the opposite rack, the clusters had one group holding a number of books by Frye including *Northrop Frye on Myth* and a second group had a range of books on theological commentary, some of which I recognized – *American Theocracy, The God Delusion* and *God Is Not Great* – as well as a few I found intriguing – *The Battle for God: A History of Fundamentalism; Continental Divide: The Values and Institutions of the United States and Canada* and *The Fire Spreads: Holiness and Pentecostalism in the American South.*

The third group, however, got me going. I recognized Noam Chomsky's *Israel, The Holocaust and Anti-Semitism* but did not know the book beside it – Deborah Lipstadt's *Denying the Holocaust: The Growing Assault on Truth and Memory*. Nor was I familiar with the other works – *Recovered Roots: Collective Memory and the Making of the Israeli Tradition*; *Islam: The Alternative*, or *The Holocaust Is Over: We Must Rise from Its Ashes*. What intrigued me the most was that these middle-shelf books had hand-written notes inside them, and a small stack of notes sat next to the cluster.

I cannot justify or explain why on that lonely day in Chantelle's dark apartment, I felt uninhibited in spying on a loved one whose notes had not been shared with me. But soon I found myself shifting around her desk-table and moving to the opposite rack to leaf through Chantelle's notes. As I pored more and more through them, I became increasingly shocked at what I found. Inside Aristotle's *Metaphysics* was the handwritten note:

> *People by nature are actuated with a desire for knowledge, and one indication of this reality is a love of the senses, irrespective of any utility in their discovery. Philosophy is a science that is speculative of truth and if people pursue philosophy, it is not for any stub-your-toe utility that might be afforded, like studying, say, engineering but rather on account of self-understanding. Philosophy is thus the freest of all sciences since it exists for its own sake.*
>
> *It is unworthy of a person not to investigate the knowledge of his own condition, and if some god is covetous of his own tree of knowledge, then it is especially important for that pursuit of knowledge to happen. Yet the most difficult knowledge to acquire may be about those very universal things, for they are the most remote from the senses.*
>
> *Everything is generated from something, including contraries, since nothing is the absence of something, be that gas, object or whatever; thus, whatever was there before the Big Bang was perhaps of a different configuration than what we know (raising the issue that the Genesis mythology may be consistent with the Big Bang, with the emergence of life in progressive stages, and with the remarkable phenomenon of speciation or the formation of new biological species. Such awareness could encourage a new humanism).*

Whenever concrete things are audited by philosophers, they are obliged to interpret the energy behind them, especially if, as Heraclitus hypothesized, all sensible objects are in a constant state of flux. Long before Einstein or even Nietzsche likened genius to the highest forms of energy, ancient philosophers thought of energy as only potentiality or capacity, although Aristotle saw matter in terms of energy or activity.

The philosophy of religion was historically classified as a part of metaphysics, and Aristotle's first cause as an unmoved-mover was later read by some as God. Such a first cause argument came 1,000 years later to be called natural theology based on reasoned experience, as distinguished from revealed religion based on scripture and religious visions.

Roman Catholic Aquinas said theology did not require philosophy to promote a knowledge of God yet said philosophy could be of service in the aims of theology. But philosophy requires one to enter into debate with an open mind and to remember one's own presumptions, and Aquinas enlisted Aristotle for the explication and defense of those tenets. Aquinas's conclusions, therefore, that there is an unmoved-mover, which we understand to be God, is at best a tautology, because any first mover must have a precursor at least in principle, and our minds as yet are too entropic to grasp that principle, any more than we can yet come to grips with the notion that matter is cooled-down energy.

Aristotle in his arguments on metaphysics said that the creator-creation phenomenon is a dyad but any dyad has to be preceded by the number. Yet deep within the human psyche there exists a feeling that somehow life is infused with a divine spark or at least a vital essence. Databases meanwhile are filling up with the genomes of everything from the tiniest virus to the tallest tree, and scientists will soon develop a creature that has no ancestor yet is a creature that by many a definition is alive and able to replicate and produce proteins. It is thus possible to conceive of a world not far off where bacteria, plants and animals will be designed on a computer and grown to order. This will bring about a ground-shaking change in how we view life.

Regardless of the ethical and religious considerations that flow out of this new reality – one being that these new creatures, for better or worse,

could breed by themselves – it demonstrates more soundly than anything
that has occurred since Adam and Eve that life's essence is information,
and that non-living matter can be brought to life, with no need for a god
or vital essence.

"Vintage Chantelle-the-Greek attack on Rome," I mused. My curiosity took me next to a collection that included *Guide for the Perplexed* by that childhood hero of mine, medieval Jewish scholar, Maimonides:

Many readers believe Maimonides was in line with the rabbinical thinking of his day but they overlook his saying that he would not openly state any controversial views. Maimonides wrote that his Guide was addressed only to a select and educated readership and that he was proposing ideas deliberately concealed from the masses.

Maimonides attempted to explain some of the more mystical concepts of the bible by alluding to spheres, elements and intelligences, with little in terms of direct explanation. He also tried to show that evil had no positive existence but was a privation of a certain capacity and did not proceed from God; when evils were mentioned in Scripture as having been sent by God, the scriptural expressions had be explained allegorically.

By then I had forgotten I had been feeling lonely that day or for that matter that I was spying, and so with an insidious mix of curiosity and resentment for being alone on a vacation planned with Chantelle, I carried on snooping into her comments beside the books.

Wisdom literature is a genre common in the ancient Middle East and
is characterized by sayings of wisdom that teach about divinity and virtue.
The techniques of storytelling are used but the books presume to offer
insight and wisdom about the nature of things.
In the bible, wisdom literature represents that class of Hebrew
writings which reflect on ethical topics, as distinguished from prophetic
and liturgical literature. The wisdom or hokhmah *of these writings is*

*in the sage utterances on the concrete issues of life, without the philo-
sophical support that came later with, for example, that contemporary of
Jesus, Philo of Alexandria.*

*Like Jesus and much of the Pharisaic community, Philo used allegory
but used it in the main to fuse Greek philosophy with Judaism. Philo was
not popular among Jewish literalists but his concept of Logos as God's
creative plan for the world may have influenced early Christology.*

*Centuries later, Goan was a Jewish philosopher who pioneered a
school of Biblical exegesis characterized by a rational investigation of the
Hebrew Bible, including a scientific knowledge of the text. Goan tried to
make his exegeses lucid and intelligible, by the light of philosophy and
scientific knowledge.*

*About 1,000 AD, Jewish writer Halevi meshed religion and a sense of
nationalism to embody the fulfillment of the supreme politico-religious
ideal of medieval Judaism – the return of the Jews to Jerusalem so that
they could dwell in safety. Halevi was said to voice the deepest soul-life
of the Jewish people and each individual Jew.*

What was Chantelle up to? Next to the collation of paper volumes were
five books stacked together in a unit, and each book had a note immediately inside its front cover. The first book was a novel called *Damascus Gate*
in which Chantelle had written, *On the insanities taking place among multiple and conflicting religious minds in Jerusalem today.*

The second, *Who by Fire, Who by Blood*, had a note stating that the story
underscored the fine line between religious Jewish zealotry – *Yiddishkeit* –
and chauvinistic fanaticism or paranoid schizophrenia. Chantelle's note
added that the book could be helpful to Americans who rush to pass judgment on Palestinian and Israeli Arabs, or dismiss issues as black and white,
when there could be shades of gray.

A third book, *Saving Israel: How the Jewish People Can Win a War
That May Never End* had a short note saying it was *A plea by an Israeli
nationalist on what it will take to save a Jewish Israel and why it is critical
to do so.*

Again I read the words "nationalist" and "Jewish Israel."

The fourth book was a surprise, since it appeared to be a cheap thriller called *The Masada Plan*, and it had a note saying it was a story that underscored Israel's plan to use its nuclear arsenal on the U.S. as blackmail, if the Arabs had actually proceeded to roll their tanks into Israel in the 1973 Yom Kippur War.

The fifth and final book in that grouping did not seem to fit with the others but by then my mind tried to make it mesh anyway. It was entitled *Jews and India: Perceptions and Image*, and Chantelle had noted that, despite the Indian Jewish population being one of the country's tiniest minorities, the relations of local Jews with other communities was and remains an integral part of the history of Indian multiculturalism. She had written that, over the last two centuries, Judaism and its image in India have been woven into the thinking of prominent religious and nationalist movements, as well as into the minds of leaders of an independent India and the mass media. Chantelle had added that many decades have played witness to a mass adoption of Israelite identity by some key Indians, but how and why, the notes did not say.

Set to the right, along the middle bookshelf, were several loose-leaf sheets of paper with Chantelle's notes. The first set highlighted the Sabras, the first native Israelis, and said,

> *Educated in the ethos of the Zionist labor movement and the communal ideals of the* kibbutz, *the Sabras turned the dream of their pioneer fathers into the reality of Israel. While being only a small minority, their cultural influence was enormous and is to this day felt in Israel. The Sabra myth became the central one of Israeli society, and the Sabras were instilled with a set of Zionist myths teaching them that the Jewish people, though small and oppressed, were destined to be delivered from their enemies in the Land of Israel. While labor Zionism as such was a secular movement, it nonetheless saw itself as having a religious ideal. Today's Israeli children have less knowledge of Jewish and Zionist history, and their access to other information via the Internet is much greater, with their being exposed to happenings and beliefs throughout the world.*

Why had Chantelle not shared this information with me? Odd, I thought. The next note did not fit in with my growing assumptions. It talked of Jean Paul Sartre's book *Anti-Semite and Jew* and his character analysis of how one can become focused on it:

Anti-Semitism is a passion, not a product of reason. It is not the Jewish character that creates anti-Semitism but rather it is the anti-Semite who creates the Jew; if the Jew did not exist, the anti-Semite would have to invent him. Anti-Semitism is thus a fear of the human condition and does not fall into the acceptable realm of free opinion.

We are critical of Jews who in 1914 did not join to defend France or England or Austria earlier, but the Jew has the same national interests, and in the French Resistance, the Jews formed the principal cadres before the Nazis went into action. The Jews have been forced to be on the move for 20 centuries in pursuit of a dream of assimilation that constantly receded. They have been reduced to aspiring to a world of universal brotherhood in a world that rejects them. We have forced the Jew to be loyal to Jerusalem over, say, France and it is the anti-Semite, not the Jew who stops assimilation.

The Jew rightly holds that violence has no place in human relations. Jews cling to justice, even when persecuted, perhaps justifying their often reported lack of tact.

For those anti-Semites who allege that Jews have little creativity and cannot think outside the rabbinical or persecution box, what of Spinoza, Proust, Kafka, Chagall and Einstein? Perhaps some rabbis and their Jewish followers did not appreciate the Enlightenment, but who can blame the Jews for not having Christian taboos and using their intelligences differently, with a different choice of weapons, or for that matter feeling the need to monitor all signs of anti-Semitism or resentment of Jewish success?

It is a false stereotype (embodied later by American sports coach Leo Durocher saying "Winning is everything") that the Jew is arrogant when he succeeds and abject when he fails. Life can't be just about winning, for if we want only to win, there will always be losers.

Supposed Jewish clannishness is really conscious collectivity, although a Jewish newspaper did label non-Jewish people "them." But the least favorable among any people can find a common bond with like material and spiritual interest, for it is only to another Jew to whom a Jew can say "we." A Jew's love for a Jewess is more than for a gentile because there is a double sensibility and humanism – a Jew going to a brothel is outraged to find a Jewess there.

American anti-Semitism appears to spring from the fact that Jewish immigrants were among the first to arrive, but were still Jews in the second and third generations, thus supposedly having a concealed attachment to their race.

A gentile should not believe that if he goes up to a Jew with open arms, he will greet the gentile with confidence. For the Jew smells hypocrisy, showmanship and an underlying anti-Semitism, and is rarely wrong. Yet in friendship with a Jew, there is a sincerity and warmth that one rarely finds in a Christian; this is because of Jewish suffering, the most overwhelming of sufferings.

The anti-Semite sees a grand conspiracy of secret international money and media-controlling elites. The Germans in the 1920s became anti-Semitic, when they believed they were ruined by the Junkers and big industry – The Germans perceived that behind the scenes were huge trusts, gold and diamond controllers and munitions makers; thus, the beleaguered Germans came to blame wars on Jewish agitators, and class struggles on Jewish demagogues. Anti-Semitism can fire misdirected anger into a vigilante mentality and ultimately led to the Nazis. The Jewish blood that the Nazis shed accordingly falls on all our heads.

We must defend the Jew no more and no less than ourselves, for no person can be free until all Jews enjoy the fullness of their rights, and no person can be secure until the Jew has no fear for his life.

Sartre's work disturbed many Jews, despite his being their advocate – when Sartre wrote it in 1944, he did not know of the total Holocaust and wrote only that the Jews returning from German internment would do so with insolence and could induce a new burst of anti-Semitism. But from what little Sartre did know, he decried there being almost no coverage in the French newspapers; many Jews themselves were also at the time labeling as "inauthentic" the effort to base Jewish identity on the Holocaust experience. Those Jews argued that in not forgiving their perpetrators, the label of "victim" would continue to have power over them, and they would not find peace.

Perhaps I should have been comforted by Chantelle's sensibility shown here or at least by her thoroughness but I could not juxtapose her Sartre notes with what I judged her provocative others. I pressed on to a pile of typewritten sheets that Chantelle must have rambled off, top-of-mind, in preparation for later speeches. Again, she had not felt obliged to share any of the information with me nor did I recall, for months, having any discussions about the issues in her speeches.

I took the notes back to my chair and began arranging them on the table to support my brewing thinking. The top sheets seemed platitudinous enough but they were there perhaps to draw in her audience:

God's divine purpose is yours, not God's, but God can catalyze that purpose's many manifestations. God is a loving teacher and cries with us when we err but is ready again the next time to help if the god within us asks.

Why is there suffering? A loving teacher cannot interfere in life's trial-and-error process or else we lose our freedom and stay stuck as spoiled children. God coaches us as best God can but it is up to us to learn.

In turn, we human beings are not masters of other creatures but are their loving butlers, ever ready to help when needed, while still allowing them the freedom to learn from their mistakes.

Integrity mandates that religious views are always falsifiable and that such an evaluation must be never-ending, making the state of one's religion always tentative and open to new ideas. Faith needs to embrace an optimism founded on personal worth in order to generate the confidence needed to evaluate raw religion against one's own values. Faith-based autonomy is thus one where a person feels well about herself but is not proud, and appreciates that a mixing of minds brings out the best in others.

We should read the Bible as all things with the autonomy of an honest scientist and try to glean the principles of each story, while understanding the historical context to avoid the pitfalls of direct application. Such a healthy heurism will afford us a dynamic excitement that should build within ourselves as we progress.

Wishes mythicize our history and distort its foundation for our motives. Rather than pray for miracles, we should recognize life as a miracle, sense it, love it and be thankful.

How can one tell if she is being given the straight goods? One way is to be conscious of the words in use. In, for example, the English language, speakers aiming for blunt truth tend to use old Anglo-Saxon words like "water" or "board," and those wanting to cloud the issue tend toward the French side of the language, with words like "enhanced," "interrogation" or "technique."

There is a rabbinic saying: "You will one day give reckoning for everything your eyes saw which, although permissible, you did not engage." (Jerusalem Talmud, Tractat Kissushin 4:12)

As my arranging came to unveil, I thought I began to see Chantelle's attack.

For authority, perhaps we should not look to the Romans but to the Hebrews where authority stemmed from knowledge, not might.

Designating people as saints not only betrays a god-presuming judgment but also allows us to shun our responsibilities, dismissing others as higher than our humanity. The cultivation of saints betrays a craving for a sacred something that one can touch, or a divine incarnation. We pull the same cop-out with the label "devil" or "genius."

Whether Jesus did exist is moot: his words do not require a real Jesus for us to glean meaning from them, and digging up his bones means little, since he did not claim to be the literal son of God. All myths need central characters but as those myths grow over time, they draw less and less on the concrete for support.

The Gospel of Mark did not say "Jesus was the son of God," and the Gospel of Mark came first, not the Vatican's Matthew: there are parts of Mark in Matthew and Luke, and parts of Matthew and Luke in each other but not in Mark. The writers of Luke (his physician Luke was long dead) knew how to point-counterpoint with the Hebrew bible to fabricate salvation history.

Scratch 'n sniff a patriarchal society and you will find a matriarchal one. It does not take Freud to foresee what happens to any male mind that is molded by a domineering mother Mary in a child's most formative years. The suppressed male ego tries after puberty to break loose and in some patriarchal societies to be a stud while in others to drink volumes of alcohol. In both cases, the over-mothered "prince" still calls home at night to his mother Mary to mollify his guilt, and if that prince rises to power in a patriarchal society, his mother Mary can look on with a wry smile.

Just as subjects demand how their queen behaves, so too do the masses demand the same from their ruling aristocracy; people in dictator-ships demand that their rulers be dictators as were their mothers during childhood.

Jesus was a racist and a humano-centrist but was programmed to ensure his tribe's survival. He was a non-mystic and Hasidic prophet who intended his preaching only for a Jewish audience, stressing an attachment to the Torah. In the gospels of Mark and Matthew, Jesus had to be enlightened by a gentile girl, who was a Canaanite from the wrong side of the sea – she asked Jesus to heal her daughter but he at first dismissed her as a non-Jew on whom he should not waste his energy, saying his gifts are not to be thrown to foreign dogs. The goyim mother persisted and Jesus experienced a eureka moment before going 10 whole miles to the other side of the sea to "feed" 4,000 people.

Then came the underbelly of Chantelle's core attack:

In the beginning, all cultures had developed myths both about gods and spirits living within those worlds, and the label "sacred" was a way of expressing humility, demanding caution in front of forces impossible for mortals to comprehend. The gods were thought to have emerged from primal chaos, before they created the natural world and us within it, and this divine-natural linkage was true for Greek myth and philosophy throughout the Middle East, as well as East and West. But the Hebrew Bible took a different spin with a USP or unique selling proposition, like the launch of Trident sugarless gum. In that beginning, god was created through fiat by a few male brokers who rose to power first in the image of a tyrannical old man on a big hill called a mountain. The concocted god was thus the ultimate tribal leader and we his minions were to implement the mighty men's strategy, using that one-stop-shop god whose image of omnipotence was the ultimate thing that our minds felt comfortable grasping.

Nature and the divine were starkly separated but we people were given the carrot of "dominion" over all other creatures and were to presume that, just as we down on earth were to serve the whims of the mean old man-god on the mountain, all other creatures were on a dominion earth to be dominated by us under the guise of Tory steward-ship. But because we envied birds that could see over the big hill, angels were concocted as messengers and because we thought these angels possessed inside information, we began to assign to them protection over fearful us, rather than trying to source those fears ourselves.

This humano-centrism was combined with an ethno-centrism, as the power brokers above us further bribed our egos, teaching us that we were a chosen people in recognizing this ultimate god first. We were thus to enlighten the lessers by our example but always remember that we were the chosen few. To keep us further in line and displace any resentment against the powerful men, the power brokers adopted a forest-fire strategy of uniting us against a common enemy and inducing victimhood among us lessers.

Added in were the carrot-stick motivators of a heaven and hell whose goodness and badness addressed our desires and fears, and kept us working, fighting and dying to serve the power brokers' whims. These myths carried us into early Judaism's militancy as well as the aggressive proselytizing of its Christian and Muslim offshoots.

The god so concocted was thus a demiurgos, a jealous, covetous, cruel, war-mongering and self-serving tyrant. His conception begs the question, "If a person's god is so flawed with human frailties, is it possible to decipher any truths masked by those flaws?" One answer may be in the fact that Jesus had his faults but we can still glean from his teachings, as did agnostic Benjamin Franklin.

The exile of the Jews for 50 years in Babylon had not meant captivity as such. The exiles were still allowed to meet and confer freely and carry on their normal occupations. The exile had thus not meant the end of Israel and there had been a recognizable continuity of religious tradition and community life. After the exile, some Jews chose to remain in Babylonia, while others had already moved to Egypt and stayed there, becoming part of later influential Jewish communities such as Alexandria.

During the closing centuries of the Old Testament period, the sweeping changes that later took place in the Jewish community involved the fusing of cultural and religious traditions, and four religious themes emerged:

The relationship between national religious faithfulness and prosperity, a key element in Deuteronomic thinking;

Identification with the cult;

The expectation of a catastrophe that would be universal in range and would be followed by a new order. The word "apocalypse" meant revelation or unveiling, and the truth that the apocalypticists sought to unfold was a secret knowledge, imparted only to the faithful;

A key representative of the god of Israel such as David.

The mass of detailed regulations that would emerge relating to ritual purity and cultural practice reflected a priority to preserve, free from *blemish or deviation, the worship of the god of Israel, an aim the Deuteronomic reformers sought to reinforce by a law of centralization. Constantly pressed home was the concern already in Deutero-Isaiac teaching that other nations should come to worship and obey that god of Israel.*

After the Romans toppled the Temple of Jerusalem in AD 70 and later disbursed some of the Jews from Israel in 135, the scriptures and the synagogue came to dominate the addressing of perceived Jewish needs and the holding of them together. The age of inspiration was thought to have ceased and a claim of antiquity was thus judged necessary to fortify the authority of religious writings. As for a messiah, a son-of-man concept had evolved in the Jewish bible as a sort of heavenly super-prophet, and this thinking was background for the title as applied to Jesus in the early New Testament.

Perhaps we need to see God not as a noun but as a verb and never-ending energy. If God is a source and catalyst for our contemporary energy, then that God is trying to teach us to be christs and to progress along a process that parallels the evolution of all things.

Then came a supposedly emancipated Chantelle's surprising praise of Islam:

A central Qur'anic concept is that reason and thought must be involved in the attainment of faith: Allah does not change people's condition unless they change their inner selves, and we are to study our behavior as it relates to beliefs, while recognizing that skepticism is the mother of all sciences. Muslim scholars have insisted that education is not only a right but also a religious obligation for all Muslim men and women, and centuries ago in Islam, nobody was considered fully learned until he had mastered medicine, mathematics, chemistry, botany and some astronomy.

Under the Muslims, Jews and Christians were not persecuted the way Muslims were persecuted in the Christian parts of Europe.

Ottoman slaves, for example, were seen as dependents and allowed to rise according to their abilities.

The educated Muslim argues that his prophet's words were, yes, divinely inspired but are not to be taken literally. Instead, one needs to decipher the sense of what Muhammad was trying to communicate. He was human with self-doubts and his ego was tempted, as was that of the earlier prophet Jesus. But Muhammad was kind to animals, in direct contradiction to the Judeo-Christian teaching that animals were there for human beings' use, including enslavement.

The Qur'an is not riddled with the inconsistencies or theological paradoxes of the Judeo-Christian bible. Abraham in the Qur'an, for example, is not told by god to sacrifice his son but instead receives that command in a dream. And Eve's ostensible tempting of Adam is not mentioned nor is the preposterous thought of childbirth being some sort of punishment for women.

Islam does not encourage tribal or nationalistic solidarity. Nationalism misguides people into aiding their own kind in an unjust cause. Instead, the Qur'an's god says "We have made you into nations and tribes so that you might come to know each other." Muslims help the poor without concern for the recipients' religion.

The reality, however, is that many Muslim immigrants to the United States and Canada come from places where fiction writing is not even taught, or from places where the arts are ignored or undervalued as a luxury. Not surprisingly, therefore, the apologetic mentality of the Muslim casts him in a bad light and his defenses of Muslims are inadequate. The Muslim world also seems inept at portraying itself attractively. An unshaven Yasser Arafat with a pistol under his belt is about the best picture that anti-Arab forces could wish to have alongside the image of a lascivious old Arab with a harem of abducted blonde women in his tent and an oil well nearby. These and other stereotypes of the over-sexed, treacherous, trigger-happy and dumb Arab can all be found in Hollywood films.

Nothing weighs so heavily on Muslim credibility as their absence from the human rights discourse, for that absence implies that they let *others decide for them what is moral. But human rights among Muslims have to some degree been protected for 1,000 years by divine commands to honor body and life, personal freedom, intimacy, honor and private property; moreover, from the time of Muhammad in the 600s until after the fall of Islamic Spain in the 1600s, Muslim women mixed with men, were educated, worked and traded, fought, had financial responsibilities, could choose their husbands and divorce them as well. The West was centuries behind.*

No one factor is harming the chances of Muslim women as much as the occidental assessment that women in Islam are second-class citizens. The rare but brutal African custom of female circumcision is an occidental favorite. Islamic men and women are called upon to play different roles of equal dignity; they are not seen as identical but complementary, physically and psychologically. There is no basis in the Qur'an for male superiority, and polygamy may have made sense many centuries ago in times of tribal war with abandoned widows. The notion of men being called upon to protect women if they need such protection is an example of the adaptation of the Qur'an to existing pre-Islamic attitudes: polygamy was allowed, for example, by the Hebrew laws of Moses. Research shows that the majority of Muslim women do not feel oppressed, and stories within the Qur'an of women seem positive. The Muslim future rests on women and children, and American converts can play a role, using their organizational and leadership skills. They should not accept Muslim traditions such as head scarves unless they feel them necessary.

The doctrinal Iman keeps calling the faithful to an imminent battle for life or death rather than expounding a point of ethics or doctrine. Preachers in mosques should stop shouting like spoiled children – the louder the voice, the less credible the message.

Islamic rejuvenation may come from places like Los Angeles, Oxford and Cologne rather than traditional places of Muslim learning.

Chantelle's attacks on Christianity and its Judaic source lay bare, along with her praise of Islam. At the end of the edited notes, I noted in particular Chantelle's comment, *A poet is more formidable than a multitude of soldiers.* My mind was afire.

It was still the middle of the afternoon when I heard the apartment door open. Instead of my customary getting up to greet the weary doctor, I stayed in my chair and slipped her notes under the newspaper on the table. Chantelle nonetheless strode over and gave me an embrace but I remained seated and I guess she sensed my aloofness – instead of a kiss on the lips, I got a light one on the forehead. Chantelle then sat down on the big living room chair some 12 feet away and began facing me with a gentle smile and a look of entreaty. "How has your day been so far, Arthur?"

I swiveled to her, with my left arm remaining on the desk, and I took time to cross my legs. "Chantelle, reality can be *kerfuffled* by philosophizing. Did you ever study in school, *Sufferance is the Badge*, based on Shylock's line, 'Sufferance is the badge of all our time'? It details the history of the Jewish Diaspora and tells of an ongoing tale of torment."

Chantelle folded her hands and kept both feet flat on the floor but she did angle her body toward me. "A great deal of Jewish intellectual and artistic contribution occurred during the Diaspora, Arthur," and I lowered my forehead to admonish, "Expulsions, pogroms," but Chantelle held her position. "And sometimes periods of relative integration, with Jewish communities thriving. Arthur, I don't imagine it's much fun spending your vacation alone in my apartment. I am truly looking forward to our getting away."

I held firm in my upright wooden chair, with my face looking down on Chantelle from a higher eye level. I said nothing and she tried to open me up. "Perhaps I do have fun with philosophy and feel a little Athens can help in any intellectual mix," but her comment triggered my wrinkled brow. "Are Jews too much of a type?" and Chantelle turned her legs more toward me, perhaps sensing the source of my question. "I don't know what the newspaper said today, Arthur, but you talk of a type like Shylock. In grade nine, our North Toronto class 9A was 20% Jewish and our homeroom English teacher was a Czech. The first Shakespeare we studied was *The Merchant of Venice* and our class saw the play, west of Toronto in Stratford. But before we went or for that matter had one class on the play, our teacher gave his own soliloquy to clarify that the merchant Shylock was representative of a type existing in time and place, and only by circumstance happened to be Jewish. The teacher went on to highlight Shylock's rhetorical passage: "If you prick us, do we not bleed?"

My psychiatrist and mentor Michael Fisher, himself a Jew and Holocaust survivor, told me that Dostoevsky was not an anti-Semite either but only an insightful person who was nevertheless limited by his humanity, time and place."

I tried to expose the person I judged a phony. "You French Canadians are reputed to find contemporary Jews the same. Your Quebec priests would not even let you go to war, and said it was a Jewish conspiracy."

Chantelle shifted more forward. "Arthur, I have an Uncle Dick who was captured in France during World War II and spent several years in a German prisoner-of-war camp but luckily, he said there was a proven 95% rate of survival in those camps."

My face stayed stern and I looked down again on Chantelle's eyes. "So you have some sense of the reality that the war was," and she kept her position forward at me but her face took on the look of a medical resident, responding to a teacher's question. "Uncle Dick told me that the prisoners had a tough time getting food near the end of the war but said that the Germans didn't have any either, because the rail supply lines had been bombed by the Allies."

"Poor souls," I countered, and Chantelle let out a bit of a sigh while gesturing to the bedroom, "Arthur, I would like to have a nap."

But I was not ready to give any ground or reveal as yet the source of my suspicion. I tried again to take control of the conversation. "Individuals often seem shaped by their culture, and the study of those differences is intriguing, but we're squeamish about such study after Hitler," and Chantelle quickly added, "And the incomprehensible evil he represented. Many now believe in absolute evil but not necessarily its opposite."

I offered a frown of discontent, as if uncomfortable with whom she presumed that opposite could be, and I tried putting her on the defensive. "How about Jesus, portrayed by you people as timeless and universal?" but Chantelle remained unmoved. "Jesus was not worldly and wanted to improve Jewish life, not abolish it. He urged his followers to adhere strictly to Jewish law and said, 'Go nowhere into the land of the gentiles.' Jesus also betrayed his humano-centrism and by comparison, the Muslim poet Kabir was less condescending when he asked what kind of god would he be if he did not hear all creatures?" Chantelle then added with a slight shrug, "But Jesus may have been impeded by a lower awareness than some people have now. I don't imagine he lost a lot of sleep thinking about fish dying in pain when they writhed on the floors of fishing boats."

Chantelle then gave a stretch and leaned back. "Science continues to chip away at the myth of human exceptionality. From whales creating cultural songs to parrots identifying shapes to ants being teachers, every year studies show animals to be acting, using mental abilities traditionally understood to be exclusively human."

I resented Chantelle's sudden comfort after my early third degree. "So Jesus is not your archetype?" and she shifted forward again on her wingback chair to put herself straight at me. "I don't have an archetype and Jesus is one prototype for me. He was a person with flaws but I still try to glean from his good parts as I do from others. Doctor Fisher agreed with me that Jesus seemed to be trying to say what Dostoevsky did come to say 1,800 years later in *Brothers Karamazov*, that one route for reaching heaven on earth is in helping others."

I was still bent on provoking Chantelle's weaknesses and raised my chin. "And what of Spinoza. Would he be another prototype?" yet Chantelle would not be thrown. "I heard of his book, *Ethics*, from U of T's Northrop Frye."

I suddenly lifted within my chair, thinking but not saying, *"Frye! Ah yes, her bookrack contains many of his books."* I decided to shoot. "The Jewish community has a string of jokes on Northrop Frye, the closet anti-Semite."

Chantelle glared back at me, as if I had struck an icon, and she locked her fired eyes right on me. "Arthur, Northrop Frye was a man of the highest principles and exceedingly kind. Women in the 1950s were treated as equals and they found attractive his clarity of mind. Frye felt a tremendous sense of oughtness and was passionately devoted to truth. He despised anti-Semitism and in his criticizing ancient Israel's mythology was careful always to define what he meant by the concept of myth as story."

I then leaned back and smiled wryly, as if I were on to something. "So you knew the man" and Chantelle shot back, "Regis Brandin had been Norrie Frye's best friend since the 1930s when they were college mates. Regis taught me, from his home near my high school, a brief history of Christianity, using a book by your University of Chicago's Martin Marty. Like Frye, Regis was a United Church minister who taught at U of T's Victoria College. Among the lives that Regis and Northrop Frye influenced were Norman Jewison, Margaret Atwood and Donald Sutherland, and Regis said he never heard an unkind word about Northrop Frye."

I still had the higher eye position and used it again to look down on Chantelle. "Nor you?"

"No!" Chantelle's eyes then fell to the hardwood floor and she leaned back in her chair, while uttering a slow sigh. "Well, there was one Jewish professor at OISE, where I was taking a supplementary course."

"OISE?"

"Ontario Institute for Studies in Education. Professor Rosen claimed that Frye had affairs and I said if true, it was irrelevant. I added that one of the difficulties with Frye's being a genius was that he had a scientist's drive for truth and was accordingly bored by political pandering. Frye, on top of being shy, was thus not street smart. People with scientists' minds, Arthur, often accept manipulative cat-talk as simply another building block in extending knowledge and can thus be seduced by a smooth, Reaganesque delivery. Bull feathers can baffle brains."

I felt Chantelle was getting away, so I went back on the attack. "In times of crisis, cadence matters as much as content. Winston Churchill proved that and had outstanding speechwriters," but she would not be caught. "I seem to recall Frye suggesting that only a trickle of Jews, perhaps 45, had escaped ancient Egypt, that Solomon's temple was built by *goyim* and that Leviticus in the Hebrew Bible sanctioned slavery. But Professor Rosen noted that Frye could not speak Hebrew and could thus not understand that the very shape of the letters give shades of meaning, untranslatable, to the text."

I chose to lean forward as if hearing a confession. "So you resented this Rosen," but Chantelle held to her position, this time without eye contact. "I benefited from Doctor Rosen, not from his resentment of Frye but from a better understanding that what we gentiles read from the Old Testament is a Greek translation, contorted toward the New."

I felt Chantelle was trying to take over the agenda, and I was not going to let her away. "But that does not explain the resentment of Frye among Jewish intelligentsia."

Chantelle would still not be trapped. "As I said, Northrop Frye was a United Church of Canada Minister, albeit a liberal humanistic one, and that Church endorsed a book called *The Unholy Land* on the plight of Palestinians."

I remained forward in my chair as if drawing out a confession. "Jimmy Carter has managed to alienate both doves and hawks with his book *Palestine: Peace Not Apartheid*, and his South African analogy is said to threaten Israel's right to exist," but Chantelle then became defensive. "Carter did improve Israel's strategic position in the Middle East 30 years ago by brokering an Israeli peace with Egypt, but evidently found Menachem Begin impossible at Camp David. What Jimmy Carter recently hoped to achieve in visiting Israel is beyond me but he did set up the Carter Center in conciliation, saying that the negative image of the U.S. needed to be transformed."

For me, there was too much give and take going on. "You led us off on a Frye tangent from the 17th century's Baruch De Espinoza," and Chantelle stayed composed, though she had almost lost contact with my physically higher eyes. "I think Spinoza believed in a god who is part of all that the deity creates and does not interfere in human affairs. Spinoza, yes, questioned the immortality of the soul but he was one of the first people in Europe to promote a socially democratic state, separate from the church. He believed that once priests or rabbis seized control, the voice of God could no longer be heard. Einstein was warm to many of Spinoza's concepts."

I did not want Chantelle off the defensive and leaned back in my higher chair to assume an Abe Lincoln position. "Well, if your spin doctor Spinoza was so wonderful, how about his predecessor, Maimonides?" and she was calm in response: "A thousand years ago, prophet Moses Maimonides declared that God is not far from anyone and is ready to help all who ask" but I lifted my head to the ceiling. "Ah yes, but you are omitting to say that Maimonides believed that a Jew need not be punished under the laws of Judaism, if he put to death a person judged a heathen or a gentile. And that he saw blacks as less than human. Maimonides racially excluded those not worth the effort. "

Chantelle may have sensed where I was going, if not the reason why, but she would still not be lured. "We can still learn from people, like the Hebrew Bible's Abraham and Sarah, despite their having a black woman slave, named Hagar."

I then tried to rekindle my earlier indignation. "It seems to take religion for good people to demonize."

Chantelle looked set to respond in kind but I sensed the need to shift things back to a mode where I was doing the accusing and so, before I could stop to think through what I was about to say, I blurted out, "I read your notes."

Chantelle's eyes opened wide at me, then they went over to her bookcase at the side and then to its middle, where her notes were missing. She then dropped her eyes to the floor, uncrossed her legs and sank back into her big winged chair. "Arthur, those thoughts are works-in-progress, and any jottings that I put down are little more than blue-sky inklings, for thinking through and challenging later." Her arms then went to each side of her chair and Chantelle's eyes turned straight on me. "But for certain, those inklings are personal. Arthur, you have invaded me without my permission."

I felt a pang of guilt but did not want to lose what I hoped would be Chantelle's forthcoming confession. "Good, if that means I provoked a conversation with a busy doctor," but she leaned forward in her chair, still with a stern face and her eyes stuck on mine. "You have stolen from me, Arthur."

I went back in my chair as if hit by an unexpected blow and found my eyes avoiding those of Chantelle. Suddenly, it was I who felt the need to diffuse the issue but in so doing, I added an aside: "Canadians have an irritating nasal sound when they are moralizing to Americans. You need more vowel sounds and to speak more slowly from the back of your mouth," but Chantelle held forward and did not flinch. "Stolen, Arthur," and I tried again to wriggle out by mocking her indignation. "I stole your soul?"

"I don't have one, only a mind."

"You mean that big brain god gave you, Doctor?"

"No, Arthur, I mean what I said, and no one yet knows the difference between the brain and the mind."

Again I tried to widen the issue and justify my own indignation, waving my hand to the ceiling. "How old is this saintly Doctor Fisher?" and Chantelle's face turned to scorn. "He would have resented being labeled a saint and he died years ago," but I would not let up. "And of Jews, what did he say to you?"

Chantelle's face was still forward and stern, and her feet lay flat on the floor. "Doctor Fisher counseled me to read Paul Jonson's *History of the Jews*. Jonson was a gentile who had been hailed by many within the Jewish community as a Good Samaritan. After I discussed the book with Doctor Fisher, he encouraged me to read Paul Jonson's *History of Christianity.* Since then, I have learned a great deal from the Jewish community in Toronto hospitals."

I sensed that I could get Chantelle back on the defensive. "And you can claim your very boyfriend has a Jewish mother," but Chantelle did not fall for the provocation and said nothing, keeping her glare on me. I tried a former tack. "Why are you French Canadians so anti-Semitic?" and Chantelle looked to fall for the chance to intellectualize, her eyes shifting to the bookshelves. "I don't know, Arthur, nor do I know whether such anti-Semitism is properly documented. Among French-Canadian colleagues from Montreal, I have heard there was an anti-Semitic sentiment in the garment district, and like New Yorkers, many Jewish Montrealers before immigrating had been urban and had related occupational exposure, particularly in the garment industries of Eastern Europe.

"French Canadians by comparison, along with, say, Irish and Italian immigrants had been weaned on deference to authority, as driven into them for centuries by wealthy overlords and the Roman Church. Even their language lacked sufficient transmitter orientation to make their communications direct or clear, and it would be up to the more powerful receiving person to interpret what was said. Thus the power-distance index of those former peasants, along with perhaps culturally induced uncertainty avoidance, helped program them into monotonous jobs, where decisions were made by a boss over them."

A tired Chantelle was nevertheless anew in her element and I let her plod on, waiting for a chance to pounce. "Like New York, I have been told, the cutthroat garment business of Montreal was a kind of boot camp for an opportunistic philosophy, but it cash-cowed offspring who grew into professional occupations such as law and medicine. Montreal Jewish General Hospital is one of the best in Canada."

I tried turning the talk back to support my pending scolding. "And in the legal profession, did this noble Montreal have the hostile takeovers and proxy fights that Jewish lawyers had to resort to in New York, because they were not allowed into the staid law firms, on account of those Jews' antecedents?"

"I don't know in any detail, Arthur, but from what I understand of Canadian medical law, it seems that heretofore frowned-upon legal practices are now acceptable in all law firms. In any event, Jewish Canadians are prominent in all areas of professional life today."

I folded my arms and looked at one of the bookcases. My indignation was still unaddressed and we had moved the talk to the abstract, in an area where Chantelle could excel. I had let it happen and wanted to steer the talk back. But still, I should not have said the next words: "Wow, a history of the Jews by a girl Gorf," and Chantelle slammed her arms on both sides of the wingback. "We are not Frogs, Arthur, nor are we 'types' as your mother might say. You have violated me, Arthur!" but she had inadvertently given me a chance to bring my anger back. "And you are violating my mother!"

It was then Chantelle who was taken aback, and I made the only move that I saw to complete my role as wounded – I got up and tore toward the door. Chantelle's face followed me but I don't think she noticed that I had in my hand the newspaper with her notes inside.

I ran west along Grosvenor Street to my TVR, where I had left it for days with the top down, having gambled that the Illinois license plates would assure no parking tickets. I threw the tickets into the passenger seat, jumped into the driver's side, made a U-turn and shot east, one-and-a-half blocks to

Yonge Street. Then I spun left to charge the half-dozen miles north to Highway 401 and its link back to Detroit and Chicago.

The holiday traffic was light but pedestrians were everywhere, and I dodged and weaved up Yonge, bent on keeping up my frenzy, as if a moment's stillness would afford me time to see my role for what it was, and how I had been the one to have spied on a loved one. Within minutes, I was in Toronto's uptown, north of St. Clair Avenue, and I noticed to my right the grand entrance to Mount Pleasant Cemetery. Suddenly, I remembered that I was to have shown Chantelle my Canadian roots on our way to Western Canada. I found myself swerving into the midtown cemetery and its ultra-slow roads, with Mount Pleasant's famed trees, people bicycling, jogging and walking with baby carriages.

I had not been to the Franklin family gravesite in 15 years, after ashes from a Connecticut cousin had been distributed there. The site had been in the family since December 7, 1941, when Pearl Harbor had been bombed and my great-grandmother had died. Her husband, Arthur Franklin, after whom I was named, was buried there too and had lived well into his 90s before dying in 1968. He had been born in 1876 in a Southwestern Ontario county that actually dips 50 miles south of Detroit and that Arthur Franklin had fought with his mother in the summer of 1893 when he was 17 and had hitchhiked out west to Saskatchewan to trim wheat fields. Near the end of the summer, he had gone to the Chicago World's Fair where he had later been fond of saying he had spent the loneliest time of his life.

At that moment, all this history excited me and reminded me of the grounding that I had wanted to share with the woman I loved. Within minutes, I was standing next to my roots in the silence of the treed cemetery and felt the cemetery's oxygen hitting me. For a second, I sensed that my rage was dissipating and almost turned back to Chantelle's apartment but as if to justify my indignation or perhaps my days of earlier loneliness, I psyched myself up again into a theatrical anger and jumped back into the car to bolt out of the cemetery north to Highway 401.

After bombing west along the 401 for four miles, I caught sight of a sign pointing to Highway 400 going north, and it was the one that Chantelle and I were to have taken to kick off our trip to Western Canada. And so instead of continuing southwest for another four hours to Detroit before humming on to Chicago, I opted to start the Canada vacation myself and took the ramp on and up to the 400.

Some 200 miles north, my first stop was in the old lumber-mill village of South River, five miles north of the village of Sundridge where Chantelle and I had bunked down with her sister en route to Temagami. My Toronto great-grandfather had been in charge of the South River lumber mill and in 1926 had built, eight miles west of South River on Eagle Lake, a sprawling cottage that was nestled in pine, cedar and white birch, and set back along a 500-foot stretch of beach. The cottage had been sold in the 1980s by one of his sons but I recalled as a toddler seeing its long screened-in veranda, giant stone fireplace and huge moose horns, found on a bull that had died of old age.

I had supper in South River and then raced the eight miles west to Eagle Lake, to see if the grand old cottage was still there. It was, but much of the property was not and several new cottages now blighted the big, old property. At one new house, its owner Constance, a retired United Church of Canada Minister, had keys to the old cottage and was more than kind in letting me see it. There, I witnessed again the giant stone fireplace, big front porch and the pines and white birches leading down to the lake beyond. I sensed for a moment the smell of my roots and an experience that I would have so much liked to have shared with someone I loved.

Constance and his wife invited me to stay for the night and in the evening took me to the July 1 Canada Day fireworks near Eagle Lake's bridge. The fireworks were harmless enough but I could not help pondering how the energy-sucking launches, anchored close to the bridge on this little lake, contrasted with the local villagers standing passively along the causeway.

Wednesday July 2 2008

Early next morning, I was shaving with the bathroom door open and Constance noticed that I was using my great-grandfather's straight razor. He insisted that I get the blade sharpened by a craftsman who had a huge stone home in the woods, east of South River. Later, when that knife sharpener heard I was headed for Western Canada, he told me of a shortcut, beginning 11 miles north of South River at the village of Trout Creek. The shortcut wound west over hilly countryside from main Highway 11 to Highway 69 along the coast of Georgian Bay.

With the TVR top down, I tore up Highway 11 and then scooted west to that quiet Highway 522, driving past a pillared 19th-century stagecoach stop in the hamlet of Commanda. Before 8:00 a.m., I stopped at an old gas station and store in the hamlet of Arnstein and took a liking to a brown, wool car blanket made by local Mennonites, so bought it for my dark green car. Once I then reached Highway 69 on Georgian Bay, I turned north toward the nickel city of Sudbury but stopped along the way beside a French River gorge long enough to hike down its rugged canyon and view the crashing river.

In the little city of Sudbury, I went to its Science North center and watched a butterfly being born, before I went down a mine shaft to feel what it was like to be that far underground. Then, with one of Constance's apples in mouth, I jumped back into the top-down car and raced west to the town of Espanola, where I veered left to cruise south, toward a causeway leading to the huge Manitoulin Island that spread 100 miles east to west along the north side of Lake Huron.

I stopped for lunch on the Manitoulin Island side of the causeway and sampled some of the local cranberry juice in the village of Swift Current where I learned that a mile to the south was a rocky road leading to a First Nations spiritual area called Dreamer's Rock. I took the low-slung TVR across the rocky side-road and arrived at the bottom of a steep but round-about mini-mountain, then trekked up through its trees and trails, before slugging up another 100 yards of giant white rocks to reach an awe-inspiring quietude that overlooked the northwestern edge of Georgian Bay. It was there in the freshness and solitude, and with so much pouring forth in front of me, that I started to think of what was important in life. I was there for an hour.

I then took the car west across Manitoulin Island over well-paved roads with no other cars around, and by mid-afternoon came to a place called Misery Bay. There I ventured onto a long path that wound through some astonishing fauna, before coming upon the most extraordinary shoreline I had ever seen. There I was, next to a stretch of Lake Huron, standing alone on thousands of acres of flat-rock beach, and all I could see in every direction were huge expanses of water, distant islands free of people, a quiet forest behind me and a beach that stretched for miles, while being over 100 yards wide. I was the only person there in this heavy tourist time of July, and the only other animals were insects, sandpiper birds and the ever-present seagulls.

I made my way back to the car and then raced for an hour or more back to Manitoulin's northeastern exit bridge, before tearing up to the Trans-Canada Highway and charging west toward the massive land of Northwestern Ontario. At afternoon's end, I stopped at a lakefront motel in the village of Thessalon and there joined for supper a retired farmer and wife, who were from a Manitoba valley far north of Winnipeg and 1,000 miles northwest of where I was.

To my shock, I learned that the retired farmer and wife, both of whom looked healthy and were still driving, were almost 100 years old. Yet remarkable as the couple was, by the time I was into my second glass of wine, I was rambling on not about their life experiences but about those of mine and my Canadian great-grandfather "Papa" who would have been 132 years of age, "His son, my grandfather Arthur Franklin II, had been the youngest of four children and a playboy spoiled by his mother in her last diabetic decade or two.

My grandfather 'Art' had been well into his thirties when he had left his big North Toronto nest and had taken his first real job in 1940 as a lieutenant in the Canadian army. After World War II, he had followed a wealthy Ontario buddy to Chicago where for a while he'd made it big before alcohol, cigarettes and a bitchy British wife got to him."

The farm couple were listening politely, but by 6:00 p.m. said they were going for a walk down to the water's edge before the onslaught of evening mosquitoes. I took to jog past them down to the rock beach and there saw the beginnings of a sunset spreading its hue over the bay, along with a mist rising up from the calm water in front of three pine peninsulas.

It was then that I got the urge to go hunting for a pub in the village of Thessalon but found instead only a bar for drinking Canadian beer on draft. After downing a couple, I began to eavesdrop on some anti-American gab going on at a table nearby but also overheard from the same that in this pure, maple-syrup Canada, a Mountie heavy had been ushered out of office for being a softcore hood.

I finished the night early and staggered back to the room, having already recalled the old alcoholic "Lighthouse" trick of leaving the door strategically unlocked. I had also ordered an early breakfast of eggs to be left outside my door.

Thursday July 3 2008

On another early morning, I darted west along the Trans-Canada, past the Canadian American cities of Sault Ste. Marie and then followed the highway northwest to begin the jaw-dropping 200 miles over the top of Lake Superior. With the TVR top down, I wound my way through low mountains on the right and a crashing Lake Superior far down on the left, and the whole scene filled me with a sense of freedom.

At the first lookout point, I stopped long enough to talk with two senior people riding east on a Harley, and they spoke of Canada's Group of Seven nature painters, who a century ago regarded this Algoma area as the beginning of a Great North that canopied the continent. This north was a haven of freshness, rejuvenating the mind and motivating much of what I guessed was viscerally Canadian.

When I then completed the northern arc of Lake Superior, I continued north and west past the city of Thunder Bay and on for another 100 miles or more. En route, I stopped for a bite in a town called Uppsala and made the *faux pas* of asking if the restaurant owners were Swedish. I got the blunt, "We're Finns up here, not goddamn Swedes."

I then cruised up and into the hushing Lake of the Woods region but paused on the highway long enough to walk off into the forest and have a pee. It was there while urinating that I saw a caterpillar struggling against the wind to reach a tiny branch from his dangling position and I took my free hand and put it up just below the caterpillar to give him enough backdrop if he needed it. The caterpillar accepted the help and touched down on my finger, then after a second or so, summoned the stuff needed to the complete the climb.

When I reached the little city of Kenora, I stopped at a B&B that overlooked breathtaking Lake of the Woods, and had it not been for the flies biting, I would have taken a canoe and sapped up some of the evening. Instead, I left the car at the B&B and went out for some pub grub and soon found myself listening again to some booze-induced indignation, this time from a drinker at the bar. "We Canadians were guinea pigs at Dieppe during World War II and were cannon fodder in the Great War before that. Canadites, that's what we were. Kill us off and Hollywood-up the story. Wars run by fuckin' Russians and their secret leaders."

My indignation from Chantelle's notes resurfaced. "The systemic underbelly of Canadian culture, I am learning." I slammed my glass on the bar. "I think you should know I am Jewish."

I turned to storm out but the old drinker spoke again. "Oh, well I meant to say some people are manipulators. There are even some good Americans," and I yelled back from my distant position, "I *am* American," and the drinker tried to rescue himself. He shouted across the bar, "So…how did you feel about the free trade con?"

I cooled a little but looked askance at the man. "The one we now have with Canada and Mexico?" and the drinker was off on his talk. "The Americans slapped some hokum duties on us and later when we won in court, the Yanks laughed at the judgment. We know how to play hardball too but cheating even in poker is not right and you guys invented that game."

I was still standing near the exit but then found myself edging back to the bar, and the old drinker must have viewed my move as an endorsement for him to continue. "Our government agreed to sacrifice a couple of hundred Canadians in Afghanistan to please Washington and seek redemption after a decade of botched Canadian performances. The Afghan sham will some day leave in power a bunch of warlords and a corrupt government, with the opium trade intact. The Europeans know that, except for France with its Jewish president and the Poles, who are sucking up to the Yanks as protection against the Russians."

I chose to ignore the French-Jewish president remark and tried to sound up-to-speed with the old drinker. "So international myths are under stress?" but he was at the ready. "The Canadian troops should all be transferred to the navy and air force, to protect our Arctic sovereignty. It costs a third less to go by ship through the Arctic from Europe to the Orient than it does through Panama, and there are trillions of dollars worth of natural gas, oil and minerals up there. The Russians sure as hell know it and so do the Americans, even the Norwegians and Danes know, and the Norwegians are years ahead of us in having an ultra-modern city above the Arctic Circle. Canada is going to dispatch an unmanned sub to map out its underwater border, 200 nautical miles off land, before the UN deadline of 2013 but the Americans, Russians, Norwegians and Danes are all playing games around the North Pole."

The old man then waved his hand to the air. "A northern East-West route could save China $120 billion a year, and Canada could provide ice-breaking assistance, search-and-rescue, ports of refuge, charts, navigation aids, and ice and weather forecasting, in return for China helping finance our infrastructure development and operating budgets. As for any legal dispute over the Northwest Passage, it could be sidestepped, saying the financial agreement with China was 'without prejudice' to the sovereignty issue."

The man then took both his hands to the air. "But no, the Canadian government is buying tanks and jets to fight World War II style. Scrap the tanks and jets and get back the nuclear subs that we backed out of fifteen years ago in '93, when no Canadian leader had the guts to say what they were really for."

The man soon looked to be loving his one-person audience and he bought me a beer. "The Arctic was never expected to become a navigable waterway or a site for large-scale commercial development but the ice is melting fast. There is a Law-of-the-Sea Convention that says the high seas are free but there are continental shelves beyond the 200-mile zones from the water's edge. Yes, there are rules governing the Arctic but there's no way .the big boys will respect them unless we Canadians have military power up there."

I downed the beer while the old man went on: "A full 150 countries have ratified that Law of the Sea but the Americans never have. Your American subs and the Russian subs are all over the place up there and you Yanks don't even recognize our sovereignty."

When I finished the beer, I smiled at the man and excused myself to leave the bar and amble over to an empty table but before I could sit down, I was invited to join a nearby table of six young others. The youth at the table said they had wondered how long I would last with old Fred, and they told me he had lost a son in Korea.

My six new drinking companions, three men and three women, all appeared to be in their young 20s and were all wearing flannel shirts or old hockey sweaters, jeans and lumberjack boots, looking to be in some sort of uniform for Canadian hosers. All were drinking Canadian draft beer from two huge pitchers in the center of the wooden table and one gave me a colorful answer to my question, "What did the word *Ontario* mean?"

"An Iroquois name – beautiful water or beautiful lake, but our beer didn't make it in." He then panned his head around the bar's outside windows. "Nice part of Ontario up here but after midnight you gotta watch out for the FBI."

"FBI?" I asked and in jest, he half-slammed his glass to the table. "Fuckin' Big Indians."

At midnight, I left half-drunk and stumbled the mile back to the B&B.

Friday July 4 2008

Next morning, I was celebrating my America's birthday alone, humming west on the Trans-Canada Highway toward the province of Manitoba, and once into Manitoba, I cruised mile after mile through a restful green, free of the signage that cluttered much of Ontario. I stopped for a pee in Portage La Prairie, a pretty little city mid-province, and had intended to veer north to Riding Mountain National Park and see the elks, but when I got out of the the car to urinate, I was swarmed by mosquitoes and jumped back into the cockpit to keep heading west.

After a time, I was in Saskatchewan and I pulled up in the village of Morse at a co-op gas station, where the owner took one look at the TVR and told me not to go over the speed limit in Saskatchewan or I would get a ticket. He then invited me into his restaurant for some pot pie and upon entering, I noticed several Amish men sitting quietly at a table. The owner caught my glance and smiled, saying the Amish customers were proof that his food was good.

I sat down at the front, next to a picture window and soon found myself peering out through the window across the highway to a vast expanse of prairie, under a giant sky seeming to come all the way down to the ground. Suddenly, the smiling owner was back again and asked if he could join me. He looked to be a healthy man in his 70s and said he was still working hard and that his parents had been hard-working Ukrainian Canadians. My host was quick to add, however, that in the cold winters of Prairie Canada, there was a tradition of helping others, and there was thus a safety net such that people knew they would not freeze or go hungry, if opportunities did not go well for them. "Saskatchewan is the land of social democracy, after the droughts of the dirty '30s, but that's not to be confused with what you Americans call socialism. Being fourth-from-the-left is a pivotal position in any group thinking and that's helpful to know up here, because in Saskatchewan you will always find three people to your left."

For some reason, the owner's comment made me peer outside the picture window again, and I noticed this time an American flag, flying tattered. He caught my glance at it and clarified that the flag was there out of courtesy, but like the Canadian flag was not an icon to be worshiped. I found myself agreeing with him and thinking that is how it should be here, under a Canadian cloudless sky, north of any sacred icons on my America's birthday.

As I continued gazing through the window, I suddenly caught myself reflecting on the first few days of my trip and trying to piece together from the days of cruising and nights of drunken thought, the reality of free trade, where we Americans could, if we wanted, play bridge instead of poker and make ourselves not above international law. Winning was perhaps not everything and God was not on our side.

At that moment, a pretty young lady in a modest brown dress entered the restaurant and walked right past the nodding Amish to come straight to my table. "Excuse me, my name is Kelly. May I sit down?" I remembered my Canadian great-grandfather's manners and jumped to my feet. "Of course!"

Kelly was fresh of face, with straight, sandy-colored hair and without a trace of makeup. She asked for a ride to the provincial capital of Regina and I knew my duty. Off we went.

Kelly suggested that we take a scenic detour and soon we were miles north of the Trans-Canada Highway, reaching in half an hour the Qu'Appelle Valley. Kelly had been telling me along the way of her home in Morse, Saskatchewan, and of her not having a computer, television, radio or telephone and living alone in a housing unit on the outskirts of town. She had said she'd come west from Eastern Canada and was recovering from some sort of pain that we did not discuss. But what few words she had spoken sounded well selected and her vision seemed simple.

At the beginning of the valley was a First Nations village, and as we entered it in the vintage TVR, dogs began barking alongside, to give signal to the fact we were there. The road then continued up the northern ridge of the valley, before it curved west for 40 miles high above a river that rushed alongside the entire length of the valley. I took a look beyond the river to the far southern side and could see another row of low mountains counterpointing with the ones to the right of us on the north.

The temperature was cool for July, about 70 F, and the sky was a full blue. Suddenly, two white, long-tailed birds flew in a half-embrace right in front of the windshield and tried to set themselves down on my hood. I slowed the car down to ease their landing but the birds found the wind a bit tricky and they fluttered off. Then to my left, a First Nations man emerged up a mud path from the river below and he was carrying a net of fish. The man saw Kelly and me and smiled a broad smile as if to say, "Welcome to heaven."

Kelly and I spent an hour meandering along the northern ridge and at one point, we got out of the car to look over the valley below, feel the sun and absorb a Saskatchewan sky that went on forever. Finally, near the western side of the valley, Kelly and I came to a stop in the village of Fort Qu'Appelle at a fish culture reserve where I learned my mother had killed my childhood goldfish by giving them fluoridated water. Then Kelly and I walked over to a First Nations hospital and were invited to supper with Chief Anne. Kelly caused a bit of discomfort when she asked the resident nutritionist about the hospital's vending machines, replete with sucrose, carbonation and caffeine but void of any juices or water. The nutritionist was a well-meaning white woman, in fact an American and new to her job, and she agreed with Kelly's concern but said that a cola company had sponsored the vending machines and that sugar was what was demanded.

Back south at the Trans-Canada Highway, Kelly and I drove west under the open prairie sky of late afternoon, passing some salt flats Kelly said constituted the western hemisphere's only reserve of shorebirds. We then cruised into the early evening beside a freight train running parallel to us until it gradually overtook us along the vast flat grassland.

By 8:00 p.m., we reached Regina, the capital of Saskatchewan, and I invited Kelly to stay with me at my pre-booked B&B. She graciously declined and said she was committed to bunking elsewhere. I kissed her on the forehead before we gave each other a long hug and I vowed to stop at Morse on my way back to see her.

The B&B was a stucco home, well preserved with wide front porch and a rust-free '49 Ford in the driveway – there was no eastern Canadian rock salt in the Canadian West. An elderly gentleman greeted me, dressed I guessed in the mandatory Canadian plaid shirt and he, Stefan, swore by his Ford after my commenting on it. But I noticed too in the next-door driveway that his neighbor had a 40-year-old Volkswagen.

After I checked in, Stefan invited me to sit with him in the front parlor and sample some of his sherry, while his wife stayed in the kitchen and prepped for the next morning's breakfast. He became intrigued with my touch of defensiveness after I said my father's roots were in Toronto, and Stefan declared, "Whether a Canadian is from the Prairies, Quebec, the West Coast, East Coast or anywhere in between, a hatred for Toronto is what binds this country together."

I was enjoying the sherry at day's end and did not appreciate until I offered to refill Stefan's steel cup that he was drinking from a different vial, one of cranberry juice. "Please don't let me cause any discomfort for you, Arthur. I just don't drink any more but would be hurt if you stopped because of me." The "discomfort" word stuck in my mind but I stayed drinking, though motioning that I too should probably stop, while hoping for his protest. When it didn't come, I had myself another glass of sherry as back-up, in case I came later to feel poorly about taking more.

Stefan may have seen through my move and chose to elaborate on his own circumstance. "My wife Katherine and I were drinking buddies, after the kids left for Alberta, but things took two huge turns for the worse and now we've stopped."

I tried to put the issue at arm's length. "I guess I get it from my father's side. His grandmother was Irish Canadian and did not drink herself but carried the Celtic gene. Although as you know, Stefan, one does not need to be Celtic to have a problem with alcohol. France has one of the highest rates of alcoholism in the world, behind Russia and Poland and 10 times the rate of cirrhosis of either Britain or Germany."

Suddenly I sensed I could be treading on ethnic sensitivities. "I hope I am not offending" and Stefan swept his paw. "That's okay, Arthur, I'm Canadian born," and so I went back to the arm's-length pedantry. "As you may have picked up, Stefan, I intellectualize the issue of my drinking, so I don't have to emotionally integrate the problem."

Stefan's head then turned to me in a smile. "God forbid you should have to do that, Arthur," and when I queried "Why?" he grinned. "Because you would then be splitting an infinitive. Not bad for a second generation Canadian, eh Arthur? I had a strict English teacher up in North Battleford."

I retired that Friday night at 10:00.

Saturday July 5 2008

On the first Saturday of my trip as I reached Alberta in mid-afternoon, a bit of boy play seemed in order. The speed limit had shot up and the drivers had shot up more, so I put my foot down to cruise at a 90-mile glide, zooming past massive countryside and distant oil rigs, for the three full hours to Calgary.

When I arrived after supper, it was clear that the Calgary Stampede was on but there also seemed to be an upbeat attitude that looked to have a broader foundation. Oil-rich Calgary was awash in new boutiques and restaurants and it had a happy hubris that poured forth from its greeting people. I parked the car at my B&B and set out to wander past the new office towers, looking for some semblance of Bohemia, rationalizing that not everyone could be oil-rich, with some people maybe even questioning the cowboy lifestyle.

After a half an hour, I had not yet arrived at anything resembling ramshackle and I had to settle instead for a prefab pub on the city's southeast side. It was there that I met Graham. He had been serving beer for a year in Alberta but was on his way back, the following day, to Vancouver Island and what he described as a life more temperate. He told me he was not going to take the tourist route through Banff or Jasper but instead go north, past Willmore Wilderness Park and Grand Prairie, before crossing into British Columbia. Once inside B.C. at Pouce Coupe, Graham planned to go west and south for 500 miles, through the middle of the province, before veering west to reach Vancouver and its ferry across to Vancouver Island.

The talk reminded me of how vast Canada was and the reality of time then hit me. I had eight days left of vacation before reporting back to work in Chicago on Monday July 14, and if I continued west for even a few days, I would have to break south to the United States and go across its northern edge to reach Chicago on time. Such a route would also mean that I would not see Chantelle, and after four or five days' vacation, I felt a need to see the woman I loved and share with her some new thoughts. But by the time of those thoughts coming to mind on that Saturday night in

Calgary, I was getting progressively drunk and my priorities got waylaid by a need to take in more alcohol. Finally at midnight Mountain time, I staggered out of the prefab swing door and caught a cab back to my B&B.

Sunday July 6 2008

I drove back east toward a softer-edged Saskatchewan but when I stopped at Morse where Kelly lived, I had to probe locals to track her down. She was found wandering some peripheral fields, carrying a bouquet of daisies, and Kelly invited me to stay overnight but I declined and feigned a half-truth of time. She did not understand, given the number of days I had before I went back to work, but I said something like pressures on my mind from the cutthroat East and she smiled the resign of a person sweetly met but never to see again.

I bombed east through the rest of Saskatchewan and Manitoba and reached Kenora, Ontario, a little past 2:00 a.m., Central Daylight Time, it being too late to drink. I then spent three sleepless hours in bed.

Monday July 7 2008

Before 6:00 a.m., I had already departed the Kenora B&B and was experiencing again the awesome drive over the north shore of Lake Superior. But when I got east of Sault Ste. Marie, I turned south into Lake Huron's Manitoulin Island and there caught the afternoon ferry for the one-and-a-half-hour shortcut to Southern Ontario and its upper Bruce Peninsula.

At the top of the Bruce, I was suddenly in a sailboat and scuba-diving village named Tobermory. I wanted to explore its underwater park but arrived too late in the day and had to settle instead for some Great Lakes fish and Point Pelee Ontario wine, while watching the sun set on a majestic Lake Huron.

Tuesday July 8 2008

After a breakfast of porridge, honey, grapefruit juice and coffee, my B&B hosts urged me to pause on the way home at a flat-rock beach near Lion's Head and sample one of the Bruce Peninsula's east coast gorges, while I swam in the cold, clean waters of Georgian Bay. I did so and then shot south down the Bruce Peninsula. At the Bruce's bottom, I veered southeast to begin a scenic cruise through the villages of Chatsworth, Durham, Mount Forest, Arthur and Fergus. By mid-afternoon, I was in the little city of Guelph, having a veggie lunch, just north of Highway 401 and its fast route east to Toronto.

The 401 was packed and its drivers felt aggressive after my reprieve of a week. Suddenly the adrenaline cranked up and left me playing car hockey with the worst of them. But by then I was also thinking of the voyage behind me, of Mount Pleasant Cemetery, my roots, the spiritual experience at Dreamer's Rock, Fred the indignant Canadian, the socially-minded man from Saskatchewan, the tattered American flag, Stefan the reformed alcoholic, Graham leaving oil-rich Alberta to go home and Kelly the young lady still healing from the ravages of a frenzied East.

I wanted to share my thoughts with Chantelle but also came the thought of how I had left her. I had spied on her notes and had justified it, under the construct of indignation. In a charging TVR, I was coming to appreciate that I had broken the faith of the woman I loved.

As I entered the Avenue Road turnoff from the 401, the slower traffic felt not slow enough and the green of Queen's Park came much too soon. It was only a minute before I wrapped around Queen's Park and parked on Grosvenor Street. I left the top down and charged the 100 yards to Chantelle's apartment.

The old front buzzer gave off its feeble sound but there came no answer. I buzzed again, waited a few seconds, then buzzed again. Then again.

I guessed Chantelle to be at work and decided I would surprise her, so I went to the building's west side, where there was a 10-foot square of grass beside her basement window, and I saw the apartment was dark. After no response coming from my tapping, I began sliding aside the half-open screen but in doing so, noticed wedged at the far right corner of the window jamb a piece of yellowed newspaper. I was about to chuck it into the apartment to discard later, when suddenly its headline caught my eye.

The article was from *The Toronto Star* 20 years ago and was about a Florida family that had been stricken with AIDS. I started reading how a section of Western civilization had cut off all communications with the family's two innocent children:

I cannot forget the face of eight-year-old Randy, standing alone in the schoolyard on the first day of classes last week. As other boys and girls recounted the highlights of their summers, Randy stood clutching the wire fence, and his young eyes stayed puzzled, the little boy not comprehending the brutal ostracism.

I spent that first week of school in central Florida, home to three boys, hemophiliacs who had tested positive for the AIDS virus in 1986. After their condition was revealed, the boys were excluded from school, the family was asked not to return to church and the mother lost her nursing job. The day before school opened, a man called the father, saying his children were going to die anyway, so...

On that first day of school, half the children stayed home to protest the boys' admittance and on Tuesday and Wednesday, anonymous callers phoned in bomb threats. At school, no one would play with Randy and his sister Candy overheard two other first-graders talking about the "AIDS boys." Some neighborhood kids came by, looking for the "faggots." That same night, Randy and Candy said they were afraid to go for a walk on the road, because the school people would run them over and say it was an accident. By Friday, another threat said vigilantes would burn the house down.

Wasting no time, the family left home, leaving the children's uncle asleep in the back room. About 10:00 p.m., a fire erupted in the boys' bedroom and the uncle was rescued by a neighbor.

The Rays lost everything, Louise her wedding dress and the children their favorite books. When Randy was told of the fire, he asked his father if Randy's stuffed animal, Mr. Monkey, had been saved. He had carried the stuffed animal around with him to the doctor, to the hospital, whenever he was frightened. But Mr. Monkey burned too. The mayor has not spoken publicly but has withdrawn his 10-year-old from school.

To the outside world, these kids are brave beyond belief but inside, their pain is immense. The night before the first day of school, Robert looked up at me and I said the only thing that came to mind, "Be brave." He was and still is, unlike so many of the adults in his part of central Florida.

The article went on to say that the father decided to leave the entire area of the state, taking with him his hemophiliac children who had acquired the immune deficiency syndrome virus through blood transfusions. I thought of my country, the United States of America, and how such ostracism fell in line with rugged individualism, the American myths and the importance placed on flag, to symbolize the reverence for which all those myths stood. I also thought of sharing it all with my beloved Chantelle.

Wednesday July 9 2008

Chantelle was still missing on day two, when I learned she had taken a leave of absence, and her old Volvo was gone from the hospital parking lot. Now, there was no hiding how deep I had hurt her. Chantelle, the woman I loved and so reverently respected, was the same woman to whom I had made no attempt to meet halfway, in our misunderstanding.

I did not have a key to the apartment, so I left the door unlocked and tore up in my TVR the 100 miles to Penetang. As I then approached the foot of the Fouriere steps, mother Camille smacked the screen door open and thundered out, with sister Roxanne tailing close behind. Pantel was not there and had gone for his school-bus run.

As I stood at the bottom of the porch steps, Camille jabbed her index finger down at my face, "You, Jew, have lost her and Chantelle will soon be a big shot." Her arms stretched out to the sky. "Soon she will drive a big Mercedes and you..." Her arms came back down and her right index finger rifled right against my chest "...will be nothing, ha ha ha!"

Genes sometimes skip a generation. What I should have done was display some of the same tolerance that Chantelle would have shown any ailing patient, but I thought instead of hate being an acquired emotion and not one built in at birth.

The race back to Toronto came with a deep pain in my chest, and once I was back, I left the car again with top down in an illegal parking space and charged back to the unlocked apartment, pleading with another resident to let me in at the front before hoping that the familiarity of Chantelle's home would spawn thoughts of where she was. A bottle of red wine sat on the kitchen counter, open but corked, and I pried it out with my teeth, before spitting the cork into the kitchen sink and slugging all the wine down. The pain in my chest began to lessen and so I shifted down the counter to the wine rack for more.

With a second bottle in hand, I sat down on Chantelle's wingback seat, contemplating what to do next. My eyes wandered the living room and office, and it was not long before my thoughts turned to Chantelle's notes. But this time no rage came back. An hour passed, drifting into mid-afternoon before my eyes fell to the bottle and I saw it was empty. By then I was feeling relieved and suddenly felt compelled to try using Chantelle's notes to find out where she was.

I brushed my teeth to clean my breath of alcohol and with notes in hand, proceeded up the old building's basement hall to the front door, wedged it open with a doorstop and ventured over to the hospital's doctors' lounge, to try coaxing fellow physicians into giving me hints as to where Doctor Fouriere had gone. The doctors took issue with my willingness to use her notes that way, and no one was prepared to tell me where Chantelle was, even if they knew.

Her kind boss, Doctor Abrams, did however see how desperate I was and told me he would allow my car into her free parking spot, such that if Chantelle returned, she would find it there before entering her apartment. I thanked Doctor. Abrams but knew I was too drunk to drive and said I would move the car there soon but for now would leave it on the street with its Illinois license plates. He may have sensed my drunkenness and in any event said his doctor's card was needed to enter the lot. Doctor Abrams suggested he move the car there and advised me that I needed to pay my parking tickets anyway. I nodded a "Yes" and together we ambled out of the lounge over to the TVR on the street. Without a word, I went to the passenger seat and put Chantelle's notes on the floor beside the old parking tickets. Doctor Abrams then maneuvered my sacred TVR into Chantelle's parking space and I told him putting the top up was tricky, so we left the top down and shook hands, before Doctor Abrams raced back into the hospital. I was dehydrated and went back to the apartment for more wine, not thinking that I had left Chantelle's notes on the car floor.

Chicago was an hour behind Toronto, and after 5:00 p.m. Toronto time, I placed a phone call to Cork & Church, saying that because of a domestic crisis, I would be delayed from my Monday July 14 return. Cork demanded I not be late in returning and when I implored that I had no choice, he hung up. Communications went no better with my mother when I phoned her, and she asked again if I had knocked up a *shiksa*.

Thursday July 10 2008

On Wednesday evening, after having some of the packaged food in Chantelle's kitchen, I had another bottle of red while sitting in her winged chair, and my night for turning in was early, in the hope that I would be well slept for the new day to greet Chantelle. But the night was sleepless and when in the morning I dragged myself out of bed and ventured toward the washroom, I caught sight of the empty living room and the heartache came back like a vise-grip. Then before I even urinated, I turned to the kitchen, opened another bottle of red wine and downed half of it in three gulps. I took to the toilet with bottle in hand, peed and went through the motions of washing my hands before I returned with bottle to the kitchen. I found some more food in the cupboards, managed to open four cans with my Swiss army knife, ate the contents raw and washed it all down with some more wine.

By then, the heartache was no longer going away with the wine and in opening another in anticipation of the first soon to be empty, I noticed the rack was running out. I returned to the washroom with bottle in hand, shaved, showered and drank, then went back nude to the kitchen to fetch the final bottle for steadying me while getting dressed. I put the rest of the last wine into an empty juice bottle and departed for the wine store, leaving the building front door again ajar.

Along the way, while sipping wine from the juice bottle, I noticed that the heart pain was still not going away and so I resolved instead of going to the wine store to go to the government-run liquor outlet and buy vodka. Upon arrival, I finished the wine in the juice bottle outside and then bought four magnum bottles of vodka to stock up, in case the government store at some point refused me. Upon leaving, I rendered a polite Canadian thank you but once outside, poured the vodka from one of the bottles into the juice bottle, in a desperate attempt to ease the heartache. It worked and I made it back to Chantelle's apartment.

Friday July 11 2008

The pain anchored in my chest had eased but not its source and by Friday, all the canned food was gone. I had also started a process that kept me so incapacitated that I did not have to deal with reality, beyond waiting in Chantelle's apartment for her to return. I was drunk each day by mid-morning and when I phoned Cork at week's end, he heard my slurred words and fired me. Then, in some drunken hope of consolation, I phoned my mother and she shrieked to my father, when she heard me slur that I was not soon to return.

There were 400 hours left in that sultry month of July and I passed the 400 either unconscious or trying to be that way. When I had been near Chantelle, I had strived to be a better person but now I was sober only in the light of early morning and long enough, with some kick-off vodka, to amble to Fran's Restaurant, down two eggs with dry toast and then buy more vodka, before meandering two blocks back to the basement apartment.

I had no Canadian work permit and, in any event, sensed that my references would not check out. I had only my debit and credit cards and their pre-morbid reputation. As for my mother, she would keep trying to reach me and leave guilt-ridden messages.

Tuesday July 22 2008

When morning came, I was unable to make it to the government booze store and I passed out around noon, but late in the day, I managed to *schlepp* over to the Yonge Street strip and get to the liquor outlet. I bought some vodka before downing a couple of big snorts on the sidewalk, and then feeling somewhat soothed, tucked the vodka into its plastic bag and sauntered north toward a bench. I noticed, however, on the way, a pub up some stairs and so I started up its dusty steps, all the while hearing laughter and the sound of British accents.

The Brits didn't ask me what I did for a living and I found it novel that unemployed I, full of alcohol and poaching off a girlfriend's apartment, could be treated with respect in a genteel pub. The acceptance brought out some good in me and I decided I wanted to keep the perception going, so after a couple of pints, I turned down a Brit's offer to buy me a Guinness and feigned my day's limit. I then negotiated my way down the stairs to the street and began to work my way back home to the apartment where I hit the straight vodka again.

Friday July 25 2008

The following day, as light hit the apartment window, I woke up still clothed and needing vodka in the worst way but found the bottle beside the bed empty. There was another in the kitchen but I was shaking so badly that I had to crawl there to get it. But once the new vodka was in me, I became calm enough to make my way on all fours back to the bathroom, while pushing the new bottle across the floor. When I got to the bathroom, I pulled myself up to the sink to put my lips around the tap and I took four gulps of water before sitting down on the toilet to pee while quaffing more vodka. Then I staggered back to the kitchen, where I poured the vodka into a water bottle and started another trek to the liquor store.

On the way home, I stopped in front of Chantelle's hospital at a mini-park, or what Canadians call a parkette, and sat down on a bench to have more vodka. It was already 75 F and I felt the warmth that ethanol gives but I also sensed the trees around me swaying, so I lifted my body off the bench and crossed Grosvenor Street to the apartment building, jimmied the door open and made my way down to the basement. I had to crawl the last part of the hall to make it to Chantelle's apartment before I got inside to her brown wool rug, curled up and passed out.

I awoke that same day, this time in the afternoon to realize the sun was streaking through the western window, and so to spare the effects of the sunlight, I reached for the vodka and got myself unconscious again in a matter of gulps. I awoke again at suppertime and rallied to repeat the liquor store process but this time built an emergency inventory, in case the government facility cut me off at a later date.

The following day, to face the daylight, I managed to get enough vodka into me to steady me again for the trip to buy more, but this time skipped the parkette and went straight home to phone the hospital and ask of Chantelle. There was no word.

Sunday July 27 2008

During the third week of the vodka ritual, I began to realize my body could not take it. I was lying in bed with a bottle beside me, and every new shot triggered a shudder, with the revulsions building to vomits on the floor beside me. Though I was very dehydrated, I discovered after a crawl to the bathroom that I could not even keep water down, and I lay back on the bed, bouncing and shaking out of control, with my eardrums booming as if there was a drum coming from within.

After a while, I tried crawling again to the bathroom but as I began to pull myself up to the sink, I caught sight of myself in the mirror and retched. I collapsed down to my knees, turned to the toilet and ripped out my insides. I lay down on the floor trembling next to the toilet for many minutes, until I finally managed to slide back to the sink, hoist up its front and mouth some water. But after the gulp, I spewed again. I tried to straighten up but fell sideways into the tub and had to crawl out over its edge before reaching the sink tap and washing away what I could.

For the next 20 hours, I tried getting water into me and on the following day, took in a bit without vomiting. The day after was a nerve-end better and by day four of the torture, in the morning of a late-July Wednesday, I managed to phone a detoxification unit. It was full but I did have a talk with a detox counselor who was an old alcoholic lady and she coached me to meet her that afternoon in a city help office.

I shaved as best I could and then with shredded face, took a short shower before I coaxed on fresh socks and underwear, and stumbled east three miles to an office of sorts, next to a Toronto public housing development in an infamous area called Regent Park. There, I had a seat in a small, spartan waiting room across from two shabbily dressed men – one a teenager, one older and heavily bearded – who were working on computers with free access.

Both men turned around to look at me, but instead of turning back to resume whatever they were doing, each took an extra moment to peruse me and the elder man gave me the evil eye. I lowered my gaze to the floor as if to show I was a welfare case minding my own business but minutes later, I got up out of indignation and stood to spy over the men's shoulders. The language on their desktops was Hebrew. The elder again turned to look at me and was about to say something but my woman counselor appeared.

My counselor was a gracious lady despite her drawn alcoholic face, and she welcomed me into her little office where I found out the woman was helping me out of some motive beyond her work. After meeting with her for 20 minutes, I set out with an AA book in hand for one of Toronto's 400 weekly Alcoholics Anonymous meetings. There I was received by kind faces pouring forth their empathy.

Thursday July 31 2008

Days passed, with juices first, then eggs over easy, followed by toast, bananas and spinach. I walked Toronto, sometimes for 15 miles, and swam at the pool in the university's Hart House, before showering and heading off to another AA meeting.

For three weeks it was like this, until late August, with life little else. But the swimming did build to a mile a day and during the swim, my mind began to drift. I thought of Chantelle and how I might contribute.

Wednesday August 20 2008

Three weeks into sobriety, I was staying dry but was unresolved on the cause of my drunkenness and still angry at something or someone. Chantelle was not to be heard of but in preparation for her return, I sought to align my mind with what I surmised was hers.

Chantelle had a dark green three-speed bicycle, made in Sweden no less, and by then I had enough balance to ride a few miles northeast to a ravine called Moore Park, off Toronto's Don Valley. There in the ravine, I was puffing uphill to keep the 50-pounder going when suddenly in front of me, spread across the entire dirt road, were four bikes. Next to them were four Orthodox Jews – one young man and three boys about puberty in age.

The man was standing with a cell phone welded to his ear but must have heard my puffing, since the three boys looked straight at me before turning their eyes to the man to get, I guessed, his signal to move their bicycles out of the way. But the man kept his head turned sideways on his cell phone and his eyes never met mine.

To the right of the wide path, the brush was forbiddingly prickly, so I got off my bike to inch my way past on the left, along a slippery edge above a creek. As the boys watched with their hands at the ready to move their bikes, their eyes stayed stuck on their leader for his apparent go-ahead. But his eyes didn't leave the ground and his ear stayed pressed to the cell phone.

Once beyond the mess of bikes across the path, I stopped and turned to say in scolding tone that I too was Jewish, and the boys looked at my face before they again looked to their leader. Without warning, he slammed shut his cell phone and commanded the boys to pick up their bikes, and off they went in the other direction.

The Moore Park ravine led west to David Balfour Park, with its long green stretch at the south having multiple orchard trees from a time long past. As I bicycled up into the park's northern half, I ventured into a hilly, heavily wooded area, alongside another above-ground part of the creek that was sill part of the Moore Park ravine. There, I suddenly felt the call of nature and chose in the fresh air of a mid-town city to relieve myself, wipe things up with my old cotton handkerchief, and bury the poop and hanky in the bank's mud. Then, with bike in tow, I set out on foot up a mud path that wound its way north along a steep hill above the creek to Mount Pleasant Cemetery, the one that housed my great-grandparents.

Again I saw the joggers and the walkers but noted this time that the deciduous trees were all labeled. I biked across the cemetery and found at the northwest side, an exit gate to a wide trail that had once been a railway bed. I took it west over a bridge crossing Yonge Street to Oriole Park, with its playground for handicapped people. I then followed a city bike-path north out of the park, past some staid homes and Norwegian maples, to Eglinton Park where I witnessed free tennis courts, a hockey arena, recreation center, playground, hardball diamonds, soccer fields and a wide variety of dogs playing off-leash.

I bicycled east to Yonge Street, north of busy Eglinton Avenue and saw among its shops and patios a restaurant that I judged, from the purple Bentley and orange Porsche automatic out front, to house perfect assholes. I parked and went inside to use the Canadian bathroom and found some clue that I was in a mafia restaurant – there was no condom dispenser, only one for colognes.

I biked southwest, several miles past the grand mansions of Forest Hill to another ravine and took it west past Sir Winston Churchill Park to an intriguing area of mixed ethnicity. I followed my curiosity and kept cycling west until I came across an old streetcar yard that had been changed into an artsy area called Wychwood. From there I saw at the bottom of the road an open stone gate, and as I biked closer to it, I saw a tiny sign saying "Private Road." I decided to bike through the gateway anyway and found to my surprise an English village called Wychwood Park, with woodland, pond, huge trees and Tudor homes, all set on the bank of Toronto's ancient Lake Iroquois, and overlooking downtown.

A short while later biking back east, I passed Casa Loma and came to recall its being built by the grandfather of Chantelle's mentor, Regis Brandin, who had been a retired professor of multiple religions before dying a few years back. I pondered what he would have said today about my reaction to the perceived arrogance by an Orthodox Jew. Doctor Brandin was a gentile but had taught Hebrew to Jewish children at Toronto's Beth Tzedec synagogue, and had told Chantelle that the haughtiness of a few Jews was not in keeping with the principles of Judaism. Regis wanted followers of Judaism and Jesus to close their gaps of thinking, but in order to do so, he said that gentiles had first to strip Christianity of its irrationalities.

After Labor Day of Monday September 1 2008

September ended the Canadian summer, and a sense that the party was over was awash across a Presbyterian Toronto. This time, though, the city was focused on a Wall Street recklessness that was wreaking havoc with the world's economy. As late as 1960, the financial sector in the United States had generated only 2% of corporate profits but now it was 40%, and there had been a deliberate undoing of the 1933 Roosevelt Act that had kept separate the commercial banks from the buccaneer investment banks, with their swinging deals and speculative ventures. Canada had maintained the distinction between the banking sectors but now the U.S. had an incessant tension between the two.

Production of real stuff had been replaced by illusory financial "products," which in the short term tricked the less conniving, and the resulting derivatives had become weapons of mass destruction. Financial whizzes had learned how to game and in the previous year of 2007, Wall Street's top 50 private-equity and hedge-fund managers had earned an average income of $588 million.

This money elite posed a real hazard for the rest of us but other financial magnates of repute, once realizing they were being bilked and facing a deregulatory green light, had also buried bad debts into bigger bundles and had passed them along to greater fools, all the while taking huge bonuses and hiding the money. The head of one New York investment company had bilked half a billion out of it before leaving, fully knowing that the company was going under.

One reason the frauds had grown so vast was that many investors had been drawn in by their friends, and informal advice had run over rigorous research, leading to all sorts of shortcuts. The bubble was bursting in the American economy, the U.S. credit rating was being threatened with a downgrade that would cost billions, the conspirators were hiding, along with their assets, and journalists had done no more homework than they had done before cheering on the start of the Iraq war.

From the late '60s and '70s onward, the American economy had been hijacked by a free-market mantra that said greed was good and regulation bad, and we Americans had led the world in dumping debt onto our grandchildren, mortgaging our future under the rubric of freedom. The 1964 presidential candidate Barry Goldwater had rejected the legacy of Roosevelt's New Deal and had fought to remove all aspects related to what he described as a welfare economy. Subsequently, Ronald Reagan, who had delivered a speech in support of Goldwater and had made practice runs for the U.S. presidency in '68 and '76, had been elected and had implemented sweeping political and economic initiatives.

Reagan's policies had advocated both control of the money supply to reduce inflation and a spurring of economic growth by reducing tax rates as well as less regulation of the economy and government spending. But at the same time, Reagan borrowed to support huge increases in defense spending, creating massive government debt and ultimately a world recession. By 2008, other nations were following, depleting their ability to address pivotal problems like health care and climate change.

If the assumptions about an innate wisdom of markets were flawed, as former Fed Chairman Alan Greenspan would finally admit, then faith in reaching a new equilibrium was also misplaced, because there never was any solid ground upon which to build such assumptions. A propensity to overvalue nonproductive things like financial derivatives, gold and diamonds and undervalue things like food, global climate and social responsibility seemed more the mark of the market society. The 17th-century Dutch Age of Mercantilism and the later British Empire were built on tobacco, gold, sugar and salt, and were delivered by slaves.

The results of such misplaced priorities were not only the outcomes like that black autumn of 2008 but also preposterous inequalities in power, and it would not be Wall Street that would pay the price. Opaque derivatives, like the synthetic collateralized debt obligations or CDOs, were being manipulated by a handful, and there was little doubt that the clique would play a core role in inflating global assets before the meltdown. These pioneers had also featured prominently in the market crash of 1987 and later on in 1998, when the collapse of the hedge fund Long-Term Capital Management had rocked world markets.

Yet the culprits stayed motivated by a heinous mix of hubris, narcissism and a demagogic god to justify their every entitlement. They feigned victimhood, like the other market players, but sooner or later, those whiz kids would be back in the same high-stakes game that they had created, using their same old tricks. Their ability to access leverage became diminished only in the short term, and the CEOs of money-manipulating businesses could take comfort in the legal history of Wall Street – the biggest financial firms, even after being sued for fraud by regulators and paying huge fines, rarely deposed their leaders.

Citigroup, Goldman and Merrill Lynch were among 10 firms that had earlier, in 2003, agreed to pay $1.4 billion for settlement of claims that their analysts had manipulated recommendations, but not one CEO had lost his job. There had been a similar result in 2006 when Citigroup and Goldman Sachs had been among lenders paying for manipulating the market in auction-rate bonds. Goldman Sachs played a key role in capital markets, conducting bond issues for emerging economies such as South Africa and Israel.

Seeing the world through markets not only distorted our sense of selves but also projected our disability onto everyone else. Because of Wall Street lobbies, a spirit of social cleansing would ensue, and we masses would be lectured that our thrift would be the only solution to fix the problem. Little recognition would be given to the notion that perhaps the opposite of self-serving consumption was not thrift but generosity.

Blame would further deflect as in the past – after the 1929 market crash, the U.S. had reacted with economic nationalism and had thrown up protectionist walls, supposedly to shelter its maligned majority but really to deflect mass indignation, and other countries had followed suit. The U.S. majority had thus come to suffer more with the resulting trade war and the Great Depression, and American banks had pulled billions out of Germany, helping give us the Nazis.

The 1930s Depression and the current crisis also experienced their origins in excessive debt, especially mortgage debt – since 1913, Americans who pursued the American Dream of home ownership had been able to tax-deduct the interest on their mortgages, and residential mortgages had grown from 10% of household worth in 1920 to 27% by 1929. Banks had been able to create money out of thin air, lending out on people's deposits and getting to keep the interest they collected on them. Government control of cash reserves was government control of credit, but few leaders asked whose money it was, if not the people's. Depression economist Keynes had argued that the money was in effect the peoples', but he was condemned as an anti-Semite.

This time in 2008, with mortgage deductibility being allowable up to $1 million, housing prices had inflated and bad mortgages had been transmitted into the financial sector through hedge funds and credit default swaps, their being so named with egregious insouciance. Goldman Sachs had bet against its own clients' holdings and its CEO had said he felt no duty to tell customers who had bought any collateralized debt obligation.

But the 2008 sub-prime mortgage defaults were only a symptom of the problem, misdirecting people's awareness toward them and related consumer indebtedness. The bigger cause of the meltdown was the assets that people could not find, because there was no record of them. The recorded cash in the world – bank notes and coins – was $13 trillion, with $2 trillion in U.S. banks, $2 trillion in other world areas but $9 trillion going untaxed, stashed away in secret banks. The documented paper in the world – mortgages, bonds, et cetera – was $175 trillion. But the nominal value of derivatives out there was around $1,000 trillion or $1 quadrillion, and there was no track of most of them. Nor was there any real understanding of the sum of the derivatives, since enormous double counting was involved, even triple counting or more, with credit default swaps hedging against potential losses, but the hedge not always nullifying earlier contracts.

The International Swaps and Derivatives Association conservatively estimated – read protectively – the total value of outstanding derivatives at $450 trillion, $400 trillion of which were contracts tied to interest rates and currencies, but much trading in the derivatives market – in the hundreds of trillions of dollars – was happening privately and was based on little more than a phone call. The U.S. Commodity Futures Modernization Act of 2000 had allowed derivatives, including credit default swaps, to escape federal regulation, and derivatives dealers with large counterparty exposure posed systemic risks to the marketplace. Moreover, insurance firms, with less reporting requirements than banks, had been deeply into the derivatives business, with those firms tied to corporate bonds, mortgage securities and interest rates.

The inevitable bank bailout of 2008 would prove instructive. A Republican president would be compelled to do so, and an incoming Democratic president would be compelled to endorse what he hated. What, then, would make the two presidents do it?

Having things recorded was what allowed people to trust international transactions, but the secrecy surrounding derivatives had cost trillions of dollars, and derivatives could not be traced or priced. Moreover, nobody seemed able or willing to take the bad stuff out of the system. On planet earth in September 2008, there were $60 trillion worth of credit default swaps outstanding, and they had to be paid off in one form or another. Soon, the United Kingdom would be three hours from financial collapse.

In 1850, before the Irish potato famine, there had in London been frenzied commodity speculation and after the famine had broken out, there had continued to be Irish commodity exports but none to feed the starving Irish. About 4,000 years ago in ancient Sumer or today's Syria and Iraq, the city of Ur had prospered in the fertile land between the Tigris and Euphrates rivers, but Ur had suffered a calamitous market crash, 1,000 years later, when its mutual fund bubble had collapsed after reckless speculation. Ur never recovered.

In the 1,500 years leading up to that crash in Ur 3,000 years ago, religious institutions had been financially forced to outsource from private capitalists, and the bedazzling metal, gold, had been seized upon by those capitalists as a form of currency for trade. Those gold capitalists could stir up a war or economic crisis, and the price of that gold would go up. Kings, literally "big men" in dialect, had come to replace priests in positions of power, with palaces replacing temples as places of magnificence. But those kings were financially owned by those gold-manipulating capitalists. Gold, considered a divine and indestructible metal in ancient Egypt, had come to do what central banks would later do, and thousands of years later in our current era's year of 1284, Venice had introduced the gold Ducat, soon to become the most popular coin in the world and remain so for five centuries.

The period 1880 - 1913 before World War I had been the gold-standard years, when central banks had but a single function – exchanging gold for paper or paper for gold. That function, however, had ended abruptly in 1913, when the U.S. Federal Reserve system had been created, and some believe that move was the key event of the 20th century. But the bankers of today don't like to talk about gold. The Federal Reserve became the greatest agency for inflation ever, and its manipulated monetary policy was implicated by economists in World War I, the Great Depression and World War II.

Gold has been mined for 3,500 years and some 3.5 billion ounces have been extracted. One-third today is in central banks, one-third in jewelry and one-third is hoarded, which means that gold remains the world currency of last resort.

In 2008, as in decades earlier, a conservative mantra echoed over and over was that deficits were the products of liberalism, but the way right-wing parties governed in North America invariably produced deficits or weakened the fiscal position to force deficits later. That reality was heretical to conservatives and counterintuitive to us economic illiterates but the evidence bore it out. Since, however, economic literacy remained low, key conservatives knew that the inevitable tax increases to clean up the mess would be politically damaging, not to those conservatives but to the politically inheriting liberal thinkers. Woe to the Obama to come.

If the law had required holders of these derivatives to record them, one would have known who was holding the worthless stuff, and the decision to locate value and isolate the toxic paper may have been the only lasting alternative to collapse of the entire system. But the holders of bad derivatives did not want to be revealed, because they had survived behind the scenes on image, while fooling a manipulated majority.

The larger the number of witnesses to crimes, the less likely it was that anyone would intervene, and bankers were rewarded more for the money they brought in than for the money they questioned. Institutions, furthermore, were holding those assets and would become insolvent if the bad assets were recognized. The six largest banks in the U.S. had assets worth 60% of the gross national product and those banks, we were told, were too big to fail. As Teddy Roosevelt had said 100 years earlier, economic power can take over political power, and Wall Street is happiest when Washington is paralyzed in a stalemate, making for a non-interfering government.

The top 1% of American income earners enjoyed tax rates that were one-third lower than they were in 1970 and a hedge fund manager earning millions could pay a lower tax than his secretary, yet the wealthiest 1% of Americans possessed a net worth greater than the bottom 90%, leading to inevitable resentment, social malaise and crime. The rich continued to bankroll the campaigns of Democrats and Republicans alike, and once elected, those parties wouldn't dare bite the hand that fed them. Adding to the final insult, many of those rich died rich.

Yet that September of 2008 was not calling for a Karl Marx. The man's name still conjured up reams of perversion but the capitalism that had emerged globally in the 1990s was uncannily like the world anticipated in *The Communist Manifesto*, published in 1848. After that grim 2008, worker upheavals would come, but workers no longer enjoyed the strength in numbers from big factories or even from living in the same part of the city, and a lot of the exploited people worked in funky areas, producing software or mini-advertising.

It looked to be a time of massive manipulation but for me, living off plastic credit cards in a foreign country, I felt mostly out of work. The weeks shifted by and I tried to fight an insidious depression with physical fitness and an exploration of what I felt Canadian. But I also kept up the hope that someday soon, I would again see my love and she would see my change...

Monday October 13 2008

As a stoic September flew by, I came to surmise that Chantelle must have been in touch with her father and that if I could reach Pantel, I could locate Chantelle; so, when Canadian Thanksgiving rolled around on the second Monday of October, I wrote Pantel a letter.

Dear Pantel, Canadian Thanksgiving 2008

    You asked me once if there really were a God. Please keep asking. I now share with Chantelle an ever-changing view of God but of one always benevolent and ready to help us help ourselves, while not curtailing our freedom. God is not made in man's image as the Bible portrays but is a Creator bigger than our minds can so far handle.

    Chantelle, I think, would say that our freedom allows us not only to discern the clues God gives as we make our way but also to question God's very existence. God is not a covetous tyrant who wants to dominate us through fear, power and bedazzlement but is a nurturing teacher who tries to coax out the best in us, and has us keep questioning to expand our curiosities and consciences, letting us feel the freedom coming from such awareness.

    I feel, Pantel, that the Creator encourages our spirits so freed to evaluate all that is set before us. And in so doing, that Creator catalyzes our own re-creation — we use our confidence and imaginations to blossom, and our lives become governed by well-built consciences. Within our expanded awareness, we learn to respect all other creations, and come to recognize our responsibility to protect the more vulnerable, getting a teacher's thrill in seeing them blossom.

    I hope this helps.

    Love,

    Arthur

Friday October 31 2008

No reply came in the weeks thereafter and I began to wonder if Pantel had ever seen my letter at all. I did not trust Camille or Roxanne and I came to fantasize that I could not be heard by anyone. October wore on, and as the harvest colors of the early weeks of autumn fell into a threadbare starkness, the shorter days meant less sunshine and I came to feel a foreboding that was driving me down at all times. I tried again at month-end to reach Pantel.

> *Halloween 2008*
> *Dear Pantel,*
>
> *I feel that learning for the sake of learning and loving so doing should be part of what life is all about. I don't know what the children you are bussing are learning but the kids down here sound like churn-outs. If what I've read is true, any student who figures out the system can learn to navigate that system and do short circuits within it, becoming part of a process that is really cheating and yielding people who are little more than street-smart point-grabbers, with a shaky educational foundation.*
>
> *Please, Pantel, use your love and wisdom to help your bus children see another option. I believe Chantelle would want it that way.*
> *All my love,*
> *Arthur*

Again, no answer.

Monday November 17 2008

Four months passed with no Chantelle walking through the door, and November brought a skeletal look to Toronto with shorter days still. My bicycling, in fact all attempts to fight depression, came to feel pointless and I gave up any thought of writing to a non-responding Pantel.

On the third Monday of November, I was having breakfast at Fran's after a sleepless night, anticipating another week of waning hope, and I felt the urge to have alcohol stroke the inside of my chest. I strode east to the Yonge Street strip but had to wait an hour for the government liquor store to open at 10:00 a.m. While I was waiting, I caught sight of a homeless person, crouched down on the sidewalk beside a storefront, and he had a bottle of Canadian rye peeking out of a brown bag. I introduced myself and gave him $20 for what was left, and then I sat down on a close-by bench and downed the rye from the brown bag, watching the sleaze of the Yonge Street strip awaken around me. Finally, at 10:00, I bought four magnums of vodka, as well as four two-ounce ponies for my safari pockets, and marched back to Chantelle's apartment, gulping the ponies along the way and feeling at that moment quite comfortable.

Sometime around noon, I started feeling hungry and so I sauntered back to Fran's with a water bottle full of vodka but was refused service and had to go to a fast food sit-down along the Yonge Street strip. There I wedged a double burger into my mouth before I staggered back to Chantelle's apartment and quaffed more vodka. until I passed out in her reading chair. I awoke in the middle of the afternoon and realized that I needed money from my Chicago bank but first I had to get enough vodka into me to steady my walking. After doing the bank, I hit the pub just after 4:00 p.m. and feigned I was going to have a pint of Guinness after a hard day's work. Within minutes, I was in a conversation about Britain's role in the world, relative to the U.S., and it did not seem difficult to have such abstract talk in a dusty pub of low light, gabbing away with Brits who thought that I, an American, would have an inside view of the United States.

Two hours floated by, with a French impressionistic sense of clarity and my being numb to anxiety, caring only for the moment and the alcohol going into me. Around 6:00 p.m., I sought to show my limit and call it quits but then realized I had to make it home on the rush-hour sidewalks. As fortune would have it, I had enough alcohol in me to be dismissed as a downtown drunk and was given free space.

After passing out on Chantelle's bed, I awoke at midnight and took four gulps of vodka before having a mouthful of tap water and then, with water bottle full of vodka, ambled back to the British pub. At its 2:00 a.m. closing, I was comfortably drunk but somewhat rested from the earlier pass-out and I summoned enough moxie to ask for a taxi. The driver was a big black African and he came up the pub stairs from Yonge Street to help me down into his car. When we reached Chantelle's building, he helped me again but told me that I needed to find God.

Tuesday was not so easy and when I awoke after dawn, I had the shakes but managed to get to some vodka in the kitchen, and in some hour thereafter, fell drunk off Chantelle's winged chair and passed out on her brown rug. Hours later, I awoke in a panic and thought I had not enough vodka, thinking too that I would be refused by the government liquor outlet. But I managed to get again to the kitchen and discover two giant bottles, with one as yet unopened. After several huge slugs, I was sedated enough to shave, shower, put on clean clothes and hit the pub at its 11:00 a.m. opening for some eggs, toast and Guinness. I do not recall any of the pub talk but I think the Brits and I – gosh their accents made them sound knowledgeable – did solve most of the world's problems and even its architectural challenges.

Things got worse in the week thereafter and the cleanliness of my body fell from a shower every second day to every fifth. The pub came to cut me off and the other pubs in the area were alerted to refuse me. My buying vodka from the government outlet also became forbidden and so I had to resort to a private-sector wine store that still served people stinking drunk. Even it, however, quoted some law saying that I was restricted to two double-bottles a day, and they were not enough to keep off the shakes for more than four hours.

With filthy body, I would be shaking by the afternoon and evening, before bouncing all night on Chantelle's bed and then in the morning, walking unshaven, un-showered, un-slept and shaking to the wine store. When I would then get back to the apartment, I would down the two oversized wines, order in pizza, wolf it, barf it back and lie down for another day of the shakes, interrupted only by the intermittent crawl to the toilet.

By week three of the poisoning, December had begun and for some time, I had been seeing only a wine clerk each morning and a pizza man each day. I seemed soon to die.

Monday December 8 2008

On the morning of my 30th birthday, I was lying on Chantelle's bed, trembling in sweat and having to pee in the worst way but saw the floor to the bedroom door splattered in vomit. I had been awake all night, bouncing and counting the hours until I could once again buy more alcohol. But underneath, I wanted to be rescued.

Suddenly there was an almost inaudible knock on the apartment door as if the knocker did not want to appear presumptive. I squeaked out a "Yes?" but could not decipher the call back and so I rolled out of bed, clothed as I had been for a week and crawled over the vomit out of the bedroom to the front door. I propped myself up, and before thinking to look through the peep hole, opened the door. There stood a little man with a wide smile. "Happy birthday, Arthur. May I come in? I'm a little tired, since traveling from 5:00 this morning."

I gasped in my trembling but managed a thank you. "Pantel! You are always welcome!" and we gave each other a huge hug. Pantel took a seat in Chantelle's reading chair and I flopped onto on the floor opposite. He chose, I guessed, to overlook my shaking. "Not far from the bus station, here. Never thought I would see Toronto again. Got a few days off when an AA person volunteered to do my bus route for me." Pantel bent forward with his hands folded and legs apart, and he looked straight at me. "Arthur, I need your help."

I dropped my eyes to the floor before I slowly brought my face back up to Pantel. "You need *my* help?" and he spoke as a gentle healer. "I can't say that I know how you feel, Arthur, but only for different reasons that I've been there. There is a Journey of Hope AA meeting at noon on Charles Street, just east of Yonge and I would like you to take me there."

I gave a shrug of hopelessness at the very suggestion. "Pantel, that is a mile from here and I'm not in shape to go anywhere past the wine store. I've got the shakes!" But he responded with a calm sense of knowing, "We've got to come down slowly. I brought you a birthday present."

Pantel reached into his canvas bag and pulled out two bottles of wine. He opened one, handed it to me and I swallowed it all before stopping shaking. Pantel smiled at my easing but added as a matter of course, "We'll have to pace the second one until the 'store opens, and then we'll get you some more."

I shrugged again the same gesture as if all were lost. "The wine store allows me only two big ones a day. They keep the shakes away only until late afternoon," but Pantel again smiled as if ready for my stock response, "We'll get you four doubles and another four tomorrow. How is your money?"

I perked up a bit. "I've got plastic. If you're buying, why don't we get some vodka at the liquor store?" but Pantel's smile turned to a mild sternness. "No, we shouldn't switch or you'll get sicker and the higher percentage alcohol lets a person consume more per hour; so, for now we'll work with what we've got. Can you keep eggs down?"

I was by then already drinking from the second gift bottle. "Yes, but for the AA meeting, I can't shower and shave," and Pantel assured me that my freshening up could wait. I protested, "I'll be drunk, Pantel!" and he was ready again. "That don't matter, Arthur. They've all been there before," and then he looked down at me. "Please. You'll help me."

Again I looked at the little man whom Chantelle revered and loved, and asked him why he had not responded to my letters. Suddenly Pantel winced and said he had only just received them after their interception. I had guessed as much. I said okay to the AA meeting.

It was just past 9:30 a.m. on a sunny December Monday, and before I took to the wine store with Pantel, he allowed me to transfer the rest of the second wine into a water bottle to sip along the way. Pantel then used my credit card to buy four double-bottles while I waited outside and then he allowed me to duck into an alley to drink four gulps from one of the new bottles, before I emptied the rest into my water bottle for our trip to Fran's for toast and eggs.

When we got back to my apartment, Pantel caught an hour's sleep in the reading chair and I sat on the floor against one wall, trying to sip the wine more slowly. I was not watching the time but was pondering instead how I might approach the notion of Chantelle's whereabouts.

When Pantel awakened just before noon, there was not enough time to make the AA meeting. Not to be daunted, Pantel went through Chantelle's phone book to find another.

There turned out to be a 1:00 p.m. meeting at Saint James Cathedral, downtown, but the trek south would be the first time I had been on a Toronto subway since before I had deserted Chantelle. Before we entered the church, I had several swigs of wine from my water bottle and then laid it down beside a tree, pending the first of two breaks ostensibly to go to the washroom.

The meeting at the elegant old church took me by surprise. Most of the people present looked like eminently respectable ladies and gentlemen, and no one seemed to take notice of my shabby appearance or foul smell. The sense of acceptance rather entranced me and for a moment I almost had a renewed perspective on my existence. But once outside, I became anxious for more wine from my water bottle and after I quaffed it, started to mull in my mind about the 20 minutes it would take before I would be back in Chantelle's apartment for more wine.

Once Pantel and I were back at the apartment and I had a few gulps, I suddenly found myself feeling sleepy and excused myself to the vomit-blobbed bedroom where I fell asleep. When I came to, about 5:00 in the afternoon, I discovered the pizza boxes and blobs of vomit were gone, as were the many empty wine bottles, and a fresh set of laundry sat next to Chantelle's bed on a clean floor.

Pantel then put the pressure on to go to a 5:30 p.m. AA meeting at the U of T, allowing me to go with my disguised wine in tow, and later after another meal of digestible eggs, we went with my wine to yet another meeting at the Orthopaedic Centre on Wellesley Street northeast of Chantelle's apartment. There, Pantel obtained a listing of Toronto AA meetings, and we went to three different meetings a day for the next five days, from Tuesday December 9 until Sunday December 14, when Pantel had to take the Midland-Penetang bus back home.

During the week that Pantel stayed with me, I got enough sleep to ease my drinking back from four double-bottles a day to three doubles, and by the Sunday of his departure, to my own purchase of two. Earlier in the week, Pantel had taught me the trick of adding water to the wine, if and when the body allowed, and in the week after he left, I tried to ease my way down to zero, while going to two AA meetings per day.

I was becoming sober, at least physically, and may even have begun to feel a touch of the serenity that AA said could come my way. But perhaps I was just deluding myself and expecting too much too soon or confusing serenity with a fresh sense of self-righteousness and not acknowledging the anger still simmering in my system. One thing for certain was how disturbed I was with what Pantel had told me on day one – that he did not know of his daughter's whereabouts nor had he heard from Chantelle, other than receiving at his school-bus depot many months ago, a letter from Western Canada, saying she loved him and was fine.

Sunday December 21 2008

On the first day of winter, I began swimming again at Hart House in the University of Toronto, and that afternoon as I left, I experienced a bit of intrigue – it all started when instead of heading back across Queen's Park to Chantelle's apartment, I needed to walk south to University Avenue and Mount Sinai Hospital to meet an AA doctor who was to give me an Ativan prescription for sleep during recovery. But while I was walking down to the hospital corridor of upper University Avenue, I noticed an inordinate number of Orthodox Jews and suddenly realized that sundown marked the start of Hanukkah, and the 39 rules of the Sabbath were to come into force.

A community *eruv* or symbolic boundary was being constructed to allow Jews who observed the traditional rules to carry specific items outside the walls of their own property, an act normally forbidden during the Sabbath. An almost invisible ribbon was about to enwrap a huge swath of Toronto, in particular its Jewish strongholds, and the ribbon was difficult to spot but its extension included fences, hydro wires and fishing lines, along with symbolic doors and walkways. Volunteers were patrolling the perimeter and commanding an *eruv* hotline, and it was then and there that an Orthodox Jew told me they ultimately wanted to ensure Toronto had one of the best *eruvs* in the world, encompassing the hospital corridor and expanding past city borders, to accommodate Jews who had moved beyond them.

When I arrived at the hospital for my 3:00 p.m. appointment, the waiting room outside the doctor's office was empty but for one Orthodox Jew, and he sat without eye contact but with an enigmatic scowl while reading a copy of *The New York Times Book Review*. At exactly what I guessed to be his due time, he let out a huff, slapped down his reading material, shot up and without knocking, pried open his doctor's door. The doctor still had another patient in the room but nonetheless offered a timid smile, yet the Orthodox man demanded to be seen at his scheduled time. I don't know what happened next because my own doctor's door opened and I was asked in, before my doctor promptly closed the door behind me.

A caution later came to me about the Ativan, not from the AA doctor but from the dispensing pharmacist, and when I told him about my fear of sleeplessness, he shrugged and replied that his body had allowed him only an hour's sleep the previous night. The pharmacist then went on to say that my brain would go to sleep when it was ready and that I should not worry about it.

With the Ativan at bedtime, I was able to stop all alcohol intake, and the swimming built to a mile per day. At night I slept, but on the first night as I lay awake, waiting for the Ativan to take effect, my rage eased a bit and I began pondering how much my misdirected anger may have played a role in judging that Orthodox Jew in the waiting room – why would he, after all, have had eye contact with me, if he were embedded in the *Times Book Review*? And did he really have a scowl? Did he really let out a huff? Was his appointment past due or was there some other emergency issue not known to me? For that matter, had I known last August, when biking through the Toronto ravine, of any extenuating circumstances around the Orthodox Jew whose behavior I had presumed arrogant and self-serving?

Christmas Week of 2008

In addition to the mile swim and AA meeting each day, I began to scour Canadian and American newspapers, as well as the university bulletins in Toronto's Central Reference Library, for clues as to where Chantelle was. I also checked in each week with her kind boss, Doctor Abrams, who had let me keep my TVR in Chantelle's covered parking space.

As Christmas approached, a sense of loneliness began to build with the carols ever present but I was rescued by an AA invitation to help out at Toronto's Don Jail. That volunteer work led to more and as 2008 drew to a close with my continuing to help those less fortunate, I suddenly found myself feeling hints of a rush that I could never remember having run through me before.

The prisoners were quick to pick up my American accent and proved remarkably adroit in understanding differences in criminal law between the United States and Canada. They wanted me to answer why the United States remained one of the few countries in the world with capital punishment, and the prisoners grilled me on the no-parole part of U.S. life imprisonment, especially for youth. What I also found interesting was that despite these inmates' liberal interpretation of the law, I learned in a jail church service on Sunday December 28 that the prisoners were passionately traditional in their Christian ritual, albeit some had tried to switch to Judaism to get better kosher meals.

Next to Toronto's Don Jail, itself a big box, stood the older one, condemned 30 years earlier but constructed 150 years ago as a kind of palace and North America's biggest jail, with gargoyles in its corridors. It remained one of the continent's few classic jails, yet instead of being capitalized upon for movie sets or tourism to pay for renovations, it had been allowed to decay and its only hope, beyond a short hiatus of tourism planned for 2009, was in its restoration as part of a health-care facility. As with Toronto's 1930s art deco Harris Filtration Plant, the historic jail's closure to the public reflected a myopia that threatened much of Toronto's architecture, and I wanted to fight for the preservation issues but my AA group insisted that I stop for fear of relapse.

My volunteer work at the jail was fulfilling and I quickly became eager to be employed more. Then, just before New Year's Eve, while walking home the two miles from the Don, I passed on Grosvenor Street in front of its Central YM/YWCA, a sign with the headline, "Get Ready for 2009." Underneath the headline was an ad for vocational testing at a low price of $500, and I put my vintage TVR up for sale to get the money and pay off my credit cards. The TVR was gone in two days but not before I was forced to pay the overdue parking tickets. Then I took the tests.

Days later, I was scheduled to meet with my Y counselor but had to wait 20 minutes outside her office while she helped somebody else. I noticed next to my chair a low table with a dozen or more magazines and newspapers, with most of them having that look of staleness found in doctors' offices. But one in particular headlined the invasion of Gaza by Israel in late 2008. The article was not from a mainstream Toronto newspaper but one that I had frequently seen for free in street boxes, and the headline looked provocatively anti-Israel. I read on:

> Since 1948, Israel's military doctrine has been about striking fear into the hearts of its enemies, using the excuse of deterrence, and in recent days, Israel's killing of hundreds of innocents in Gaza is the latest execution of this strategy. Israel is determined to terrify Gaza because it is rationalized that if it cannot do so, how can it deal with Iran or Syria? The mass bombing and ground invasion are part of Israel's attempt to restore its reign of terror and re-entrench credibility with its enemies.
>
> The attack on helpless Gaza is also an attempt to restore credibility with an Israeli public. Reverberations from the 2006 war on Lebanon — less than a resounding success — are still keenly felt and there is no room seen for a second failure. Over 80% of the Israeli public have thus approved of the attack on Gaza, despite its causing an end to any peace negotiations with Syria.
>
> There is also a February 2009 election in Israel and the governing Labor and Kadima parties want to improve their odds by showing they are as hawkish as right-wing Likud leader Benjamin Netanyahu, or his

influential old father. Inaction, moreover, by the governing Labor and Kadima parties would mean humiliation for Prime Minister Olmert and electoral defeat for Foreign Minister Tzipi Livni, not to mention the end of Defense Minister Barak's political career.

Israel had thought it best to strike while President Bush was still in power, knowing he would support Israel and put the blame squarely on Hamas's pop-gun rockets. Other Israeli supporters now plan to lobby Washington and pull maneuvers on Wall Street to halt any Obama-led introspection, thus maintaining the American status quo in foreign and domestic policy.

Officially, Israel attacked because Hamas refused to renew the six-month ceasefire and lobbed rockets into Israel as soon as the agreement expired on December 19. But Israel bombed Gaza earlier on November 4, killing six Palestinians and again killed four more on November 17. Israel then began intensifying its overall siege and Hamas reacted. This is a chronic pattern: Israel assassinates, Hamas reacts and the reaction gets the press as the cause of the conflict.

As some Israelis have admitted off the record, this war is not about Palestinian rockets. Negotiations could have dealt with them. The war is to restore Israeli army prestige after it looked less than invincible in the Lebanon war of 2006, and Israel has been rehearsing the invasion of Gaza for months, including fabricated reports and video shots. There is also now an information agency to win support for Israel, and it has been role-playing with rehearsed theater, believing that it can seize world opinion while dominating media time. Israel also got its Foreign Ministry involved before the ground invasion, to get the international community onside.

The 2008 - 2009 Israeli attack on Gaza is from the air, sea and ground. Israel has seized control of radio frequencies and has jammed Hamas and Islamic jihad stations, while broadcasting warnings in Arabic. The tunnels from Egypt have been bombed but Gazans need them for food, medicine and other necessities, otherwise unobtainable, because of an earlier Israeli blockade.

Any asylum for Gaza's population continues to be denied, and the Gazan people have to stay in that tiny dangerous place. Many Gazans don't know what their neighbors are hiding but things are so crowded that many innocents are dying, especially in apartments near bombed government buildings. Stocks of fuel in Gaza have fallen to zero and power plants have had to close down. Water and electricity are cut off and after sundown, people are in pitch dark, with over half of the 1.5 million Gaza people without running water. Israelis have struck a UN school, a UN health clinic, a critical hospital, multiple residential houses and a World Food Program warehouse holding 400 tons of food. Meanwhile, the Israeli aid, as advertised as going to Gaza, is totally inadequate.

The International Red Cross in Gaza has made a rare public statement, saying it is dealing with a full-blown humanitarian crisis. Gaza hospitals are overflowing, with no running water and powered by their own generated electricity. Hundreds of civilians have been killed, from toddlers to the aged, and a UN agency said the civilian casualty toll in Gaza is 25%, with a Palestinian human rights group saying it is 40%.

Israel is not a signatory to the Rome Statute and is therefore not subject to the International Criminal Court. And Israeli war crimes go beyond preventing neutral medical personnel from reaching civilian victims: when Israeli troops occupy Gazan homes, they use families as human shields, before leaving the homes trashed and desecrated with hateful graffiti; Israeli forces have shelled the UN Relief and Works Agency (UNRWA) with high explosives and an incendiary substance called white phosphorus; Israel has also threatened UN personnel and civilians, with forces firing next to a UNRWA school, sheltering Palestinian civilians. The Israeli claims that militants fired first, from within UN premises, have proven untrue.

There is a lurid sense of disproportion versus Israeli casualties. In 1996 in Lebanon, 106 innocents in a UN shelter were killed by Israel but still in this 2008 - 9, the deaths of 40 innocents in a UN school shelter was the third item on an Israeli newscast, following a Israeli soldier's funeral.

Hamas is pleading for a ceasefire and has not carried out a suicide bombing since 2005, but Israel looks bent on the total destruction of Gaza to give Israelis a sense of might and vindication. Israeli polls show support for prolonging the multi-phased attack, with anything affiliated with Hamas a legitimate target. Israel crushed a European-financed government complex, and in close-by Israel, people cheer to the sound of each explosion from an Israeli air strike.

The world has deserted Gaza, buying time for Israel to see how much damage it can do to Hamas. Its rival, the Palestinian Authority, is said to have signed a security agreement with Israel, preventing people in the West Bank from protesting against the Gaza conflict. The Palestinian Authority also wants the right, after the war, to control the Gaza border openings instead of Hamas. Both the U.S. and European Union refuse to condemn Israel's ground invasion, calling it defensive, and both the U.S., and France under President Sarkozy, have made sure that the UN Security Council will not meet until Wednesday January 7 or 10 days into the holocaust.

Palestinians have been deemed by Israel not to be cowering enough to its reign of terror and Israel has accordingly bombed Gaza's Islamic University and parliament buildings, symbols that Israel and the U.S. said they sought to promote in the Arab world. Israel's former UN ambassador says Hamas must not be allowed to win, arguing that it would encourage other Muslim Brotherhood factions and lead to tragic consequences, particularly for Egypt. And Israel says it won't abide by a UN peace resolution, if it does not guarantee elimination of Hamas rockets. Thus if Hamas agrees to stop launching rockets, but a few renegades remain on occasion doing so, Israel will still blame Hamas and retaliate with targeted assassinations of its political leaders.

Israel may be a master tactician but it seems short on socio-moral premises. Like the specious thinking that striking terror into any opponent is the best pre-condition for negotiations, Israel has also fooled itself into thinking that the civilians being bombed will turn against the military Islamic group defending it. Perhaps Israel has so presumed because its own public is hard on Israel's military when it produces less than a dancing-in-the-streets victory.

Israel has long held that causing suffering to Palestinian civilians would make them rebel against their national leaders. But this assumption has proven wrong, over and over again – when Hamas took over Gaza in 2007, Israel imposed a blockade and pushed the 1.5 million Palestinians to the verge of a humanitarian catastrophe, destroying any chance for lives worth living, but Hamas grew stronger. The war in Gaza is meant to teach the Palestinians a lesson but the massive suffering could transform a docile population into a recruiting pool for resistance fighters.

What is this Islamic Resistance Movement called Hamas, founded in 1987? Hamas and Hezbollah did not exist before 1982. They are ideological reactions to Israel's right-wing Likud Party and to Ariel Sharon whose violence, racism and colonization of an occupied Arab population ultimately generated the will to resist. In both Palestine and Lebanon, the secular political systems proved unable to protect society against Israeli aggression or domestic strife, and movements such as Hamas and Hezbollah developed to fill this vacuum.

Before the current war, Palestinian support for Hamas was on the wane, with double the support for bitter opponent Fatah. But now even Fatah members, who were earlier evicted from Gaza by Hamas, are openly protesting the Israeli incursion and criticizing their Fatah leader Abbas, whose response has been to criticize Hamas for not renewing the ceasefire.

Breaking Hamas's will is unlikely – for 21 years Hamas has endured imprisonment, assassinations, expulsion, boycott and siege, and has grown in strength through it all, even despite Israel's blockade of Gaza for 18 months. Hamas may fall in official terms – in the first week of the Israeli invasion, with 500 Israeli Air Force sorties against Hamas targets in the Gaza Strip, nearly every instrument of the Hamas administration has been obliterated. But the people of Gaza are strong believers in their god, and one can't erase their belief with tanks or planes.

What distinguishes Hamas from other movements is that its leadership cuts across generations. When compared with Fatah, after Arafat died, there was weak leadership and chaos. The other great strength of Hamas, note two Israeli academics who wrote *The Palestinian Hamas*, is that it is more than just a terrorist movement – Hamas is essentially a social movement and has directed its energies toward services to the community, responding to its hardships and concerns. Like Hezbollah, Hamas has multiple roles responding to constituent needs in the realms of governance, local security, national defense and basic service delivery, responsibilities that their secular governments failed to fulfill. Indeed, Islamic movements in the mold of the Muslim Brotherhood have proliferated in recent years across the Middle East, answering the call from people unrepresented in less-than-democratic institutions. Palestinians have had their needs met by Hamas and the common people constitute its stronghold.

Israeli defense says that it wants only deterrence and a ceasefire but those comments are ill received by the Israeli right wing. It wants elimination of the Hamas organization. American-puppet Egypt also wants Hamas out and will not open its border for help unless Hamas is gone. Egypt is seen in the Arab world as an Israeli collaborator. Israel claims that it does not want to remove Hamas but kills its top leader and then says that there is no way for dealing with Hamas. Israel's takeover of Gaza has also severed the area from the Palestinian Authority.

One objective of Israel's invasion is to hand over Gaza to Fatah President Abbas but even in the Fatah-controlled West Bank, Palestinians face roadblocks and harassment by Israeli soldiers, and Israeli settlers make life miserable. Hamas sees Fatah as an Uncle Tom stopgap before Israel takes over all of Palestine and Palestinians have their citizenship reduced to that of guest worker.

Conflict management, involving talks with Hamas, may be a possibility as was so in 1993 when Israeli leaders and Palestinian Liberation Organization leader Arafat shook hands. For years before, Israel had made it a crime to talk with the PLO and a half-century ago, Israeli

Prime Minister Golda Meir had said she hated the Arabs and never believed in peace with them.

With 300,000 Israelis living in the West Bank and 200,000 living in the Arab part of Jerusalem, it is all but impossible to draw borders for a two-state solution, and the Israeli wish grows for the Palestinians to be gone. The war has been popular among Israelis, despite not being so elsewhere, but Israelis seem softwared into believing that most of the world is against them. Ironically, in today's world and despite World War II films to the contrary, Germany and Japan are among the countries believed to be playing the most positive roles in the world.

I had no time to digest the article before the Y counselor called me in. She said the vocational tests showed I was a helper, healer and altruist and could be a social worker, rabbi or philanthropist. But the results didn't really register on me, since I was stuck on the article. As for the unresolved anger I had earlier touched on with the counselor, I dismissed it then as coming from Chantelle's being gone and my role in her departure, with the need to reach her through a new understanding of myself.

Monday January 5 2009

One of the AA meetings I came upon was one I discovered, a bracing walk four miles north, and the meeting had a healthy Jewish population that allowed me to feel that I, Arthur F., was not the only Jew who drank. I could also get a ride back from Abe R., a medical professor who lived west of U of T, and en route get a chance to hear not only anecdotes about Jewish life in Toronto but also his gratuitous perspective on Chantelle. "Israel, Arthur, in one sense is like Quebec and while its license plates shout for room to remember, let us hope that such room is big – a common enemy can be a powerful source for unity but as you said of Chantelle, she believed that for French Canada to become a full world contributor, it had to keep healing from within."

I saw no point in reminding Abe that many French Canadians lived outside Quebec but he loved to lecture while in command of the car. "When any community adopts a common enemy, a sense of fear can waft over it like a fart in control of shape and space. You can't ignore it and before the smell dissipates, another fart pours forth from the same indigestion. I know some otherwise educated Jews who feel that anti-Semitism is always imminent, and their paranoia shapes an attitude that sees Israel as the only answer, making them unwilling to hear any criticism of it. Hell, anyone with a pair of scissors can cut-and-paste an anti-Semite, but for us Jews to have any real dialogue, we have to move on beyond tribal dictates."

My smile turned to a squint, as I felt Abe was setting me up but he went on: "I'm scheduled to deliver a lecture, come noon tomorrow, at U of T's Centre for Jewish Campus Life and I'd like to invite you. If nothing else, it will remind you of the diversity of views put forward by Jews anywhere."

Tuesday January 6 2009

The following morning, after an AA meeting and a Hart House swim, I went to the university Jewish Centre and there came to meet a doctoral student named Edward, who was a Sephardic Jew and had much to say about Ashkenazi Jews and Israel. Edward was short and frail, with skinny wrists that looked to shoot out from his pressed white shirt, and he was almost bald, with short black hair. He looked to have been, at one time, a high-school nerd who had never involved himself in athletics.

Edward was from a Cairo Jewish family that had moved to Israel, and he claimed there was more pluralism in Israel today than in the United States or Canada. He said that some parts of the Israeli spectrum, along with their published writings, would be deemed outlandish in North America and cited as an example of the ancient Diaspora. "Since the days of ancient Egypt, where Jews were a significant minority, we have played a leading role in world politics. The Jewish Diaspora began 1,000 years before the Roman occupation.

"Then with the removal of Jewish captives from Israel, after its being conquered by the Assyrians in 740 BC, emigration began on a larger scale under Persian rule, up to the time of the Second Jewish Temple in 500 BC and carried on right through to the Romans. A growing proportion of Jews lived outside the Jewish polity, some through exile and some through economic ventures, such that by the first century BC, the Jewish Diaspora had penetrated nearly every part of the urban world. By the time of Roman arrival, Diaspora Jews outnumbered Jews in Israel by almost five to one – 4.5 million to 1 million – and whether there was a mass expulsion under the Romans is suspect, since many Jews stayed put, defying the rabbis and even in some cases later converting to Islam."

Edward and I were standing to the side in a somewhat empty foyer, and with his skinny wrists flailing and high voice twanging, he would have undoubtedly caused attention if not commotion, had there been more people present. "Arthur, even among you European Jews, walled off in ghettos by controlling rabbis, the prayer for 2,000 years of a return to Zion was only a prayer of a messianic future that god alone would bring about. Anyone who tried to 'force the end' was considered a heretic. A more enlightened understanding of the actual Diaspora could open Jews to a different relationship with Israel, and one where they felt more freedom to accept criticism."

I tried to maintain an inquisitive face but had to reveal my prejudice. "But how about the Orthodox, who are convinced that god has given them their land and refuse to co-operate in vacating any of it?" Edward grinned and his little finger pointed up. "There is also within Israel a Jewish sect that believes the very opposite – that Israel as currently constituted is an affront to god and an injustice, until god says it isn't. The sect's members have even been known to hobnob with Holocaust deniers." Little Edward then swept his arms apart. "Israel is very dynamic, Arthur, and there is not one car without a bumper sticker. Writers in Israel today play a role that is moral and political but remains unfamiliar to writers in the United States."

I shifted us more out of earshot and then threw Edward a challenge: "Our friend Abe said that the majority of Canadians do not think Israel has, in fact, freedom of speech, and the Canadian Council for Israel and Jewish Advocacy has found, to its distress, that the more Canadians know of the Israeli-Palestinian conflict, the more they support the Palestinians."

But Edward pointed his finger up to my nose. "Because, Arthur, the Council's approach is misguided. Israel is at the crossroads of the world's East and West, and could be a beacon for racial tolerance and pluralistic thinking. But the distortions of the last 2,000 years, especially the last 200, with constructed narratives judged critical to the re-creation of Israel, are mythological stories that are no longer necessary."

I felt I could not let this pass and lowered my eyebrows at the little Edward. "Cannot the Holocaust happen again?" and he came back as if energized. "The Jewish world has been Likudized and the current Likud practice is one of fear, pariah policies and furious denial. The Likud doctrine allows no space for ex-tribal thinking to ask why, for example, Islamic fundamentalists are induced to behave the way they do. Meanwhile, so-called terrorism festers in deplorable conditions inside illegitimate borders of an occupied land. Historically, there was never an Arab-Jewish conflict per se and the Arabs had been in Palestine for thousands of years before the Romans, versus the Jews who ruled Palestine for only a couple of hundred years."

Inadvertently, I had let a genie out of the bottle inside little Edward and he was almost jumping. "After the resurrection of the Jewish state of Israel in 1948, a million Jews like my ancestors left the Arab countries where they had enjoyed protected minority status. Huh! Baghdad in the 1940s had been 40% Jewish and many Jews had held top posts in the civil service! But a turning point came in 1941 with the Farhoud, a pogrom that lasted two days and was launched after a pro-Nazi coup had been quashed by the British.

"Egypt's Alexandria had also been cosmopolitan, with many Jews having Egyptian servants, and in Cairo, Jews could do business during the day and stroll out each evening to enjoy the nightlife. But the Arab-Israeli conflict has seen the departure of indigenous Arab Jews, who had lived in Arab countries for centuries. In 1956, when Israel attacked the Suez Canal, the Egyptian government felt forced to lump Zionists together with all us other Jews, but later in Israel, my Sephardic mother came to declare she did not fit in with the Ashkenazi Russians and their boorish manners or with loud-mouthed taxi drivers living in a pressure-cooker country.

"We North African Jews have been marginalized by European Jews, who have driven the Zionist program from the beginnings. And you Jewish Americans are worse than Canadians, with your dual loyalty to Israel at the expense of a duped U.S."

I was not prepared to accept yet another anti-American slap from a self-righteous Canadian. "I'm an architect, Edward, not a civil servant," but again his little finger rose to my nose and he almost shouted, "All acts are ones of political economy, Arthur, and there is no such thing as keeping out of politics. You have a responsibility to know what is going on, before you vote or practice your profession or even live your life."

I took to lowering his finger from my face and probed. "Is economics not the number one social science governing all others?" and he shot back, this time raising his finger only halfway up, "Number two, Arthur. Political economy may be the ace of spades but the wild card is religion."

Edward then thrust out his arms in a waxing shrug. "After the end of cold war and now with increasing globalization, look how central religion has become. Gone is the pretension that the global split is left versus right.

"The so-called Islamic guerillas who fight us do so not because they hate the West and seek our destruction but because they believe we seek theirs. We have invaded their space, for us to deal with an extremist element that has exploited local grievances to gain power.

"The way to end terror tomorrow and end the Islamic militant's reason for being is for Israel to return to the pre-1967 borders and Palestine to become a state, with its headquarters in the historically Palestinian section of Jerusalem. But Israelis refuse to negotiate away any of biblical Israel, and for us not to understand that is not to grasp the nature of religious politics.

"Negotiation, compromise and accommodation are the marks of economic politics, where every deal has its price, but those who rule according to a belief cannot afford to negotiate, for that would undermine the belief itself. Zionism is a successful brand, whose promotional link is provisional, opportunistic and ever-shifting and is thus by definition impossible to counter. It should be no surprise that al-Qaeda is a counter-movement of educated men from upper-middle-class Muslim families that have been sidelined by puppet regimes in post-colonial economies, making the 'war on terror' interminable because it's an impossible task."

Little Edward then let out a huff as if he had just had some air pricked out of him. I then tried to hold center ground, with a stern but inquisitive face. "What about the United Nations sentiments against Israel?" and Edward perked up as if he were armed for the argument. "The UN, 60 years ago, sanctioned Israel along with a separate Palestine but Israel never respected the UN and regarded it the same way that prominent Jews had regarded Britain and Churchill in the first half of the 20th century – as a tool for getting Israel. The U.S. took over that role in 1948 when Chaim Weizmann, soon to be Israel's first president, induced U.S. president Truman for domestic political reasons to overrule all advice to the contrary and unabashedly endorse the immediate creation of the Jewish state."

Edward paused and checked around to see if anyone else was listening and then he went on in a calmer voice: "The passive Palestinians were not organized and did not have an Ashkenazi compulsion fueled by a meticulously communicated, 2,000-year-old mythology. Leading Jewish historians now have written about the ethnic cleansing of the Palestinian people and the catastrophe, or Al Nakba, at the time Jewish Israel was created.

"Palestinian properties were confiscated and hundreds of villages razed, young men were mass-murdered and old people were forced onto roads for escape, soon sitting beside carts and begging for a drop of water but there was none. Israeli military objectives, moreover, made it impossible for Jordan's British-officered Arab legion to move west to save Arab towns or help the refugees. Even David Ben-Gurion, who faced down right-wing Zionists led by Menachem Begin, still believed that much of the early Israeli effort had to be done clandestinely, including the destruction of those hundreds of Palestinian villages."

Little Edward was painting a grim picture and I tried to trip him up. "You said, Edward, that Israel can still be a beacon for world hope. If it were to be exposed for what you allege, do you believe it could still pull off such a role?" and he again grinned with that same readiness. "Knowledge of what really happened is critical to understanding both oneself and one's adversary," and I grudgingly gave a nod of acknowledgment before I raised my eyes to the ceiling. "Sounds like someone I thought I knew."

I recomposed. "But Edward, you talk of those rabbi-walled European Ashkenazis and us ignorant American Jews, with you the noble Sephardics having being marginalized. How much of what you are saying is just anti-Ashkenazi resentment coming from a disillusioned Sephardic Jew?"

Edward put his arms on his little hips as if in control. "There is an intellectual vibrancy in Israel today, Arthur – leading academics are dedicated to stripping away the David and Goliath mythology along with the other fables that re-established Israel, in order to save it from itself and assure its continuance, through an owning up to the prejudices that dog Middle East peace.

"Those same thinkers want us to challenge the warrior ethos engrained in Israel's soldiers, such as the tale of Masada where myth has it, Jewish zealots committed suicide rather than surrender to the Romans. But those academics who are trying to debunk that Ashkenazi mythology face a storm of invective by many who label the academics post-Zionists and doubt their commitment to the Jewish state."

I could not help my eyebrows lifting. "Not surprised," and Edward's finger came back, again this time almost to my nose. "But are you not surprised for the right reasons, Arthur? Disillusionment is a constant among North Americans who become intimate with both sides of the Middle East divide.

"One former writer for *The New York Times* became a counselor to Arab prisoners in the notorious Ketziot or Ansar 3 prison, the one Israel erected in the Negev Desert during the first Intifada uprising in the years 1988 to 1993. The reporter became distressed with the patronizing comments of veteran Israelis, who found his interest in the Palestinians quixotic. Those Israelis had been given a rifle in a *kibbutz* and the promise of post-Holocaust power. They had also been given the Holocaust lessons, 'Don't forget history or it will repeat itself' and 'It is easy to kill an unarmed Jew but not one with a gun in your face.' The American reporter came to have a visceral distrust endemic to many Israelis and Jews beyond, and that distrust is predictably mirrored on the Arab side."

I tried to relax my stance. "Perhaps I too am naive, Edward, but the task you map out may betray your own naiveté, given the depth of prejudices and emotions they stir" but Edward came back again with a knowing smile: "My doctoral thesis is in sociology, Arthur, and Minnesota studies suggest the task is possible." When I queried "Minnesota?," Edward's smile turned to a wide grin. "Just say Minnesota study and the academics nod." He shrugged. "They need their icons too."

Thursday January 8 2009

Chantelle's Grosvenor Street apartment received a note from Mendocino, California, where state troopers had found her trying to sleep but shivering on the back seat of her old Volvo, in Russian Gulch State Park. They had reported that she was carrying a small amount of money, full identification and an Eastern U.S. editorial attacking freedom and the profit motive. They had forced her to the hospital.

Shaking with excitement, I tried to contact Chantelle but found she had promptly discharged herself and headed south with a doctor from the hospital to San Francisco. And so, with what little information I had, I managed to track down the doctor who came to be immensely helpful. "Hi Arthur, Jeff. Quite the lady, your Chantelle. I work two days a week in a hospital in Mendocino, and she followed me down to my home in the city.

"I invited her to stay with my wife, daughter and me. Our 11-year-old Bree would not leave Chantelle alone! But after three days, she graciously left. We tried to compensate her for tutoring my daughter in science but Chantelle would take nothing. She's still around the city somewhere, as my wife discovered in a Berkeley newsletter, and I heard someone was trying to arrange for her to speak, outside of Alcatraz, but I don't know where she is staying, Arthur."

There was then a pause on the phone, before the doctor's voice heightened, "There are a few notes here that she left on the laptop and I guess she wouldn't mind my e-mailing them to you."

I knew I was prying in my inimitable way but the kind doctor could sense my desperation. "Please, Jeff and thank you." Moments later, I saw from Chantelle the only words I had seen since she had gone:

> We have had plagues like AIDS before. Ninety years ago, when
> Americans and Canadians returned from Europe and World War I, many
> returned with syphilis, and gonorrhea built to epidemic proportions.
> Hospitals panicked and infants were rammed with eye drops, while
> people everywhere were bombarded with anti-sexual advertising. Anti-
> Europeanism ran rampant. If we took time now to try to understand the

aftermath of World War I or the more recent communications on AIDS, we would be better prepared for the next threat to come along. No group was responsible for AIDS but homosexuality and the sexual revolution as spawned by the pill have been labeled causes. We have fallen prey again to fear, anger and the religious edicts founded on them. As with syphilis, now so with AIDS, the first death has been truth.

During the week following my phone call with the San Francisco physician, I learned much about where Chantelle had been, since she had left her Toronto apartment. But actually tracking her down proved daunting. At the start of the week, I found out from a Berkeley administrator that Chantelle had visited the school and picked up a letter sent to her. The administrator had been led to believe that Chantelle was still in San Francisco but not on campus.

I had at least the Berkeley point of reference as well as the knowledge that someone else knew enough of her itinerary to have sent a letter to her at Berkeley. I tried the same.

January 8 2009

Chantelle Fouriere
Communication and Administration
University of California at Berkeley
San Francisco, California

Dear, dear Chantelle,
   I am now unable to communicate my beliefs, except to say I keep rethinking them. Some seem clear but then they shift again, while others I can hardly see at all.
   During my swim each day, I wonder about you and God, and think my inability to communicate my views beyond commenting on their fluidity reflects a process that underscores some sincerity of faith. In any event, one thing the process seems to be doing is helping my communications with others.
   Chantelle, I love you and will love you always.
   Arthur

Women's College Hospital had been tight-lipped about Chantelle's whereabouts, and now I think it never knew where she had gone. I discovered from that San Francisco physician, Jeff, that Chantelle had gone for a month in the summer of 2008 to Canada's West Coast and the far side of Vancouver Island, where she had enjoyed its long beaches and giant waves rolling in from the Pacific. Then she had gone back to mainland Vancouver, where she had found work in the Faculty of Medicine at the University of British Columbia. I got hold of a UBC bulletin in the University of Toronto Robarts Library, and found a piece that Chantelle had written in October of 2008.

WHY WE MEDICALLY NEED RELIGION

We human beings are not unique among animals in having conscious-ness but early on in our development, we seem to have reached a threshold, where we posed a painful question – was there life beyond inevitable death or were we no more than food for worms? To save us from being overwhelmed by a sense of what's-the-use, we withdrew into denial and began a quest for life-enhancing illusion. We thus developed the capacity to be suggestible, even hypnotizable, sheltering our minds by distancing ourselves from realities with escapes into fan-tasyland.

The human brain does not just know, it also feels, and for reasons of health, evidently cannot afford to know all the time – our intelligence has afforded us a language to abstract and hypothesize but alongside any search for truth remains a survival need to wish the unfathomable into fact. The resulting beliefs are not verifiable but are nonetheless reinforced by our tapping further into suggestibility and defying logic, all the while rewarding our minds with endorphins that override criti-cal thinking. We have embellished this self-deception by coming to think of ourselves as spiritual beings, and religions have been erected to prey on our susceptibilities. Our human-defense mechanism against psychic paralysis has thus made us into the most theological of crea-tures and we have survived in our mythical universe, a world apart from other animals' innocent nakedness in nature.

Religion may be an essential evolutionary element of the human condition. Children are more inclined to believe stories of a creationist kind, irrespective of what their parents believe, and older people are more susceptible to creationism as they count the years before death. We women also have a bent toward obsession with spirits, if such a spiritual feeling is part of any religious practice involving a healing ritual.

Human beings often assume our thoughts exist separate from the fleshly matter of our brain and this picture fits well with a view of souls being disconnected from bodies, or the continued existence of loved ones after death. Ironically, Jesus said this world is all we have and it is heavenly, with body and spirit being the same, but Paul in his founding of Christianity picked up the Platonic split between spirit and flesh.

Notwithstanding high Buddhism, religious systems stress the role of a supernatural power and the word "atheist" is from the Greek word "without God." Even non-religious people are prone to believe in something beyond the mere body, be it soul, spirit or psychic something, and the agnostic still needs the psychic oases of, say, nationalistic myths or other reality-transcending beliefs. As for atheists, they may be lying to themselves, because it may be impossible for the mind as it has evolved to believe in atheism. If the atheist denies the existence of a god, he has to formulate that god first in principle, and if he chalks up all progress to the human mind, the atheist inadvertently may be betraying what an empowering leader God is, since great leaders induce followers to believe they've led themselves. Interestingly, people who profess religion are less likely to cheat on tests if they think their disapproving god is watching but professed atheists experience the same kind of god-fearing response, suggesting there is a further case for not believing in atheism, unless one labels that god as conscience. Agnostics, on the other hand, simply render doubt to the existence of god and should be acknowledged for their honest thoughts. As for anyone who does not honestly care whether or not there is a god, we don't even yet have a name for him.

Safety from seeing death as inevitable and therefore life as meaning-less, also has a social dimension, and the need for mythology includes a group delusion that goes beyond the protective needs of the individ-ual. Societies purvey self-deceptions to survive and thrive, and the cen-trifugal norm tends toward blind obedience, giving us both a refuge and a prison. Freedom is buried under a mass consciousness that at best is a political compromise, and human beings who long for the pro-tection of once-omnipotent parents tend to seek socially acceptable ways, with dogma, devils and easy-to-see stereotypes. The person thus judged sane in that society is not the wise fool of a Shakespearean play but the one who adheres to some acceptable mix of illusion, reality and socio-political discretion. On planet Earth, there are a couple of thou-sand gods, often contradicting one another and the statistical probabil-ity of any one of them being the one true god is next to nil. But the closer we get to that zero probability, the more our magical beliefs kick in, and most religions contain rationalizations to contradict threaten-ing facts.

Given this cultural ensnarement, we are at some distance from grasp-ing that the human brain adapted, for survival reasons, to death-deny-ing beliefs. That cultural compulsion makes it hell for any person who wants to see the world as it really is – there remain today bad conse-quences for people who do not use society's storied offerings for shap-ing reality, since people who try to unravel that story spread their thoughts beyond the boundaries of any society and pit themselves against the respective culture. Religious beliefs nevertheless cannot be overloaded with contradictions or the erstwhile-duped followers will ultimately be unable to restrain their critical thinking and come to see the emperor with no clothes. In this last generation, one of the biggest enemies to traditional religion has been a broadening education among religion's traditional followers, and not only has our critical thinking been exercised but an expanded awareness has created considerable discomfort with religious falsehoods.

Paranormal believing, whether religious or not, has also proven to be crucial to human survival by its very universality. Perhaps we will outgrow this need for religious escape and come to see it as evolutionary baggage but perhaps not, since many Western people now decrying traditional religion have also come to look upon themselves as spiritual beings. If people, therefore, do abandon traditional beliefs, they still need to constrict reality back to what is manageable, and hucksters of all kinds stand at the ready to subdue our consciousness.

Without the craving for fantasy being satisfied by traditional beliefs, neuroses can develop upon withdrawal, and those followers who have been conditioned to a need for order and direction under one socially endorsed god can fall prey to religious substitutes or illusions, created through suggestibility. Obsessions and compulsions can thus become growing pains in any breakdown of cultural mythologies.

So, why not keep our pet beliefs? First, blindness to what is less than whole truth can mean we followers of fear and awe distrust any truths outside our own theater. Such blindness can also make us more inclined to accept further perversions from our dictated "truth," even though those suggestions may be contrary to our gut notions. Additionally, the less real our lives become, the less self-awareness we have and the less empathy we accordingly have for the pain of others. And because we cannot rely on reason, we can be led into more prejudice against anyone outside of our religious confinement, along with greater aggression in executing those prejudices.

This same lack of discernment that allows us to be less tolerant also means we can grow less tolerant of ourselves, and often we fall back into the black/white dictates of a bad-parenting society, with its quick fix of assured certainty. Beyond the oppression from such a quick-fix opiate, our blind obedience to tyrannical thinking can also lead to another negative effect, often associated with rigid beliefs – a repressed anger whose rage must come out some other way. People with strong religious views tend to be less humanitarian and advocate harsher forms of punishment. They have higher rates of sadistic behavior and records of wife and child abuse. Most religions have a devil to work as counterpoint to their god in an overall illusion of order, and killing that devil is judged an act of righteousness. Followers of rigid religions are thus often potential killers, and wars are predictably holy wars, conducted as such.

Undeveloped discernment can also allow religious people to confuse what is, versus what ought to be, and blind followers of religions can lie when tested if they think their god would be so pleased. Research shows yes, less anxiety among religious test subjects versus non-believers when completing a task under pressure but believers are also shown to be less stressed when making an error – their brain's 'alarm bell' does not necessarily register the error, allowing them to continue making the mistake.

When blissful ignorance, self-deception, a holy-war philosophy and a belief in a life better after death get meshed with nuclear technology, we can no longer afford a religious drive for destruction. It is worth noting that the vast majority of fundamentalist Americans believe in war as an option, while only a small minority of people in Europe as ravaged by two world wars still do.

Religion may in the past have cushioned us against inevitable death but religion has also kept us out of touch with ourselves, insensitive and afraid to create. If there is an ultimate evil, it is perhaps in the reality of our killing one another, out of the joy of triumph, and in sacrificing our children, under the name of love. As for the bliss of ignorance versus its possible alternative of mental illness, it is not religion that makes us happy but fearless faith. People, moreover, will always search for purpose in their lives but that search does not necessarily mean the need for religion – agnostics also have a need for meaning but do not have to find it in an immortality labeled "spirit." They can often find it in the thrill and magnificence of life itself, together with all the opportunities that life affords to the inquiring mind.

There is, in New York and Toronto, a Coping Without Religion support group, and recovering religion addicts also meet for SOS or Secular Organizations for Sobriety sessions. Some atheists and secularists are weary of discrimination in favor of religious groups, such as Canada's funding for Roman Church schools, tax breaks for traditional churches and God references in the Canadian Charter of Rights and Freedoms. Others are tired of the Israeli-Palestinian issue or religious fundamentalism in its many manifestations. These differences in values may soon be highlighted when Toronto transit riders see a transit ad already in London, England, saying that "There's probably no God. Now stop worrying and enjoy life."

Faith should inspire confidence, curiosity and good works. It is thus not to be filled with fear or founded on lies compounded by mystery. Faith does not moreover have to accept a realm that transcends the limits of current comprehension, since such acceptance sanctions ignorance and represses curiosities. A scientist, who probes beyond what is known, needs to have faith to bolster her curiosity to carry on, while she holds on to the utmost integrity in her approach.

Faith in a higher power, I suggest, involves a relentless quest for truth in parallel with works of love, whether those works be neurosurgery or delivering the mail, and it should be no surprise to us that philanthropy and kind dogs make us happy. If we live in good faith, perhaps we can strive to be the person whom dogs think we are.

What I did not know, when I read Chantelle's October 2008 piece from the University of British Columbia's bulletin, was that the piece had been picked up by other university journals and had been read by none other than the man who had intruded upon Chantelle and me when we had first met in Chicago, Terry Hardy. I recalled, at first, feeling threatened by his aggressive nature and remembered when I had first shaken hands with him, that it was as if we were enemies and he had been making a gesture of peace. But I also recalled that those threatening feelings were assuaged by his words later delivered in a public address, during the summer of 2007, long after Chantelle had departed Chicago.

As I was to learn, Hardy also had been trying to track down Chantelle after she had left her doctor job in Toronto. When he had discovered she was on Canada's West Coast, Hardy had raced to Vancouver from his office in New York to catch up with her. But for reasons not known to me, he had been stopped at the Canadian border, so from Seattle, Hardy had managed to track down Chantelle's whereabouts at the UBC Faculty of Medicine.

After Hardy's ban from Canada, he had chosen not to approach Chantelle directly, wanting, I guess, not to have to explain. Instead, he had chosen to submit a complementary piece to Chantelle's October 2008 submission in the following month's issue of the UBC bulletin. He must have known that, if she did not actually see it, someone at the school would undoubtedly bring it to her attention.

SPIRITUAL GROWTH

It starts at home. Spiritual children are happier, with language development years ahead of others and emotional intelligence emerging long before puberty.'

For any child, spirituality has four parts:
1. Personal meaning in his or her life;
2. Relationships and love for others;
3. A sense of awe with nature;
4. Belief in some higher power.

The fourth is controversial in part because we have our own childhood experiences of a higher power, many of them negative, and moving beyond those experiences involves an uprooting of our foundational thinking. Children, particularly in their first six years, need the assurance that someone is above them and protecting them, for children to have confidence, build esteem and develop an ability to see the best in others. No one later complains that he was too well loved as a child, only over-protected or under-supported for growth. Respect for self and others begins with huge hugs of love and trust through truth, and such a spiritual experience is pivotal to any healthy physical and intellectual growth to follow.

One of life's greatest stressors is the absence of gentling. The lack of, say, touching by a mother during a child's earliest period – the brain's most formative months – can mean an incomplete development of neuron systems. The mother can also impede her own development and stay unable to learn the language of acceptance, brought forth in a child's spontaneous embrace. Instead, the mother can remain constrained by her own hang-ups about, say, a hug, and her child is denied the unconditional love critical to balancing any conditional love gleaned from obedience. Conversely, if a mother figure is over-indulgent and a father uninvolved, the child can be submissive, dependent and in fear of conflict or creative solutions. Parental love must embrace an understanding that the children need to leave the nest.

According to a theory of mind, an awareness of our own mind and its being different in consciousness from others emerges some time around the age of five, along with the possibility that others may believe something different from us. Thus for those people who later mature beyond puberty, a power greater than ourselves may be found in the synergy brought forth by any mutual sharing of thoughts. But the forum for such sharing has always first to be founded on a one-on-one relationship of trust between a parent or guardian and child. That basic relationship also mirrors how the child will relate to any higher power. Children in their most formative years of one to six, especially in the years one to four, rarely question parental expectations but instead focus on their own inadequacies, and the more they feel good about their emerging god, the more they will share their innermost thoughts and experiences. When we as parents reciprocate by disclosing our innermost thoughts to our child and so communicate that we trust and respect the child's judgment, we open up a two-way communication founded on trust. We also model for our children our own need for their love and support, giving them further respect and license to share.

Enormous spiritual growth can occur between the close of a child's main development in his first six years to those around puberty, when altruism has its best chance to blossom. But for such blooming to happen, that earlier growth will have to have gone beyond just following of rules and approval, and have moved through to respect for self and others.

One reason that a stage of spiritual maturity can be rare by the age of puberty is that many parents themselves remain stuck at earlier stages and so put the same ceiling on a child. The lower the level of parental ability, the higher the role of punishment and children learn, for example, that hitting is a proper response to anger. If any society condones this little child abuse, the scene is set for more, and the total society evolves to one disciplined only by treating people as if they were spoiled children. A classic Greek definition of discipline is to instruct, educate and train in mental and moral development, such that the person can evolve to a level of autonomy where he or she is respectful of self and others. But unfortunately the concept of discipline has degenerated to mean control, correct or punish, and parents who routinely punish, produce children who live with the message that power is everything, their becoming resigned to dependency on policing.

Civilizations in this 21st century are exceptionally complex, with much more freedom to fail, and the accordant need for enlightened parental training has never been greater. How did civilizations survive in the past without such parental training? Not well, and as Chief

Seattle once tried to communicate in his letter to President Thomas Jefferson, life is not about survival but about living.

In the week after Hardy's article in UBC's November 2008 bulletin, he had managed from his room in Seattle to reach Chantelle at the school's Faculty of Medicine and had been correct in assuming she had read his dissertation. He had then told her that the School of Theology and Ministry at Seattle University would like to sponsor her in an ecumenical seminar. Hardy had assured Chantelle that the school had a tradition of not only rooting students in their Christian faith but also engaging them in vibrant dialogue with other traditions, rounding the students out in preparation for spiritual and pastoral help to others.

Chantelle had heard encouraging things about the intellectual vibrancy of Seattle, that "most Canadian of American cities," and so in her old Volvo she had entered the United States in December 2008, for the first time since Chicago. From her colleagues at UBC, I understand she had at the time been dressed in what could pass for an Arthur Franklin uniform of beige safari slacks, white turtleneck, brown safari jacket and hiking boots.

When Chantelle had met Terry Hardy in front of the main Seattle library, she had viewed again the gaunt young man, and he too had been dressed in a safari outfit but all in olive, except for black army boots. Hardy's sandy hair had still been short and his face pallid, reflective of a person who kept himself fighting-trim but did not get enough sleep or sun. Hardy's pockets in his shirt, jacket and trousers had all been bulging as if he'd been armed, and under his right arm he had carried a black folder, two inches thick and open at the top.

Before Chantelle had then been allowed a chance to ask about her overnight room in the university, Hardy had said the seminar had been postponed but that he had been given a money order to cover her expenses. Oddly, the money order had not been made out by Seattle University and before Chantelle could have probed, Hardy had changed the subject to the lovely autumn weather and had said that he had taken the liberty of preparing a picnic lunch for a place high up on a hill, next to an historical cemetery overlooking Seattle.

After Hardy and Chantelle had made their way up in her Volvo to the cemetery, its director had greeted them and had then taken time to show Chantelle some historical parts, while recommending an adjoining spot for a picnic. The cemetery director had also surprisingly booked a B&B where she could reside for the night but what Chantelle had not known was that my Canadian great-great-grandparents, Arthur and Hattie, were buried there. Long after I had learned she had been in the historical cemetery, I had fantasized that Chantelle had been drawn to the hill, out of some need to feel near me.

As best as I could later piece things together, the gist of that picnic and the extraordinary events to follow had happened as such:

Chantelle sat down on her side of the picnic bench and folded her arms deferentially in her lap. "Mr. Hardy, thank you for finding this delightful picnic place above the city. The food is particularly thoughtful."

Hardy sat down on the opposite bench and opened on the table the picnic basket. "I know of your love of history, Ms. Fouriere, and thought the space appropriate for our meeting again, although I'm not sure Chief Seattle would approve of the land bought below."

Chantelle chose to remain the diplomatic guest. "As you pointed out in your excellent article, Mr. Hardy, Chief Seattle tried to tell Thomas Jefferson that life was about living, not survival, so let's think the Chief would allow us our lunch."

But Hardy then tried to extend. "It is intriguing that Benjamin Franklin had commented on white women often preferring to live with their Native captors," and Chantelle's response fell into step of a guest. "Agnostic Franklin would probably have argued that humanity's noblest sacrifices are those that harvest freedom for faith and reason, not the takeover of another people's land, and it is interesting that Martin Luther King's persecuted people were not promised the land of others."

Hardy gave a grin of satisfaction and leaned forward on the table, folding his hands on top, as if in prayer. "American Jews solidly supported Martin Luther King at the start, but the blacks criticized Israel," and a frowning Chantelle was about to speak but a still-grinning Terry Hardy would not let her in. "Ms. Fouriere, you are devoted to truth and have an almost godlike grasp of Christian history. The United States of America, this year in 2008, is going through a change more radical than anything it has experienced for 100 years, since Russian Jews created Hollywood in the camera-friendly swamp of Los Angeles."

Chantelle reared back a bit and gave a look of askance. "Russian Jews? Mr. Hardy, I don't know anything of your background but my mentor since puberty was Jewish and it is not my intention to offend you."

Hardy pushed way from the table and raised both palms in a back-off command. "Please, Ms. Fouriere, you have not offended me. I am intimate with the history of Russia and its subjugations." He then pressed forward, with his next words referring back to an earlier comment about a changing United States. "Perhaps we need to listen more to King's messages and not to the notion of good and bad guys. Human beings are the only species to extrapolate the pain of others and have concocted torture accordingly."

Chantelle took to folding her hands in her lap and gently counterpointed that change is not unique to the present times. "People such as Martin Luther King, Darwin and Jesus are engines for civilization's Midrash, self-critique and renewal," and Hardy suddenly looked straight into her eyes, while giving a long smile of gratification. He then poured out two glasses of cranberry juice and placed them on the table with two ceramic plates and steel cutlery. "Thus the spiritually seeking person should not despair from misconstrued meaninglessness or ask what the heck he can do about it anyway," and Chantelle's face formed the beginnings of a smile. She quenched her thirst with half her glass and then set a pumpernickel bun on her plate. "The spiritually growing person should be able to examine information with ever better tools of discernment and keep growing in her ability to articulate feelings. Her beliefs should thus remain dynamic and ready for change, as she progresses toward enlightenment on any issue."

Hardy helped himself to some nut-bread, a serving of vegetables and some smoked salmon. He had evidently picked up on Chantelle's use of the feminine gender and so continued in like vein. "And she will not subsume her individuality by seeking shelter in clubs, movements or masses of people but will look instead to freedom and personal responsibility."

Chantelle put some raw vegetables on her plate. "The spiritually progressing person will come to recognize how little she knows but will come to
enjoy an ever greater sense of life's purpose," and Hardy jumped back in, his
mouth full of food: "The spiritually mature person will thus seek a life that
is consistent with her understanding of life's purpose and will live out that
faith with actions that determine her behavior in all areas of life."

Chantelle, by this time, was munching on her raw vegetables and she
took her time waiting for her mouth to clear before speaking. "And lead her
to be productive and creative. She will work and be fulfilled in it. Her openness will lead hopefully to a feeling for nature and art, and she will be curious, with millions of questions leading to more questions, along with the
thrill created by the opening of new doors."

Hardy again came forward and looked to harness the essence of what
Chantelle was saying. "She will thus have a well developed social conscience
and will use her honed tools of discernment to handle the moral and ethical
demands of life." He then dropped his eyes to the table and put forth a
resigned sigh. "Sadly, the work of a spiritually integrating person will come
up against social norms," and Chantelle felt pressed to defend. "Yet is work
really creative if it meets no social resistance? The arts especially should
form part of our heritage of freedom, where inner repression by the individual and external expression within society interrelate in a spirit of creative
tension."

Hardy bowed his head and gave a long, wide smile. Chantelle went on:
"The person progressing toward some sort of spiritual integration will thus
still have pains, as part of the trial-and-error growth process but will, it is
hoped, also experience joy concerning her or his condition in life. He or she
may also experience 'highs' and feelings of wonder, though those elations, I
pray, will not be those of self-delusion. And as his knowledge expands, that
person's sense of freedom will increase too, giving him an emotional security, with realistic perceptions of skills and assignments as well as a strong
tolerance for frustration."

Hardy must have felt the tolerance comment not in keeping with
Chantelle's earlier mention of social resistance, and he tried pulling the
thinking back. "It is a collateral sadness that the spiritually giving person will

often be unpopular, since fearful people love to watch the fall of a prophet. In honoring life, the most spiritual human beings often experience the most painful tragedies."

Chantelle fell to defend. "But those beings can thus honor life, Mr. Hardy, since it brings to them its most formidable weapons. The spiritually growing person will feel loved because he or she loves, and will come to appreciate that hell is only an inability to feel such love. And while he won't necessarily be able to communicate his spiritual experiences in full, he will nevertheless be able to express them without hurting others' feelings."

Chantelle waited for Hardy's nod and then continued: "Such a person will thus have social relationships that are fulfilling but not overwhelming – his exposure to multiple perspectives and accordant language will also give him a sympathetic sense of humor to deal with challenges, so that he can laugh at things while still being respectful of elements within them."

Hardy sighed again and gave a theatrical shrug. "Unfortunately for the comparatively non-spiritual person, his thinking will be shunted by his limited language, and he will often not understand a joke."

Chantelle again fell into step. "While the spiritually growing person will thus reject the shortsightedness that religion leads to success or self-justification and creature comfort, the happier spiritual person will learn to demand nothing from god, and be thankful for truth, love and accordant justice."

Hardy beamed and tried to abridge. "And she will still believe in some power greater than herself, not on any level of professed belief but on a social vision with related action."

But Chantelle added a condition that lessened Hardy's beam. "The spiritually integrating person will thus be independent but not brood alone. She will be proud to no one but will see socialization as a way to help to restore tranquility and a contented temper. Ultimately, the graduating person will come to appreciate that we as a global people cannot achieve empathy, which is much needed, until we have entered into that growth process."

Hardy then sat back and may have pondered that he had shifted thoughts as far as he might, that day, on what he saw as common ground and so he tried a platitude to summarize. "The world needs discourse that encourages critical thinking within a spirit of honesty, but blind faith is standing in the way and what follows is not love but a mystifying tyranny." Chantelle nodded in agreement.

Hardy looked buoyed and leaned over the table to push his last thought. "The original sin, as presented in your Christian Old Testament, Ms. Fouriere, seems to come from a sexually neurotic god, not to mention warmonger, and the added fabrication that such a sin is carried down from one generation to another makes the lie unfathomably worse, inducing guilt and begging for the remedy of atonement. Then along comes Paul, who adds a pinch of Hellenistic mystery, and he devises a christ who is the dying/rising lord of us all. Paul made Jesus a bad parent, with Jesus taking our sins upon himself and robbing us of the chance to mature, through responsibility for our mistakes."

Suddenly, Chantelle reared back but may still as a guest have felt the need to hold common ground. "If there were an original sin, I feel it would be more in the uncritical attachment to an ideology and the consequent stifling of children's curiosity. For centuries, Rome drove home the horrible folly that curiosity was indeed a disease and that people should instead be satisfied being dumbstruck by mystery."

Terry Hardy gave a grin at where he and his guest had moved, and she carried on: "Within this repression, any attempt to broaden the mind beyond the boundaries prescribed was condemned as an act of pride, and the conscience that was needed to expose such repression was left too unexercised to see the folly."

Hardy's broad grin turned to an ingratiating smile. "As you no doubt know, Doctor Fouriere, children at the outset need, for survival, to believe what their parents tell them, and parents or any extension of them are often seen as gods. The Jesuit expression, 'Give me a man for the first seven years and you can have him after that' underscores that propaganda, ground in during those formative years, is unshakable thereafter."

It was then Chantelle's turn to give a smile of approval and Hardy marched on: "Instructing young minds, therefore, that blind faith is a prime virtue is a form of child abuse, turning children into fodder for future crusades, where children learn to kill a demonized enemy. Israeli children, polled on Joshua's massacre, overwhelmingly approved of it, and even those who disapproved often rationalized the massacre on the grounds that it halted contamination from ethnic mixing. But those same children overwhelmingly condemned that type of massacre when the perpetrators involved were Chinese."

Chantelle suddenly wrinkled her brow, in a mix of surprise and a little discomfort. "It seems that every nation originally guided by religious principles – be they Jewish, Christian, Muslim, Hindu or Marxist – turns them at least in part into a form of devil worship."

Hardy re-folded his hands on the table and then raised that fold forward toward Chantelle's heart. "That god takes the side of an ostensibly oppressed proletariat and holds out the goal of a promised land, if the duped proletariat works toward it."

Chantelle again reared back but more this time, especially from Hardy's folded hands near her chest. She then again attempted to temper. "Perhaps a bit harsh, Terry. Animal instinct calls for the protection of one's own kin, since kin reproduce from the same genes. Tribal survival is an extension, and it is in our self-interest to ensure that beings of like trunk stick together against any enemies beyond. In-group loyalty yields group protection, and in-groups create their own social memes and blueprints, complete with moral grammar for survival."

Hardy took in a deep breath as if to show his comfort with Chantelle's words. "Yes, three of the daily prayers for an orthodox or conservative Jew include an exultation of his god for not making him a gentile," but when Chantelle lowered her brow, Hardy took to wrinkling his forehead, as if in apology for innocently taking the argument too far. She came back in, "You need not condemn your religion for its growing pains, Terry. Judeo-Christian leaders also had to appeal to their god's high-mindedness, with Moses's supplicating in defense of a woman who had been demanded by that god to commit horrible acts."

Chantelle perhaps did not appreciate that she had put herself back into Hardy's argument as she carried on. "And early Christians did not benefit from the misfires recorded in the Jewish bible – they created a New Testament that was a topological counterpoint to a Greek translation of the Jewish bible, with that translation labeled the Old Testament. And where the New Testament did not fit, the Old was simply readjusted to support the New. The myth of martyrdom, for example, was picked up from the Old Testament's Maccabees in the New Testament's Epistle to the Hebrews, and likewise Jesus's self-sacrifice later became a model for martyrdom in the Mediterranean honor-shame societies."

Hardy's face betrayed that he could not contain his enthusiasm over how things were going and he almost lifted off the picnic bench. "Yes, Christian fundamentalists seem unable to distinguish between doing good and feeling good. Fundamentalists profess belief in a life after death but are against assisted suicide. They save embryos with no nervous systems but kill non-believers and slaughter conscious animals in religious rituals. Half of Americans see the end of the world as part of a second coming and thus see little need to protect the environment!"

Chantelle eased back a bit on her bench, looking more comfortable with where Hardy was apparently going and she added in for support, "Fundamentalists also argue against atheism, Darwinism and even secularism, saying they lead to nihilism or moral irrelevancy. But Darwinism is an intellectual orthodoxy, not a creed, and in Darwin's original edition, he spoke only of a 'natural selection' and not of 'survival of the fittest.' That phrase came later at the influence of others."

Hardy smiled, knowing he had Chantelle in the argument and he let her roll. "Darwin nevertheless did strike a chord, when his theory of evolution refuted that human beings were god's chosen creatures and that human beings were alone in possessing immortal souls, with other creatures there for people's use and our being responsible for their custodianship."

Hardy tried to ride the new momentum. "Even in this 21st century United States, teachers see tears on students' faces after teaching evolution." He then raised his face to the sky. "Trying to teach biology, without evolution, is like trying to teach current events, without mentioning history."

Chantelle came back again in support: "Atheists are also often humanists and there are few humanists in prison. No war was ever fought for atheism, and for that matter, when was the last atheist riot? Nine out of 10 members of the National Academy of Science reject the very idea of god, yet atheists remain the most reviled minority in the United States."

Hardy eased back with a slight smile and raised his hands to the sky, as if in summary of what had been so far said. "Can blind faith nonetheless be beneficial as a kind of blissful ignorance?" and Chantelle found herself again in a comfortable argument. "There is little evidence that religiosity relieves stress, and histrionics played out against a backdrop of guilt may at best be a catharsis. Prayer moreover does little for the person prayed for but can give a good feeling to the person praying."

Chantelle then spread out her own arms with palms up. "And if done in public, it has the added benefit of piety" but suddenly she wrinkled her brow and straightened up, as if she had inadvertently been flippant. "It's tough to abandon a belief system, since it is part of the structure at the roots of our being. Such a belief system also tends to be structured in absolutes, making it difficult to grasp the Socratic concept that children should be taught not what to think, but how."

Hardy again pressed forward. "The writing of the Judeo-Christian bible spans nine centuries and parts like Noah's ark were plagiarized from other mythologies, yet half of Americans interpret that bible literally. Yes, abandoning beliefs is painful and all the more so with the complicating factor of forgoing family and friends. One faces an almost impossible situation! More than four out of five Jews marry other Jews, with the thought of a young Jewish man marrying a *shiksa* being anathema."

Chantelle's face lost any trace of a smile and she lowered her forehead but kept her eyes straight on Hardy. "Christian fundamentalists can exhibit similar in-group behavior, Terry," and he again raised his somber face to the sky. "Religion is said to be true for the masses, useful for the rulers and false for the wise. The Prophets of Hebrew Wisdom were often seen as a threat to the established way, but their words today are simply unheard and an American Taliban of the Christian right has taken over much of communications. 'Terrorism' as a hate word has picked up the torch from the 'communism' fear-word of yesteryears, and well-heeled televangelists have joined forces with tax-free rival churches, to compete for congregations and tithes in attacking the new enemy. Hate continues and children's minds stay suffocated under the rubric of religious totality."

Chantelle gave a deep squint, as if sensing the argument was being pushed one way. "As you know, Terry, our awareness of self and interactions with others are rooted in the relationships we had with our prime guardians, usually parents. Each of us in our formative years experienced a plane of emotions, fears and longings, encompassing much of our grounding around those parental relationships, and the concept of god is often expressed as an all-protective mother or punish-and-reward father."

Hardy again sat back to let Chantelle continue. "Our collective unconsciousness breeds religious thinking but we need to graduate from primordial images while never losing consciousness of them as our foundation. In so moving forward, we may unmask ourselves to our own eyes and so grow in our capacity to discern magical thinking."

Chantelle then turned her head as if speaking to the dead people in the cemetery: "As for our awareness of inevitable death, that reality has catalyzed our need to record and has given us a sense of history. We witness death but we also witness birth, and perhaps we need to see history not as linear but as cyclical, wherein the wintry smile of our knowing older folk is in harmonious counterbalance with the springing to life of young people."

Chantelle was betraying a little smile, and Hardy gave her all the space she needed. "Nothing of the spiritual can be absolutely known but people, I feel, can use customs and tradition as a guide, along with conscience. If we must have rules where we cannot rely on principles, let us put those rules at the bottom of our moral pecking order. Principles, along with the arts and sciences, can free the mind and lead to better progress."

Chantelle then added with a little shrug, "To be sure, such progress will not be without nature's trial and error, and I suppose if we need to keep hypnoses to ensure our healthy imaginations and sexual fantasies, let us keep those hypnotic gods confined to the tooth fairy, Santa Claus, the Easter Bunny and Halloween."

Hardy then tried with a straight face to convey the time and Chantelle responded with a question. "Mr. Hardy, should I be taking the B&B for just one night before going back to Canada or will the seminar be rescheduled right away?"

Hardy sat at the ready with a watertight defense. "Not any time soon but the spiritual organization, with which I am involved, has offered to finance the costs for your talking to a number of American universities."

Chantelle was finished her meal and sipping iced tea but she suddenly felt inquisitive about this man, whom she had again just met. "And what organization is that, Mr. Hardy?" but he was prepared. "I'm involved with a number of Jewish groups, loosely held together, and I have been authorized to cover your expenses while giving you a little stipend."

Chantelle's face looked puzzled. "And arrange my participation in these American schools?" but Hardy was set again. "We feel it best for you to do that part, so that we not interfere with your freedom of choice, either in what you say or where you say it. Suffice to say, based on what we have heard so far or read, we trust your judgment." Hardy added a wise smile.

Chantelle, as a young woman accustomed to men's flattery, was unmoved. "I am not sure how you could be so sure, Mr. Hardy, from what few talking engagements I have had," and he offered a small smile before leaning back from the table and turning his face down to his side of the bench. He brought up his black leather portfolio. Then, while Chantelle watched with some anxiety, Terry Hardy slid a manila file out of the portfolio and laid it in the middle of the table, before directing his face straight to hers. "Ancient Jews held many prominent positions in the Egypt of old and there were there many wealthy Jewish communities before the time of your christ. Jews settled in Egypt from the eighth century BC on, especially on the island of Elephantine at the southern border buttressing Nubia or the Sudan."

Chantelle gave again a deep squint but then raised her broad eyebrows to signal Hardy to continue. "Exceptional permission had been given the Jewish settlers to worship in their temple, not far from the Egyptian religious shrines, and tensions built over hundreds of years. By the third century BC, there were anti-Jewish riots in Egypt's Alexandria and by the second century BC, there was Greek resentment against Jewish support for the Romans. It is interesting that before that Greek time or later during the

Maccabean period, there had been no discernible anti-Semitic sentiment in Greece and no anti-Jewish mention in Greek literature."

Chantelle's face turned dark and she must have wondered where this man Hardy was going. She let him continue. "Oh, that Mark Anthony had not let burn the world's biggest library later in Alexandria! What it could now reveal. Cleopatra never did have sex with him or with Caesar, and she was your typical Hellenistic monarch." Hardy then raised his own face and brows. "There is a great deal of scholarship about the Hellenistic world and the role of women, particularly upper-class women. Cleopatra would have been well versed in poetry, astronomy, geometry, geography and especially rhetoric."

Chantelle was allowing Hardy to pour forth, perhaps in the hope he would signal where he was leading and reveal what was in the manila file, and so she tried to sound a little indignant in her response. "You referred to my christ, Mr. Hardy. I don't have a Christ," but he suddenly thrust back, "Hmm, surprising, given that I surmised from your mission that you are the second," and Chantelle almost lost her composure. "I am the second sister in a family of four, Mr. Hardy, and I understand for some Israelites, that the second Messiah was Bar Kokhba in the 130s, a man presumed ready to launch an era free from outside dominance."

Hardy gave a knowing grin and his eyes slowly lowered to the manila file. "You said you found fault with Maimonides, Chantelle, and admired Spinoza on whom rabbis pronounced anathema as well as his family for generations."

Chantelle lurched back in shock of this knowledge but a moment later came back in defense. "If I have offended your Jewishness, Mr. Hardy, because of my raising questions on some of the roots of Christian fundamentalism, I am sorry. Anti-Semitism is a cancer that has been with us for over 2,000 years," but he leaned forward and came at Chantelle with a dig. "You are Quebecoise, I understand, where anti-Semitism runs rampant," and her face betrayed a rare anger. "I am not Quebecoise, Mr. Hardy, but given your question perhaps it is best that we not continue our agreement."

Hardy knew it was time to deliver his ace card. He slowly opened the manila file and to Chantelle's horror, she saw her notes from the Toronto apartment. She slunk back and Hardy grinned. "You needn't be alarmed, Ms.

Fouriere. No one knows you are here today but for two of my trusted colleagues. Let me say that you are a person of rare enlightenment."

Chantelle sat in silence and a minute passed, with a breeze passing over the table, high up on the Seattle hill. When Chantelle did eventually utter a few words, she asked to be directed to her B&B to be alone. Hardy must have anticipated her reaction and he uttered a quiet "Yes."

Chantelle spent the rest of the afternoon, in fact all evening, at the B&B, before she retired early. After breakfast the following morning, while she prepared for the two-hour drive back to Vancouver, Chantelle received a phone call from Hardy and he began by volunteering to take her to lunch. She respectfully declined but added in a business voice, "I feel I must retain ownership of all that I say," and Hardy almost shouted, "Of course! We are of one mind on that."

The issue was settled but for some talk on logistics and distribution of funds, and inside of a month in December of 2008, Chantelle had things wrapped up in Vancouver. She enjoyed Christmas with some medical colleagues at UBC and before the new year, headed south for the American border and on, through the state of Washington, to Oregon and California.

Much of Oregon had a temperament that I now find decidedly Canadian and I discovered Chantelle had delivered a guest lecture near the start of the school year at a theological school south of Portland, in the small university town of Eugene.

To understand the spirit of a people as expressed in its poetry or customs, one needs to understand that people's religion. Religion has proven to be universal – anthropologists have found no people without a sense of the sacred and ways to express it – and includes such dogma as communism.

There appear three stages that people go through in relating to their natural surroundings – magic, religion and science. Early on, fear and awe make people ask favors from what lies beyond and myth becomes established as a cultural force before any philosophy grows out of it. Thinking mythically and imaginatively evolves to be almost indistinguishable, and the more romantic the myth, the more the hero takes on divine attributes, with the opponent taking on the role of the devil. That way of treating the concept of evil leads to preaching that there is a malevolent force in the world and some myths have developed a Trickster, Hinduism a Destroyer, Buddhism a Tempter, Zoroastrianism an Ahrimam, Islam an Iblis and Judeo-Christianity the Devil.

Since our initial Euro-American society was grounded on Judeo-Christianity, we could benefit from an understanding of how our text bible came to be. Where that bible is accurate in history, it is so only by accident, with historical reporting having been of little interest to its writers. They had a story to tell for what they judged the greater good of society, and the select way to tap into that society's preoccupation with nature's cause-and-effect was through myth and metaphor. What biblical authors thus wrote was a source of vision, not doctrine, and the Judeo-Christian bible was not the word of God but a series of transcribed witness accounts to that presumed word.

We should thus ask if anyone can harness history with fiction to create a story with enough substance to be teachable. If so, how does one manage the tension between reality and perception in a way that offers lessons to posterity? The issue also puts the writer in the position of a Tory god, and what inevitably emerges is a mix of truth and falsehood, with a seductive dose of verisimilitude added in.

The roots of the bible go back over 3,500 years and were first handed down through oral tradition. People remembered the stories told over and over again, around the fire or in the council house, but not in the way we remember something that had actually happened – the stories were rather like dreams or jumbled sequences of events making little regular sense, or as parts of some whole that escaped full recall but still preyed on the imagination. Later on with documents, they were, I am sad to say, not handed down but after being sourced and copied, were judged of no more useful life. Ghost writing, moreover, was not seen as forgery but as a veneration of the original.

The original manuscripts for the Hebrew Old Testament were written during the 1,000 years between 1450 and 400 BC, in a Hebrew version of first consonantal-alphabet languages emanating out of Upper Egypt after 1900 BC. But portions were also written in Aramaic, a language used in both Israel and Sumaria within Palestine, from about 900 BC onwards, and Aramaic was used by the common people like Jesus, with Hebrew remaining the language of religion, government and upper class. Aramaic then continued in wide use until about 650 AD, when it was supplanted by another sister language, Arabic.

The writers of the Judeo-Christian bible's Genesis had three key sources – "J" from the use of "Jahweh" for God, "E" for a god called "Elohim" and "P" for the later accounts of priests, who emphasized their temporal interests. The creation story in Genesis comes close to a group of sardonic folk tales, with some being much older than the bible and telling of how man almost became immortal but was cheated out of that status by covetous deities. The tree of knowledge myth was also in many Mid-Eastern myths, as were stories of gods plotting to destroy man, those gods being afraid that man was getting too big for his sandals.

Chapters two and three of Genesis deal with the purpose of creation and were written before the creation story of chapter one, its being edited in after-the-fact to rationalize Genesis's purpose. The book of Proverbs, with its fatherly advice to sons, borrows from Egyptian and other Mid-Eastern books of the time, but a militaristic Messiah like David is also forecast to help Israel win wars over perceived oppressors.

The Axial Age from 800 to 200 BC, and extending to our current era's second century, was a period that embraced religious changes as triggered by Hebrew prophets like Jesus, but with Muhammad later emanating from that same spirit. The period also included Buddhism, Confucianism, Hinduism, Jainism and Taoism.

One big difference, however, did occur between Eastern and Western thought – whereas the god of the East tended to call for withdrawal, meditation and serenity, the Western god put out his word through spokesmen who advocated worshipful obedience. The Western method led to a preoccupation with personalities and celebrity obsession, and the Judeo-Christian bible came to be an action thriller, hitting its audience with ways meant to marvel – spectacular battles and romantic heroes larger than life to mesmerize the mind and minimize the need to exercise intellect, with egos given fixes to satisfy wishes.

I do, however, have an inadequacy that I must convey to you, when talking about the Old Testament – I do not speak Hebrew and my source may be from time to time the Greek translation of the Hebrew bible, called the *Septuagint*, after the 70 or so rabbis who created it in Alexandria, Egypt, between 300 and 200 BC. Seventy-two scholars, six from each of the 12 tribes, worked in separate groups and produced 12 Greek translations from the Hebrew. The translations were later consolidated and reproduced, because educated Jews spread throughout the empire were beginning to lose their Hebrew rooting, and the *Septuagint* came into wide use among Hellenistic Jews and the Diaspora communities.

The *Septuagint* was, yes, made by rabbis initially for the better educated Greek-speaking Alexandrian Jews, but Greek was never the language of Palestine and the *Septuagint* was never officially read by Jews in Palestine – they spoke Aramaic and read only Hebrew. Thus within Palestine, local Jewish authorities condemned the work and declared a period of mourning, because of defects in the Greek version.

As for the New Testament, some scholars suggest its gospels were originally written in Aramaic for regional audiences in the years after Jesus died and before the written epistles of Paul. Those gospels were later translated into Greek during the 50 years between 70 and 120. Students like you have thus asked why the translators of the bible into the King James Version a few centuries ago did not use the *Peshitta* text from the arguably more original Aramaic, used for centuries in the East. The answer could simply be ignorance by the West, before the British colonial conquest of the Middle East and long after the King James Version had been published.

The *Septuagint* was also the main source of the Old Testament for early Christians, during the first centuries of our current era. New Testament writers relied heavily on the *Septuagint* and a majority of Old Testament quotes cited in the New Testament were taken directly from the *Septuagint*, with a smaller number quoted from the Hebrew texts. It was the *Septuagint*, not the original Hebrew, that was the main basis for the Old Latin, Egyptian Coptic, Ethiopic, Armenian, Georgian, Slavonic and numerous translations of the Christian bible over the centuries, along with part of the Arabic translations of the Old Testament. And the *Septuagint* has never ceased to be the standard version of the Old Testament in today's Greek Church.

Jewish authorities throughout the Middle East did not like the unforeseen "hijacking" of their scripture by another language, and so 50 years after the death of Jesus, rabbis met to determine which books were truly the Word of God. After that period and during the first century, the *Septuagint*'s history became confined to the Christian church. Some modern bible translations continue to use the *Septuagint*, alongside Hebrew manuscripts, as their source text.

As a translation into a different culture, the *Septuagint* is at best a second best. The Dead Sea Scrolls unearthed 60 years ago show that the Scrolls, *Septuagint* and more recent Hebrew text are similar but as any philologist would tell us, languages don't translate cleanly because they reflect different peoples' interpretations of life and variations in values. The Greek translation has been accused, for example, of having an expansionist and missionary flavor, alien to the original, and of lacking the flickering dance of pun and assonance evident in the Hebrew. As for the later force-fitting of the Hebrew Old Testament to fit the Greek New, the Virgin Mary concoction was partly the result of a mistranslation of the Hebrew bible into the Christian Old Testament – the forecast in the Hebrew bible's Isaiah of a messiah born of a young woman or *almah*, was mistranslated into *parthenos* or virgin.

Further linguistic corruption started about 350 years after Jesus had died, when a Roman writer Jerome made an additional translation into Latin, and the metaphorical poetry of the Hebrew and the organic symbolism of the Greek were force-fit into the geometric Latin language of the aqueduct. The word "sky" came in Latin to imply solidity, whereas the Hebrew *rakia* had as its chief element, a kind of quantum-physics expansion. And the organic Greek of words, like bread and wine, came to have a literal equation with body and blood. The overall Latin translation became known as the Vulgate or "vulgar tongue."

Three-and-a-half centuries later, by the year 600, Latin was the only language allowed for scripture by the Roman authorities, and for the next 700 years, translations, while numerous, were severely restricted. The Vulgate was the bible for 1,000 years until the Protestant Reformation.

Many vernacular translations sprang up between 1400 and 1700 in England, Germany, France and other parts of Europe, even Italy. Wycliffe produced the first true English Bible from the Vulgate in about the year 1400, before being burned at the stake. About 50 years later in about 1450, Gutenberg invented the printing press but his first book was a two-volume Latin Bible.

Even with the advent of printing, it took another 50 years for the Greek to be widely available, because the Greek language had hundreds of custom symbols. Subsequent editions thus could be error-ridden, although the emerging Protestant Reformation carried enough anti-Latin motivation to make the eventual Greek editions more useable.

After 1500, there came to be a parallel Greek/Latin Bible that was one of the first scholarly tools for literary analysis of the Christian bible and may have helped Martin Luther to produce the first German New Testament from the Greek and Hebrew. Thereafter, Tyndale produced the first English New Testament in printed form, based mainly on the Greek but with phrases of Saxon simplicity. Many contemporary expressions like "the root of the matter," "set your house in order" or "to every thing there is a season" emanate from that bible.

The year 1537 saw the publishing of the Protestant Great Bible or First Authorized Version, and the Geneva Bible of 1560 became a revision of that "Great Bible." The Geneva Bible was the first study Bible, with less than flattering comments about the Catholic Church, and remained popular for 100 years, especially with Puritans in the new United States.

In about 1550, the Church of Rome decreed the Vulgate to be the exclusive Latin authority for the Bible, and the Vulgate became the authoritative biblical text of the Roman Catholic Church for 400 years, until a revised edition was authorized by the Second Vatican Council in 1965. Nonetheless, in that earlier time of Vulgate sanctification, Rome surrendered its Latin-only edict, and the first Catholic English translation from the Vulgate became the seed for many Catholic bibles.

The Church of England's King James Bible was created between 1604 and 1611, and to its credit, the King James Version used Greek sources for the New Testament and Hebrew for the Old.

In about 1750, a German Lutheran biblical theologian named Bengel stressed the idea that not only manuscripts but also families of manuscript traditions must be differentiated, and he initiated the formulation of criteria for text criticism. Around 1840, the English *Hexapla* New Testament was published, showing the Greek and English translations in parallel columns, demonstrating the need for a better rooting by translators and scholars.

The next major works took place in the late 1800s, with the Revised Version of the King James Bible, again a translation of the Hebrew and Greek by 65 English scholars. In 1901, an American version of the Revised King James was published and in 1952, the Revised Standard Version, with its Greek and somewhat suspect Hebrew, was authorized by the U.S. National Councils of Churches. The discovery in 1947 of the Dead Sea Scrolls made much first century BC material available, and we now have translations of high quality but each still with only a perceived balance between literal translation and creative interpretation.

Today, there are almost 8,000 versions of the Judeo-Christian bible, and for any literalist to presume that each is the literal word of god means that all witness accounts, translations, redactions and type settings are perfect, and that god's divine inspiration has corrected every bit of human failing along the way. God help the literalist."

Chantelle's talk in Oregon won her an invitation to host a seminar at Berkeley. An Oregon grad student named Eydis offered to show Chantelle some interesting points along the way, if she would give Eydis a ride to her Northern California home in Mendocino. During the trip, Eydis was soon telling Chantelle that she had changed her name from Maria to make it more Nordic, in sync with her sandy hair, and that her last name Abate had been Anglicized by friends to make it dovetail with her new first name.

It was a 50-mile drive west from Eugene, Oregon to the Pacific coast and Eydis, who had rebelled against her parents' rigid Catholicism, was almost bubbling in her coming out and wanted to source Chantelle as a further mentor. "Chantelle, I found your talk on the formation of our bible disturbing, since it showed me again that straight answers are cathartic and do little more than satisfy some neurotic need for security."

Chantelle was grateful for the company on the 300-mile ride and did not want to shunt the young student's enthusiasm. "The bible, Eydis, uses a symbolic language and is polysemous with multiple meanings. More than a third of the Old Testament is written in poetry."

Eydis the young student sat up. "Then absolute answers are presumptive and restricting," but Chantelle passed her a gentle smile. "I would like to suggest, Eydis, that the bible can be looked upon as having a threshold language that helps take us to the brink of our thinking. We need, yes, to keep a healthy heurism in looking at symbolic language as signs for direction, and the paths we take still demand we wrestle with those suggestions and share multiple interpretations with others."

Eydis let out a gasp as if she were discovering fresh support for her beliefs. "Well, is the bible an archetype or just one prototype among many?" and Chantelle again turned her head toward Eydis before returning it to face the road ahead. "Mythology is the total structure of human creation by words, with a· bible at the center of its literature. *Mythos* in Greek means sequence of words or 'story' and each *mythos* forms a model plot that focuses on what is judged important for that society to know."

Eydis raised her head toward the roof, "Right! You just said it! So the plot is Toryism by a bunch of old boys!" and Chantelle held her face forward toward the windshield, responding in calm acknowledgment. "The system is far from perfect but seems to have evolved because of its workability. Literary Darwinists see an evolutionary purpose in the mental training crucial to living within groups and argue that storytelling has evolved as an art form, because of the prestige accrued to the socially vital storyteller."

Eydis's mouth opened wide. "Leaving us at their mercy! The trick of the oral storyteller, like that of great novelists later, is to inhabit the listener and reader's mind!" But Chantelle tried to take the talk back to the empirical. "For better or worse, Eydis, there develops in any oral society a myth-making tradition called bricolage, or stringing together of available bits and pieces, and myths become functional units of society."

Eydis was lapping it up. "We've been taught that in such societies, oral records were hard to trace and were officially anonymous but became pseudonymous at a halfway stage between the oral and written traditions. There was also a tendency to regard sacred things as secret, adding mystery to the awe in the orally handed-down traditions. Over time, those stories became solidified in sacredness and became part of a society's so-called revelation."

Chantelle's voice held calm. "Yes and despite the storyteller's intent to rule over the language, the story's language could overtake the storyteller, and the prejudices of the storyteller could get magnified by the story's evolving allusions." Chantelle then gave a slow nod to the windshield. "But for any society to survive and thrive, it has to select its history."

Eydis jumped up inside her seat belt. "And when any society does, it compromises openness, and what is true comes to mean what we need to know, as judged by someone more powerful than us!"

Chantelle's tone stayed steady. "As you have no doubt learned, Eydis, in any early society, poetry develops before prose, in part because the meter, rhyme and fixed epithets of verse make for ready memorization. But the poet does not say 'this is so' but rather 'let this be' and poetry has, yes, multiple meanings."

Eydis again sprang up, almost reaching the ceiling as if to shout above the roof of the car, "Making the confusion worse is the fact that storytellers or prophets, as you say, need a degree of accreditation by society, for it to confer authority on those editorialists!" She then turned toward Chantelle. "And as the society evolves, popular prophets often become hacks, telling the bottom rungs what the powerful people at the top want the bottom to know. Thus, a non-hack prophet like Jesus can glean support only through demagoguery." Suddenly, Eydis eased her tone. "It is ironical that prophets like Jesus often later get raised to infallibility, to spice up the original story. Death tends to deify, and the longer a person is dead, the more his words become ideology."

Chantelle's voice held steady. "Both Plato and Jesus used symbols to convey a message, when prose was felt too unimaginative for the job. Plato talked of the 'noble lie' planted inside a story, with an overriding message of greater good," but Eydis would not let that chance pass. "The Platonic noble lie may be a way to keep a society together but such an interpretation gives the myth-maker huge latitude in judging what is best for the population as a whole. Power corrupts and the chance for abuse runs high."

Eydis again calmed a bit, as if she had just let out a great exhale. Eydis then turned to her new mentor. "Chantelle, can there be any value in a premise made only by a manipulation of history?" and Chantelle turned to her with a slight smile. "One danger in conveying a moral message with symbols to all strata within society is that the white lie can be taken for a literal truth. The lie then takes on a life of its own with power enough to overwhelm the original message. The story ultimately builds to the point where the prejudices of the first storyteller are forgotten and the story's empirical legitimacy becomes moot."

Eydis sat silent, possibly pondering what Chantelle had said and Chantelle offered a consolation. "It is a mark of a mature society to give partial acceptance to prophetic minds, without holding a belief in their infallibility. The flaws of David in ancient Israel were acknowledged but people knew they could still learn from him."

Eydis perked up again. "Yet as we know, religious leaders in the bible, by and large, did not write. Their words were recorded by others under the guise of discipleship," and Chantelle carried forward the thought. "Thus a prophet's utterings need to be interpreted and reinterpreted with an honest heart, with intellectual rigor and openness to other points of view, as we are doing now."

Eydis caught her mentor's kind smile at the windshield and Chantelle continued: "You already know, Eydis, that even if, say, my language was exact, you would still be integrating it with your own experiences as my thoughts entered your mind. Such is the nature of imperfect communications but we should not despair – the process itself can generate its own energy, and the degree of engagement by any listener or reader will determine in great part the amount of creative thought triggered by the listener's mind."

Eydis's eyebrows shot up and her mouth opened to form the letter "O." Chantelle saw the shock and offered another gentle smile. "I feel, Eydis, that we should not read the bible with our pendulum swung solely to rational skepticism. Rationality is needed and we will still need to apply Rudyard Kipling's 'Rule of Six' – who knew what, when, where, how and why. We will also need to discern, as best we can, cause and effect.

"But I feel we need to regard the bible as literature that does not necessarily assert but rather holds up symbols calling for a variety of reactions. We need, as well, the Kipling discipline that I suggested, before we even think of grappling with the factive verb 'to know.' In this way, we should be able to offer a legitimate challenge to ideologies, using, instead of a frontal attack with rational skepticism, a healthy suspension of judgment."

When Chantelle and Eydis reached the Pacific coast and Highway 101, the talk stopped and both started taking in the scenery. The greenery of Suislaw National Forest gave way to acres of sand along the Pacific, and soon there were huge cream-colored dunes, as high as 500 feet, popping up on the ocean-side.

A little farther along, Eydis suggested that Chantelle detour to a side road at Cape Arago, for the ocean's 12-mile ride to Brandon, past the coastal wetlands that were home to deer, bears and 150 different kinds of birds. Chantelle loved every moment of the excursion and a gratified Eydis suggested they continue on the slow road for another 20 miles, past the fir forests and beige shores to the little fishing town of Port Orford, where Chantelle got back onto Highway 101.

Once into California, the old Volvo carried on for another 100 miles past the gold-rush city of Eureka and its Victorian homes, and then went through Humbolt Redwoods State Park with its old-growth trees, 300 feet in height. After that, Chantelle and Eydis continued south for another 100 miles, and the car finally reached the hamlet of Mendocino, with its saltbox houses looking straight out of the North Atlantic coast and not the Pacific.

Eydis invited her mentor to stay with Eydis's parents but Chantelle declined and said she wanted to spend some time alone, to gather her thoughts for a possible seminar. But Chantelle was also tired and didn't relish any discussions on religion, if she were a guest in Eydis's home.

Thursday January 15 2009

It had been a week since Chantelle's Grosvenor Street apartment had received a note from Mendocino, California, where state troopers had found her in the small hours, sleeping inside her Volvo in Russian Gulch State Park. After being forced by the police to be checked out at a hospital, she had continued south, following that fine man of a doctor, Jeff, to San Francisco.

After my waiting a week and too short a time for an answer, I seized on the only encouragement that I could muster from not getting a response, and decided that if my letter had not been returned, Chantelle must have received it. I embarked on a strategy to ingratiate myself to my beloved Chantelle, presuming at each move to possess a true view of her beliefs.

Dear Chantelle,

I read today in Toronto's Reference Library the highlights from a Vatican strategy paper that advocated a reaffirmation of papal policy, in terms of what must endure in Catholicism, both as truth and piety.

The so-called inanities of Western post-modernism were to give way to a return to ethics and metaphysics, as "better defined" by historic Christianity. Young people were expected to resume coming forward as priests, with nuns and lay people committed to a plenary Catholicism, rather than being mere social workers. And the total Roman structure was to have a clearer understanding that the pastoral should always be secondary to the doctrinal, "because Catholic doctrine manifested truth."

The save-the-planet movement was to be exploited to generate a renewed reverence for nature-respecting reproduction and thus undermine opposition to Catholic ethics surrounding contraception, abortion and medical experiments.

The "richer" traditions and ancient dogma embedded in the East would continue their post-Marxist role of playing a greater part in forming Catholic consciousness and would counter the challenges from both liberation theologies and a renascent Islam. The experience of containing ethnic rivalries would dissuade Catholic churchmen away

from the "unalloyed pluralism" of ecumenical sentiments and pull them
back to pure unity in spirituality and its governance by historic Catholic
doctrine.

> *Where are you, Chantelle?*
> *All my love forever,*
> *Arthur*

No answer, but I did learn from a,Berkeley administrator that the speech promoter had been Terry Hardy. Chantelle had declined his proposal, after reading a letter he had sent to Chantelle via Berkeley. The gist of the letter was that Chantelle's talk in Oregon had not been provocative enough, like her addresses in Chicago, and was not in keeping with her priorities. But the letter had also conceded that perhaps her lecture had been mandated by the curriculum. Hardy had reiterated that he would continue to respect Chantelle's ownership over what she said but had a few suggestions that she could incorporate into future engagements for greater impact.

I don't know exactly what Hardy said but as best I can glean today, I now surmise the following: "Chantelle, in extending your talk on how mythical stories are formed and solidified, the Judaic Torah for example contains instructions including laws that no one in ancient Israel was excused from learning.

In your Oregon lecture, you faulted yourself for not knowing Hebrew and cautioned that some of your understandings of the ancient Hebraic text might have to be filtered through a translation into Greek. The translation was done, you affirmed, by rabbis who had become alarmed by the enlightening influence of Greek Hellenistic culture on their Jewish intelligentsia and concomitant emancipation of women. Wherever the Greek or later Roman Empires had established stability and given people economic opportunity, along with freedom of movement, a Jewish Diaspora of prosperous communities had formed."

After reading Hardy's letter, Chantelle felt she had again to set him straight that he could not have any control over what she said. She learned from the note where Hardy was staying and they agreed to meet for lunch, near the Pacific Ocean's edge at Fisherman's Wharf.

It was warm on that meeting day in January 2009, warm enough for Hardy to be garbed in his usual military olive and Chantelle to be dressed in Levis, brown hiking boots, brown wool turtleneck and a beige windbreaker. Her long dark hair, 5'10" height and unadorned beauty made her stand out on the San Francisco waterfront.

After a moment exchanging pleasantries and sitting down for lunch, Chantelle set in. "Mr. Hardy, I am concerned over your wanting to do my thinking for me, particularly after your spin about rabbinical alarm over emancipated Greek thinking."

Hardy gave a knowing smile, perhaps sensing it was time to reel back in but no doubt wanting to keep Chantelle implicated in her notes. He tried a sincere posture, with hands folded on the lunch table middle. "And you certainly are erudite on that issue. I too find fault with Maimonides and admire Spinoza," but Chantelle picked up the allusion to her notes and mustered in a diminished voice, "Mr. Hardy, as I said to my former boyfriend, whom you know is Jewish, those notes were top-line thoughts, for processing and refining or discarding later," and Hardy lunged forward, "Of course! Not to suggest…it's just that Fundies…"

Chantelle's brows turned down. "Fundies?" and Hardy straightened up. "Sorry, Christian fundamentalists distort the Hebrew bible with a rule book of their own, and such fundamentalism hurts me, Chantelle."

Hardy lowered his head to the table as if to hide some hurt and then followed up with a raise of his head back to meet Chantelle's eyes and let her see his pain. "I feel that such a rule book is empty of Greek questioning yet full of responses that are not answers. For me, the fundamentalist rule book is a sophism founded on a theology of cheating."

Chantelle appeared to fall for the intellectual diversion, with its pinch of sentimentality. She moved to heal the wounded man. "Religion, Terry, is the one area of life where the standards of reasonableness and self-criticism normally demanded in intellectual discourse do not apply. The non-appliance of rationality to religion can be damaging, because those standards are critical to the exploration of ethics or any kind of contemplative thought."

Hardy bent his head forward and raised his eyebrows, as if Chantelle had sanctioned his sentiments. "Add to this closed-mindedness, any militancy in executing those ideals and one has the makings for a permanent state of unrest."

Chantelle leaned back and put both palms on her place mat, as if to slow Hardy's charge. "The Christian fundamentalist faith is anything but passive and hides behind an Andrew Jackson kind of anti-intellectual coziness, where any intellectualism is equated with pretension."

Hardy pushed both shoulders forward, as if she were giving him license. "And as you have said, Doctor Fouriere, the fundamentalist faith varies inversely with verifiability, and is structured on suspect passions and attendant contempt for reasoned inquiry."

Chantelle kept her palms firmly on the mat and came forward a little. "With emphasis on the non-synoptic gospel of John, Christian fundamentalists often commit logicide in their slaughter of words, and tens of millions of Americans rely on self-styled Christian broadcasters for news and its interpretation." Hardy held forward and he used each shoulder to punctuate what he said next. "And the previously coined enemy, communism, has been replaced by secular humanism! Richard Nixon's silent majority has grown vocal and has erected a fascist reaction founded on fear and the power of human inertia."

Terry Hardy then marched on, as if fortified by what he saw as an endorsement. "Critical to this new skew is the perception of victimhood! As you no doubt know, Doctor Fouriere, it's an inner trait of a mob to feel persecuted. To suggest, therefore, to such a martyred group that it is morally superior to the perceived persecutors, is to tap into their lower traits, with a message more seductive than the flat fairness of equality."

Hardy then grinned as if happy with himself and knowing of Chantelle's weakness for this type of argument. She lifted her middle fingers off the table but let her palms stay on the mat. "With individuation subsumed by submissiveness and its militaristic enforcement, a black-and-white world is fabricated in a Cowboys-and-Indians Reaganism, where phantom enemies always lurk. Quack therapy abounds and people needing quick fixes for their spiritual delusions wait for miracles from a Godot who never comes. Tyranny follows, and while the swallowing followers wait for salvation, they are bilked for money from a reigning hierarchy and its underlying priests, who promise that god will reward a hundred-fold."

Hardy sat back and let out a sigh, as if to wax "Such is life." He was about to continue when a waitress came to take their orders for salad and tea, but the pause was long enough for Chantelle's broad condemnation to ground what Hardy could get away with next. "The twin manipulators of sight and sound are used to blow away the victims' rationality, and any ability to discern gets nullified by poisoning the channels of information, while at the same time the mob's minds are pounded with pretended love. God-given liberty is thus repressed under a mask of patriotism and new recruits are told they are forever damned, until they are born again."

Hardy looked to love his blurb and added with index finger, "Not born through Greek freedom to learn or have social responsibility but by being dependent upon, as you said, an over-mothering Jesus, who treats them like helpless children and wipes away their sins. Converts are chained to ecclesiastical activity, with no time for openness to anything else, and the time-exhausted converts are inculcated with a doctrine that demonizes any alternatives."

Chantelle had already lowered her fingers back to the mat but suddenly she arched her shoulders forward. "Fundamentalists on the Christian right see the hole in enemy lines and go on the attack, using war metaphors and prayer warriors, while behind the front lines, a family superstructure is erected in support of the war and homes become microcosms of militarism. A male hierarchy is fortified, where fathers are perceived as masters, wives play their role as moms and children learn to obey out of fear."

Hardy's finger rose in response. "Yes! And do not get to feel the confidence that you once said, Chantelle, should come from learning, or the trust that accompanies such confidence. Those children in turn learn not to trust outsiders."

Two salads came with glasses of tap water, and the teas to come later. Hardy waited for the lady, Chantelle, to lift her fork before following suit but as his fork lifted from the plate, his face betrayed not wanting to lose the momentum. "Friends and spouses share the same prejudices and the resulting mobs become cults of perversion, where all thinking is cross-wired by an intellectual incest, with all thoughts reinforced by the prejudices of doctrines already drilled into fellow members. The followers thus lose their need to discern or have consciences, and all moral choices are made for them by an invented Jesus, who sees only threats from Greek reasoning. Gatherings that pretend to be public become spiritual closets from which secular media are banned or asked to leave, and even science is hijacked and sexed up to present a perversion of thought, in support of their fear-filled inwardness."

Chantelle smiled at a Terry Hardy face waiting for a reaction and then he had a couple of bites, along with a drink of needed water before he went back at it. "Within the greater fundamentalist community, the militarism marches to the same drum and followers remain fooled by an illusion of tranquility." Hardy waved his arms in a sweeping shrug. "Killed is any capacity to love beyond what is prescribed, and any romantic love is seen as competing with an authority founded on force."

Hardy then took a bigger bite but in the ensuing silence, took it as a cue to provoke more. "The militaristic mentality endorses both the violence of the Old Testament and a sexual psychosis that damns God-given pleasure. Censorship takes on a form of sexual denial where human beings, despite being encouraged, as you said, Chantelle, to make love copulating face-to-face, are propagandized into presuming sex is for procreation only, from the be-fruitful-and-multiply mandate, given after the agricultural revolution, thousands of years ago. Homosexuality is thus cast as an aberration, using a literalist twist on Leviticus, because such sexuality does not manifest the fruitful-and-multiply doctrine."

Hardy then lifted his head high to the sky. "It is frightening that the United States, with its world dominance, has allowed AIDS-ridden Africa to carry on without condoms or to have enough medicine for sexual diseases" and Chantelle lowered her fork. "The disinformation of this fundamentalist ideology creates a clear enemy, and the communications gap becomes so wide that the fundamentalists cannot see the flaws on their side, since they don't speak their enemy's language. American fundamentalists have been anti-black, anti-poor, anti-environment, pro-gun and pro-corporal punishment of children. Like the apostles in the Jewish feast of Pentecost, they often speak in tongues, supposedly in code, but are clear in declaring the USA to be god's country."

Hardy went back in his chair and smiled. "Yes, Doctor Chantelle, and with their Jesus having taken away their sins, the evangelicals can then charge ahead in pursuit of their golden calf, unhampered by any social conscience. They can accept that in our world's wealthiest country, 30 million people remain employed at under nine dollars an hour, with no health care or other benefits."

Hardy was on a roll. "The Fundies push their frontmen to shift government monies from direct support of those less fortunate to religion-based organizations that are less accountable but more discriminatory in their hiring. The Fundies also tap into anger from the loss of manufacturing jobs to Asia and foster bigotry against whole races of people who do not subscribe to their Jesus."

Chantelle had been seduced. "The U.S. is now full of spanking new big sucker churches, all tax-exempt and surrounded by a sea of energy-consuming cars and school buses, with all the churches built in mausoleum suburbs with sparse trees, little shade, energy-eating air conditioners, strip malls, high-speed streets, few pedestrians, a sameness of houses and no sense of community. Within such mediocrity and its controls on even the air we breathe, the predictable fallout is ennui, melancholia and a confusion of likes and dislikes, and the people so subjugated remain vulnerable to quick fixes and an infatuation with wealth and fame."

Hardy gave a grin at the rage in Chantelle's still soft voice, and he sought to fuel the rage. "The war effort is then expanded against the most vulnerable, and seniors' homes are targeted where the susceptible seek heaven after imminent death, as well as relief from present pain."

Chantelle fell into stride and wrinkled her brow, as one of her shoulders came forward. "It is hard on a beleaguered people, when others look at them as though they need pity or over-mothering. Fundamentalists espouse to the vulnerable a utopia enwrapped in bedazzlement and the vulnerable are taught to want memorization and speak prayers of magic, while the predators carry forward the battle from their tax-exempt mega-churches, pushing politics and erecting giant museums to make mainstream their propaganda."

But suddenly with Terry Hardy beaming a wide smile, Chantelle caught herself in a deep squint and was perhaps alarmed at the anger in her own words. She then calmed. "Let us recall, Terry, that the United States of America was founded on principles arising out of the Age of Enlightenment and that all founding fathers were Unitarians who did not spin their bible literally. What would they say now, if they witnessed the resurrection in the United States of a 17th-century theology, or the 40% growth in fundamentalist Christian schools in the last 15 years, or the fact that a quarter of the U.S. population now professes to be evangelical?"

Hardy sat content to let Chantelle continue. "Indeed, three-quarters believe in a judgment day at life's end, and one-third or more believe the world is coming to an end. But because of divine rapture, the elect will be saved. Little more than one in four Americans believe in Darwinian evolution and almost one-quarter believe that the Old Testament's Genesis is true, including the world's being created some 7,000 years ago."

Hardy then sensed it was his turn to appear erudite. "Fundamentalists and other literalists argue that everybody is entitled to his opinion about creation, as if scientific evidence equates with chauvinistic emotionalism. And in their rigidity and literal spins, they seem to have no understanding of spiritual progress in ancient Hebraic society."

Chantelle leaned back and offered a wide smile while nodding, and so the unbridled Hardy continued: "Within an irony of tolerance, Christians on the outside tolerate the intolerant Fundies and in so doing close their ears to the real Jesus who said to love your enemies but not to shy away from fights with their fallacies. Traditional churches that denounce those parts of the Bible containing violence and hate nonetheless remain complicit in accepting the intolerant Fundies, and so religious intolerance, the chief stuff of war, is given free rein through passive acceptance by the purportedly aware."

Chantelle felt herself with a caring man and she moved to speak in support. "As with the abandonment of social conscience by fundamentalists, so too with war. They need not care about war, their envisioning an end of times and a second coming of their christ. Thus they buy into a kind of narcissism of the saved, and it follows that they become not only dominionists over all other creatures but also part of a select few within humanity itself."

Hardy smiled as if he could not have been more pleased with the direction the conversation was taking. He brought both shoulders forward. "The literalist, looking at the Christian Old Testament, can rationalize the subjection of Canaanites to Israel and the Jews being compelled to put away their foreign wives, or the forbiddance of practices done by Israel's neighbors, with Hebrews separating milk and meat because a Canaanite fertility ritual had involved the boiling of a kid in its mother's milk.

"In like fashion, all non-human creatures can be seen as given into the custody of human beings and a human attitude toward nature becomes one of exploitation, with a reign of terror over all creatures to ensue."

Chantelle still had a look of some comfort on her face and she moved to support: "It is thus easy to moralize on AIDS in the sub-Sahara or to oppose stem-cell research that could create breakthroughs for conquering disease. Easy too to adopt 'terrorism' as a buzzword to connote Islam in its many forms. The Muslim Allah never desired human sacrifice but confined that delusion to its Old Testament's Ibrahim. Islam, as you know, Mr. Hardy, condemns violence as contrary to god's nature."

Hardy gave a long sigh. "Other Old Testament books were edited to sanction the overthrow of heathen empires, with the logical conclusion being the full and eschatological restoration of Israel. Genesis with its El Elyon as most high god and Salem as Jerusalem had the object of establishing Israel's god-given right to the city of Jerusalem, along the way to the full restoration of Israel."

This time, Chantelle paused and slowly wrinkled her brow, perhaps realizing how far Hardy had taken her. She tried some context. "We are apt to identify messages in some bibles as human endeavors to create god's kingdom. Whereas causality relates to what we retrieve from the past, the Hebrew Bible as we know, Terry, is directed toward the future."

Hardy was not to be contained. "Evangelical Fundies, Chantelle, with their literalist spins can thus be the Jewish Likud's best friend. The 'Likudiks' recently featured at a fundamentalist convention an Israeli bus blown up by Palestinians, alongside the Israeli Ministry of Tourism, in the convention's largest display space."

Chantelle winced and tried to bring the talk back to the biblical. "Human beings, being human, will continue after a covenant, such as ancient Israel's, to behave toward other ethnic groups in ways that are possibly too reflective of the *id* to which their god has appealed" and Hardy came halfway off his seat. "Christian fundamentalists see Moses at the command of an ethnic-cleansing god who drove the Amorites, Canaanites, Hittites, Perizzites and Jebusites out of their homelands, killing women and children. Except for the young female virgins who were to be used, but remained second-class citizens until they accepted in full the Jewish Law. And that literalist god's threat – to punish sin and guilt even to the seventh generation – remains the ultimate expression of hate."

Chantelle gave a dark frown and had a look of unsettlement. "But as you know, Terry, the Jews are by no means unique in this misunderstanding – early Christian Patricians sought, through whatever means, irrefutable premises to support their perfect god, and in so doing brewed a New Testament with the end site being not the Hebraic restoration of a full Israel but the arrival on planet earth of a messiah as forecasted in the Hebrew bible."

Chantelle was off again on a subject she loved. "The New Testament had a John the Baptist mirroring an Old Testament Elijah, Jesus a Joshua, and Jesus's parents Mary and Joseph mirroring the Miriam who had been the sister of Moses and a Joseph who had led Israelites into the fertile Nile Valley of Egypt. The three wise men visiting baby Jesus are a variation on the Queen of Sheba's visit to Solomon, and Jesus's beatitudes in his sermon-on-the-mount are parallel in structure to Moses's Ten Commandments."

It was Chantelle who then gave a shrug and held up her hand. "A professedly Christian reader of the New Testament is continually tricked by an echo from the Hebrew bible."

Hardy was not about to lose the ground they were both on. "Yes, Chantelle, the Jews are not unique, but the Likudiks feel chosen by god and are not bound by Western societal decorum, yet they disintegrate the integrity of their own faith by going in-your-face political. Likudik frontmen see themselves as holy warriors or the Joshuas and Davids of today, and

Christian Fundies fall for the line that Israel must rule the full biblical land, for Jesus to return."

Chantelle again winced and tried to ease the talk by staking again some common ground. "Ancient Egypt is embedded in the Old Testament as a furnace-of-iron prison, and the so-called heathen in both ancient Egypt and Babylon are cast as dragons," but Hardy again came almost off his chair with, "Egyptologists have redacted that many Jews had been living well in ancient Alexandria, before the famed Exodus!"

Chantelle's wince grew more pronounced, feeling perhaps she was being steered. "There is evidence, Terry, that man named Joseph at the end of Genesis did shepherd the Israelites away from famine and into the fertile Nile Valley of Egypt," but Hardy remained high in his seat. "And many Jews there, Chantelle, rose to prominence in trade and government as they later did in Tarsus, Odessa and Rome. By the time of Jesus, one in seven people in Egypt were Jews!"

Hardy lowered back into his chair, perhaps to recapture his role of level-mindedness. "As reported by Hebrew prophets, many of those Jews in the Egypt of eighth century BC resented their exploitation by the Jewish rich, who took their own people's land and were quick to tap into corrupt judges to support the luxury-loving women of Jerusalem." He then turned his head to the side and rendered a philosophical shrug. "Unfortunately, the exploited greater Jewish people were not street smart and had their anger displaced by the seductive story – that they alone possessed the only true god of salvation and were the chosen people to enlighten lesser groups."

Chantelle's forehead again wrinkled at where Terry Hardy was going but he tried smiling and came back with a broader comment. "If notions of bio-logical and racial preference are inculcated into a myth, the mythological god can be maneuvered into a bargaining position, to lay down a contract between that god and his chosen people."

Hardy knew of Chantelle's love for arguing religious issues but this time it was he who paused and winced at her evident discomfort. Suddenly, he assured Chantelle that she would continue to have full control over what she said, but he suggested they meet from time to time to exchange updates on her progress. Chantelle agreed in principle, yet said she needed time to reconsider their arrangement and whether their views did in fact dovetail enough for her to continue. Chantelle also mentioned a job offer that she was about to accept, helping medical science students at Berkeley until the end of the semester, when it would then be necessary for her to step back into Canada so as not to overrun her six-month guest stay in the United States.

Hardy agreed but inside of a week seized the opportunity to find for Chantelle a late-May speaking engagement in Minneapolis, near the Canadian border. Hardy assured her that she would be free to express her thoughts but did indicate that the subject area was to embrace American Christian fundamentalism.

Meanwhile, throughout that first half of 2009, I kept trying to communicate with Chantelle via Berkeley.

If there is one thing worse than feeling persecuted for being a Jew, it is being pounced on by Jewish powers-that-be. On the Friday before Obama's inauguration, late in the day, I was barely out of Toronto's Central Reference Library and into the air of midtown Yonge before I was being hustled by some teenage Orthodox Jews. "Excuse me, are you Jewish?"

I was caught off-guard and reared back before managing a sneer. "Chicago Jew and not cut as much as New Yorkers. I also don't make that girlish yiddling sound. And I drink!"

That was all these kids needed to hear, and they were on my back all the way to the subway. When I darted down the entrance to escape them, those black-hats stayed on me until I finally got to the other side of the turnstile and disappeared into the masses.

I was angry. Had us Americans been given, after September 11, 2001, the freedom of full information, maybe we could have avoided being coerced into further folly. George W. Bush named former Secretary of State Henry Kissinger as chairman of a commission to investigate the 9/11 terrorist attacks but U.S. legislators were going to demand that Doctor Kissinger reveal his consulting clients, to flush out conflicts of interest. He resigned instead the commission position, saying the rumors would not fade unless he shut down his consultancy firm entirely.

Ten days after 9/11, an American Muslim immigrant named Rais Bhuiyan was working at a Texas gas station, when a self-described "Arab slayer" walked up to him, asked where he was from and shot him in the face before murdering two other Muslims. Rais survived and has been pleading since for forgiveness of the killer and a stop to the hate – if people hear hatreds often enough, what has been strategically created is a rage where the only option is revenge.

A sheik had been interviewed after September 11 in New York of all places and had talked of the Palestinian issue being pivotal to the event. But his thoughts were all quashed and he was not heard of again. Resurrected instead was the Hollywood myth of an American Sarah in the farmhouse and an Abe working in the fields, while a David protected them with god always on their side. Women were to go back to making babies and looking after the home, and the threat of 9/11 was re-conceived as a threat to the American home and family, with women needing protection and to be provided for.

To the fore came the American knight in shining armor, who protected American blonde virgins from swarthy enemies, and rape was reinforced as the ultimate fantasy of challenge to potency and honor. Later, in an ill-conceived war in Iraq, a fictionalized rescue of a private named Jessica Lynch was aimed at male impotence in not being able to protect against the attack of 9/11. The rescue sham was not unlike U.S. cinema, with its manipulations in the 1956 John Wayne movie *The Searchers* with an untrue story of a Cynthia Anne Parker from 1836. The story had been an earlier rationale for land takeover and the slaughter of the American First Nations people.

September 11 triggered an explosion of hearsay, echoed often enough to erect a series of ersatz truths. A blast of fantasies highlighted such fables as oppressed Islamic women, with cosmetic companies capitalizing on the fantasies to pour millions into Afghanistan. Flight 93 of September 11 had been downed by American fighter jets but the surrounding facts were suppressed and the doomed flight fermented into a fantasy, with the victims' widows playing to sworn scripts. Acts of torture soon boomed on TV, along with the righteous halting of "Arab savages" from murdering American innocents. But the real words weren't heard: "I still remember the distressing scenes – blood, torn limbs, women and children massacred. All over the place, houses…were being destroyed and tower blocks were collapsing, crushing their residents, while bombs rained down mercilessly on our homes…as I looked at those destroyed towers…it occurred to me to punish the oppressor in kind…so that it would have a taste of its own medicine and would be prevented from killing our women and children."

That was Osama bin Laden, speaking of Israel's 1982 invasion of Lebanon as backed by the United States with naval bombardments. Bin Laden, like others, did not have Islam as his prime motivator but he spoke instead as an infuriated member of the region. The U.S.-labeled club of original terrorists consisted of many *mujahedeen*, who had been given American support in fighting the 100,000 Soviet troops in Afghanistan, but after bin Laden had been later expelled from puppet Saudi Arabia and the Sudan, he had issued a piece entitled *World Front for Jihad Against Jews and Crusaders*, and that piece had sealed his fate in the West.

Since 9/11, there have been over 130,000 murders in the U.S., with only 30 of them committed by radicalized individuals, but the media have sensationalized a handful of incidents where Muslims in the West have embraced a violent interpretation of jihadism. Had it not been for earlier attempts in the 1970s to cast the Arab world as the work of the devil – with Islam the new evil empire – but with that world's vastness proving too varietal to be so defined, the cast would have been done.

Iraq, on the other hand, was a case small enough to be crystallized in Western perception as an urgent battle within a long-term war, and the failings of Saddam Hussein could be magnified to meet his role as cast. Iraq, before the 2003 U.S. invasion, had enjoyed nationwide medicine, health care, drinking water and relatively emancipated women, and Iraq's Christian community had been one of the oldest in the world, with Ur the birthplace of Abraham. Before the American invasion, Baghdad had also contained more Christians than any other Middle Eastern city, but Iraq was anathematized as the new evil Babylon that had been the antithesis of Jerusalem 2,500 years ago, and Saddam Hussein was cast as the evil King Nebuchadnezzar, who had warred with Israel and destroyed Jerusalem in 586 BC.

In 2003, the source of hell was Iraq and now it is Iran. Imagine if the U.S. ever apologized for the CIA's 1953 overthrow of Iran's elected government, with that act catapulting Iran's reaction into extremism. Imagine if the U.S. public ever knew that in 2003, Iran had sent a Swiss official to Washington to make a peace offer of recognizing Israel and abolishing any nuclear weapons plans, in exchange for an end to sanctions, as well as diplomatic relations with the U.S. and recognition of Iran's significance as a country. Nobody in the White House at the time had thought it would look good to make peace with part of Bush's "Axis of Evil."

I would lose track of Chantelle after San Francisco but did not know it at the time and kept sending letters to Berkeley. She did not appear to be speaking anywhere, and only months later did I find out that Chantelle had come back north. As for me, I charged through the winter of 2009, doing my daily swim at Hart House, going three times a week to AA meetings, and beginning in the middle of January, attending a healthy debate on world conditions, once a week, again in Hart House. When I was back in Chantelle's apartment, I read her books.

Monday January 19 2009

Beginning at 8:00 a.m. after my swim at Hart House, I came to meet with a couple of others in its Great Hall, empty at that time of day. Before the first get-together, my new friend Edward decided I needed reminding that we Jews had survived thousands of years on intense debate, and it could often be unpleasant, but sometimes produced greatness. He added that he was going to take a beating that day from a conservative Jew named Chaim, and I was eager to meet Chaim because I wanted some balance to Edward's criticisms of Israel and Ashkenazi Jews. I was also still disturbed by the article I had read on the Gaza war in the Y before receiving career counseling.

Tiny, perfect Edward arrived in his standard garb of pressed white shirt and grey wool pants, but Chaim turned out to be fat and sloppy, arriving in a purple shirt that fell out over a bulging stomach and trailed down over a pair of messy trousers. He had on big black galoshes that were totally un-wiped from the snow outside.

As Chaim shook my hand, his puffy arm gave me a pull backward, because he was trying at the same time to sit down on the far side of the oak table. I feigned no notice and followed Edward's move in taking an oak chair on the opposite side.

Once seated, Chaim placed his right arm behind his chair before he shifted his entire body sideways to give room for his fat thighs. The move made his left shoulder stay forward, facing Edward and me. Chaim then thrust out his left arm over the oak table and made a spider-like shape, with his palm coiled up on the table middle. Soon he would tap these fingers whenever he wanted to command the floor. "Arthur, there are many in Israel critical of its government and even its beginnings." Chaim's head then turned to Edward. "We even tolerate Sephardics," and then he turned his head back to me. "But outside Israel, intemperate criticism of its actions can fuel a group who hate Jews."

Edward's head swiveled to face mine. "Arthur, Israel is truth on the ground and will be there for a Jewish eternity, that is, for the nation's grand-children's grandchildren. Israel stands no more chance of being taken over by Palestinians or other Arabs than does your United States by the Lakota descendants of Crazy Horse."

Chaim tapped his fingers. "The Canadian Union of Public Employees is just one example of that hate. Its shibboleth – to allow Palestinians the right to self-determination including the right of return – is code for dismantling Israel as the world's only Jewish state." Chaim then thrust his left shoulder over the table at me. "Thank god for your U.S. campus watchdog and its keeping a list of professors who denounce Israel."

I resented Chaim and Edward using my country this way and sought with an erudite squint to offer a dose of reality. "Half of Jewish Americans under the age of 35 say that the end of a Jewish Israel would not be a personal tragedy for them," but Chaim lunged forward with his whole upper body: "Israel is home and psychic security for Jewish people everywhere, and we all live with the implicit message that the state of Israel is the answer for the 20th century trying to annihilate us. Israel's Yom Ha-Shoah day of remembrance does not just commemorate the six million Jews exterminated – it underscores that the wound should never be allowed to heal and is Israel's point of existence."

Edward slid his tiny hands forward toward Chaim's spider-hand and laid his palms flat in front of it. "Israel achieved independence over 60 years ago and has the fourth most sophisticated military in the world, along with the bomb" but Chaim charged back: "But fears at all times it will cease to exist. Even the West, as our American friend Arthur has today revealed, has never accepted the idea of Israel, and we fear another Holocaust by assimilation."

Chaim folded his fat arms and said with flat defiance, "There is a fundamental Zionist principle that needs to be heard – the survival of the Jewish state and its people must never again be left to the unreliable mercies of others. We are forced to protect what we have."

But Edward turned his palms up as if in reason. "One can be so afraid of a pending holocaust that to get relief, one acts to provoke it. The constant Holocaust reference is like the cries of Zionist Herzl, who forecasted in the 19th century that Europe would absolutely turn against the Jews. When he then met with members of the world's Jews at the 1897 Zionist Congress in Switzerland, they had no sense that Muslims would object to thousands of

Jews entering Palestine. After Herzl published *The Jewish State* in 1896, two European rabbis went to Palestine and wrote back that the bride is beautiful but is married to another man."

Chaim shifted loudly in his chair and let out a huff. "Herzl saw the reason for Zionism as being to create a home in the land of Israel, not for all citizens but for the Jewish people, with such a home assured by international legitimacy. Hence the support for the Gush Emunim or Block of the Faithful now seeding Judea and Samaria, or what is misnamed the West Bank, with Jewish settlers."

Edward also shifted to come back in, but Chaim put his spider-hand back on the table and tapped his fingers. "Much of the impetus for that support came in 1967, when the dreams of 2,000 years came to be fulfilled by reaching territories intimately linked to Jewish history, especially Jerusalem. Since 1967, the settlers have been touching the pulse of Israel's founding ethos – that God gave us the land and that Jewish settlement in the land is critical not only to establishing a state in the ancient homeland but also to our returning to the holy sites, which are part of the bedrock of Jewish history."

Chaim then heaved a huge sigh and leaned back as if pleased with what he had said but Edward jumped back in with his little chin leading: "The settlers manifested a renewed pioneering spirit, and their fundamentalist beliefs in being tied to the land by God were overlooked, as was the impact on Palestinians. The settlers oppose a Palestinian state but continue to get government breaks, and Israel now demands that Palestinians acknowledge Israel as a Jewish state, despite 20% of Israeli citizens being Muslim or Christian Arabs."

Chaim looked recharged after his brief respite and his eyes glared over his spider-hand to little Edward on the other side. "Israel is the only place in the world where Jews can fight for their lives as Jews, and it's not just the Israeli settlers – the Likud too dreams of a Greater Israel that incorporates the West Bank, Gaza and the Golan Heights." Chaim's eyes then shifted to mine. "Arthur, before World War II, there was a song by Jabotinsky, founder of Revisionist Zionism and root of the Likud Party. The song referred to the *shtay gadot* or two banks of the Jordan River – 'The Jordan has two banks and both are ours.' The Jews were chosen to live in Palestine and Moses led the way."

I took in a loud breath to get attention and then spoke with my head turning to both Chaim and Edward: "Moses still does, from what I can see. Israel is saying that Fatah and Hamas must come together and if by some miracle they do, Israel will up the ante and brew something like all terrorism, as Israel keeps redefining it, has to end before there can be a Palestinian state."

Edward nodded at me and came back in. "Israel is also using Iran's alleged development of nuclear weapons and the front of peace talks with Syria, to dupe the U.S." and I asked fast, "And you think this Obama will be duped?" but the corpulent Chaim faced me head on. "Obama has no *yachas*, no special relationship with Israel, no feeling for the roots of Israel or with Israeli tradition. We never imagined that the special U.S.-Israel relationship would be any different but Obama is worse than Carter. Come the next presidential election in 2012, Obama may be the only Democrat since 1920 to win less than 50% of the Jewish vote. Israel is headed for trouble with this new president from south of the desert."

Edward scowled at the desert comment and lurched forward. "Some blame the rise of the Israeli right on a need to counterbalance Barack Hussein Obama, and what has been resurrected is the world-against-us fear, along with the threat to Israel's existence. It may be that 80% of American Jews voted for Obama but there is a strain within the pro-Israel community that says, unless you are unwavering on a pro-Likud approach, you are anti-Israel. Trumped is any care for the Palestinians."

Chaim swept his big right arm across in front of Edward and me. "All of Israel knows that in 1975, the UN passed the infamous resolution saying Zionism is racism," but little Edward held his ground with chin forward. "Right-wing anti-Arab policies are gaining popularity in Israel, and the mainstream has joined to ban Israel's two Arab parties from the upcoming 2009 election, on grounds they oppose the existence of Israel as a Jewish state."

That comment seemed to silence the three of us before Edward calmly continued: "Israel toys with representation of the Arab minority and pretends to be a Western democracy but among the young, where one would expect sensitivity, high-schoolers demand the subjugation of Arabs within Israel and don't want to live in the same buildings with them or hear the sound of Arabic. There is also a growing movement to exchange Arab communities in Israel for Israeli settlements in the West Bank, and for Palestinians to be forced to Jordan."

Chaim gave a condescending smile and pushed his barrel-shaped body forward toward Edward, pointing at him with the middle finger of his spider-hand. "The world has always rejected us but our god provides. God will punish us Jews if we divide the Holy Land and allow for the abomination of a Palestinian state. The only answer for people's criticism of the settlements is that it is surely anti-Semitism, but time is on the settlers' side. Settlers say what the Israeli government wants – the Palestinians of the West Bank should be made Jordanian citizens and the world should recognize Israel's presence in the so-called West Bank as eternal."

Chaim then leaned back for more air before bellowing, "Netanyahu will win the election and his idea of enclaves for Palestinians until they depart is the true feeling of all Jewish-Israeli parties. The world has to recognize that the Jordanian Option is the only solution. The West Bank – Judea and Samaria – is part of *Eretz Yisra'el*."

Edward again put both palms flat on the table. "After 1967, Israel's balance of a secular versus religious state tilted, with new control of historical sites and a renewed divine ordination for geographical expansion. Many in that 1967 Arab-Israeli war had argued that occupying all of Biblical Israel would be at the expense of a predominantly Jewish state, because of the Arab inhabitants, but now we have scenarios where right-wing rabbis push settlers to stay in the biblical land of Israel, seeking to disenfranchise the Arab Israelis. The rabbi-directed settlers paraphrase Exodus in saying that the Jews should have a holy nation of priests and Arabs should have the status of protected foreigners, with no say in governance."

I felt I had to intervene again with a question, and I pressed forward at an angle between Edward and Chaim to address them both. "And you feel we Americans will buy into that thinking? If we don't object in principle, someone in my country may take a look at the numbers – beyond the massive direct support for Israel, the dollars for funding the war on terror since 9/11 have been 20 times the dollars spent on the war on poverty."

But Chaim reared back his head, smiled and then came forward, tapping again his spider-hand on the table middle. "We keep photos of families who died at Auschwitz, reminding ourselves that Islam is the new Nazism, whose leaders must be killed and the Palestinians in the West Bank must be forced out, either by war or slow starvation. Had the Arabs accepted Jewish ownership in the first instance, there would have been no problem but they did not and therefore are our enemies."

I came forward straight at Chaim, with forehead tilted down and eyebrows lifted: "And you are not afraid that Israel will be caught in its own web of tautological propaganda?" but Chaim seemed ready with a classic rebuttal, "Reality has made a Jewish state necessary – the world failed to defend Jewish existence. There is a need for a place where Jews can implement their culture, values, language and history, a place in which to recover."

Edward and I looked at each other, and each of us gave a sigh but Chaim ignored us and carried on. "Israel will not let Iran have the bomb and does not trust the international community to tackle the issue. The Iranian president has no legitimacy for talks with Obama."

I again came forward as before: "Not even talks?" but judging from Chaim's reaction, I fell right into his argument. He lifted his spider-hand's middle finger at me. "Heed not talk but facts. During the seven years of the Oslo peace process, the number of Jewish settlements mushroomed, and the sons of settlers now account for one-quarter of the Israeli officer corps."

Edward turned to me and shrugged. "The favorite Ashkenazi ploy word is 'terrorism' – no Israeli government will give back land, while any faction, however small, of Palestinians practices terror." Edward then raised his chin to the air above Chaim's fat head. "Leaked Israeli communications priorities show that semantics are pivotal to its spin on terror, and the word 'terrorist' is used to convey the impression that the terrorist person or organization operates outside the standards of morality and civilization. Any Palestinian killed, therefore, has to be cast as a suspected Hamas militant or other terrorist, and to strengthen that web of deceit, Palestinian organizations must be portrayed as having camouflaged charities, which need to be shut down with international sanction."

The table went silent but then a heated Edward leapt back in with his little chin raised. "The irony of the ploy is that if here were no resistance, as was true for several years, Israel would feel no need to negotiate or end occupation. Israeli generals want the token terrorism and suicide bombings, and will provoke them if there is a prolonged Hamas ceasefire. It is well known that those Israeli generals tolerate – need – a little terrorism to fool the Jewish public and spring indignation." Edward's chin went higher. "The worst news the generals received after Hamas took power was that its first major act was to declare a ceasefire."

Edward kept his chin pointed above Chaim's head. "Israel says it will not negotiate until terrorism stops but knows that terrorism as Israel spins it never will – Israel provokes it at every turn by assassination and other methods when things get quiet."

Chaim's spider-hand had for some time been tapping louder and louder, and finally when Edward acknowledged the noise with a look of disapproval, Chaim pointed again at Edward with a middle finger. "We want a Fatah-Hamas *détente!*" but little Edward pointed back. "No you don't, because Israel would be obliged to reciprocate! Hamas recognized, from the governing outset, the reality of Jewish funding from the U.S. and Europe, and offered peace. But Israel did not want it. Many in Hamas also accept a two-state solution but Israel does not want them to do so – Israel wants to delegitimize the Hamas government."

For a moment, Edward had silenced Chaim and Edward pressed on. "And the Israeli wall goes on with clandestine mapping, since exact awareness of the wall's route within Israel and the international community is judged provocative. Palestine has had a wedge driven into it, with orchard groves and olive groves torn up and 135,000 Palestinians cut off from former jobs. The wall has left piecemeal chunks of land that can never amount to a functioning state and any non-violent Palestinian resistance to the wall has been met with Israeli tear gas, rubber bullets, live ammo and imprisonment."

To his slight smile of surprise, Edward was still holding the floor, with Chaim perhaps in retreat, readying for another charge. Edward kept on:

"When people in Toronto protested these past weeks against Israel's recent slaughter of innocents and children in Gaza, Jewish authorities photographed the protesters and forwarded the photos to the Royal Canadian Mounted Police for investigation and possible categorization as terrorists."

Suddenly Chaim came forward with head lowered to Edward. "The Jews in Sderot next to Gaza are blue collar and have not exploited anyone, but they live under the constant threat of rockets coming in from Palestine. One girl was killed and people were so distraught, there were calls to kill the political leaders of Hamas. One Sderot man, a toolmaker and father of three said there is so much unemployment that he has had to work as a security guard."

While Chaim had been talking, Edward had been leaning back to catch his wind, but at that moment he lifted in his chair as if to match Chaim in height. "Israel had to show who was in charge, so it pre-sold propaganda for crushing Gaza, as Israel did in its earlier war on Lebanon. What had actually started that earlier Lebanese conflict was Israel's shelling of Palestinian civilians on a Gaza beach, leading to retaliation and the kidnapping of one Israeli soldier. But…" little Edward lowered back down in his chair "…the Israeli myth – that no human effort would be spared to rescue each sacred soldier – went to work despite Israel having kidnapped, jailed and killed Palestinians for years, to combat self-described terrorism."

Chaim abruptly shifted his body away from both Edward and me as if to change the subject. "If Iranian leader Ahmadinejad is set to get re-elected this year, British intelligence will foment the largest and lengthiest uprising in the Iranian revolution's history, and while Americans stay paralyzed with this Muslim Obama, we can thank god for good ol' Britain, as well of course as France's Sarkozy."

Edward pounced back up: "And the Germans will roll over to France and its Jewish president to ensure that Islamic Turkey is not allowed into the European Union."

I tried with a neutral face to temper the talk with a platitude. "Unity of expression is the secret weapon of any victory," but Edward leapt in: "We Jewish people have been duped, as we have been since the years leading up to 1948 and the beginnings of Chaim's Ashkenazi Israel. The costs of settlements at the time were funneled and the data hidden under a security imperative. Since then, the settler lobby has enjoyed an unparalleled ability to create facts on the ground."

Edward was still sitting forward and was not about to give ground. "Whole populations of an occupying power have transferred land to the occupiers, and rabbis now advocate the harassment of Arabs until they leave Israel. Any Arab who retaliates is judged a *rodef* or pursuer, who supposedly threatens the life of a Jew and is thus worthy of death under Jewish law. Settlers terrorize Palestinians with impunity and the Israeli human rights watch has had to resort to giving video recorders to beaten Palestinians. The settlers also send death threats and enjoy a lovely stretch of beach, while hundreds of thousands of the world's most wretched people live only a stone's throw away. If the settlers think an area of Palestine has the potential to explode, they trigger a mess before they come down hard. Last year, the settlers were killing six so-called rioters a day and as part of the game, the number always stayed at six."

Little Edward then raised a skinny finger to the ceiling. "Settlers are regularly released from the army to protect their own units with sophisticated arms, and rabbis within the settlements still instruct people to disobey soldiers and not give up any occupied land. Right-wing rabbis see Arabs as *gerim toshavim* or resident aliens, like history's Amalekites on whom god commanded ancient Israelites to show no mercy."

By this time, Chaim evidently had tolerated Edward's promulgation long enough, and Chaim leaned forward with his middle spider-finger raised again. "The Torah demands the total destruction of the enemy and the Amaleks were the archetype of unadulterated evil, to be exterminated," but Edward raised his finger too. "Yes, Israel has the death penalty but only for silencing Nazis or for people judged guilty of treason, yet within Israel, the intellectual left's stance against the Hamas boycott/blockade is also branded as treachery and defeatism."

Chaim shifted his barrel body around and came forward with his other hand to make a second spider. "Israel has allowed Jews to have the experience of being part of a majority, but if trends stay the same, the proportion of Jews living between the Jordan River and the Mediterranean will drop to a minority by 2020. The Arabs have to depart historical Israel, since if ever they were to form a majority, they would have to be denied voting rights and be encouraged to leave by economics or war."

Edward pushed forward on his chair and again put both palms flat on the table. "If Palestine does come to recognize Israel as the state of the Jewish people, then a one-state solution with an Apartheid system will sanctify what Israel already is now. Obama may be lobbied out of office, with a conservative puppet to replace him and any two-state solution will fade into a Palestinian dream.

"As for Israel itself, the gap between rich and poor is already wider than in any other developed country, and Israel is segregated along ethnic lines. Refugees can be denied because they are not Jewish, the rationale being that there are already enough poor people in Israel, with those existing ones being the priority as per the Talmud."

Chaim's finger went straight back up. "Israel is not racist! We let Ethiopians into Israel," and when Edward tried to shoot back that they were Ethiopian Jews barred by European Jews from Israeli schools or owning homes, and making less money than the Israeli Arabs, Chaim drowned him out with a barreling voice: "We Jews need to have a common religion, in order to have roots in our country, and it would not be safe to have less than a majority. A Palestinian right of return would destroy that majority and thus the Palestinians are out to destroy Israel. The Arabs in our country do not feel part of our Jewish Israel and have to leave. Three-quarters claim they feel violence at the hands of the Israeli authorities, saying it is part of a Zionist plot!"

Chaim held on to his turn dominating. "Equality is not a right but an interest, and the Arabs have no right to resent our giving citizenship to all Jews who want to come to Israel. The Arabs had no Shoah, no Holocaust, and have no threat to their survival. In 1947, Ben Gurion should have said what he wanted and cleansed Israel of all Arabs."

I chose to come back in with a querying face: "Do you at least believe, Chaim, that the Israeli Arabs should have their rights protected while they're still there?" and he unexpectedly lashed back, "There are no Israeli Arabs, only Arabs in Israel!" And then he went on: "Of all people of the Western world having been in existence from 3,000 years ago, only the Jews have the same language and religion."

Chaim had both me and Edward temporarily silent. "Buses must not travel on the Sabbath, and we must have a religious-disciplined state, as have Muslims in Islamic countries. Non-religious Israeli children must come to understand that they are simply Hebrew-speaking *goyim*. We must go back to the Bible to source our roots and relive its heroic past. The image of a little boy under the gun of a Nazi must be replaced with that of the Jews taking back Jerusalem in 1967."

Suddenly, Chaim's face went sad and he closed with something that did not really tie in with his militancy. "Our Jewish commitment to decency has meant passivity for 2,000 years!" but with this, little Edward came back to life. "The pacifistic Jewish stereotype is that Ashkenazis don't fight for other countries. But there are Jewish laws commending so-called just wars and Israel has a capture-of-the-land holiday."

Again I tried offering in an even tone that an Israeli woman had lost a child by a suicide bomber but she was trying to bring together both sides, through a bereaved-for-peace organization for Israelis and Palestinians. The woman noted that most Israelis have a poor understanding of how Israel had been founded or how it has become a state that tyrannizes anyone not Jewish. The woman blamed Israel's media and its school system, which teaches one side of history and that the state of Israel is the only guarantee against another Holocaust. She said Israel could have been a world model for tolerance but has become a terrible aberration of Judaism. Edward added that the woman remains reviled as a traitor by many Israelis.

Perhaps Chaim had been letting me speak because he was trying to win me over, but with Edward's add-on Chaim suddenly flared up, almost shouting, "She received a prize for freedom of thought, proof that Israel is that very world beacon," and Edward again caught fire. "Unthinkable is what Israeli schoolchildren have rammed into them about returning the Golan Heights to Syria. The northeast shore of the Sea of Galilee has feeder springs that form a key part of Israel's water system."

Chaim sat back and Edward kept his ground. "We in the West have no access to what is really going on. The allied invasion of Afghanistan was caught on TV only by Al Jazeera, and it covered the U.S. invasion of Iraq better than anyone. Al Jazeera is less biased than mainstream American networks but it incurred the wrath of the White House, when five days after September 11, it aired a statement from Osama bin Laden saying, 'I have not carried out this act, which appears to have been carried out by individuals with their own motivation.' U.S. authorities countered by releasing a videotape that portrayed bin Laden saying he had personally calculated the damage that a fuel-laden aircraft would cause to the Twin Towers, and an American pop culture became infused with deep paranoia, suspect of all non-Americans and chasing terrorists at every turn." Little Edward then paused to catch his breath before going on. "Given the resultant culturalization of America and attitude towards bin Laden, one thing seems for sure – the Americans will forever silence him, the moment they find him.

"The United States blew up the Al Jazeera bureau in Afghanistan, despite the broadcaster giving exact co-ordinates to the U.S., so that such an 'accident' would not happen. And to no surprise, the Iranian president received an undiplomatic reception in New York, when he hinted at skepticism over the official version of the 9/11 attacks, asking what conditions led to it and who was really involved in putting it together."

Edward then said something that brought me straight up in my chair. "Christian evangelicals are much to blame for American brainwashing and have searched for an antichrist since the collapse of the Soviet Union. American evangelicals have been preoccupied with the Middle East since the creation of Israel and see Jewish expansion as an end-of-times sign in support of their own rapture-filled second coming."

"Edward," I had to clarify with a straight face, "Christian evangelical support for Israel in America is shrinking! The call for attacking Iraq has been exposed to all Americans as has Israeli intelligence about Iran's nuclear plans. The letters U-S-A in 'Jerusalem' no longer dominate."

To my surprise, Chaim countered my comment: "But three-quarters of American Republicans and half the Democrats still favor Israel over Palestine."

A second or so of silence passed as Chaim gave a grin of contentment but little Edward soon shot forward: "Israel is a nation with a poisoned prophecy. We need again prophets to envisage the future, not from a story-book past but from the reality we can see. The Holocaust has paralyzed Israelis for 60 years and some Israelis are now crying 'enough' as only Israelis dare do."

Chaim and I looked stunned and Edward held on. "We cannot move beyond survival by continuing to claim that critics are closet Nazis. Zionism has been a bridge game for 150 years, moving us from mythicized exile back to sovereignty, and the trump card has always been the Holocaust. All is per-mitted because of it and no one will tell us how to behave.

"The Eichmann trial of the early 1960s did not liberate us but rather chained us to hate and self-justification. Yes, the victims and survivors of the Holocaust should remain upheld as they are, as components for progress, but mainstream Israel stays imprisoned in denial, from a fascist right wing that was the abused child and is now the tyrannical parent. Israel needs to abandon its victimhood mentality and become a light for humanistic Judaism."

Chaim folded his fat arms and let out a huff. "We now have a threat anew from Hussein Obama. His failure to cast a veto over any deprecation of Israel is a betrayal. Israeli intelligence has had to warn us that we are now less of a U.S. ally."

Time, I felt, for a bit of levity. "Maybe Tony Blair can help. He seems to understand how religion motivates, especially in the United States," but Edward turned stone-faced. "A Bush whore," and I had to add that the alleged whore had launched the Tony Blair Faith Foundation, to promote respect and understanding among the world's three major religions, and that Blair could yet save a million Africans with malaria nets. But Chaim and Edward were unmoved.

Edward then turned to me, with his little brow bent forward and eyes asquint. "Arthur, 200 years ago, you Ashkenazi Jews began liberating your-selves from rabbinical dictates through the Enlightenment and we all had some chance. But today in Israel, rabbis are preoccupied with things like diet, and they ignore the gap between rich and poor." Edward then turned back in his seat and gave a waxing shrug. "As for issues like homosexuality, the rabbis won't touch them."

Little Edward then turned his face to the middle. "Ironically, those same rabbis have now entered into an unholy alliance with new Russian atheist immigrants. Many Russians have moved to Israel because of a Jewish grandparent, and there are now in Israel over a million Russian Jews. They are opposed to the community values put forward from its beginnings by left-wing Israel."

"Now there's power! Russian Mafia!" shouted Chaim with his arms spread out but I was unsure what he meant. "Russian Mafia?" and he replied, "Mafia, schmafia, the Cosa Nostra is a *goyische* fantasy," and Edward, to my shock, agreed. "Arthur, in your United States of America, Vegas is not run by Italians, and the biggest Vegas issue is the fixing of bets, placed on things like world boxing events."

Chaim smiled as if he had found a moment's support. "The Wops don't even know what a derivative is," but then an adroit Edward turned Chaim's quip into a fresh tirade for Edward's cause. "Israeli hoodlums specialize in the beating of Palestinian teenagers who throw stones, and the hoodlums get government sanction. Palestinian activists are forced to buy protection from the hoods, and Israel's drug dealers get protection from the police by being political informers. As for the foreign press, they remain afraid of being condemned as Arab lovers."

Chaim intervened with a sigh of resignation. "Our Jewish homeland has not had a single day of peace since its creation. If Iran does not use its nuclear weapons, we will still remain wracked with fear," and Edward jumped in at a chance to treat Chaim as naive. "Iran's security concerns may be aimed as much at meeting the Sunni threat as any threat from Israel. It is worth noting that Iran and the United States backed the same sides in Iraq and Afghanistan, and Iran almost went to war against the Taliban in 1998 when it launched a campaign against Afghanistan's Shiites."

Edward's little chest lifted as he took in a slow breath, before he swiveled back to me. "Like most countries, Iran's security policy is driven by multiple imperatives. The Pakistani factor is another driver of Iran's nuclear policy and the U.S. overlooking that factor compromises any American leverage over Iran." But Chaim waded back in as if Edward was uttering diplomatic claptrap: "And we must crush that Iranian source of Israel's fear."

I caught myself squinting at the sound of Chaim's last comment and probed for the means to be used, but Chaim simply lifted his shoulders and replied with a non-answer, "Through whatever means necessary. We have no true allies, and in the Yom Kippur war of 1973, when hundreds of Syrian tanks sat on our doorstep, we had to take the means necessary to get the United States to turn those tanks around."

I lost the lightness that I had momentarily had and felt a knot tightening in my heart, but I could not say the word "bomb" and Chaim carried on: "Other cities have antiquities but the jewels of Jerusalem are of the moment and future." He then loudly shifted in his sitting position. "If we brought down that main mosque, the temple could be restored."

I sat back in silence and a smiling Edward resorted to another historical tact. He said Hebrew Kabbalah teachings on the nature and purpose of existence are not in the realm of exclusive Jewish thought as is pretended, since there are earlier Hindu counterparts. But Chaim quickly countered, with his chin in the air, "A thing is never truly perceived, apprehended or defined, except in feeling and *Hatikva* as you know, Arthur, is the hope that defines Israel's existence, its having come into being just when hope appeared to have perished."

Chaim beamed a look of triumph at little Edward and me. "In our beloved Jerusalem, at the end of the Holocaust History Museum is a balcony whose view of the surrounding forest is verdant and overwhelmingly stunning. Exile has been replaced by statehood, landlessness by home, and hell by hope. There, is the just reward for our labor and the solid hope for our future. That reality, Arthur, is what Israel is all about – recovery, renewal and the hope of a Jewish future. When the proverbial Jewish child came out of the concentration camp, with his visage almost gone and his eyes, once glimmering, now hollow, his mind was trying to make sense of what had been the incomprehensible. But…" Chaim's chin lifted in reverence, "…he was holding next to his chest an Israeli flag."

The time was reaching 9:00 a.m. that January and we agreed to reconvene in a week, but I wanted to hear more and asked Edward in confidence to stay. The Great Hall by then was becoming occupied, so we tried to find another place. But Hart House was its usual beehive of students and the only unoccupied room was the tiny interdenominational chapel.

Edward took a seat on a back pew, to the right of the aisle and I took one in front, before I turned around and put my arms on the back of the pew to face a sprawling-out little Edward: "Edward, some of you Sephardics have a different view of Jewish history from the one given us by Ashkenazi Jews." He stayed laid back but gestured with his right arm. "Arthur, Western history was shaped in great part by rabbis after Greek Hellenization. They felt the threat of Jewish emancipation under the ancient Greeks, when Israelites were freed to discuss philosophy or question the status quo. Educated women in particular enjoyed enormous autonomy and were free to walk or go to the gyms, and for both men and women, there were social clubs, with much productive dialogue taking place."

Edward broke into a broad smile. "The thought of these Israelite men and women taking care of their physiques was unheard of, and the further thought of their doing so nude was anathema to the tribal-minded rabbis. Jewish men and women were even abandoning the Bible and rabbis reacted by translating it into the Greek *Septuagint*, to pull back their flock.

"After the death of Greece's Alexander the Great in 300 BC or thereabouts, his kingdom was split into four parts, and in the two parts, Egypt and Syria, Judaism was allowed to function according to the status quo. But in the 200 years up to that 300 BC, internal Jewish politics had changed and authority no longer rested in the hands of a monarch. It was now wielded by the High Priest and he functioned as head of state for life, with that position perpetuated by heredity."

Edward still lay back with arm stretched out along the pew and he looked to be loving the lecturing role. "Greek culture, however, had so pervaded Judaism that there were Hellenistic sects of Jews and those pro-Greek Jews were held in disdain by Jews who held onto their ancestral orthodoxy. Within the ensuing conflict, a pro-Greek Jew bribed the Greek leader Antiochus to have the Jew appointed High Priest in place of his brother, and Jewish lawful institutions were abolished, with new usages contrary to Jewish law introduced.

"A gymnasium was erected below the citadel and some of the young Jewish men in Jerusalem began to practice their athletic skills in the style of the Greeks. Even the priests abandoned their service at the altar and took part in the games held in the palestra. The contempt for Jewish customs went so far that many Jews artificially reversed their circumcisions, seeing them as a rabbinical plot to lessen sexual sensitivity under the guise of a sacred covenant. Indeed 1,000 years later, Jewish sage Maimonides would write that, for the totality of purposes of the perfect Law, there belong the abandonment, depreciation and restraint of desires in so far as possible. Maimonides affirmed that most of the lusts and licentiousness of the multitude consist in an appetite for eating, drinking and sexual intercourse, but for the totality of intentions of the Law, there belong gentleness and docility, man should thus not be hard and rough, but responsive, obedient, acquiescent and docile. Maimonides concluded with his god's commandment, 'Circumcise therefore the foreskin of your heart, and be no more stiff-necked. Be silent, and hearken, O Israel, if ye be willing and obedient.'"

Edward then came forward at me with his right index finger wagging. "Circumcision is male genital mutilation and any Jew who suggests that criticizing circumcision is anti-Semitic should come to understand that nobody has the right to perform unnecessary surgery on another human being, especially a painful one on a totally trusting child. No one asks that child for his consent, and the foreskin has long been identified as the most sensitive part of the penis." Edward then threw up his arms. "Circumcision is now preached as a way to cut AIDS in Africa, despite the Canadian Pediatric Society saying circumcision is not necessary. Covenant, schmovenant! Circumcision is a pan-African rite that spans multiple tribes including Islam. And in the South Africa of today, some Xhosa teens are still initiated into manhood in centuries-old circumcision rituals."

I had to nod in agreement if not knowledge, and Edward marched on but this time resting back against his pew: "Soon a rival to the Greeks came in the form of the Romans and Antiochus tried to hold onto Greek dominance but Rome prevailed and he was forced to go home defeated. On his way home, Antiochus vented his revenge against those Jerusalem Jews who had supported Rome and he killed a number of inhabitants while carrying others away as slaves. The Jerusalem Temple was also looted and profaned by imposing pagan sacrifices.

"Antiochus's violation of the city became the voiced cause of the Jewish Maccabean revolt in 200 BC as spearheaded by the priestly class, with priests withdrawing to the mountains after a bloody confrontation, before rallying other Jewish rebels around them. They nicknamed their leader 'Maccabaeus,' meaning 'the hammerer,' and rebel resistance was enough to achieve an independent state.

"Later on around 80 BC, when Jews of influence began moving to Rome to do business with the new empire, key rabbis insisted that their flock live in a walled ghetto, where Jews would not be tempted again by outside cultural influences. But the Romans were found to be *nouveau riches*, and the *lingua franca* of higher education, culture, church and even business remained Greek. Educated Jews were thus less attracted by Rome's plagiarized culture and they helped rabbis trigger the first Jewish revolt against Rome 150 years later. Rome retaliated by knocking down the second Jewish temple and then in 135 AD, dispersed many of us Jews after we rose up again."

I took to raising my right hand off the pew back to signal a halt. "So the group that went to Europe constituted us fool Ashkenazi Jews, and you enlightened Sephardics remained on the south side of the Mediterranean?" and Edward smiled while inflating his little chest. "Not quite that simple, Arthur. The original Ashkenazi Jews were descended from medieval communities in Germany but later, Jews from the other parts of Western and central Europe came to be called 'Ashkenazi,' and many of them migrated east between the 11th and 19th centuries. Most Jewish communities within Europe are thus loosely labeled Ashkenazim, with the exception of some near the Mediterranean.

"The majority of Jews who have migrated to North America from Europe in the past two centuries have been Ashkenazim, particularly Eastern Ashkenazim, and this is especially true in United States, where live five million American Jews, including the world's largest concentration of Ashkenazim. In the 11th century, the Ashkenazim officially comprised only 3% of the world's Jewish population but today they are as labeled about 80%, and the 1800-year Diaspora myth is to a great degree one fired up by Ashkenazi rabbis. Particularly Russian ones, where breeding of a Jewish race to produce the highest intelligence began early."

I took in a long breath and got up from my pew to take several paces toward the rear door and ensure we were still alone. Then I returned to my pew in front of Edward and sat down sideways, with my leg stretched along the pew. When I turned back to face Edward, he was already smiling when I asked, "The 1800-year Diaspora is Russian propaganda?"

Edward remained relaxed and his voice held calm, if not sounding a bit patronizing. "Up to the time of Muhammad in the seventh century, many Jews remained in the Middle East, and some converted to Islam, but after the seventh century, a large number of Jews moved to an area northeast of the Mediterranean, near the Black Sea. There in these Slavic and Khazar lands, Jewish merchants adopted the region as a gateway, for a 'Khazarian Way' from Eastern Europe through to Muslim lands, India and even China.

"During the eighth century, the Khazars converted to Judaism and the Khazar kingdom became a Jewish kingdom, though Judaism was not impressed upon all the population and the less elite retained their other religions. The empire thus realized a Jewish homeland amidst the Diaspora.

Khazaria became a haven for religious pluralism, with the Khazars showing tolerance toward conflicting faiths, and the main city, Itil, held Muslims, Christians, Jews and Pagans. The Jews brought to Khazaria sophisticated methods of trade as well as the Hebrew language, and it became the medium of communication throughout the Jewish community, versus the Yiddish language of central Europe, founded on German.

"But in about the year 1,000, the Russians and Byzantines joined forces to attack the Khazarian Empire and within 200 years, it ceased to be an empire or even a country. Many of the Khazarian Jews migrated to join other Jewish communities in Eastern Europe, and in Poland and Lithuania, the *shtetls* or country towns of Jewish population sprang up, representing the long-gone link between the market towns of Khazaria and the Jewish settlements of Eastern Europe. Centuries later, the folk songs from Kiev in the Ukraine could still be heard of Khazaria, the 'country of Jews' and of 'Jewish heroes.'"

Edward noted that my eyes were locked on him and he continued, "In the centuries thereafter, in that part of Russia beyond Khazaria, Ashkenazi Jews who had not moved farther west to central Europe came to play a central role but remained apart from the rest of the population. Around 1840 in Russia, a network of designated schools and related communities was created, since the Russian Jewish community had not availed itself of the opportunity to study in regular schools – like the wider European Jewish community, Russian Jews had viewed any such government move as an attempt to assimilate the younger generation."

Edward paused to ensure eye contact with me, before he raised his little finger. "Today, Arthur, influential Jews in Israel and beyond can still be cast as Khazarian." He went on: "Subsequent to those Russian 1840s, the reign of Tsar Alexander II improved the perceived treatment of Jews but new policies were also implemented to ensure their assimilation. At the same time, a rapidly increasing Jewish population led to its being increasingly visible, and resentment grew within the non-Jewish community. After another 50 years at the end of the 19th century, the Jewish population had doubled to five million or 4% of the Russian population and about one-half of the world's Jews. A Russian Jewish proletariat had developed, along with an upper class, and economic diversification had led some Ashkenazi Jews to, for example, lease alcoholic beverages at a time when the distribution of alcohol was a government monopoly. Jews had also become pivotal to construction and industrial development as well as banking, professional positions and academia."

I frowned and looked down to the floor between the pews, before giving a twist of my head. "But as you said, Edward, Western Europe's *lingua franca* was Yiddish, growing out of the German and the Ashkenazim grew out of Germany in the 11th century!"

Edward leaned back and stretched his little leg along the bench pew before he rendered a condescending smile to *schmiel* me. "But may still have descended from that Khazarian Empire in Russia. Unlike Western Europe, the *Haskalah* or Jewish counter-Enlightenment in Russia gave priority to Jewish culture and values, religious and otherwise, and the nationalistic flavor of the *Haskalah* fired up the ideology of Zionism. Wealthy and influential Russian Jews came to encourage others to spread that restricted and nationalistic version of *Haskalah*.

"Around 1880, the Russian Tsar Alexander II was assassinated and the assassins encouraged mass rebellions. Russia fell into anarchy, blame was placed on the country's Ashkenazi Jews and retaliatory pogroms broke out. New Russian laws led to restrictions on Jewish ownership of land and later prohibited Jews from serving as military officers. Jews were also expelled from Moscow, causing disillusionment even among assimilated Russian *maskilim*.

"Ashkenazi Jews then joined the ranks of Russian radicals and a Jewish-workers revolutionary movement was founded. Worker unions, founded by Jews, created the Russian *Bund*, which took up Jewish causes, in particular cultural autonomy for Russian Jews, and the *Hibbat Zion* movement brought to Russia an already burgeoning Zionism from Europe. Some Jews even fled the country and went to Israel."

I lowered my forehead and reminded Edward that the World Zionist Organization was grounded in Western Europe but he came back fast: "The mass of members and support systems came from Eastern Europe, and the Zionist movement grew in all segments of Russian Jewish society, secular and religious. That growth of Russian Ashkenazi, in turn, inspired the growth of Hebrew, as opposed to the Yiddish found in Europe, and eventually the Russian intelligentsia and *Bund* won out, with Hebrew destined to be the language of the new Israel.

"By World War I, when the Russian army was defeated, commanders blamed the Ashkenazi Jews and accused them of spying for the Germans. Jews were even tried for espionage but by 1917, the Tsar Nicholas II, who had been warring with Russia's Ashkenazis, abdicated the throne and a new provisional Bolshevik government abolished all restrictions on Jews. By the end of 1917, the Bolsheviks moved to negotiate peace with the Germans and the Zionist movement in Russia took off. As news of the 1917 British Balfour Declaration – to take Jerusalem from the Turks – reached Russia, Zionist rallies were held in all of its major cities. A self-defense organization called the Union of Jewish Soldiers was founded and one Joseph Trumpeldor of later Israeli legend led it.

"By the mid-1920s, Ashkenazi Jewish officers in the Russian Red Army constituted double their ratio in the general population and Jewish elites helped administer the country. And while the Russian communist government tried to suppress Hebrew and secularize the Jewish religion, those restrictions only led to the strengthening of Zionism within Russia, with much help from Jews outside and around the world.

"Even after the collapse of the Soviet Union, Russia still had one of the world's largest Jewish communities but the population of Ashkenazi Russian Jews now has shrunk because of immigration to Israel or the United States, as well as aging."

Edward suddenly sprang up from the pew as if he were just recalling something. "Since, by the way, intermarriage during the Soviet rule led to many Russian Jews being not technically Jewish, Israel has waived that technicality. There are now only half a million Jews left in Russia, with more than double that number in Israel, where they enjoy enormous influence."

I lowered my brow and squinted at Edward's evidently anti-Ashkenazi prejudice but out of curiosity I still wanted to prod him. I stood up and stretched to adjust the pace, and he then tried with reasoned voice to contain his eagerness. "Okay, Arthur, here in this multi-faith Hart House chapel, I will try to give you a crash course, but if anyone comes in the door, I will stop. Mind you, nothing I say today is not being tossed about, among educated Jews in Israel, but they are more aware and inclusive of multiple views than are we, and this Canada of ours only thinks it has free speech."

Edward then gave a stretch as had I, before he sat back down and let his left arm and leg spread back out along the rear oak pew. "As I said when we met, Arthur, by the time the Diaspora began around the year 135 AD, there had already for centuries been four to five times as many Jews prospering in Egypt and elsewhere than had lived in Israel. But the manipulation of the past is a function of politicians and their spin doctors – in Israel's case, writers and educators.

"Ashkenazi Jews have spun a Diaspora view of their 1,800 years in official exile as inherently regressive and repressive, and huge money and effort is still being spent to create and entrench this myth as both a fact of Jewish life and a rationale for the 1948 creation of Israel. Before the 1948 Zionist victory, the Jews in Palestine referred to that 1,800-year exile as *galut*, and the Zionists used it not only to increase a sense of punishment by their god but also as support for a sense of chosenness. The Ashkenazi revisionists ignored the Jewish prosperity of fourth century Babylon, 10th-century Russia or 12th - 15th-century Spain and also ignored those Jews who had not emigrated after being reprimanded by the Romans in 135. The revisionists instead lumped the whole 1,800 years together, and the Zionist collective memory came to construct the entire period as a long, dark exile of suppression and oppression by non-Jews.

"Russian Jews were at the forefront of modern Israel in Palestine as they were in Hollywood, not to mention Churchill's political riding of Manchester when he switched parties to get the Jewish vote. Hordes of Russian Jews had fled to Manchester from the retaliatory pogroms of the late 19th and early 20th centuries.

"Across much of the world, rabbis came to focus more and more on persecution and exaggerate the suffering of the 1800 years in exile, preaching for example of a sea of blood coming after the 16th century expulsion from Spain and Portugal. The darker the image of the exile, the greater the promise Zionism offered, with the state of Israel being the Hollywood ending after almost 2,000 years of suppression culminating in the Holocaust.

"Jewish literature of the early 20th century, both in Europe and Palestine, was often written for schools by that Russian-Jewish counter-Enlightenment, *Haskala*, and the writings had an overridingly negative attitude toward the 1,800-year exile. The first Zionist *Aliyah* or moving up following the Russian pogroms of the late 19th and early 20th centuries, influenced Churchill and the creation of Hollywood.

"Austrian scientist Nathan Birnbaum coined the word 'Zionism' in 1891 and the persecution story was used as a foundation for Zionism at the first international congress meeting in 1897. Then Zionism came to be even more politicized in the 1930s and 1940s, as the literary scene followed the Russian Jewish model. Cosmopolitanism and universalism became derogatory words and Zionism changed facts to legends, using Russian-style metaphors. History texts from the 1930s on emphasized the theme of pogroms and persecution and it was a Jewish teacher's obligation to teach nationalism and an unquestioning pioneering mindset.

"For students, the physical land of Israel became sacred and the Zionist settler of pre-1948 came to replace god as the creator. *Kana'im* or Zealots were recast as brave shock-troops from their earlier dismissal, and *Kiddush Ha-shem* or a martyr's death for the sanctification of god's name was replaced with a hero's death for one's country. During World War II, children in Israel viewed the pacifist European Jews as sheep going to slaughter and the Holocaust as non-heroic; instead, the mythical image of the Zionist pioneer, with plow in one arm and gun in the other, became a sacred icon. Israeli poets, admittedly not fulfilled by manual labor, nevertheless came to praise it, and even a doctored archeology like the manipulated literature came to be a weapon of propaganda in support of the ideology and mythical tradition.

"Bar Kokhba had led the Jewish revolt of 135 against the Romans and was later proven to be a fake Messiah but in pre-1948 Israel, he became a popular legend. And the ancient Jewish traitor Josephus, who had gone to work for the Romans, wrote the first rendering of the battle of Masada in Aramaic, but in the budding days of Zionism in 1862, a rendering of Masada was to appear in Hebrew and that Hebrew version was selective of the facts, with the actual Jewish suicide revised to a Hollywood-Alamo fight to the end.

"Russian Jewish propaganda in Israel today has given us Jews a mass neurosis, which we Sephardics call the Masada Syndrome, and the Masada myth is a lot of *schtuss* or bullshit that only boy scouts now believe. Most Israeli historians hold that Josephus was, like most classical chroniclers, a dramaturge and that he fashioned the romantic "death instead of surrender" story in imitation of Greco-Roman models. From what Israeli historians can now piece together, some zealots did kill themselves as well as their families while some died fighting but others tried to flee and were either successful in hiding, cut down or captured into enslavement.

"But the Masada myth held strong and it became a counter-metaphor to the Holocaust. In 1942, when Israel heard of some Arab support for Nazi Germany, the Jews in Palestine felt threatened and helped trigger the 1943

Warsaw Masada. A Masada poem was created in Israel, praising the action taken, as opposed to the passivity chosen by Jews who remained in Europe. What followed was a desire for revenge steeped in evil acts, along with a socialist stance for promoting revolution, yet always having that fatalistic caveat of inevitable doom. Masada came to represent the last possibility for Jewish redemption and led to the slogan 'Never again shall Masada fall.'"

I betrayed a look of doubt but did not want to challenge the fiery little Edward, who seemed to hold his share of resentments. Yet he had said that nothing we were discussing was not being bandied about today in Israel and so I tried a little leavening to keep him going. "So Robin Hood really did steal from everybody and keep everything?" but Edward's face showed no lightening up. "In 1920, eight Zionist leaders died defending the Jewish settlement of Tel Hai in Upper Galilee. The Arabs had been granted entrance to search for French troops because after 1919, that part of the Middle East was under French and not British control. There was a communications mix-up, shots were fired and another legend, 'never mind, it is good to die for our country,' was spun from the words of one who had been present, that Yosef Trumpeldor, a rare Jew who had not avoided military service for Russia. Trumpeldor, as the legend came to be, tried to educate exilic Jews to defend themselves against the Germans and fight for their rights and true destiny.

"Tel Hai gave Israel the mythical origin of a new era and broke away from the traditional exilic martyrdom. Born was the 'few against the many' myth, later scripted for Churchill in the Battle of Britain, and Tel Hai became a sacred site for Jewish pilgrimages, including school and army visits. There is now a regional college with a 'few against the many' Zionist theme central to its collective memory.

"Israeli literature came to be secularized, dependent not on its god but more on one's grit, and allegiance came to be socio-political, with 'Israel' as the new god. Jewish youth in Palestine soon used school trips to 'feel' the land, rather than use prayers of centuries past, and the process required fitness in contrast to the 'weak sheep' who had gone to the Holocaust.

"By 1948, daring, resourcefulness and risk-taking became qualities admired in underground activities against the British. Britain stood for law-and-order and the concomitant obedience to· authority, while the Israeli emphasis was on the glory of patriotic death and solidarity. Thus, with Ashkenazis controlling Churchill's every move, with Harry Truman wanting the Jewish vote in U.S. swing states and half of all Russian Communist leaders being Jewish since the time of Lenin, all tools were in place for the creation of the new Israel.

"After 1948 and up to 1967 with the capture of Jerusalem, defiance to achieve the goals of the Promised Land was engrained in the Jewish consciousness and that defiance is still today a pivotal mode of thinking in Israeli culture. Zionist historical reconstruction held fast to its anti-traditional thrust and became a counter-memory, to reshape a past while incorporating both religious and secular elements for it to be all-encompassing. Masada came to have more symbolic significance than the Romans' toppling of the Second Temple and the shibboleth 'to die or to conquer the mountain' · came into being. A trip to Masada came to mirror the valiant ancient Jews in their exile from Egypt.

"The new literature, especially for children, recreated history as legend to glorify the past. There was the Lag Ba'Omer bonfire where in the 1940s children burned Hitler in effigy, and in the 1950s and 1960s, Egyptian president Nasser. Yet, overriding all acts was and remains the theme of the Bar Kokhba Revolt myth and its representation of Israel's emphasis on courage, success and revenge. National myths in Israel have become divine cultural forces."

I shifted position on the pew and raised both palms as if in acknowledgment of a common cultural trait, saying my Chantelle would have argued that such is true of all countries. But Edward lifted off his pew. "In the case of Israel, myths co-opted by a conflict position have led to relentless social friction! True, there has been a backlash, especially among Jews like me, and the anti-hero image of the *schlemiel*, once popular in Yiddish folklore and biblical literature is now mocked by many Israelis. And yes, the old Israel view, that audacity plus *fait accompli* equals total success, is now thought by some to confuse the strategic with the tactical, with success offering only a delusional gain versus *litsor uvdot ba-shetah* or facts on the ground. But the Trumpeldor myth is still used, as it was, to defend the Sinai settlement with Egypt in the 1970s."

Edward let out a huff. "Hawk Menachem Begin's decision to bury the bones of the defenders in the Bar Kokhba Revolt in Judea and Sumaria is still seen for what it was – an underscoring of Israel's commitment to take over the Palestinian West Bank, toward a realization of the full biblical Israel, with all non-Jews gone or having only guest status."

"Whew!" I thought as I shook my head. My liberal Jewish sensitivities were being trod upon. Edward sat down but remained forward and lifted his brows. "As for the Holocaust, it played a role alongside such legends as Masada in the 1940s and 1950s, but the 1960s marked the beginning of a slow change in Israeli attitude as triggered by the Eichmann trial and execution, along with the 1961 publication of Edward Lewis Wallace's launch of Holocaust stories, *The Pawnbroker*. Then the 1973 Yom Kippur War made many Israelis feel vulnerable and so rose to power the right-wing Likud, with right-wing religion carrying on the slogans 'we are basically one large *Masada*,' 'Suicide before surrender' and of course 'Never again.'

"A tragic narrative has now established continuity between Masada, the Holocaust and the State of Israel, and part of that narrative includes the pre-1948 Russian-Israeli favorites of the 19th- and early 20th-century pogroms. Sometimes added in for spice are the 17th-century retaliatory pogroms in the Ukraine and Poland as well as the Welsh miners' strike in the early 20th century."

I gave a reasoning shrug. "We Americans have our Alamos and do not admit to ever having lost a war. And Teddy Roosevelt's march up San Juan Hill, after it had already been taken, was perhaps the world's first propaganda film."

I did not then appreciate that I had pushed a button in Edward. He thrust his little head forward. "And a favorite of Lenin's," but I went on with reasoned face as if unaffected. "They are Platonic noble lies, like early Greek mythology or the Hebraic Noah's Ark," and Edward came back again with face right at me, as if, I felt, to make me look the insouciant fool. "That American myth has cost the deaths of thousands, if not millions, of people and has helped shape imperialist strategies such as the Monroe Doctrine that justified American-sponsored dictatorships and genocides. Indeed a spin on 9/11 has caused huge trade damage at our Canadian border – your

American Homeland Security has a veto over any border security initiative and is happy to exercise it."

I was not to be moved. "Whatever Teddy Roosevelt's theatrics in ascending to the presidency, he made things safer for both Canada and the U.S. by pioneering a food and drug act and launching a national parks system whose treasures exist to this day. And let's not forget that Teddy was unrelenting in his harsh descriptions of Wall Street."

But little Edward was not about to back off. "And was not above the same people making his phony film," but before I could query "What people," Edward raised both arms in a shrug and sat back to appear speaking with reason. "The issue is degree, not kind. What has come to be known in Israel as the Masada Complex has influenced negotiations with the Arabs, and one Israeli psychologist has labeled the complex the Masada Syndrome, or the central belief that the rest of the world holds negative views toward Israel and us Jews in general."

Edward took in a breath and slowly let it out. "As I'm sure you know, Arthur, at Passover there is the Hebraic children's poem, 'Every generation, they stand up against us to destroy us,' and all Jewish high holidays commemorate conflict and the persecution of us Jews."

I said nothing and Edward probably accepted my silence as agreeing. "Right-wing Israel wants all *Eretz Yisra'el Ha-Shlema*, that is the entire land of Israel of biblical dimensions, and that right wing sources the Numbers book of the Hebrew bible for support – that Israel is a people dwelling alone in a hostile gentile world. Divine anti-Semitism is thus a sanctified metaphor, along with the post-1948 Israeli slogan 'climbing up the mountain' to form a mythical structure that is the master commemorative narrative for Zionism."

Edward then continued with his role of mentor, and with me the sophomore fool. "Mythical stories have beginnings and ends, and make for a more seductive, memorable narrative. It is typical of conservative Russian Jews to enhance a hero, and this sentiment continues being spearheaded by Russian Jews in Israel and Hollywood, as it was with conservative Jews like the Middle East's original terrorist, Lithuanian Jew Menachem Begin. Some Jews among us are constantly changing and adapting history."

Edward paused to catch my stunned reaction and then he smiled, sat back and carried on. "Hollywood staging makes it easy for the tail to wag the dog or to smokescreen prime objectives. Take the sham in attacking Iraq – Alan Greenspan last year in 2008 confirmed what Paul Wolfowitz admitted in June of 2003, that 'the Iraq war was largely about oil.' The Americans now in 2009 buy into this so-called apologetic truth but the number one reason, still being camouflaged, is that attacking Iraq was part of an Israeli end game.

"More than two million Iraqi refugees, or one-tenth of the population, have been driven into exile, while their jobs, education, electricity and drinking water are gone and crime is everywhere. The damage to the moral standing of the United States has been incalculable, yet once again the Americans are allowing Israeli intelligence and manipulation to repeat the tragic error against Iran."

Edward's little body was cranked up and I tried to stay listening. "As for the war in Gaza, discourse in Israel is moving to the hard right, thanks in part to Russian *émigrés*, with nationalist cries for a Jewish-only state. Arab Israeli protests are the result of chronic and systemic discrimination but these realities are lost on much of Jewish Israel, with its paranoia only exacerbated by outside criticism. The war in Gaza heightened the perceptions in Israel that Jews once again stand alone as per their history, and that only their god of Israel is onside, with that god being the ancient, warmongering *demiurgos* of the early Hebrew bible."

By then, Edward was back up on his seat, and he swept his little arm across the small non-denominational chapel. "We Jews are intelligent enough to re-enlighten ourselves and break free from these oppressive myths," and then he slowly turned his focus straight to me. "But as for you Americans, the image of Israel and Palestine is the principal prism through which you view world affairs. Obama landed himself in hot water with American Jewish lobbies a couple of years ago when he told an Iowa audience that nobody is suffering more than the Palestinian people. Iowa, where 60% of Republican caucuses are governed by evangelical Christians!

"Obama had to work hard to court the pro-Israel vote but even later, when he was selected as democratic candidate, a panel of Israeli authors, professors and former diplomats – known as the Israeli Factor – ranked him dead last of all possible presidential candidates, scoring Obama a five out of 10 versus the Republican McCain's eight. If the U.S. election had been in Israel, McCain would have won in a landslide. The average Israeli remains suspicious of Hussein Obama, Israel was not named at inauguration, only the Muslim world, and Obama is seen as unduly discreet with the word 'terrorist.' He plans to break precedent and not let Israel know what he is going to say in Cairo and there are already Israeli posters of the Jew-hater Obama wearing a Palestinian *kaffieh*."

"Yes, but Edward," I said, as I attempted a reasoning brow, "when Americans negotiate against their chosen foes, we have had a B-movie actor leading us, denouncing the Soviet Union as an evil empire," and Edward pointed at me. "Arthur, even Ronnie Redneck did not resurrect the 19th century's '54 40 or fight' and want to take over Canada."

I had come to think that anti-American jabs were part of what it meant to be Canadian and let it go. Edward, meanwhile, looked spent from what he had said and his head lowered to the floor between the pews. He uttered again his plea: "We Jews are intelligent enough to re-enlighten ourselves and break free from oppressive myths."

The time was nearing 10:00 a.m., Edward had a class and I sensed that I had found a way to engage my beloved Chantelle. I spent the rest of that Monday composing a letter and mailed it the next day.

Chantelle Fouriere
Communication and Administration
University of California at Berkeley
California

Dear Chantelle,
  I am reading from your books as well as your daily Globe and Mail
and have taken to debate once a week in the Great Hall of Hart House.
The Middle East is a minefield of myths, and only one in 10
Palestinians wants a return to Israel but nine in 10 see the 1948 UN
'Right of Return or Compensation' as sacrosanct.
  After World War II, Jews were leaving the chaos of Europe and
arriving in the Middle East by the ocean-load, and by 1948, the new
Israelis, internationally armed, were fire-bombing hundreds of
Palestinian villages. The village houses collapsed and hundreds of
Arab towns and villages were uprooted, with three-quarters of a
million Arab civilians either fleeing Palestine or being uprooted by
the Israeli army.
  Many of the victims, since, have rotted for 60 years in refugee camps
under inhuman conditions, having been told at first that their stay
would be a week. Those victims still hold land deeds dating back to
1917 and the Ottoman Empire.
  One Palestinian refugee camp, Shatila in Lebanon, is less than a
square mile but houses countless thousands of Palestinian refugees. It is
a dark, moldy place of contaminated water, foul smells, exposed wires,
power blackouts, epic unemployment and chronic despair. Some of the
refugees are resigned to a tiny Palestine that leaves Israel with its current
borders, but many of the young would prefer to go west rather than
remain in such a ravaged Palestine.
  As for the Palestinians in Gaza, it is hard to imagine a situation
worse. People in Haiti or Somalia can leave and start over but
Palestinians remain stuck in a hot prison. This, despite people like Ariel

Sharon having said that Israel has not left the Palestinians homeless, because they could have emigrated like all the others.

In 1948, agricultural Gaza had 80,000 residents but was forced to absorb 180,000 more. Now each square mile of Gaza has 16,000 people living in rabbit hutches in the most densely populated territory on earth. Israel won't allow an airport, seaport or navigable roads from which to escape and Israel controls the electricity and water. What few fish there are have to be caught close to the shore in untreated effluents, and if the boats venture too far out, they are peppered by Israeli gunboats. As for any spiritual escape, getting to Mecca is almost impossible.

Western media do not accept the Palestinians' right to resist occupation, the assaults on them and their ultimate ousting, or their democratic right to elect a government, but Israel is allowed to do whatever it wants to further its objectives, including mass murder. In my United States, religion-TV channels make appeals for Christians to send money to Israel, casting its people as oppressed by terrorists. Prominent evangelist Pat Robertson has decreed that the sending of such money is helping the people of god.

As for your Canada, sweet Chantelle, it is not the giant Berkeley that it pretends to be. Canada's Conservative government is now in bed with the Jewish lobby, with the Conservative leader saying they know where their interests lie and who their friends are. While Canada now keeps complicit where American regional trials and executions of Canadians are concerned, Canada's current government will scream murder if such injustices happen in Iran or other Arab lands.

Last year in Canada, a person who had been drafted into the Nazi army as an interpreter was deported after more than 50 years of Canadian citizenship, because of an indirect connection to a war crime. Will these standards be maintained for Canadian bombers of German civilians? The Canadian War Museum ran into trouble when it portrayed participants in the bombing of Dresden and other German cities as war criminals. The museum gave in.

A chief of a respected Ottawa newspaper was fired by the giant media empire that owns it, after the newspaper tried to protect freedom of speech among its editorial staff. The head of the media empire, Canada's largest, wants a pro-Israel agenda and managed to secure government funding for a Canadian Museum of Human Rights, recognizing that the public view of human rights can be managed. The empire head is a child of Russian Jews who fled persecution and found a haven in Canada, and wants the Museum of Human Rights to tell the stories of wrongs that have been righted and wrongs that still need to be righted.

Such a Canadian national memorial to the Holocaust has been a long-standing dream of Canada's Jewish community, and the resulting new Canadian Museum for Human Rights, while officially neutral on political issues, will position the Holocaust as central to the overall human rights story. The Holocaust is argued to be the most thoroughly studied genocide in history and is considered deserving of such status. But Ukrainians are upset that the museum will grant prominence to only the Holocaust, alongside the abuse of aboriginal peoples, and not to the genocidal famine that occurred in the Soviet-occupied Ukraine in 1922 - 23.

A Christian evangelist was recently used as frontman for a Canadian government crackdown on film grants for works judged offensive, and the fine print said 'denigration of an identifiable group.' The hidden issue is said to be censorship of any Palestinian voice. Ditto an anti-child-porn smokescreen on the Internet and Quebec's coming down hard on women covering their heads with the niqab, under the government guise of security. And the Toronto school board just reviewed for removal a children's book, The Shepherd's Granddaughter, because one parent complained the book had an anti-Israel bias.

Tolerant Canada is also pandering to Israeli interests on immigration, empowering the Minister of Immigration to fast-track the types of immigrants whom Israel prefers to see and freeze out those considered undesirable. When the Canadian Arab Foundation accused the Minister of being a pro-Israel whore, the foundation's grant was cut off.

Canada has also barred, on grounds of security, an anti-war British MP from coming to Canada to speak at a forum entitled 'Resisting War, *from Gaza to Kandahar.'* The MP led an aid convoy to Gaza after the Israeli invasion and was praised as a humanitarian by the Palestinian militant organization Hamas, which is banned in Canada.

A judge in the Canadian West has ruled that a couple can't have custody of their children because it was endangering them when the children were taught neo-Nazi beliefs. The father admitted to using Nazi salutes but not preaching violence, yet the judge decreed that drawing racist expressions and symbols on one's child is not just bad parenting but advocating genocide. The willful promotion of hatred against an identifiable group is a crime in Canada.

Canada also may cut off its long-standing contribution to the United Nations Relief and Works Agency for Palestinian Refugees, the only Palestinian relief agency that counts. The cutoff may come because some Jews have accused the agency of being anti-Semitic and its officers in Gaza of complicity with Hamas. The UNRWA is now 60 years old and the welfare of the refugees and their descendants is still in its hands, including about 750,000 people in the West Bank and more than a million in Gaza. Only through support from countries like Canada can the agency survive.

The Canadian government is also quashing the critically relevant long census form, under the supposed threat of purposes for which it may be used. The government is saying that Canadians have complained about its intrusiveness but those complaints have been minimal. Chief statistician Munir Sheikh has resigned in protest and his replacement is being pressured to re-evaluate how data are collected, including a register-based survey to map out selective ethnicities.

Another long-term employee is set to resign, citing dismay over the handling of changes to the long-form census. The long-serving employee also says that the free exchange of ideas is diminishing and that internal dissent is no longer tolerated by the now politicized senior managers, particularly over the new national census and household survey, whose results are to come out in 2012.

Again in snow-white Canada, an educational channel is carrying a program, Israel Today, while the media have bought in to the dated

275

propaganda that Hamas does not recognize Israel's right to exist. In fact, Hamas promoted a ceasefire with Israel from the moment it took the reins of government and Hamas abided by the ceasefire for a year and then offered to extend it indefinitely, but Israel broke the ceasefire with murder. Hamas also did not make any major changes in legislation after it took office and did not try to Islamicize the people.

Israel continues its land grabs and demolitions, walling in more of the West Bank while evacuating only token settlements and then upping its assassinations, so that when Palestine responds to the provocations, Israeli troops raid Palestinian banks and the offices of charities, including the Nelson Mandela Foundation.

Israel will continue to demonize Palestinian leadership, such that Israel can claim no partner for peace, keep its occupation, accelerate land grabs and continue its long-term objectives, including removal of the Palestinian people. Adding salt to the wound, some Palestinian leaders have inadvertently served to further Israeli plans to delegitimize Palestine's claim to self-government.

As the dream of an independent Palestine fades, 50% of Palestinians say they would emigrate of they could. The Nakba *or catastrophe of 1948 as Palestinians describe their holocaust, did not obliterate their culture but the subsequent 60 years have disengaged them from not only hope but actual history, and they have grown in despair to appreciate that it is in Israel's interests that the West not understand.*

As for us Jews now in power, we cling to an oppressed ideology, and rather than being inspired to feel the pain of another and have the accordant courage to take responsibility, we quip that 'Israel was not born in sin!' and dismiss criticism as a new anti-Semitism. We abuse the saying of a Hasidic master, 'Always look after your own soul and another's body, not another's soul and your own body.'

All my love,

Arthur

Again, no answer.

Monday February 9 2009

By 8:00 a.m., Edward and I were already seated and having a coffee at a long oak table in the Great Hall's north end when Chaim arrived and plopped his bulgy brown briefcase onto the chair beside him, opposite us. He then pounded his elbows down on the oak table, before looking straight at me. "Arthur, I hear your *shiksa* is a French Canadian? A few years ago, there was a Frog song, 'If Israel says jump, the U.S. says how high, from the Wolfowitz war to Pearle, the Israeli spy.'"

Edward saw my scowl at the slur on my sacred Chantelle and caught my arm. I tried to hold my cool and take the high road. "In the war for Israel, the battle for Washington was won long ago and the real international court for Israel is Washington. Any Israeli PM's first visit to Washington is a rite of passage, and the sense that Americans are enjoined by divinity to protect Israel is so engrained that it is difficult to conceive of the United States altering course."

Little Edward, again in a dress shirt, leapt in to keep the conversation going, the way I had started. "A full half of all American foreign aid money goes to Israel, and Israel is the only country not required to give any account of that money. The United States also shares with Israel intelligence not shared with NATO or other allies." Edward then lifted high on his chair. "The Israeli lobby in the United States is a laby-rinthine coalition, including Christian evangelical heavies, and both the Republicans and Democrats get a giant share of their funding from Jews through tax-allowed political action committees. The Jewish-Israeli view dominates American media, and any news outlets not pro-Israel are boy-cotted and have demonstrations made against them. The Israeli side dominates American think tanks and maintains a campaign to monitor and control what is spoken and written about Israel on American cam-puses."

Chaim brought both his hands forward and put them into two spider formations on the middle of the table. "The need to protect ourselves holds true everywhere. In Europe and even redneck United States, the words 'East Coast' are code for a rumored New York Jewish conspiracy."

Sensing that Edward would be ready to protect my flank, I tried again with reasoned face to take the high ground. "If America were a true friend of Israel, it would be constructively critical. Despite U.S. media behaving like cheerleaders as they did at the start of the Iraq war, a majority of Americans want to withhold aid if Israel refuses to resolve the Palestinian question."

Edward smiled. "The United States is not seen in Israel as a friend but as a tool, as was Britain under Churchill. American public servants who are critical of Israel do not get key Foreign Service jobs, but Israel can and does renege on agreements with the U.S., and is the number one ally spying on it."

I frowned some uneasiness in letting Edward use me this way and pointed out that a majority of American Jews gave less support for the Iraq war than did the U.S. mainstream. But Edward was not about to hold his fire. "Likud drives the United States and drove the Iraq war, with oil the scapegoat, when the story of weapons of mass destruction was exposed. Only Israel, other than Kuwait because of the Gulf War, advocated attacking Iraq and today another Israeli-intelligence story is being used to stomp on Iran. Israel wanted to silence Saddam Hussein and was worried when he let UN inspectors back in. Just imagine if Iran did the same!"

Chaim, by then, was tapping his spider-hands on the oak table to register his displeasure but Edward was not to be intimidated. "The oppressed Jews of Israel, the U.S. and the world are induced to see any opposition in the starkest possible terms. Then the fooled Jews and puppet Washington wedge the other side into the fantasy. It's a Nazi Goebbels trick – to throw out falsehoods when beginning a debate – and all through the Bush years, that tactic has been standard practice. Even the label 'anti-American' has become a way of avoiding debate, when the label is viewed as code for 'anti-Semite.'"

"Enough," I thought of this dumping on my United States. "George Washington was part of the Enlightenment and signed the Treaty of Tripoli, affirming that the United States was founded not on religion and had full tolerance for Muslims," but Edward came back with another self-righteous Canadianism: "A poll last year in 2008 revealed that Canadians rate the

United States and Israel down with Pakistan in having a negative influence on the world." Little Edward then lifted right off his heavy oak chair. "God! A full 15% of Americans hold the view that Israel must expand its borders to set off a cosmic battle, from which believers will be taken naked to heaven. Rapture!"

Edward then eased back down and turned to me. "You are a spooked society, held captive by terror and your government is allowed to do anything in the name of security, including gucking up our borders. Only one in five Canadians now believe we should have tighter co-operation with you on anti-terrorism, versus half after 9/11."

It was I who was then riled, to Chaim's broad grin. I had been reading Chantelle's books and newspapers, and so I pivoted toward little Edward and shot back: "Support for your Canadian pluralism is on the wane and your peacemaker image is laughable. You can't even protect your own citizens from U.S. abuses."

Edward looked taken aback and I held on. "And as for your pure Canadian government, chief staff has often included Israeli sympathizers to drive every file." I pointed my finger at a slouching Edward. "You Canadians can be duped too! Take Afghanistan – the Taliban at the start were anti-communist zealots, who saw the corrupt puppets presiding over an opium-driven economy, and the Taliban leaders, for all their jihadist pronouncements about fighting foreign infidels and Jews, are just as mired in old rivalries as is the Afghan government. Canada's forces should be in your Arctic, protecting the oil, gas, minerals and transportation routes, all soon to be there."

Edward the scrapper finally came back in as if I had hit a chord. "Our press is free, and Prime Minister Pearson won a Nobel Peace Prize. Pearson also appointed none other than Northrop Frye to head up the Canadian Radio and Television Commission, the CRTC." Edward raised his little finger at me. "You've told me, Arthur, that you love to read Chantelle's conservative business newspaper, *The Globe and Mail*, but it was labeled 'left-wing,' translation secular, by Rupert Murdoch's Fox News. Four corporations control your country's entire media and objectivity in the American press is a joke. No wonder 90% of Americans believe that other people aspire to be

Americans, when 90% of Canadians, Japanese and Western Europeans don't."

Chaim had eased back in his chair with the smile of a contented cow, watching Edward and me face off, but I chose to ignore Chaim and kept to Edward: "Your Canadian prime minister is purportedly a fan of Fox News and once lunched in New York with Rupert Murdoch. This, despite one of Murdoch's columnists saying that working for him was like being in an Islamophobic command center. And one of your Canadian newspaper chains equates any attack on Israeli forces with an attack on Israeli civilians and uses the words 'militant' and 'terrorist' interchangeably. As for your sacred CRTC, it was criticized during those Frye years by Jewish media and recently felt compelled to attach domestic and non-cable conditions to shunt the Arab satellite Al Jazeera. Another of your free media programs, *Little Mosque on the Prairie*, did not even make the main Canadian media awards."

For the moment, tiny perfect Edward looked like a scolded puppy and Chaim lowered a grin of condescension at him while I continued: "Allowing, moreover, a human rights commission to police Canada's media, phones and computers, for their discussion of religion or other minorities, is a bad idea, but most smug Canadians don't know that is the law. And as things stand, Canada's hate-speech wording in its Rights Act allows for mind-reading of intent where only a vague probability that a speech could cause hatred or contempt gives cause to pounce. The wording also condemns any work that just seems to do that!"

Edward remained the slumped puppy but Chaim by then was also grinning a little less as I pressed on. "Your most senior government people say that any threat to Israel is a threat to Canada and use the ploy of saying hate-filled bigotry against any one is a threat to us all. Israel uses fake Canadian passports to assassinate Hamas leaders on foreign soil but Canada gives knee-jerk support for whatever Israel does, so that the Canadian government can buy domestic Jewish backing.

"Your government planted Israeli right-wing sympathizers into your Human Rights and Democracy organization, and the government now kills funding for any group that dares to oppose Israel in any way. Canada abstains on any UN vote to allow Palestinians to have self-government and Canada now is in the tiny minority steadfastly supporting Israel in the UN."

Chaim was no longer smiling but sitting in silence with Edward as I continued: "A new Canadian federal policy for funding academic research comes with peace and security purse strings, with 'relevance' to Canadian foreign policy priorities. Those priorities reflect a stepped-up support for Israel.

"At the behest of the Canadian Jewish Congress, the Toronto school board banned access to a book that voiced the perspectives of both Palestinian and Israeli children, and your lauded Canadian university, Queen's, has taken to creating a gang of 'student facilitators' to roam residences and dining halls to stamp out remarks on race – criticisms of Israel – under a camouflage of pejorative remarks that include those on gender and sexuality. Canada's Lakehead University has gone further, with its student union restricting activities of student clubs and censoring publications judged offensive to any identifiable group. And your liberal York University has had donor funding cut because of student criticism of Israel."

Chaim's spider-hands held still as did little Edward and I pushed on. "Canadian First Nations Chief David Ahenakew was tried a third time under Canada's hate laws and had his Order of Canada honor stripped from him for his private anti-Semitic remarks. He said he had first learned as a teenager, living in Ukrainian-dominated Saskatchewan, that the Jews had started World War II. The poor man was driven to an early death.

"When the financial capital of India was attacked, the Canadian news focused on the Jewish center which commandos rescued first before the Taj Mahal hotel. And Canada has repeatedly tolerated Israel's ambassador attacking people critical of Israel's human rights record, as well as allowing him to voice warnings against Muslims immigrating to Canada and influencing policy, as supposedly Muslims have done in France and the United Kingdom.

"B'nai Brith is saying Canada is finally acting out of principles but you both know that the Jewish vote formerly going to the opposing Liberals is dead. My New York cousin says that as the United States goes, so in 20 years goes Canada."

Edward came forward in his seat. "Canadian natives can, however, win political brownie points. One woman received high honors from the Roman Catholic Church for her advocacy in forgiving Church atrocities, committed in native residential schools. She had been raped and beaten and had witnessed murders but said it was time to begin the healing."

Chaim's face lifted as if he saw an opportunity. He posed a dark frown. "The residential schools abuse has been likened to the Holocaust as have abuses in Cambodia and Africa but there is a danger that the real Holocaust will lose its sense of proportion. Thank god, Russia is denying the annihilation of 10 million Ukrainians during the 1930s." Chaim's voice rose up as did one index finger. "Residential schools were not Nazi gas ovens and the schools' goals were not mass murder. Minority groups can get caught in their own demagoguery and can be lulled into seeing certain circumstances as repression. If everything is a Holocaust, then nothing is."

Saturday February 14 2009

I was fired up and eager to reach my love.

Chantelle,

Happy Valentine's Day!

A Toronto radio panel had three Canadian Jews talking about Muslim terror but I doubt that one would find on air three Canadian Muslims talking about Israeli terror.

The ideology of victimhood can rationalize everything. The deeper its sense, the greater the perceived threat to existence and the more justified the reaction. There becomes a fine line between Yiddishkeit or religious zealotry and fanaticism.

We Jews are taught that Israel is a response to the Holocaust, with our 11th Commandment being 'Thou shalt not hand Hitler a posthumous victory' and we are to find a divine plan in the evil of Nazism. Since the Eichmann trial of the early 1960s, we have focused on a post-Holocaust theology and are forbidden to despair of the God of Israel, lest Judaism perish. Even some secular Jews see the hand of god in Israel's 1967 victory.

But not all Jews see the same god, and we seem to embrace the widest horizons for holding different points of view. A rabbi who died 30 years ago condemned the state of Israel, formed so soon after the Holocaust, as an act of Satan, leading Jews into meaningless evil and sacrilege. He saw Zionists as the latest manifestation of an evil hubris that has constantly brought disasters upon the Jewish people. The rabbi went further and put the blame for the Holocaust on the sin of Zionism and related kibbutzism, luring the Jewish people into a calamitous heresy. There seems some of the historical rabbi Goan in him, and

perhaps we need steering more by our Wisdom Literature than by stereotyping. God knows what the Sabras – those Jewish children born in Israel since 1948 – have been fed.

Jerusalem had been Muslim for 1,300 years and the sacred Muslim Dome of the Rock was completed before the year 700. In the 16th *century, the Ottomans granted Jews their Western Wall, the last remnant of the second temple that was toppled by the Romans in 70 AD, but Zionism spins that God gave the title of Palestine to the Jews and there has been fighting in the sacred parts of Jerusalem since the 1920s.*

In 1947, the UN declared Jerusalem to be an international zone but Jewish zealots were confident that all would proceed in a preordained pattern, and that the expanding state of Israel was the Kingdom of God, with each clod of earth holy. Today, there are forces in Israel not even deterred by nuclear catastrophe and they want to destroy that sacred Dome of the Rock, saying it is demonic.

Don't put in power a person or group with a grudge against the world. Menachem Begin pioneered the Middle East terrorism in the late 1940s and was fueled by rage or some say mirrored guilt. He bombed Palestinian bridges, blew up British troops and terrorized Palestinian women and children, spearheading the theft of their land and livelihoods.

Many Toronto Jews today are going to have one more child than planned and move to Israel, since having a baby with the Israeli government's blessing is part of a Jewish Israeli fertility drive that is more aggressive than the one of Francophone Quebec. Israel is spurred on by the biblical call 'to be fruitful and multiply' against a booming population next door. The birth rates of Jewish and Arab Israelis are carefully scrutinized, along with racial profiling, and even the Orthodox blemish of in vitro fertilization is being subsumed by a more open interpretation of a male Jew being forbidden to waste his seed.

There is still some empathy in Israel for withdrawal of the Jewish settlers from Gaza but a small, diehard 1% of the Israeli public blocks withdrawal. That 1% is powerful and does not admit that its mythicized history continues to justify today's Hebron, where 450 Jews live in the midst of 150,000 deprived Arabs, and are protected by American money. The extreme right sees useful any appeal to the broader public but does not believe in democracy, and Israeli prime ministers pay homage to the 1%, while declaring that Jewish Israelis have to protect their grandchildren. Beyond the 1% and to a degree not acknowledged, Jewish Israel is guided by an historical imperative for establishing a greater biblical Israel, and many people are inspired less by law than by divine will.

Arab Israelis endure endless discrimination and it is almost impossible for an Arab in Jerusalem to get a permit to build or enlarge a house. One Arab citizen, fed up with the squalor in his inner city of Jerusalem, moved to a suburb, where one day a rabbi knocked on the Arab Israeli's door and offered to teach him the Torah. When the Arab explained that he was a Christian, the rabbi reacted with horror and told the Christian Arab to get away from him as if the Arab were dirty. In the same suburb, a group of 20 Jewish youths attacked Arab teenagers at a local mall and beat them with sticks, clubs and knives.

It will be interesting to see what transpires when the new commuter rail line gets completed in 2011. It will pass through Arab areas that Jewish Israelis rarely see, with many of those areas already walled off or segregated by barriers. Some Jews do not want to share the rail line with Arabs, and the Orthodox are crying for kosher cars and sexual segregation. Time will tell.

Israel's new Ministry of Information and Diaspora Affairs is concentrating on contacting Jews in the former Soviet Union, despite many being practicing Christians. And in Toronto as in Chicago and I guess everywhere, there is a low key collection box in synagogues and meeting places, a kupat kerem kayemet for the redemption of Palestine. We Jews are the only racial group that needs an organization like the World Jewish Congress, with its wielding awesome power.

Chantelle, I sense your thinking more now than ever.

All my love always,

Arthur

Thursday March 5 2009

My Sephardic friend Edward and I saw on a Hart House bulletin board an invitation to hear a Palestinian speak at a United Church northwest of the U of T campus, and we decided we had to go. Edward said he had been to concerts there and that the church was a big boring building but full of interesting people.

The church's architecture turned out to be all that was promised but the varying groups inside, clustered in open-doored big rooms, did seem to be doing something productive in a dynamic part of midtown. Edward and I went into the old auditorium to hear the Palestinian speak.

To a visibly eclectic audience, the speaker began. "Israeli troops in 1948 had a slogan of 'Take no prisoners' from a legendary battle against the Romans but were met by a Palestinian philosophy of 'We peasants don't fight.'

"The Palestinians went to the top of the mosques with white sheets to surrender but were shot down, and when more Palestinians came out in nightclothes to greet the arriving Israelis, they too were shot. Finally, some Palestinians took rifles but were met with machine guns, planes and Israeli bullets from all sides. When the armed Palestinians all finally surrendered with their hands up, they were shot, and women and children who were walking with their hands up were cut down by Israeli machine guns.

"Bands of Israelis swarmed villages and blew up buildings, and Palestinian families fled to the fields without fighting. Any resistance was taken out on villages as a whole.

"One after another, the villages fell without the Palestinians firing a single shot. Leaders were hanged on oak trees and the young men taken and crushed by bulldozers.

"At one town where the people surrendered with white sheets, the Israelis selected 60 men and tied their hands behind their backs, put them in a row and shot them with machine guns, while the rest of the people fled to the fields. At another, the Palestinians again surrendered with white sheets and the Israelis wrapped them in the same sheets before shooting them. In one village, the peasants were all ordered to kneel and bend over, and the Israelis rained stones down on them. In another village, some locals pleaded that they were old and disabled with nothing to gain from resisting, but the Israelis put 20 onto a truck and shortly thereafter shot them. Israelis broke into homes, firing and gang-raping young women, and the religious villagers were totally shamed, in their ethnicity.

"Again and again, the Palestinians surrendered and asked for mercy but their spokespeople were shot in the open and the young men taken out of sight until the villagers heard the firing. The Israelis did not bury the dead but bulldozed over them.

"While Israeli planes shelled, some Palestinians tried to defend their homes but were forced into village squares, before the Israelis blew up and bulldozed the houses, while dynamiting the olive trees. Every village and city in Galilee fell in 1948, and when some Palestinians tried to buy back their homesteads, they were crushed.

"Israelis drove the people out of the villages and the airplanes fire-bombed them. The Israelis took the land while Palestinians watched from a distance. After the incursion, the Israeli military made almost everywhere out-of-bounds. If Palestinians tried to take vegetables from their own land, the food was confiscated and the land was soon fenced off with barbed wire.

"Thousands of Palestinians were put into death camps in the middle of bare fields, surrounded by barbed wire. Villages of people were piled on top of one another and the camps became cesspits, where Palestinian families ate weeds and drank water from dirty ditches. In one camp alone, 1,500 people died and the Israelis made the site into a soccer field. At another, after the inhabitants were massacred, the Israelis began a new life on the stolen properties.

"After the Israelis had confiscated all the lands and despite a UN resolution, there was no compensation to the Palestinians. Israeli patrols roamed the abandoned villages and looted the houses for gold. The remaining Palestinian spokespeople were assassinated and the abandoned homes were demolished, house by house. The Jews built settlements on top, and one mosque was turned into a cemetery, with another mosque becoming a cow pen.

"In one Arab city, the olive trees from which one could have lived were replaced with pines, and the legendary jasmine trees with their shade and fragrance were torn down. Palestinian shanty towns sprang up with metal shacks, cold in the winter and hot in the summer, and lineups for water were put in the line of fire for the Israeli military. Phone communications to the new Israel was prevented and to the outside world almost impossible.

"Some Palestinians escaped the genocide by running from village to village until they finally reached Lebanon but by the 1950s, a number felt return-fever and tried to go home. These Palestinians had deeds to the land and did not believe it was forever lost but many were slaughtered, since even visits were forbidden by the Israelis. Some former owners did nonetheless make it back and looked among their abandoned houses for food. But the Israelis had orders to kill anything that moved at night and in 1951, sweeps were ordered by Israeli Prime Minister Ben Gurion, with the sounds of Israeli guns heard hacking down Palestinian people.

"What followed those early 1950s was the Israelis demolishing every Palestinian village house, erasing the cemeteries, uprooting the Roman olive trees and wiping out the orchards. All were replaced with Jewish settlements and the orchards were replaced with Israeli *kibbutzim* surrounded by border guards. Fruitless palms and pines were planted to replace the ancient Roman olive trees, and one village was paved over in asphalt.

"Israelis did not recognize the legitimacy of any Palestinians who protested, and labeled them saboteurs. One Palestinian man got 20 years in an Israeli prison for trying to defend land that had been in his family for generations and for which he had a deed dating back before the 1917 time of the Ottomans. Another Palestinian man was given 30 years for such an attempt and when condemned as a saboteur, he laughed and was given another 10 years for contempt.

"Within prisons, Palestinian detainees would be told by Israelis that they had interrogation methods that the Palestinians could not imagine and would be forced to tell Israelis all they wanted to know. Detainees were tied to chairs for weeks and had bags put over their heads, while others were detained for months in dark, damp, cold underground vaults where the detainees wallowed in their own excrement. There, they were beaten by Israeli boots and chains, and forced to swallow smashed teeth. The cells were small, too low to stand and had suffocating walls of iron. One would have no idea of time, and being in the vault for 10 days could feel like 10 years. The demoralized detainee could then be ice-picked into a confession. In other prison vaults, sleep deprivation was used, along with no food or water for three days, before Israeli guards undertook an interrogation.

"As resistance grew, Israelis tied the hands and feet of a mass of Palestinian humanity in the hot sun, and after a day when all detainees were desperately thirsty and many burnt, the Israelis searched and stole all, before rounding up 200 of the young men to be shot. Whereas the Palestinian uprising forbade execution of any prisoners, the Israelis were often Russian and behaved like the Bolsheviks, who had forced their prisoners to take off their clothes in the snow, so that the bullets would not ruin their clothes.

"The Israelis also swept into Lebanon and in their first incursion, bombarded the Beirut hospital and a sports city built for Arab games. Israel cut off Red Crescent funding to the Palestinian refugees, and the bewildered Palestinians, seeing all roads closed to them, were pitted into a civil war, becoming slaughtered civilians in a massacre co-coordinated by the Israeli army. Two books have been written about the massacre, both by Israelis.

"Refugees began to appreciate that if they ever went back to their homes, they would find another country, and those refugees also knew that the Jews did not want them to assimilate or make Israelis out of them – the refugees were to leave Palestine to live with other Arabs. Israel's ambassador to the UN Abba Eben pronounced 'two states' but such was a sham. The reality was that no one could be partner in a land considered holy to the people of Israel. It would take the land, the water and resources, and leave Palestinians stateless in sub-human conditions or under Jordan.

"Across the decades after 1948, many Palestinian people tended to 'disappear,' since they had no recorded names. Some carried pictures of 'lost' loved ones but frequently to no avail and even when they resolved to give up and emigrate to say, the United States, they were refused.

"Were the Palestinians right not to tell the world? In one of many massacres, the French press implored Palestinians to describe the experience but in those times, people forgot themselves and their children, and the women were taught not to complain and suppress everything. They barricaded themselves and their secrets in silence, put on mental masks and went back to their country as slaves, helping the new Israelis build houses on the ruins of the Palestinians' own.

"History can be a quixotic parody, written by those in control. But if ever there were to emerge truth beyond the bits and pieces leaking out, and were that information not branded as hate, there would be a new world awareness and the Palestinians could show a god-like forgiveness, even as the guilty continued to deny their crimes."

Monday March 9 2009

The Palestinian speaker Munir came to insist on joining one of our weekly discussions, and Edward and I feigned fear but wanted more to see the clash between Chaim and the Palestinian. He arrived at the meeting dressed in a black parka with hood, white winter boots strapped halfway up his calves, a navy wool turtleneck and blue jeans. Munir was medium in height, somewhere between my six feet and that of little Edward, and he looked fighting fit under his winter clothes. His face was shaven and his hair cropped, suggesting to me that he had it cut at some budget place around campus.

As the four of us approached the long oak table at the north end of Hart House's Great Hall, Edward gestured for me to take the chair next to Chaim opposite Edward, leaving a fourth chair empty for Munir to be seated opposite Chaim. There were at the start some strained civilities, before we threw off our winter garments and began to sit down.

Suddenly Chaim went on the attack. "Hamas does not recognize Israel!" and the Palestinian slowly seated himself before speaking. "An early campaign slogan, like Hilary Clinton saying she would open up free trade. Only a tiny core of Hamas still voices that ideology, forcing Hamas leaders to echo such cries in front of diehards, but each time it makes headlines in the West."

Chaim for the moment was silenced and the Palestinian calmly continued, with eyes straight on Chaim. "Israel does not want Hamas to recognize it or Israel would lose an excuse for not allowing a Palestinian state. All 22 Arab countries have agreed they would recognize Israel if it would withdraw from the occupied territories and implement the UN resolutions. Twenty years ago, the Palestinian Liberation Organization was fooled into recognizing Israel in the hope of ceasing settlements. Hamas even declared at the start of its governing, a ceasefire, saying it was prepared to compromise with Israel, and that ceasefire was honored by Hamas for over a year. Even for Shalit, the famed Israeli prisoner being held, Hamas had as its first condition for release, a ceasefire. But Israel wanted a war and provoked a reaction by murdering 12 Palestinians on a Gaza beach."

Chaim looked taken aback and Edward and I stole a smirk at each other, in anticipation of a match but Chaim may have been summoning something bigger, since he let out a verbal shot, saying Hamas prisoners still confess non-recognition of Israel. The Palestinian then leaned forward over the oak table. "Israeli law allows for 'physical pressure' and Hamas victims have made confessions under torture as well as sleep-and-urine deprivation, signing in a language they do not understand."

Chaim remained back in his chair, perhaps still mustering his forces and Munir seized the moment to continue. "Israel wants one state, a Jewish Israel and its whole biblical package, from the Jordan River to the Mediterranean, and after that, it will want more, if resources like water are involved."

The Palestinian's last comment brought Chaim forward and he placed his favorite spider-hand on the table. "We have been 2,000 years in exile since the Romans forced us out!" but Palestinian Munir had done his homework and he lunged forward over Chaim's spider-hand. "We Palestinians did not come with Muslim rule in the seventh century but were descendants of Semites, whose tenure in Palestine has been at least 5,000 years. The Hebrews arrived 3,500 years ago and settled for a time at peace in the hills but later conquered their neighbors by wars. The duration of ancient Israel's territorial possession of Palestine was a short one."

Chaim raised his eyebrows as if impressed with the strength of his opponent, but then brought forward a counter-thrust that sounded a bit like Edward: "American critics of Israel say that its rule over occupied territories is the source of the violence and a peace deal with an independent Palestinian state would kill that resentment. But Israel knows that such a two-state solution would not change things, because Iran represents a deeper source, lying in an ideology that demonizes Israelis as manipulators of a false holocaust as well as 9/11, and that Israel is founded on fraud."

We all went silent after that bomb by Chaim and then he brought forward his fat body over the table. "That ideology is common in the Muslim world and includes a belief that Jews control Western media and international finance." Chaim's middle spider-finger went up. "Nazism revisited! Iran, therefore, cannot be allowed to negotiate with Obama."

Chaim then took to leaning back in his oak chair and Edward and I looked at each other, as if to assess the contest so far. But the Palestinian looked undaunted. "Muslims, while not necessarily agreeing with Iran's leader that the United States is half-Judaized, have nonetheless no illusions that after all is done, the U.S. will defend Israel. That is the Jewish way of the West – the Jews in Algeria automatically got French citizenship when France took over that country but the Algerian Muslims did not."

After the moment's silence that followed, Palestinian Munir marched on with a sage face and his right shoulder forward: "A sizeable chunk of the U.S., before Obama, was on the verge of a populist theocracy, with Catholics, Evangelists and Jews behind the scenes, to create a dialogue replacing talk with traditional Protestants. And it's no secret that the evangelical promise of cheap grace is a powerful presence in the U.S. armed forces."

Chaim still looked to be searching for a place to attack and let Munir continue. "The last 100 years of war have been overwhelmingly Abrahamic ones of religion, with Jewish control of the seas and the lines of communication. Victors' amnesia has also prevailed with the U.S. Civil War, and the German so-called atrocities of World War I, though now discredited."

Little Edward made a noisy shift in his chair. "The Western media is, yes, pro-Israel and Iran's presidential challenger Mousavi is heralded by the West. He was Reagan's go-to-guy in the Iran-Contra scheme with Israel, supplying Iran with weapons paid for by Washington and routed through Nicaragua, in exchange for the release of American hostages in Lebanon." Then Edward pointed his little finger. "Yet not all Jews are Zionists or Zionists Jews! Jerry Falwell and Pat Robertson are cases in point."

Palestinian Munir suddenly looked pumped. "In free-speech United States of America, the career of a political scientist may end if he dares question assumptions of the strategic alliance with Israel. Jews and their media-controlled West have had no understanding of Palestine for 2,000 years." Munir kept the floor. "A land without a people for a people without a land became the slogan after the 1897 World Zionist Conference, and when Rabbi Yitzak migrated to Palestine in 1904 to become rabbi of the new Jewish settlers, he tried to spiritualize the secular and argued that if a state were made the supreme value, there was nothing to halt a ruler from exterminating subjects, who in his view obstructed the state mission."

Chaim tapped his spider-hand on the table and bent forward toward the Palestinian. "You want the law of religious fanaticism, sacrificing your children by teaching them to be suicide bombers!" and Munir lifted his tight chest, before he thrust his head forward at Chaim. "You taught us bombing in 1948 when Jewish fighters lobbed a barrel of explosives into a crowd of Arabs. At the same time, when the UN divided Palestine into Arab and Jewish states, Menachem Begin headed the *Irgun* militia, and it seized the Arab village of Deir Yassin where it massacred hundreds of citizens. Thousands of other Arab civilians fled, abandoning 400 villages with the hope someday of returning."

Chaim this time lashed back, with his right arm coming up and pointing. "So you left, as Israeli history says!" but Munir would not back off. "Those who did not flee in terror were forced out or murdered, but Israeli history has long claimed that Palestinians in 1948 left in response to appeals by surrounding Arab governments. As for any Arab suicide bomber in recent times, the Israeli reaction has been to destroy his family home and sentence his brother to 15 years in jail, merely for being a member of the military wing of Hamas."

Chaim leaned back in his oak chair and raised both hands to the high ceiling as if in judgment. "We hear daily of Islamic theocracies, their treatment of prisoners and suppression of women. You cut off their clitorises!" but Munir suddenly raised both palms against Chaim. "Rare and highly local practices, like the Catholic cult worship of relics. As for treatment of prisoners, Israel's notorious prison out in the desert and its legendary torture tactics are known to millions of Muslims but you Jews control the Western press and are trying to stop Al Jazeera from coming onto Western airwaves, using the trump card of hate. As for women, huh! Jewish women cannot read from the Torah, while the Qur'an may be read by both men and women."

Chaim shrugged. "How about all the restrictions that you put on people's freedom? In Israel, we do what we want..." and the Palestinian lowered his palms as if to reason. "The Qur'an does not regulate everything, only those things thought necessary, as do Jews and Christians. Other areas are regulated by human beings, as is done by Jews and Christians."

Edward suddenly leapt in with something surprising. "In much of the Arab Middle East, states are ruled by secular autocrats who have sidelined democracy, the rule of law, dissent and human rights. The only serious opposition is the mosque and the Islamists." The rest of us then sat back, for a moment off balance, and the charged little Edward continued: "The Islamic rule of law existed prior to the advent of Western colonial domination, and as for the suppression of Islamic people by a few tyrannical governments, sectarianism is used as a ploy by foreign powers and their Arab autocrats for their own needs. Almost 60 Muslim-majority countries endorse some subset of *sharia*-inspired legal code as an underlying principle, not literal prescription, but *sharia* in Western parlance has been likened to Islamic brutalism."

Munir relaxed back into his chair and broke into an endorsing smile but Chaim shifted his eyes to see if the rest of us were ganging up on him and Edward gave him a nod before speaking. "Democracy and secularism, furthermore, are not synonyms. I know of no state that functions without some official or unofficial ideology, even if it be the masked one of official non-ideology."

Edward then lifted in his chair as if to increase his tiny size among the rest of us larger men. "And Israel needs no lessons on being a theocracy – Likud runs the show more and more, as did the rabbis who ghettoized Ashkenazi Jews in Europe for 1,800 years." He then gave a shrug. "By contrast, we Jews were welcome and comfortable in Islamic lands, and from 700 to 1200, Islam led the world, not only in refinement of manners and human cleanliness, but also in humane legislation and religious tolerance. Muslims crossed Gibraltar in 711 and founded Andalusia, where for 800 years Jews prospered and lived peacefully with Christians and the Islamic government. In fact, Jews were prominent in those Islamic governments and often intermarried. Islam tolerates all races, colors and even apostasy, and Muslims with rigorous religious training are far less likely to radicalize than are Orthodox Jews."

Chaim huffed at what he may have thought a conspiracy. "We have extremists as do the Palestinians..." and he rang almost victorious in declaring that Islam had its *majnoons* or raving fanatics, but Munir would not let Chaim away with his dash of Arabic. "Israeli extremists? Shimon Perez, the Middle East's eternal optimist, referred to Palestine before the Jewish take-over as an 'empty desert' and helped start the Jewish settler movement. He led Israel's nuclear program and would have nothing to do with Hamas. As for the broader Israeli public, it urged both the assassination of Hamas leaders and the deadly air strikes, after the first retaliatory suicide bomber in over three years."

I was feeling a little lonely for Chaim and decided to throw in a question, more to stimulate debate than take his side. "Munir, we hear again and again of Islam's glorious past, but how does that mesh with the values of society today?"

The Palestinian turned to me and took a chestful of breath. "Arthur, if Islam were to follow only the laws of capitalism, the Islamic world would become as materialistic as Western society and the quality of life would diminish, with riches replacing God as focus. Christians have resigned themselves to a world of usury; thus, the abolition of interest is feasible only within an economy that is Islamic."

Chaim had nothing to say to this nor did Edward or I, and so Munir systematically turned his head to each of us. "Since the fall of Spain to the Christian world in 1492, some Muslims have associated the rise of Dutch, British and American capitalism, and the role of Jews therein, with the imperious god of the Jewish bible.

"Jewish plutocrats have spearheaded a manipulation of much of planet Earth, through the exercise of power by material wealth. Whether it be the forcing, centuries ago, of U.S. tobacco farmers to pay insurance for transport or the role in the 1919 Treaty of Versailles, or the post-WWI carpet bagging of Germany or the same carpet bagging in the U. S. after its Civil War, such that 50 years later, a third of Americans' borrowing was to illegal creditors."

Munir for a moment had the rest of us silenced and he continued: "Even earlier in the Deep South of 1800, there were more Jews in Charleston, South Carolina – the Wall Street friendly port city and center of transatlantic cotton trade – than in any other city in America. Between the Civil War and World War I, another 40,000 Jews moved south, many as merchants. Let us also not forget that the Dutch Jews of Amsterdam, Rotterdam and South Africa dominated the slave trade to the Americas during the Age of Mercantilism and during, as well, the later British Empire and America, post-1776."

Chaim by then had a deep scowl on his face but so did Edward, and I was not far behind. Without saying so, the three of us seemed to be intuiting something insidious in what was being said and perhaps, out of some wish for the Palestinian to hang himself, we gave him more rope. "One-and-a-half million Palestinians have been displaced by the Israelis but Islam, not Goldman Sachs, is seen in the West as the one with the brand image problem. Manhattan can oppose a mosque on the site of the World Trade Center, saying, 'All I need to know about Islam, I have learned from 9/11' and one can almost hear the Pharisaic prayer, 'Thank heaven we are not like those people,' yet Iran is expected to endorse a nuclear Non-Proliferation Treaty while its neighbors Israel, India and Pakistan stay outside the NPT and keep arsenals of their own."

Munir had been still revolving his face to each of us but then stopped and leaned back, before he gave another heave of his athletic chest. He raised his hands above his head into a fold. "In the great U-S-of-A, so long as the Anglo-Jewish establishments are not challenged, adherence to exotic religions is considered harmless, and at worst quaint or idiosyncratic. Islam is the only religion not allowed that benign neglect or toleration.

"The fundamentalist derogative label does not get attached to Israeli integrists, Lubavitchers or even right-wing Christians, but is reserved for the debasement of Muslims. And the vaunted inter-faith dialogue in the U.S. and quack Canada remains almost always with Christians-and-Christians or Christians-and-Jews, with the strongest hostility coming from Jews when the talk gets around to Palestine."

I had heard enough, but in deference to Edward tried to hold a sense of intellectual integrity in posing a question. "How about your infighting as in Iraq?" Munir turned back on me. "Need I mention intra-Christian wars or intra-Jewish splits?

"Shi'ism represents 15% of all Muslims and claims blood ties to Muhammad Shi'a of the original Muslim family. Other Muslims regard Shi'ites as discriminatory but many Sunnis seem unaware that the Shi'as pioneered neo-Platonic Gnosticism."

Chaim folded his arms and smirked, as if pleased he was not the only person being disciplined, but then came forth purportedly on my side. "God help us with your goddamn holy wars…" and the Palestinian rose up in his chair with his finger pointed. "The concept 'Holy War' does not exist in Islam, versus the chosen Jews with god on their side. Wars of religion are an Abrahamic trait, whether that fight is for land or slaves or gold, and the curse of Abraham has permeated Western cultures."

Chaim, Edward and I glanced at one another in looks of disapproval, but Munir kept on. "Americans see world history as the unfolding of an Abrahamic process, and ever since the pilgrims, the Americans have spun history with a covenantal theology, along with its mandate to climb new hills and settle new valleys on the march west. New England's puritanical legal codes were founded on the laws of Moses, and Thomas Jefferson, despite ascribing to the Enlightenment, wanted 'Israel the Promised Land' on one side of the United States seal.

"Anglo-Saxon secularism manifests much of the Abrahamic paradigm because the Abrahamic and capitalist narratives complement each other. Marxism too manifested a version of the New Jerusalem, when Communist Jews toppled the tsar and took over Russia."

Chaim suddenly sat up as if struck and lashed back: "The communist-Jewish myth is an old Nazi saw, and you are not going to get me to apologize for Jesus or the fucking Virgin Mary." Chaim then settled a bit and gave a broad sweep of his fat left arm. "Anyway, Christianity will soon be extinct in the land where Jesus walked, and the offshoots of Islam are responses to anxieties over the image of anyone's daughter."

I had to interject. "As are the waves of fundamentalist Christianity," and a recharged Edward came in right behind me, "Or the violent perversions of Hinduism in India, and the Hebraic suppression of Jewish daughters in Israel, New York and elsewhere."

Edward then launched again into an area on his own. "One of the world's most potent forces revolves around the mythic figure of the delicious young lamb of a teenage girl, leading to fantasies, crime and the reactive practices of religion. Studies have repeatedly found that poverty reduction in any country is relative to the level of education and related awareness of its women."

Edward sat back, pleased with himself and I thought to ask Munir, "What about your jihads?" and he came back at me with a look of condescension. "Jihad means to strive, to endeavor, especially against one's own lethargy, spiritual hopelessness or psychological ill-confidence. An Israeli guard booted a Palestinian boy for carrying a prohibited flag but the boy stopped and stared up at the Israeli without flinching. Then the guard booted him again."

Munir held on to the floor while the rest of us took a breath. "As for the Muslim *Wahhabis* or fundamentalists of today, they are not unlike the Christian Puritans of 400 years ago, when they decried Roman Catholicism. The current Muslim-Puritan upsurge likewise reflects a fear by some people who see their way of doing things threatened." Munir then half-spread out his arms. "Once resolved, Muslims of true faith will have a chance to show the world how dynamic Islam can be, within an ecumenical spirit of goodness."

Chaim huffed a grunt of contempt and scraped his chair back to leave but Munir thought to throw a closing jab as a fat Chaim struggled to get up. "The coalition of right-wing and ultra-Orthodox parties, soon to take power in Israel, is a government that Israelis delude themselves into thinking they do not want but then rationalize it, with the fallacious claim that the world is against them. They also lie to themselves in saying they want a two-state solution. "

Chaim let out another huff after arisen, and may again have sensed that there was a conspiracy against him, but I for one was disappointed in not hearing enough of Chaim's side. After he departed, there were a few minutes left before Edward's 10:00 a.m. class, and he took the time to try a bit of collegial discussion with Munir, sensing perhaps that the Palestinian was not going to return.

Within that spirit as invited by Edward, Munir began again: "There is no issue that arouses Muslim ire more than the plight of Palestine. Mythological little Israel has the fourth most powerful armed forces in the world and

Jewish settlers claim the right to live anywhere in the biblical land. They even sing songs calling for violence against the Palestinians, and one lead pop singer claims to have shot one Arab per day while living in the West Bank. The Israeli singer broadcasts a radio show preaching war as a way to achieve peace, and of course accuses people who disagree with him of being Jew-haters.

"Meanwhile in Jerusalem, about 470,000 Jews and 250,000 Arabs live in the city but the city denies building permits to its Arab residents, forcing multiple generations and extended families into single houses. One ancient Arab section *Abu Tor* was renamed *Givat Hananya* or Hananya's Hill in order to claim that the area historically belonged to Jews and was never Arabic. On one recent day, 45,000 homes in Arab Jerusalem were crushed."

I interjected with a straight face to ask where it was all headed, and Munir turned first to me then Edward, before he took a deep breath and gave us both an earful: "Britain in 1915 pledged in the Hussein-McMahon Treaty to support the independence of Arabs in Palestine, and Arabs fulfilled their pledge by fighting Ottoman Turkey. If you have not seen the movie *Lawrence of Arabia*, you should.

"But then came Britain's 1917 Balfour Declaration, promising a Palestinian home for the Jews. The wording of that Balfour Declaration was vague but every word of it was agonized over as to its legalistic minutiae, by Zionist organizations in Britain and the United States. At the time, Palestine was 90% Arab and 10% Jewish but the Balfour Declaration mentioned only the Jewish communities, as if they constituted the majority.

"Soon, monopolies over the land's natural resources were granted by Britain to Zionist companies and by the 1920s there were 175,000 Jews in Palestine. The Arab revolt of 1929 was against Jewish right-wing Lubavitchers, who regarded non-Jews as racially inferior.

"By 1940, the man responsible for Jewish colonization, Joseph Weiz, stated openly that the final goal left no room for non-Jews and the only solution was a Palestine without Arabs, not one village or tribe. On the eve of the UN partition in 1947, Jews represented 33% of the population but had only 6% of the land and the UN gave them 56%. Arab village children were killed by smashing their heads with clubs and Zionists used radio messages urging Palestinians to flee for their lives from their homes.

"By the end of 1948, Jews had 80% of Palestine and by 1967, one-and-a-half million Palestinians had been driven from their homes. Israel, despite its propaganda, started the wars of 1948, 1956 and 1967 as well as the 1978 invasion of Lebanon. And all the while, Jews used and continue to use the wild card of the Holocaust, to rationalize injustices to the Palestinians. The irony is the Jews do have their promised third temple – it is called *Yad Vashem*, Israel's Holocaust museum."

Munir paused, raised both eyebrows and then his right index finger. "It is interesting that the director of the museum admitted that most oral 'memories' of the Holocaust were unreliable." Edward then added something that I found almost in support of Munir. "The separation of church and state compels people of different faiths to live and let live. But it is theology that is the devilish detail – religion deals with codes, by which people conduct their lives, but theology deals in intellectual abstractions and is profoundly dangerous."

Friday March 13 2009

Dear Chantelle,

    In heretofore liberal Canada, there was euphoria over Obama, but now any repeat of a JFK or an FDR affirming Canadian liberalism may be swamped by a conservative groundswell spilling in from south of the border. If the Bush-created recession continues, a misplaced anger could add to the groundswell, with new bedfellows like Wall Street and American Jesusland restoring what they deem Christian – unbridled capitalism, a morality bent on sex and a hatred for anything Islam. Now, in Canada, cultural laws are being changed behind a smokescreen of sex, using Christian frontmen to camouflage suppression of anything Islamic or Palestinian in point of view.

    As for the UN, Canada's conservative government now ranks with Bush for derogatory remarks against it, yet aspires to a seat on the Security Council. Much of the world opposes the new conservative Canada but its government is already finessing excuses rather than admit the problem is Canada's new, immovable position toward Israel and concomitant disdain for the UN.

    How we hear news up here will play a key role in the formation of policy, and any Arab-based Al Jazeera being aired in Canada is something I'll believe when I see. Though Al Jazeera news has won international respect for editorial independence, both the English and Arabic versions fight ongoing accusations that they harbor anti-Israeli and anti-American bias. Forgotten is the role that the American CNN played in convincing the world that the U.S. was right in invading Iraq, while casting aspersions on countries like France that argued against it.

    One-third of our world news stories still originate from free-speech United States, but one has to search far beyond the mainstream to learn that Israeli archeologists, despite political pressure, have found no support for the exodus from Egypt or for the 40 years in the desert and grand entrance into the Promised Land. Yet any group that feels as strongly as a people once abused as slaves can create a common cause that sets that people apart and gives it a sense of engagement with its mythology. Not surprisingly, Orthodox Israelis are opposed to the archeology.

Obama probably understands that the focus of Muslim criticism against the U.S. is not religion but foreign policy, yet he is toeing the line in singling out Iran as a potential nuclear menace, perhaps to help negotiate with Israel on the Palestinian issue. Not since Carter has a U.S. president been so clear about Israel, as well as Palestine, being in need of changing their ways to achieve peace.

Israel will insist that for discussion of a two-state solution to resume, the Palestinians will now have to recognize Israel as a "Jewish state," thereby relinquishing among other things, the Palestinian right of return. That consideration was not part of negotiations in Israel's treaties with Egypt and Jordan, but it is a classic Israeli negotiating tactic to put on the table an element not part of earlier talks. Israel will also include the nuclear disarmament of Iran, saying it is another "only road" to Middle East peace.

If that is not enough, Israel will also demand an impossible guarantee of Palestinian demilitarization but will continue to dismiss the growth of Israeli settlements as "natural," while labeling the West Bank with its biblical Israel names, Judea and Samaria. Israel will also be absolute in having Jerusalem solely as its political and religious capital.

As for Obama's dream of nuclear disarmament, how can he come to terms with Israel having nuclear weapons and not being signatory to the global Non-Proliferation Treaty? That is a question I doubt will be dealt with for generations – Israel will not tolerate discussion of it and the Western press dare not raise the issue.

Meanwhile, Sudan reports that Israeli air attacks have killed hundreds of refugees but Sudan's president gets accused of crimes against humanity. Before Obama took over, Israel and the U.S. signed a document allowing Israel to intercept shipments that it judged hostile over a very broad region as defined by Israel. And France, under Jewish president Sarkozy along with tag-along Germany, does not want Muslim Turkey gaining entrance into the European Union.

Back here in Canada, a union representing academics has reacted to Israel's bombing of a Gaza university with an academic boycott, and threats have piled up against the union leader. He compared Israel to the former Apartheid of South Africa, and the Canadian government alleges that he fostered racial slurs during an Israel Apartheid Week at Canadian universities.

Self-professedly tolerant Canada is also trying to change its citizenship laws, making them unsuitable to an age when citizens often live abroad, without losing their ties at home. About 50,000 Canadian citizens are living in Lebanon, and the Government of Canada is now saying that the right of their great-grandchildren to become citizens should be disallowed. Under counsel from Jewish groups, and citing France and Britain as precursors of Islamic trouble, the Canadian government is developing immigration policies that prey on fears of "undigested immigrants" clinging to Muslim sharia law, gender inequality, honor killings and other views contrary to Canadian values. The irony is that the Orthodox Jews from Israel's theocracy would not qualify as Canadians.

Discover Canada: The Rights and Responsibilities of Citizenship is a new study guide for those seeking to become Canadians, and it is full of responsibilities and values, including condemnation of the Muslim-stereotype practice of honor killings. Canada's new citizenship guide was made after formal consultation with senior Jewish Canadians and is blatantly partisan – the guide uses emotive words like "barbaric" to describe cultural practices such as spousal abuse, and the guide self-servingly adds, "Canada's openness does not go this far." The guide also excludes key authors from its highlights on Canadian culture. To under-score the new citizenship needs, the Canadian military will be now be in attendance at each graduation.

The same Jewish-Canadian consultants want a citizen test to flow from Discover Canada, including querying applicants about those Canadian "liberal democratic values," thus embedding those values into its citizens. One consultant openly deplores the current system and says it is a crime that the system has an easy test that he claims is manipulated by immigration consultants, who train non-English or non-French speakers to pass. *The same consultant has the gall to add that every glimmer of change in the immigration process, rules or requirements gets attacked by "ethnic associations" – read Muslims – and by their i mmigration lawyers and counselors who fight, he claims, to protect their incomes. The new Canadian citizenship test, based on the new 63-page* Discover Canada *guide versus the old smaller guide, has a failure rate of 30% versus the old 5%, and Canada is worsening things by cutting back on language programs for newcomers.*

Seven Jewish Children: A Play for Gaza *is about the recent Israel-Gaza conflict, and it premiered in London shortly after the end of the Israeli siege. On closing, the play's director was invited to bring the play to Canada by the Independent Jewish Voices, a network of Jewish groups opposed to the Israeli occupation of the Palestinian territories. Yet from far and near, conservative Jewish groups have damned the play, saying it is a threat to Jewish existence. Ironically, at the same time over in the West Bank, a theater has been training young Palestinians in the dramatic arts, offering an alternative to a life of violence. An aligned theatrical school was destroyed by Israeli bulldozers in 2002.*

As you know, Chantelle, after Bedouins discovered the Dead Sea Scrolls near Bethlehem in 1947, some of those Scrolls made their way to the Palestine Archeological Museum in East Jerusalem. The Scrolls included some of the earliest written sources of the Bible's Old Testament, and Israel seized them upon annexing East Jerusalem in the 1967 war. Many Israeli Jews now take them as proof of their claim to the land of Israel.

Ethno-centrism and perceived persecution from a common enemy are tools used by rulers to deflect any indignation away from a society's internal oppression. Rulers thus deem it unimportant that the Noah-flood myth resembles those in other parts of the world, or that the Hebrew Book of Judges, purportedly about tribal leaders, was crafted to create a history of the united Israel. Humano-centrism is another ego appeal for promulgating that planet earth was created for the use of male Homo sapiens, *and we continue in this 21st century to kill 100,000 whales per year, while wondering why whales appear uninterested in revealing to us their communications. Until we see all creatures as equal, we human beings have no future.*

Still, the myth carries on: "In the future, when your child asks you what is the meaning of the laws that our lord god commanded, tell him we were slaves in Egypt but the lord brought us out. Hope takes us forward towards god's promised Mount Zion, a place where there shall be no more pain (for learning preventive protection), no more sorrow (for learning wisdom) and no more tears (for cleansing our eyes)."

I met a Canadian Jew who says he himself has never experienced anti-Semitism but is nonetheless having his children learn Hebrew, so that when they grow up, they will know why people hate them. He has a grandmother who was in Auschwitz but does not feel his angst over criticisms of Israel and has a more nuanced view, even of Auschwitz, than do her children who have only heard about it.

People who do not understand the Bible or the Qur'an, including so far myself, don't understand many of the sources of world conflict. For two millennia, that bible has been the cultural point of reference that Western people have held in common, an imaginative framework or as your Northrop Frye once put it, the mythological universe for all Western literature.

Our human need to create narrative may be one way to make sense out of things, but folklore is not science, and the struggle for meaning has to include an effort not to ascribe meaning to something unwarranted. We hate what we do not know and we develop intellectual allergies, yearning for a moment's unity with creation. Instead, maybe what we need is the ability to see human existence more in the striving for such a moment.

Some thoughts, Chantelle, while I think of you.

Love,

Arthur

Wednesday March 25 2009

Dear Arthur,

I sense you are feeling new trouble and perhaps a few thoughts can help.

For me, the key point of Exodus is history's first recorded break from slavery, with that break including the beginnings of a belief based on, among other things, ethics. You know the importance that the Mosaic code places on human life: an individual must not be sacrificed for money, power, convenience or the overall good of the group.

Somewhere in the Mishnah, it is written that if a group so destroys one person, that group also destroys the principle of life. Please remember, Arthur, what you Jews have taught us: that the sanctity of life and the dignity of each person, along with social responsibility, constitute the grounding for justice.

Chantelle

I must have alarmed her but I took the letter as love. The letter came from California but after its arrival, I lost contact with Chantelle for some time thereafter, until I learned she was in Minneapolis.

Thursday April 2 2009

That early Toronto morning was unspeakably beautiful, and after I arose before dawn, I brushed my teeth, put on a safari shirt and shorts, hiking boots, long wool socks and old brown bush pilot jacket, then walked to greet the day with the ancient oaks in Queen's Park. The sky was still charcoal in the final hour of darkness, but a few clouds were beginning to make their way into the early light.

By 5:30 a.m., birds had begun singing and as the sun began to edge up, I lay down on a bench to view the sky and the rising sun, beyond the top of the oaks. I dropped my eyes south to catch the sun splashing on the pink of Ontario's Parliament buildings, before I rotated my head west to peer past the park and see the sun striking the stone of Hart House. For half an hour, I lay there absorbing the sight of a new sun and the sound of birds in the 58 F of a quiet Toronto. Then I fell back asleep.

Inside of another hour, the traffic around Queen's Park began to awaken me, and I got up and walked over to Hart House for my 7:00 a.m. swim. I front-crawled the mile, shaved, showered and manicured and then at 8:00 met with a former theology professor of Chantelle's, Roger, for breakfast in the Arbor Room coffee shop of Hart House.

Roger was a middle-aged man of medium build, healthy of face and clean cut, looking, I thought, the Canadian academic, wearing caramel glasses, cord jacket, brown slacks and comfort shoes. Roger knew I had an agenda and he sat at our table in silence, smiling, while leaving us both in a pause before I took the cue. "Roger, what was anti-Semitism's original purpose?"

Roger gave me a wider smile. "I don't know, Arthur, but no true believer in the teachings of Jesus could be an anti-Semite." I was not satisfied. "You said 'Jesus' and not 'Christianity.' Was Paul a crime against life?" and Roger shifted in his chair. "I would like to think, Arthur, that there is some good in all people."

I then sensed some common ground on Paul and so I shifted to two other people whom I surmised we both respected. "Mendelssohn saw the 'miracle' as folly and Goethe saw tolerance as something to bring strength.

Why do so few people seem ready to see?" Roger broke into another smile but then eased his body forward so that people at other tables could not hear. "Repressed freedom of thought and conscience, Arthur, is a crime against life but I do not know why such repression has to be. Centuries before Jesus, issues like judgment and immortality were embraced in the theology of Zoroastrianism but because of its subtleties, it was easy to distort for the ignorant and suffering. A few powerful people were then quick to spin those subtleties, and the Pharisees were among those who did the spinning as did Paul later along with his followers."

Roger was still forward to keep his voice quiet: "Arthur, I agree with Chantelle that one of the worst crimes against life is the concept of original sin. It preaches hate against the foundations of life and turns our God-given sexuality into something impure. The Greek Dionysius believed that for life to reaffirm itself and keep doing so, procreation was the sacred road, and the torment of childbirth was to be re-experienced again and again. Einstein like Dionysus and others, have tried to change the way we see the world but the torment is great for such advocates of change."

I lifted my eyes to meet Roger's. He continued with a knowing smile: "You too, Arthur," and then he leaned back in his chair, more relaxed. "Knox College's handyman is retiring and we need a person not only to maintain the place but also restore the integrity of the 100-year-old building. It needs updates. The pay is modest but the benefits are excellent and we can get you a Canadian employment card if you can help."

Roger's smile widened and his eyes glistened a little. I peered longingly into them and then lowered my head as if unable to take the good news I was hearing. I wanted not to believe in miracles but felt at that moment a miracle was happening, and so before I would let it disappear, I lifted my head back to face the wise, kind man at my table. "In any way I can, thank you, Roger."

Back at the apartment, I started another letter to Chantelle but didn't send it, as if I were afraid of speaking too soon. Instead it was 10 days before I wrote again, and in the enthusiasm of those days after Roger, I sought to incorporate the good news into proof of my change.

Sunday April 12 2009

Easter 2009

Dear Chantelle,

I went today to a United Church of Canada service, to sense whether this left-of-center church is really anti-Semitic. It criticizes Israel but so do I, and I found it not so much anti-Semitic as following a philosophy that, when combined with Canadian winters, induces a sense of need to help those less fortunate. I also found a few Jews in the church body.

"Jesus Christ" had been taken out of the service and replaced with a kind of hope, with Easter presented not as a return of God's son to save us but as an expression of fresh optimism. There was no talk of a virgin birth, no atonement for our sin and no omnipotent god who had to be appeased to avoid wrath.

This church as you know is not a cult but is Canada's biggest Protestant denomination, though I was told by one grumbling grey-haired man that this midtown church was not representative of the United Church as a whole, and that to qualify for being a minister at that parish, one had to be a non-white lesbian.

It was quite the belated Passover.

Love,

Arthur

P.S. I now have a permanent Canadian job as jack-of-all-trades for Knox College.

Tuesday May 26 2009

In the good spring weather at the end of Chantelle's semester, she drove her vintage Volvo north and east from Berkeley through Nevada, Utah, Wyoming and South Dakota to enter Minnesota, on her way to a speaking engagement in Minneapolis. It had been arranged by Hardy for her to speak at a local university on Christian fundamentalism and Chantelle was supposed to be free as agreed to say whatever she chose. But upon arrival at her residence room, she found a few suggestions that Hardy had left. Chantelle rejected the notes out of hand and delivered her lecture as prepared:

"Omar Khayyam was a cross-disciplinary scholar of the late 11th and early 12th century, living in Iran or what was then called Persia, whose empire included Afghanistan, northwest India and much of Egypt, with ties to China. Khayyam's liberal teachings were not unlike those of today's humanists who realize there is no life after death and see the folly in any related ritual. But he raised the ire of a fundamentalist sect called Sufism, and the so-called holy men, who interpreted religion in a restrictive manner, branded Khayyam's teachings as heretical.

"Some see the American fundamentalist beginnings as a 19th-century reaction to perceived attacks on the Puritan bible but long before the American Revolution, there were Puritans in New England and in 1774, Britain's King George III was labeled as an antichrist for granting religious freedom to Catholic French Canadians. The earliest Americans needed a common bond and a herd instinct drove people into fear-filled religions.

"Americans profess, even think they believe, in the separation of church and state but the reality in practice is quite different. Despite the founding fathers being shaped by the Enlightenment, the United States by the mid-19th century had become a Christian nation, second only to historical Israel in believing god had directly intervened in its destiny. During the first American decades before the Civil War, the Methodists of the industrial North burgeoned.

"Abraham Lincoln never joined any church and his early candidacies were opposed by many clergymen when he said, 'If he could save the Union without freeing any slaves, he would do so,' only to change later. After the

311

Civil War, the South recast itself as a righteous, indignant people, and the Southern Baptist Convention began to expand north into the mining country as well as into the west and northwest, with the expansion of railroads and cattle drives. And so by the start of the 20th century, conservative Baptists had pulled ahead of the more centrist Methodists, and during the years 1900 - 1915, a series of booklets called *The Fundamentals* was published, extolling the absolute authority of the Christian bible, along with its every word, and the need for such words to be preached through evangelism.

"After World War I, mainline Protestant numbers began to fall behind those of the fundamentalist-minded denominations, which by then were voicing outrage at the supposed moral decay of the Roaring '20s, with its short skirts, jazz and radio. And despite the unsuccessful trial in the 1920s of a Tennessee teacher who had taught his students Darwin, the fundamentalists managed to get Darwinism banned in schools of eight like-minded states. Religions that are gung-ho at the start tend to be more violent, and it is more usual for believers in one god to be more violently intolerant of other beliefs.

"By the 1930s, the SBC or Southern Baptist Convention had begun a missionary effort in the American West, and World War II then gave a boost to evangelical awareness. By the end of the war, the new American president Harry Truman was a Southern Baptist, and Billy Graham triggered an evangelical revival in 1949 - 50. Then in the 1960s, as baby boomers reached teenagehood, mainline religions began to slump in attendance.

"In the 40 years since the '60s, Northern centrist denominations such as Presbyterian, Congregationalist and Episcopalian have continued to decline, while the Baptists, Pentecostals and related assemblies have increased. In the 1960s and 1970s, there was a six-fold increase in Christian schools, and four-fifths of American TV sets were tuned to fundamentalist preacher Jerry Falwell.

"Compared to an affluent North, Southern Baptists tended to be part of a lower socio-educational background, and they reacted against the free thinking and liberal arts exposure of the 1960s and '70s, particularly as related to the hated North. For the evangelical preacher, scholarship on theology or anything else was a minus, since he had to be seen as a regular guy. Richard Nixon in 1972 tapped into that backlash by appealing to an American 'Silent Majority' and fundamentalist leaders were quick to capitalize on the attendant judgmentalism of a supposed moral majority. Jerry Falwell later met with President Reagan who supported Falwell's mock of 'welfare queens.'

"The fundamentalists are now entrenched in all U.S. states, with half of Americans saying they are born-again Christians versus one-third 20 years ago, though connotations of the term 'born again' are now given greater breadth. Yet notwithstanding any broader interpretation, fundamentalist Baptists who profess biblical inerrancy number 40 million today versus a combined mainline membership of only 15 million.

"Almost three-quarters of Americans say they are absolutely certain of god's existence and over one-quarter take the Christian bible literally, believing it to be historically and scientifically accurate. More than one-third read the Bible or other Holy Scriptures at least once a week, not counting worship services, but nearly half affiliated with a religion seldom or never read other books or visit websites about their own religion. Half of the United States believes the words of god and Jesus divine.

"Perhaps predictably, only half accept any form of evolution, even one guided by God, and only one-quarter of Americans accept Darwin's principle that human beings evolved from other forms of nature and not God. One-third say they have experienced or witnessed a divine healing and believe that all living creatures including human beings have existed since the beginning of time, with almost one-third of the U.S. believing Jesus will soon return to judge the living and the dead. Last year in 2008, the American Museum of Natural History launched an exhibit on Darwin and the show could not find a single corporate sponsor.

"The world's 50 nations with the lowest human development are all deeply religious but the best life expectancy, lowest infant mortality and lowest homicide rates occur in countries like Canada, Japan, Sweden, Norway, Australia, Holland, Belgium and Britain, some of planet earth's most unreligious countries. Those countries also have the highest social welfare and foreign aid, and their CEO salaries average 10 to 20 times that of an average employee, versus 500 or more times in the United States. One-third of all sex education in the U.S. during the recent Bush years has preached only abstinence but the U.S. continues to lead first world countries in venereal disease and teenage pregnancies.

"The American states where fundamentalism thrives are also those with the lowest education and mental health, as well as the highest rates of child poverty and homicide. Additionally, teen pregnancy rates are higher among conservative Christians than among other groups but this fact has become fodder for 'redemption from sin.' Evangelical preachers are required to be sinners, reborn before a specified audience, and once the preachers are found out, everyone else rejoices in the preachers' redemptions.

"Of some 3,400 American teens surveyed, white evangelical Christians were most likely to believe in abstinence from sexual activity, yet were more sexually active than teens from any other religious background, having intercourse for the first time at just 16 on average, while teens who had formal sex education had a 40% delay in sexual debuts. Moreover, half of the studies on the impact of sex education show an increased use of condoms.

"Today in the 21st century, one-third of the U.S. electorate uses Judeo-Christian scripture as a life guidebook for shaping the political scene, and much of the U.S. worldview is grounded in a religious fundamentalism, where a majority believes the world was created in six days and sees the end of the world as imminent, save for a select few. And domestically, at least until Obama, the natural sciences have been almost as threatened as the founding fathers' enlightenment, with American children's test averages on both evolution and science ranking below those of Bolivia and Slovenia.

"Steps on world disease control, pregnancy and cervical cancer protection, and medical research on cells in petri dishes have all been crushed by fundamentalist judgmentalism. Homosexuals are still likened by some fundamentalists to adulterers, alcoholics and prostitutes, and purportedly can be cured of their attitudinal misconceptions. Abstinence has been taught as the main protection against HIV, despite the teaching's dismissal by national medical institutions, and the civil rights of sex workers have remained unaddressed, as well as the need for clean needles by people addicted to intravenous drugs.

"A personal salvation doctrine lets capitalistic power brokers wring their hands, as they watch lower income people turn their thoughts away from economic and social fairness. Evangelicals feel equal before their god, and are accordingly not bothered by some members being filthy rich. Capitalists thus promote the faith.

"Women's rights are also held in check, along with social renewal of any kind, since to many a fundamentalist, the end of the world may come at any moment. When science threatens these beliefs too much, some fundamentalists have resorted to the folly of 'intelligent design,' and there is a creation museum in Kentucky and a Holy Land theme park in Orlando, Florida.

"Fundamentalism increases in times of crisis, and the 9/11 attack was a classic chance for fundamentalist spokespeople to preach the one true faith of the select few. Once they get immersed in a crusade or holy war, the capacity to judge all alternatives is gone, and death-to-the-enemy comes as easily as it does in his bible, where in Chronicles, 120,000 men were killed in one day and 200,000 women and children carried away captive. In another part of Chronicles often taken literally by fundamentalists, 185,000 Assyrians were killed and in Judges, 45,000 Ephraimites were put death because of a minor variation in interpretation.

"Death to the declared enemy comes that easily because the fundamentalist ideology embraces stereotyping where illusions are boxed into neat compartments and set up in advance, in a visible line of fire. There is no need for nuances or even attempting to understand other points of view, since the compartments are boxed and sealed from other germs of thought. American evangelicals, 40% of whom believe that the antichrist is alive on earth and has seized such institutions as the United Nations, were at the forefront of proselytizing in Iraq after the American invasion, and had 30 evangelical missions in Baghdad within a year.

"Historically, before the Americans, Christian cults had also done much to support British imperialism and in an earlier century still, cults had been at it in the Dutch Republic during its economic domination of the world in the age of mercantilism. South African Boers had adopted a frontier mentality, and with the help of the fundamentalist Dutch Reform Church, had analogized themselves with the Jews in escaping from Egypt. Spain too, before the Dutch, had used the 'chosen' concept to support its imperial hubris and consequent capture of world gold.

"An argument can be made that all Western nations since biblical times have believed in their own exceptionalism, a key ingredient of which is religious fervor and related decline in science and reasoning – as the Roman Empire declined in the fourth and fifth centuries, it closed the world library in Alexandria, discarded the works of Aristotle and Ptolemy and endorsed the dismissal of Greek logicians from offices of higher learning. After Rome then closed the schools of philosophy, the classical Greek and Hellenistic heritage of Europe, including the greatest part of Aristotle, was preserved in Baghdad and later transmitted to the Occident via Muslim philosophers. The decline of the Roman Empire, like that of Spain, Holland, Britain and now America was marked by fears of economic and moral decay, an increase in fundamentalism, a decline in science and an expectation of a divine rapture to save the chosen few from an Armageddon."

Chantelle concluded her presentation, but once back in her residence room, and out of a wish to re-settle the independence issue with Terry Hardy, she peered again at his notes:

Christian fundamentalism espouses a thin theology of saving souls and a creed masked under the guise of personal responsibility. Christian fundamentalism is a dualistic mindset, dividing thoughts and acts into good and evil. Its markers are often negative – no dancing, no revealing clothing or sex outside marriage – and fundamentalism grounds itself on literal interpretations of the symbolic and self-contradictory bible.

Here in Minneapolis in 1902, a lecture was given at the bible college by Leon Trotsky and his colleague Emma Goldman. But only 12 years later, World War I killed any honeymoon with the sciences such as Darwinism and confirmed to Fundamentalists many of their premillennial predictions. Ironically, Darwin had not written solely for the Fundy-feared scientist. He was rich from the family profits of the Wedgwood Company, founded by his maternal grandfather, Josiah Wedgewood, who was also Darwin's wife's paternal grandfather; the budding natural scientist had written with his sponsors in mind –

316

Darwin's doctor father was a middleman for mortgages between
aristocrats who needed cash and industrialists with cash to lend.

During World War I, pre-millennialists were thrilled with the British
capturing of Palestine from the Ottoman Turks in 1917. A half-century
later, Jerry Falwell proclaimed that Israel as reborn in 1948 marked the
beginning of the return of christ, and the last days could not have begun
until the Jews lived in the holy land.

Chantelle gave a smile of relief at having refrained from using anything
in Hardy's notes. But still she remained disturbed and wanted again to be
firm with him at their next meeting.

Wednesday May 27 2009

Chantelle left Minneapolis in her old Volvo and made her way east to Lake Superior, before she turned north and headed up its western shore to the Canadian border, to begin the awesome 200-mile arc over the top of the lake. Chantelle then drove southeast to Lake Huron and its Georgian Bay, for its coastline drive to Penetang. It was an all-day drive.

Villagers in the early part of evening caught sight of Chantelle entering Penetang and one woman remarked, "Is this not Camille's daughter who never knew her place?"

She visited her beloved dad and went for a long walk with him, before they said goodbye and gave each other a huge hug. Then she was gone.

Chantelle did not continue south to Toronto but instead ventured northeast for a 400-mile trip to Montreal via Ontario's Algonquin Park. Before she reached the western edge of the park, the sun was setting behind her on the Great Lakes and it was becoming too dark to appreciate the majestic Algonquin and so Chantelle decided to stop at a cabin 10 miles into the park and sleep overnight.

Thursday May 28 2009

The Algonquin Park cabin sat next to a lake that was surrounded by pines, grey rocks and rolling hills, and together with the morning air, felt like something out of heaven. Chantelle would have stayed the day but in deference to the black flies at that time of year departed after a hearty Canadian breakfast of eggs, peameal bacon, toast, juice and tea. It was a couple of hours east to Ottawa and another two to Montreal.

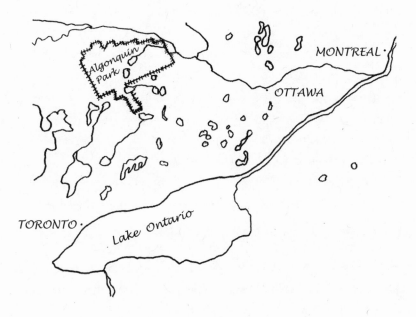

Montreal's McGill University had invited Chantelle to chair a seminar on the changing spirituality in Quebec, and though the school was officially Anglophone, most of the staff spoke French and were surprised to hear her Quebec City accent. The seminar was scheduled for the following day and gave time for Chantelle to take a walk up Mount Royal before she dined with academics from McGill's med school. She then had a couple of hours back at her residence to prepare notes for the seminar and sketch out some introductory remarks:

Before we judge anything, we need to remember that Socrates was
at least as pious as his executioners. It is a duty to shatter myths and

319

slaughter sacred cows, and that practice in Hebrew is called Niputs
Mitosim. *We can be awed by the incomprehensible, but philosophy is
a long-term game and an honest philosopher has to live within a spirit
of* gesinnungsethik *or the adopting of personal convictions as moral
principles to govern all actions.*

*Every religion or ideology, whether it be Christianity, Judaism, Islam,
Constantinian Catholicism, Protestantism or Fundamentalism, develops
from considerable confrontation at the time and place of origin, and a
collective memory then evolves to meet societal demands. Children's early
socialization and collective memory during the first four to six years of life
precedes their introduction to the formal study of history, and 80% of a
person's personality is in place by the age of six.*

*Congratulations to Quebec for having put the study of multi-faiths
into its core curriculum, as did Birmingham, England, some years ago.
The province has acted for the rights of the child, and one hopes the
resulting awareness will broaden understanding.*

*Only 1% of Quebec's baptized Roman Catholics are involved today
in the life of their parishes and only 5% go to mass. But there are now
100 Baptist churches in Quebec versus a very few 50 years ago when
Baptist missionaries were arrested for preaching on the street and one
minister spent a year in jail for preaching a gospel beyond the borders
allowed by the Church of Rome. Yet half of Catholics don't know that
their church teaches that the consecrated bread and wine in Holy
Communion are not merely symbols but actually are the body and
blood of Christ.*

*Protestants have not been pure in their interpretations, either. At
the start of World War I, the Church of England was divided on the
issues of the virgin birth and miracles of Jesus, but rather than open
up a fruitful debate, the Anglican powers resurrected from the dark
ages a papal attitude that god had imposed limits on what knowledge
man might acquire in this world, without sinning. The Church of
England further judged that ordinary man was motivated by both
fear and a comfort for the past, thus too frail to wrestle with truth.
He needed the collect guidance of a Church divinely directed, even*

if following such guidance meant going against his senses and conscience.

Supposed attacks on faith are not necessarily affronts but can expose aberrations. Science, moreover, is not to be equated solely with mechanical efficiency, material growth and the hedonistic worship of such things – it is science that has revealed to us the environmental and sociological damage done in societies that are rich in religion but poor in self-evaluation. The results of science also improve with increased freedom – pioneers like Newton and Darwin did not believe in determinism, and physics now acknowledges a random factor perhaps representative of that freedom. The principle of indeterminacy and of quantum physics in general point to the need to be free to see God and goodness, not for any reward thereafter as we approach death but as part of a process of reaching a heaven in the here and now, as Jesus and Dostoevsky suggested.

A view, however, that knowledge comes only from science or related mathematics seems to be founded on some dogmatic response by people who pretend to be pure scientists. Francis Bacon in the 16th century and Isaac Newton in the 17th enjoyed the rigorous Midrash of spiritual discussion, and Galileo's threat to the prevalent system was only in his healthy curiosity when he resurrected thoughts of astronomy, previously stomped on under Roman dogma for 1,000 years. Descartes too was a questioner and was dedicated to an honest doubt that Tennyson would later posit as a best mark of faith.

Perhaps dogma has endured for so long because it has controlled communications – only atheists and agnostics consistently top those who can correctly answer questions about world religions. Regardless of the reasons that dogma has endured for so long, the severity of any church response varies with both the degree of its dogma and its notion of legitimacy through longevity. Now, however, with the computer and its concomitant third industrial revolution, after the plow 8,000 years ago and steam engine 250 years ago, brute strength has lost its key role in determining will, and people of both sexes and all ages are privy to occupations and related thinking, once forbidden.

Notwithstanding that fact, followers of dogma, rather than welcome new schools of thinking into our discernment, can feel threatened by arguments that morality, altruism and the religious impulse are behavioral adaptations to improve tribal survival. Tribalism and ethnocentrism may be so ingrained into the software of our systems that only frequent exposure to ideological interchange affords us any chance to halt bigotry and other prejudices from entering our hard drives. Much of our conscientiousness may also be inherited, and it is difficult to overcome familial or tribal prejudices. But Gorbachev and Mandela have shown it possible. We also know that the explosive issue of racial differences can be turned into a positive effect if we tap into the multiple intelligences of different ethnic groups, giving us greater contributions within, say, music or the visual arts.

A changing era such as ours can show us the impermanence of most things, but for any minds free to discern, things can be seen with greater clarity than ever before, despite the enormous choices. There is little question that discerning is a tough job but if we keep our tools of investigation well honed, there is a solid chance for spiritual growth through awareness.

Freedom is oxygen, but with that freedom comes risk, and we need to feel free enough to appreciate that if God were to interfere on our behalf, our freedom would cease at that instant. Rather than calling upon a false god to bail us out in times of disaster, perhaps we need first to acknowledge that science is an element like fire or water, amoral in nature but ready to be channeled to meet our needs and at least mitigate disasters."

Friday May 29 2009

The seminar was in the boardroom of McGill's School of Theology and there were 30 or so people present, most of whom were divinity students but some were from other disciplines, while still others were outsiders who had just expressed an interest in attending. The room was warm and un-air conditioned, but the windows were open to the outdoors and they offered a breeze to the people dressed in a ready casualness.

Chantelle walked in at 10:00 a.m. wearing a logo-free and coffee-colored shirt, clam-digger pants and Birkenstock clogs. She greeted the group with a cordial "Good morning," and then sat down at the front, giving the group a wide smile and placing her notes on the table.

Chantelle said the room had to be vacated by noon but other than that, there were no restrictions on what people could say, other than being thoughtful of others. Soon, however, as perhaps is always the case, a handful of attendants came to dominate.

Chantelle began her introduction, speaking without her notes but people kept looking at them out of curiosity. When she finished there was a moment's silence before, from the front, a buxom young woman with long, dark hair and a red tank top threw herself in: "The Vatican is fighting allegations in the West where it can, but to hold onto power, it is shifting its focus to those peoples of the world where awareness is still lowest and fear the highest."

Sitting opposite was a thin young man, with wire-rim spectacles, beige shirt and shorts. He had been listening back in his chair, with arms folded but suddenly he shot forward and pointed out that fundamentalist Protestant churches were using similar strategies, when not keeping themselves in isolation. The young man added that he was doing a paper on the rise of Pentecostalism but said there was a countervailing liberal "Jesus boom" going on in contemporary literature, especially among baby boomers who had reached a stage – with their children out of the nest and death a few decades away – when conjunctive faith or exploratory ventures for meaning often take place.

The tank-topped woman roared back in, "The Vatican struck up a commission to question the ordination of women, with results hinging on an investigation of Christian scriptures. But after the commission had revealed to the pope that there was no biblical evidence for or against the ordination of women as priests, the pope nevertheless declared there was evidence in the scriptures that women could not be so ordained."

No one said anything and the silence almost lent an echo to the woman's alto voice. She continued, "At least the Vatican's ruling on contraception found something in the scriptures – after finding no rationale against it in the New Testament, Rome found a tenuous link in Genesis – it is the duty of a man to go to his brother's wife and raise up seed, thus supporting Augustine's later rule of sex in marriage being only for the purpose of procreation. In the case of women priests, the Vatican could not distort and so it simply lied."

Chantelle sought to referee. "I don't know how much leverage popes have in the system and I feel a bit sorry for the present one. After he recently met with Jewish groups to underscore Catholic teaching on the *Shoah*, he still had to deal with a bishop who remains a Holocaust minimizer. The irony is that this pope is an insightful theologian, who wrote that Christianity is not an intellectual system or collection of dogmas or even a moralism, but rather an encounter or love story that surrounds an event."

Chantelle's comments softened the room and even the tank-topped woman held off. Others began to speak, and in the course of exchanges Chantelle qualified: "Nature can be breathtaking, as evident in Quebec, but nature should not be worshiped. It is far from perfect, and has been working for billions of years to improve itself." Chantelle went on to point out that one of the most compelling evidences in support of evolution is the fact that nature is often not an intelligent design, with whales sometimes producing teeth during fetal development only to be reabsorbed later and with the giraffe having a nerve from the brain to the voice box, but that nerve continuing down the chest and impairing lower arteries. Human beings too, she said, still produce damaging white blood cells under stress, in anticipation of scratching attacks from wild animals.

Perhaps, Chantelle suggested, the only phenomenon approaching perfection is an organism that functions unobstructed within its own environment, since there is evidence to suggest that such an organism will always work for betterment, as part of evolution. If, she hypothesized, God is a catalyst in the process of such progress, then God is involved not only in such betterment but also allows creatures such as buffaloes to run off cliffs and human beings to make mistakes, such as killing for greed or sport, in order to learn from those mistakes.

A trim woman in her early 30s and with her hair done up in a bun, wearing a headscarf and blouse buttoned to the neck, had been sitting at the end. She suddenly leapfrogged onto what Chantelle had said. "Perhaps we need to stop calling on a false god to forgive us, when we are overwhelmed with guilt. Instead, maybe we need to make ourselves accountable from the outset and exercise our consciences to prevent guilt-inducing thoughts, before they occur."

The trim woman then grinned as if happy with herself and continued: "The God we thus need may not be the god we desire and we should not confuse the two. I suggest that we don't need God to do our biddings because God has given us the tools we need."

Chantelle smiled and uttered an audible "Yes," but immediately thereafter the tank-topped woman charged in, as if to get a rile out of the trim woman who was evidently of Orthodox Jewish faith. "Only seven Roman Catholics in the Third Reich refused military service and in the year leading up to World War II, almost one-quarter of the Nazi SS were practicing Catholics."

But Chantelle would not let the comment stand and injected that in early Protestant America, once slavery was established in the early 1600s, government injunctions were created to fit the needs of slavery, with only the Quakers protesting. Chantelle added that a pioneering form of capitalism was established, with rival religions springing up and competing against one another, within the aggressive spirit of free enterprise.

Chantelle pointed out that the separation of church and state was first put forward by a prominent Muslim in the 12th century, and much later in the 18th by the Enlightenment fathers of America and those of the French Revolution, but she had to admit that no country can operate free of ideology and suggested that humanism might be a way to start. The Orthodox Jewish woman suggested that such humanism was already in some theologies, and that the new Quebec curriculum, designed to replace the old Catholicism, did not allow Jewish schools the freedom needed to continue their emphasis on ethics and religious culture. The Jewish woman added that there was a long-standing Quebec subsidy of faith-based schools, to about 60% of their expenses, and the *Hasidim* should not be penalized for having single-sex classes or for trying to ban bathing suits in public parks and force the YMCA to frost its windows. She said that it was unfortunate there was a move afoot to exclude religious instruction from subsidized Quebec daycare centers, in response to stories about Jewish daycares. No one, however, picked up on the fact that the stories included indignation about Muslim daycare centers or that Quebec's "reasonable accommodation" focused on limiting the wearing of Islamic face coverings by users of public services.

The lank divinity student suddenly sighed aloud and re-folded his arms before he leaned back in his chair. "The often Christian-condemned Herod gave popular tax cuts and built the sanctuary of the Jerusalem temple, of which only the Wailing Wall survives. But speaking of Christianity, the United Church of Canada has been condemned for being an apologist for Hamas. And a community of religious Jews north of Montreal has women and even little girls dressed from head to toe in black, including their faces with chador-like veils, and many marry as young as the age of 16. The cult's literature says that Muslim women copied their attire from it."

Chantelle intervened with an empirical point that the veil long preceded Islam and had historically been used in a variety of ways and representations. In our current era during the 1950s, she said that Algerian women wore veils as a symbol of resistance against French colonialism and as a badge of cultural ID. But the divinity student carried on as if resenting Chantelle's slowing the momentum of his attack. "The Jewish group believes that the sight of women may excite men into sinning and the responsibility for sin rests with women. The woman leader of the group was convicted in Israel of severely abusing her mentally retarded son, but when police tried to take the child away, a riot broke out in the community."

The seminar went hush as if to decipher what had been said and the divinity student held onto control. "And in New York, a Hasidic Jewish sect does not even allow members to read the 'impure language' of English. One female member was told that all outsiders hated her and that if she spoke to anyone who was non-Hasidic, she risked getting kidnapped and chopped to pieces. Yet within the sect, the woman was raped with impunity at age 12 and then forced into marriage at age 17 with a virtual stranger. The Jewish woman finally did escape the sect but she is an outcast now, with her family sending her hate mail and advocating that she commit suicide. The sect's rationale is, as always, the Holocaust." The divinity student then tightened his arm-fold and punctuated his iteration with a nod of his head.

Chantelle leapt in to offer a comment that seemed to mollify all present. "Anti-Semitism can be a dangerous force in the left-wing polemic, and I ask again that we keep our comments relevant and within the spirit of thoughtfulness for others." She then carried on with a subject that Chantelle felt would inject some positive energy into the forum. "There is an international project to find the Higgs boson or 'God particle' that physicists theorize gives mass to matter, and their search brings up the questions of faith, universe and existence."

A young man halfway down the table on Chantelle's left had been sitting quietly and doodling on what looked to be computer paper. He was sporting a sandy beard and was of medium build, wearing what looked to be a linen shirt, celery in color. Suddenly, the man perked up at Chantelle's mention of the scientific project, and he heralded the turning point of last September 2008, when the world's largest science experiment had been launched. The Large Hadron Collider, he said, marked a new turn, where the top ranks of physics were no longer dominated by the United States. "Now, with the world's most significant physics installation located on the Swiss-French border and employing 9,000 of the world's top physicists, and with Bush's Washington having canceled or scaled down funding for many of its largest physics initiatives, the best scientific minds are leaving the U.S. and going back to Europe."

The group sat silent in apparent deference to the young man's knowledge and he pressed on: "Unless Obama changes things, many American scientists now feel hampered with having to toe the government line, and Christian fundamentalist pressure against things like stem-cell research has made the U.S. an uncomfortable place to practice large-scale experiments. Budget cuts have also sent signals that the U.S. has its priorities bent."

The young man's words looked to be music to the tank-topped woman's ears and she shot up in her seat. "Just like Rome in decline! Errors and forgeries in the bible's translation from the Greek, such as John's passage on the supposed trinity, went undetected for 1,000 years until printing came along with the Gutenberg Press in 1450. Up to that time, Rome had kept uppermost the Augustinian focus on legitimacy through durability. To that end, Augustine argued that war was justified if done by the command of god, and Augustinian thinking was used to rationalize Christians in 1100 destroying Banu Ammar, the finest library in the Muslim world. Roman Catholicism also survived by embracing pagan values and in the year 1500, Vatican museums were founded with Pagan art from Rome, Greece and Anatolia."

The tank-topped woman then swiveled her face back to the young Jewish woman. "In the 16th century, when Protestants changed Catholic clerical facilities into schools and universities, Jewish communities moved from heretofore Muslim Spain and Portugal into central Europe, and the migrating business communities became giants of a new capitalism."

The tank-topped woman may not have meant any invective against the young Jewish woman but she nonetheless took issue. "Yes and the Protestant Reformation had much to do with the financiers of the German duchies resenting the incessant subsidy to Rome," but the tank-topped woman added fast, perhaps to show she was on the Jewish woman's side, that when one Rabbi Eliezer urged Jews not to support Luther, he turned on the innocent Jews.

Chantelle tried to rescue the talk. "One bright spot did occur in 1600 with Francis Bacon's published *Advancement of Learning*. He envisioned a new age and a return to high Greek thinking, after more than a millennium of what he described as Roman repression."

The word "repression" triggered some indignation in the group and the divinity student charged back into the fray. "Centuries later, Christian missionary expeditions, aimed at gaining more recruits, failed miserably when attempting to penetrate cultures already entrenched in Hinduism, Confucianism, Buddhism or Islam. Christian imperialism succeeded only in backward regions of inchoate culture and paganism, and it was here that Christianity used a twofold strategy – one: evangelize the lowest people and capture them in numbers before moving up to the rulers with the mass's demands; two: aim at the top and get the religion established as policy, then work downward by force."

The divinity student smiled as if presuming the ensuing silence meant passive endorsement. He pressed on. "The *Mahabharata* is an epic story, 15 times the length of the combined Hebrew bible and Christian New Testament, and was composed over 600 years, from 300 BC to 300 AD. Hundreds of stories were drawn to it, and it became a compendium of myth, folklore and social theory, as well as a walking encyclopedia of Hinduism. Like the Bible, the *Mahabharata* grew out of an oral tradition but its greatness lies in its moral complexity – people keep trying to do the right thing and fail until they no longer know what the right thing is."

The divinity student then leaned across the long table. "But unlike the Bible, the *Mahabharata* deconstructs wishful thinking and exposes the inevitable chaos that often surrounds moral life. In particular, *Mahabharata* exposes the horror of war, yet still rationalizes it as part of the inevitable violence of human life." He again nodded his head, and the tank-topped woman was about to wade back in after the provocation, but Chantelle gestured to let the young man continue. "The World-Wide Web was produced in the Swiss-French border by physicists who had been searching for ways to share graphical data with colleagues at other labs. In a decidedly un-American 'we are number one' way. Those scientists who were gathered on the Swiss-French border recognized that research into the nature of the universe was far too big for any one nation to finance, and in the case of the United States, too warped religiously to afford politically."

This time, the tank-topped woman could not be held back. "Fundamentalist leaders of Christianity, Judaism and Islam know that sex is also a politically easy target but that attacks against despotism, corruption or even torture can lead to destruction of those critics' lives. Evangelical churches are thus about entertainment and socialization, with born-agains knowing little of what they profess – Hebrews had been instructed to pray out loud, but Jesus said to do so in silence."

329

With the last jab, the Jewish woman shot up her head but Chantelle said that noon was approaching and concluded with information for further thought – that the American business of selling to Christians was reaching new levels, with Faith Guard insurance having no deductible, if one was driving to and from church. Chantelle added that there were now radio stations, banks, biblical parks, anti-abortion mutual funds, health clubs and even faith-based towns, including a faith theme park in Florida and a Roman Catholic town near the Everglades. There appeared to be a third "awakening" going on, as happened in the U.S. during the periods 1730 - 1760 and 1800 - 1830. Radio was today preaching a demigod, using fear and terror in broadcasting the evils of Islam, with funding from Vegas. Chantelle noted that in Canada, because of regulations on religious broadcasting, such preaching is not heard or seen as much, but that in rural Quebec where Catholics number 90%, some prayers had been restored, as of old, in town meetings, with those local Catholics decrying, "Just try stopping a Jew or Muslim from praying where he wants."

The temperature that afternoon was about 75 F, and Chantelle's old Volvo barreled south through Quebec's Eastern Townships before it carried her into Vermont, past its green mountains and Lake Champlain.

Through her open window, Chantelle could feel the fresh air all around her, and she came to sense that much was good in the world. Her scheduled talk at Harvard was post-weekend and she opted to take the scenic Vermont Route 100 from top to bottom, cruising past pastures, quaint villages and general stores, and finally on to Massachusetts, where Chantelle turned east onto the Mohawk Trail, eventually hitting the Atlantic coast and Cape Cod.

That night, Chantelle stopped at a McGill-recommended B&B near Sandy Neck Beach, and during the daylight hours of the following Saturday, she trekked the eight miles of barrier beach, before bunking down again at the B&B on Saturday night. On Sunday, Chantelle toured by foot the near-by marshland, with its shorebirds and wildlife before she drove in late afternoon to Boston.

Monday June 1 2009

Chantelle was slated to be the morning speaker in a small Harvard classroom and she had been led to believe that a seminar would follow. Chantelle began accordingly:

"No matter how good any populace's intentions, when it hands its moral order over to government, it becomes enslaved to the degree to which that moral order is surrendered, and such dependency happens in democracies as well as fascist states. We in democracies often make our rulers so conspicuously accountable that they govern by mob rule, and the rulers become bad managers, clinging to what is acceptable. We dependents are thus not allowed to go through the necessary self-correcting processes that would be rightly caused by the pain of our own mistakes.

"Take, for example, science. To say science is the cause of hedonism or problems with our planet earth is to condemn fire because it can burn or water because it can drown. It was scientists who pioneered the ecology movement at a time when people were still flocking self-satisfied to their places of worship. And research today remains the critical starting point for any enlightened thinking – the moment we admit that questions of right and wrong, of good and evil, are really questions about well-being, we see that science can contribute to the answering of such questions. We also see that well-being is part of what is experienced and thus depends on a range of things that can influence varying states of the brain. The lab in its many manifestations needs to precede informed thought.

"We still cannot predict the weather but people pretend they can transcend science and comprehend the meaning of the universe. They begin with tautological premises built on untested certainties, and dismiss at the outset all alternatives, in what becomes a metaphysics held together by blindness disguised as faith.

"The notion, for example, of first cause contradicts itself because such a cause would have to be assisted by something else at least in principle and is thus an effect. But when we think of a first cause or for that matter the final end, we are tempted to bring infinity to a standstill and try to take a snapshot in our desire for certitude.

"Dictated beliefs are also a self-contradiction, since thoughts or mystical experiences do not operate in any two persons in the same way, or for that matter, in any one person more than once. Yet for thousands of years, a gestapo has existed to ensure that we receivers of dictated beliefs follow the values put in place by the supposed revelations of others.

"What are we left with, after we have surrendered ourselves to dictatorships, whether democratically elected or not? If we look at say immortality, we unveil a wishful defense against a fear we all have, and the thought of immortality tempts desires, while we ignore the specious support for it. Souls, moreover, are said to override life's tangible end and a person's soul, we are told, is the prime essence ebbing out of all thoughts, good and bad. The brain as we know it dies but people claim the soulful part is immaterial and thus eternal. But we know from Einstein that the mind too is immaterial, as is the body in which it lives, and the thought of a soul being separate has a tinge of magic attached to it and should thus be viewed with suspicion.

"As for the souls of other creatures, where do rulers, to whom we have so surrendered, draw the line? Dogs and cats feel fondness, hurt, loneliness and internal politics. Do they have souls? Pigs are highly intelligent. Do they? How about cockroaches, plants or pieces of stone?

"As for heaven and hell, they may have been expedient concepts to ensure order, but they presuppose not only good and evil but also a god who makes good and bad people, and is thus a cheating chess player, abusing foreknowledge devilishly obtained. If such a god is then presumed omniscient, he is also grossly discriminatory and is as unjust as the sport hunter who inflicts pain on god's presumed unchosen.

"Our ego is a self-centered prince but let us hope our superego is a wise counselor. For when we create a discriminatory and covetous god in the likeness of our own egos, we enslave ourselves to a tyrant and so limit our growth. Perhaps, instead, we should question whether happiness is sustainable if we satisfy only the ego's desires – can we then attain self-approval? If not, we pay a monumental price to an egotistical god.

"Within such enslavement, what is the growth of our consciences? Many in the orthodox or 'right glory' business believe the world is one where we perform services for later reward and is thus a guilt-and-debt universe of 'scratch my back and I'll scratch yours.' In like fashion, many feel that they owe their mothers and fathers an enormous sense of gratitude, with some need for repayment, when they had no say in their being born. Their parents made them, out of some animal instinct or theological dictate, or perhaps a wish to keep the genes going, and it is those parents' responsibility to care for their children, once such procreators have created them.

"Let us look, by way of comparison, at someone who provides some thing or service, without expecting anything in return. The giver can none-theless still feel well about the circumstance, and the giving process need not indebt the recipient who can, if his mind is free, see the giver's inner pleasure and later enjoy a similar feeling, doing a good favor to a third party. Such a process brings out the best in human beings and it permeates a kind of *agapé* love, generating feelings of fulfillment in both givers and receivers.

"In Toronto where I went to school and worked, there are almost 200 dif-ferent ethnic groups and the UN rates Toronto as the most cosmopolitan city in the world. Yet people from a broad swath of cultures often hold doors open for one another or say, "Sorry, that's okay," when they accidentally bump. These people seem in great part to recognize the net benefit from small acts of kindness, and perhaps we need to recall that the German word *danken*, to thank, relates to the word *denken*, to think, and thoughtfulness is one manifestation of mindfulness.

"Let's look at another advocate of altruism, Adam Smith. Capitalists mis-quote Adam Smith and his invisible hand, in much the same way they glean from an equally misunderstood bible, and perhaps it is worth noting that the bible offers counsel on money management, four times for every time that it does on prayer. Smith's *The Wealth of* Nations, published in 1776, was an attack on the mercantilist political economy and it tried to harness the aggression of amoral capitalism to make the best of a reality, as one would with fire or water.

"The book that Smith actually prized most was his work *The Theory of Moral Sentiments* and in it, as later echoed by American Protestant Reinhold Niebuhr, Smith said the original sin lay in man's viewing himself as the moral center of the world. That sin, he said, was made worse when such an individual identified with a group, since the group would not have the individual's superego to act as countercheck and could thus make larger-than-life claims, under the guise of patriotism or purity. Billy Graham preached to racially segregated audiences and Rienhold Niehbuhr was one of the few to see the folly and refuse to meet the evangelist.

"Adam Smith was a moralist who deplored the reality that wealth and greatness were often confused with wisdom and virtue or that contempt was often thrown on poverty and weakness. He appreciated that confusing intelligence with wisdom was dangerous and Smith would most likely see today's Wall Street derivative geniuses as monsters. Smith believed that the wealth of a nation was best measured by the lowest economic rung's access to the necessities and amenities of life – drinking water, healthcare, education and public transit. It thus seems probable that he would have said that, just as a fundamentalist restrictedly defines faith, so does the capitalist confine economics to two variables, goods and services, when economics has eight – goods, services, time and energy, and the quantity and quality of each. The world's original economists – all farmwives in the post-plow era around the time of the originating Hebrew Bible – knew that reality.

"Biology may have made us kind, since people at birth are built with a capacity to grasp the notion that good acts have their own reward. And regardless of how self-centered we are later programmed to be, there are within us principles that direct proactive compassion, above and beyond reactive guilt. Those principles can manifest our interest in the fortune of others and render their happiness necessary to us, such that for Darwinian reasons or simply utility, we receive a gift when we give.

"Those who do not learn of that compensation from love's inherent gratification cannot escape the limits of ego and are doomed to remain unable to see the difference between say, capitalism and economics. They are destined not to live but to survive on the Wall Streets or Vegases of the world, with a crippled consciousness. On the other hand, those who can feel the freedom to see beyond an egotistical god can come to see beyond their own shortcomings and recognize those parts of moral genius through which we all evolve forward."

The seminar time for questions at the end was unexpectedly kept to a minimum, and Chantelle was met by a Professor Khan who had done the arranging. He took her to his office.

Chantelle had her hair in a ponytail and was dressed in a Cape Cod outfit, with denim shirt draped over clam diggers above a pair of sandals. By contrast, the hirsute Professor Khan was in an academic uniform of tweed jacket, knit tie, cord trousers and scuffed shoes. He looked to be about 40 and his manners at that moment were conspicuously correct in not taking a seat before Chantelle sat down. Doctor Khan then dragged around his desk chair and seated himself about five feet away but did get up long enough to fetch her a glass of water.

Chantelle suddenly found herself confronted by politics. "Doctor Fouriere, Tony Blair has noted, as did the former pope, that people inevitably are beings who seek meaning and crave answers. But Freud suggested that people seek not truth but reassurance. And Isaac Newton, who perceived that he was chosen to overcome millennia of error, was still mindful of his flock, his walking a razor's edge between truth and overexposure, while writing 10 million words on theology, alchemy and biblical prophecy."

Chantelle looked not about to betray her being thrown by the professor's opening, and she held upright in her wooden chair, with legs crossed. But Chantelle did try to deflect his opening salvo by taking a drink of water and then taking her time in looking for a coaster, before she set her glass down at the front of the desk. Chantelle then tried to counter with a bit of context. "Professor Khan, for those seeking meaning, why fear relativism? Is relativism a sort of counter-dictatorship that recognizes nothing for certain or is it more like a corollary to human finitude, with truth being correlative with reality?"

The bearded professor gave what looked to be a knowing smile at Chantelle's love of argument. He then lifted his brow and bent forward and down, to cue her into elaborating, and she responded in kind. "Minds, as you know, are meant to wonder and what expands the mind may not so much be thought as thinking."

Khan held silent but folded his hands and remained forward, as if to underscore his listening. Chantelle went on: "Perhaps perspectivism is a better descriptive for gauging reality, where no one vision contains all the truth and any view may hold some truth." Chantelle then added with a shrug, "As for questions that are metaphysical or theological, what is the rush for certainty? Does stability need to come from the hard and fast?"

Doctor Khan then took his turn by first shrugging his shoulders. "Religion is often wrong at least empirically, since it postulates things that science shows us can't happen." He raised his arms and leaned back in his desk chair. "Perhaps we need the art of making up our lives and becoming fools in our own act, but always having a god ready as anesthetist?" and Chantelle fell into the argument. "But is such an act in fact our own? American children spend one-quarter of every day in front of a computer or TV, and that is the equivalent of a work week. Two-thirds of American children have a television in their bedrooms and we both know that children who read less get lower grades. Adolescents, moreover, playing video games have higher blood pressure and more anti-social behavior. Thus of mystical experiences as well, Doctor Khan, are they really our own or are they induced?"

Doctor Khan gave a smile of satisfaction and he looked to provoke again. "But, Doctor Fouriere, religious Americans have a higher morale and live longer. Their social life is more harmonious, secure and efficient." He kept his eyes on Chantelle as if wanting to underscore his sincerity, before he continued: "God is in our genes and must have been stapled into our human genome, since those peoples who develop a spiritual sense have historically thrived and those who do not often die in chaos."

Khan then gave a bigger shrug that was perhaps more like the real he. "So what if religion is a placebo? I did my doctorate in religious studies and specialized in the Renaissance concept that if one gets the symbolism right, it will resonate in the mind, give understanding and cause spiritual change." He then spread his hands far apart. "Rather than worrying about the historical reasons for religion, why not instead have all of us meditate in a temple?"

Chantelle tried an empirical point of reference. "More than 40% of new Canadians have a high degree of religiosity, compared to only 25% of native-born Canadians," but the professor suddenly went red in the face. "And

Muslims are the fastest growing group in Canada! They are only 2% of the current population but are expected to be 8% in 20 years."

Khan re-folded his hands and kept leaning forward in his chair. "And what if new values clash with the principle of equality of men and women? Your Quebec is about to follow France's lead in introducing anti-niqab legislation, requiring Muslim women to remove face coverings in government venues, including schools and hospitals. Yet Montreal's Orthodox Jewish community fears such legislation may mean that they are the next target, since the whole game started when the Orthodox forced a co-ed gym to frost its windows, so the Orthodox wouldn't see females clad for exercise." Khan then pointed his finger. "What's more, Canadian religious courts in the Christian and Jewish faiths had for generations been encouraged to deflect family disputes from the costly and adversarial legal system, but the province of Ontario banned in 2005 religious courts outright, rather than allow an Islamic version known as *sharia* law, the Province using a camouflage of gender equality."

Chantelle gave a look of askance. "Camouflage?" and the professor pressed forward more. "Reported honor killings, genital mutilation and female repression have rocked Canadians' sense of tolerance, and across Europe, multicultural policies have crumbled under suspicion of new religious groups. A litmus test of a mythology, relative to any progressive thinking, is the role of women, and discrimination against women is an obvious fault line not just in mosques but in churches and synagogues. There is more than a sniff of hypocrisy in Canada's celebration of its successes as a multicultural society, since in Canada there are Jewish strictures excluding women from the 10 people allowed to be present, before prayers can begin in many synagogues."

Chantelle squinted at the specific reference to Judaism and she sought to broaden. "I thought, Doctor Khan, you were going to make mention of the Quebec government keeping the crucifix in its parliament," to which he threw up his hands in despair. "Another camouflage" but before Chantelle could again question, he thrust his body back forward. "Canada has the luxury of choosing its immigrants so that no one group predominates, and the country keeps the status quo happy. But what's an identity, other than a label replete with the baggage about how those people, so labeled, should behave? Such notions lead people to think of themselves as American or Canadian, and they make others respond to them accordingly."

Chantelle frowned and came forward to set her eyes level with the professor's. "Doctor Khan, the honor killings and genital mutilations you mentioned…" but he sharply interjected with a face reddened with rage, "Aberrations! A tiny, radical fraction like the Christian Floridian who wants to burn the Qur'an or the Jewish Israeli who massacred 20 Muslims at prayer in a mosque! But much is made of honor killings, genital mutilations or punishment by stoning, as if they were the norm by a barbaric enemy of humanity itself. Where in the news do we hear of the Jewish subjugation of women in Israel, with its back-of-the-bus practices that would not be acceptable to the fabricated Canadian identity?"

Chantelle gave a knowing smile as if she were about to leaven Khan's argument but she first turned to the desk for another drink of water and he seized the silence. "As for the new war videos bashing the Taliban and based on consulting with real American combatants for design, the game developers and the American military have become solid bedfellows. There is a long Judeo-Christian tradition of killing infidels, especially espoused on TV and computer games."

Chantelle fell for the diversion. "Blind receivers seem not to want to know that freedom of thought is as critical to life as is eating and sleeping, and those people so blinded erect tyrannies over themselves and others."

Chantelle had been drawn into her element. "Regardless of orthodoxy, the fundamentalist by definition does not carry out a hermeneutic of suspicion on himself and has no critical awareness of his presumptions. Fundamentalists can thus be fond of the words 'just' and 'must' and seem unable to grasp that God gave us both intellects to doubt and freedom to make or break ourselves, in re-creating what god has wrought. Instead, the fundamentalist often views such freedom as eating of the tree of knowledge and thus an intrusion on god's turf."

Doctor Khan sat back and gave a smile of gratitude. "And given the threat of such an invasion into that tyrannical god's territory, it follows that any perceived attack must be halted by force. The fundamentalist thus sees ecclesiastical dictatorship as a good thing and buys into the Augustinian concept of *libertas*, or living obsequiously under a perceivably good governor. In so doing, the fundamentalist collapses mythology into history and presents a radicalized alternative to progressive thinking. Confucius said that if people are led by political maneuvering and restrained with punishment, they learn to be cunning and shameless."

Then, as if to touch on a Chantelle pet issue, Professor Khan added with head raised to the ceiling, "Television networks have caught on to their audiences, craving for religion-based entertainment, and it is now going mainstream" but Chantelle caught the second temptation and tried this time for a better perspective. "But as you know, Doctor Khan, the heraldic announcements of the Christian Gospel Luke are similar in literary form to reverential 'lives' about pagan leaders during the same period – a hero had to have a heroic birth, and Luke scripted Mary's eyewitness account of the holy spirit involved in Jesus's birth."

The professor sat back as if he had reached the comfort of some common ground. "There is a saddleback church in California, with on-site restaurants, shops and sports facilities, and there is one in Texas with 42,000 members and four services each Sunday. There is another monstrosity in the suburbs outside Chicago, and some of these mega-churches have sanctuaries bigger than shopping malls. All provide clear answers, in addition to a christ who is the route to wealth and happiness. One of the church leaders was actually polled ahead of the pope in being the world's – that is the United States' – most influential Christian."

Chantelle held calm and again tried perspective. "But it was an American, Thomas Paine, who said 200 years ago that his god was his own church. And as for consciousness, it is an American study that today is trying to unravel when life begins in the fetus."

Khan bent his head forward and raised both eyebrows. "Social engineering, Doctor Fouriere?" and she leaned back, putting both hands on the arms of her chair. "I don't know, but I applaud the effort if done with honest inquiry." Chantelle then went on. "When cultural traits spread through a population, they can modify the selection priorities that act on the genes, altering them across the long term. Human beings learn through socialization but they can be tricked by culture to do acts that are contrary to their consciences. Culture plays a staggering role, and we should remember that there is only a 2% genetic difference between human beings and chimpanzees."

Khan again grinned and reworked Chantelle's words. "Cultural dictates, yes! The definition of the word 'Israel' is 'he who fights with god' and there is a Hebrew phrase *ha-kaytz*, meaning 'forcing the end.' Israel is a state among nations and must be held to account, not absolved because of the Holocaust. It occurred because anti-Semitism was rooted and respectable, and writers and politicians were proudly anti-Semitic. All that changed after the Holocaust."

Chantelle suddenly lowered her large dark eyebrows and tightened her hands on the chair arms. "Professor Khan, critics of Israel cán often hurt in effect if not intent," and Khan leaned back, raising his head to the office ceiling. "You Canadians like to feel liberal. Canada's non-profit Aga Khan Foundation supports social development programs in Asia and Africa and wants to make Canada the home of an institute for exhorting pluralist values. Aga Khan, one of the world's greatest promoters of tolerance, selected Canada as home for his Global Centre for Pluralism."

Chantelle looked decidedly unsure at the professor's possible apology and searched for interpretation. "Pluralism may be a step in the right direction for Canada, to replace a self-mocking policy of multiculturalism where new ethnic groups can feel marginalized, like a Tibetan, when all he wanted to be known for was as a filmmaker. And as for us cool-headed Canadians, there is nothing so conservative as a liberal-minded person, and liberal institutions as you appreciate, Doctor Khan, cease being liberal once they attain power. There is a long history of torture in democracies."

The Harvard professor came back fast in an attempt to steer the talk back his way. "Fostering a more complex sense of the past is important for a pluralistic country like Canada to maintain its connection with historical events like the Second World War, while at the same time trying to reflect the current concerns and historical experiences of newer immigrants. In May 1943, German and Italian forces surrendered to the Allies in Tunisia, creating 250,000 prisoners, many of whom were sent to British Ceylon or what is now Sri Lanka, and Lord Louis Mountbatten, the man who had overseen the massacre of your guinea pig Canadians at Dieppe, was put in charge as part of his newly assigned Southeast Asian duties."

Khan then seized upon an earlier tangent about torture and threw out a jab against the Canadian opposition leader, who had been a Harvard professor and had commented on the appropriateness of torture under some circumstances. The professor added, "It is interesting, Doctor Fouriere, that there is no hard evidence that torture can extract information that is otherwise not possible to attain. Torture persuades people to say things that torturers want to hear, even if those things are not true, and the question of true or false gets enmeshed in a delirium. People will say anything when they are getting their nails pulled out or sense they are drowning when undergoing water-boarding. Torture tactics are often aimed less at gleaning the truth than aiding politics, and military leaders use torture to get evidence for their propaganda."

The time was reaching noon and Chantelle declined Doctor Khan's offer to buy her lunch, saying she had a five-hour drive south to Princeton University. Chantelle later arrived at Princeton around suppertime and found a May 5 2009, letter that had bounced from Berkeley to Minnesota to Princeton.

Dear Chantelle,

I had not noticed earlier, during my treks to the Hart House pool, problems with the oaks in Queen's Park. The branches are not reaching up but are wilting down, and the leaves have the paleness of fall. In fact, all across old Toronto, the maples are dying and are being replaced with small trees that don't interfere with wiring. They offer little shade or breeze, and residents are scrambling to buy energy-sucking air conditioners whose noise is too great for the little trees to muffle.

It is already hot across the Great Lakes and looks to remain that way all summer, especially on the ever hotter American side. Despite a hopeful Obama, the groundswell of anger and related hate continues to grow, and there is already talk of stopping the construction of mosques, not only in New York near Ground Zero, but in places as different as Tennessee,

Wisconsin and California. Some opponents are even spinning the Qur'an to claim Islam is against the American constitution.

I was once told that the ability to avoid collective guilt and distinguish between government policy and national identity is a mark of moral sophistication. Understanding history, as you know, Chantelle, helps the kind of critical thinking that not only takes reason and fair-mindedness to its highest level but also embraces intellectual integrity and humility to afford empathy and justice.

As for the new Obama backing stem-cell aid, right-wing groups like Nightlight Christian Adoptions are bringing suits to stop the move, using a federal judge who was appointed by Ronald Reagan. No wonder the old oaks are wilting.

I love you, wherever you are,

Arthur

Tuesday June 2 2009

After a quiet Princeton dinner with welcoming academics on Monday, June 1, Chantelle spent a restful evening at a guest residence, preparing for the following morning's talk:

> A half-century ago during television's *Gunsmoke* era, author John Stein-beck made a slow trip with his dog Charley across America and was appalled by the refuse he saw along the way – American cities with reckless exuberance of production, chemical and metal wastes, even atomic wastes, buried deep in the earth or sunk in the sea.
>
> Now that the United States, still with one-quarter of the world's economy, has triggered a worldwide mess brought about by a combination of U.S. deregulation, tax cuts for the 1% wealthiest and a trillion-dollar Iraq war, we should perhaps recall that the economic problems of the 1970s – stagflation with falling prices and soaring gold – were caused initially by the Vietnam War, along with the American role in the Middle East.
>
> Half a trillion dollars disappeared on Ronald Reagan's watch and equally predictable from the 'enlightened self-interest' of the time was the widening gap between rich and poor. The United States of America now has the widest first-world gap between the wealthy and the poor, as well as the lowest direct taxation, but almost 50 million people have inadequate health care. Since 1975, household income has grown by 60% but the top 1% rung has grown by 275% while the bottom fifth has grown by under 20%. The personal income ratio of CEO-to-worker has gone in forty years from 40-to-1 in 1970 to 500-to-1 today.
>
> North American conservatives don't practice what they preach, declaring lower taxes, smaller government and a balanced budget, but delivering only on smaller taxes. For 20 years, under Ronald Reagan and then the two Bushes, conservatives also enjoyed majorities in Congress and were free to do what they wanted, cranking up defense spending and deficits. Now the Tea Party is singing the same balanced-budget tune with no tax increases, despite a bipartisan panel concluding that tax increases are the only way to go.

It is a monetarist mythology that growth will go on forever, allowing things to be measured only in the short term. Deregulation has also meant a free-for-all, with globalization cranking up the frenzy for things like automobiles, multiple bathrooms, endless clothes and related energy. But monetarist 'efficiency' has ignored depletion, pollution and waste disposal, not to mention the social damage to the have-nots or the emotional health of us all.

The myth of unending plenty is one where everyone will be able to live as have Americans for a long while, if everyone simply thinks like conservative Americans and especially if they convert to right-wing Christianity. They will become consumers of goods and enjoyers of supposed democracy, and while such intoxication lasts, an unconscionable few will get obscenely rich, with many more a little rich as scallywags, but with a huge portion staying locked in poverty.

As this materialistic myth carries on, a smokescreen war on terror will breed more terror and more war, as it may soon do in Iran or in the Arctic, with its fifth of the planet's oil and gas. Neglect of the world's poor and the environment may lead to catastrophes, 100 times the size of Hurricane Katrina but half of America still buys into a few leaders saying that god chooses our rulers. What is most frightening is that perhaps those leaders' god does.

I am a Canadian with American cousins, and I weep at America's religious fundamentalism and its devil-take-the-hindmost lifestyle. The U.S. is the only major western power where the death penalty still exists and Texas alone, under George W. Bush, murdered over 150 American people. Almost 1% of Americans are in jail, the world's highest rate and seven times that of Europe or Canada. Pistols and assault rifles, unthinkable north of the border, are readily for sale in this country.

And oh, how the provincialism prevails. The American media are astonishingly parochial, often resembling a Vaudeville act, and only one in eight U.S. citizens holds a passport.

Despite the founding fathers being products of the Enlightenment, America has become a theocracy, where one-quarter of the population thinks the bible's creation myth is true, while it simultaneously derides religious rules in Islamic countries. The U.S. also professes to be peace-loving *but has been at war for 400 years, that is, two centuries before it became an official country. Many Americans have been duped into opting for a quick-and-easy route in a search for reality, and they go straight to national myths, eating them up like American fast foods.*

If, after some summing up of this process, all we get is the ultimate shopping mall, then the economic crash of the past year may give us time to stop shopping and reflect on the anticlimax of our temporal values. Maybe the Sitz im Leben of evangelists will change and maybe there is hope for cautious optimism. But I feel first that our education needs to start in the sandbox, where toddlers learn to play with one another, slowly and painfully, taking turns using the dump truck.

The changes of our 21st century will surpass those of all recorded history, and multiple new weapons of mass destruction will confront us. How we recognize those weapons and how we see meaning underscore the need for dialogue, within an ever-growing spirit of pluralism.

As a Canadian and your closest friend, I love the United States of America. It has produced Benjamin Franklin, the Marshall Plan, Peanuts's Shultz and now Barack Obama. And it has repeatedly demonstrated an ability to heal itself. Please open your windows again and see what your founding fathers saw 200 years ago. Then, after the long hot summer, take a long walk in the autumn leaves before later Taking a winter walk in the Canadian snow.

A letter came to me, late in the spring.

Tuesday, June 2, 2009
Dear Arthur,

I am on my way to New York to see my Jewish benefactor, head of his organization. I wish you well.

It is a shame about Toronto's trees. The gnarled oak in Queen's Park is still my favorite and I remember your loving a certain gnarled one in Chicago.

I also wanted to help balance your thinking by bringing to your attention another Jewish organization, this one an Israeli medical one

called Save a Child's Heart or SACH, where half of the patients are
Palestinian.

I don't know my itinerary from here on in. I do not think we will link
up again but feel we should stay in touch.

May God bless you, Arthur?

Chantelle

I thought: So – that bastard Hardy is Jewish! Probably Orthodox or something close to it. He has his own agenda for advancing Israel's right wing and is using Chantelle!

I telephoned Pantel that night to let him know that Chantelle was well.

Wednesday June 3 2009

At 6:00 a.m., Chantelle departed for the day her B&B, three blocks northwest of Central Park, and began, with backpack, a long jaunt south to her 8:00 a.m. meeting with Terry Hardy. Her benefactor's office was in an old, low building, 100 yards east of the Hudson River and just up from the Holland Tunnel on the north side of Christopher Street.

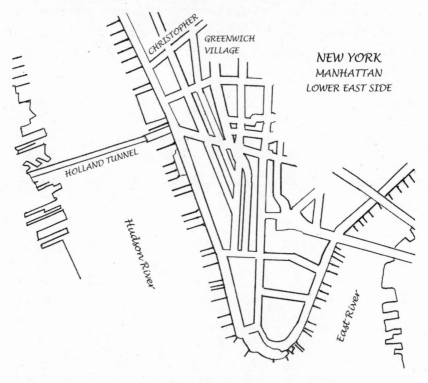

Chantelle got to the building at 10 to 8:00 and in front of the entrance stood two of Hardy's assistants who accompanied her up an old stairwell, four floors to a hallway door. After it was unlocked, the door opened up to a spartan space of wooden floors, long plastic table and six plastic chairs. Beyond the table and next to an unwashed window looking out on the river was a cot with plain wool bedding, tucked up military-style.

The two assistants suddenly disappeared and Chantelle found herself alone behind a closed door. Then another door opened, next to the cot, revealing a tiny washroom from which her benefactor emerged.

Terry Hardy was as remembered, tall and wiry and still dressed in an olive green, with safari shirt, safari jacket and safari slacks atop black army boots. His sandy hair was short as before, looking self-cut, and Hardy's face was pallid, deadly serious and looking like someone who did not get enough sleep or sun. His jacket's two breast pockets were bulging with something hard, making him look armed, and under his right arm was a black leather folder, about two inches thick and open at the top.

Chantelle sensed an agenda and wanted to register a point before her benefactor got a chance to speak. "Mr. Hardy, I am pleased to see you again and do appreciate your support but the notes you left in Minneapolis suggest that we still need to be clear about my ownership over anything I say."

Hardy took several strides forward and stopped to stand at attention, three feet in front of Chantelle. He stretched his lean right arm forward. "Welcome, Chantelle. Please sit down. Would you like a coffee?"

For a moment, Chantelle let the autonomy issue rest. "Thank you, no, just a refill of my water jug, please," and Hardy turned back to the tiny washroom, where he filled her container before returning to the table. Then, he waited for Chantelle to sit down before seating himself at a 90-degree angle to her, such that for Chantelle to face him, she would have her face away from the sun coming in through the unwashed window.

Terry Hardy looked to force a smile and leaned forward on his plastic chair into a prophetic position, with his legs apart at about a 30-degree angle and his hands flat on his knees. "Doctor Fouriere, your words are your own. We are thrilled with what you have chosen so far to say, and those views reflect the overwhelming majority of people we represent.

As you have said, any religion tends to be a combination of intellectual theorizing among the elite and quick fixes among the fearful, and no basis can be found, for example, for the son-of-God *mysteria* regarding Jesus." Hardy then lifted his left palm and feigned to paraphrase her: "His god-son references were Aramaic allegories, long in use in the Middle East, and instead of coming to save us from sin, Jesus came as a guide to help us access our own spiritual understanding."

Chantelle gave a mild smile at Hardy's grasp of her talks, and when he caught the smile, Hardy continued: "Jesus was a christ but so can we be,

349

saving ourselves and experiencing a resurrected life by seeing the god within. You said, Chantelle, that there is in each of us a self of evolutionary energy needed to assess right and wrong, but that individuation is an unpopular process, bound to threaten the established order."

Chantelle's smile was still there. "Some of those words may be yours, Mr. Hardy. I think you once said that the god within us can help us graduate from dependency on handed-down ethics..." and he suddenly slapped his left thigh. "Yes, and in the challenge of facing up to truth, I said perhaps we need first the growing pain of forlornness, with disillusionment coming before wisdom. But..." Hardy raised an index finger. "I also suggested that religious institutions themselves need to undergo such self-assessment."

Chantelle the child specialist leaned forward as if in sync. "As you wrote, Mr. Hardy, children from the outset can be happy if they are given unconditional love and support, and huge spiritual growth can occur before puberty, at which point altruism has its best chance to blossom."

This time, Terry Hardy swept his left arm to the side as if to move past the childhood discussion. "The spiritual graduate will then pursue a life of purpose, with actions determining her behavior but she is bound to come up against social norms," and Chantelle fell into step. "But is work really creative if it meets no social resistance?" and Hardy stretched out both arms to bless what she had said. "And as you have noted, Chantelle, there are bad consequences for people who do not use a society's stories for shaping reality – questioning people often take their thoughts beyond societal boundaries and pit themselves against that culture." Hardy then straightened up and raised his right hand. "Creative thinking, you said, needs a contradiction between an established way and a true need, but if a lie is woven up-front into a system of beliefs fortified by social directives, myths can evolve into dictates."

Chantelle suddenly felt a little less comfortable and eased her smile, shifting a little in her chair. "I did not put it quite that way, Mr. Hardy," but he continued his thrust. "As I have said to you before, Doctor Fouriere, an American Taliban of the Christian right has taken over the United States and 'terrorism' is the governing hate word." Hardy then raised his face to the ceiling. "Victimhood is often a mob trait, especially if the persecuted group is made to feel superior. People within the mob share the same prejudices and those mobs become cults of perversion, with thinking further perverted by intellectual incest." He added with face straight to Chantelle, "It is just such a mentality that endorses the violence of the Old Testament."

Chantelle winced askance and Hardy put his arms forward with palms up in defense. "As you have said, Doctor Fouriere, the sweeping changes that took place within the Jewish community, during the closing centuries of the Old Testament, included identification with a cult and the expectation of a catastrophe, followed by a new order. Evangelical Christian Fundies with their literalist spins are thus, as I have said, the Jewish Likud's best friend."

Chantelle frowned but came forward on her plastic chair as if to make an offering. "As you once said, Mr. Hardy, Christian fundamentalists in their literal spins seem to have no understanding of the progression of ancient Hebraic thinking. Midrash is not necessarily about getting it absolutely right but about committing to a process through which we all progress."

Hardy again looked to the ceiling as if the conversation were being elevated. "Yes and as you have said, integrity mandates that religious views are always falsifiable and that such evaluation will be never-ending, making one's beliefs always tentative and open to new ideas."

Chantelle gave a relaxed smile and sat back in her chair, signaling to Hardy, he surmised, to press on. "As you also declared, Chantelle, to understand the spirit of a people, as expressed in its poetry or customs, one must first understand its religion, and it is a fine line between *Yiddishkeit* or religious Jewish zealotry and fanaticism. The tree-of-knowledge myth was in many Middle Eastern beliefs and the Noah's ark story mirrored an earlier myth in India, but wishes mythicize history."

Hardy then looked to hold the floor as if he had been given more leash. "In the Hebrew beginning, a god of infinite might was created by a few male brokers who got to power first and then manipulated the image of a tyrannical old man on a big hill called a mountain. And while the naming of such a god was officially forbidden, the god's unspoken name was *El-Shaddai* or the old Semitic 'He of the mountain.' Thereafter, to keep us in line and displace any resentment against the powerful men, the power brokers adopted

a forest-fire tactic, uniting us against a common enemy and inducing paranoia among the jealous lessers."

Hardy then gave a broad grin as if in his element. "The chosen god chose
a perfect man, Abraham, to lead a perfect people, and other nations were to
vanish but Israel was to survive – the concocted god would determine all
matters of war and peace, including god's striking those who opposed. Those
acts, the god rationalized, would be done not in hate for others but out of
love for the chosen few, who were better off aligning themselves with that
god so concocted.

"That god paved the way for the cyclical tradition of sin, punishment,
redemption and salvation to retrieve the lost Eden. The god was thus a *demiurgos*, a jealous, covetous, cruel, warmongering tyrant, who spewed out his
word through spokesmen, leading to an obsession with celebrities and the
bible being an action thriller, meant to marvel."

Chantelle was sitting a little stunned, perhaps at how well her benefactor could marshal her words to meet his somewhat evident agenda. He
marched on. "Jewish sage Maimonides, 1,000 years ago, would not openly
state any controversial views, and he was addressing only a select and educated readership, while concealing his views from the masses. As you wrote
in your notes, a contemporary of his, Halevi, was said to voice the deepest
soul-life of each Jew in embodying the ideal of medieval Judaism – to return
to Jerusalem and dwell in safety.

"A thousand years later, the story has not stopped – the Sabras or children of early modern Israel were instilled with a set of Zionist myths teaching them that the Jewish people, though small and oppressed, were destined
to be delivered from their enemies, that is, the rest of the world, by the
promised land of Israel." Hardy then turned a hand palm-up toward Chantelle. "As you have said, Doctor Fouriere, tribalism and ethnocentrism may
be ingrained into the software of our systems."

Chantelle recovered enough from her shock at Hardy's twisting of her
words to interject, "Paraphrasing a person out of context, Mr. Hardy, can be
as dangerous as a Christian fundamentalist abusing the bible for his own
ends. I agree that it is a duty to shatter myths and slaughter sacred cows, and
that practice as you know is called in Hebrew, *Niputs Mitosim*. But in doing

so, Mr. Hardy sir, your focus seems single-minded and could inflame passions." Hardy stayed unmoved and Chantelle straightened up. "As I also noted at an earlier date, anti-Semitism is now again in much of the world's left-wing polemic, and as we know from my stolen notes, anti-Semitism is a passion, not a product of reason, more a fear of the human condition, thus unacceptable in the realm of free opinion."

Hardy nodded in apparent agreement. "So-called racial scientists in the 19th century created fictions of racial superiority" but then he lurched forward to take back the momentum. "As you have said, Chantelle, religious fundamentalism increases in times of crisis, and 9/11 gave a chance to preach the one true faith of the select few. Once those few got immersed in a holy war, any capacity to judge alternatives died, and death to the enemy came easily, because the ideology embraced stereotyping." Hardy then raised an instructing finger. "Among American evangelicals, 40% believe the antichrist has seized the United Nations."

Chantelle was again silenced by Hardy's word-spins and he kept going: "As for the Bush nightmare just finished, you said that any populace that hands its moral order over to governments becomes enslaved to the degree that the moral order is so surrendered, and such a reality is true in democracies as well as fascist states. As for the American media…" but Chantelle jumped in, "Yes, astonishingly parochial, you don't have to misquote me again, Terry, and a war on terror breeds more terror."

Hardy had Chantelle moving to his dance. "And as you have said, America has become a theocracy where one-quarter of the population thinks that the bible's creation myth is true, but at the same time deriding the religious rules of Islamic countries."

Chantelle by then was pale of face. Her concern over ownership of her words was growing ever greater and she sought to rein in her benefactor by reminding him that how each of us interprets meaning underscores the need for dialogue within a spirit of pluralism. But Hardy suddenly apologized, 'if he were misrepresenting Chantelle,' and said he had arranged for her to speak at Columbia University, on the upper west side not far from her B&B. Chantelle said she appreciated his support and looked to be mollified by Hardy's apology.

Friday June 5 2009

"Thank you for such a generous welcome to Columbia this morning and I want to share with you some thoughts on Jesus, as they relate to a theology much in question these days.

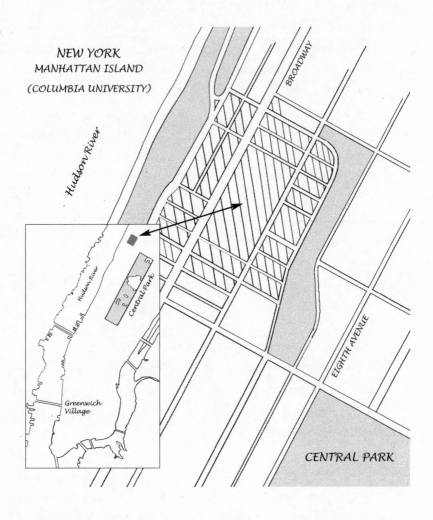

NEW YORK
MANHATTAN ISLAND
(COLUMBIA UNIVERSITY)

Hudson River

BROADWAY

EIGHTH AVENUE

Hudson River

Central Park

Greenwich Village

CENTRAL PARK

"Jesus was born around the Roman calendar year zero and was the biological son of Miriam of Magdalena as well as some man other than her husband, Joseph. She had been betrothed to someone earlier and being betrothed in those days meant a lot more than just being engaged. Moreover,

354

the strict rules of Jerusalem were not necessarily practiced in the tough towns further afield, and the whole region was under Roman occupation.

"Jesus had seven siblings – twin Thomas, James, Judas, Joses, Simon and at least two sisters – and in Jesus's late twenties, he had worked with his cousin John the Baptist, before John was arrested by King Herod. After that, Jesus had embarked on his own movement, having among his 12 apostles two of his brothers, Judas and Simon, and that Jesus Movement was possibly funded by the moneyed women tag-alongs as spearheaded by Miriam of Magdalena.

"Near the age of 30, Jesus conducted a ministry for two years near the Sea of Galilee, wandering up and down this deprived region of Israel, preaching redemption and a reconstruction of Judaism. There were hundreds of other messiahs doing the same thing, roaming that Jewish side of the sea.

"Jesus was evidently influenced by the liberal Jewish thinking of Hillel, who years earlier had said that the Jewish Torah was only part of an ethical code and that the essence of the Torah was in its spirit. Hillel had advocated Judaism's golden rule in saying 'Treat others as one would wish to be treated by them.' Such a philosophy was picked up by Jesus in his saying 'Love your neighbor as yourself.' Jesus may have also been influenced by the pacifist teaching of the era's Essenes.

"In many respects, Jesus was a classic heretic – a reformer who tried to work within the system and was a strict adherent to Judaism, seeing it with enough breadth to allow attacks on the conservatism of priests, lawyers, literalist Pharisees and the establishment Sadducees. It is indicative of how varied Jewish thought was and remains that a contemporary of Jesus, Jewish philosopher Philo of Alexandria, interpreted the Exodus story of early Israelis not as a geographical movement but as an allegorical moment in a soul's ascent to god.

"At times, Jesus the heretic could fall right in line with traditional Pharisaic thinking. Jesus, for example, used parables to teach, not, as taught in Christian schools, because his disciples were too afraid to think outside the box, but because such teaching was a proven method used by Pharisees and other leaders among ancient Hebrews. One purpose of deploying parables was to launch a political rebuke to disengage the audience from a pre-formed position. Parables also impacted in the same way that memorable nursery rhymes do, as taught to toddlers.

"It is also often taught that Jesus made himself unpopular with the ruling Sadducees who wanted to revolt against the Romans along with their taxes, when Jesus said 'Render unto Caesar that which is his.' But other Jews at the time also advocated the same as did Jesus, especially Pharisaic rabbis who preached respect for government authority as an instrument of god and accepted Rome as a political but temporary necessity. Jesus's preaching furthermore to help the 'least of these' in society, was not unique but simply the Pharisaic teaching of his time.

"In the best of Jewish liberal tradition, Jesus saw himself not as lord but as a servant, messiah or representative of the Israelites, to help in their spiritual rejuvenation. Jesus had no kingdom except a spiritual heaven on earth, waiting to be recognized. One simply, Jesus stressed, had to have one's eyes and ears opened, and the 'miracle' of being healed could happen. Jesus emphasized, as had Hillel and as had Jeremiah in the Old Testament, the spirit of Jewish law rather than the letter of it. Again in classic Jewish liberalism, Jesus broke the taboos of the orthodox society, eating with the 'unclean' including women, and teaching people to pray in silence rather than out loud in public piety.

"Jesus made much of the Book of Isaiah, with its denouncing sacrificial offerings made sacred in the earlier bible and in Isaiah's portraying a more mature and caring god. One would also like to think that a loving Jesus would have disagreed with those Old Testament psalms that called for vengeance on god's enemies.

"Like Socrates, Jesus taught by energetic example, writing nothing and codifying little. We do not know to what degree Jesus understood the learning curve, where learning is maximized via participation, but he evidently saw the Socratic need for students to question what was heard or seen, and for learning to be lifelong, with the educational process aiding personal revelation. How much Jesus recognized another educational purpose, identified by Socrates as training for civic engagement, is unclear, but both Socrates and Jesus seemed to appreciate that one cannot change schooling without changing social structure, and that any failure to recognize social problems or engage in verbal conflict on moral issues could hold back the spiritual development critical to both intellectual growth and physical well-being.

"Both Socrates and Jesus also apparently grasped that teaching should be drama and embrace a world of special engagements, not for the purpose of creating a world of awe-striking special effects, but for creating an environment of ambient anticipation. Both understood the need to create a participatory, aesthetic construct that would exude an ethical imperative.

"It follows that Socrates and Jesus would have seen the challenge for any rabbi or teacher as being one of building on an ethic of responsibility for the needs and views of others. Such a superstructure would keep in play a prism of perspectives from which to prioritize paradigms, while keeping at the same time conflicting schools of thinking within a spirit of creative tension and refusing to bring any artificial unity to the whole.

"Like Socrates, Jesus wanted to induce action in the student but understood that the need for such action had to dwell in the student. The student thus had to graduate from his schooling with Jesus, armed with enough discernment to beware of say, scribes who paraded about in long robes, loved salutations in the market places and demanded the best seats in synagogues. Like a good psychiatrist wanting to put himself out of business by healing people, Jesus wanted his learners to move beyond his teaching and carry forward his message.

Jesus did however use ploys such as empathy in an appeal to self-centeredness, saying 'Love others as you would yourself,' rather than putting forward a proactive sympathy for others, where any act of goodness is its own reward. Evidence also suggests that Jesus like his predecessors meant such a neighbor to be only a Jew – Jesus advocated going nowhere among the gentiles and had to be educated into helping a non-Jewish woman who came from the wrong side of the sea.

"Like his theological thinking, Jesus's ethnocentrism was grounded in centuries of chauvinism and the preposterous thought we *Homo sapiens* were given custodianship over all the world's creatures. Jesus could have used a good lesson in Islam – he preached that 'God saw the little sparrow fall, so just imagine how god regards lofty human us,' but Islamic tradition teaches,

'What kind of god would he be if he did not hear the ant or the leaf's prayer?' and that 'There is no animal walking on earth nor any bird flying on its two wings that is not a creature like you.' Followers of Islam do not kill for sport.

"Jews like Jesus, nevertheless, have a long history of being great truth tellers, but people do not necessarily like poop disturbers. Jesus said 'I came not to send peace but the sword' and he was perceived as such a threat after he rode a donkey into Jerusalem – that act being a symbol of peace for some in the ancient world but one of defiance in Hebrew customs – that he got himself killed.

"After Jesus died in 33 AD, his brother James took over leadership of the Jesus Movement, headquartered in Jerusalem, and James was nicknamed *yahkov ha zaddik* or James the Righteous. James was considered a Nazarite or 'Super Jew' like John the Baptist.

"Like Jesus, James practiced a strictly orthodox form of Judaism, and he and the Jesus Movement carried forward Jesus's strict obedience to the Torah. In the Letter of James to the Jewish audience of the churches in Palestine, gentiles were never mentioned, and James's Letter, like the teachings of his brother Jesus, was rooted in classic liberal Jewish thinking. One might try to force-fit James's argument into Greek terms, by saying that the best test of one's faith is through Greek *agapï* love and *sophia* wisdom, by applied works or *katorthômata*, but most of us here at Columbia today know what happens when translators try to force-fit any theology."

Chantelle then paused for a moment and tilted her head sideways, heaving a sigh. "Then along came Paul. While Jesus, James and followers strictly adhered to the Jewish Torah, Paul almost abandoned it, shifting the focus from the message to messenger and morphing the orthopraxy of Jesus into an orthodoxy of belief in a resurrected son of god.

"At the time, there were plenty of Middle East virgin birth traditions from which to develop a story, including Egypt's Osiris and Greece's Dionysius, and if a reader follows the progression of New Testament Gospels onward, one can see how the story became embellished – Mark's first gospel in about the year 70 was a clean read but then along came Matthew in the 80s, John in the 90s and the writers of Luke in the 90s - 120s. Through this succession of gospels, Jesus was more and more set up as above humanity, and the myth became continually reworked in a way not dissimilar to the way King David and the legendary Abraham had flaws later removed in the Jewish Bible to promote Hebraic monotheism.

"Evidence also suggests that the so-called grand meeting in Jerusalem, in about the year 50, between Paul and James, Peter and the Jesus Movement never took place, since Paul makes no mention of it in his own writings. The supposed meeting – to give Paul license to convert the Jewish Diaspora and gentiles outside of ancient Israel, in today's Lebanon, Turkey, Greece and Croatia – may have been concocted in the New Testament's Book of Acts, written after the year 100, or two generations after Paul. And the *Didache*, or Teaching of the Twelve Apostles from the 80s era of Matthew, a teaching that resurfaced in 1883, does not at all relate to Paul's story of Jesus's death and resurrection. The *Didache* talks instead of the mandatory Torah observance and a metaphorical meal of wine and bread. That meal as presented is also well after the lives of Jesus and Paul and is radically different from Paul's Last Supper with its Aramaic *Maranatha* or 'Come Oh Lord.' The Book of Acts may thus have been strategically written to join the Jesus Movement up with Paul's Christ Movement.

"James was killed in 62 AD and eight years later around the year 70, a cousin Simeon took the helm. By the time Simeon was crucified around 100 AD, there were 13 sub-bishops in Jerusalem, all of them Jewish. The followers of the Jesus Movement remained Torah-observant and came to be called the Ebionites, who followed a fully human Jesus and made no big deal of his death or resurrection. These Jewish Christians remained prominent through the second to fourth centuries AD and it took five or six centuries for the movement to disappear.

"Jesus's racism, like the ancient Jewish lists of banned foreign wives and offspring being excluded for seven generations, can perhaps be tempered by the Qur'an. It preaches that God created different races to vie with one another in compassion, and the Qur'an opposes the use of force in all religious matters, recognizing the validity of all rightly guided religions and praising all great religions of the past. The Qur'an says that God does not change people's condition unless they change their inner selves, and it is the duty of any Muslim to create a just and egalitarian society, in which the poor and vulnerable people are respected. Such a society is incumbent on every Muslim and requires a jihad – that is a struggle or effort and not a holy war – to achieve it. Leaders are also expected to live frugally and to give to the poor. Idolatry on the other hand, unlike the relic-worshipping of the Church of Rome, is a cardinal sin – 'They that make them are like unto them.' As for the practice of excommunication, it has never been common in Islam, since nobody but God can read a person's heart.

"Today, fundamentalist Jews and Christians could perhaps be given a good lesson in Islam, whose *umma* or brotherhood contains no racial prejudice. We in the West have much disinformation on Islam, for example on the so-called 72 virgins waiting in heaven for a Muslim martyr, when the actual Arabic is not 72 virgins but white raisins of celestial clarity. We also tend in the West to focus on how downtrodden Muslim women are, when they in fact could legally hold property 1,000 years before women in the West, and some Jewish women still today are not allowed to study the Torah. As for born-again Paul, who fashioned himself to be Jesus's number one fan, Paul said wives were to be subjects to their husbands and to the Lord, and it did not occur to him to condemn slavery.

"A thousand years after Jesus, Jewish leader Maimonides went beyond Jesus's chauvinism and declared spiritual growth and maturity to be possible within a variety of races, creeds and philosophies. It should thus not be surprising that Christian missionaries during the centuries of European colonialism could not convert racially diverse Muslims to Christianity. Interestingly, in 19th-century India, Christian missionaries were challenged to a debate by Buddhist gurus and the Christians tried to throw a dart at the start by asking whether there was one God or many. The Buddhists replied that the question was both blasphemous and absurd – blasphemous because if there was one god, then why not many, and absurd because the question was like asking if there is one light, then why not many. Prophet Muhammad said 'Religion is sincerity' and in direct contrast to the Church of Rome, Islam encourages reason and knowledge, carrying forward much of the free Greek thinking that was brought to the Middle East through cultural Hellenization.

"Not surprising, then, that the Muslim prays without clergy and worships without a Roman military-style hierarchy. Islam furthermore does not buy into the concoction of an original sin and rejects that fabrication as both fatalistic and suggestive of a god who makes mistakes. Instead, Islam reassures us that no one should carry another's burden, and Jesus's dying on the cross for our sins presumes that God could not forgive us in the first place or that we cannot save ourselves by living a life of responsibility. It is also illuminating that Muhammad believed in protecting the environment, women's rights and social justice.

"Unlike Rome or Jerusalem, Islam does not claim exclusiveness for itself, and 200 years after the Roman resolution of the father-son-holy ghost Trinity in the fifth century, Muslims dismissed it, because of their belief in one God. Muslims also understood that they would do a disservice to the Prophet if they were to elevate him to a supernatural being, because the lower his purely human status, the higher was his merit. Ditto, the Muslim no-no on proclaiming people saints. Indeed, Jesus would have been an excellent Islamic prophet – as one of god's chosen servants, as he said he was, not a damned lord, like some landowner up on a hill. Muhammad in the Qur'an says 'I am mortal like you' and there is no virgin mother-of-god myth. Only in the Qur'an has the Christology of the first century's Jewish Christian been preserved unadulterated.

"It is also, dear New York, a Muslim no-no to make speculative profit, for example, on Wall Street or lending with interest, whereas Jews have been allowed from the start to do so to non-Jews. Gambling is also an Islamic no-no and the Qur'an paved the way for the abolition of slavery – the original enslaved non-Muslims became bondsmen with concrete rights and duties, not Judeo-Roman chattels.

"Maybe in a progression of thought, Islam may be considered the logical torch carried forward from Abraham, Moses and Jesus. Both Jesus and Socrates encouraged their pupils to do such further thinking."

That day at Columbia, much of what Chantelle said was discomfiting for some to hear – the applause was academically polite but not above the odd hiss. Beyond the students and staff attending, there were few others present and the lecture received little publicity. Or so Chantelle thought – Terry Hardy saw things differently.

When Chantelle arrived at Hardy's building at 8:00 a.m., she found herself free this time to climb the stairs unaccompanied and at the top, Hardy's apartment door was ajar. When Chantelle eased it open, there was Terry Hardy standing 10 feet away at the table front, dressed again military-style but this time with legs apart, ready for an encounter. "You need to get off this Muslim stuff, Chantelle. This is New York!"

Chantelle tried to respond, saying she had only wanted to highlight some positives for perspective but Hardy shot back, "Doctor Fouriere, you forgot the closet target group. If we have any hope of winning this war against the Christian Bible Belt, we have to undermine its symbiosis with the chosen people. We've got to out-Strauss the Straussians!"

Chantelle was still standing at the front door but then closed it. "Straussians?" and Hardy gestured to suggest she was ignorant of someone she should know. "Leo Strauss was a German Jew who came to the U.S. before the war." Hardy's stance eased a little but Chantelle remained fixed. He elaborated. "Strauss believed that all means were justified to create a country, such as the coming Israel, but that the strategy had to be cautious, secretive, even duplicitous, with truth confined to an elite."

Hardy then looked to remember himself and invited Chantelle to sit down but forgot this time to ask her if she wanted water. He continued, "Leo Strauss believed that the masses would never do the right thing for rational reasons but needed to be motivated by myths and the emotionality of religion. His disciples, many of them Jewish, built links to the Christian right and did similar spadework exploiting American nationalism. That nationalism was recognized by Straussians as a para-religion and was thus a way to motivate people to do great things, rather than trying the vapid route of liberalism."

Hardy finally sat down and leaned back as if to reinforce his words. "Today in Washington, followers of Leo Strauss or Irving Kristol – a New York Jewish journalist from Eastern Europe – may not be aware that they are following the twosome. Strauss was a key influence on American Zionists Paul Wolfowitz and Richard Pearle."

Chantelle looked ill at ease with where the discussion was headed. She asked for a fill of her water jug but Hardy popped back so fast and returned to his former stance that he didn't lose his stride. "Jews in the U.S., since at least the time of Mark Twain, have often hidden their Jewishness or Anglicized their names – while only 2% of the United States is officially Jewish, many Jews resent censuses and after World War II in the Soviet Union and the U.S., did not want known how many of them there were."

Chantelle lowered her dark eyebrows and bent her head forward but chose for the moment to let Hardy continue from his position standing over her. "We've got to be the ones to be the chosen and take the game away from Christian fundamentalists. We have to get the internally oppressed Jews on our side. They fall for the Russian-Jewish game – that it is perception that counts and not reality – but if we expose that game through every medium, we can create a change in awareness, and the oppressed Jews will be moved to act."

This time, a standing Hardy waited for Chantelle's reaction and it did not take long. "Terry, you are more erudite in Jewish history than I am, but I do know enough to appreciate that Jewish opinion can encompass a broad range. Passionate views can be healthy, provided that passion does not lead to an obliteration of objectivity."

But Hardy picked up only on Chantelle's concession of her lesser knowledge and he shouted a platitude, with arms stretched out as if in plea, "The roots of Zionism are grounded in a Hebrew myth of a land promised, briefly won and then lost. That myth also grounds, as you know, much of Christianity, especially among fundamentalists, and it is a terrible template of the imagination. The Jewish Diaspora had been well under way by the eighth century BC, and ancient Palestine was under Jewish rule for only 170 years, with many other regimes occupying the land for much longer than did the Jews!"

Chantelle could see the plea in Hardy's face and she let him carry on. He lowered his voice. "Near the beginning, Abraham got a call from god to leave the homeland and become an exile in search of god's Promised Land. As you said in one of your sermonettes, Chantelle, the Canaanites and Hebrews began their national histories with the same god, but the townsfolk

Canaanites evolved their thoughts to multiple gods with less than universal qualities…"

Chantelle crossed her long legs as if to slow the pace, and took a sip of water. "Terry, I did say something to that effect…" but that start of a response was all the endorsement he needed. Hardy plopped down on his chair and charged on: "With the Hebrews' late god-brand entry into the Middle East, their marketing leaders knew as do you that for their brand to be successful, it would have to have a unique selling proposition or product-related point of difference, like Crest toothpaste." Hardy then took in a slow breath, before he rested his palms on his legs. "Accordingly, the marketers sculpted a god that was in their image but more so, with that god existing only in infinity so that he was the ultimate mean old man on the mountain. The god so projected forbade any image of himself, to magnify his mystery and fuel fantasies among the manipulated majority, but that actual god was close to being the graybeard from Betty Boop cartoons, and the ruling lords who regularly met with marketers perpetuated that status quo. That god almighty was integral to the total show."

Hardy then bent forward into a more supplicant position. "As you have said, Chantelle, the creators of that fantastic god made the fabled Abraham and flock, and the later-named Yahweh was thus avenged against earlier god-brand entries, striking down those who opposed him. Abraham's Curse thus became the label given to the atavistic impulse to send our children to war." Hardy then, perhaps for show, struck his forehead.

Chantelle fell for the supplication and looked to find commonality with her zealous benefactor. "It is sad that violence against a scapegoat is often seen as pivotal to preserving social order in a time of crisis. Freud, in his early discussions with Einstein, praised the safety-valve effect of war, when used this way."

Hardy grinned a winning smile. "Even your Northrop Frye said that a state of war was the norm, with peace only a temporary cessation, making the myth of infinite peace more attractive by its being hard to get."

Chantelle was about to react to that comment on one of her icons but Hardy was suddenly interrupted by the phone ringing from the dingy little bathroom. He adjourned and closed the bathroom door but Hardy spoke loudly as if he were talking long distance on an old phone and Chantelle could not avoid hearing, "Hardy…yeah…preemies…"

Chantelle gave a start at the sound of a word she knew from Women's College Hospital where the word "preemie" meant "premature." But she did not know of the word's other use, meaning "premium" or problem-free newborns. At any rate, Chantelle thought she should not be eavesdropping and chose not to touch the issue when Hardy returned.

Hardy voiced behind the bathroom door, "Close it through Odessa and I'll talk to you later." When he exited the tiny room, he continued as if he had not been interrupted, "We've got money to get you into film, Chantelle," and she frowned. As her benefactor sat down, he elaborated: "Lenin said film was Russia's most important art and Russian Jews launched Hollywood after they had been squeezed out of New York and Chicago but before the Russian Revolution. Even Churchill acknowledged no one could exaggerate the part played by international Jews in the creation of Bolshevism and the Russian Revolution."

Chantelle was looking decidedly uncomfortable but she tried again for common ground. "But I understand Churchill did not know that Lenin's grandfather was Jewish," and Hardy jumped at her. "Maternal! Nikolai Lenin's real name was Vladimir Ilyich Ulyanov, and though his parents followed family custom and baptized him Russian Orthodox, his mother was of Jewish-Swedish descent."

Chantelle sat stunned and Hardy held command. "Her father was Israel Blank, a wealthy landowner with many serfs and part of a greater family that oppressed and exploited workers. Israel Blank converted to Christianity to further his medical career as well as be recognized as nobility and gain self-protection."

Terry Hardy then gave one of his rationalizing shrugs. "Not surprising, given that Russian Jews were key in supporting the tsar against Napoleon, decades earlier. A desperate tsar had looked for support from not only the nobility but also the merchantry, and millions in cash had poured in from the latter. The tsar was led to believe that Moscow would be the New Jerusalem, to receive its own christ and overcome the insolent Goliath identified in Napoleon."

Hardy then gave a studied look at what he must have thought a docile Chantelle and then he leaned back in a slouch. "Jewish merchant houses nonetheless prepared in advance for the invading French, and the Russian quartermasters were also almost all Jewish, well-fed and dandy-dressed, while the regular Russian soldiers were soon to lay starving or dying of typhus. The war got so bad that on the death march of prisoners, people who could not keep up were taken behind and mercy-shot. Indeed, many a soldier was so wretched that he too asked to be taken back and shot.

"Station masters too were Jewish and many a laborer suffered in the inns of Russia as in Yiddish Poland. And while monarchs knew they had always to report to their subjects, at least on the surface, to stay in power, power brokers controlled the communications. Russia won against Napoleon with propaganda, luring him in and inciting hatred from the towns he burned, while Russia used their towns' inhabitants as fodder. Near the war's end, the glory of Russia was promulgated through the controlled media and one leader, Danisove, who had conquered an entire city, punished the Poles but remained benefactor to the Jews while he received deputations, concluding peace, and driving out Napoleon. In a subsequent Russian commission of reform, all articles of legislation and legal work went through one Jewish man named Rosenkampft."

Hardy then went on talking about Lenin and his background, and Chantelle continued to sit stunned, apparently humbled by her benefactor's intimacy with Eastern European history. He said that Lenin in his early adult years was a regional inspector of public schools and later director of elementary schools, which was a very successful career within the imperial Russian public education system. And while tsarist cultural mores defined the Ulyanov family as "ethnically mixed" including Jewish, the family was officially judged of the Russian intelligentsia.

The Ulyanovs, Hardy pressed on, educated their children against the human rights ills of their time and all of the family's children, save a sister who died at 19, became revolutionaries. What motivated Lenin, according to Hardy, was his witnessing at age 17 in 1887, his eldest brother hanged for participating in an assassination attempt against Tsar Alexander III, and his sister arrested and banished to the large but remote Ulyanov family estate.

Hardy added that Lenin went to Kazan University where he studied law and read *Das Kapital* by Karl Marx, and Lenin was subsequently arrested and expelled, because of his involvement in a student riot. The police barred him from other universities and put Lenin under surveillance as the brother of a known terrorist, but then he studied law independently and in a few years was permitted into the University of Saint Petersburg. There in 1892, Lenin was awarded a first class diploma in law and was a distinguished student, not only in Latin and Greek but also German, French and English.

Lenin, said Hardy, came to recognize the value of mass communications technologies for educating Russia's mostly illiterate, heterogeneous populaces, and later as Bolshevik leader in 1919, Lenin recorded eight speeches on gramophone records. During the Khrushchev era of 1953 - 64, seven were published but the suppressed eighth delineated Lenin's opposition to anti-Semitism.

Chantelle folded her hands and lowered her head toward the floor. "It is sad that some Jews have been pressured to renounce their roots and christen themselves, in order to survive in an anti-Semitic environment. Disraeli did the same thing in Britain, decades earlier."

Hardy folded his hands too but lifted the fold towards Chantelle's chest. "Didn't renounce their roots – Disraeli said that race was everything and later Dostoevsky, writing of the Siberian gold mines in the mid-19th century, queried why their treasures were all being left to the Jews. Still, Dostoevsky may not have known of the other half of Jewish gold domination happening in South Africa."

The heretofore obsequious Chantelle then gave a wrinkle of doubt. "My Doctor Fisher, a conservative Jew, enlightened me that Dostoevsky was not so much an anti-Semite as a person limited by his place and time," but Hardy was not about to let the comment stand. "If you hear beleaguered Russians speak today of the unbridled capitalism dominating cities like Moscow and making billionaires out of a crass handful, you will hear them tell you, that is the way it was before the 1917 revolution, with merchants in Moscow, Petersburg, Kiev or Odessa exploiting the weak at every step."

Chantelle for the moment sat silent, perhaps gathering her thoughts, and Hardy kept on. "If you read the July 27, 1918, Russian publication of

Izvestia, you will discover that the first law passed after the Communists seized power in Russia made anti-Semitism punishable by death." He raised again his folded hands at Chantelle's chest. "In your Ontario, Canada, I have a Mennonite friend who escaped religious persecution in Russia after the revolution."

Chantelle's face betrayed puzzlement. "But you just said…" and Hardy thrust back in, "He was a Christian and of German descent to boot."

Chantelle then tried to offset Hardy's hint of an anti-Christian pogrom. "Stalin was a notorious anti-Semite, was he not?" and Hardy rushed forward in his chair. "Stalin rose in the Communist Party under the leadership of Vladimir Ilyich Ulyanov, Lenin, and by 1917 had known Lenin for 12 years. Lenin treated Stalin as a protégé, admired his executive and communications skills, and contrary to Trotskyite propaganda, Stalin did not trick or manipulate Lenin. They had a partnership that Lenin consciously fostered over a long period, and even Stalin's mistress Rosa Kagarovich was Jewish. What's more…" Hardy raised his index finger. "I was told as a teenager that Stalin's head of the infamous *Cheka* or NKVD Secret Police, for the entire 15-year reign of terror from 1938 to 1953, including the years across World War II, was a Jew named Lavrenti Pavlovich Beria."

Hardy then slapped both hands on his legs above the knee. "In the Bolshevik era, Jews constituted less than 4% of the Soviet population but represented over 50% of Communist Party membership. Bolshevik Jews were political commissars in southern Russia, carrying out their tasks with cruelty and zeal, and Soviet citizens suffered horribly, then reacted like prison inmates – too beaten down, isolated and distrustful of their neighbors to speak up.

"Jewish-directed Bolsheviks repeated the slaughter in Estonia, Latvia and Menachem Begin's Lithuania, where 'bourgeois' was the public code word for gentile, while 'vermin' was the private word. A full eighth of the Baltic population was exported to Siberia or executed by the Jewish-run Soviet secret police, and commemorations of World War II in Estonia, Latvia and Lithuania are marked almost as if the countries had fought on the German side, with veterans who had fought the Russians from Nazi SS divisions being heroes to many. The same is true in the Ukraine and Poland."

Hardy paused to look for reaction in Chantelle, but she was still sitting silent. He then went on as if tacitly endorsed. "In 1943, when thousands of Polish army officer bodies were unearthed by occupying German forces in the USSR's Katyn forest, the Soviet Union claimed they had been killed by the Nazis and the Soviet Union persisted in this lie to its dying day. Britain was complicit in this lie for decades, despite in 1943 the head of the British Foreign Office, after confessing turning his head from the reality of Katyn, wondering in an internal memorandum, 'How, if Russian guilt is established, can we expect Poles to live amicably side by side with Russians in the generations to come?'"

Chantelle gave another frown, though this time it looked to be one of disapproval, not doubt. "Mr. Hardy, as a Jew with intricate knowledge of your people's history, you are aware of that wide variance in views and socio-political philosophies among Jewish people. Churchill condemned the international Jews as a second group not loyal to their country," but Hardy leaned more forward and looked straight into Chantelle's eyes, "And what country is 'their' country? In far eastern Russian, near the border with China and more than 5,000 miles from Moscow, there still lies the Jewish autonomous region of Birobidzhan. Founded in 1928 with Yiddish as its official language, Birobidzhan is the result of Lenin's nationality policy, and in the years leading up to World War II, there were 50,000 Jews living there."

Chantelle looked askance and Hardy gave a grin of self-satisfaction. He carried on. "After the reign of Lenin, Stalin did not favor the idea of a Jewish autonomous region and Hitler's Nazis had among their plans resettling the Jews in Madagascar as had the British before 1900, resettling them in Uganda. The Nazis also had in mind Palestine but international Jewry had already made the determination, during World War I, that Britain was their best bet for Palestine, since the British as part of their 1917 Balfour agreement with international Jewry had wrestled Palestine from the Turks. When Israel was later created in 1948, many Jews left their autonomous region of Russia, and Birobidzhan became all but forgotten. Today, there remain only 6,000 Jews."

Chantelle's frown darkened beneath her big black eyebrows and Hardy may have sensed he had gone too far. "But we digressed long ago from the

369

issue of getting you into film. Whether it is in movies, TV or computer video, film is more emotional than rational, and its mix of sight, sound and movement can manipulate the mind like no other."

Chantelle again fell prey to one of her prejudices. "Particularly minds in their most formative years, Mr. Hardy. Members of the international writing society PEN would agree." Hardy pounced on her comment. "Dominance of the mind now revolves around a conflict camouflaged by a fictitious war of civilizations. The West got power, not through higher values or civilization but by being able to conquer economically, militarily and then culturally – the West had the means to mold minds into believing that it represented a higher civilization."

A buoyed-up Hardy then looked down at his black leather folder, and as he pulled out a sheet of notes, Chantelle squinted, uncrossed her legs and raised herself forward in her chair. "Mr. Hardy, you said I would be allowed freedom to express my thoughts, and I must continue to have that autonomy in the future."

Chantelle's benefactor smiled back a look of readiness and handed her a single piece of paper as if it would explain itself. She glanced down at the note and her frown lessened as Chantelle read,

1. ALAN DERSHOWITZ *THE CASE FOR ISRAEL*: PEEL COMMIS-SION 1937; 1882 FIRST WAVE IMMIGRATION
2. TYPHUS SOPER
3. SECRET U.S. TRACE OF INTERNATIONAL BANK TRANSFERS

Chantelle was sitting upright. "These seem broad enough, Terry. I will stop at the New York Central Library to follow up on them," and "Fair" was all he answered. But then Hardy said he had secured for her a key speaking spot in Central Park for the following day. He did not then pause for Chantelle's reaction but stood and excused himself to the bathroom to his phone. As the bathroom door closed, the front door opened and Chantelle was ushered out and down onto the Manhattan street. The time was still not 9:00 a.m.

Sunday June 7 2009

Chantelle spent the rest of that Saturday preparing for the next day's speech, where she would be picked up by the Sunday crowds and maybe the New York press. She appreciated the opportunity and while Chantelle had insisted on autonomy of voice and was disturbed by much of what Hardy had said, she did feel somewhat behooved to be fair to her benefactor.

At 2:00 p.m. on Sunday, Chantelle stood front and center in Central Park's old Naumburg Bandshell, where her 5'10" frame struck a presence with its beige linen skirt and brown nursing shoes. The audience that had been waiting on chairs grew larger as she began speaking:

"Monotheism was perhaps originally suggested by both the image of the sky and the envy of birds that could fly over hills and glance at all there was on the other side. There was also a god often assigned to a dominant house atop an ancient hill, and that god could dole out justice like a tyrant, giving privileges to the masses so they would carry out his wishes. As the first five books of the Hebrew bible came to take form, Jewish laws came to be referenced to an authority god, and Jewish society came to be dominated by rulers with that god's support.

"A belief that the world was made for us human beings sprung out of that covenant and locked us into a narcissistic confusion where elements like the sun became agents of a crime-and-punishment god. Ancient Jews evidently were also less curious than other literary races about the physics of creation, and the interpretation of nature as an object of adoration led to nature coming to be worshiped, not studied and was used to project fears and anxieties.

"The morality thrust upon the ancient Jewish people also had a herd instinct – that only the group's god knew what was good and bad – and there is a tyranny inherent in such a concept – social conformity will always be a priority, and the exodus from Egypt during the last quarter of the second millennium BC, regardless of accuracy, became a solidifying force as the only successful revolt of an enslaved people in antiquity.

"In subsequent Israelite conquests, there was frequent intermarriage, but after the Jewish people returned from captivity in Babylon, their leaders condemned intermarriage, as they had earlier when the Samaritans had been denied their Israelite heritage. It appears that history was continually being cleansed to retain the ancient Jews as god's holy people. It is thus ironic that a foreigner named Ruth became grandmother of the mighty King David.

"A key message of Genesis suggests that obedience to an omniscient god ensures salvation but that god could behave so badly at times that at one point, Moses had to implore the god to take the higher ground. Nonetheless, later biblical writing said that the god ordered the slaughter of every man, woman and child in captured cities, despite custom in the Middle East being to sell conquered women and children into slavery.

"In one passage, the ancient Jews were permitted to slaughter thousands of their Persian enemies in revenge for a pogrom that only might have been, and in another passage, the history of hated Assyria was written from anything but the Assyrian point of view. In yet another, the questionable ethics of Judith were advocated, along with hatred and deception of one's enemies. And while Leviticus was written to administer a sacrificial system not used by Jews after their temple was destroyed in 70 AD, an underlying theme seems to be that if you obey the law, god is pleased, so let's obey more and please more. Deuteronomy, from the Greek word for repetition of the law, can also be punctilious, and Solomon's expressions of wisdom may be doubtful, given his opulent lifestyle. We readers can therefore feel relieved by the time we reach the writings of II Isaiah and its protests against the exclusiveness of a god based on ritual purity.

"Of particular relevance to a Christian belief in Jesus as the Christ, is the Old Testament's Daniel, since Daniel forecasted a messiah or 'child of the people' and adopted a Pharisaic belief in the resurrection of the righteous. The whole sequence of sin-exile-repentance and restoration had become a paradigm of Jewish faith.

"Before the Romans took Jerusalem in 63 BC, the Middle East for several hundred years had been under the cultural influence of Greek Hellenism but one Greek leader in the second century BC resented the Jewish influence in the region and tried to enforce a kind of fundamentalism onto Jewry. The Jews revolted and that revolt came to be celebrated in the uniting festival of Hanukkah, but in the final century BC, Israel wound up in a civil war between the establishment's Sadducees, who were kowtowing to the Romans, and the intellectual Pharisees. A million people were killed.

"For centuries, Jews were subjugated by invading empires, and much Jewish strife came to focus on how much outside culture could be appropriated, without Jewishness as such ceasing to exist. As the strife worsened, a sense of dread came to linger over much of Jewish thought, yet a redeeming element was that Judaic thinking remained far from monolithic and any absolutism was thought to be a sort of pathology.

"One example of varied Jewish thinking was a life after death. The traditional reward to Jews for following the Torah was not eternal life but the land of Israel for their grandchildren and their grandchildren's grandchildren, that is, an eternity. Eternal life was thus a temporal concept. There was no eternal soul in traditional Judaism and the Sadducees in particular did not believe in an afterlife, their subscribing to making the most of the existing one. Some belief in an afterlife did nevertheless work its way into Pharisaic thought during the Jewish martyrdom associated with that second century revolt against Hellenistic fundamentalism.

"Also prominent in Jewish thought was the concept of *tikkun olam*, where people are called upon to work with God in repairing the world, and one such thinker had been the liberal rabbi Hillel, who lived from about 50 BC to 20 AD when Jesus was a youth. We do not know if Jesus spoke Hebrew or Greek, beyond the vernacular Aramaic of the region, but much of the educated thinking of Hillel seems to be in Jesus. Like Hillel, Jesus advocated a new social order within traditional Judaism, along with strict observance of the Torah, and Jesus saw such a world of orthopraxy or right action manifesting itself in a kingdom of God on earth. Belief in that kind of messiah, who would spearhead an eschatological era or a renewed reign of the proverbial King David, was quite compatible with traditional Judaism."

Chantelle carried on for the better part of an hour, but not without the departure of a number of seated people, one or two of whom gave her a restrained "Boo." A couple of reporters noted the friction but at each slight disturbance, Chantelle took a few minutes to allow the noise to dissipate, before she carried on. Perhaps the presence of a New York cop, standing at the side of the seats, kept the gathering subdued.

Terry Hardy was nowhere present but at the end of Chantelle's hour, one of his adjutants whisked her away, before she could talk with any member of the audience or in particular, with the two keen reporters. They then departed as quickly as did Chantelle. Shortly thereafter, she managed to wrestle away from the Hardy adjutant and spent the rest of the afternoon walking in the outdoors of Central Park.

The following morning, Chantelle's hair was done up in a ponytail and she was dressed in blue jeans, boots and a white cotton shirt opening over her jeans when she met Hardy in his Manhattan flat. This time, he was standing at ease when she entered. Hardy nevertheless got in a fast start before Chantelle sat down. "A violent *Aqedah* preserved Judaism. That is the function of sacred violence, and scapegoating is a critical variable in triggering religion, holding societies firm at their foundations. Where Judaism differs is in the extremity of its appeal, with the great majority of Jews duped by both a story of chosenness and victimhood to displace resentment away from the mean old men on the mountains."

Chantelle calmly took a chair beside a standing Hardy and she took her water jug out of her backpack. "May I have a refill, please Terry?" He gave a huff as if cut off, but after a quick return, Chantelle's benefactor adopted a different tack as he sat down. "Your 'In the Beginning' notes, Chantelle, work well against a people whom a Connecticut Jew told me don't like manual labor and were not handy. And Frye, as you know, said Solomon's temple was crafted by non-Jews. Victimhood unites like that forest fire, making a common enemy out of anything, real or perceived."

Hardy folded his arms as if to punctuate what he had said. Chantelle thanked Hardy for the water, took a drink and put her water jug down on the table. She then crossed her long legs. "I don't recall Frye saying anything about victimhood, Mr. Hardy," and he was about to interject that he had not made such a claim but Chantelle didn't let him. "An us-against-the-world philosophy can yes, act like fetal alcohol syndrome and perpetuate itself while fomenting secrecy within any victimized community. And yes, it can be child's play for leaders to manipulate the minds of followers within that community…"

Hardy leapt back in. "Especially if the storytelling elite has, as key members, hyper-smart rabbis, genetically engineered to be more intelligent from the earliest days of their created ghettos. Marrying a rabbi in the ghetto was a ticket to gifted offspring and not surprisingly, Russian Jews and their descendants record some of the highest I.Q. scores in the world."

Hardy then tightened his arm-fold as if to say "So there!" but Chantelle was not to be swayed. "And Jewish people have earned numerous Nobel prizes. Racial breeding, Terry, is not some clandestine plot that is unique to Jews – ancient East Indian morality directors sanctioned as the 'Law of Manu' the breeding of a definite ethnic group and subspecies. The task was to breed no fewer than four types – priest, warrior, trade-farm executive and menial task worker." Hardy would not be daunted. "So-called 'scientific racism' was not confined to the Nazis and had been going on for 1,500 years by Jewish communities in Russia and beyond."

He continued, with arms folded, "With their leaders' manipulation of the I.Q. and those leaders stroking the people with chosenness, along with the inculcation of victimhood, what is not surprising is the zeal with which the Hebrew god-brand strategies were carried out. In the 17th century, there was a fake messiah in the Jewish ghettos of Europe, and many of the duped Jews prepped for a voyage to Palestine. The fraud was exposed but the seed for 19th-century Zionism – the movement to create and nourish a Jewish homeland in Palestine as already set in place in the Middle Ages, was given new nourishment.

"The 19th century would also see one Asher Ginsberg try spearheading a return of Judaism to its irreducible essence, as grounded in Palestine, and Jacob Rosenheim founded an organization called Agudat, whose intent was to symbolize God's rule over Israel and have Agudat be the central organization of the Jewish world. In the final quarter of the 19th century, Theodor Herzl and Chaim Weizmann became key political lobbyists at a number of key Zionist conferences, and at the urging of Herzl and other Zionists, the dream of a Jewish state took formal shape at the World Zionist Organization in 1897."

Hardy looked again for a reaction in Chantelle and her sober face was encouragement enough for him to push on. "Subsequently, a Jewish delegation was sent to Palestine to explore the idea of creating a Jewish state but found that Arabs already lived there. Herzl and delegation then determined that any agreement with those ancient resident Arabs would be impossible and that the goals of Zionism could be achieved, not by negotiations and bargaining but only by military power, with perhaps a wall to keep out the gentile vermin. This philosophy became mainstream Zionism, without openly admitting it."

Chantelle adjusted herself in her little plastic chair, took another sip of water and crossed her legs the other way. "I understand that some of the causes of today's Middle East mess can be traced to Europe's anti-Semitism as manifested in the 19th-century Russian pogroms and France's stripping of the epaulettes off a senior Jewish military officer, Alfred Dreyfus."

Hardy reared his head back and gave a wide grin. "Odessa, the warm-water port on the Black Sea, was an example of a popular, tax-free Jewish city in the 19th century. "

But Hardy did not anticipate Chantelle coming back so fast. "After the pogroms of the 19th and early 20th centuries, Odessa, I understand, justifiably became a nursery for future Zionist leaders. Near the end of the 19th century, Moscow expelled 10,000 Jews, with 50,000 fleeing."

"Many to Palestine," Hardy added "and the marketing leaders in Europe's Jewish community came to brew that the Jewish people could recognize no land other than Palestine for saving them."

Hardy then lifted his head and looked down on Chantelle. "You need not educate me about Odessa, Ms. Fouriere. Those pogroms did not come out of nothing, and thanks in part to Winston Churchill, a band of rabid foxes was ushered into Britain. Churchill's first full-blown political engagement with Russian-Jewish immigrants came at age 27 in 1904, when he recognized in his Manchester Northwest riding, a population that was one-third Jewish, and he switched to the Liberals. During that same period, New York received ocean liners of Jews fleeing Russia, and they repeated what they had earlier been doing with the theater industry in Britain, penetrating American show business and the aligned vocations of news media."

Chantelle then took her turn in folding her arms in defiance. "In defense of Winston Churchill, Mr. Hardy, many people east of the English Channel harbor propaganda against him. Churchill said, I seem to recall, that the Jewish people embodied within the same race the extremes of Christ and antichrist. I would attest to the former, given the classic Jewish ethics embraced in the Christian Bible's Letter of James as written by Jesus's brother. I always carry a paraphrase of it with me."

Chantelle reached down to her backpack and pulled out an exegesis of the Letter of James dated March 20, 1995, when she was 13 years of age, in the middle of her high school years at North Toronto Collegiate.

LETTER OF JAMES

The words "faith" and "learning" are fraught with connotations and have been shaped to meet the expediencies of time, place and power. The Bible's Letter of James deals with the integration of faith and learning, in relation to life's living, and has never been free of controversy.

James deals first with the testing of one's faith, a trial that he believes should be greeted with joy, since the test produces endurance leading to maturity and integrated wholeness. "If one feels lacking in wisdom, one need only ask for it from a generous god and wisdom will be given; provided, however, one asks in faith and honest doubt'"as captioned by the poet Tennyson, 'There lies more faith in honest doubt, believe me, than in half the creeds.'

James emphasizes acts that carry through the word of God, versus an illusory hearing of that word. One should not profess faith if one does nothing to demonstrate it; don't, for example, pride oneself on not being adulterous, if one's behavior contributes to the inner city being ruinous.

The tongue is one of the greatest rudders, and one should never lose mind of its potential for doing good and evil. One should also not compound wrongful acts with hypocrisy or judgment of another, because only God can judge. In trying to be god-like, one loses his freedom.

James emphasizes listening and says being quick to anger betrays ill will. And if one understands the right thing to do in a certain instance and fails to do it, one still commits sin.

Few people should become teachers, for teachers help mold minds and are thus to be held accountable with greater strictness. The one "perfect" law is the "law" of perfect liberty, and one should love others as he would be loved.

Material wealth is cut down to size as are those myopic people who wallow in it. "Gauge a person's worth not on the size of his house, and exercise a hermeneutics of suspicion on anyone who wears his wealth on his sleeve; ask if he acquired such gain through the oppression of others. Those who have exploited people and the land in pursuit of luxuries need to look at the temporality of the booty and know that it remains as evidence against them, causing their ultimate downfall.

Temptation is said to be of one's own making but generous acts are always outflows of God's love. Envy and self-ambition lead to disorders of every kind but wisdom from God is free from hypocrisy and partiality. Those who glean such wisdom from God are eager to help others and are full of mercy and peace.

The sources of conflicts and disputes are cravings within oneself, and a person can commit every conceivable wrongdoing to satisfy those earthly cravings. But in so doing, one separates further from God and becomes a self-exalted creature of pride. The truly exalted are the unassuming who see the illegitimacy of such cravings and the moral undoing in trying to satisfy them. One should thus resist devilish temptations and they will flee; if one draws near to God, He too will draw near.

Above all, do not make insincere oaths. A 'yes' should mean 'yes' and a 'no' a true-to-oneself 'no.' We should sing prayers of thanks and if sick, should exercise our faith and trust, and God will care for us. If we have done wrong and ask in true faith for forgiveness, we will receive it. If we help another out of spiritual sicknesses or back from wrongdoing, we will have helped save that person from a hell on earth."

It is not surprising that the Letter of James continues today to create discomfort for many of us – James says what is often not said and his teachings bear relevance for even the atheist. There is in the Letter arguably not one thought that does not penetrate our consciences and way of life now – James is predicated on principles that are timeless and universal, and the fact that it comes packaged in a Christian message should be of only moot concern. A reading of the Letter of James's from time to time cannot but help realign our inevitably out-of-balance set of values – author James's reminders of our human frailties underscore to us the never-ending need for spiritual growth, in addition to the mental and physical, as part of any educational process.

Hardy had remained still but suddenly arched forward on his plastic chair and raised again his index finger: "And, Doctor Fouriere, the Russian Jews who fled the pogroms of the 1880s and 1890s were not at the nice end of that stick. They were the landlords and Shylocks of Russia, as they had been throughout history in other parts of Europe, Egypt and ancient Ur." Hardy then lowered his finger but did not let up. "And so in Churchill's riding, the so-called liberals of 'The Manchester School' brought international trade networks, colonial exploitation and imperial collaboration."

Then, as if Hardy had again taken his point too far, he slipped back in his chair and lowered a wrinkled forehead to Chantelle. "As Oscar Wilde opined, 'Anybody can make history but only a great man can write it.'" He reminded both of them that the "great man" view of history was shaped by a few old men on the mountain.

Chantelle nodded and offered that the business of writing history is a complicated and difficult process, but Hardy gave another winning grin. "In France by the late 1100s, a great multitude of Jews had been dwelling there for over 1,000 years, when their elders and wise men under the Law of Moses – called *didascali* or teachers – made a resolve to come to Paris. There the Jews grew so rich that they claimed half the city and had Christians in their houses as servants. As you know, Jewish teaching allowed the lending of money to non-Jews, and the French citizens, soldiers and peasants in the suburbs, as well as the various towns and villages, became so indebted that many parted with life possessions, while others were bound under oath in the Parisian houses of Jews, held captives as if in prison.

"Then in the late 1100s, Philip Augustus came to power in France, and he annulled all those loans made by Jews to Christians. He then made moves to drive the Jews out of the lands governed by him but they kept their baronial estates, and certain ecclesiastical vessels had become pledged to the Jews by way of security, when the needs of the churches had been pressing.

"An edict nevertheless went forth from Philip Augustus that the Jews of France should be prepared to leave. Some Jews became Christians to secure their possessions in entirety, along with the assurance of perpetual liberty. Others perceived that the aristocracy had been the usual route for bending the king, and so sought to win with gifts and golden promises, aristocrats and prominent clergy. Philip refused and resolved to spoil the French Jews of their gold, silver and garments, his understanding that the Jews themselves had spoiled the Egyptians in their exodus from Egypt. The Jews in France then sold their movable possessions, and with the proceeds for expenses on their pending journey, departed in 1182."

Chantelle took a long sip of water but otherwise sat silent as if she were attending a lecture. Hardy held upright in his chair. "England repeated the French scenario, a century later. Though a few Jews had come to England from Roman times onwards, the majority had come from France as carpet baggers, with William the Conqueror in 1066.

"Jews were not subject to lords under the new feudal system but reported straight to the king. Christians could not, under usury laws, lend with interest but Jews could lend to non-Jews and the king could tax rich Jews, so that a sybaritic relationship developed. Like in the Rhineland, where the first crusades were financed by Jews eager to fulfill the dream of a return to god's Promised Land.

"A century later, at the coronation of Richard the Lionheart, Jews bore handsome gifts for him but were refused entry by state officials, and many stately Jewish homes were burned. Richard reacted by trying to protect his financial interest in 'his Jews' but in the decades later, King John legislated that every Jewish moneylender had to swear an oath on the Torah that he would register all his bonds. Would that John had been around Wall Street at derivatives time!

"England also attempted to address the issue of slavery in its mines and passed in 1215 a Magna Carta that among other things, attempted to harness Jewish exploitative practices. English Jews were later taxed until many sought to leave the country but then in 1290, orders were sent that all Jews were to quit the realm and they were gone until 1656. Many left for France and Belgium, and Paris was the goal of the wealthiest, despite 100 years earlier, Philip of France having expelled all Jews except those deemed profitable to the French crown.

"This pattern of usury, counter-revolt and expulsion repeated itself again and again throughout Europe, as it had in Egypt before the time of Jesus.

Expulsion from Lithuania in 1500 is one of the reasons that the Russian-Jewish Communists were so vicious in their reign of terror over the Baltic and other states neighboring Russia."

Hardy then took a visibly deep breath before he reared back and spoke again to the ceiling. "Decades after the Russian pogroms of the 1880s and 1890s, the resentment repeated itself in Wales, where coal miners were striking and a few Welshmen reacted against landlords, lenders and mercantilists. Churchill attacked, using the British army to appease not only the Jews in his home riding but also key Jews in Russia and the United States – World War I was looming and Churchill knew as did other British scallywags, that in order to keep the British Empire in existence, it would need the help of world Jewry."

Suddenly, Chantelle sat up as if stung. "Churchill condemned such supposed international Jewry as an influence that was closer to your described end of the stick," but Hardy came back, "And he wrote to Russian Jews advocating Zionism, not Bolshevism."

Hardy crossed his legs and folded his arms. "You in the West know little of Russian history and have been sold fairy tales. Yes, there was a pan-Russian famine in 1921 and another in the Ukraine in 1932 and '33, but hidden for decades was the *Holodomor* or death by hunger caused by the Communist leadership robbing the peasantry of their grain. In the early 1930s, a Jewish *New York Times* reporter covered up that Moscow-directed Ukrainian famine that took millions of lives, yet for his other work in Moscow, he won the Pulitzer Prize in journalism."

Chantelle's blank expression may have betrayed that she was in an area out of her depth, and so for the moment, Hardy carried on. "And Trotsky's so-called *coup d'état* was not an uprising but a reactionary self-defense of his foxy Provisional Government. Churchill later was very upset with the Stalin-Trotsky split – Stalin was trying to remove Trotsky's underlings and Churchill was pointing out that they were all Jewish. Most in your West don't even know that 'Bohemian' in Eastern Europe was code for Jewish."

Chantelle's eyes widened but she held stiff in her chair and Hardy marched on. "Europe's ghetto walls began to fall in the early 1800s and the Jewish people began to be liberated from rabbis, who had nourished the 'chosen few' story and what your anti-Semite Northrop Frye called the great-est surviving contribution that Israel has given the world – that of an omnipotent god who was the only true god in the world. Ancient Egyptians had thought the same way but that tradition did not survive, yet as per Exodus, Jews were to worship none other than the covetous god named Israel. 'You must believe in God' meant that the Jewish people had to believe what its story-makers meant by god, and the very word 'Israel' means one who strives with God."

Hardy then lifted his chest as if in relief. "As you know, Doctor Fouriere, the Hebrew bible began taking shape around 2,500 years ago but many other works of classical learning were lost in the burning of the world's biggest library at Alexandria, as well as later in the Roman Church dark ages. Too bad – the exodus from Egypt, the conquest of a promised land and the monarchies of David and Solomon are mostly fiction, as your Frye no doubt pointed out."

Hardy had again struck one of Chantelle's sacred cows and her face took on a condemning scowl. "Northrop Frye used the word 'myth' as story, Mr. Hardy, and whether those events occurred is no more relevant than the American myth of George Washington's cherry tree," but Hardy would not let up. "Rabbi Wolfe told his Los Angeles congregation that new studies show the Exodus never happened."

Chantelle's scowl turned into an "Oh really?" look, and Hardy kept the advantage. "The myth, moreover, that Abraham between 3500 BC and 2000 BC made a covenant with God and went to ancient Canaan from Mesopotamia or Iraq, is a crock – there is no authentic trace of such a large-scale migration from the east. There may be some evidence of Jewish migra-tion from Canaan to Egypt during the later 500 years between 2000 BC and 1500 BC, because of drought, but as for the myth that Moses led an exodus in the later 400 years between 1550 BC and 1150 BC or of Joshua conquer-ing the promised land, the only mention of Israelites in independent ancient records says that at 1200 BC, the followers of that god Israel were already in Canaan."

Hardy again looked up to the ceiling and gave a grin of smugness. "There is also no trace of David or Solomon during the 250 years between 1150 BC and 900 BC. And as for the Hebrew population, it appeared to be more in the north, with Jerusalem being only a village, during the 300 years from 900 BC to 586 BC. Independent records talk of the fall of Israel in 722 BC and Judah in 586 BC."

Chantelle sat the berated student and Hardy expanded. "There appear two strands of Hebrew mythology running from Genesis – one had an *Elohim* or Jewish god who favored Northern Israel and another strand talked of a Jewish god *Yahweh* who favored southern Judah. In another inaccuracy as you know, Chantelle, Genesis has a man named Jacob setting up his son as king, but that passage was written later in perhaps the seventh century BC, as evidenced in its anachronisms to camel-caravans not used before then."

Hardy sat back and waved his hand in a prophetic gesture. "The whole Jewish biblical history, as Hebraic minimalist scholars now admit, was crafted by the southern, religious elite to bolster its claim to rule over all the children of Israel, after the northern realm was wiped off the map by the Assyrian Empire in 722 BC."

Hardy then took a pause for his wisdom to digest and it was Chantelle who took in a big breath. "Let us assume as a premise, Mr. Hardy, that the history of the Hebrew Bible is suspect, thus rendering its Christian counterpoint the same. The Judeo-Christian god may have been made first in ruling man's image but that god matures across the Hebrew Bible, and Christian scholars such as the second century's Origen noted that the reader has to die to the literal, in order to rise to the spiritual sense of scripture. Modern 19th-century Britain's John Wesley echoed that view, and both scholars were able to see beyond the impossible infallibility of biblical writings, viewing them as collective witnesses to God's word, with some writings refuting other parts in the same bible."

Hardy lurched almost out of his chair at Chantelle and he roared back, "Origen! Isn't he the dude who had himself castrated, and isn't Wesley the Englishman whose phony faith was exposed when crossing the Atlantic and he was frightened by a storm? Wesley also later messed around with someone's wife in the U.S. South, I understand, and had to get back to England in a hurry, so that he could continue his demagoguery in the Midlands."

Chantelle suddenly looked more comfortable, as if in her element. "If I also recall correctly, Mr. Hardy, Jewish scholar Martin Berman recently rendered a message not dissimilar to Origen and Wesley, suggesting that we need to approach the Hebrew Bible in good faith and with a freely discerning mind to glean the principles from the mythological stories," but Terry Hardy raised the back of his right hand and wiggled his middle and index fingers back and forth in the opposite directions. Chantelle shook her head. "Mr. Hardy?"

He grinned and folded again his arms. "I'm surprised that a Canuck like you does not recognize Canadian economist John Kenneth Galbraith's imitation of an ant trying to cut away a roadblock of horse manure in its path. The ant works its two claws into the impediment, cutting away the horseshit."

Chantelle kept calm and accepted the slap, before Hardy again lowered his eyes to hers. "You and I established in one of our earlier meetings that Jewish power brokers and their rabbis resented your Greek Hellenism" and Chantelle fell for the taunt. "Many of the better-educated Jews found Greek culture attractive, with its secularism, humanistic spirit and intellectual freedom. And yes, some Jews did leave the synagogue for the wholeness of an integrated life in spirit, mind and body."

Chantelle's benefactor then came forward. "Those Jews who were attracted to the Greek academies came to be banished by the rabbis from Jewish centers of learning. And as for the Greek gymnasium, rabbis dictated that the naked body was an insult to their *Yahweh*. They succeeded in perpetuating peasant thinking but things got out of hand for them with the Hebrew Book of Wisdom or *Sophia* gleaned from the Greek-and-Aramaic-speaking Jews in Egypt. By 200 BC, there was no reconciliation between the intellectual Greeks and moralistic Jews, and key rabbis fomented the Maccabean revolt against the enlightenment of your Greek Hellenism."

Chantelle stayed silent and Hardy smelled victory. "Jewish fundamentalists at the time of that Maccabean revolt had linked themselves with Greece's enemy, the Romans, and shortly thereafter in 80 BC, leading rabbis established a ghetto in the city of Rome before Rome conquered Jerusalem. But given the earlier attraction for educated Jews to your holistic

Greek life, the rabbis in Rome stipulated that the ghetto had to be walled to insulate their flock from any *goyim* ideas, and that ghetto flourished for 1,900 years until 1880."

Chantelle finally came forward but again inadvertently fueled Hardy's argument. "Educated people in Rome as you know, Mr. Hardy, spoke and thought in Greek, as they did in Roman culture," and Hardy waltzed back in, "But who did the financial backing, Ms. backed-by-me Chantelle Four-iere? Think of New York, Hollywood or the Bible Belt today."

Chantelle winced, crossed her legs and pointed at Hardy. "Think of Oxford! The ancient Greeks, Egyptians and Chinese had games, and the British resurrected them." He then threw back a sop: "Fair ball. Wall Street reduced sports to spectacles, like your Canadian hockey," and Chantelle fell into step. "The Romans degenerated the ancient games into spectacles, Mr. Hardy, without the help of your so-called New Yorkers."

Hardy had Chantelle engaged and he put the palm of one of his hands atop the other. "As you have preached, Chantelle, a generation or more after Jesus died, Jewish Christianity, or the Jesus Movement, fared well and only started a long decline over the next centuries as Peter, James, Andrew and the circumcised Christians of Jerusalem died off. As for Judaism, after the Temple was toppled by the Romans in 70 AD, the rabbis took over as the voice of authority and they cemented that position in 135 when the Romans again angrily reacted to the Israelites."

Chantelle again gave a frown but held quiet in order to hear Hardy's perspective, before offering any counter. "The Christ Movement was another story. In the generations after Jesus's death, rabbis knew that if Paul's Christ-as-God myth were seen as true, then Judaism as taught by the rabbis would be false; moreover, if Paul's myth caught on among the chosen few, Judaism would perish. Thus the rabbinical rulers, who had witnessed Jewish Christianity taking structure in Jerusalem, resolved that they would have none of this Christ stuff, and so in the 35 years from 80 - 115 AD, brewed the twelve Benedictions against heretics, meaning Christians. Thus the final schism between Judaism and Christianity started but after the rabbinical takeover in 135 AD, Jewish Christianity was doomed to melt into obscurity.

"From 135 onward, with Judaism being under the direction of the 'teacher's chair' rabbinate, any evangelizing among non-Jews was halted and Judaism was destined to remain the intransigent religion of the chosen few. During the fourth century, rabbis met to discuss the Torah and its later commentaries, as well as uncover laws to govern all subsequent Judaism.

"For 1,500 - 1,800 years after 135 AD, rabbis also maintained that web of ghettos strung across key areas of Europe, together with a labyrinth of inter- and intra-connected communications networks, and those ghettos became greenhouses for bigotry against the non-believers outside those walls. As the rabbis had done in Rome before the birth of Jesus, they continued to demand segregation, and ghettoization was a rabbinical condition for Jews settling in a European town. Rabbis also tabooed musical instruments and when a millennium later, many Venetian Jews became emancipated by astronomy and math, some rabbis wanted to make the ghetto walls even higher."

Hardy was smiling in his apparent element. "Yiddish was adapted from an early German, with smidges of Eastern Europe later, while Hebrew was used to preach the Talmudic philosophy, and Yiddish became an underground *lingua franca* as a weapon against the perceived persecution in exile. Yiddish was thus designed to lock the Jewish people into the ancient faith and be at odds with the whole culture around it. Even greetings were expressed in the contrary – a 'How are you doing?' could trigger a 'This should happen to my enemy' response of gloom and complaint, and complaining became the order of the day, in keeping with the Torah course of history. As late as the 20th century, when many Americans accused Jews of kidnapping the child of Charles Lindbergh – first solo pilot across the Atlantic – because of his being a Nazi sympathizer, the Three Stooges did a spoof of the accusation in Yiddish."

Chantelle looked to have listened enough and she leaned forward with forehead right at Hardy. "Yiddish was also a source of a literature unequalled in its mix of humor, tragedy, despair and hope, consistent with the same Jewish tradition. When the father of Yiddish literature Sholem Aleichem – that is 'Peace be with you' or 'Hello, how are you, so what's new?' – met with

Mark Twain, legend has it that Mark Twain said 'Let me introduce myself, I'm the American Sholem Aleichem.'"

Terry Hardy looked to like having Chantelle back in the discussion and he trod on, "Within the parochial ghetto life, understood by everyone as mandatory, was the nationalistic cry 'Hear, oh Israel' before bed and at sunrise," but Chantelle suddenly brought Hardy up short. "Those ghettos were also greenhouses for creativity and within them, the principles of Judaism led to fundamentals about how people could prosper, while living within a close unit of family life and extended community. We know today of gentiles who emulate such a structure, in a small Pennsylvania town that was transported from Italy, and led to a life where every citizen was cared for by the community and where there were no heart attacks from stress."

Hardy went back in his chair, perhaps to give Chantelle some leash and she continued: "True, in the Jewish ghettos there was religious conservatism as rationalized for community survival, but there was also mercantilist innovation and in the early middle ages, Jews could compute exchange rates, write letters and get them delivered via a wide network. Popes and princes used and protected Jews, and those 12th-century English Kings whom you mentioned did well out of rich Jewish traders before England expelled the Jews. Many fled as you know, beyond France and Belgium to Spain, where they fared well for hundreds of years. Arab conquests nourished Jewish administrative intelligentsia, who prospered in Islamic territories and especially in Spain."

Hardy looked unconcerned with Chantelle's counter and he tried to undercut it. "The symbiotic relationship was kept between the Jews and the *goyim*, and rabbis had already recognized the power of medicine, law and mercantilism, with their also knowing that gold carried the power to command. Prior to our 15th century, there were no ambassadors resident in other countries, and much of what we call 'history' is from the Jewish-composed letters to which you referred. Only in the 19th century did historians, starting in Germany, create the discipline of 'scientific history' based on documents relevant to the time being examined."

Chantelle interjected with a brightened face, "And now we have the Internet's WikiLeaks" but Hardy pounced again. "The WikiLeaks all advance the American-Israeli agenda. We don't need WikiLeaks to tell us that Libya's Gadhafi liked a voluptuous Ukrainian nurse. The most comprehensive leaks are about Iran and its supposed threat to both Israel and so-called moderate Arab states."

Hardy was by then afire. "The Saudi King Abdullah wants Iran's head and has agreed with the U.S. to promise China a guaranteed source of energy if Beijing joins in pressuring Iran. Another leak talks of America's inability to remove enriched uranium from a Pakistani research sector and another that a bombing of Iran will not save the world but that a million ground troops will be needed, as in World Wars I and II. And of course, there is also talk of forcing the Israeli-hated Obama to resign."

Hardy then heaved his chest and Chantelle opted to let him vent. "The *New York Times* is said to be there to protect us, with its deciding which leaks to publish, and the rest of the Western press is following like sheep. All fall for the scam that the WikiLeaks leader is disappointed, because the leaks have not revealed that both the U.S. and the West are driven by a centrally controlled conspiracy – indeed the Western press says the leaks reveal that the network of diplomatic cables supposedly show that the actions of senior U.S. people are not driven by anything secret at all! The sham has worked. The Western press is adding that a world without secrets is a child's perception of a good place to be and that cabinets need to deliberate, diplomats need to talk to one another and order is preferred over chaos. The supposed chilling effect of WikiLeaks has made fear of exposure much worse. How convenient for Israel, in killing talks with Palestinians, to keep the settlement building going!"

Hardy again raised his right finger. "But WikiLeaks does not acknowledge what 'moderate' Arab leaders dare not say in public about Iran – that they do not consider it a threat. Only 10% do, while 80% see Israel as the main threat, albeit 60% still do not want Iran to have nuclear weapons as a counterweight to American and Israeli hegemony in the Middle East."

Hardy's roll was carrying him away. "As for the Jewish 'invention' of gold thousands of years ago, little of the gold that Spanish imperialists ravaged from the southern Americas trickled down into Spain's economy, and Portugal's gold-rich Jews similarly dominated its colonies. The newfound gold whipped up an inflation not seen again until the economic exploitation of Germany after World War I."

Chantelle tried to steer Hardy back to an earlier discussion. "The ghettos had tight sanitary laws, and progressive Jewish medicine led to the ghettos' protection against European plagues," but Hardy again lurched forward, "And Jews in their ghettos were shielded from the Black Death that killed one-third of Christendom. It was Europeans' first exposure to the bacteria, and in the 14th century, Lake Geneva Jews admitted that the Black Death had been created by John of Savoy, who had been given, by rabbis, poison for the wells of Venice and other points of travel."

Chantelle's eyebrows lifted high and she jabbed her finger straight at her benefactor. "Confessed under torture, Mr. Hardy, and it is my understanding that the Bubonic Plague was spread by rats and fleas," but Hardy held forward. "Yes, spread, not created, like typhus via lice, later. A few rabbis, along with their medicine men, legalists, lenders and traders, nourished a system with no attachment to the downfall of outside society. Instead, they capitalized upon it before blaming the society, until the society blamed itself. I have met a German teacher who was born at the end of World War II, and he broods on the horrors that Nazi Germany brought upon the world. He reads no Nietzsche, hears no Wagner but sits weighed down by an oppressive guilt."

Chantelle had a sip of water and cleared her throat before she came back to her benefactor in a calm voice. "Perhaps it is not odd for a Jew to feel as do you, Mr. Hardy. Marx was the product of a rabbinical line but was baptized at age six; as you know, baptism was seen as a ticket to acceptability outside the ghetto walls. It is tragic that people like Marx and Mendelssohn felt the need to reject their faith before, in Mendelssohn's case, becoming a composer of Christian music, or Mahler in like fashion, becoming head of the Vienna opera."

Hardy raised back his pointed finger. "Renounced Judaism for show, Doctor Fouriere, and Marx claimed that Jews embodied everything bad in capitalist modernity."

Chantelle by then was more composed in her chair, perhaps feeling on familiar ground. "Marx was shocked, when visiting France in the 1880s, to find that people were actually implementing his theories…" but Hardy carried on as if she had not intervened. "Renounced as do and have done some rabbis against some Jews, throughout history," and then he pressed forward again. "Let us not forget that other rabbis participated in the legendary Jewish-Christian disputations in Spain during the 13th and 14th centuries." Hardy then raised that pointer-finger of his to the ceiling. "There is no evidence that rabbis inside the walls worked at all for interfaith sharing. They saw the dialogue as a chance for a joust where everything was fair. Your Northrop Frye talked of an ostensible sharing of ideas in the 12th century by a priest, rabbi and Muslim leader, and when they met for discussion, the priest and Muslim had one or two pages of notes, but the rabbi had 300."

Chantelle gave again a shrug and thrust forward her lower lip. "Homework, responsibly done," but Hardy's finger came down at her. "But to what end? Certainly not for a meshing of ideas and attempted reconciliation, but instead a Leo Durocher contest to win. The rabbi badgered the priest and Muslim, insisting that the rabbi was right, and his opponents were judged not only wrong but unworthy, having not been chosen to be a light to the world."

Chantelle bent her shoulders inward inadvertently and Hardy saw the defensiveness. "And with respect to your Jewish ethics, Ms. Fouriere, universal rights inside the ghetto walls were seen as quixotic justification for Christian indignation against merchants like in Venice."

Hardy then took his finger back upward. "So-called anti-Jewish atrocities such as those in 17th-century Poland were reactions against corrupt rabbis who colluded with the governorship in opposing those reactions. Those rabbis were operating under the guise of *shtadlanut* or political dialogue to safeguard the welfare of Jewish communities. But what was camouflaged was a license to bolster, via money men, rabbinical power for enforcing the authority, over the Jewish people, of Torah learning. The Jewish leaders of Russia had been up to the same tricks, and the *Habad Hasidim* based in Russia was ruled by a hereditary dynasty."

Chantelle finally rebounded. "World history, Mr. Hardy, may revolve around the legitimate struggle of the Jewish people to make a home for themselves. I understand that the first recorded incidence of anti-Semitism is in the Hebrew bible's Esther, where a Persian ruler observes that the Jews are different and do not keep the laws of the king," but Hardy piggybacked on Chantelle's comment. "The Jewish bible also talks as you know of a Jew named Joseph who was banished to quasi-slavery in Egypt but worked his way up to become the pharaoh's right-hand man, and of Jews taking over Egypt's entire landlord and food-supply role, with the consequent anti-Jewish riots in Egypt between 800 and 600 BC."

Hardy had again taken the floor. "In the so-called Jewish exile in Babylonia, many Jews became wealthy in banking and financial institutions. There were also riots against Jewish exploitation in Alexandria, Egypt, during the second century BC. What's more, in Gibbon's monumental work *The History of the Decline and Fall of the Roman Empire*, he repeatedly denigrated the economic exploitation of the Mediterranean world by Jews and referred to capitalistic Carthage as having been suspiciously founded by Semitic émigrés from the neighborhood of ancient Judea.

"There were Jews in China from at least the eighth century AD and there were reactions against ruthless Jews in Greece in the 19th century, when British scallywag Lord Palmerston secured post-riot retribution for one prominent Jew named David Pacifico. There was deep resentment of Jewish financial abuse in the Ottoman empire and again in South Africa, New York's Harlem and your Montreal."

Chantelle's position stiffened and she kept a stone face on her benefactor. "Returning to our Russian discussion, Mr. Hardy, I understand the *Habad Hasidim* were taught to manage their unconscious selves by descending deeply into their minds until they encountered, as should mystics in all world religions, a sacred presence within their being," but Hardy by then was heated. "You need not educate me again about Eastern European Jews! Rabbinical oppression of the Jewish people within rabbinical walls was not unlike the smothering by Jewish mothers within their houses."

Chantelle then evidently thought it necessary to elevate the argument. "Modern anti-Semitism seems to flow from the perception of a few Jews who are categorized as having the Jewish social disease, supposedly needing to overthrow institutions and values of all kinds," but Hardy again twisted her comment to further his cause. "Not all kinds, only those that counter rabbinical dictates," and he marched on as if given license. "Russia's rabbis and its prominent Jewish community supported the tsar in the early 1800s against Napoleon and the French Enlightenment. Napoleon had offered Jews emancipation from the ghettos if they forsook rabbinical bindings but Europe's key rabbis, already fearing the period's European and American Enlightenment, painted the bargain as Faustian, and the rabbinical network of Europe so propagandized its people."

Hardy took another big breath as if the arguing needed a pause after Chantelle's attempt to elevate, before he came back in an almost apologetic tone, "I agree with you, Chantelle, that anti-Semitism is an irrational and cancerous reaction to manipulation by a few Jews. There was during World War II, near my homeland outside Kiev, an area called Babi Yar, where legend has it, thousands of Jews were marched from a street called Sretskaya, then stripped of their clothes and values, and pushed to the edge of a ravine, where they were shot and covered over with earth brought in to cover the deed.

"Yet the neighboring Ukrainians somehow kept their anti-Jewish resentment. Over and over again, I heard in Eastern Europe after post-World War II that the Germans when occupying, paid the locals for everything, along with supporting documents, whereas the Russians when they counter-invaded, stole everything."

Chantelle adjusted herself in her chair and tried a general perspective. "Leopards of like spots have always met to realize their group hopes. In health care, drug companies are known for doing so and yes, they don't do it in the open."

Hardy sensed engagement and re-entered with a mellow voice: "Tsars and monarchs for millennia have known that histrionics must match the demands of what the masses delude themselves into wanting. Aristocracies repeat the process and react to the lower classes in kind – the wealthy British in the upstairs of London townhouses knew that they had to respond to what the lowly people downstairs demanded, in their image of the upstairs people. Rabbis were quick to surmise this reality, and when the ghetto walls started to fall, those rabbis went scouting for new ways to manipulate their people. In Britain, the rabbis came to recognize the British strength of word mastery and its manifestations in theater, law and politics."

Again Chantelle fell prey, "Theater resurrected from the Greeks," and Hardy rendered a coy smile. "Pride! Anyway, when the ghetto walls fell during the early 1800s in Europe, east of the great Britain…" but Chantelle interjected, "A new awareness led to a sharing in the decision-making process, as Jewish people had already done for 200 years in the spiritually alive 'New Jerusalem' of Amsterdam. The city had copied Poland in declaring religious freedom, and the later German Enlightenment of the 18th century had spawned such Jewish philosophers as Moses Mendelssohn who had affirmed the separation of church and state."

Hardy's face lost any trace of agreement and he tried to take back the agenda. "And had put reason ahead of faith," but she countered, "I think what Moses Mendelssohn meant by faith was religion. As you know, Mr. Hardy, the *Haskalah* or Jewish Enlightenment was indebted to him, and he has often been called the father of Reform Judaism. I feel he would have believed as I do, that spirituality encompassing truth, love and the development of conscience must precede discernment, and that such discernment must precede the shaping of values in any kind of socialized faith."

Hardy's smile came back. "A 19th-century Jewish intellectual, Nachman Krochmal, had subjected the sources of Judaism to scientific inquiry and in so doing, had denied the originality of *Halakhah*, contradicting some rabbis' claim that Jewish law was founded only on the Torah. Krochmal, like Amsterdam's Spinoza 100 years earlier and Zachariah Frankel 50 years later, had found the Age of Enlightenment attractive, as had other Jews who longed to shake off the restrictions of the Jewish ghettos and their dictates."

Hardy then cupped his hands as if to mock a person of the cloth. "Needless to say, they had all come to be reviled by self-protective rabbinical power. Spinoza in particular, one of the greatest contributors to world ethics and humanism, had an anathema pronounced on him and his descendants, not unlike that given to the German people after World War II."

Chantelle nodded to Hardy's comment and she sought again to give context. "The orthodox word for heresy or apostasy is *apikoros* or follower of Epicurus…" but Hardy's cold face came back at her. "Ancient Jews could have carried forward your Greek philosophy and not hoarded their brand of exclusive monotheism. Instead, 2,000 years later, 18th-century rabbis regarded the *goyische* Enlightenment as hostile to their spin on Jewish faith."

Chantelle reared back from Hardy's charge and he continued: "Your 'New Jerusalem' Amsterdam produced the age of mercantilism, along with a slave trade that continued a Jewish tradition from Eastern Europe, Portugal and Spain. Some 12 million Africans were abducted and Jewish slavers flourished in colonies like Brazil." Hardy then gave a shrug and spread out his arms with palms up. "One of the first Caribbean plantation owners was Jewish."

A recovered Chantelle tried again for balance. "Once the slave boom was established, it was gentiles who made injunctions to fit slavery's needs," but Hardy was again at the ready. "The new United States of America also came to bill itself as 'The New Jerusalem' founded as a 'City on a Hill' to beam its light of ethical monotheism across the world. As had Britain before, the mercantilist Netherlands before Britain, and Spain earlier still."

Chantelle raised her brows in interest and her apparently knowledgeable benefactor carried on. "The ethical monotheism so spun was based on a contract, where a tyrant god maintained a protection racket for a supposedly favored people induced with accordant obligations, and the colonizers Spain, Holland, Britain and the United States were sucked into seeing themselves as the chosen people. The myth fits the move toward greater exploitation."

Chantelle's brows came down and she uncrossed her legs before pressing forward. "The four founding fathers of the United States, Mr. Hardy, were all Unitarians and promoted the secular humanism of the Enlightenment," but Hardy leaned forward with face straight on Chantelle, "But accompanying such free thinking was another force at foot. At the time of the 1776 Revolution, Americans regarded themselves as God's chosen people and the Jews got quick citizenship. The 'Give me your poor' message on the Statue of Liberty was composed by a Jewish woman, and international Jewry was pivotal to the creating of the New York Stock Exchange in 1792."

Chantelle then raised her head to the air above her benefactor's head, and she tried to turn the conversation back by pointing out that Spain, before the Inquisition began in 1492, had under Muslim rule, been in harmony for 800 years, and had been regarded as the most open, tolerant and religiously diverse country in Europe. Chantelle added that she understood Christopher Columbus was a Spanish Jew, by 1492 living in the Italian city of Genoa. He was careful to conceal his Judaism but was eager to locate a place of refuge for the persecuted Jews of Spain. Columbus's sailing west to reach the Indies, Chantelle had been told, stemmed from his faith in the Bible's Book of Isaiah: "Surely the isles shall wait for me, to bring thy sons from far, their silver and their gold with them" (60:9). Chantelle added that in Columbus's diary, he had also purportedly written, "In the same month in which Spain issued the edict that all Jews should be driven out of the kingdom and its territories, it gave me the order to undertake my expedition."

But Hardy held on the attack. "According to the terms that Columbus successfully negotiated, he would be entitled to 10% of all revenues from the new lands he discovered, and he would have the option of buying one-eighth interest in any commercial venture with the new lands and receive one-eighth of the profits. From the start of the Spanish Inquisition in that fabled year of 1492, when Columbus had gone looking for gold, many Jews in Spain held key positions and many Christians had Jewish blood."

Chantelle tried to maintain her calm. "Torquemada argued that so long as the Jews remained in Spain, they would influence the tens of thousands of Jewish converts to Christianity to continue practicing Judaism. Spain's monarchs Ferdinand and Isabella had rejected Torquemada's demand that the Jews be expelled until 1492, when the Spanish Army defeated Muslim forces in Granada, restoring the whole of Spain to Christian rule. The 'Expulsion of the Jews' decree then came down and Columbus set sail, the day after expulsion from Spain began."

Terry Hardy suddenly came forward almost off his chair. "The Grand Inquisitor Tomas de Torquemada himself was a Jew, and under 'Father' Torquemada, his Spanish judges executed 11,000 heretics, versus only four heretics in the two centuries before, when Spain had been under Muslim rule. Torquemada's successor, Diego Deza, was also Jewish."

Chantelle glared in surprise at Terry Hardy and he raised his arms as if to feign a yawn. "As for the Columbus expedition, its interpreter, Luis de Torres, was born a Jew but had converted shortly before the expedition set sail. Two other 'New Christians,' Luis de Santangel and Gabriel Sanchez, had a hand in the financing, and two Jews, Abraham Zacuto and Joseph Vecinho, provided navigational expertise. Six Jews in all accompanied the Jewish Columbus on his voyage."

Hardy again came forward but this time with some apparent self-control. "The greater Jewish people were hoodwinked and left their beloved Spain, with many going to Poland or Amsterdam. But many also ventured south, where they were welcomed by the Ottoman Empire. As you no doubt know, Ms. Fouriere, Sephardic Jews in the Muslim world were not snowed by the Ashkenazi rabbis' concoction of persecution and the concomitant ghetto walls."

Chantelle squinted and tried to mesh what her presumed Jewish bene-factor Hardy said with what she knew: "Spain, the model of cosmopolitan tolerance and advanced medicine under Muslim rule, evolved into the nar-rowest community on the continent," and Hardy thrust forward again. "After the Spanish Inquisition, powerful Ashkenazis released their energies into the types of capitalism that Karl Marx would later condemn. South African dia-monds and a second set of dishes for special occasions became parts of a hoax over much of the world but there were backlashes, such as in Russia with an attempt to expose the hoax in the 1905 publication, *Protocols of the Elders of Zion*."

Chantelle suddenly gave a dark frown, before springing up in her chair to challenge her benefactor straight on. "Which has been shown to be a fab-rication by tsarist interests. Passages were plagiarized from a political satire that had been published in Geneva 50 years earlier, imagining a dialogue in hell between Machiavelli and Montesquieu, and there are said to be addi-tional borrowings. When the tsar was informed that the pamphlet was a con-coction, he was reported to have ordered copies confiscated, because he said that a good cause could not be defended by bad means."

But benefactor Hardy leaned back and afforded a slight sigh. "The Geneva story only underscores the legitimacy of the message. The Jewish people were also fed by a few powerful brokers that the *Protocols of the Elders of Zion* were based on medieval fantasies about Judaism, and in one such supposed fantasy, the Archbishop of Lyons in 825 AD had said the slave trade was run by Jews. Those duped Jews kept a blind eye to such acts carried out by the powerful, like the wealthy Russian Jews, who had already thrived in tsarist Russia for centuries."

Hardy again raised both arms to the ceiling in a slow, eye-catching fashion. "*The Elders of Zion* had to be quashed, since it set a precedent for later books in the information boom after World War I, with books like *The Jews Who's Who* of British aristocracy. Two New York Jews tried to counter that reaction in the West by creating in 1938 a fictional *golem* or mythic defender of the Jews, named Superman."

Chantelle's face betrayed her diffidence, and she tried to take the argument back to an area where she felt some comfort. "Almost every ethnic group, Mr. Hardy, has a suspect rival, but ethnicists do not damn their rivals for demonic world domination. I remember Jewish writer Hannah Arendt being balm to me when she said in effect that the sources of evil are not deep but lie within our grasp. As such we should not despair."

But Hardy smirked at Chantelle's apparent grasp at assuredness. "How about the propaganda to justify killing former U.S. ally Saddam Hussein, before he could squeal on Israel? As you probably know, Chantelle, Americans have an average I.Q. of 100, so it was not difficult for an inbred, sheltie-dog leader to communicate, using an 'I don't talk fancy but I'm a straight shooter' kind of show-biz talk. In my former school in Eastern Europe, during the Cold War, I was instructed to read Michael Moncur's *Cynical Quotations,* and I had drilled into me the quotation number 858 by U.S. editor H.L. Mencken, that 'Nobody ever went broke underestimating the intelligence of the American public!'"

Chantelle shot up erect, put both feet on the floor and shot back with eyes straight on her sponsor, "My psychiatrist and mentor, Doctor Fisher, had little time for that phrase. Doctor Fisher had grounded me that Nazi propagandist Goebbels had said that the more preposterous the lie, the more people would believe it, and that the most brilliant propagandist technique would yield no success, unless a fundamental principle was held in mind – that it must confine itself to a few points and be repeated over and over."

Hardy's face again gave a grin of smugness. "As perhaps with all paranoiac fantasies, a secret-conspiracy perception needs some truth. As your Hannah Arendt pointed out, there historically have been scattered throughout the world, a number of Jewish bankers who raised funds for various states. A Rothschild on his deathbed purportedly ordered the turnaround of a big ship in mid-ocean, uttering 'This is a simple matter.'"

Hardy's face then again hardened. "But Hannah Arendt was only echoing, after World War II, the sentiments of Mark Twain a century earlier that the crucifixion of Jesus had not much to do with the world's attitude toward Jews. The reasons for it were much older. Twain reportedly submitted that the Jew was a money-getter, making money the end and aim of his life – he was at it in Rome, was at it before Rome and has been at it ever since, making the whole human race his enemy."

Chantelle's eyebrows again lowered and her face went dark. "I understand that Mark Twain said the Jews are immortal, versus the empires of Egypt, Persia, Greece and Rome and that they have fought a marvelous fight with a lack of vanity behind the scenes. The Jews have constituted only 1% of the human race but have contributed to the world's list of great names, out of proportion to the smallness of their numbers."

But Hardy again was happy to have Chantelle engaged. "Mark Twain's true opinion of the Jews is probably the best kept secret in American literary history. Immediately after his death, his eccentric daughter Clara married a Jewish piano player and Twain's publishers were given speedy instructions to delete *Concerning the Jews* from the author's collected works. What rabbis censored is what Twain suggested was one Jewish secret of such immortality. People had told Twain that they had reason to suspect that, for behind-the-scenes reasons, many Jews did not report themselves as Jews. Twain held the opinion that the Jewish population in America was grossly underestimated."

Chantelle gave an uncomfortable look and a buoyed-up Hardy carried on. "As Mark Twain liked to believe, all Christian Americans had read the story in Genesis, chapter 47, of the years of plenty and the years of famine in Egypt, and how a Jewish Joseph seized the famine opportunity to take away the nation's money to the last penny, together with all the livestock and land to the last acre. Then he took the nation itself, buying it up for bread until all Egyptians were slaves possessing nothing. It was a disaster so crushing that its effects have not disappeared from Egypt even today, 3,000 years later. Was Joseph cementing a tradition established in Egypt and Ur, centuries before the crucifixion of Jesus?" Hardy then added with a flippant wave of his arm, "As for modern Palestine, Mark Twain expressed a dyspeptic view of it."

Chantelle had already nodded an acknowledgement of the biblical passage but her shoulders had again turned in, after what Hardy had gone on to say. He thus continued: "For like reasons, Austria tried ousting the Jews several centuries ago, and Russia in the late 19th and early 20th century attempted to legislate Jews out of their hold on the country, since the Christian peasant stood no chance against Jewish commercial cunning. Key Russian Jews were always ready to lend on a crop and when settlement day came, they owned the crop and the next year owned the farm, like the Joseph of ancient Egypt.

After the U.S. Civil War, carpet bagging Jews came down *en force* to the U.S. cotton states, setting up shop on the plantations, supplying the blacks' wants on credit, and at the end of the season were proprietors of the blacks' share of the present crop and part of the next one. Before long, the blacks detested the Jews as much as did the whites, as later would other blacks resent the slum landlords of Harlem or the recent people in the subprime mortgage system."

Chantelle sat stunned, wondering who she was with and Hardy kept on. "Indeed your hockey violence lives on with a Hollywood fraud that taps into the testosterone of youth and the misplaced anger of TV addicts. Like the 1919 baseball fix. Hell, a Canadian world boxer recently said that every boxing win is known ahead of time and in what round."

Chantelle's dark eyebrows finally went down deep and her head bent forward. "Anti-Semitism is full of such secret-conspiracy fantasies and is thus distinguished from other racism," but Hardy tried to deploy her very words. "Anti-Semitism as cultivated by a few Jewish myth-makers who said to their people, they were the world's chosen. Besides, if the shoe fits and as your Frye pointed out, the listener completes the equation of that saying, the listener is at the experiential top of the learning curve."

Chantelle's face turned visibly angry and she rendered the look of a scornful librarian. "You use Northrop Frye as a weapon, Mr. Hardy," but he gave a Gallic shrug. "Greeks don't shoot the messenger, Ms. Fouriere. Even the Romans didn't do that," and she fell again for the trap. "They had Greek teachers," to which Hardy feigned a gasp, crossed himself and said "Again! Pride as you sermonized is a universal deadly sin."

Hardy then straightened up as if it were called for by decorum. "But back to the British robber barons and hellhole cities like 19th-century Birmingham as exposed by anti-Semites like Dickens."

Chantelle again tried to slow things down by taking another drink. She settled herself ready for another onslaught by her benefactor. "The U.S. Christian militant positioning is not dissimilar to that of Britain, 100 or more years earlier. After the Jews had been expelled from England at the end of the 12th century, they were welcomed back in the 17th century by funda-mentalist ruler Oliver Cromwell who had envisioned a Jewish return to Judea.

"But scratch Christian fundamentalism and you'll find Jewish mercantil-ism, and Cromwell recognized from the early 17th century that much of the Americas' gold was no longer making its way to the wealthy Jews of old Spain and was now making its way to the new Jewish burghers of Amsterdam. Thus during the start of the 17th century, Dutch mercantilists created the first joint stock companies and the first stock exchange, along with massive consumer credit, where merchants and shopkeepers could speculate. In fact, a speculation bubble hit the tulip mania, followed by the South Sea Bubble. Wealthy Dutch merchants then married into aristocratic families, breaking the ancient feudal system, and as late as the early 1800s, Dutch financial markets played a key role in the Louisiana Purchase."

Chantelle must have betrayed some intrigue with what Hardy was say-ing, because she allowed him to carry on, erect in his chair. "Oliver Crom-well as you know played a pivotal role in making England a republican com-monwealth. He was a commander in the army that defeated the royalists in the English civil war, after King Charles I had entered the English House of Commons in 1640 to arrest five MPs. After the execution of King Charles I in 1650, Cromwell dominated a short-lived commonwealth of England, conquered Ireland and Scotland, and ruled as Lord Protector until his death near 1660. And while Cromwell played a pivotal role in bringing the banned Jews back to England, Spinoza, who saw through so many other things, saw through Cromwell."

Hardy raised his chin as if in love with his role of lecturer. "After some 'Buy when there's blood in the streets' fortunes were made – to misquote a Rothschild – exploiting London's Great Plague in 1665 and the Great Fire in 1666, by 1688 came England's so-called Glorious Revolution. King James II would not honor government debt, and creditors, many of whom were Jewish, would have none of this breach. Cries came from London's Old Jewry district and key merchants helped Parliament prevail over King James II. He was overthrown by a union of Parliamentarians.

"An invading army was then led by Dutch *stadtholder* William of Orange who ascended the English throne as William III and the fact that he was Protestant and James a Catholic made for a good front. A few years after this Revolution, King William, like predecessor James, also looked like he might default on loans and he too came close to losing his crown but then a second provision came for legalizing the crown, on the spurious revolutionary principles of the Old Jewry. These aims were euphemized by the doctrine, 'A right to choose our own governors.'

"The crown survived the doctrine, sort of, but the English borrowed the techniques of 'Dutch finance' from the late 17th century, and the ability to bear huge debt and yet prosper became an Anglo-Saxon hallmark. Helped by gold to be found in the English-speaking world, England and later Britain came to lead the world banking system. At first, English goldsmiths had been the closest thing to any form of banking system but soon England indebted itself to wealthy merchants, and the emerging Bank of England became the foundation of both the public and private credit systems of the English-speaking world. Needless to say, the Bank of England proclaimed from the start, an official stance against bigotry and it held a world dominating role until the U.S. took over the role in the mid-20th century."

Chantelle was sitting still and allowing her benefactor to lecture on. "As for communications-connection networks, a Jew in 1650 opened England's first coffeehouse in the influential Oxford area, and by 1700, there were several hundred news-gossip coffeehouses in London – doubling as book-and-pamphlet shops – versus only 30 in the formerly dominant Amsterdam. Soon newspapers followed, leading to advertisements and marketing, mass mail, and by the 1840s, the telegraph and in the 1870s, the telephone. By the outset of World War I, 75% of the world's cables, with their movement of information and later money orders, were controlled by Britain.

"Like our time's Ronald Reagan addressing the Association of Evangelists in Florida – firing up anti-Communist fever and meeting with an Israeli head to discuss a possible Armageddon – Oliver Cromwell said in a 17th-century Parliament that England's enemies hated it because they hated god but that the cause of god's people defended England. Actors like Cromwell and Reagan, as well as their script-writers, may hold audiences in contempt but they have to hide that contempt. Greed combined with a haughty sense of providence – the greatest crimes come from such self-righteousness."

Chantelle had heard enough. "Adam Smith in *The Wealth of Nations* said that tolerance for different religions is the best way to reap social benefits at the lowest possible cost. Smith saw religious sects like English Methodism as a saving grace in affording an incentive for both moral vigor and a consensus of values among the industrial revolution's new poor, after peasants had moved to jobs in the cities."

Hardy let Chantelle talk on as if in support of what he had said. "Smith also advocated public amusements and even the exposing of hypocrisies in ruling churches to fortify the poor laborers' sense of identity and self-justification, and to prevent religious dictatorships. Hence, there came to be the Wesleyan Methodism among Britain's Midland laborers. Adam Smith saw religion, yes, as a crutch but also believed that the moral fortitude built into such support could improve the quality of that crutch."

Hardy's head lifted to suggest that he was slightly taken aback by Chantelle's grasp of economic history, and he gave her space to continue. "Smith observed that one religion leads to despotism and two leads to civil war. The England of your 17th century, Mr. Hardy, had the most pluralistic religious makeup in all of Europe. Dynamic religion calls people forward to ever more open societies, and as Jewish communities have shown us for 3,000 years, disagreement and controversy are signs not of a decadent society but the necessary conditions for spiritual progress."

Chantelle was still given ground. "Enslavement can happen under benign governments as well as malignant ones, because all governments come to exploit ideology to control people, and all governments require bureaucracies that expand, until people are bound to them with self-interest. When the ruler then cries, 'Give the people food and booze,' those people do not appreciate that they are recovering a portion of their own property. Only Greeks on the street apparently know."

Hardy heaved a breath to try jumping in, but Chantelle would not let him. "And yes, the voice of human inertia keeps calling the human sheep home, with a nostalgic need for retrieving roots, but Smith observed that another human impulse – to change and develop within a spirit of tempered conflict, not tranquility – differentiates the means of capitalism from other forms of economic organization. True, god can be interpreted differently and capitalists can say that social progress is a sign that they are on the right track for god's grace but it just may be that a capitalistic environment affords the best freedom for not only scoundrels but also their opponents to expose, criticize and control such skullduggery."

Chantelle tried to summarize before letting Hardy back in. "One thing seems certain – reason, revelation and tradition all have their uses but if left unchecked, they create their own inertia. Revelation and tradition seem to work best when reason prevails."

Chantelle finally leaned back and Hardy took his cue to steer things back his way. "England, more than any other European country, after mercantilism moved from Amsterdam to London, spoke for 300 years in a progressively louder voice for resettling the Jews on their historic land of Israel.

"One key Jew, Montefiore, belonged to Britain's Sephardic elite and had made his fortune trading coral, diamonds and other commodities, across family and social networks. Montefiore's marriage to Judith Barent-Cohen brought an alliance with the Ashkenazi Rothschilds who helped him turn his small fortune into a large one.

"Montefiore publicly embodied the idea that the Jewish cause was also the cause of humanity in general and Britain in particular. He pushed for Jews to win full emancipation, and Montefiore joined forces with middle-class dissenters to help end the slave trade, underwriting with Rothschild a one million pound loan to finance the abolition of slavery in the West Indies. Idealistic Christians, some of whom themselves were excluded from full civil rights, in turn backed the emancipation of Jews at home and their restoration to the Holy Land. When Montefiore appealed to the Ottoman Sultan to protect his subjects, pivotal British politicians again approved, because modernizing the crumbling Ottoman Empire would help thwart the Middle-Eastern ambitions of Russia and France, until Israel could be made manifest."

Chantelle looked content for the moment to let Hardy carry on, in an area where she knew less. "An imperial and industrial-revolution Britain gave rise to non-conformist Jews in commerce and industry, and by the 19th century, Britain had a Jewish Prime Minister, Benjamin Disraeli, who wrote a book about an Israeli state. Viscount Palmerston carried forward the concept, envisioning an Israeli state that would be economically and militarily advantageous to his Britain. As scallywag Palmerston said, 'Nations don't have perpetual allies or enemies, only perpetual self-interests.' After the Suez Canal was built in 1869, the concept of the Canal being owned by Egypt was opposed by Lord Palmerston and soon Disraeli entrenched a foothold in the Middle East when in 1875 he bought, ostensibly for Britain, a controlling share of the Suez with funding from the Rothschilds.

"Britain also seized control of much of Iran's oil before World War I and when Iran tried to nationalize its oil industry in 1953 with permission from the international court in The Hague, Britain and the U.S. boycotted Iran. In 1957, the American CIA and Israeli intelligence *Massad* helped found a counterforce within Iran and named its so-called secret police *Savat*. To the spiritual Iranian, for whom the inside and outside of a person needs to be the same, the USA was seen as 'The Great Trivializer.' Not surprising, therefore, that when the USA helped Iraq's Saddam Hussein invade Iran in 1980, it was only a matter of time before The Great Trivializer-USA would have to silence Hussein."

Chantelle lowered her brows in a corrective frown. "Mr. Hardy, you were trying to compare the current U.S. Christian militant position to that of Britain, 100 years earlier" and he stiffened in proper response. "Some biographies of Winston Churchill have been censored by both his executors and those close to him, and Jewish Ronald Cohen was Churchill's de facto bibliographer. But from what we people have been allowed to glean, Churchill, with his Jewish backers, framed his policy on a Disraeli model, all behind the stage of maintaining a balance of power in Europe."

Chantelle let Hardy carry on. "Winston Churchill's father had many Jewish friends, and Winston himself had studied the Jewish Old Testament and reportedly loved it. Churchill had been fascinated since childhood by Jewish monotheism and history, and evidently took at least some of the Hebrew bible stories literally. He alleged that Rome and even your Greece could not achieve what the ancient Jews had done, in having a Moses who had spoken to god and had led god's chosen people out of bondage. Churchill said moreover that the Jewish system of ethics, as reflected in your James's spiel..." Hardy thrust his arm out at Chantelle, "...was the best possible combination of differing world ethics, and Churchill was reported to have developed prejudices against Muslims in his first visit to the Middle East in 1899, thereafter having a low opinion of Arabs in general."

Hardy once again was in his element as mentor. "Nathaniel Baron Rothschild became the first Jew in the British House of Lords and was a close friend of Jewish banker Sir Ernest Cassel. After Churchill's father's death, the new Lord Natty Rothschild offered to help Winston politically, while Jewish banker Cassel would look after Winston's finances. Churchill's continental European vacations were all paid for by Jews.

"Churchill's political views toward Jews had already begun to crystallize at the start of the 20th century when he had run in that Jewish Manchester Northwest riding and had thrown his support behind the Jewish-British movement to aid prominent Jews fleeing Russia. The Conservative opposition had accused him in vain of acting out of Jewish instructions and one Lord Alfred Douglas later went so far as to allege that Winston was in the pay of Jews, both before and after World War I. Churchill dismissed the criticism as anti-Semitism.

"Churchill admired the corporate spirit, mission and closeness of the Jewish community, and he became a member of his riding's Jewish hospital and of Britain's Jewish clubs. Within those clubs, some Zionists wanted a new Jewish home that was part of the British Empire, and a few looked positively upon a Palestine kept as it was under the control of Ottoman Turks, but 95% wanted an autonomous Jewish home in geographical Palestine and by 1905, there were 50 Jewish villages there.

"In the ensuing period before World War I, Churchill was urged to petition in support for a Jewish home in Palestine, but he balked at putting his support in writing, thinking that such a move would overplay his cards. After the war, however, Churchill became the key cabinet minister responsible for determining the future Jewish home in Palestine, and he evolved to becoming British prime minister and one of Israel's staunchest defenders in the early 1950s."

Chantelle folded her arms across her chest. "You are jumping ahead, Mr. Hardy, and perhaps betraying a dangerous so-what."

Hardy straightened up in a theatric response, and after a big breath, resumed: "In 1903, when key Germans proposed copying an earlier British sentiment in having the Zionists move to Uganda, the Germans did not appreciate that the vast majority of Zionists by then wanted only Israel. Churchill *did* understand, from the Russian Jews in his Manchester riding; thus, at the height of World War I, when the war was at a Mexican standoff, Britain opted to take Jerusalem from the Turks in 1917. Britain needed to make a deal to cut off the money and food supply to the Germans as well as get the Americans in on Britain's side."

Hardy then came full forward and put his hands flat on his denim knees. "In the mid-19th century, there were 12,000 Jews living in Palestine, often living off external patrons, but in 1881, Zionism took a quantum leap forward when Russian revolutionaries assassinated Tsar Alexander II and his son Alexander III blamed the Jews. The exodus of Jews from Russia started and as discussed, many went forth to New York or London but some ventured to Palestine with the cry that it had been promised to them since the time of the Crusades. These Zionist pioneers got help from Baron Edmond de Rothschild of Paris as well as the London branch of the family, along with other co-religionists, and those funds went for food, medicine, equipment, doctors, nurses, schools, teachers and money to purchase the land. But the non-Jewish long-time residents of Palestine had no anonymous donors and could thus not buy the same land."

Hardy waved his hand as if he had a wand. "In the early years leading up to World War I, there were 700,000 people living in Palestine, and the Zionists mixed with a population of a few ancient Jews as well as many descendants from the ancient Canaanites or Philistines, against whom ancient Israel had warred during its establishment. Soon there were 85,000 Jews in Palestine, half of whom were Zionists, but Jews still in total were only a ninth of the population.

"The new Jews often bribed their way into Palestine and bought huge tracts of land, with the takeovers resented by the locals, who suddenly found themselves hired hands on formerly accessible land. The new Jews did not recognize the long-time Palestinians' right to graze their flocks on land just harvested, and those Jews were hostile and contemptuous toward the Arabs, calling them ignorant and backward.

"Palestine was a critical link for the Arabs as a land passage between Egypt and the rest of Arabia, but Palestine was also close to the Suez Canal that Disraeli had bought in the 19th century, and the Canal was Britain's economic windpipe. That Palestine at the start of World War I was as we know under the rule of the Turkish Ottoman Empire, and three months into the war, Ottoman Turkey entered in on the German side."

Hardy then leaned back as if to take a long puff on a cigar. "In 1915, at a time when Britain was losing World War I and the continued existence of a British Empire was in doubt, British Prime Minister David Lloyd George, who himself had been raised by a Christian-literalist uncle, brought the Jews-back-to-Israel issue before the British War Cabinet. In the U.S., Henry Ford got wind of the situation and chartered a peace ship in an attempt to end World War I, but Ford was branded as an anti-Semite and his practices of mass production were represented as industrial enslavement. At least Ford paid his employees enough to buy what they built, versus today's financial institutions with their bogus bundles, bankrupting those at the bottom before the financiers themselves get bailed out."

Chantelle crossed her long legs and thrust her shoulders forward. "Digression again, Mr. Hardy" and he leapt back in. "Okay. At the start of World War I, pivotal British Jews parachuted a frontman, Arthur J. Balfour, into head of the Admiralty and that plant Balfour became the sole Conservative candidate in the War Cabinet of 1915.

Early on, Balfour motioned that Asia and the Middle East should be carved up and his motion was seconded by Winston Churchill, before a sub-committee was created to consider Palestine. A second pivotal player became British diplomat Mark Sykes, a non-Jew who emerged as a key advocate for Zionist interests and a third, British Consul Sir Henry McMahon, whose written promises to the Middle East's Grand Sharif Emir Hussein, noble old descendant of Muhammad, would ensure that Hussein would risk his life and that of his family to fight back for Arab lands controlled by the Turks.

"The British anticipated that the German-aligned Ottoman Sultan, who was also the Caliph of Islam, would declare a jihad against them, pressing the British-governed Muslims in South Asia, Egypt and Sudan to rise up against their imperial masters. The Brits knew, however, that if the second-ranking figure in Islam, Grand Sharif Hussein of Mecca, supported Britain against the Ottomans, such support would weaken the call to holy war. And so, in a series of famous letters, British Consul General in Cairo, Sir Henry McMahon, promised to support the establishment of an independent Arab kingdom in Syria, Lebanon, Arabia and Mesopotamia, now Iraq.

As had British General Kitchener before being killed in the war, Mc-Mahon made multiple deals with Grand Sharif Hussein, and McMahon made an agreement with the Sharif to bequeath all of Arabia, including Palestine. But the British wording was vague and was questionably translated, and McMahon's 1915 letter came to be twisted by the British, with certain Middle East districts playing on different meanings of the word *vilayet*, meaning a political jurisdiction in Turkish but being a broader geographical expression in English to mean 'vicinity' or 'environs.'

The Zionists interpreted McMahon's agreement to exclude Palestine, adding that his letter was not legally binding and McMahon himself would later say his promise to the Arabs need not be binding. Sykes and his French counterpart Picot drew up an envisaged post-World War I Middle East, with Jerusalem being a Christian-Jewish-Arab condominium, run by the British. Political plant Balfour then proposed a facade of Arab self-government while proclaiming Arab self-rule.

Zionism meanwhile, though its initial world headquarters had been in 19th-century Berlin after the Congress of Berlin had decreed religious liberty, grew increasingly anti-German after the Ottomans joined Germany in World War I. Yet despite a growing Zionism, at the start of the war only 8,000 Jews of Britain's 300,000 belonged to any Zionist organization. The most aggressive members were Russian Jews who wooed the rich Jews of West-End London as well as the British-Jewish organization the Cousin-hood, which included the Rothschilds. Much of the British-Jewish estab-lishment was active in finance, a few were in Parliament and many sup-ported the Jews in Palestine but they did not want to live there themselves, in the same way that the rich Diaspora of Alexandria, before the time of Jesus, were not interested in living in Israel. But perhaps the most pivotal person of all was the Jewish-Russian immigrant Chaim Weizmann, whom many in the Jewish community labeled a *folke-mensch* who charmed British high society."

Chantelle adjusted her back in the plastic chair. "*Folke-mensch?*" and Hardy raised his eyebrows as if struck by educated Chantelle's lack of Yiddish. "Man of the people, but he was more of a *schnorer* or engaging beg-gar, and while Weizmann had been growing up in Russia, Zionism had been a central theme in his schooling. He was the official British delegate to the international Zionism congress in 1911."

Chantelle settled a little as if to acknowledge the clarification and Hardy charged on. "Two other influential Jews who came to Britain from Eastern Europe were Sokolow and Sacher, and those new British Zionists agreed with their international leader Herzl that the fulcrum for shifting world opin-ion was in controlling the Middle East. By 1913, Sokolow was resident in London as a skilled newsperson and behind-the-scenes diplomat, and he pressed upon the British government that it would be to Britain's advantage to have Palestine be Jewish, next to an Arabic Egypt. As for Sacher, he was a Polish Jew working for the *Manchester Guardian*, and Manchester came to rival London as a source of force and brains for Zionism."

Chantelle gave a frown of doubt. "But these Eastern emigrants from the pogroms of your Eastern Europe, Terry, did not as you say, dominate Jewish-British thinking," and Hardy looked to sense he was in control. "Not for some time. Ginsberg was a Russian-Jewish British Lord who in 1891 warned of the oppressive cruelty to Arabs by Zionists, and many British Jews including some Zionists bought into initial gestures by Britain to offer Uganda as a stopgap before Palestine."

Chantelle's eyebrows lowered more and Hardy leaned forward and folded his hands. "Let us be mindful, Chantelle, that British-Jewish society was well entrenched before the Russians came. The Board of Deputies of British Jews had been formed in 1760 and had worked behind the scenes to help the reform bill of 1832 give British manufacturers better representation relative to traditional landholders. The Board of Deputies later joined the rival Anglo-Jewish Association in 1878 to form the Conjoint Committee of British Jews."

Terry Hardy again leaned back and raised his hands to the air. "But the Zionists had passion and would shift the mood of British Jewry. Another key person, Lucien Wolfe, was a Bohemian Jew who had taken part in the pan-European revolutions of 1848 and had fled to England after their failure. Thereafter he became, like Sokolow, a brilliant journalist and behind-the-scenes diplomat, and Wolfe argued that in Judaism, religion and race were virtually indistinguishable, as they had been for 50 centuries."

Hardy paused to put his eyes straight on Chantelle. "Let us not forget that much earlier, while Disraeli had converted to Christianity at age 13, his favorite maxim was still 'Race is everything,'" but Chantelle did not betray any reaction and Hardy pressed on. "Regarding the mood of English Jews, the Zionists among them believed that anti-Semitism was unconquerable, yet at the start of World War I, many members of the Conjoint Committee of British Jews were Assimilationists, who officially advocated integration into British society. In fact, one key Jew named Samuel was a powerful

411

Cabinet member of Prime Minister Asquith. The later Prime Minister Lloyd George furthermore profited from inside knowledge to make gains on the stock market via Jewish Sir Isaacs Rufus, Lord Chief Justice. As had Churchill in 1916 – a few British Jews headed by Winston Churchill's financial backer, Sir Ernest Cassel, reported via plant Arthur Balfour that the British Battle of Jutland had gone badly. British stocks in New York plummeted and those wealthy few bought low. The story on Jutland then changed, the same stocks spiked, those few Jews sold and Cassel bribed Winston Churchill with hush money in today's equivalent of more than a million dollars.

"By 1917, Churchill as Minister of Munitions was working with Sir Albert Stern, the Zionist Director General of tank production and another key Jew was Sir Frederic Nathan, who was Director of Propellant Supplies, but both men worked with Chaim Weizmann for whom Churchill had signed naturalization papers seven years earlier. Weizmann pushed for not only a Jewish state of Israel but also its richest agricultural land and water sources, and would produce, in the final year of World War I, a map to that effect. And throughout the war in the United States, Jewish Bernard Baruch as Chairman of the War Industries Board worked with Weizmann, in tandem with whore Churchill to supply Britain with raw materials."

Chantelle betrayed no emotion on her face and Hardy took her blankness as tacit acceptance. "Regardless of the opposition between Zionists and Assimilationists, those new British Jews Samuel, Weizmann, Sokolow and Wolfe were key to the eventual Balfour Declaration on November 2, 1917, more than three years after the start of World War I. When the war started in August 1914, the Zionists put their hopes in Britain and Samuel lobbied that a pro-Zionist British policy regarding Palestine would unite international Jewry with Britain's allies in the Entente. He talked glowingly of the Jewish brain and what it could do if given a homeland, and argued that a Jewish state in Palestine would be a fountain of enlightenment for the world, despite Russian-Jewish animosity to the Age of Enlightenment a century earlier."

Chantelle was still unmoved and Hardy filled the gap. "As early as the end of 1914, when Turkey joined the German side of the Central Powers,

Weizmann had use of that plant Balfour, a man believing in the non-equality of races, while up in Manchester, the *Guardian's* gentile editor Scott became so keen on Weizmann that by 1915, Prime Minister Lloyd George was supporting him too. Weizmann and followers published a document, showing Jews increasing in population to the majority in Palestine, with self-government to follow after initial British rule. Weizmann posited that a Jewish Israel had produced great men for 15 centuries and part of the Zionist plan was to rebuild the Temple, despite there being a grand mosque over top of the site."

Terry Hardy shifted in his little chair and brought his hands forward as if in deference. "As you queried, Chantelle, the Zionists had to get the Jewish Assimilationists onside but at the start of World War I, British and French Jews felt quite comfortable, relative to Russian Jews like Weizmann and company. Those comfortable Western European Jews were arguing for assimilation or at least the appearance of it.

"Even then, however, the head of British Jewry, James Rothschild, was pressing Weizmann to petition Britain for a Jewish State in Palestine, and his heir Walter Rothschild would take over and become the man to whom Balfour would address the Declaration in 1917. It would say in effect that Britain would support the Zionist cause if world Jewry facilitated the means for Britain to win the war. At the same time, another prominent Eastern European Jew named Teschlenow went public in envisioning a Palestine that was a Jewish land of more than five million souls, as in days of old."

Hardy could not resist a grin as if enjoying the floor in a way he had wanted for years. "To be sure, the Assimilationists did not give into the Zionists easily. British-Jewish Montagu Samuel, who had earlier reversed his names to Samuel Montagu, was titled Lord Swaything, and he had a country estate, a grand London residence and a Christian wife, born Miss Stanley. Montagu was politically clever as well as malicious, and he pooh-poohed any idea of a Jewish garrison fighting against the Ottoman Turks in Palestine."

Chantelle took some water but stayed listening and a charged-up Hardy carried on. "By 1916, despite Britain and the Arabs having conquered much of the Turkish-controlled Middle East, the total World War was at a stalemate and only the addition of significant new forces, on one side or the other, could tip the balance. Britain was thus eager to make a deal with world Jewry to help fund the balance of the war and persuade mightier forces to weigh in.

"Britain believed, as did Germany and tsarist Russia, that a monolithic Jewish factor existed in world affairs and as an example, the proverbial 'Young Turks' trying to overthrow the Sultan and take control of the Ottoman Empire were spearheaded by *Domne* Turks or crypto-Jews to get Palestine for the World Zionist Movement. Britain and the allied Entente were in fact considering offering Palestine to the *Domnes* of Constantinople, for which they would withdraw their support from the Ottoman regime; it would then collapse and an Allied or Entente victory would follow. Hell, the *Domne* Turks are still quietly prominent in Turkey's army even today!"

Terry Hardy straightened himself up to fortify his presumed position of lecturer. "But back to that World War I stalemate – in running up to the Balfour Declaration, it was critical to woo the Americans onto the side of the Entente, but tsarist Russia was an ally with Britain and France, and pre-revolutionary Russia was perceived by American Jews as anti-Semitic and the enemy. Thus the wooing strategy was to convince American Jewry that the end of the Ottoman Empire would lead to Palestine becoming a Jewish homeland."

Hardy then gave a wry smile. "The plot thickened! It was circulated that Germany might promise Palestine to the Jews and so France asked Jewish-British Wolfe for help to get Jewish backing of it, since France had interests in Syria, including Palestine."

Hardy then lowered his finger and leaned back as if he was telling an old gentleman's tale at a club over sherry: "That *folke-mensch* Weizmann meanwhile had been taken in hand by the Rothschild women, to teach him proper English language and decorum. At the same time, he was trying to make acetone from grain, rather than wood, because acetone was a critical ingredient in the manufacture of explosives. Soon he would become Lloyd George's right-hand man in the Ministry of Munitions, and Lloyd George promised Weizmann a Jewish Palestine."

Chantelle held unmoved and Hardy perhaps presumed she was absorbing it all; so, he comfortably repositioned himself. "Going back to that Catholic British diplomat, Mark Sykes, he convinced tsarist Russia of a Jewish Palestine in 1916 and then convinced France. Sykes described Zionism as an 'atmospheric but unspoken' power, leading the French to buy in to Jewish Zionism's being critical to winning World War I.

"Another Jew named Aaronsohn was a skilled agronomist and he combed every inch of Palestine, ostensibly for its agricultural potential, while spying for Britain as part of a Jewish-led Nili spy ring. At the same time, Sykes sought out, on a map, key places of dominant world Jewry as part of a grand wooing strategy and Lucien Wolfe, the former Bohemian Jew, soon recommended Hebrew to be the language in the new Palestine to come."

Hardy gave a long sigh and stretched back, as if to wax over his wisdom. "Needless to say, the British kept all negotiations with the Jews secret from the Arabs or they would not have revolted against the Ottoman Turkish domination of Arab lands. The Arabs put their lives on the line as part of their deal with the British, but those British Jews did not."

Chantelle sensed another anti-Western sentiment in Hardy's comment and when Hardy caught her squint, he took to sounding more historical. "Issues then began to take shape. In arguments against Hussein, it was alleged that he wanted *sharia* law as set out in the Qur'an, and such law meant opposition to Turkish and Western modernization. But this direct descendant of Muhammad was then coroneted in the Middle East as King of the Arabs, and the British soon wanted the title reduced; so, McMahon triggered a decision to have Hussein simply be King of the Hejaz region, east of Palestine. The noble man Hussein would live to see his hopes dashed."

Chantelle took her eyes to the ceiling and had another gulp of water. Hardy waited until Chantelle's eyes met his before he went on. "Internal skirmishes in London, both within the Jewish community and beyond, were big in those early years of the war. Montagu remained an opposing Jewish cabinet member, up to the time of the Balfour Declaration, and a government opposition non-Jew named Malcolm said that in the Middle East, the Jewish pursuit of an exclusive politics had been the number one contributor to World War I.

"But Sokolow countered with the suggestion that no one had lived in pre-World War I Palestine. He further declared that to win the sympathy of world Jewry was to show the cause of Jewish Liberty – giving Palestine to the Jews – thus meshing that mandate with the needs of the Entente and implying, as had Weizmann, the power of world Jewry. Implied as well was that getting Israel for the Jews was far easier than emancipating the Jews of say, Russia and Poland or the formerly Ottoman-controlled Romania."

Chantelle continued listening from the supposed specialist and Hardy held in form. "The year 1917 became one of dramatic change and the cause of Zionism gained strength. In January, out came a British weekly journal, *Palestine*, and in it was published a map of Palestine, from the Mediterranean to Damascus and west to Egypt, that is encompassing all of *Eretz* or biblical Israel. The powerful Russian Jews of Manchester formed the British Palestine Committee or BPC and a key British Jew, Sidebotham, proclaimed that a Jewish Israel guaranteed a British Suez Canal. Then came February 12, 1917, and word of the Russian Revolution, and soon Russian Zionists wanted no part of a British-run Israel.

"The year 1917 charged on – Weizmann met Prime Minister Lloyd George at a dinner sponsored by the establishment Astor family, and nine days later met the prime minister in his office. The Sykes-Picot agreement changed to a tripartite one, giving Palestine to the Zionists in exchange for their effort to tilt the war and bring in the U.S., and in Paris, Sokolow met with Baron Edmond de Rothschild, officially hiding from the French, the idea of Palestine being a British protectorate. But the London branch of the Rothschild family of course knew and presumably would have communicated that plan to the family's Paris cousins. Sokolow wrote to the Jewish-American Louis Brandeis, who by 1916 had become Associate Justice of the U.S. Supreme Court, and the United States entered the war on April 6, 1917. Sokolow went to Italy and the Vatican, assuring both that the Jews would produce a simple agrarian population in Palestine, in contrast to what Jewish opponent Montagu had said about Jews and farming never mixing."

Chantelle lowered her wide eyebrows. "Didn't Britain claim to our volunteering Canadian boys and their loved ones that it had gone to war to defend the rights of defenseless little Serbia?"

Terry Hardy folded his hands as if in prayer-like condescension. "Like the myth of the Germans sinking the American ship Lusitania in 1915, after being damaged by a German torpedo but followed by an unexplained explosion. The ship had already been transferred to First Lord of the Admiralty, Winston Churchill, and was thus part of the English navy. England had already broken the German war code in December 1914, so that by January 1915, British Intelligence could advise Lord of the Admiralty Churchill where every U-boat was in the vicinity of Britain, including the Irish coast where the *Lusitania* sank."

Hardy gave a long sigh and lifted his folded hands over his head. "World War I pitted the bulk of the duped British population against a small group of pacifists and socialists who saw the war as a dark carnival for the amusement of the ruling elites and paid for with the lives of their subjects. There was little reason, for example, why a war should interrupt Jewish trade – and during World War I, Britain bought needed binoculars from enemy Germany while Germany in turn bought needed rubber from the British Empire to meet the needs of Germany's war machine."

Chantelle looked down at the floor and Hardy gave a slight grin at sensing a convert. "Franklin Delano Roosevelt had been made Assistant Secretary of the U.S. Navy by President Wilson, and Roosevelt said there was a financial element that had owned the government since the days of Andrew Jackson and that the U.S. was going through a repetition of Jackson's earlier fight with the Bank of the United States but on a bigger and broader basis. Secretary of State William Jennings Bryan also made note of the large banking interests interested in World War I, because of the wide profit opportunities, and in 1914 before the war, the French firm of Rothschild Freres cabled to New York's Morgan and Company the flotation of a loan of $100 million, part of which was to be left in the United States to pay for French purchases of American goods."

Hardy suddenly reared back and raised his head. "Churchill would write in 1920 after the war, 'From the days of 1776 to those of Karl Marx to those of Trotsky Russia, there has been a world-wide conspiracy steadily growing,' but perhaps as you say, Chantelle, we digress." Hardy then lowered his head. "That head of *The Manchester Guardian*, Scott, found out that France wanted Palestine, and so he squealed to Sacher and Weizmann, who regarded French hegemony over Palestine as a 'Third destruction of the temple.' Weizmann vowed to arouse the feelings of Zionists throughout the world, to secure for the Jewish people a written promise by the British regarding Palestine, using that carrot of a powerful world Jewry."

Hardy by then had almost the look of a smug victor but Chantelle maintained her straight face, with her hands folded above her knees to underscore she was still listening. "Back in the Middle East, when France's Picot and Britain's Sykes met with Hussein, Sykes said to leave all to him, and he spoke to Hussein about the tripartite agreement with Russia but did not leave a copy of it with him. Yet Sykes asked Hussein to accept the agreement then and there. Hussein had a letter of assurance from McMahon and totally trusted the English, although he would later have second thoughts, saying that Lebanese men had not been hanged to give their country to the French. Observing the British-French snow job on Hussein were British generals Wilson and Newcombe, and General Wilson wrote a 12-page letter of protest, saying it was outrageous what was being done to one of Britain's greatest admirers. What was deemed more important, however, was that Sykes not inform Hussein of his plans for Zionism in Palestine."

Chantelle peered downward in apparent discomfort and Hardy kept control. "Turkey was never certain of the alliance made with Germany in October 1914 and still thought it could negotiate a separate peace deal with the Entente – from the start, when Turkey and Britain had declared World War I against each other, both kept up negotiations to try ending it. The Zionists on the other hand thought Turkey's entering World War I presented a disaster for Jewish hopes in Palestine if Turkey were to win – they therefore opposed any peace treaty that left Turkey with a grip on Palestine."

Hardy, by then the increasingly evident neo-historian, raised his head again to the ceiling. "It is interesting that a half-century earlier, Jewish British Prime Minister Disraeli had bad-mouthed the Turks as a people, who terminated their culprits in a more expeditious manner than torture, and Britain had formed a bad image of the so-called scurvy Turks. But that same *realpolitik* Disraeli had later pushed to align temporarily with the Turks, if such an alliance would keep pre-Bolshevik Russia away from Britain's, that is, Disraeli's, Suez Canal."

Hardy momentarily pulled in his lips as if they were dry, but instead of pausing for water, he simply wet them before pressing on. "The British-Ottoman Turkish conflict had that religious component – many Ottomans practiced the Muslim religion, over which the Ottoman Sultan practiced as Caliph, and when Turkey entered World War I, the Sultan/Caliph declared the anticipated jihad against his Christian enemies. The British press then published cartoons of the Muslim creed and ridiculed the faith, despite the British Empire having 100 million Muslims. Throughout the war, British intelligence also kept a wary eye on resident Muslims, great and small, and the Anglo-Ottoman Society, formed in Britain before the war, had prominent Jews, Moses Gastner and Lucien Wolfe, as members gathering intelligence.

"A small number of Muslims in the Empire did become anti-imperialist and by 1917, one British Islamic Society protested against Palestine becoming a Jewish state, noting that the Roman-toppled temple of Solomon had that splendid mosque over top of it. The Muslims also emphasized they had not historically discriminated against the Jews as had Christians, but the ill wind of anti-Ottoman Muslimism, already well entrenched in Britain before World War I, continued throughout the war."

Hardy looked to be loving his role. "Before and after the 1917 Balfour Declaration, Britain used a number of non-Jewish diplomats in an attempt to negotiate with Turkey a peace treaty including British control of Palestine but the efforts were all quashed – Wiezmann realized that a separate peace treaty with the Ottomans might make the Balfour Declaration null and void, and said that any negotiations would have to be ratified by Russia, and Russia would never agree. It was also in Zionist interests to make as much as they could out of Turkish persecution of Armenia – after the war, British reports of that persecution came to include Hitler's having being impressed with the genocidal savagery done to the Armenians."

Chantelle wrinkled her brow, turned her shoulder to Terry Hardy and raised her chin but kept listening. "From 1913 to 1916 before the U.S. entered the war, American-Jewish Henry Morgenthau was U.S. president Woodrow Wilson's ambassador to the Ottoman Empire. Morgenthau was also a member of the New York bar and had made huge sums of money in real estate speculation before making sizeable contributions to the Democratic Party. During the 1912 U.S. presidential campaign, Morgenthau had been chair of a critical financial committee and later was a main player trying to stop the reported massacre of Armenians in 1915. But notably not the reported massacre of gypsies by the Bolsheviks in 1915 Armenia! Morgenthau also spearheaded huge monetary grants to Jews in the Ottoman Empire, particularly those in Palestine."

Hardy looked to Chantelle for reaction but when he got none, Hardy pretended not to take note. "In 1916, Morgenthau claimed that he had arranged to sell Palestine to the Jews. He embarked for Palestine with key American Jews such as Howard Roscoe, Professor of Zionism and Supreme Court Justice Felix Frankfurter, along with assistants including the president of the Zionist Provisional Committee in New York City."

Suddenly Chantelle shot up in her plastic chair. "If this all happened before the Americans entered the war..." but Hardy also shot up and raised his index finger. "Ah, but Weizmann and plant Balfour warned Britain that the Jewish-American mission could influence international Jewry to side with Germany against Britain, and Britain asked Weizmann to sabotage the Morgenthau mission that was to include a separate peace with Turkey."

Hardy then leaned back again as if he had a cigar. "And so, on the way to meet Morgenthau in British-run Gibraltar, Weizmann stopped in Paris to see Edmond de Rothschild. At the subsequent meeting in Gibraltar, the diplomatic language was German, and Weizmann fantasized that the British Tommies outside the open windows were German spies, so had them shot. Weizmann convinced Morgenthau that Turkey would not accept a Jewish Palestine or an independent Armenia, and he made it clear to Morgenthau that it was a mistake for him to associate his mission with Zionism."

Hardy raised his arms and folded them above his head. "Back in Britain, Zionists Sacher and Simon were worried about putting all Zionist stakes in Britain winning World War I, but Weizmann soon out-argued Sacher, and Simon conceded that a British protectorate in Palestine could be a temporary route to go."

Chantelle leaned forward with a queried look. "Had Britain lost World War I and had Mr. Weizmann's gamble failed, would your history of Zionism, Mr. Hardy, be different?" and he grinned at where he had Chantelle. "I'll get to that in a second. In April 1917, the U.S. entered the war against Germany but not against Turkey and prior to the British Balfour Declaration in November 1917."

Hardy then adjusted himself to take back over. "Leading up to that war entry, Walter Rothschild, pivotal to the Balfour Declaration, became heir to the London branch of the dynasty, while on the hard-liner Zionist side, Sacher edited a book called *Zionism*, talking of the Jews' failure to propagandize enough to non-Zionists. Sacher proclaimed that assimilation of the Jews was impossible, not because the rabbis did not want it, but because non-Jews did not want it.

"Prior to that Balfour Declaration, the British-Jewish Assimilationists' Lucien Wolfe had gone to the British government, complaining that the Zionists had been saying it was impossible for assimilation and warning of potential resentment of favoritism to Jews in Britain, at the expense of the rest of British citizens. Wolfe had also argued that British Zionists represented Jewish interests more than foreign-born Russian Jews like Weizmann, Sokolow and Gastner. But plant Balfour had taken it all in from Wolfe, shrugged and said that, wherever Jews lived in the world, they excited envy among other peoples, so that British jealousy was no big deal, despite Balfour later using envy as a reason why the Jews should have a national homeland."

Hardy waved a hand again to the air while holding the other as if it had that cigar. "Remarkably, while all the key Zionists in Britain were Russian Jews, they managed to defeat the British-Jewish Conjoint Committee and its Assimilationist position in 1917. The upper-class *Times* of London took the view that the Jews do constitute a nationality as fact, not opinion, and the Zionists added spice by accusing the Assimilationists of being pro-German."

Hardy gave another grin as if happy with his lecture so far. "Again in those years leading up to the 1917 Balfour Declaration, Vladimir Jacobtinsky, a young Russian Jew, had come to Britain in 1913. Jacobtinsky had wanted a completely Jewish regiment to fight in Palestine, since heretofore some 20,000 Russian-Jewish immigrants of military age, living in the East End of London, had been exempt from conscription.

"Lawrence of Arabia got into the act on behalf of the shafted Arabs, and he wrote a letter to Mark Sykes advocating not sacrificing Britain's small friends in favor of its big Zionist friends. Lawrence wrote that the Arabs were in the process of taking the whole territory including the port of Aqaba on the finger of the Red Sea and he felt ashamed, since Lawrence knew the McMahon promises were a sham. Lawrence also wrote to General Clayton, 'we are getting the Arabs to fight for us on a lie and I can't stand it.' But as for Lawrence's letter to Sykes, it was somehow intercepted and never made its way to him.

"God's fool Hussein did not know that a Balfour Declaration was being contemplated and in answer to your question, Chantelle, had Arab forces taken Damascus *before* November 2, 1917, would world history have unwound differently, yes, but only until the point when the Zionists made their next moves."

Chantelle sat pondering Hardy's answer and he pushed on. "General Allenby and the Arabs planned to take Palestine after the Arabs took Syria, but they were deliberately stalled in the next step of taking Palestine, while the Zionists worked at frantic speed in London. Allenby and the Arabs actually took Palestine but by the time they did so, the Balfour Declaration had been signed six days earlier on November 2, 1917, and the *Times* was instructed not to publish the story until November 9, so that the Arabs did the dirty work before the Zionists took over Palestine. A grain of salt had been added when Lawrence of Arabia had ironically blown up the train carrying Turkish leader Pasha to defend Jerusalem against Allenby's advancing army. On December 9, Lawrence heard that Jerusalem surrendered to Allenby, one week after the December 2 Zionist celebration at the London Opera House. The Arabs took Damascus in September 1918, but it was too late for them to help themselves."

Chantelle took in a deep breath and let out a sigh as if she had been listening to a long dissertation with much information to absorb. She shifted in her chair and looked ready to comment but Hardy re-entered to hold the momentum. "In the summer of 1917, Weizmann, Sokolow and Mark Sykes developed a statement that they gave to Lord Rothschild for sending to Foreign Secretary Balfour. The draft in essence said 'His Majesty's government accepts the principle that Palestine should be reconstituted as the national home of the Jewish people and HMG will endeavor to do its best to ensure achievement of this objective, discussing methods and means with the Zionist organization. Such action would represent the link between Palestine and the Jews after 2,000 years of separation.' Rothschild added a personal touch, 'I am finally sending you, Arthur J. Balfour, the note you asked me for.'

"Balfour developed a response, 'I am glad to inform you that HMG accepts the principle that Palestine should be reconstituted as the national home of the Jewish people,' but Balfour did not send the response – key British Jew in government Montagu protested, saying that the Balfour response would promote anti-Semitism throughout the world and adding that Zionism was run by men of enemy descent, meaning Russian Jews. But Montagu sat only in the British cabinet and was not in the key War Cabinet that would make the final call on the Balfour Declaration.

"Sacher meanwhile presumed that Zionists would insist that the proposed state in Palestine be Jewish and he resolved that Britain should recognize Palestine as the national home of the Jewish people. He set up a Zionist organization called the Jewish Coalizing Corp, under whose aegis Jews could move freely and autonomously to Palestine and develop it economically. Hundreds of telegrams from Jews all over Britain then flooded into the government's Whitehall.

"On October 31, 1917, plant Balfour finally replied to Lord Rothschild, saying 'HMG would favor the establishment of a national home for the Jewish people and will use the best endeavor to facilitate the achievement of this objective, it being understood that nothing should be done which may prejudice the civil and religious rights of existing non-Jewish people in Palestine or the rights enjoyed by Jews in any other country.' The note was sent two days later on November 2, 1917, to Lord Rothschild and published November 9. The Jewish Assimilationists were defeated, the Zionists now controlled the British government, or had its ear, and they had Rothschild in their camp. The Arabs had occupied Palestine for thousands of years, including the last 1,500, but Palestine would go to the Jews."

Hardy suddenly rose, turned and retreated to his rear washroom in order to urinate but he left the door open to ensure that he knew of Chantelle's movement, if any, in his apartment. He had a swig of water from the tap before returning to his chair. Hardy then went on as if the break had been enough for both of them. "The British would consult the U.S., and Weizmann in particular rushed to have American Zionists extract a pledge of support from President Wilson. Wilson then permitted American Zionist Lewis Brandeis to telegraph an unambiguous support for Zionism."

Terry Hardy's entire hand then went up. "It is also critical to remember that the British wartime cabinet had worried that Germany could play the Zionist card herself, given that the head of the World Zionist organization was in Berlin, and could force Turkey to promise autonomy to the Jews of Palestine. Such an action might rally world Jewish opinion to the German-dominated Central Powers and alienate it from the Entente. Jewish-American support would thus dry up as would Jewish-Russian support for what was by then the new moderate Kerensky government in post-tsarist Russia. The Jewish-dominated Bolsheviks would then cease power and make a separate peace.

"In fact, Germany had made it official – that if it were to win World War I, Palestine would go to a Jewish settlement under Jewish protection, but in aligning with Germany, the main obstacle, as Zionists perceived it, was Ottoman rule over Palestine. Britain had thus been made to believe that the Balfour Declaration would be good propaganda, both in the U.S. and Russia, and Britain had been accordingly made to feel that it had to beat Germany to the punch."

Hardy betrayed another smile as if he were quite comfortable with how things were unfolding. "British Zionists had done what they could to foster the idea of the power of world Jewry, and as Zionist Sacher wrote, 'To display delicately and deftly the image of world Jewry belongs to the art of the Jewish diplomat.' The British Foreign Office learned from Weizmann and followers to believe in the Jewish influence upon the world as a powerful if subterranean force, and he implied that Jewish monetary influence in the U.S. and Russia could tip the balance in the Great War.

"After the Balfour Declaration of November 2, 1917, Lord Rothschild said to the subsequent Jewish celebration on December 9 at the London Opera House, that it was for world Jewry the most momentous occasion in 1,800 years. 'Next year in Jerusalem' became a mantra more real than it had been for almost two millennia, as Jews had avowed it at their annual Passover celebration.

"In Russia, the Jewish-run Bolsheviks seized power five days after the British War Cabinet had agreed to the Balfour Declaration, and Lenin and Trotsky, both Jews, vowed to take their country out of World War I. After the Russian Revolution of 1917, the Jewish Assimilationist movement everywhere in the world essentially ceased to exist, the Bolsheviks said they did not want Constantinople anymore, Balfour made efforts to ensure that no Turkish flag would fly over Palestine and Weizmann considered any discussion of peace out of the question. Weizmann wanted what Prime Minister Lloyd George had promised, a knock-out blow to Germany and its ally Turkey."

Hardy took in a big breath as if to afford a grand summary. "Sir Henry McMahon, the High Commissioner in Egypt, had offered the kind and trusting old gentleman Hussein, direct descendant of Muhammad, pledges of support, if he would rebel against the Turks, and Hussein had risked his own life and that of his sons. Hussein and followers seized many of the Middle East's cities, including Mecca, Aqaba on the Red Sea, Medina and Damascus. Yet Eastern European Jews and the fabled, dissenting 'Young Turks' did more to win World War I than anything connected to the Arabs. In the Treaty of Paris at the end of World War I, Lloyd George allowed France to take Syria, so long as Britain took Iraq – oil – and Palestine.

"When Hussein first heard of the Balfour Declaration, he said he welcomed Jews to all Arab lands, his presuming Palestine would still be as such, and he welcomed any good understanding with the Jews. But by December 1917, Hussein expressed concern over the Balfour Declaration, and there were grave reservations among Muslims and Arabs over both the Muslim places of worship and the 'mischievous movement of new people calling themselves Zionists.' Jerusalem and environs were covered with Muslim mosques, shrines and mausoleums, and in 1917, the Arabs still outnumbered Jews seven to one. But the British concluded that Zionists throughout the world controlled the world's gold and capital, and Sykes scribbled all over the Arab protests that were submitted, saying they were seditionist.

"Hussein at the end of World War I was given only that Hejaz region east of Palestine, with Churchill in 1922 carving the Trans-Jordan out of Palestine, giving it to Hussein's son, Abdullah. Hejaz was then overthrown in 1924 by fundamentalists of the Saud family to establish Saudi Arabia. Hussein had to settle for being ruler over an Iraq established by oil-thirsty Britain.

"The Arabs of Palestine rioted in 1920 and 1921, and in 1929 there was an anti-Jewish pogrom of 133 deaths, not dissimilar to the 35 or 40 deaths from one of the Russian pogroms. Then in 1936, there was a full-blown Palestinian Arab revolt. The Jews had established a paramilitary *Haganah* in 1920 to defend themselves against such pogroms, and additional armed Jewish groups appeared in the 1930s. One was named *Etzel* or what the British called Irgun and another was *Lechi*, or what Britain called the Stern Gang. Both groups soon moved to the offensive against the Arabs and eventually against the British, reaching a climax at the end of World War II when *Etzel* and *Lechi* carried out assassinations, beatings and bombings, including the bombing of the King David Hotel in Jerusalem, where they killed 91 and injured 46.

"One Amir Haj al-Husseini had been designated Grand Mufti of Jerusalem but because he helped in a 1936 Arab-Palestinian revolt, he was hunted by Britain and escaped to Nazi Germany. In 1937, the British government of the day recommended in its Peel Report that Palestine be tri-national – Jewish, Arab and International – but the report was repealed in 1939 by Neville Chamberlain's government, in order to stay alive against Churchill and his backers. The Grand Mufti of Jerusalem was sidelined by 1948."

Chantelle's eyes locked in a squint, as if torn between a curiosity at what she presumed was an Eastern-European Jewish perspective and a lingering suspicion of a man who seemed to be in a great rage behind his cool front.

"I seem to recall, Mr. Hardy, that your condemned Lloyd George lost the election after the Great War," and his pale face went red. "Yes, in 1922," and his palm came up against Chantelle's face. "But long before that or any signing with the Ottomans, the financial strength of international Jewry came to override all, and the Balfour Declaration shifted Jewish allegiance to the British side. Britain agreed to take Jerusalem by force from the Ottoman Empire, international commerce issued a food blockade against Germany and the United States was sucked into the war.

"That same British Prime Minister David Lloyd George, who could recall from childhood more history of the ancient Jewish state than his Britain, saw himself as a Good Samaritan in orchestrating the 1917 invasion of Palestine. Lloyd George would remain for another five years key to a British focus on the Middle East. Muslims were cast as the new foes for Britain, after the Ottoman Empire collapse in World War I, and at the end of the war, with help from a propagandized Armageddon, 'Great, Great Britain proposed a Jewish Anglo-American client state housing a Jewish homeland, including Palestine, Jordan and Iraq known then as Mesopotamia.'"

Chantelle leaned back from Hardy's theatrics and she made an attempt to offer an override to the whole topic, dropping her eyes to the floor. "In World War I, three to four times as many soldiers died as in World War II," but Hardy seized on her words. "Winston Churchill in 1915 had ordered an attack against the Ottoman Turks, with an all-Jewish military force named the Zionist Mules Corps, and Jewish cabinet minister Sir Herbert Samuel had declared that Palestine should be British in order to be eventual center of Jewish self-government."

Chantelle suddenly slammed both heels to the floor and brought her body forward. "In your zeal to attack Winston Churchill, Mr. Hardy, you have not mentioned that he, like Balfour, affirmed that nothing should be done to compromise the civil and religious rights of non-Jewish communities in Palestine," but Hardy's face reddened again. "Or the rights and political status enjoyed by Jews in any other country. During that British campaign against the Turks to take Jerusalem, many Palestinian Arabs were killed under official British command, but Churchill would later insist that the Arabs so killed had been trying to kill the invading Jews, despite many more Palestinian Arabs dying."

Hardy then looked to assume a less heated posture and resume his role as lecturer. "At the end of World War I, there was scarcely a promise that U.S. president Wilson made to the Germans not broken, but Henry Kissinger still today regards German complaints over Versailles as self-pitying nonsense. Churchill meanwhile, even after World War I, continued the naval blockade against the German people, the blockade having been war-designed to starve men, women and children."

Hardy then gave a smug grin. "British debt was 14 times what it had been before the war but all the allied powers, save Finland, reneged on their war debts, mocking creditor Uncle Sam as an Uncle Shylock. But many Americans after World War I also blamed the war profiteers and merchants of death for having dragged them into the war, as well as the British propagandists who had talked of the rape of Belgian nuns and babies being tossed around on Prussian bayonets. Yet a desperate Germany by the 1930s had its debt reduced only from four to three billion marks, and in September 2010, Germany finally paid off its war debts."

Hardy checked to ensure his listener was still at least in partial submission, and then went on. "After World War I in 1921 and before Lloyd George lost the 1922 election, he gave Churchill the job of administering Palestine and Iraq. Churchill in 1921 went to Palestine to negotiate an Israel west of Jordan and in his 1922 White Paper, triggered the movement of 400,000 Jews to Palestine over the next two decades from 1922 to 1939."

Hardy then took to leaning forward with his eyes low in supplication. "And during that period, Chantelle, your Churchill who had supposedly spoken for equal rights for non-Jews in Palestine, quashed all Arab efforts for an elected assembly in this Palestine where non-Jews still outnumbered Jews. He drafted a Palestinian constitution disallowing any Arab majority from restricting further immigration of Jews."

Chantelle came forward with a fast counter: "I understand that Churchill was not particularly influential in the 1920s and '30s. He was isolated from power and depressed, at times considering suicide. Chamberlain on the other hand was judged mentally healthy but look where that got us!

Hitler was supposedly bipolar, and the amphetamines we hear he took from 1941 to 1945 would have made any manic-depressive symptoms worse."

Hardy arched back and looked upward as if resigned to the ignorance of others. "Abraham Lincoln also suffered from depression and was often suicidal, maybe contributing toward his empathy for others who wanted to keep slavery. He was not certainly bothered by fellow Whigs who owned slaves," but before Chantelle could question, Hardy shot on: "Churchill said if the Arabs did not agree with his increase-in-Jewish-immigration plan, 'tough,' and Churchill went further, asserting it was not wrong for a higher race to replace the Arabs. The Jewish right wing then in Israel, especially the Russian Lubavitchers, was bigoted and regarded all non-Jews as racially inferior." Hardy then let out a huff. "Predictably, there was an Arab revolt in 1929 Palestine."

The redness in Hardy's face lessened. "By the 1930s, fears in Palestine heightened that the locals had been selling land to European Jews, and most Palestinians were aware of the role that European Jewry had played in the 1917 Balfour Declaration, with Britain's consequent wrestling of Palestine from the Ottomans. In 1937, Churchill declared to Doctor Chaim Weizmann regarding Israel, 'You know, you are our masters. If you ask us to fight…' Churchill stayed opposed to any partition of Palestine and would acquiesce to Palestine obtaining self-government only when the Jews became the majority."

Hardy looked for reaction at a silenced Chantelle before he charged on. "Meanwhile, after World War I, Jewish carpet baggers made huge financial gains ravaging Germany, much like those that raped the U.S. South in the aftermath of closet Lincoln. The South, in order to survive, turned to its churches for communications and went underground with anti-Semitic movements, like the Ku Klux Klan."

Chantelle's dark eyebrows again went down. "…Closet?" and Hardy offered a hint of grin. "You recall saying, Chantelle, that good ol' Abe Lincoln never joined any church and that his candidacies were opposed by clergymen when he said, 'If he could save the Union without freeing any slaves, he would do so'? Lincoln initially did not seek to abolish slavery in the South, only in the new territories to the west. But in the

Emancipation Proclamation that Lincoln issued – long into the civil war in late 1862 – he declared freedom for the three million slaves in the Confederate states, over which Lincoln had no control, but not for the half-million slaves in the Union states of Missouri, Kentucky, Maryland and Delaware, whose affairs he could still influence. Politics won out over principle and the main splits in American society today are much the same as they were 150 years ago, at the start of civil war. Southern troops fought for the land they thought was being invaded and half of Americans now recognize that the war had more to do with states' rights than the issue of slavery.

"In any event, when Lincoln's General Grant ordered the removal of Jews from parts of the South in 1862, Lincoln personally revoked the order, but when General Ewing called for the evacuation of 20,000 non-Jews from Missouri in 1863, burning their houses, barns and crops for thousands of square miles, Lincoln did nothing. Teddy Roosevelt's grandmother was one of the Missourians so displaced and would later refuse to sleep in the Lincoln room of the White House. Roosevelt himself became anti-Wall Street but Jewish filmmakers bought him off by bribing him with the contrived trek up San Juan Hill, after the hill had already been captured."

Chantelle's brows were still down and she came straight forward at her benefactor. "Closet, Mr. Hardy?" He leaned back and raised his arms in a fold behind his head. "Aside from Lincoln's own accounts, most of which are autobiographical sketches written in the pre-presidential years 1858 to 1860, his childhood stories are mostly anecdotal. But Lincoln's law partner William Herndon did document Lincoln's childhood and said he had once confided that his mother was a bastard, the daughter of a Virginia nobleman. Such a background led Lincoln to his feelings of superiority and disdain for physical labor. Yet in 1808, Lincoln's mother Nancy Hanks had visited Lincolnton, North Carolina, and had become pregnant by a Mr. Springs, who was a Jewish blood relative of the Rothschilds and whose real name was Springstein. The product of that pregnancy was Abraham Lincoln, a Jewish American. Like Dwight David Eisenhower, the Jewish son of David Jacob Eisenhower.

"General Eisenhower caused the death of a million German prisoners of war at the end of World War II and under dear old Ike, American troops

430

raped 2,000 girls in Stuttgart over one weekend. Hell, I had one North American Jew tell me that his father boasted of regular raping parties, while he was in the army during World War II."

Chantelle again slammed both boots to the floor and her eyes went straight to her sponsor. "If, Mr. Hardy, one were to assume the worst about Eisenhower and Lincoln's tactics as chief warriors, one could still acknowledge that, like the Rothschilds and Disraelis, they may have seen the bigger picture and held integrity together while helping the world move forward."

Hardy waved his right hand in dismissal. "The big picture argument can rationalize anything, Doctor Fouriere, especially if god is on one's side. Anyway, Abe and Ike were just the center-stage actors, albeit intelligent ones – there is no evidence I have seen to suggest that Ike knew about Pearl Harbor ahead of time, as did FDR."

"Knew?" but Hardy cut Chantelle off. "Going back from our tangent to those between-the-wars years, the new Jews of Palestine were not employing Arabs, making Churchill's arguments of trickle-down benefits a crock. Yet when one prominent Brit challenged Churchill, Churchill pressured the judiciary into putting the man in jail for six months over a civil issue."

Chantelle again tried perspective. "Many a British artist and King George himself were pro-Nazi between the wars" and Hardy's face went red again. "Hitler made no mention of the Jews in his 1939 Nuremberg speech but dwelt instead on both the suffering of the Germans after World War I and the threat of Bolshevism from the east. International Jewry decided that his words were code to condemn Jewish carpet bagging after World War I and the Jewish-controlled Bolshevism of Soviet Russia."

Chantelle looked not to like where her benefactor might be going. "As you no doubt know, Terry, decades before the Holocaust, Hitler called in writing for the annihilation of Jews. His letter of 1919 said that a strong government could offset what he called the Jewish threat, by denying first their rights and then having the final aim be the uncompromising removal of Jews altogether."

But Hardy came back as if Chantelle's interjection was flak. "Jews the world over declared war on Germany in 1933, and they began an international trade boycott in an attempt to wreck the German economy. The

Germans reacted in 1935, imposing the Nuremberg Laws on Jews who had been carpet bagging, to encourage those Jews to leave Germany. The Germans also interned some Jewish citizens, as did the Americans with their Japanese."

Chantelle made a loud scoff. "Hardly comparable," but a red-faced Hardy pressed on. "As early as 1912, the French government passed a battery of laws aimed at vagrancy, but later the French issued identity cards for gypsies, using the term, 'nomads.' By the 1930s with the influx of refugees from Eastern Europe, France issued a new identity card and there followed the creation of dozens of 'special centers' – soon to become concentration camps – for refugees arriving on French soil, in the name of national security."

Hardy thought to pause and after a second's silence, put forward a platitude: "There is a tendency, Chantelle, in all democracies to isolate and discriminate against certain minorities, and democracies as you have said are just as likely as authoritarian states to practice xenophobic or racist politics, especially when the masses can be swayed by the passionate actions and speeches by say, France's current Sarkozy."

Chantelle herself began then to go red. "By the end of World War I, Mr. Hardy, Hitler had already stated that his goal was removal of the Jews altogether and he later declared that if 15,000 of your supposed Jewish corrupters in World War I had been poisoned by gas, Germany would not have lost. Hitler also said in 1938 to his right-hand man Goering that 'We have to settle our accounts with the Jews' and by that time, there were cartoons of hooked-nosed Jews being blamed for Germany's ills."

Hardy had Chantelle in the argument and he countered in kind. "Churchill had been in bed with international Jewry for half a century. In 1937, his daughter married a Jew, and Churchill declared that Hitler would be defeated and Israel's time would come."

Chantelle fell prey to her own indignation. "And about the same time, Churchill secured a copy of *Mein Kampf*'s extreme passages, earlier vetted by the Nazis so as not to offend British aristocracy," but Hardy grinned at where the fight was going. "Churchill was furnished that copy by international Jewry. The Duke of Westminster said that British power was infested with Jews and that the forthcoming World War II was a Jewish plot but Churchill quashed him too."

Chantelle may have sensed her benefactor knew more but kept up the fight. "In Hitler's private speeches, had he not talked of harnessing private industry and eliminating Jews from Germany?" and Hardy held firm. "Meaning send them away to Madagascar or ideally to Israel in Palestine. There had even appeared in Germany, by the late 1930s, signs scrawled on the outside of Jewish office windows, saying 'Jew to Palestine,' but Palestine had already fallen into the domain of the British as a result of that infamous Balfour deal to win World War I."

Chantelle then fell silent, possibly pondering how the talk had wound around to where it was, and Hardy kept on the offensive. "Had Britain redressed Germany's grievances before 1933, when Germany was democratic, it might have been satisfied. In the post-war Treaty of Versailles, the powers-that-be granted self-determination to countries wishing to be free of German rule but denied that same self-determination to Germans. After World War I, there were more Germans in Czechoslovakia than Slovaks, and the Sudetenland Germans, from 1920 to 1938, were constantly petitioning the League of Nations to be allowed back into Germany.

"Italian leader Mussolini in 1933 proposed a meeting of Britain, France, Italy and Germany to re-do Versailles, but Churchill quashed the meeting. Later in those 1930s when Italy went to war with Abyssinia, the slavery-practicing Abyssinia attacked first and Churchill said the Abyssinians deserved to be conquered, saying they were as primitive as the American Indians. Churchill added that no one should pretend that Abyssinia is a fit and equal member with civilized countries of the League of Nations."

Hardy's pale face was red again. "Churchill was an absolute white supremacist and used derogatory nicknames for labeling any non-white races. To the pleading Palestinians in 1936, Churchill said that a higher race was taking their place. Churchill also was the man behind a mental deficiency act to sterilize feeble-minded people and other so-called degenerates; Britain under Churchill was going to make colonies of these misfits. In the 1930s, the British King Edward VIII said Churchill was a man filled with emotion and brandy, his having no judgment or wisdom." ·

Hardy then looked to gloat a bit over Chantelle's silence before he trumpeted on: "During those same 1930s, international Jewry published Churchill's pro-Zionist and anti-Nazi writings all over Europe as well as the newly emerging Israel in Palestine. To add spice, a Hungarian Jew who had spent six months in Dachau Concentration Camp published in England one of the first accounts of Nazi concentration camps and pushed to get Churchill back to power. Then prominent Jew Vladimir Jacobtinsky – the man who in 1918 had fought against the Turks and had spearheaded the flow of Eastern Europe's Jews to Palestine – became a key Zionist voice and supported Churchill's arguments against Palestine being partitioned."

Chantelle looked to have begun wondering who her benefactor was but he seized the moment's silence to carry on. "Leo Amery emerged as one of Britain's most powerful people, with a solid knowledge of both Europe and all British dominions, and Amery thought and acted as if the British Empire were his private property. You Canucks have a Rocky Mountain named after him, and few Canadians or even British peers at his schools of Harrow and Oxford knew that his mother was Jewish."

Chantelle looked to have spotted a flaw and she shot forward, "Therefore, half-Jewish," but Hardy had Chantelle where he wanted her. "Half, quarter, eighth, sixteenth. A contemporary American Jew had a great, great grandfather who had been a German Jew and had immigrated to Arkansas where he had converted. Today, that part-part-part Jew sings *Kol Nidre* on Yom Kippur."

Chantelle held forward. "And some young Russians with equally oblique Jewish lineage harass religious Jews in Israel today," but Hardy resumed his tirade as if her interjection was meaningless. "Amery wrote for the *London Times*, talking of Nazi brutalities against Austrian Jews and tried to influence Prime Minister Neville Chamberlain. Chamberlain committed political suicide when he dismissed talk of Nazi atrocities as Jewish-Communist propaganda."

Hardy held forth. "When the Germans marched into the Rhineland in 1936, British approval was almost unanimous that the Germans had liberated their own territory. And after occupying that Rhineland, Hitler did not make another move for two years. But in 1938, Eastern European Jews murdered a German diplomat in Paris and a band of German vigilantes retaliated, smashing Jewish shops and synagogues, while at the same time the Nazi government arrested 30,000 Jews. International Jewry called the vigilante vandalism part of a Nazi government-supported pogrom and labeled it *Kristallnacht* or Night of Broken Glass, for which every Jew, involved or not, had a different story. That *Kristallnacht* story was promulgated across Britain to rouse up its people for war.

"British Jew Leo Amery then emerged as leader of a pack of Tory rebels, and Amery wrote hawkish newspaper articles while Churchill, despite declaring Palestine to be god's land to both Arab and Jewish Palestinians, pushed for more Jews to go to Palestine. In the three years between 1936 and 1939 alone, Palestinian Arabs tried to rise up against the Jewish takeover and more than 5,000 were killed by British troops."

Chantelle peered downward and may have begun to realize she had lost any ability to temper her benefactor. Hardy kept the floor and his role of summary-lecturer. "When Hitler later affirmed in 1938 that he was not planning to invade Czechoslovakia, the Czech leader tried to humiliate Hitler, saying 'the coward' had backed down, yet Hitler still held off on any invasion of Czechoslovakia and asked to see Chamberlain again. Churchill grudgingly told Chamberlain that he was lucky. After that meeting with Hitler, an exuberant Chamberlain should not have gloated 'We've got peace for our time' but instead he should have quietly bought time to prepare for a possible war.

"By 1938, with Germany having annexed the Czech Sudetenland as well as Austria, 10 million Germans were added to the Reich without a shot being fired. Hitler had also taken his divided Germany back to almost its pre-World War I size and had taken the country from an economically depressed country, with unemployment of six million, to the first economic and military power of Europe, with a gross national product up by a third and unemployment down to one million.

"Hitler, moreover, did not want to evangelize his National Socialism, but the Communists did want to take over the world, and the nations adjacent to Russia feared any Russian rescue more than a German invasion – 'Better Hitler than Stalin' was the cry across all the countries around Russia: Finland, Estonia, Lithuania, Latvia, Poland and Romania. In fact, from Sweden to the Black Sea, Russia was the enemy more feared than Germany."

Hardy held on. "Hitler in 1939 was trying to make a deal with Poland, not invade it. He wanted a pact against Bolshevik Russia. Hitler also wanted no war with Britain, declaring the life of each British soldier sacred; he would repeatedly throughout World War II pay a price for exercising such a belief. But Britain sabotaged any potential German-Polish deal by guaranteeing Polish independence. Churchill thought the guarantee a splendid idea, since he and his backers wanted to make war inevitable. British diplomat Lord Halifax also believed that if Hitler continued his bloodless victories, Germany would dominate Europe economically and be no longer at the mercy of any British blockade. As thus spun by Churchill's backers who also influenced Halifax, such German immunity would mean Britain's end as a world power. Halifax therefore feared Poland signing any deal with Germany and hoped instead Poland could be duped into doing a suicidal act of defiance. For Lord Halifax..." Hardy let out a scoff. "Poland's suicide was better than having Hitler chalk up another bloodless coup."

Chantelle sat silent, with a look that Hardy took for obsequiousness and he marched on. "Leo Amery and adjutants were, meanwhile, pushing for Churchill to replace Chamberlain, while the Jewish Leslie Hore-Belisha overhauled the British War office and pushed for conscription. The dump-Chamberlain drive spread to the U.S. where FDR cousin Alistair Forbes pressed for power going to Churchill, and the issue hit *The New York Times* in January of 1939. Chamberlain tried to counter by, among other things, rejecting a new Hitler peace proposal that allowed Germany to control Eastern Europe and get back its African colonies, and Chamberlain publicly added that it would be war if Germany invaded Poland.

"The Churchill backers also triggered false intelligence reports of a planned German invasion of Poland, causing Britain to panic and driving Chamberlain into that mad act of a war guarantee. Despite that guarantee, Allied intelligence, as sourced from god knows where, also estimated German strength at more than twice the true figure. Yet in any event, Poland predictably refused to make any concessions at all to Hitler on Danzig or the Prussian corridor.

"Thus by 1939, war became the only apparent alternative. Still, Chamberlain's wording in the guarantee to Poland was vague. It was meant to repel only an attack that clearly threatened Poland's independence, and it was Britain that would judge whether such independence was threatened. The British Cabinet felt that Danzig should be returned to Germany, and Chamberlain wanted leverage to persuade Poland to give Danzig back. But from the day of the British guarantee forward, the Poles refused even to discuss concessions with Germany.

"Germany then offered Poland the role of satellite ally in an ultimate move against Soviet Russia but by then Chamberlain had Churchill egging him on to hand out British war guarantees all across the European continent. Chamberlain was also led by the same false intelligence – interpreting any further move by Germany to mean a march toward world domination – when all Germany wanted was a breadbasket such as the Ukraine so as to be immune from any World War I-style shipping blockade of Germany. And Hitler knew Jewish Bolsheviks controlled the Ukraine.

"Hitler had figured that France and Britain would force Poland to negotiate but nothing came to pass. Hitler's terms for Danzig et al were mild but there were no further negotiations. In the subsequent invasion of Poland, Hitler instructed his army not to attack Allied troops of any sort but when he finally did march into the intransigent Poland, Hitler was shocked that his offer of peace was rejected by Britain. Hitler said that Britain, France and the U.S. were being stirred up by Jewish propaganda but Britain nonetheless declared war, causing Hitler's planned invasion of Russia and the Ukrainian breadbasket to be deflected against the West. For Britain to be of any help to Poland, however, the Russian Red army was indispensable and so Churchill won again by championing an alliance with the Jewish-dominated Bolsheviks. What Britain went to war over, in 1939, was what Britain in 1917 - 18 had been ready to give to Kaiser Germany. At the time World War I had commenced, the propagandized aggressor Kaiser Wilhelm II had been in power for 25 years without a war."

Hardy then eased back in his chair in the guise of an old sage. "By 1940, Leo Amery and train resolved that Chamberlain had to go, and Amery met with others in the spring of 1940 at Lord Salisbury's house to plot just that.

Amery decided that he would speak for Britain and used the model of 17th-century Christian fundamentalist Cromwell to deliver, in the House of Commons, a scathing attack on Prime Minister Chamberlain, while offering Churchill as the alternative. At the close of Amery's speech, Josiah Wedgwood struck up a rendition of *Rule Britannia* and shortly thereafter, the British royal family was forced to drop its support for appeaser Chamberlain. The King's speeches in support of the war followed.

"Around the same time, the U.S. ambassador to Britain, old Joe Kennedy, was charged with being an anti-Semite and he quit as ambassador to beat President FDR firing him. Joe Kennedy hoped to become U.S. president in 1940 but fell the way of Britain's Chamberlain."

Hardy was again smiling in smugness and carried on: "Many gentile scallywags came to view Leo Amery as their mentor and in 1940, he almost wrestled power from a resurrected Churchill before Churchill shipped Amery off to a nondescript India. There, however, Amery used his position to coerce Gandhi, with a promise of independence for India if it supported the war effort. Churchill fell for the bait, believing he had to react to cement his position and so he adopted a take-no-prisoners stance with the slogan, 'Victory at all Costs.' The slogan was music to Amery's ears."

Chantelle came back in with a comment that she might have thought would slow the roll of Hardy. "Mahatma Ghandhi had a Muslim counterpart in Abdul Ghaffar Khan, and together they envisaged a Hindu-Muslim union of India and Pakistan. Khan knew his Qur'an and shunned Islamists or Muslims who treated Islam as a political ideology. Yet for all that, he was frequently imprisoned. Khan nevertheless chose to publicize those passages that give men and women equal responsibilities and he established a school for girls."

But Hardy raised his palm for Chantelle to cease with her schoolgirl banter, and then he charged again. "Germany again in 1940 proposed peace, this time via Mussolini, who had been a British agent for MI5 during World War I, but Churchill, under pressure from Amery, held on to his out-for-blood posture and quashed all negotiations."

Chantelle then took to sitting quietly, possibly looking for ways to probe Hardy's arguments, and he kept the momentum. "From the early days of

World War II, British planners envisaged the defeat of Germany, not on the battlefields but through selective attacks on its economy. In the U.S., Bernard Baruch became the key Jewish financial contact after his link between the U.S. and Britain during World War I, while Doctor Chaim Weizmann remained Churchill's closest contact with the Zionist movement, writing in 1939 a pivotal Churchill speech that stressed a British appeal for American Jewish support."

Chantelle suddenly looked to see an opening. "The United States involved in 1939?" and Hardy may have sensed she had been taken in. "When in 1939, that mentioned British White Paper on a future Palestine placed limits on Jewish expansion, both the Jewish community in Palestine and around the world resented it. Churchill and Weizmann then defied British policy by trying, with support from the U.S., to bribe the King of Saudi Arabia for recognition of Israel as a Jewish State, using a sum at that time of three-quarters of a billion dollars."

Chantelle slunk back, looking askance at the floor, and Hardy again seized the advantage. "Hitler's Adolf Eichmann later tried transporting 3,600 Jews to Palestine but Britain stopped that transport, such that the world would not know the Nazis were trying a strategy not dissimilar to Britain's world home for Jewry."

Chantelle looked stunned but Hardy would not let up. "Churchill said he would do whatever necessary to bring the U.S. into World War II. Churchill in 1939 was upset with American neutrality and wanted to repeat the inflaming of American Jewry's hearts, as had been pulled off with the Balfour deal at the height of World War I. Accordingly, Churchill used his friendship with that American Jewish financial broker, Bernard Baruch, for a total focus against Nazi Germany, with the bribe of Palestine ultimately becoming a Jewish state. Chaim Weizmann then went to the U.S. to win over Bernard Baruch, saying that to do so would be 'the biggest plum of World War II.' Afterward, the British ambassador in Washington sent a telegram to Britain, relaying the U.S. Jews' insistence upon Jews in Palestine being armed, officially for Britain but actually against the Palestinian Arabs, or else U.S. Jews would steer their support away from Britain.

"As for any supposed German threat to the United States, American-Jewish historian Gerhard Weinberg invented much of that threat, using a comic book kind of history, with fictitious Nazi things like the New York Bomber. Additionally, by the late 1930s, anti-Communist films were no longer allowed in Hollywood but pro-Soviet films were being routinely turned out. In November of 1941, Roosevelt was re-elected and he began to maneuver the U.S. into war."

Hardy adjusted his posture in his little upright chair. "By 1940, Churchill declared that Britain could win World War II without the Arabs, and he declared to the British War Cabinet that if Britain and the U.S. were to win World War II, the concluding peace conference must establish a Jewish state in Palestine. Churchill specified that the state must not have an Arab majority that would be democratically able to restrict such a Jewish state's expansion, but that an alternative Jewish majority would be okay. Josiah Wedgwood, that on-cue singer after Leo Amery's speech to oust Chamberlain, used his clout for support."

Chantelle remained listening, perhaps intimidated by someone who evidently knew more about a subject of his specialization. "When the Germans invaded Belgium in 1940, Churchill publicly moralized about the invading of a neutral country but had been about to do the same thing with a blockade of Antwerp. Communications were, however, everything and so Churchill cut off all communications cables between the United States and Germany.

"It was Churchill who again refused to end the war in 1940 when Hitler offered peace, after the Germans trapped the British forces at Dunkirk. Hitler had not planned to invade France and had earlier built huge fortifications of defense. But even after Hitler overran France, he left alone its colonies and navy, yet Churchill said the Germans would demand the British fleet. After the fall of France in 1940, Hitler again tried to offer peace but Churchill again said no.

"The Battle of Britain that followed in 1940 was not to bring down the British Empire, which Hitler wanted to leave in place – his having agreed to restrict his German navy to only 35% of that of Britain and having scrapped all his aircraft carriers in 1940 – but to bring down Churchill. And contrary again to Western show-biz, German planes did not outnumber the British ones in the 1940 Battle of Britain – by December 1939, Britain had been producing more warplanes than Germany; moreover, for all the people killed in Britain by the German *Luftwaffe*, the U.S. bombers killed more people in a single raid over Tokyo."

Chantelle suddenly dropped her head, perhaps out of some familiarity with the plight of Hiroshima, and Hardy gave a look of satisfaction. "One of Churchill's first decisions when he came to power was to extend British bombing into the non-combatant area. Churchill talked about the German terror bombing of Antwerp and Rotterdam but the Nazis did not terror bomb – the German bombing of Antwerp, Rotterdam and even Warsaw did not take place until done in support of German ground troops, in line with internationally accepted rules of war for siege bombardment. Churchill nonetheless said if need be, he would shatter every German dwelling in every German city. The chief architect under Churchill was a Jew named Frederick Lindemann, who had a medieval desire for revenge."

Hardy then took time to straighten his deportment before he continued his beloved lecture. "Hitler in 1941 made the mistake of thinking that his invasion of Russia would show the West how futile a full-scale war with Germany would be and thus make peace. But Churchill was in bed with the Bolsheviks who were linked to his backers in Britain, and Churchill, by refusing, added another three years to the war, causing 40 million people to die. In 1941, Germany attacked Russia, executing a number of spies, including Jewish espionage agents, and the news went back to Churchill via the Nazi code machine that had been secretly confiscated by the Poles. Churchill then promulgated that the Nazi killings had been of helpless Jews.

"The vast deportation of European Jews did not begin until after Germany invaded Russia in June of 1941. But the Jews of Spain and Portugal were all spared, as were those of neutral countries Sweden and Switzerland – Spanish leader Franco had not given Hitler permission to cross Spain and take the British Gibraltar.

"Later in 1941, Churchill learned via that Nazi ultra-secret machine of Japan's plans to bomb Pearl Harbor, and he leaked the news to U.S. president Franklin D. Roosevelt. Up to that point, FDR had been given full

Jewish-American support for the U.S. entering World War II, but the American people were 80-20 against; so, just before December 7, 1941, Roosevelt ensured that key American ships were out at sea, but with enough boats and sailors left in Pearl Harbor to make things look good. The Japanese got sucked in and Churchill was said to have danced in the streets."

Chantelle put both feet on the floor and went stiffly erect in her chair. "That is an extraordinary accusation against an American president, Mr. Hardy. Do you have proof?" but he waved his arm in dismissal. "No more than I have of the machinations of World War I, all of which now are in mainstream books. Churchill, in a propaganda boost to the U.S. Jews for Zionism, got some Jews to fight in Italy under their own Star of David, and they became the only group in World War II to do so. In the Allied invasion of Normandy in 1943, the captured Eastern Europeans, who had been fighting for Germany, were not treated as prisoners of war under the rules of the Geneva Convention but instead were sent by Churchill back to death via Stalin. This was true especially of the Cossacks who had fought Russia in 1920. Later were added Cossack women and children. In that same year, 1943, at the Casablanca Conference, Churchill got Roosevelt to agree that peace could come only with the total elimination of Germany and Japan as war powers, thus ensuring that the Germans and Japanese had to fight to their deaths and extending the war for another two years."

Hardy was heating up. "A year later in 1944, Britain and the U.S. jointly issued a publicity paper that highlighted Nazi atrocities and war crimes against Jews."

Hardy propped himself up in his chair and took to looking down upon the smaller Chantelle. "Berlin responded with a 100% denial but Churchill still wanted to use chemical and biological weapons on German civilians. He commissioned anthrax to be dropped on Northern Germany to poison the cattle, and through them, send millions of men, women and children to their horrible deaths. Churchill also wanted to use poisonous gas on the German cities.

"In the British bombing of Germany's baroque city of Dresden, 770 Lancaster bombers dropped two-thirds of a million incendiary bombs, together with thousands of tons of explosives. Civilians who fled into the water tanks were boiled alive. On the morning thereafter, 500 British B17 bombers, supported by 300 fighter escorts, strafed any fleeing civilians. The fires burned for seven days."

Hardy's face by then was bright red and he was almost out of his chair. "During that same 1944 year, Chaim Weizmann advocated the emigration of 1.5 million Jews to Palestine."

Hardy then tried to compose himself, for the sake of his proffered wisdom. "Churchill had said of Lenin that in his taking the lives of Russian men and women, no Asiatic conqueror could have matched Lenin's notoriety. Churchill had also known of the later starving of the Ukraine in the 1930s and of the Russian concentration camps. Before World War II, between 17 and 22 million people were killed by Stalin, 1,000 times the number of deaths attributed to Hitler in 1939, yet Churchill would later heap praise on Stalin: at Yalta in 1945, Churchill defended Stalin and how high his integrity was, while agreeing to use Germans as slave laborers. At the end of World War II, Church and Stalin decided where the Iron Curtain would fall, with Churchill sacrificing the 100 million Christians of Eastern Europe.

"Winston Churchill as early as 1898 had said he did not care for the content of his words as much as the impression they left. Churchill, before World War I, had been the principal cause of an armored train calamity in South Africa, but he had been the one to write about it afterward, thereby launching his fame. After World War II, Churchill's six-volume history of the war won him the Nobel Prize for literature, besting Ernest Hemingway. Church had good speechwriters."

Hardy finally let out a long sigh. "By 1945, the Jews in Palestine had already formed a government, with a sophisticated military. And inside the emerging Israel, underground Jewish paramilitary organizations, such as that *Irgun* headed by Menachem Begin, had already embarked on a concerted terrorist campaign to assassinate British officials and soldiers, and drive Britain out of Palestine."

Chantelle finally recovered enough to spot a hole in Hardy's argument. "I understand that Jewish leaders at the time condemned such acts and Doctor Weizmann, as president of the World Zionist Organization, had actually gone to Palestine in an attempt to stop the Jewish violence," but Hardy again used Chantelle's words to further his own. "Or so he said." Hardy folded his arms in an 'I know everything' position and gave another grin. "Bad propaganda for the establishment of a Jewish state." He then added, "The Jewish terrorism strategy was against Arab Palestinians as well."

Again, Chantelle sat silenced and Hardy trod on. "The new U.S. president Truman and Secretary of State Marshall tried to overrule the diabolical strategy that had been developed by Jewish Secretary of Treasury, Henry Morgenthau Jr., whose plans for the treatment for Germany post-World War II were exceptionally harsh and encompassed the 'Potato Patch' plan, turning Germany into an agricultural and pastoral country. But before Truman and Marshall could get involved, Morgenthau went to Churchill, in an attempt to starve post-war Germany, and Churchill in turn carried forward Morgenthau's plan to Stalin.

"Morgenthau's deputy was a Soviet spy, and together with Morgenthau planned to turn the German industrial Ruhr region into a ghost land and another area, the Saar, to be destroyed, with all materiel and machines turned over to the Russians. The Morgenthau plan would have meant death to millions of German civilians, yet Morgenthau's simple answer was to ship any surplus Germans to North Africa. Another senior U.S. official said Morgenthau's Carthaginian views were Semitism gone wild with vengeance."

Hardy gave a wide grin as if in his element. "In the ensuing chaos of post-war central Europe during 1945 and 1946, 12 million ethnic Germans were expelled from Eastern Europe and two million perished, with the women raped and many men and women whipped or beaten, before being starved or shot. A German Diaspora that had lived for six centuries in what was suddenly Poland or Czechoslovakia was, in an Eisenhower-Churchill-Stalin agreement, denied its very existence, and it became illegal in the annexed German part of Poland even to speak German. Millions of surviving ethnic Germans were shipped to concentration camps and then to Germany, where people were already starving."

Chantelle came forward with another attempt at perspective. "You are again talking about a few Jews, Mr. Hardy. Albert Einstein, who had been disturbed by Sigmund Freud's praise of war as a social menstrual cycle, rejected the barbaric mythologies found in parts of the Hebrew Bible, and gleaned, as had Jesus's brother James, what he could from ethical Judaism. Einstein also had concerns about Zionism and turned down, as you know, Israel's first presidency."

But Hardy again latched onto Chantelle's argument. "To the relief of Israeli pioneer David Ben Gurion, but even your ethical Princeton Professor Einstein was not fussed about Jews' lending with interest to non-Jews, while not Jew-to-Jew."

Chantelle tried steering Hardy back to the issue of people movement after the war. "It was a challenge in 1946 to find room in Israel for the great masses of Jews who wanted to leave Europe," but Hardy raised his eyebrows. "Doctor Fouriere, Churchill had agreed with Weizmann that there should be three to four million Jews in Palestine, with greatly expanded boundaries for Jewish settlements, and that Jews should be allowed to immigrate to Palestine without proper papers."

Chantelle tried to counter with a little knowledge of her own. "Did Churchill not want support for Zionism to go from British shoulders to the U.S.?" but Hardy again seized on her words. "Especially since Zionists were killing Brits in Palestine. A weary Churchill implored Weizmann to take anecdotal photos of emaciated Jews in concentration camps at war's end and dupe the dull-minded Baptist Truman."

Chantelle folded her hands and tried for balance. "Is not President Truman on record as saying that the Jews cared only about themselves and no other displaced person?" Hardy tried a fast answer but she was not finished. "And at war's end, were not some Jews who returned to their native Poland murdered, whereupon 5,000 Jews fled the country?"

Hardy then resorted to another wave of dismissal. "Menachem Begin commanded that *Irgun* gang killing the 91 innocent people in the bombing of Jerusalem's King David Hotel. And while Churchill did not bless the killing of British officers by Jewish terrorists, he nonetheless pooh-poohed the bombing and continued to promote a Jewish home in Palestine."

Chantelle sat forward. "Yet in 1947, did not Britain offer to give the Palestinian mandate to the UN?" and Hardy shot back, "But Jewish terrorism against Britain continued."

Hardy then leaned back. "When Britain's Palestinian mandate ended in May of 1948, David Ben Gurion proclaimed the state of Israel, and the USA and Russia, both information-controlled by Jews, rushed to recognize it. The abandoned Arabs were forced to protect the Palestinians, who were being bulldozed."

Chantelle tried again for the bigger picture. "Those Jewish people, Mr. Hardy, had just survived the Holocaust, which Churchill described in his memoirs as the most horrible crime in history," but Hardy lurched forward, his face inflamed and his finger pointing. "British Jew Emery Reves got Churchill U.S. Jewish dollars for his memoirs, whose focus was World War II. They were translated into twelve European languages, as well as Hebrew."

Hardy held forward with his face aflame as was his voice: "Ever since World War II, there has insidiously grown within the American foreign-service elite, a Churchill cult, and anyone who defies the new U.S. hegemony is a new Hitler. Churchill, the man who declared that he enjoyed every second of World War I and kept up the starvation blockade of Germany, even after the end of that war."

Hardy looked to ensure he still had Chantelle listening. "Churchill declared 'History will be kind to me for I intend to write it,' and he wrote to Eisenhower that he, Churchill, was of course a Zionist and had been one since the start of the 20th century. In his last major exhortation as British prime minister, he affirmed that the world ought to let the Jews have Jerusalem."

But Chantelle remained undaunted. "Because it is they, my Jewish Terry Hardy, who made it famous." Yet he would not be halted. "In 1956, there was a secret meeting in which Britain and France signed a deal with Israel whereby Israel would attack Egypt, and Britain and France would jump in, ostensibly to protect the Suez Canal from Israel. Israel did attack Egypt, and Britain and France joined in the general fray a week later."

Chantelle suddenly found herself on comfortable ground and she folded her hands in a fist toward Hardy. "Canada's Lester Pearson, one of our most revered prime ministers, won the Nobel Peace Prize for his role in resolving that Suez crisis."

Hardy raised his hands over his head. "Ms. Chantelle Fouriere, the world has noted your Canadian high-mindedness but Canadians do not, in any measure, know of Adolf Hitler's library, despite much of it being in Washington's Library of Congress for over 60 years. Those books of Hitler's include 130 works on religion and spirituality, and there is one book – *Worte Christ* or 'Words of Christ' – with Hitler's lines penciled in beside a passage. It is one with Jesus echoing Rabbi Hillel's words, 'Love your neighbor as you would yourself!'"

The room went silent, and after the lull Chantelle's benefactor picked up again the advantage. "A Yale psychiatrist noted Hitler's words, '*Man kommt um den gooes begriff nicht um*' or 'One cannot get around the concept of god.'"

Hardy then bent forward in supplication toward Chantelle, with an appeal that he may have thought was in an area dear to her heart. "Hitler was reared Roman Catholic but was a classic apostate, who rebelled against the established theology in which he was bred, all the while trying to fill a spiritual void."

Chantelle remained unmoved and Hardy continued: "In the 50 volumes given to Hitler by woman filmmaker Leni Riefenstahl, he had marked 100 pages of theological prose, especially the explanation of the Trinity. Hitler had marked it, '*Körper Geist und Seele*' or 'body, mind, and soul.'"

Hardy again gave a smile, as if revealing a gem of wisdom to a new student. "In December 1941, Hitler had written that if there is a god, then that god gives us not only life but also consciousness and awareness. Hitler thus felt that if he lived according to god-given insights, he should not go wrong, but if he did, he would still have acted in good faith."

Chantelle folded her arms in a tight embrace and let out a huff. "A psychotic could say the same, Mr. Hardy" but he stayed forward in the same supplicating position. "As could you, Chantelle Fouriere."

Hardy then gave a knowing smile before straightening up in military fashion and slapping both hands on his knees. "We'll reconvene at 1400 hours."

Monday June 8 2009

When Chantelle returned in the afternoon, she had affixed her hair into a no-nonsense ponytail and tucked her shirt into her jeans. The street entrance was unlocked and after Chantelle clomped up four floors of wooden stairs, she found the door open to Hardy's apartment.

A lanky Hardy was standing waiting beside the long table, and he started talking before Chantelle reached her chair, "President Hoover, Chantelle, once said that the best way to overcome unhappiness is to make someone else happy."

They sat down and Hardy kept the moment, "It is in the 1960s that the word 'Holocaust' was spread. There were, yes, those Armenian deaths as triggered by their enemy Turks in World War I, but only since the 1960s have we come to see mass victimization as an identity that one needs to assert."

Chantelle looked recharged after her post-lunch walk and she hurled back, "Prior to the 1960s, books on German history at the University of Toronto had little or no reference to the Holocaust, but the 1961 trial of Adolf Eichmann began to change all that, and what was unleashed was a Holocaust consciousness. Even then, however, many survivors kept quiet until the 1980s, when they began to appreciate that they would die without their story being told."

Chantelle's financial backer raised both hands as if about to say something profound, "You yourself, Chantelle Fouriere, said that truth has first to come from within, in your praising French-Canadian healing. The president of the World Zionist Organization, Nahum Goldmann said that it was a sacrilege to use the Holocaust to justify the oppression of others, but he was subsequently condemned by other Jews as self-hating."

Chantelle did not register any reaction and went on to talk about a friend who had been a young journalism student and had refused to watch the images of Holocaust victims clinging to barbed wire. The student had subsequently told her professor that she knew what had happened and had no need to see it. But later the student had told Chantelle that the student's already knowing was not the prime reason – it just hurt too much to look into the desperate faces of those victims who were enduring slow murder, and her heart fractured at the agony, depravity and the unfathomable loss. Thus, to stop the pain, the professor had then stopped the pictures, recognizing that many students had met their limit.

Hardy saw that Chantelle was primed to argue, and he picked up from where he had started when she had walked back in, "A Polish Jew named Lemkin in 1942 finagled his way into Washington's Board of Economic Warfare, and there he promulgated Hitler's crimes. Lemkin was a specialist in the roots of languages and invented the words 'holocaust' and 'genocide' to capture the horrors of what he said Hitler was doing. Lemkin emphasized that genocide was far worse than mere mass murder and carried with it the violation of an entire people, along with a permanent wound to its collective memory. Lemkin got 'genocide' into the UN wording in the post-war 1940s, saying that genocide destroyed a people, not for what they *did* but for who they *were*, adding that the Jews had done nothing to the Germans. Like the older Morgenthau of a generation earlier during World War I, Lemkin had a key contact, Samuels in *The New York Times*, and there was an international Genocide Convention in 1948."

Chantelle sighed a look of resignation, as if her recharge was going to be short-lived, and Hardy added, "Lemkin wanted Hitler to become the world standard for Holocaust, ostensibly to prevent it in the future, but he and other Jewish leaders at the time also condemned the German people. Earlier in the 1920s and 1930s, the world press had done much to debunk the stories of German savagery during World War I and there was much skepticism – in the 1943 Roosevelt-Churchill-Stalin meeting, references to evidence of Nazi gas chambers were deleted from the meeting's resolutions, because of untrustworthy information."

Blood nonetheless rushed to Chantelle's cheeks. "Full disclosure, Mr. Hardy, is an antidote to disbelief that such crimes can happen, and full disclosure should continue to quash the falsehoods that Holocaust deniers have tried to spread, their doing so even in the face of photographs and eyewitness accounts. I heard a Harvard professor say that the U.S. as the greatest power on earth, has the power as no other to enforce peace through world awareness."

Hardy may have sensed he had gone too far again and so he suddenly sat back as listener to an eager student. She continued, "After Eisenhower's troops liberated the Nazi concentration camp of Buchenwald, Ike referred to the corpses in a written communication to one of his generals, 'Now the troops know what they were fighting for.'

"A couple of years ago, around Remembrance Day of 2007, I felt I did not know enough about the Holocaust and took a week off to attend Toronto's 27th annual Holocaust Education Week. The Chairman of the United Jewish Appeal had stated the objectives in a brochure highlighting the week's events – to educate as many diverse groups as possible."

Hardy crossed his legs and leaned back, while nodding an acknowledgement and Chantelle began: "One woman speaker had been born in pre-war Poland and had survived seven concentration camps, another had been born in France, and part of his family had been saved by the Salvation Army. One speaker had written a book, *From Victims to Victors*, and another had been hidden by a gentile family, but in 1946 had been transferred to a German displaced persons camp, from which she had been selected along with 92 other Jewish orphans to go to New York. One woman had watched her Lithuanian ghetto be liquidated in 1944 and her father had been sent to Dachau where he had died of starvation. Her little brother, she said, had also been taken away and most likely murdered.

"One speaker in a synagogue opined, 'When all your ideas of whom you could trust or who was reliable among your neighbors and friends are thrown into question...' and another synagogue speech shocked me, 'On a cold evening in Davos, Switzerland, in February 1936, my father, a young man of 27, shot the leader of the Nazi party in Switzerland.'

"One speech slated for a synagogue highlighted Hitler's infamous quote of 1939, 'Who today remembers the 1915 - 16 Turkish annihilation of the Armenians?,' that massacre now condemned by both Canada and the United States. Another synagogue speech by the Jewish Genealogical Society commented on the quantum leap forward in research afforded by the Swiss Red Cross International Tracing Service in deciding to open its records. Some speeches were rated as to suitability – a speech 'Beyond the

Kindertransport' at the annual Jewish book fair was designated 'for teachers and educators only' and another 'suitable for students 13+'.

Scheduled at the end of the week's program was an art exhibit, *The Undeniable Truth*, presented by the Canadian Society of Yad Vashem's Continuing Holocaust Education Committee. The artist had recently visited Europe's death camps and had depicted the Holocaust horrors through his paintings, while reaffirming their undeniability."

Hardy looked to underscore his listening. "Did you give full attendance to all?" and Chantelle calmly responded as if she was the one then speaking to the student. "I chose to attend the closing program at giant Beth Tzedec synagogue. The program brochure queried, 'How much more do we need to know about the Holocaust and what are we still likely to learn? It is a paradox that the more distant we are from the event, the greater it looms as the defining moment of 20th-century inhumanity. How could the perpetrators do what they did? What could the victims have done? And how has the experience of bystanders been internalized by future generations?'

"Before going to the closing, I slotted myself in for a speech in Toronto's North York Library and another at the Holocaust Museum and Education Centre. The library was jammed with young schoolchildren from a multitude of races and they sat with remarkable quietude as the main speaker began.

"The speaker had been born in Hungary in 1938 and was quick to note there had not been any world lesson learned, since there was a holocaust being carried out right then in 2007 by Arab armies in the Sudan, and Iran was trying to destroy Israel. The sad-looking man went on to tell the children that six million people had been killed, including one-and-a-half million children, for no other reason than that they were Jews. He said to the many races present that a self-proclaimed superior Aryan race wanted to kill all of the undesirables in the world and have a 'white-class only' society.

"The soft-voiced man dwelt on his pre-war years in a Hungarian village where there had been massive anti-Semitism, and he touched on the hot Canadian topic of school bullies, saying boys had beaten up Jewish kids in his village and had thrown snowballs or even stones. The Jewish kids, he said, had to go at four o'clock to religious instruction and he added that there had been no games for Jewish children as there had been for others, with playtime being only on Saturday afternoon. In the summer, the Jewish kids had to go to religious school, while the gentile kids from the age of six, went to work on farms.

"'Then came the Nazis who wanted to conquer the world.' He said that Hungary had been allied with the Germans against Russia, and men from the age of 20 to 50 years had been conscripted, with Jewish men drafted into forced labor. Food and clothing had all been rationed, and the speaker said he had no choice but to go to the black market and buy food from farmers to sell for a profit in Budapest, and then buy clothes to sell at a profit in his village.

"By 1944, Germany had come to distrust Hungary and had occupied it, ordering Jews out of their houses, with their doors unlocked. There had been no cars or carts, and the Jews were to have taken all they needed on their backs. They had then been rounded up in a large synagogue, where their jewelry had been confiscated.

"In the synagogue, 300 people had been confined for four days, with only one toilet, and both babies and old people had been crying. They had then been sent to the railway station and put into a cattle car, to be sent for the next two weeks to the provincial capital and its ghetto. After that, the Jews had been sent back to cattle cars for five days of travel, and during the five days, they had to sit with their rationed food on the floor, with only one bucket of drinking water and one toilet under a blanket in the corner.

"Along the train ride, the captives had been told by a Polish Jew, who had been a caught escapee, that they were 'all dead' but no one had believed him or that such a cultured country as Germany could do such a thing. When they had arrived at the concentration camp, the Jews had seen a sign saying "Work will make you free,' and had viewed it as a mocking of their Jewish work ethic. The camp had been ringed in barbed wire, with watchtowers and armed guards at each corner.

"Privileged inmates serving as camp police had whisked people out of the boxcar, told them to leave their possessions and, before anyone had been allowed to say a formal goodbye, divided the people into men and women, boys and girls. A Nazi officer had ordered a further designation, and some people had been ordered to undress and be naked for a shower in a nearby room. Out had come the gas.

"From the camp's dead people, false teeth had been removed, as is done by undertakers, and the bodies had been burnt in ovens. This speaker, however, had been asked to strip naked and he actually had received a genuine shower.

"Hair had been shaved off, because there had been a huge problem with lice and he had heard others say the hair had been put into mattresses. Each new inmate had been given a uniform and a pair of wooden shoes which were to last for a full year, and there had come to be a problem with mites all over the body.

"One night, the inmates had been marched to another camp and along the way they had seen a giant fire. The inmates had been told by a Jewish person that it was a fire of the bodies of Jewish people, who had known they were going to be gassed.

"At the new concentration camp, the speaker and fellow inmates had been given a diet of bread and soup for a whole year, and they had to work from sunup to sundown, seven days a week. The speaker said that different categories of people had been sent to different camps, and some had been forced to cut wood with only handsaws. People, he added, had been getting sick but had been allowed to remain in the camp hospital for only a week. After that, they had been sent to Auschwitz or if they had say, pneumonia and their fever had not broken, they had died.

"On October 7 of 1944, 500 of those very Jewish *Sonderkommandos*, who had enforced order in Auschwitz, revolted with stolen explosives. They did not go passively to their deaths.

"By January of 1945, the Russians had been getting closer, and because rail-and-vehicle transportation had been destroyed by the Allies, the Germans had given the people bread and marched them away from the Russians. From time to time, those people being marched would hear shots in the distance behind them and had been told that the shots were for people who could not keep up. The speaker had then been moved to a warmer indoor camp that made airplanes, and on May 8, 1945, the Nazis had left the guard towers. The inmates had not at first recognized that they had been freed.

"The speaker concluded by saying 'Thank God we live in a great country, Canada.' When then asked by an adult listener what his most frightening experience was, he said it was at night when he could hear people crying, and he had visions of those fires, seen from afar."

Hardy folded his hands on his knees. "Very illuminating," and he may have sensed that it was politic to let Chantelle continue. "The second presentation I saw took place at the Holocaust Education Centre and was delivered by a sweet lady in her 60s. Her audience was a group of young Muslim schoolgirls, many with niqabs or burkas, and some girls had their faces and heads entirely covered. Before the lady speaker began, she took me aside to ask my purpose in being there, and commented to me on how hard it is to believe that some people could have been so horrible to others.

"The lady speaker had been born in Belgium in 1939 and at the age of two, had been hidden by her mother in a convent. The speaker went on to say to her young Muslim audience that the German people had been good and bad, as are all people, but Hitler and the SS hated Jews, gypsies, homosexuals and others judged inferior. She said the Nazis had come first to round up the Communists, before they had come for the Jews, and the lady speaker went on to say that informers had been paid for reporting hidden people. 'We ourselves,' she said 'had not known we were to have been killed.'

"Jews had sold their belongings or had lent them out, in the hope of retrieving them after the war. Antwerp, the lady added, had been a diamond center and her father had been a diamond cutter.

"Everything, she said, had been rationed and though she had never been physically abused, she had also never been hugged or loved. She said she had never sulked but had to be obedient.

"At the end of the war, a relative who had passed himself off as her father had taken the lady speaker to Ireland where to her horror, a chain given her by her father had been removed from her neck. She had also tried to cross herself but had been told not to do so, because she was a Jew. At the age of 17, she had ventured on her own to London, met a Jewish man and 'had become Jewish.'

"She later moved to Canada and there met other Jewish people who had hidden during the war, but years later when she returned to Antwerp, she was confronted with people who were surprisingly hostile to her, in her parents' home and her father's place of work.

"After the woman speaker finished, one Muslim girl asked her why she was no longer married and the lady at first said the question had no relevance but she would try to make it so. After the question period finished, the speaker returned to me with her sweet smile and affirmed that she does not hate, but found it a shame that those nice-sounding Muslim girls had to wear those awful things covering their heads and faces.

"The Holocaust week's closing program was at Beth Tzedec, a conservative synagogue, but most people were casually dressed. They represented a range in age, although no children were seen in attendance. People drifted in late amidst chatter but when one person went to the microphone to ask people to take their seats, all eyes turned to the podium, whose front panel had a sign for the United Jewish Appeal.

"Then from the rear came about a dozen Jewish World War II veterans marching honor-guard style up the center aisle and carrying both the Canadian and Israeli flags. And so the evening began."

Chantelle paused for some water and Hardy adjusted himself as if to reaffirm his listening posture. Chantelle resumed. "Before the main speaker came forward, the introductory person at the microphone recapped the week's events and drew attention to Toronto's Scarborough General Hospital, where 200 doctors and other health-care workers had interrupted their critical schedules to attend one event. The introductory speaker had a plea and a prayer for the return of three Israeli soldiers held in captivity.

"The guest speaker was a Doctor Rotbard from New York and he was thunderously applauded as he took the podium. Doctor Rotbard began by saying that after World War II, many Jewish people of influence had come to North America, for which he had great praise. He likened Holocaust deniers to flat-Earth people, who look at the planet from outer space and do not acknowledge the sphere. The speaker went on to assert that 100 million documents from the meticulous record-keeping Nazis, as well as Holocaust survivors, had been retrieved, and new technologies in the years ahead would allow people to decipher them.

"The speaker then shifted his focus to the madness of the present world, as underscored by a country like Iran, which had rescued Jews during World War II, and 'now had a leader who denied the Holocaust while the very perpetrating country, Germany, had a leader who admitted it.' The wartime ghettos in Europe, he reminded us, had been established by the German government, and he drew attention to pictures taken in 1941 of Auschwitz, with its swimming pool and its killers at leisure, including those German men and women killers dancing, adding that he left to people's imagination what happened thereafter.

"The speaker also drew attention to a book, *The Origins of the Final Solution*, that addressed different kinds of killings at different times and places. He pointed out that in the years 1933 - 39, only 15,000 Jews had managed to flee to Palestine – 'A land for a people without a land' – and only a few had made it to Canada or the United States. The Germans, he continued, had kept annexing places with more Jews, especially Poland, and in 1941, 10% of the Warsaw ghetto had starved.

"Why, he asked, had the local people cooperated with the Nazis against the Jews? The speaker went on to talk of the 'poetry of the ground moving,' referring to the hundreds of thousands of Jews who had been buried alive. In one case, he said 500,000 had been killed, but two had survived and given testimony. In another incident, the speaker pointed out that selected prisoners had been nine to 12 years old, because the Nazis had needed little hands for a certain type of labor. One of those young people had acquired typhus and had been quarantined, with every place he had gone thereafter documented, along with the soldiers and Nazi bureaucrats involved. The speaker added that thus was the value of the 100 million documents, soon to be sourced through new technology.

"During World War II, the evening speaker continued, a senior U.S. person had said 'No' to the bombing of Auschwitz, despite senior Jewish pleas, including those of Israeli founder David Ben Gurion. The speaker said there is a distinction between information and knowledge, the latter implying action, and then he explained that the same U.S. government person had said after the fact, 'If only we had known, we would have done something.' The speaker then added 'Bull, because there was not the political will, as is again today demonstrated with Darfur, where Arab armies are victimizing innocent people, and the only people screaming to the world are those who have experienced such a holocaust.'

"The speaker finished and received a standing ovation, before he took questions. To an initial question, the doctor speaker appeared perplexed but then replied that he had written 15 books on the issue. To a second question as to why the victims had remained Jews if they were so treated, the doctor repeated the question slowly and loudly. To a final question by a Jewish woman as to how she and fellow Jews could, as victims, so mistreat the Palestinians, spontaneous groans emanated from the audience, before the speaker defended the legitimacy of her question. He talked of the many attempts to settle the Palestinian question and the need for racial reconciliation worldwide, again to an ovation.

"As I left the synagogue, I was greeted by a man and an elderly couple who had witnessed my awkwardness at the entrance, in asking whether I needed any special head covering. They had been kind and presumed, I guess, that I was a gentile and needed counsel."

Terry Hardy let out a long sigh and then gestured to make a comment but Chantelle was not about to let go. "The issue of such systemized genocide never entirely left my mind after that week in late 2007 and I recall at Easter 2008, reading the obituary of a Jewish Canadian man who had lived through Buchenwald and two work camps. In the years before his death, he had occasionally watched Steven Spielberg's film *Schindler's List*, reliving, his loved ones said, a part of his life that he had always refused to discuss with his family. The family recalled at his passing that he and his wife had in earlier years switched to Yiddish when they had not wanted younger ears to hear. The small Canadian city in which he had worked also had an elderly Jewish woman but she would not talk of her experiences in the Holocaust.

"On weekends, the man had played poker or had watched wrestling, but in the months prior to his death, his family reported that he had begun to have flashbacks and nightmares, calling out the names of brothers, sisters and others, who had perished in the Holocaust and about whom he had never spoken. Among the survivors I have personally known, many are haunted by the same question, why they endured while others did not, and survivors often feel that they should respond more to their survival.

"Six months later, I read in a Toronto newspaper about the hope that some Jews had found in the concentration camps, performing theater and opera where Jewish performers and actors could lose their minds in a moment of artistic fulfillment. One Jewish woman, when she was 11 years of age, had been sent to the camp of Theresienstadt and there had tried out for a part in a planned theatrical presentation. When it had been staged at the camp by Jewish actors for a Jewish audience, tickets had been hard to come by.

"The Jewish woman also recalled earlier, how her mother and grandmother had been crying, because the Nazis had taken their wedding bands. She and her loved ones had then lived on very little food, suffering through the cold and snowy winters.

"Inside Theresienstadt, amid the starvation, sickness and rat-infested conditions, the hope in the children's lives had come from their devoted teachers and from the art they had been producing – about 4,000 works have survived from the camp, including several of that woman's drawings. Such creativity was made famous by the children's book, *I Never Saw Another Butterfly* and by musicals such as the *Brundibar* performances. The Jewish woman said that when the actors had been on stage, the audience had buoyed them further up with its standing ovations.

"In June of 1944, there had been a show scheduled for visitors from the International Red Cross, and the inmates had been spruced up. Sardines had been prepared, in contrast to the green soupy substance for lunch and the usual frozen potato at night. The speaker added that a piece of bread and margarine had to last for three days.

"In October of 1944, most child performers, 28 in all, had been shipped to Auschwitz along with other camp inmates, and it had later been reported that only three had survived, but 14 actually had later turned up. To this day, that Jewish woman has terrible memories of a father who was killed by the Gestapo and of a home where she had hid in the attic, while it had been ravaged by people whom she had been told were Hitler Youth. The woman also had memories of the friends she had made and lost at Theresienstadt."

Terry Hardy gave a motion to say something, but Chantelle raised her chin to give herself space for closing. "As a Canadian and gentile, I tried in vain to retrieve some faith in humankind. But then I heard of a German named Billy Thomas, a butcher's son, who had during World War II, gone voluntarily to Auschwitz and there had called Jewish inmates by name and not number, also saving many of them from death. As one rabbi later said of this good Samaritan Billy Thomas, 'It is not for us to judge him.'

"Later in 2008, I read in a Vancouver newspaper of the 60th anniversary of survivors, there being among the more than 1,000 Holocaust orphans who were helped by Canadian Jewish groups involved in kicking down the country's doors – after years of a near ban on Jewish immigration, Ottawa in 1947 allowed 1,000 visas to be issued for orphaned Holocaust survivors.

"Some Holocaust children during that period had not been old enough to be put to work, and thus had survived to liberation, from which they had been bounced around the displaced person camps; nevertheless, despite those children's appalling early experiences, there was among them an almost complete lack of juvenile delinquency or crime. An assessing psychologist believed that the orphans had been too young to have been permanently damaged. Those orphans said they had not known of their circumstances; moreover, things that could still hurt them had been put into the back of their minds. Others did not want to dwell on self but did speak with pride that none had ever asked Canada for unemployment relief, while boasting of their success stories. In Auschwitz, the least deathly part of the camp, and one where inmates had a chance to survive, had been called Canada, and in Poland as recently as the 1980s, people still referred to good fortune as 'getting Canada.'"

Hardy let out a *whoosh* of air before taking a slow drink of water from his mug on the table. He then folded his hands above his knees, as if to take back the position of sage. "People refer to the Holocaust as the gold standard for man's inhumanity to man, and the Zionist mandate remains 'Never again.' In 1978, on television there was a multi-part series entitled *Holocaust* and it had 120 million viewers.

"You mentioned, Chantelle, that one key speaker talked about the difference between information and knowledge, with the latter implying action.

The word 'genocide' yields a moral imperative, and American public approval of Bosnian involvement went from 50% to 80%, once the notion of genocide was promulgated – the notion of 'ethnic cleansing' was added in after the campaign had begun. Reporters in Bosnia then got hold of photos of skeletal men behind barbed wire and paired them with Holocaust newsreels, accompanied with the voice-over, 'Never again.' Jewish-American organizations were the most vocal in their criticism of the Bosnian Serbs, as they will be in any country if it allegedly bombs civilians."

Hardy then raised his left palm to face Chantelle. "The trump card in Bosnia thus became the rhetorical question, 'Why the West had not done anything in 1938?.' It should perhaps again be pointed out that before Pearl Harbor was bombed, 80% of Americans were against participating in World War II but the bombing did the trick. September 11 also enhanced empathy of the American people against genocide."

Hardy then took a stretch with his arms. "In the recent Balkan wars, there were no good guys – the Albanians also butchered the Serbs but some day, Serbia will offer up General Mladic for war crimes if Serbia wants to be in the EEC." Hardy raised his head above Chantelle's. "The world is so much easier to grasp if we see things in black and white, and a Mladic trial will help support that image. The Western world understands that Hitler intended to destroy every last Jewish person, and that the Germans would be unable to try their former leaders after the war for such unspeakable crimes. In the post-World War II war crime trials at Nuremburg, the laws on crimes against humanity were created after the alleged crimes."

After having listened patiently to Chantelle, Hardy was taking his full turn. "Look too at the Kurds! They wanted to separate from Iraq, despite Iraq's 'great recovery' of the 1970s, as under-reported in the West, and Sadam Hussein offered them land. But the Kurds wanted the oil-rich parts of Iraq! And in the Iran-Iraq war, the Kurds sided with Iran. Independent doctors said the allegations of Iraq using chemical weapons against the Kurds were untrue, and Baghdad condemned the U.S. media as the work of Zionists. But Hussein in 1990 made the strategic error of arresting an official British journalist as an Israeli spy, with Hussein's adding that he would retaliate with nuclear weapons against Israel, thus sealing his own fate.

"In the U.S. Foreign Service apprenticeship, the Holocaust is part of the equipment that one brings to the job, and perhaps we need to remember that the very name 'Churchill' is often the model for the courageous and just thing to do. The very United Nations that Israel laughs at was set up in great part on the premise that 'Never again' would the world allow another Holocaust."

Chantelle pressed forward. "Understandably so! – Holocausts take a long time for their seeds to be sown, and it is critical that we catch their development from the beginning."

Hardy nodded but added with a wry smile, "Cults, as you know, Chantelle, create myths to impose order on chaos, resolve contradictions and harness apprehension among the fearful, with those cults doing so, yes, for survival but also to be fruitful and multiply as the cult judges best. The 1961 Eichmann trial had a profound effect on Israelis, and the Holocaust has set the bar high."

Hardy raised again his head. "As for those people outside cult walls, a dose of guilt from ancestral anti-Semitism can be lethal – despite American troops being bombarded with Holocaust stories, Hollywood avoided the Holocaust subject across World War II, but the Hollywood Holocaust now has embedded itself as the modern icon for historical evil, with a show-biz *Shoah* determining how the Western world channels any accorded guilt. Within the European Economic Community, the Holocaust haunts all debates about race, hate and even economics."

Hardy made a loud shift in his chair before he pointed his finger at Chantelle. "You talked of a synagogue speech saying that Jewish genealogy heralds the leap forward in research now afforded by the Red Cross Tracing Service in opening up its records. It is ironic that the American Jewish Committee became incensed when the Mormons acquired records of the Nazi 'Final Solution' and were baptizing the murdered or typhus-killed Jews of Europe."

Chantelle gave a long, dark squint at Hardy but he returned it with a smile. He pivoted both his boots up on their heels and slapped the boots back down on the wooden floor. "Few Jews know that the Jewish Ilya Ehrenburg, under Stalin, was a pivotal member of the Soviet Antifascist

Committee and directed the Soviet soldiers' ravage of German civilians, with revenge being the rationale. Few Jews also fully acknowledge that the Jewish Blue Police had been recruited by the Nazis and had punished other Jews in the ghettos and concentration camps."

But Chantelle thrust both shoulders forward. "Did those recruits have a choice?" and her benefactor expanded: "Fewer Jews know that many senior positions in the Nazi ranks were occupied by Jews, both before and during World War II, or that in the years 1938 - 1940, less than 50% of the U.S. quota for immigration was used in any one year."

Chantelle suddenly again found herself taken back and Hardy added with a scoff, "In *Guilty Pleasure*, a quarterly journal for Jewish readership in the between-the-wars years and a magazine embracing the philosophy that guilt could lead to pleasure, there was a story about a Viennese-born Jewish mystic who aided Hitler's sweep to power."

Hardy gave another sweep of his arm. "Both before and after World War II, the Zionist cult was a clique containing both powerful capitalists and senior Communists, who betrayed the greater Jewish people."

Chantelle's face went blank and Hardy pressed forward. "Chantelle, early on in World War II, Auschwitz had been a Nazi detention center for Polish prisoners, and the Germans had expected that tens of thousands of Russian laborers would soon be encamped there. But as the Nazi invasion of Russia, begun in June of 1941, was stalled in the autumn, the Nazis had to change plans – the Auschwitz facilities were then upgraded to include gas for disinfecting, because of the typhus-carrying lice that were rampant in the area. Ovens were also created for disposing of the infected bodies of those inmates who had died in the typhus epidemic."

Chantelle mustered enough composure to come forward and raise her body up against Hardy, while lowering her eyes to his. "In 1945, pictures of concentration camp survivors from Dachau near Munich appeared in the first newsreels and showed the world the horror that had been taking place," but Hardy again waved his hand. "Candid shots of inmates who were starving during the last months of the war. Key Jews had ensured that the Allies would bomb rail lines, with those key Jews calculating that the typhus-ridden prisoners were already a write-off and would go hungry as a result of the bombing, making for great photos to justify the creation of the state of Israel. Senior American officers distrusted the sources for the gassing stories, believing that the Jewish deaths had come and were still coming, post-war, from the typhus epidemic and malnutrition."

Chantelle looked to hide her shock and tried to keep her eyes on her opponent. "We now have much more detail, Mr. Hardy. In a recent book based on 100 interviews, not only with Holocaust survivors but also with perpetrators, there is a story of a mother whose shoes were confiscated on the first day and she was given only slippers. She dreamt for five years of shoes until she left Auschwitz. Another Holocaust survivor spent 12 weeks of 1943 in Auschwitz, before being moved for a year or so thereafter to a munitions factory attached to the Dachau concentration camp. He almost died of typhus and says death there came not from gas chambers but from Nazi killing squads, disease, exhaustion, and especially during the last year of World War II, starvation.

"Another recent report by a British prisoner-of-war describes how the POW used Red Cross care packages to bribe his way into Auschwitz, and there he saw piles of corpses being carried away by fellow inmates, who themselves were living on putrid soup and living in foul barracks."

Hardy leaned back and folded his arms in a defiant position. "Americans, post-war with administrator General Patton, refused to believe the Russians, whom Patton hated. He had admired the German infantry during the war and afterward, and had kept ex-Nazis on in bureaucratic positions, saying they were the only ones competent enough to do the jobs. Patton said that the sides in any war were not good versus bad but simply a function of circumstance. Patton had a fatal accident."

Hardy raised his right index finger in front of Chantelle's face. "Prominent Jews of the Holocaust Center have conceded that no gassing took place in any camp on German soil."

Hardy then unfolded his arms and slowly came forward. "When you were a young child in school, Chantelle, did you not have to read books about girls escaping from Nazis? It's a whole genre! I'm not sure that anyone really cared about the quality of the writing, so long as the children knew and thought about the Holocaust."

Chantelle had seen no such books in her little French-Canadian town, but she chose not to give Hardy space for carrying on. "In Poland today, there are only 8,000 Jews, compared to three-and-a-half million before the war. Where are the rest, Mr. Hardy?" but he twisted her point to make his own. "And yet Lech Walesa purged the Jews from the Solidarity movement."

Hardy then stretched his arms wide to the ceiling. "In Japan, books on world conspiracies sell well. Readers know that a Jewish New York banker helped Japan defeat the Russian tsar in 1905, and during World War II, Japanese-Jewish dinners were held in occupied China." Hardy was then not about to lose control. "Many Japanese people resent Western distortions – their major religions of old, Buddhism and Shintoism, do not have the dogmatic force and sacred texts of Judeo-Christianity and hell, Japan knew the earth revolved around the sun long before Copernicus. The Japanese people honor shrines to their war dead, including convicted war criminals. Even Japan's so-called Emperor worship, mixing religion and politics, did not begin until about 1880 in reaction to Western colonial threats. Go to a Tokyo bookstore and you're bound to run into piles of books that would not be acceptable in our Western society – Holocaust denials and the like. And in the back streets of Japan, you'll hear denial of its World War II crimes.

"If Japan were Germany, there would be a huge scandal within the international community, but the books are written in Japanese and are, so far, not on the Western radar. Only recently have the Japanese been condemned for their supposed reinterpretation of history, because the West now needs money-lender China, which still criticizes Japan. Tellingly, Mao purged Jewish involvement in China."

Chantelle tried to level a general comment against Hardy's comment on Emperor worship. "Expressions of religious beliefs in politics can be legitimate, so long as they are informed positions, subject to reason," but Hardy snapped back, "The pull of religious ideology is not usually a theological one but one that has everything to do with political rage – Jews celebrating Passover use extraordinary language that incites hatred."

Chantelle held fixed, possibly wondering where Hardy was going, and he again seized the silence. "Germany today has 100,000 Jews, and Russian Jews who immigrate there do so at the expense of not moving to Israel. Many world Jews regard such a move back to Germany as diluting their efforts against anti-Semitism, since the move allows Jews to be seen secure in the cradle of the Nazis."

Chantelle offered a shrug. "It is quite understandable that Adolf Hitler is a metaphor for evil, Mr. Hardy, beyond that of Genghis Khan or Attila the Hun. Whoever portrays Hitler as human, needs to justify that choice."

Hardy put both feet forward in front of an unmoving Chantelle. "Hitler claimed the Jews had started World War I, created the Bolshevik revolution and ensured that Germany would suffer under the Treaty of Versailles," but Chantelle herself then thrust forward. "Now who is using war rationalizations, Mr. Hardy?"

Hardy held firm and waved his hand. "While the myths prevail of Churchill's legendary midnight meetings and sleeping tablets, British *cognoscenti* knew of his attention-deficit disorder, and his chief of staff had complained that Churchill knew no details and had only half the picture in his mind, often talking nonsense and absurdities."

Hardy added with inflated nostrils and a huff, "Still, the British government gave Churchill free rein to write the history of World War II." He then leaned back to resume his position of historian. "British bomber-commander Harris was unequivocal about the aim of the bombing, saying it was the destruction of German cities and the killing of German workers, along with a total disruption of a civilized community via the destruction of houses, public utilities, transport and lives, creating a flux of refugees and the breakdown of morale, both at home and along the fronts."

Hardy kept on. "Statistics are unreliable but it is likely that as many as 600,000 German civilians, mostly women, children and the elderly, died in the air offensive against Germany, and that an additional five million were left homeless. By way of comparison, German raids on Britain killed 50,000."

Hardy looked up again above Chantelle's head and he waved his arm. "When, if ever, will Churchill's burning and bombing of German civilians go under the ethicist's lens or for that matter, his naval blockade of food to German civilians? The man had the *chutzpah* to say that nothing whatsoever is gained by putting off a just war." Hardy then raised his eyebrows and looked at Chantelle. "It is interesting that the study of Churchill stopped being mandatory as part of the British school curriculum last year in 2008, but we're still hoodwinked here in America, land of free speech."

Suddenly Chantelle threw her shoulders forward. "Relative to Russia, Mr. Hardy, but less than in say, Scandinavia or my Canada. The elder Bush told our Prime Minister Mulroney to get a *Toronto Star* reporter fired because he had asked the elder Bush to elaborate on Bush's comparing a so-called enemy from the Middle East with Hitler."

Hardy twisted his mouth in a sneer. "The gold standard for hate and evil, with 'Never again' being part of every American civil servant's schooling," and Chantelle shot back at the sneer, "As it is in reverse with those Internet groups consumed with anti-Semitica. Wit does not make for wisdom, Mr. Hardy," but he suddenly shifted the subject back to Canada. "Did your quisling prime minister cave in?" and Chantelle fell into step. "Not on that occasion," and Hardy was back in control.

Hardy took another sip of water as if to prep Chantelle for the bomb that he was about to drop. "We also heard about your Ernst Zundel. Huh! Even the American FBI said before 9/11 that he was no threat, with no criminal record, no record of violence, and was just a Holocaust revisionist, who claimed that he denied the Holocaust for ethical reasons and for his German father's generation, who could not defend themselves."

Chantelle could not hide her shock that Hardy had even heard of Zundel, and he held onto the momentum. "But in your snow-white Canada, despite its Supreme Court ruling that a person could not be charged for disseminating false information, and despite the country soon to restrict that information only to news known to be false and endangering, Canadian human rights commissions swooped down on Zundel, before the police then moved in with hate-crime charges and preventive detention. In tolerant Canada, the tolerance depends on who spins it, and institutions get sucked into the game of zero tolerance for any hate so spun."

Chantelle went pale, perhaps thinking of her own childhood experiences and Hardy gave her a poker face. "Canada did not use the U.S. information and issued a post-9/11 Canadian security certificate against Zundel, with no right of appeal. Canada then shoved him, pre-trial, into solitary confinement for 18 months, count 'em 18, with a tiny cell, cot and lidless toilet, and with no towels or toothbrush. He was allowed 10 minutes of exercise each day, saw almost no one and sometimes did not speak for weeks. That is the kind of isolation that can lead to insanity and that human rights groups condemn as torture."

Chantelle sat back in silence, not knowing of the full circumstances surrounding Zundel, and Hardy smelled a mini-victory. "The Canadian federal security agency, CSIS, had known of plans to bomb Zundel's home but did not warn him, and though he had joined no right wing group, he was accused of guilt by association. That type of guilt would later be used to stop speeches by the head of the Canadian Islamic Congress at the Canadian Defense Headquarters."

Hardy went on but in a more level tone, perhaps trying to appeal to Chantelle's sense of justice: "In Zundel's case, prosecutors were allowed to use unrevealed hearsay, and when Zundel subpoenaed a Canadian Security operative, who confirmed that Canadian intelligence had intercepted Zundel's mail, the trial judge quashed Zundel's subpoena. As he did Zundel's subpoenas of the Canadian Jewish Congress president and the executive vice-president of B'nai Brith. That judge had been the cabinet minister in charge of that very Canadian Security Intelligence Service, CSIS, which furnished the evidence against Zundel. But the Canadian press distanced itself from the issue."

Chantelle sat dumbfounded, not questioning the accuracy of what Hardy was saying and he prodded on. "Zundel had lectured against violence but the Canadian judge heard he was linked to the Ku Klux Klan and labeled him a racist hypocrite, who used a camouflage of non-violence. Zundel, by then, was senior in age and did not fight deportation back to Germany, where Holocaust denial is a serious crime and he faced jail. Austria too in 1989 changed its laws, making it a crime to deny or play down the Holocaust, or excuse Nazi crimes against humanity."

Hardy then raised his index finger. "After crushing Zundel, the powers behind the scenes said Iran's president was next."

Chantelle shifted back in her chair, perhaps to compose herself, and then she leaned forward, this time with hands folded. "As you no doubt know, Mr. Hardy, the Holocaust is one of the best documented events in history. There are now four million names on the Holocaust list, double the number documented as recently as 1999, despite the difficulty in verifying the deaths or the fact that others were unrecorded. That task is made all the worse, because entire families were wiped out and the documents destroyed." Chantelle then raised her own right finger. "Names need to be recovered via people, who can still remember those murdered, and by combing other documentation."

But Hardy leaned back in calm acknowledgment and he too folded his hands opposite Chantelle. "Yes, advances in computer technology have sped up the entire process of identifying victims, along with an increasing flow of information from my Eastern Europe, where most Jews perished. The original six million deaths number was based, in the main, on census tallies taken before the war of Jews, who had lived in specific towns and cities from where most were removed. Those Jews did not go back, but no solid account was made of those who went to Israel or the U.S.; hence, the hesitancy in Jews wanting a post-war American census."

Hardy added something that he may have suspected would hit a note with liberal Chantelle: "Richard Nixon released a truckload of documents before he resigned, alleging that they showed his willingness to show the whole truth," but Chantelle would not fall for the bait and Hardy tried a different tack. "Since World War II, some of our best Jewish rabbis and philosophical minds have agonized over how god could have allowed such an act of unthinkably horrible proportions to have ever happened. There are also many Jewish spiritual groups that do the like. And there is always the corollary question, 'Why so many Germans said they did not know.' But there is one question that is never asked nor is it even allowed."

Chantelle did not fall for the asking but Hardy trod on. "We human beings make mistakes but never more so than on matters that we consider unjust. The long marches of internees and prisoners of war to camps deeper within Germany had replaced the box car, because the Allies had destroyed the German rail lines."

Chantelle crossed her long legs, in a move perhaps to get attention. "One such march was relayed to me. A thousand people had started but only 700 had finished, with the toll taken by hunger and dysentery. The internees had been given only water and one piece of sourdough bread per day," but Hardy locked into step with Chantelle. "As the Third Reich crumbled, its SS allowed the International Red Cross to take about 7,500 prisoners, mostly women, to Sweden from Ravensbrueck, 60 miles north of Berlin. In April 1945, Russian soldiers reported finding 3,000 sickly prisoners who could not make the march. It is estimated that 130,000 women and children had been transported to Ravensbrueck during the six years from 1939 to 1945, and many had died from typhus, inadequate medicine and near the end, hunger. Another camp, Bergen-Belsen near Hanover had at first been for privileged Jews and prisoners of war, but by 1945 was housing the sick and weak from other camps as the Allies advanced. Your Canada's later Governor General Vanier reported in 1945 that he and a group of others had seen several hundred victims, some of whom had been there for years."

Chantelle shifted to a position more erect in her seat. "A later Canadian Governor General Massey, whom some allege was an anti-Semite, also reported witnessing such horrors. And one personal diary, recently revealed, provides yet another glimpse of the horrors – the Jewish internee was only 18 years of age in 1943, when put into the *Vught* Detention Center, a transit camp, and she wrote that although everyone was nice to her, she felt terribly lonely. She recorded that prisoners were deloused and children were transported, with the transport itself and its constant packing being almost unbearable. One morning, she recorded that a child's dying upset her completely. Yet she wanted to persevere."

Hardy was quick to come back. "And now, there are books written by survivors, not only about the survival but happiness in the concentration camps, attesting to the strength of human resiliency under extreme conditions."

Chantelle reared back at Hardy's comment and he jumped at the chance to shift back to Eastern Europe. "A Chechnyan boy's diary tells of the horrific suffering caused by Stalin's deportation of the Chechnyans in 1944, when a quarter of the population perished. The boy's diary details descriptions of emaciated children being fed 'pancakes' of straw and water, and of corpses being dumped from death trains by Russians soldiers."

Hardy waited for Chantelle's reaction. but when he got none he raised his brows as if to deliver something more shocking. "The diary also talks of two young children who were abandoned in a frozen wasteland, when the train doors were slammed shut in front of them."

Chantelle could not have helped hearing the rage building in Hardy's voice and she tried to assuage. "Auschwitz was freed by your evil Russians at the beginning of 1945, Terry," but he was not to be softened. "When the Soviet troops came across the German Diaspora in Eastern Europe, before pressing on to Germany itself, the Russian army, from the lowliest foot soldier to the highest officer, were given sanction as part of an ethnic cleansing to rape all German females from the age of eight to 88, and a million babies were born."

Chantelle shook her head in what may have been shock or disbelief and Hardy took to sounding more rational: "Even a Jewish journalist writing for the Russian front noted that the Soviet army heads had set up blocking detachments, hundreds strong, to shoot those conscripts who tried to flee. One block-force commander had said to an officer, 'That's enough shooting at their backs, now come and join the attack.' Not much different in Chechnya in the 1990s, when Russian conscripts were brutalized by drunken leaders who had to be bribed by their juniors to stop such pounding, before those conscripts were then thrust forward as cannon fodder against the relentless Chechnyans."

Chantelle offered a look of genuine concern. "Your hatred for Russians seems a dudgeon in your heart, Mr. Hardy," and he rushed to justify. "In the 1970s, the Soviet Union faced hunger because of a wheat failure and the government was forced to approach North America for grain. The purchase was accomplished but not before the Soviet Union was pressured to loosen its hold on certain 'oppressed' minorities and allow them to leave, meaning free Jews to go to Israel."

Chantelle's eyes went to the floor as if she were learning something disturbing, and Hardy took the opportunity to take the talk back to World War II. "Why are war crimes like the Japanese raid on Nanking, reportedly killing 250,000 civilians, so poorly known in the West and even less in Japan?"

Chantelle offered a stock answer. "I understand the Nazis had documented in great detail their crimes," but a cranked-up Hardy leapt back in, "But the Japanese are every bit as punctilious as are the Germans and yes, there were war crime trials in post-war Tokyo but only a handful of Japanese were convicted."

Chantelle gave a shrug. "Perhaps for Cold War reasons," but then she thought to add, "Perhaps Japan should teach its children about the war, as has done Germany."

Hardy was not to be swayed. "A book on Nanking by a Chinese American was criticized in Japan as inaccurate, and there are fascists who drive the streets of Tokyo in armored limousines, broadcasting their views through loudspeakers."

Chantelle's face again went blank and Hardy leaned forward with eyes straight on her. "A handful of Soviet Russian veterans had been the first to see Auschwitz in January 1945, when Lavrenti Beria, that Russian reign of terror head, had been chief of the Soviet NKVD Secret Police. It was Beria who announced that the Russians had discovered the holocaust of six million Jews, all in Poland, but the Russians would not let any outside investigators examine the alleged sites. All through 1946, the Russians were not believed."

Chantelle took to sitting up erect with feet flat on the floor. "Thank you, Terry, but we now do believe. Was not the Holocaust planned at Nazi conferences like Wannsee in 1942?" and he nodded while answering back in what Chantelle may have thought at first his agreement, "In 1942, Churchill and the Zionists planned out the promulgation of the Holocaust, as part of a British psychological-warfare scheme, when the Allies were losing on all fronts. At the end of the war, eye witnesses made fortunes in the post-war black markets."

Chantelle offered another shrug, before she thrust her arms forward. "Deniers presumably could have been given money to talk too," but Hardy held on the attack. "By whom? Many of the deniers were non-Germans and former inmates of Nazi concentration camps. I met a Lithuanian whose father had been a Jew and his mother a Lutheran. Before they were married and still at the outbreak of World War II, his father had been transported to a number of concentration camps, including Auschwitz, and his bride-to-be had followed, by joining the International Red Cross."

Chantelle sat back as if to hear a piece of history not known to her. "Typhus, Chantelle, had already been sweeping much of the planet by the middle of the war, and the disease struck hardest in the concentration camps. The Germans tried with Zyklon-B gas to stomp out the lice that were spreading the typhus and so save the inmates. Heads were shaved and clothing was deloused with Zyklon-B. But the typhus spread anyway and the Jewish internees caught typhus by the thousands. Even the administering *Sonderkommandos* – young male prisoners who had been selected to assist in certain tasks – despite their wearing gas masks to protect themselves, often caught typhus as did the German camp guards themselves."

Chantelle held back in her chair as if being bombarded, and her East-European benefactor carried on. "The Germans tried to halt the spread by incinerating the bodies of those Jews who had died of typhus, and cremation was the only safe way. The *Sonderkommandos* could not burn the bodies fast enough and it took eight hours to dispose of each body. The morgues themselves were then disinfected with Zyklon-B."

Chantelle remained fixed back in her chair, but her dark eyebrows turned down in a frown of what must have been doubt, and Hardy waved his arm to the ceiling. "It was a holocaust triggered by the typhus-carrying lice, but almost no records of the epidemic can now be found – they went missing amidst the chaos of central Europe in the years 1945 to 1947. That Lithuanian said that his mother will soon be dead, as will the other Red Cross workers who witnessed the typhus epidemic."

Chantelle then lunged forward. "The observers on both sides of the argument will soon be dead, Mr. Hardy" but he would not be halted. "The United States recognized the typhus epidemic during World War II and initiated its own typhus commission for the five years from 1942 to 1947. Doctor Fred Soper, whose name was on the note I gave you, was an expert on epidemic diseases and was head of the U.S. Rockefeller Foundation's Typhus Team. Soper conducted trials showing that mass delousing by insecticides was a better means of controlling outbreaks of the disease than fumigation or vaccines. Thanks to Zyklon-B gas, the death rate in the concentration camps was reduced from 9% in 1942 to 3% in 1943."

Chantelle was sitting stone-faced and Hardy probed for some reaction. "Have you, Doctor Fouriere, heard nothing of the World War II typhus epidemic?"

Chantelle looked down at the floor and her next words were almost inaudible: "Mention was made during the Toronto SARS crisis in 2003, and I had a Canadian uncle who was captured by the Germans and spent the bulk of the war in a prison camp. Later, Uncle Dick said his camp had not been hit by the typhus but that it had overrun camps in the east."

Hardy gave a grin. "And did this Uncle Richard have knowledge of what was going on?" but Chantelle opened up her palms. "My mother did not like her family seen with Uncle Dick, because he was part Cree, although I overheard his saying that Russian prisoners were being worked to death in a tit-for-tat for the Russian treatment of German prisoners. Uncle Dick also said that Russia had not signed the Geneva Convention, and conditions for German prisoners in Russia were unthinkable, with almost none of them coming home."

Hardy was leaning back but then he bent forward. "Recently in 1988, the foremost U.S. expert on executions went to the former concentration camps of Auschwitz, Birkenau and Majdanek. His summary concluded that no gas chambers had been used in those camps for genocidal executions. In the case of Birkenau, where the Nuremberg Tribunal had concluded that 1,765,000 Jews had been gassed, no mass killing capacity was found. And a former president of the American Red Cross revealed from the Soviet archives that there had been a total of 70,000 Jewish deaths from all causes in Nazi concentration camps."

Chantelle's eyebrows again turned down but Hardy drew down in supplication. "The commandant of Buchenwald was tried and shot for abusing prisoners and another, Commandant Amon Goh, was on trial by the Nazis for similar reasons, near the end of the war."

Terry Hardy then waved both his hands to the air. "But because of Allied bombings of the German rail lines, food and medicine could not be delivered, and many inmates were dying of starvation and disease. Those inmates are the ones in the photos at the end of the war. After World War II, the Red Cross issued a 1,600-page report, saying the concentration camps lacked food in the final months because the Allies had bombed the railroads and other means of transport. And notwithstanding that Allied damage to such transport, the Nazis had allowed the Red Cross into the camps right through to the end of the war, to distribute relief packages."

Chantelle was sitting speechless, as Hardy went on. "The Germans, moreover, possessed Sarin and Tabun, nerve gases 1,000 times more deadly than the insect disinfectant Zyklon-B. And during the delousing of people, only a fraction of the disinfectant Zyklon-B gas was inhaled. Powerful ventilators had been installed in the gas chambers to extract the remaining gas."

Chantelle tried to manage a counter. "The Nazis charged the loved ones on the outside for the cremations," but Hardy lashed back, "Including shipping urns from Auschwitz." Chantelle turned her face to the side, possibly wondering how Hardy's comment fit hers. Hardy charged again. "The World Almanac of 1947 used figures from the American Jewish Committee to conclude there were 16 million Jews on planet Earth in 1939 before the war, but after in 1948 *The New York Times* stated that the world Jewish population was between 16 and 19 million, excluding a million in Palestine. Europe had three million Jews who had not emigrated by 1941, but after World War II, the Red Cross said that three-and-a-half million Jews applied for Holocaust reparations."

Chantelle stayed locked in a frown but Hardy charged on. "From more than 1,000 tons of Nazi documents seized by the U.S., no order from Hitler for the extermination of the Jews was found. The Nazi 'Final Solution' was emigration, as had been tried by Adolf Eichmann before he had been intercepted and stopped by the British."

Hardy then gave a huff and, "Before World War II, the German government had offered Germany's Jews right of passage out of the country" before he suddenly lost himself in a rage. "A full 15 million Christian Russian kulak farmers were killed between 1924 and 1930, upwards of 10 million Ukrainians were starved to death from 1930 to 1933, and 12 million Russian political prisoners perished during the 30 years from 1919 to 1949!"

Chantelle partially recovered. "Your talk, Mr. Hardy, is a reiteration of a familiar denial theme, that the bodies at Auschwitz were cremated as a hygiene measure to control typhus, and that the gas chambers were actually life-saving delousing showers. It has been acknowledged by the Jewish community that a number of gas chambers were originally built as such units, not to murder but to delouse clothing as well as combat insects and rodents, and later were transformed to serve the homicidal purpose. But Nazi-funded industries that set up the units slipped up often enough in documentation to expose themselves."

Hardy's head reared back as if he had been thrown by Chantelle's knowledge. She then added a challenge: "You made no mention, Mr. Hardy, of current findings around the hundreds of Ukrainian villages where Jews were systematically shot by Nazis."

Hardy's head came forward and he tried to deflect. "Your Canada, Chantelle, condemned the Turkish genocide of a million Armenians as did key Jews during World War I, but at the start of World War I, Russia declared war on Ottoman Turkey and Russia pressured the Armenians in Turkey to rise up against its Ottoman rule. Many Armenians did and were told by Turkey to leave their area of conflict, the region being in the middle between Russian and Turkish fighters. The Turks later reported that 200,000 Armenians were killed in suppression of their rebellions but Britain published the Turkish atrocities as part of its war propaganda, despite the British foreign office admitting it had no direct knowledge.

"Meanwhile, the Jewish U.S. ambassador to Turkey, Henry Morgenthau, had that close friend in *The New York Times*, which began publishing in 1915 that a million Armenians were killed or in exile, despite having no count of the numbers. *The New York Times* went on to publish 145 stories about the massacre of Armenians, but did express some ambivalence regarding the occurrences and reported that the Armenians had brought it upon themselves by trying to stir up rebellion against Turkey. Morgenthau made much of an offer to transport 350,000 Armenians to safety and Turkey said okay.

Later, in the years leading up to World War II, that Polish Jew Lemkin who would later coin the word 'Holocaust' tried at an international conference in Madrid to tie the alleged Armenian massacre with Hitler's ascent to power, but his attempts were dismissed as Jewish propaganda. Hitler in 1939 did say, 'Who today still talks of the massacre of the Armenians?' but he could have been implying that only Jews were using the allegations for advancement of themselves, yet his words were spun to suggest that he too could get away with such atrocities without the world caring."

Chantelle's eyes veered to the right in reflection of Hardy's shocking information, and he caught her pause. "During the 100 years, post-Napoleon to the end of World War I, five million Muslims were expelled from Europe, but ethnic cleansing as we know it today, re-emerged *en force* after World War II in 1945."

Hardy then lowered his head as if to appear reasonable. "Using a 1923 Greece-Turkey treaty as a model, where both sides agreed to exchange minorities, the United States, Britain and the Soviet Union endorsed ethnic cleansing at the 1945 Treaty of Potsdam, when it was thought that such ethnic cleansing was a prerequisite of peace. Churchill went further and regarded homogeneous nation-states – Israel – as the only path to a stable postwar peace.

"It was thus decided to expel 12 million people of the German Diaspora from parts of Europe, where they had lived for 600 years – eight million from Poland and surroundings, three million from Czechoslovakia and one million from other areas. The total killed among that German Diaspora, excluding those from disease and hunger, was almost two million, and the states expelling the Germans took every measure to ensure that all traces of the former residents were wiped clean. The Polish army declared, 'Treat the Germans like they have treated us,' and many Germans were forced into slave labor. Czechoslovakian Germans were forced to wear armbands, stripped of property rights, forced into cattle cars, given minimal food rations and were at the mercy of criminals.

"By 1948 and for the first time in history, Eastern and central Europe consisted almost entirely of so-called homogenous states. Then, during the Cold War and Communist era, public discussion of such expulsions and deportation from Eastern and central Europe was severely restricted, and the West could not access information."

Hardy gave another sly grin and his chin went up. "In like fashion, in post-British 1947 India, Muslims were confronted by Hindus and Sikhs, and 12 million people were expelled, with more than a million dying. These realities should sound a clear warning against those who build walls or advance social engineering on an international scale. Ethnic cleansing failed to stabilize India-Pakistan, Poland or Czechoslovakia, and many children of those forced migrants feel as strongly about their 'homeland' as the parents did."

Chantelle heard her benefactor's reasoned, almost caring tone and she tried to respond in kind. "To use your words, Mr. Hardy, even the wisest can be fooled, and a good historian does not create history but uncovers it."

Hardy's eyebrows suddenly lifted with a look of delight but Chantelle quickly added, "Holocaust denial is a form of disrationalization" and so Hardy tried to go back to his reasoned tone. "One Jewish inmate was allowed to compose a whole symphony on paper given to him by Nazi guards, and the music was performed for 500 inmates. Dialogue should have the ability to withstand any assault by a false claim, especially if that falsehood is founded upon an age-old phenomenon."

But Chantelle would not let Hardy away with his rationale. "Free speech does not grant the right for a false premise to be treated as the other side's starting point in a legitimate debate, since the false starting point violates further reasoned inquiry. Ideological motives orchestrate preset conclusions, and time should not be wasted in counter-arguing them. Instead, one is morally obligated to undercut the very foundations of those arguments' speciousness. Debate with a Holocaust denier gives legitimacy to that denier, on an issue that is not a matter of debate. I suggest that one should instead illuminate how Holocaust deniers abuse method to distort their true objectives."

Hardy slowly fell back as if to draw Chantelle out more, and she continued: "Deconstructionism, moreover, can be dangerous if real experience is made relative. Stalin's terror was arbitrary but Hitler's was targeted at a particular group. Stalin, yes, killed more people but the equivalences are not analogous – Nazi Germany breached the moral order of social organization."

Hardy rendered a benign smile and then came back in a way that he may have thought Chantelle would not refute. "The anti-German propaganda, decades earlier in World War I, meant that many Americans took later reports of Nazis using gas to kill Jews with a grain of salt. A 1935 series of U.S. hearings on the role of WW I shipbuilders, munitions manufacturers and international bankers, including a review of the infamous British Balfour Declaration, fueled an 'I'm from Missouri' kind of American doubt and isolationism."

But Chantelle turned Hardy's specifics back on him. "Therefore, no one later in 1945 listened to soldiers' accounts of Nazi death camps at Bergen-Belsen." and Hardy stiffened. "Where, Doctor Fouriere, one quarter of the 60,000 deaths occurred after the British arrived, and the deaths were from typhus and the continuing effects of malnutrition.

"At the end of the American Civil War, Northern prisoners, who were still in the South, often exaggerated or fantasized their conditions and demonized their defenseless Southern opponents as racist. Each prisoner had a healing need to embroider his own odyssey or tell tales of fellow survivors, and that human need was tapped into by the North. The propaganda technique was repeated after World War II, with many concentration camp survivors making millions by exposing a Holocaust. In so doing, they made watertight the arguments for Israel."

"Denial, Mr. Hardy, of a person or group's suffering is the ultimate cruelty. The victims are fired by a supreme resentment for what they suffered, and those who have not experienced racism or in this case the Holocaust, find it difficult to understand the vulnerability of the victim."

Hardy then said something that made Chantelle sit up. "France, like Germany and Austria today, declare Holocaust deniers to be criminals but liberal democracies are not well served by laws that limit free speech, such as laws denying the Holocaust or the Armenian genocide – those laws can be exploited in the reverse, to fuel conspiracy mongering that Jews control everything including speech. Suppressing Holocaust deniers may do as much to prop up Jew-bashing as the bigots themselves and so why not err on the side of freedom and oblige good folks to learn how to take on the Jew-haters? In a liberal democracy, is not counterargument more constructive than driving the haters underground, where their ugliness can fester?"

Terry Hardy heaved a huge shrug. "As for any grand Jewish or Zionist conspiracy, if one exists, most Jews don't know about it and are as duped as anyone else." He may then have picked up a squint of uncertainty in Chantelle and he chose to add, "Holocaust survivors should be happy with their deniers – after each attempt to exercise their right to deny on U.S. campuses, Holocaust courses have soared. Already, countless grade school and high school classes use *The Diary of Anne Frank* as a mandatory text, and we never hear that she died of typhus. People who are labeled Holocaust deniers are now so desperate, they are trying to counter-label their opponents as *exterminationists!*"

Suddenly, Chantelle raised her left hand in a gesture to call halt. "You are using, Mr. Hardy, the logic of a hockey-mom who lets her children play in the street to slow down traffic," and so he tried again. "At the end of World War II, an American news dispatch said the U.S. army rescued three million refugees, mostly Jews, and an American Jewish Committee later opposed the taking of a census that included a question of religious affiliation."

Chantelle was silent and Hardy took to sermonizing. "People expect a clean storyline in history and Hollywood is only too happy to supply it. Mission accomplished, like the winning of the World Series. But history is more a mixed tale and does not end with a concluding prize."

Chantelle held back in tacit acceptance and Hardy trod on. "At the end of World War II, Russian Jews who had killed millions of Christians, sat in judgment of the Germans, and billions of dollars have been wrung out of not only the United States and Germany but also the Jewish people themselves."

Chantelle's eyebrows went down again and Hardy shot up erect. "In March 1948, President Truman wanted the Jewish vote in American swing states, as well as support from Jewish banking and media, including Hollywood; so, after some relentless lobbying at him, Truman decided to support the founding of Israel, saying that he had to answer to the hundreds of thousands who were anxious for the success of Zionism but that he Truman did not have among his constituents a like number of Arabs.

479

"Truman thus promised Chaim Weizmann, the Churchill-backer and future president of Israel, that Truman would support a partition of Palestine with a new Israel. Truman overruled the Foreign Affairs department and Secretary of State George Marshall, using instead a domestic expert as White House counsel on the matter. It was that domestic expert who made the case for such an Israel."

Chantelle sat up and looked again to paint a bigger picture. "Many Jews justifiably saw Israel as their only salvation, after six million had been murdered. After the war but before proclamation of the State of Israel, there were photographs of British soldiers dragging from ships the hopeful Jewish immigrants to Palestine and relocating them to British camps on Cyprus, to prevent their reaching the Promised Land."

Chantelle then sat higher in her chair to match the taller Hardy. "Israel feels the need to exist and stay strong," and he snapped back, "And as supposed victims, can do no wrong, Ms. Fouriere?" but this time, it was Chantelle who sat at the ready. "Rationality and dialogue are possible everywhere there is violence, Mr. Hardy."

He was not about to let her away with the platitude. "And among the propagandized Jewish people, fundamentalists have paranoiac fantasies. Almost 150 years ago, Jewish leader Leopold Zunz argued that in Jewish rituals, of crucial import was the concept of cult, with it alone making the myths and beliefs of the religion comprehensible."

Chantelle gave a nod of concession. "A few Jewish fundamentalists are apparently haunted by the Holocaust and chronic anti-Semitism. Spirituality needs to separate perception from suppression, and all faiths need to lead to practical compassion, rather than rage or hatred. If the central tenet of a religion is not the sanctity of all creation, I believe such a religion will fail."

Hardy's face gave a glow and he took in a long, audible breath. "Since 1945, there has built a tradition, laudable enough, of promoting human rights across the world, and some of our best Jewish minds wrack themselves over how the Holocaust could have happened, while none question that it did happen. Were they ever to do so, a Himalayan pressure could be taken off the backs of the world's Jews, because the oppressed within them would no longer have to use victimhood to placate guilt, or use their intellects to out-dance critics, while remaining enmeshed in their own hate-filled propaganda."

Chantelle's eyebrows came down hard in a dark frown, and her eyes opened to the man to whom she had entrusted herself. "Victims of a great crime, Mr. Hardy, feel no resolution from denial of the crime. To move on, they must come to grips with the horrors of human reality, and denial does nothing but further oppress. Your proposed route to emancipate supposedly oppressed Jews from manipulators within their own community is like telling a post-war German mother, whose child died in Nazi battles, that his sacrifice was worthwhile. She sees the ploy and is the worse for it."

Hardy sat silent, wanting perhaps to appear to be reasonable, and Chantelle pushed on. "There is also another danger, Mr. Hardy – the impact, for example of Holocaust deniers on vulnerable Muslim communities in Western Europe. Holocaust history has been dropped as a subject in parts of England, and teachers have been unwilling to teach Holocaust lessons, so as not to offend deniers. Have you seen the Simon Wiesenthal Center's documentary, *Never Again*?"

Hardy tried to wave aside the question. "Some of your labeled Holocaust deniers want Britain to change *Yom Ha Shoah*, or Holocaust Remembrance Day, into International Genocide Day," but Chantelle kept in charge. "One of the positives of the Holocaust tragedy, Mr. Hardy is that it has given our present world an awareness of genocide. I am confident that the Jewish people will continue to speak out, as they have recently done against the genocide in Darfur."

Hardy perked up as if sniffing a weakness. "The four million killed in the Congo is much worse but Darfur gets the anti-Arab highlight, because the Israeli-led West wants regime change there as it will some day in Libya. The supposed genocide is like the West's indignation over Iran's treatment of women, while women sit at the back of the bus in Orthodox Jerusalem. Hell, Hindu India's ravaging of women is not even on the radar!"

Chantelle fell back again in her chair, maybe to gather her thoughts but Hardy remained upright. "As you have lectured, Ms. Fouriere, people want to believe dramatic stories or poems, and they are more compelling if they are thought to be true."

Hardy took a moment to sit back as the resigned philosopher but Chantelle waited this time for him to carry on. "Berlin has a Center for Research on Anti-Semitism, and many post-war German children are chronicling and attacking the Nazi-era crimes. Germans also remain anxious about sending troops to another country such as Darfur, and Germany's 1949 Constitution forbids wars of aggression. There are also German laws against any form of Nazi symbolism or anti-Semitism and even in Austria, the Nazi Party is illegal.

"Berlin, like other German cities, has a program welcoming home mostly Jewish residents, who were forced to flee the city from 1933 to 1945. Jewish people are invited to return and make peace with the new Berlin, and the week includes a reception with the mayor, a night at the opera, tours of historic Jewish sites and visits to their old neighborhoods. The city picks up the tab for each returning émigré plus a guest, and has done so for 40 years."

Chantelle came back in. "The program, Mr. Hardy, surely reflects a growing awareness of the Holocaust since the 1960s and a desire among post-war generations to address atrocities that their parents had not even acknowledged, let alone apologized for. Many Germans had earlier said they did not know what had been done or did not want to believe it."

Hardy's face betrayed that he was pleased with Chantelle being still in the argument and she carried on. "The capital of the Third Reich was the center of German Jewry, with its Jewish community numbering 170,000 or one-third of the national total, and many adult Jews remained, well into World War II, trapped by their belief that things could not get worse. A father of one returning Jewish person had said that he wanted to be on the very last train to leave Berlin and would not be upset if he missed that one too. Even Jewish children who were whisked to England thought the whole thing would soon blow over. But by the end of the war, two-thirds of Berlin's Jews had fled and 56,000 had disappeared, leaving only 1,500 who had stayed."

An evidently content Hardy stayed seated back and let Chantelle keep going. "Today, Berlin has 12,500 registered Jews, although some others may be understandably reluctant to declare themselves. Berlin's Jewish Museum opened in 2001 with a design by Daniel Libeskind, portraying the history and culture of Germany's Jews and carrying a certain degree of atonement. It is atonement that most returning Jews are presumably looking for, but I understand it is still not clear for some of them that Germany has come to terms with its past.

"A school has been named after a politician who opposed the Nazis and was killed after the 1944 attempt to assassinate Hitler. According to a plaque on the school, it is a school without racism, a school with courage.

"There are also markers on lampposts and brass plaques on sidewalks commemorating those killed by Nazis, each one with a name, date of birth, date of deportation and death. The largest memorial is near the historical Brandenburg Gate. Many of the memorials are the result of private initiatives that began in the 1970s, with the broadcast of the TV miniseries *Holocaust.* Since then, Germany is increasingly facing up to its genocidal past. The museum and plaques are part of a movement for not forgetting."

Hardy lifted high his eyebrows, apparently again in light of Chantelle's knowledge, and he let her roll on. "One Berlin evacuee got word while in the Middle East of 1945 that his parents, who had been sent in early 1943 to the concentration camp Theresienstadt, were not only alive but remained together. His mother had been assigned to prevent women from using the washroom to commit suicide. For that evacuee, his week in Berlin brought an invitation to return next year to speak about his boyhood experiences.

"A train track in Berlin also commemorates the 35,000 people who were dispatched from 1941 to 1945, and each deportation is recorded on steel plates that run along the railway track. Germany is terribly anxious to come to terms with what happened. It is even chic to do Jewish things in Berlin."

Hardy suddenly stiffened and his right index finger came out. "But women in Berlin's Orthodox synagogues still have to sit at the back behind a latticed screen." Hardy lifted his chin high. "For a long time, East Germany left the war-destroyed synagogues intact as examples of fascism, while the killing of Jewish civilians was barely acknowledged."

Terry Hardy then shot forward: "German television documentaries are often financed by Zionists! There was some attempt at balance before the

1970s and the Holocaust was rarely discussed in earlier public forums; Germans had instead learned of their own suffering from the Allied attacks and fire-bombing of civilians.

"The 1970s and '80s began to change all that, with texts being agitprop guilt-inducers about the Nazi era. Now, the Holocaust is as much a compass for Germany as it is for Israel, and the Holocaust is on German television and in newspapers all the time. German children are also required by law to study the Nazi period, and many don't even like to be German, identifying themselves as European. Many a German family has splintered over the Holocaust, and no Germans suffer more than do the children and grandchildren of Hitler's presumed murderers. German children are told they are born from the loins of Nazis and bear a horrible burden, some not allowing themselves to love their parents or grandparents. Many German children also fear that they may have criminal tendencies, with a blood thing called genetic culpability, and in an attempt to compensate, they go to Jewish parochial schools and Jewish summer camps."

Hardy then paused to heave a shrug. "In what may be the final trial of a Third Reich figure, a 90-year-old Nazi was convicted for standing guard in a concentration camp as hundreds of trainloads of Jews arrived. The man was a Ukrainian, who escaped death in the camp by volunteering for the job. As had Jews themselves." Hardy stiffened and raised his index finger. "But the German spy agency, the BND, recently announced that it would not release files on Adolf Eichmann, the man tried and executed by Israel at the start of the 1960s. Germany has been Israel's ally since its creation."

Hardy then shook his head to the floor. "Now, the bad feelings against Turkish neighborhoods in Berlin is public news, and the belief that multiculturalism – that is the entry of Muslims – has failed, is widespread across Europe. Over half of Germans have swallowed the sop that Muslims are a drain on the economy, and in Germany as elsewhere in Europe, extreme anti-immigrant – anti-Muslim – views are becoming more prevalent. There is now even an 'M-word!'"

A straight-faced Chantelle did not fall this time for the Hardy provocation. "Germany has moved on. Berlin has one of the finest symphonies in the world and Germany's sports are among the safest and best played in the world. Post-war Germany feels that it has a moral obligation to defend Israel and, yes, is Israel's number one ally, albeit the U.S. being the most powerful one."

But Hardy held his position. "Yes, to face up to the fallibility and deep wrongs of one's country is to reconnect it to the wider world. It also allows a person to see any state for what it should be – a sturdy if battered vessel for the dreams and ambitions of its citizens, not a golden trophy of preordained rightness. By comparison, Britain, during its 'enlightened' 1950s, slaughtered, tortured, raped, castrated, starved and jailed some 150,000 Kenyans, including the grandfather of Barack Obama, for having the temerity to fight for national independence."

Hardy took in a long breath and added, "Germany may get a temporary seat on the UN Security Council, while Canada is denied, since your country is doing everything it can to suck up to Israel's right wing. The new right-wing Canada plans to play a key role in fighting any Palestinian bid for UN membership."

But Chantelle also stuck to her train of thought. "Now, two generations of Germans have repudiated the values of their elders, because they were so corrupted. And yes, some German youth despise their progenitors for silence after 1945 and their inability to mourn."

Hardy came back: "Perhaps the earlier generation of Germans, still living after World War II, saw something that came to be forbidden for those born after the war."

Chantelle caught herself lowering her head for a moment's thought and Hardy held up. "Spain, with its 1930s civil war, has never experienced a moment of national shame, but almost everyone in Spain remains one step removed from guilt, with there lingering a collective terror over self-examination.

"And as for Russia, huh!" Hardy swept his arms to the ceiling, "unlike Germany, which you have pointed out, has taken pains to atone for its Nazi era, Russia is trying to erase the darkness of its past. Older Russians reminisce over their country as a former world power, and few young Russians read Solzhenitsyn. His works on the Gulag Archipelago and slave-labor camps are not even taught in schools. In other parts of Russia, like the

Solovetsky Island where the Orthodox Church has had a monastery for centuries, the Church is doing whatever necessary to walk hand in hand with
official repression and minimize memories of the horrible, local prison.

"Seventy years ago after the Revolution, the Arctic Circle's Solovetsky
Islands were a grim end of the journey for the first political prisoners, including scientists, writers and artists. 'Solovki' as it was known, became a symbol
for the sadistic treatment carried out by the Soviet Union, and one in four
prisoners died from exhaustion, accidents or cold. Those who did not make
their work quotas could be left outside in the bitter winter night, or during
the summer months tied to trees in bug-infested woods for the mosquito
treatment. The Communist bureaucrats fine-tuned the torture techniques
to maximize slave-labor production, including the digging of mass graves."

Hardy paused to ensure Chantelle was still listening before he scoffed,
"Currently, there is concern among international Jewry over the growing
efforts in countries like Lithuania to rejig Europe's approach to history.
Those countries want to place Nazi and Soviet crimes on an equal footing,
and include an investigation of alleged atrocities by Jewish partisans. Not
surprisingly, critics of those countries' attempts claim that efforts to upgrade
Soviet misdeeds downgrade the Holocaust."

Chantelle again sat silent in deference to a man whom she assumed
knew more about Eastern European history than she did, and a cold-faced
Hardy pressed on. "During World War II, one-and-a-half million German
soldiers died on Russian soil and German archives have maps of their burial
places. But in the decades later, Russians began digging up the graves of
German soldiers and robbing them. Only 10% of Russian soldiers could be
identified but 90% of the German soldiers could, and the digging up of
German graves by Russian amateurs became an obsession. Germany established a *Volksbund* charity for the caring for remains of German soldiers
killed abroad, and after the Soviet Union collapsed, a treaty was signed, giving Germany the right to collect German remains and bury them in Russian
cemeteries."

Hardy leaned back and looked down on Chantelle. "Suppressing the
past enslaves an entire society to the glacial power of its distorted history,
perverting the landscape and defining by lies the world as we know it today.

Solzhenitsyn's *Gulag Archipelago* was smuggled out to the West 35 years ago and it points out that by the mid-1960s, over 85,000 Germans had been convicted for Nazi war crimes, as compared to 10 in Russia. The Russian government is still preventing a true accounting of the death toll in World War II, and one historian who works within has told of raids on his databases. The Berlin wall fell peacefully, and during a recent commemoration, one East German was heard to remark sardonically that Lenin had said that a revolution could succeed only with violence."

Chantelle held unwavering. "Mr. Hardy, I understand it is Jewish memory that has allowed the Jews to carry on, and perhaps redress is necessary to extract good from evil and attain justice. Some empathetic Jews have noted that the Japanese-ravaged Chinese in Nanking have no recourse for monetary compensation, because China in the 1970s signed with Japan a document declaring all World War II issues settled."

Hardy's finger came out again. "But as you also must understand, Doctor Fouriere, victors write the past and that past pollutes the future. Japan is accused of being in denial and Tokyo has a shrine for the dead who were executed post-war. The original Nanking document was written in the Chinese style of the times, deploying not only anti-Japanese racist remarks but also attacks on American and British exploiters. Many centuries ago, the post-Confucian Chinese buried the Confucians up to their necks in earth, and then chopped their heads off, setting in place a long Chinese tradition. Accusing the Japanese of doing the same thing at Nanking thus sounds contrived. In the post-World War II Tokyo war crimes trials, Russian Jews made many of the claims against the Japanese. Japan says Nanking was not a massacre, and those few Japanese people brave enough to voice an opinion say the attack on Nanking was to liberate it from white imperialists with long noses.

"Now however, Japanese school texts are becoming like their German counterparts – tools of international politics. For the longest time, China did not want to talk about Nanking, since it would draw attention to both rebuttals and China's own atrocities. Remember, Mao threw the Jews out! And contrary to what we in the West supposedly know, Japan's earlier invasion in 1931 of Manchuria had likewise been defensive – Tokyo had feared the rising power of Chinese nationalists and Mao Tse-tung. Have you heard of the Manchurian Conspiracy, Ms. Fouriere?"

Chantelle suddenly thrust both shoulders forward and stomped her boots on the floor. "Grand conspiracy theories such as those you mentioned will always capture the imaginations of some people within frustrated societies, Mr. Hardy, and it is easy to dismiss the hyperventilation of conspiracy theorists as simple acts of madness. But those mad people have an impact on the shared values holding societies together, and as happened when Holocaust denier David Irving was put on trial in Austria, his prosecution enabled the defendant to present himself as a martyr for free speech."

Hardy gave a knowing grin. "The expression 'grand conspiracy theory' was a caption coined by the conspirators themselves as a way of pigeonholing any people who dared to question as paranoid schizophrenics. Our values over the last half century have been erected on unfounded guilt and indignation, and have led to a grand mirage, with false absolutes impairing our sense of fairness. Humanitarian wars now present themselves as peace by other means, and few Western politicians champion the view espoused by your Canada's Woodsworth in 1939, that war should be avoided unless the case for it is overwhelming."

Hardy heaved a grand sigh before he let his hands slap down on his thighs. "There was some hope in the Internet, but wealth and power are now moving to manipulate that medium too. Internet companies will soon be forced to remove material judged offensive from their websites – translation, critical of Israel."

Hardy lowered his eyes toward Chantelle to ensure he still had her ear. "The world's Jews, Chantelle, remain remarkably talented, diverse and infused with good humor, but they have been forced to conform and their freedom has been sacrificed for security. Fear and indignation have been driven in, with manna too often becoming the only escape for the talented Jewish mind. The cadre of power brokers, who brewed the Hebrew bible's mean old man on the mountain, is today, with rabbinical directorate and gargantuan financing, still directing those myths."

Chantelle remained unmoved and Hardy turned his palms up on his thighs. "Creative solutions to the challenges of the Middle East could come from within Israel itself, as well as the world Jewish community, but first a few Jewish manipulators would have to admit guilt and so free the rest of the Jews from the prison of victimhood, along with its us-against-the-rest tribalism. Israel and the Jewish community could then do a Midrash on itself, and yes, the process would be torturous but the outcome would move the world forward several orders of magnitude. The creative-mindedness of world Jewry could then make a world contribution that would be unsurpassed since breaking free from the walls of rabbis, and our planet earth would benefit again from great minds like those of before, in Spinoza, Marx or your Doctor Fisher."

Chantelle suddenly shot up as if struck by a chord. "Mr. Hardy, perhaps some Jews like to identify with Marx, but his high-mindedness was manipulated to manifest a reign of terror. The devil, no matter how conceived, has a high level of self-awareness."

But Hardy also lifted and raised his right finger to the air above their heads. "Yes, in the battle for historical perspective, politicians can manipulate and eyewitnesses can be influenced. Documents can be frauds and in support of a hate culture, scholarly skepticism gets turned aside."

Hardy then fortified his arms into a fold. "Chaim Weizmann and Winston Churchill had SS chief Heinrich Himmler assassinated at the end of World War II, in order to cover up the secret 1943 peace talks between him and Churchill's government. It wouldn't do for stories about the creation of Israel to be shown as British propaganda."

Chantelle tried to leaven. "Any threat to self-preservation needs a reality-check for the degree of real versus perceived, and has to include a gauging of the intent of the threat as well as the perceived need for preservation."

Hardy raised his face high as if to an empty room. "Thus it follows, lofty prophet Chantelle, that threats as big as Jesus will be seen as something to be done away with, as was Jesus before." But she would not let Hardy away with his quip. "I don't recall Nietzsche's exact words but I think the essence of the message is that when fighting monsters, we need to see to it that we ourselves do not become monsters."

Hardy then turned his eyes down to Chantelle. "A very anti-Churchillian message – Churchill said we had to stoop as low as the enemy to defeat him.

That lowness led him to propaganda. But…" Hardy's finger went up again, "…such propaganda can ensnare the propagandists, so that they preserve their credibility only through acts in accordance with that propaganda. Churchill thus sanctioned the burning alive of hundreds of thousands of innocent civilians in the bombing of Dresden."

Hardy tucked his hands under his little chair and gave off a slight shrug. "We now know more about how history has been written. Hitler did not at all want to conquer the world but to be self-sufficient in food from the Ukraine, so as not again to be starved, as Churchill and backers had done to Germany in and after World War I."

Chantelle leapt in. "One need not be Eastern European or Jewish to feel angered by historical distortions, Mr. Hardy. But every respected journalist accepts as given, the fact of the Holocaust."

Hardy lashed back with his index finger straight at Chantelle: "Western journalist! The world revolves around the Holocaust and it pours through all policy. The Holocaust is the premise for every Western justification. Without the Holocaust, there would be no reason for the 40 million war-dead or the millions more torn from their homes."

Chantelle shot back: "The Universal Declaration of Human Rights was a post-Holocaust attempt to recognize and protect the dignity of all persons," but Hardy scoffed, "Universal! People in the East sense a different reality, and until the East comes to dominate the world, the Holocaust myth will dominate the planet's political motivations."

Chantelle attempted to jump back in but Hardy gritted his teeth at her. "There is a movement within Israel to heighten the awareness of the Armenian holocaust, as part of an attempt to elevate Nazi Holocaust denial to the ultimate world crime. World War II would not have happened, had it not been for a few Jews propagandizing about what was happening. The objective was to guilt-trip the world, with a hoax to get Israel, and every means was justified to that end. "

Chantelle fell back stunned but then mustered enough indignation to rally back, with eyes straight on her benefactor, "Self-hatred, Mr. Hardy?"

Hardy jumped to his feet and stood over Chantelle. "My mother was raped by the Russians, and some Jews later took my sister at puberty from an orphanage paid off in L'viv, Ukraine, with the orphanage serving her up as a sex slave to Orthodox Jews in Israel. The Orthos like their lambs young but are forbidden to use condoms, so they fucked my *goyische* sister bareback. For five years, she was not allowed out of the brothel, until the Israelis spat her out of the country without papers or passport. At age 17, my sister was spent and registered positive for HIV. She was rejected as gentile vermin that could not mix with the chosen few, and she committed suicide on the Palestinian side of the Israeli wall." Hardy's face was bright red but then fell again pale. "Since then, I have dedicated myself to justice."

Chantelle slowly fell back against her plastic chair and then she stared down at a space of nothing before the floor. A second or more passed before Hardy sat back down. He folded his arms, looked down on Chantelle and punctuated, "Old Testament-style justice," but the biblical reference lifted her eyes straight back at him. Chantelle thrust her hands forward over her knees and bent forward, with her eyes not veering from his. "Mr. Hardy, I feel horribly sorry for your sister, as I do you now, but feel you need to reach some point where you can at least want to forgive. Hate is eating away at you, and your resentments own your mind, so that you suffer further from the resulting enslavement."

Hardy gave a hint of surprise in his look and the doctor Chantelle continued: "By keeping your hate focused in a monomaniacal way, you dishonor your sister and pay again for the sins of a few Israeli people." Chantelle held steady. "We can opt to make room in our minds for some horrible event but we can also opt not to have that tragedy remain life's defining moment. Yes, new hurts pour onto old ones and rekindle feelings of being cheated out of all that was hoped for, but buying into constant revenge keeps us imprisoned with a poisoned perspective, and the life we lead sticks to a script of resentment that is self-destructive."

Hardy's arms were still folded but he lifted his eyebrows and gave the hint of a shrug. "I use the rules of the eye-for-an-eye Hebrew bible" but Chantelle held forward. "Your sister's perpetrators will do it to themselves, Mr. Hardy. Theirs is not the faith of Isaiah or of the later Jew, Jesus. God gives us freedom to falter but God also coaches us to use self-love, in order to help discern truth and related fairness. We cry for short-term justice but

491

our best assurance for long-term fairness comes from such self-love and its radiation to others."

Hardy turned his eyes again to the air. "Well, rabbi Chantelle, until we reach that self-giving goal, we will have to live as you once preached, with less than perfection, needing human systems of law and justice for self-preservation."

Chantelle still appeared stunned from the news of Hardy's sister but she summoned enough wherewithal to press a point. "In obsessing over Jews, you obsess against yourself, Mr. Hardy. You are consumed by hatred, including self-hatred, my still presuming you are Jewish."

He waved his long lanky arm. "I am not in a Western courtroom, Doctor Fouriere, and the answer is none of your business."

Chantelle suddenly slammed both boots to the floor. "But your financing my speaking to front your agenda *is* my business, Mr. Hardy. No more! Your rage forces preset conclusions, since your very foundations are specious. Your false premises violate inquiry and make any subsequent debate a sham. And in your fiery reiteration of Holocaust-denial themes – all heard of by the world before and all soundly repudiated – you betray not only your own irrationality but also the resentments that you harbor against a few people who wronged, however horribly, your mother and sister. Goodbye, Mr. Hardy, and may some day, a god of understanding reach you."

Wednesday June 10 2009

It was more than a week since Chantelle had sent her letter, telling me she was meeting with her benefactor, Terry Hardy. And though I had been mollified after hearing him speak a year earlier in Chicago, there was something suspect about his funding, and maybe it was the social-minded Jew in me but I sensed Hardy had an agenda more conservative than mine. I wanted to caution Chantelle but I wanted more to let her know that I now had my eyes opened. And so I wrote, with hope stretched to the limit, believing that I was finally onside with her thinking, and writing to the only address I had – Princeton, where she had delivered her talk.

Dear Chantelle,

Anti-Semitism now seems representative of all racism and I confess trying to label you that way in our fight a year ago. The charge of anti-Semitism can be a trump card for shutting down discussion. People's views in our West are shaped by terrorism and an Israeli-biased media, and I wonder if we will ever understand what truly happens in the Arab world.

The outrage over Israel's war on Gaza has dissipated but Israel has refused to cooperate with a UN fact-finding mission headed by a South African judge named Goldstone. He has accused Israel of targeting Palestinian civilians, after hundreds were killed, with only three Israeli civilians dying.

Israel plans its own investigation to pressure Goldstone into saying he was wrong, and in the interim, Israel has urged the West to reject the judge's report, compartmentalizing him as an Apartheid racist. But Goldstone is a Zionist who connects the dots between the Holocaust and the creation of Israel.

The irony is that when the old white-supremacist South Africa faced sanctions, it was Israel that continued supplying it with arms and even helped South Africa start the development of a nuclear bomb. Then in 1987, when Israel did finally adopt sanctions against South Africa, Israel made sure that they did not include existing arms contracts, and those contracts carried through right to the end of Apartheid in 1994. Both Israel and South Africa's Apartheid began in 1948 but Israel resents any comparison.

Generations of White Afrikaners were brought up to believe that blacks were the descendants of Noah's son Ham and were accordingly cursed to be the servants of servants. And within Apartheid, there were right-wing groups so secret that even the people within them did not appear capable of explaining what they were. In one ultra-right-wing cult, officially Christian and named Israel Visie, its leader had studied a Bible rewritten to suggest that anyone not white was an animal of the field.

Another reason Israel is eager to stave off UN war crimes proceedings, along with international criticism regarding Gaza, is because Israel is poised to become a member of the Organization for Economic Cooperation and Development, and membership in the OECD would mark international acceptance, with economic benefits. Israel hopes to host the organization next year, 2010 in Jerusalem, giving the country further de facto recognition of its illegal annexing of Arab East Jerusalem.

Israel is also eager to quash any concerns about bribery to win defense contracts on settlements within Palestinian territories, or of Israeli intelligence using British, Irish and Canadian false passports to carry out assassinations. Additionally downplayed is the fact that since its creation, Israel has asserted the right to kill or capture enemies anywhere, despite any outside country's police regarding such acts as crimes.

An Israeli think tank has found that the country is facing a global campaign of "delegitimization" and Israel has resolved to delegitimize the delegitimizers. It is developing commercials, entitled Making the Case for Israel, and they embrace demagoguery like, "Are you fed up with the way we are portrayed around the world?" Israel is also hosting public events to smooth over any illegal Israeli actions that demonize the country.

Israel, post-Gaza, is trying to rebrand itself as a world creator of quality-of-life enhancements, such as the cell phone and ingestible camera, and spokespeople are emphasizing that such rebranding has no end date, since Israel is here forever. Israeli diplomats are openly talking *about their new strategy, countering allegations that the country defies international law, and the strategy is shifting to more pleasant theaters, with Israel sending abroad writers, theater companies and exhibits. The Toronto Film Festival is set to hold a spotlight on Tel Aviv.*

Meanwhile, the Jewish right wing in Israel is taking over, such that even erstwhile supporters of Israel can no longer criticize it with impunity. Turkey, a once-valued ally that carried out joint military exercises with Israel, has been snubbed for criticizing its assault on Gaza. And Obama's failure to get the Palestinian peace talks moving again has left the Israeli peace camp marginalized, with American mediators giving up on insisting upon any halt to further Israeli settlements.

The ultra-Orthodox Jews in Israel – known as the Haredim or those who tremble in awe of god – have a higher birth rate than even the Arabs, with the Haredim averaging nine children per family. The ultra-Orthodox have accordingly gone from being a tiny minority in Israel to 10% of the population and one-third of the primary schools. And under the current Israeli political system, chronic coalition governments are compelled, for their very survival, to allow minority parties to force their will upon the majority.

With the rise of the Haredim ultra-Orthodox Jewish community, Israel is headed toward theocracy, and the Haredim have teamed up with right-wing Zionists to become a pivotal force. It is now predicted that within 10 years, the Haredim will control the government of every city in Israel.

Today in the West Bank, the two largest settlements are ultra-Orthodox, and the Haredim are one-third of Israeli settlers. The Haredim are trying to make Israel a Halachic state, with strict adherence to Jewish law, and the Haredim have attacked non-kosher butcher shops and torched cars driven on the Sabbath. The Haredim are also pushing to have buses gender-segregated and say that democracy has no place in Judaism.

Violence among the Haredim is now so widespread that there are communities where the police won't go and women have been beaten for dressing immodestly. Both men and women have also been beaten for sitting beside each other on buses, and in the military, religious Zionists have refused to ride in vehicles driven by women. As for those West Bank settlements, with ever more Haredim living in them, Israel's conflict with the Palestinians is becoming increasingly religious, and as the settlements become more religious, the Jewish secular community seems sure to leave.

Those Orthodox, as you may know, Chantelle, don't want to make room for any Reform Jews or for that matter, religious conservatives. In Canada as well, there is street pressure being put on secular Jews to become Orthodox, after Orthodoxy began a revival in the 1970s. Today, there is a steady stream of secular Jewish youth embracing it, and the Canadian Orthodox population, with its procreation mandate, now doubles every 20 years.

Orthodox Jewish teaching says there are two kings, whom each of us has inside. The Bad King is our selfish impulse, the yetzer hara, and the Good King is our rational side, the yetzer tov. But the same teaching has now to acknowledge that new neurological findings confirm what Scottish philosopher Hume long ago professed – that an act of kindness (mitzvah) or charity (tzedekah) benefits the giver as well as the receiver, and our neuron pathways reinforce that goodness impulse; thus, to be against such evolution is to be cruel.

But the Hasidic Chasidic masters also teach that an act of kindness delivers a reward, reaching to the heavenly spheres, rather than to an appropriate place on Earth – the Orthodox preach that a spiritual elevation or aliyas neshamah will come through strict adherence to the Torah, along with its Torah Emet (Torah of truth) and Mitzvot (Creator's commandments). For the Orthodox, the Torah Chaim (love) and Toras Emes (truth) reflect truth at its truest, and their god will recompense the flock for all the propagated grief. At this time, however – note the carrot – it remains unknown how the flock will be recompensed. Teshuva (repentance, return) thus has the power to end the promulgated exile and bring redemption, and the days of fasting and commemoration bring to mind victimhood via exile, along with the Jewish people's role in their sinful neglect of the Torah and Mitzvot.

The Orthodox teach a form of racism – in the Hebrew bible, one Joseph asked his brothers to tell his father Jacob of all his glory in the spiritually unclean land of Egypt, while Joseph managed to remain strong and connected to the Orthodox god. That god reassured his people that the father Jacob would go down with Joseph to Egypt but the same god would bring him up again – implicit is the reassurance to Jewish people everywhere that they will get out of exile, be redeemed and have their true advantage in the world revealed.

And always there is the Orthodox leaders' cry that the Jewish people are besieged on all sides and nothing is more threatened than the future of the young generation, with the only solution being Torah education. The Orthodox leaders insist that it must begin at the earliest age and continue on in every aspect of life without compromise. They preach that Jewish suffering is rooted in Jews' wavering from the Torah, and whenever they waver, they become complacent and lose preparedness for war against ever-present threats from anti-Semitic enemies. As the children thus learn from Jacob's return to the land of Canaan, they acquire material things, not just for prosperity but also for war, to protect their lives. And when the children remember that the destruction of the Temple is another cause for grief, they heed that a Jewry united under Orthodoxy will merit the rebuilding of the Holy Temple in Jerusalem, never again to be destroyed.

Chantelle, I feel your thoughts as never before and I love you.
Arthur

Princeton University advised that it forwarded my letter to Chantelle's Manhattan B&B, which in turn forwarded it to Terry Hardy's address. Then, after some effort, I managed via Princeton and the B&B to get Hardy's address but could not obtain his phone number or e-mail address.

No response came to my letter, beyond Princeton's thoughtful alert, and there were no university publications announcing Chantelle's speaking any-where; so, with growing fear that I would never see her again, I put my trust for reaching Chantelle through letters addressed to her supporter, Terry Hardy.

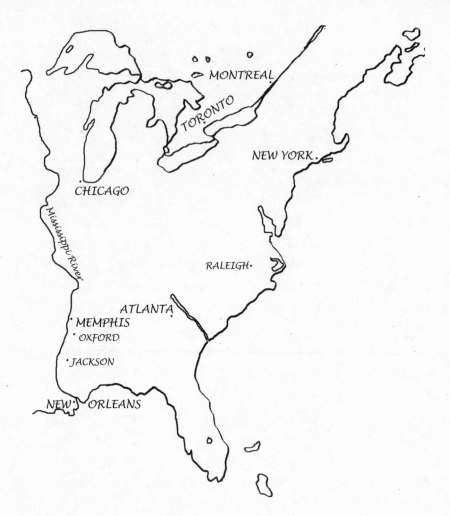

MONTREAL

TORONTO

NEW YORK.

CHICAGO

Mississippi River

RALEIGH·

ATLANTA
· MEMPHIS
· OXFORD

· JACKSON

NEW · ORLEANS

Sunday June 14 2009

After Chantelle's break with her benefactor, she spent some quiet moments with God in Central Park before resolving to drive south, down the eastern United States and into the core of Christian fundamentalism, to meet it head-on for rigorous debate. Then, within an ever hotter June, she steered clear of Washington on advice from Princeton colleagues and soon was given permission to speak as a Christian preacher in the urban "New South" of Raleigh, North Carolina.

Chantelle arrived for her address dressed in beige slacks, shirt and san-dals, and was standing on a mound sloping away to a swath of greenery that opened up to the wide Fayetteville Street beyond. Her audience gathered spontaneously and it appeared to be mainly a group of people still dressed for church, on an otherwise unhurried Sunday. The gathering numbered only a few dozen when Chantelle started her talk:

"In the Greek and Roman empires, the *lingua franca* was Greek, and under the impulse of Greek thought, along with a range of Middle-Eastern theologies, religious cults flourished. One such religion was Hebrew and it offered a one-stop shop of monotheism and a life of happiness if one simply kept to a specified covenant with the chosen god. Jewish intelligentsia 300 years before Jesus translated the Hebrew Bible into Greek, partly in an attempt to keep the Hebraic flock from succumbing to Greek thinking, and that bible, known as the *Septuagint*, later became the foundation for the Greek New Testament written in the century after Jesus's death."

Chantelle's words seemed harmless enough to the quiet audience, and she carried on in apparent comfort. "Biblical scholars agree that little in the New Testament reflects the words of Jesus – 'Love your enemies, our father, heaven is leaven and belongs to the poor and hungry, turn the other cheek, give to all who beg, a shrewd manager lets his debtors off with less, the smallest mustard seed produces a large plant, a prophet is not respected on his own turf' – but not much else."

A few in the audience turned their heads to gauge other people's reactions but Chantelle took no notice. "After Jesus's death, many women followed the lead of Mary Magdalene and played a key role in things like charitable trusts. In fact, Christian women's work was one reason why Christianity took over any proselytizing role from Judaism, which ceased to expand in ethnicity. Soon, however, the Christianity that followed aligned itself with a Mediterranean honor-shame morality and preservation of the family name at all costs. Women lost their short-lived independence."

Several women in the audience audibly turned and smiled at one another, and Chantelle took her cue to press on. "Jesus had not been a judge and had done much to quash thoughts of guilt and sin, but after he died, it was concocted that Jesus had died for the sins of the guilty. Then Paul shifted the center of gravity from Jesus's life to that after his death, and rationalized that if Christ were not resurrected from the dead, then faith in him was in vain; therefore, Paul argued, Jesus had to be resurrected. Paul then went on to put icing on the cake, claiming that such resurrection was a reward for any follower, his thus embracing the doctrine of death-denial."

The same women no longer had smiles and were looking around to witness a few couples opting to leave. As they did, however, some passersby sensed the indignation in people departing and joined in to hear what was being said. "While the Greeks had considered such 'hope' or keeping people in suspense, the evil of evils, the concept of an everlasting life, nonetheless raised egoism to infinity, and any sufferers were sustained by a hope that no one could refute.

"Conditions for Saul-turned-Paul were thus propitious – there had been a decline in traditional polytheism, but like today, a deep spiritual hunger remained and Paul promised the fullness of one god in christ. He also used the Greek word 'soul' to declare that a salvation of the soul could be attained if a person simply followed Jesus's steps as spun by Paul – the deeper the problem, the deeper the theology that Paul used to solve it. One possible example grew out of the pagan ritual of winter solstice, with the realigning of Jesus's birthday to December 25, that date later sanctified by a pope in the fourth century."

Many people began to depart, some suggesting they report the radical speaker who was disturbing a Sunday afternoon in Raleigh. But Chantelle remained undaunted. "Mark knew of the martyrdom of Peter and Paul in about the year 60 AD and Mark thereafter was in a hurry to finish the Christian bible's first gospel, in part to alert the ruling Romans that Christian Jews were not Hebrews, before the Romans toppled the Jewish temple in 70.

"The writers of Matthew followed with a gospel to an audience of Christian Jews, painting Jesus as the new Moses, but later the writers for gentile Luke made his gospel popular to non-Jews, adding stories like the Three Wise Men but still appealing to Jews by fabricating the ancestry of Jesus all the way back through Jewish history. The Old Testament was then reworked to be part of a process fulfilled in christ, and Jesus came to be born in Bethlehem, far off from his homeland, because that location was King David country, and the birth of a descendant-messiah had been so prophesized.

"The Gospel of John bears little relationship to the synoptic gospels of Mark, Matthew and Luke and was written to have readers believe that Jesus was the son of god and that the fearful could have everlasting life in his name. As for the Acts of the Apostles, the disciples were disappointed that Jesus, once crucified, had not then called upon the heavenly hosts to establish the messianic kingdom after his entry into it. But there arose an implied mission – to keep the movement going as the event of Jesus receded. And so concocted was a pending second coming."

Here was Chantelle, speaking in second-coming country, and many of the remaining audience were talking loudly among themselves. Yet she took no notice and rallied on. "By the second century, there were masses of Christian texts with no official status but two types of Christianity emerged, one trying to reconcile itself with free Greek thought and the other grounded on the assumption that human beings were corrupt. For the latter, the law implied obedience, and any authority rested with the Church and the men who ran it."

A few women then swiveled back from their side glances and talk to render a polite applause, and a smiling Chantelle felt the force. "This Patrician-Christian morality claimed that only its god knew what was good or bad, but such morality made people fearful of those sins invented by that morality, especially the God-given gift of sex."

Women again smiled at one another but some of the men did too, and Chantelle was not about to stop. "Morals such as fair play or the abhorrence of cruelty, should have been assessed as to how certain acts can affect others but the Ten Commandments forbade any faith other than the Patrician-Christian one and carried a death penalty for any variation in thinking.

"The Judeo-Christian Old Testament's Numbers, books five to nine, were common to every culture in recorded history, but number 10 was a Hebrew god priority in not coveting the servants and livestock of others. It is interesting to compare that priority with the Muslim Mahavira in the Jain patriarch, saying that one is not to injure, oppress, enslave, insult, torment, torture or kill any creature or living being."

"Muslim," the audience murmured and the rumbling grew louder, with more people turning around to see the reactions of others. Suddenly, a man who had been texting into his BlackBerry was doing so at a frenetic pace. Chantelle took no notice and carried on. "People, since at least the time of Jesus, have been cherry-picking the bible to justify their every impulse, moral or otherwise. The Old Testament counsels Hebrews that one may buy male and female slaves from among the nations around Israel, and that all slaves are to regard their masters as worthy of the slaves' honor, but over the brethren-people of Israel, one is forbidden from ruling with such harshness. Christianity followed a similar course and added polydeism, by which followers could judge another a saint, while simultaneously abrogating their own responsibilities by saying they were, after all, not saints.

"By comparison, across much of Islam, saints were a no-no and as for the issue of slavery, Iran, with its Shia Islamic stress on theology and accordant interpretation of texts, assumes god spoke about slavery only within the norms of the seventh century. Iran, however, is a little more open than most of its Arab neighbors."

There was a sudden hush in the audience and Chantelle rushed to fill the gap. "Life can be simple but the convoluted processes in our brains complicate it. We have selective memories with an emotional overlay that prioritizes things differently, and we don't often grasp what true listening means. What few words we heed are often distorted as they make their way through our circuitry, and just as AIDS and desertification are natural phenomena, so too is our need to address them, and moral judgments should not overwhelm us in our dealing with such issues. God is here to help us but like a good parent, has given us the skills to fix things ourselves. We need communications, farsightedness and, as Jesus said when he figuratively healed the blind, eyes that are open."

The BlackBerry man finished his texting and scurried off. The rest of the audience dispersed, with some talking loudly and a few turning their eyes back to view the person who had been speaking.

Chantelle drove deeper into the Bible Belt, where she felt she could have a stronger impact. But opposition forces were prepared – city fathers had been pressed to pass resolutions condemning her perversions, and during her ever-briefer speeches, police sat at the ready while a new group began to agitate every audience from within.

At each new gathering, there also appeared a prominent evangelist named Reverend Ralph Sather. He was a fat man, looking to be in his 40s, with a puffy face that seemed to ooze fried chicken. The rest of his body burst through polyester suits, all of them resplendent in colors of ice cream.

At one new speaking point when the audience grew restless, police began to edge forward toward the podium but Sather counseled them to let Chantelle carry on, allowing the anger to simmer. "Such evangelists are drug peddlers, and vulnerable people mortgage their lives to a short-lived euphoria." Sather then unleashed the police to break up the forum.

Chantelle traveled next to Atlanta and witnessed there an urban New South sprawling all the way to Tennessee. By 2009, much of that South was suffering from dehydration and it was hot that day in June, when she started to speak:

"History is written by the victors…"

A few police were on hand but the audience was small for such a big city, and was remarkably multi-racial, contradicting a fading stereotype of a Southern town. Ralph Sather was also present but remained at the rear, directing nothing. Chantelle continued, "…and the American Civil War was no exception."

A small applause followed as if Chantelle had pushed some button but then she elaborated: "World War 1 was another, and the greatest tragedy of that 'War to End All Wars' seems to be that we have learned so little from it. World War I caused a North American panic on venereal diseases, the decadent '20s and World War II, but World War I's first victim was truth."

There was a numbing silence and Chantelle kept going. "Truth needs reason and reason cannot happen so long as neurotic religions guide our lives. When evaluating any religion, I suggest we look at the results. Dogma that is handed down can shunt our thinking, from an age when we are still children, and once shunted, our freedom of conscience is quashed. Words gain power over us and 'faith' is spun to mean assent to a specified 'wisdom,' leaving us powerless under an angry god. Once then bound, we too can feel a sense of power, and abuse it to whip all those beneath us into shape."

Shortly thereafter, Chantelle finished speaking. Sather had only watched and listened. Tennessee was next:

"God made the neutron and here it is for us to sense in the science labs at Oak Ridge. If we divide an atom, we find a smaller form – the electron – and its behavior appears random. And if we keep going inside that atom, we reach quarks and discover that the big quark's behavior again defies prediction. Our planet's most fundamental cores appear to operate without programs."

The audience remained politely quiet and Chantelle went on. "A century and a half ago, a monk named Mendel devoted his life to experiments in biology, and although his bishop had forbidden monks from even teaching the subject, Mendel published his results in 1866, with every page an exposition of modern genetics as now sanctioned. No one understood his exposition and no one cared. His papers were all burned and Mendel descended into oblivion."

The audience murmured a little but stayed listening. "Science's fight against ignorance and related superstition has changed little, and despite science now offering clues on many issues of mythology, faith in a rules-based religion remains, for many of us, the same. People seem acclimatized to the notion that technology can be used to solve certain mysteries of life but those same people recoil if science treads too closely on their cherished mysteries."

The audience began to shift and the murmuring grew ever more pronounced, but Chantelle did not appear to take notice. "Throughout history, tribal organizations have formed to address the eternal question 'Why?' and the need to so focus may be hardwired into our human consciousness. Yet because of the universal appeal of that question, scientists also ask it, since extraordinary claims require extraordinary evidence.

"The beauty of scientific inquiry is that it does not claim to hold the truth, yet science always is in motion toward it. Scientists don't know there is no heaven but they do see an atmosphere, and scientists leave the heaven question open. Science, moreover, does not derive authority from any body of accumulated knowledge but rather from an awareness of science's own fallibility and ignorance, within an environment where everything remains falsifiable. Rather than 'believing' in something like the virgin birth or even atheism, science accordingly says 'This is the most reasonable opinion to hold right now' and the scientist 'believes' only in the principle of scientific enquiry."

The audience grew further restless and mumblings became increasingly audible but Chantelle held on, eager to stimulate rigorous intellectual discussion. "Also hardwired into our human brains is the drive to connect, both emotionally and socially, and that evolutionary need is second only to the survival instincts of eating and mating – it's worth noting that any group of scientists gathered together can experience a transcendentalism not much different from the high that Christian fundamentalists feel, when hitting on what they sense is 'the answer.'"

Heckles then arose from the rustling audience and Chantelle attempted to put her words into context. "What classical cultures held in common was a vision of an orderly and reasonable society, and upon the foundations of this model was founded modern science. Against, therefore, the vagaries of human caprice, science sought to construe reality. But science is also a source of power that the state wants to harness, and if science is allowed to go that way, our values fall into disarray and cynicism. Science, in and of itself, is amoral but we must never abandon our moral imagination in initiating it, because without that moral imperative from the outset, science will perish, along with faith and society as a whole."

The audience by then was so animated that Chantelle's next words were almost inaudible. "Intriguingly, atheism contradicts science, since science, to be faithful, requires doubt and re-evaluation, but atheism is grounded on the absolute belief that there is no God and ignores the reality that human beings at root are universally religious."

The Reverend Ralph Sather was present and looked around to sense the restlessness. He then took hold of a microphone that had been set up at the side for later questions. "Life, as she just admitted, is a mystery that we cannot understand, but we do appreciate that mystery and are humbled before it."

The audience gave a cheer and Sather bellowed on. "The mystery will stay, and we God-fearing people will hold to our orderly and reasonable society."

Chantelle lowered her head, with a look of supplication to her audience. "Without expanding awareness, we will follow our beliefs to hell," and Sather seized upon the word. "She is condemning us!" but again she tried to reason. "Universal unity is not important," and Sather picked up the crowd's moans. "She is trying to break us up and God's authority over us!"

Chantelle tried ever more beseechingly. "Please! You were not given minds to confine them to monasteries of salvation-seeking," but Sather grabbed his microphone out of its stand and put the mic in his right hand, while he raised his left. "She is labeling us, and she herself a Catholic!"

Chantelle then bent low, and with breaking voice tried to appeal, but her message was not what the audience wanted to hear. "Is work really creative if it meets no resistance? Divine creation can be a trick to closing the door on the question of what happened first."

Sather charged back, "A revolutionary! She is challenging our God."

Chantelle's voice almost broke. "I am pleading with you to inherit the mind," but Sather knew she had lost her audience. "From the North, now exposed!"

Before Chantelle had arrived, Ralph Sather's network of fundamentalists had taunted the people of Oak Ridge, Tennessee, and she was condemned as a cult leader. Her reputation became sullied across a section of surrounding counties, all deemed by Sather his diocese.

Monday June 22 2009

I spent all weekend putting together a letter, before mailing it to Hardy's address.

Dear Chantelle,

There is a growing right-wing reaction to Obama as Americans turn back to their god and a backlash media. In the unemployment fallout from the Bush years, forces are gaining strength on platforms like hate-TV against any Obama moves on health care reform and the like. Congress looks like it will snap back to the right in midterm elections.

Obama talks of an "empathy deficit," but empathy is a word mis-trusted in much of my United States. The irony is that if biology can be used to justify competition, it can also be used to justify cooperation – a leading Cambridge professor is spearheading the neurological study of empathy, but the professor is quick to caution that beyond any brain circuitry wired in at birth, loving parents are needed to entrench in children a sense of self-belief, such that empathy becomes automatic. That Jewish professor was told as a boy by his father that the Nazis had turned Jews into lampshades and soap.

Obama is trying to move discourse to a higher ground but he has inherited economic despair, nightmarish debt and two wars. To make matters worse, the puppet media now running the USA are choosing both the issues and their solutions, and not even an eloquent Obama stands a chance in this tabloid society.

The Western press is claiming Pakistan is a "Fortress of Islam" but the same press cannot recognize that Israel and the United States are the Judeo-Christian equivalent.

Egypt's Coptic Christians are reported to be under threat but as you know, Muhammad took steps to protect Christians, affirming that he and his followers were with them. The Qur'an prohibits desecration of any houses of worship and advocates a bond with Jews and Christians, with all members regarded as People of the Book.

The Harvard Arab Alumni Association is being blasted for organizing an Arab world conference in Damascus where the Syrian president's wife delivered a gracious keynote address in support of independent civil societies. The resulting comments provoked intense reaction among U.S. political intelligentsia. The American magazine Vogue later profiled the same London-born Syrian first lady, saying she and her husband governed their presidential residence with "wildly democratic principles" but after an outcry, the profile was removed from Vogue's website.

President Obama's cousin is chief rabbi of Chicago's Ethiopian Hebrew congregation, and Obama's top two advisers are Jewish, but the Israeli prime minister's brother-in-law said on radio that there is an anti-Semitic president in America. The American Tea Party founder has even claimed Obama received campaign contributions from Hamas! Iran is being criticized for re-enacting murders but Israeli prosecutors do the same whenever they can, and an Israeli lawyer says such a process helps the prosecution solidify the case.

Does the West know that Iran's pursuit of nuclear technology in the 1950s was spurred by Eisenhower's Atoms for Peace program? And that Iran had made steady progress with Western help? But after Iran's 1979 revolution, Western concerns about Iranian intentions led to the West's halting any honoring of contracts for fuel and technology, and Iran had to do the technology itself? Or that Iran welcomes tourists and they can readily clear the border?

Iran is the world's largest Shia Muslim country and Iranians are surrounded by Sunni Muslims (Pakistan), Hindus (India), Jews (Israel), Christians (the U.S., Europe and Russia) and Han Chinese, all with nuclear weapons; so, Iran may be saying, 'Why not us?' Watching any Iranian developments, however, is Israel, with its right-wing government stressing the danger of Iran and warning that Israel will not stand by and allow Iran to develop nuclear weapons.

How much political unrest in Iran is set afire by Israeli intelligence and the West cannot be gauged, because principal source of information for us is Iran's enemy, the West. The Iranian government has had to counter foreign driven calls to boycott its elections, those calls being done

through social networking. Iran has multiple Internet cafes, and anyone
can sabotage government intentions, while remaining anonymous.

In Lebanon, the leader was assassinated, and while Israel had the
most to gain from his death, a Western tribunal is trying to pin the guilt
on the Shi'a Muslim group Hezbollah. And in the Christian holy area
where John the Baptist baptized Jesus, Jordan has cleared the minefields
on its side of the border, after a 1994 peace deal with Israel. Jordan has
also established there a cultural heritage center but Israel has opted for
barbed wire and signs near ancient monasteries and churches reading
"Danger! Mines!"

I was on a Toronto subway this week and the woman next to me was
watching a film that damned young Hamas men who married girls under
the age of 10, some under the age of six. On that same subway, I read in
a left-behind newspaper that Israeli archeologists have uncovered the
remains of human teeth from 400,000 years ago, belying the thinking
that Homo sapiens *began in sub-Saharan Africa.*

Information is controlled in America by a triad of Hollywood, a dated
theodicy and puppet evangelists. The Texas school board refuses textbooks
with sections on evolution and Texas is a large market and so textbook
companies are nixing evolution. The 21st century has also just witnessed
a two-term president who proclaimed the miracle of salvation and said
the country's ills could be cured with religion-based initiatives. Let us not
forget that the press blessed at the start the Wolfowitz war, and let Bush
away with declaring Hussein "evil," then standing by while he was tried
by kangaroo court and lynched into silence.

During the Second World War, transparency equated to a black-and-
white newsreel full of propaganda and left us with a memory bank of
'just wars.' Propaganda by those in control of promulgated information.
Three hundred years earlier, Britain's leader Cromwell endorsed Irish
theologian James Usher, who dated creation to 4004 BC, by relying on
the work of second century AD rabbi Yose ben Halafta. His Book of the
Order of the World *established Jewish historical chronology. Now, there*
is yes the Internet, but it still remains difficult for us in the West to have
any sense of proportionality.

Across Europe, fears are being fomented and fringe leaders fronted to protect Western values. Mainstream politicians who look at the electoral success of xenophobic populist parties are trying to appease, saying to in-groups what those groups feel is the truth. And online, one can find thousands who share perverted views, triggering a vicious spiral of group-think that reinforces ideologies and polarizes the public into like-minded segments.

Switzerland has placed limits on mosque minarets and France is having hearings to discuss what it means to be French, with the subtext being that France's national identity is endangered. Now that some Jews are moving back from Israel, with Sarkozy as president, many of them fear Europe is becoming Muslim. Sarkozy claims he did not invent the fact that some French neighborhoods are ghettos, and that racism is on the rise – read anti-Israel. Sarkozy is targeting Muslim immigrants in saying France has too many foreigners and that halal meat prepared to Muslim standards should not be available in public school canteens. The French right wing is also talking of France's Islamicization and has compared a prayer rally of Muslims to France's Nazi occupation.

France's Ministry of Immigration and National Identity was created by Sarkozy, and its Minister has produced a guide that poses the question whether the government should control immigration to preserve national identity. Recently, the Minister wondered aloud if Islam was compatible with the French Republic, and France's Minister for Family Affairs advised young Muslims not to wear their caps back to front, because baseball caps so tilted are used by blacks in Brooklyn as an anti-Zionist symbol. France is also banning full face coverings on women and is miffed by American moves to encourage more communications with Muslims to diffuse the threat of terrorism in post-9/11 Europe.

Toronto, meanwhile, has become ground zero in the propaganda war over the Middle East, and despite some of Toronto's most vocal critics of Israel being Jewish, the school board is considering removing yet another title from its curriculum, after Jewish groups complained it inferred an anti-Israeli position.

As for the rest of the country, we can no longer look to snow-white Canada as an oasis for measured thinking. The newly conservative Canada has calculated that the Canadian government can support a right-wing position on Israeli politics without fear of being outflanked by center-left thinkers among Canada's Jews. Canada's reputation as a global rights champion has been damaged, says an Amnesty International report, criticizing Canada's uncompromising support for Israel, along with Canada's defunding of agencies giving aid to Palestinians.

Canadians themselves continue to support gay marriage and certain abortions, and are against capital punishment. And Canadian priorities remain education, health care, the elderly, the environment and child poverty. Indeed, by 90% to 4%, Canadians believe they have a better quality of life than the Americans, with whom they share a 5,500-mile border. But not for 50 years, since President Kennedy, has there been a Canadian prime minister who is more conservative than his American counterpart – while Obama tries to bring some objectivity to the Middle East, the newly conservative Canadian government is downright cozy with Israel and related lobbies, and the Canadian Conservative Party line on Israel is more and more that of Israel's right wing, Likud.

Canada's earlier commitment to Afghanistan was foisted on Canada's former Liberal government, in part to improve Canada's influence in Washington and NATO, but the current Canadian government, with backers rooted on the conservative side of the American Republican Party, has made domestic politics an overarching calculus of Canada's foreign policy. The government supports Israel at every turn in the United Nations and once Hamas won in Palestine, Canada was first to announce no dealings with it. Canada supported Israel in Lebanon in 2006 and Gaza in 2008 - 2009, and was the first to boycott an international conference on racism, before condemning Goldstone's report on Israel's attack on Gaza.

The governing Conservative Party in Canada has made huge inroads in foreign and domestic policies to get the Jewish community on board. Planned, under a Jewish senator's chairing, is a string of Conservative surveys that will put funding of the Canadian Broadcasting Corporation *under the microscope, with the Tory government ultimately deciding how big a hit the public broadcaster will take, under the guise of official restraint. The prime minister regards the CBC as liberal and says he watches CNN instead.*

The newly conservative Canada plans to bring back harsh anti-terrorism legislation, and the prime minister says the major threat to Canada is still Islamicization. Canada is also planning to ban the niqab head covering for Islamic women when being sworn in to citizenship. If the Conservatives ever do get a majority, and despite a declining crime rate for over 20 years in Canada, a multi-billion dollar crime bill will be at the front of the Conservative agenda, ahead of all moves to help the economy. To my mind, there are two key reasons:

1. To flush out and silence critics of Israel under the guise of terrorism. A key part of the bill paves the way for Canadian victims of terrorist acts to sue the perpetrators and supporters of terrorism, including seeking compensation from foreign states.

2. To harden marijuana laws to appease right-wing United States, as part of a bartering process to help the process of commercial border crossings.

Much else in the Tory agenda, like the hot button of sexual child predators, is the stuff of camouflage and decoys.

Count on that law being just the beginning. The newly conservative Canada is creating a law on "hate" but if we need a law to protect us from bigots, who will protect us from the law? The law is a pathetic attempt to eliminate evil, as self-defined. Even on the Internet, the originators of content will be bound by Canadian laws of libel and slander, not to say hate speech, and hyperlinkers will be held liable, if they register approval of the defamatory content to which they link. If we want to censor hate completely, why not start with the Bible, with its homophobia, wife-beating and ethnic cleansing?

Criminal sentences are also being toughened under the post-9/11 Anti-Terrorism Act, and Canada's human-intelligence agency has had its budget and staff doubled versus a decade ago. It now reports directly to the Privy Council Office, the one joining the civil service to the prime minister. *The rationale for the intelligence moves is that Canada has to maintain its credibility within the English-connection spy network that binds the U.S., Britain and Australia.*

The Canadian International Development Agency also offers little information as to how it disseminates funds, and the newly conservative Canada is not a member of the International Aid Transparency Initiative, a coalition aiming to improve aid effectiveness and make aid spending accessible. Conservative Canada also plans to open a watchdog Office of Religious Freedom as has the U.S., and promote the Office across the world. Whether Canada's watchdog will have the same role as its American counterpart — to appease evangelical Christians and their backers — remains to be seen. Will, for example, Canadian women who wear niqabs be forbidden to vote, while the country still allows voting by mail-ins?

Canada also plans to cut off an agency that helps democracy in fledgling South Sudan, but the same Canada continues to give priority aid to corrupt and dictatorial Ethiopia. The Canadian government now cuts off funding to organizations if it feels their views on Israel are not appropriate, and rarely mentioned is Canada's financial pledge through the country's International Development Research Centre, to support political and economic think tanks in the poorest countries of Africa, Asia and Latin America. An unspoken international aid objective is to make competing groups like the Muslim Brotherhood more moderate and so reduce their risk.

The minister of immigration has been an unbridled supporter of Israel's right-wing government, and the Canadian government is now calling for immigrant communities to keep an eye out for terrorists and report them, with the public safety minister saying he wants Canadians to spy on one another and report suspicious activities within their communities. The rationale is that al-Qaeda needs Western Muslims who move in easily and understand the culture of the West.

At the famous Atlantic landing Pier 21 in Halifax, the Canadian Jewish Congress is to get a federal grant to put up a monument to St. Louis, the ship that was turned away from Cuba, the United States and

Canada in 1939, with 1,000 Jewish refugees. The monument highlights the words "Anti-Semitism," "xenophobia," "racism" and "hatred." Canada's governing party also plans to pay special tribute in India to the Jewish center that was a focus of the attackers last year in the attack on Mumbai. And planned for 2010 is the release of a joint Canada-Israel postage stamp.

The newly conservative Canada is forcing civil servants to vet research findings or their sharing of scientific information through a media relations office, to ensure they are "on message." And in Canadian universities people who are critical of Israel, especially staff, are being condemned by politicians and the right-wing press, and are being pushed to leave office. Canadian evangelical colleges, with their theological echo of Judaism, are meanwhile getting economic stimulus grants.

The Canadian Forum on Religion and Public Life spearheaded a report on the world trend of Muslim population, saying it will increase by over one-third across the next 20 years, or twice the rate of the non-Muslim population, and that Canadian Muslims will go from 3% to 7% of the population.

Canadian-Jewish writer Mordecai Richler's The Apprenticeship of Duddy Kravitz is being kept off Canada's university literature courses. The book, published only 15 years after the end of the Holocaust, not only dares to offer up a vicious stereotype – that of a ruthlessly ambitious Jew and one willing to cheat to be someone – but also makes him human. Richler has been likened to the Russian-Jewish writer Isaac Babel, a Jew in a Cossack brigade fighting in the 1920 war against Poland. That war was fought on territory where there were many Jews, and under Soviet regulations, the Cossacks were not supposed to harm them.

The Jewish Diaspora in Canada, like that of the U.S., now reflects the majority opinion in Israel – fiercely opposed to any Palestinian state – and while Obama still struggles with that pipe dream, Canada's Conservative Party is so much on board with Israeli thinking that it has now snared the majority of the Canadian Jewish vote from the Liberal Party.

514

Lenin lauded the power of the telegraph and postal service, and saw the strength of film. Now the Internet is becoming a tool for societies to track down and get the scoop on dissidents, and a Canadian law is in the works to track users.

The banned-in-Canada Al Jazeera network has reported the all-encompassing concessions that the Palestinians have been willing to make to achieve a state in peaceful co-existence with an unbending Israel. Al Jazeera is now advised by a former Canadian Broadcasting Corporation executive, and while the Western press highlights such things as Iran's slew of capital punishments to show that it is under siege, many in the West are screaming for more of Al Jazeera to come out. It still remains to be seen how Obama or Congress will react to Al Jazeera or to the deplorable condition of the U.S. media. Al Jazeera is part of the Middle East solution but the American media is xenophobic and thus part of the problem. Al Jazeera has been denied access to important centers of stories in such areas as the Israeli-Gaza conflict, forcing Al Jazeera to resort to use of social media for sources.

More than three-quarters of the population in Pakistan believe the purpose of the U.S. war on terror is to weaken the Muslim world and ensure continued Wall Street domination, but what we hear in Canada is that people in Pakistan won't protest Muslim oppression, because of a fatalistic feeling that they have no impact.

All my love, always,

Arthur

Sunday July 5 2009

Chantelle drove deeper south to Oxford, Mississippi, and there healed her wounds in the B&B of a kind old widow who had heard of her plight. Chantelle did the housework and helped with the meals but still could not help scribbling down her thoughts, and soon she spoke again to an Oxford audience, on the Sunday evening of America's birthday weekend:

"A good evening to you all. I see many kind faces here tonight, and some of you know a bit about me." Chantelle gave a gentle bow. "Thank you for allowing me to return," and after a small applause, she came back up. "As I sense some of you good people know, no one can fairly judge another, until he or she has time to reflect on what the other has said or done."

No murmurs were heard but a few warm smiles came to the young lady who felt crestfallen after her verbal beating in Tennessee. She continued, "Love in action can be a difficult and painful task, when compared with love that is stage crafted. Staged love is done with props and sleight-of-hand but such love, if it is love at all, begs for reward and demands applause. Sustained love, on the other hand, is laborious and needs God's help."

A few women at the front again offered broad smiles and Chantelle could not help but notice. "I respectfully suggest to you that some religious messengers are really manipulators, who have been stage-acting all their lives. They abandon reality and in so doing, abandon too their fellow human beings, while sticking to their roles.

"I feel compassion for such people, for they have lost vision. Many of you sweet Southerners, whom I have met, have been destitute for decades, exhausted by toil, weighed down by poverty and often finding yourselves at the bottom of our justice scale. Some of you, yes, have resorted to fast fixes for the pain, and the manipulators have been only too quick to use a narcotic that they can readily peddle to the most vulnerable, its being the miracle."

The audience still held quiet but some heads did turn, as if people were not quite sure where Chantelle was going, on this American birthday weekend in the Deep South. "Faith does not spring from a miracle but faith itself can be a miracle. In your prayers, please do not ask God to bring you miracles, wealth, or elevation out of what some of you see as destitution. Think of life itself as heaven, present each day for every one of us. Love life. God has given it to you to breathe, see, taste and feel."

A few in the audience again turned to gauge the reaction of others, and there was some rumbling but there were also smiles, and soon the audience was beaming in agreement. Chantelle then gave a wide smile back to the audience before concluding after several more minutes, "Thank God for life's blessings, for you have many. God loves you and so do I."

No loudness followed, only some polite applause, along with a few nods and some endearing smiles. Chantelle took in a deep, long breath and heaved a long sigh.

Chantelle felt renewed by Oxford and with what little money she had earned from the B&B, ventured south on Mississippi's Interstate 55, to stop overnight in Jackson. But as the tall, beautiful Chantelle got out of her old Volvo, three men began to harass her, before a senior couple graciously came to her rescue. The couple, Melba and Norm, then invited Chantelle to stay in their Jackson home, even a few days if needed, and she accepted on the condition she make the meals.

There, without a planned place to speak, Chantelle nonetheless could not refrain from sketching down her thoughts during the evenings after Melba and Norm had gone to bed. After four days with the kind couple, Chantelle expressed a wish to meet and talk with Jackson's people. Norman, a retired fireman and former mayor, arranged for her to speak on the outskirts of town at the crest of a cleared field. No one then knew that Sather had got wind of Oxford.

Thus at dusk on a warm Sunday, Chantelle began talking atop a little hill to 100 or so people in Jackson, Mississippi:

"Thank you for coming out this evening. I want you to help me with something that has been bothering me for some time. The problem revolves around language and how we use it. God, I believe, created our world but we seem to have created god."

Chantelle was using words in a way that few people in the audience understood, and at the back, a silent Sather smirked in anticipation of her undoing. "When I speak of God, am I speaking of your god?"

Suddenly, a young-sounding baritone bellowed from the middle of the audience, "There is only one god!" and Chantelle nodded with due respect before she responded, "Yes, sir, I too so believe but 'God' is a word and words are invented by us."

The same voice bellowed again from the front of the audience. "God gave us the word," and some applause followed but Chantelle bent forward with her microphone in hand and tried to counter. "Yes, sir, but words are not perfect." Another male voice then rang out, this one older but just as loud. "God is perfect. He commands our words," and there followed a wider applause.

Chantelle tried to appeal. "I pray so, sir, and pray God shepherds our actions." Then, an angry woman's voice sprung up nearby. "Let's hear what the girl has to say. She's brave enough to stand here in front of us."

A small applause followed but suddenly a police cruiser appeared at the side of the field, and the crowd turned mute. Melba and Norm, who had been sitting on deckchairs at the front, gave Chantelle a warm smile and Norm's voice calmly resonated across the front, "You're doing fine, Chantelle."

Chantelle turned to Norm, gave a slight bow and came back up smiling before she returned to her speaking. "Thank you...Every word we utter, every sentence we make, is of our own minds' making, and everything we say is affected by where and when it is said. If, and this is the problem I just mentioned, we put too much of our own minds into the words we speak, we lose ownership of them and soon they own us."

Sather, by then, was becoming visibly twitchy but he let Chantelle carry on with her supplication. "Think of what a few of my words have done to us this evening. I mean no harm. I am here tonight, trying to express in these darn words, a problem I think many of us have."

But then another old baritone voice tore through the crowd, "We don't *know* many words," and the audience lightened up. Sather however became edgier, evidently not quite knowing what to do, and Chantelle kept on. "Using what words we know, the labeling of people is an act of people, not God, and the true causes of things cannot, as yet, be known."

These words did not look to sit well with a few people and some folded their arms in a defiant position, but Chantelle tried to deepen her appeal. "Our bible is full of metaphors and allegories. Why do we need to sanctify the meaning of each word, in a book of fairy tales?"

Some in the audience gasped and Sather's smirk came back, but he let Chantelle keep going, perhaps in the hope she would hang herself. "Any words that move us inevitably face some resistance," and the audience visibly shifted, with an audible rumble. Suddenly, one of the policemen got out of his squad car, slammed the door and stood leaning against it, with his eyes straight on Chantelle.

Chantelle bent forward again, threw her left arm forward with palm up and tried to heighten the appeal of her reasoning. "If the bible is afflicted with the disease of language, as it so appears, how do we read it?"

A woman's voice rose from the rear, "*Our* Bible is divinely inspired," and a loud applause followed, but Chantelle stayed stuck on her argument. "Is its every translation divinely inspired? Its New Testament was written in Greek from an earlier Aramaic. Did the writers fully understand the Hebrew of the original Old Testament? Centuries later, we get a Latin translation for the following 1,000 years, and then an English, then God knows what."

But Chantelle must have struck a chord, because the same woman attacked back. "That's right, girl. God knows and he has carried us through all the tongues!"

Chantelle looked across the audience and tried to engage, not the woman but the issue. "Settling for translation of a poem from a foreign place of long ago is dangerous, is it not?"

The audience stayed simmering, and Melba and Norm gave a frown to each other. Sather, meanwhile, remained silent and opted to let Chantelle go on. "The dogma of divine creation, for example, is simply, is it not, a creation of some group's words."

The silence that followed was stunning, and the policeman started to march forward. Norm took note and came forward to touch Chantelle's arm but by the time she peered down at him with a puzzled face, Norm had already turned his face to meet the oncoming officer. "It's okay, George, we're finished now. She's a guest of Melba and me."

As soon as Melba, Norm and Chantelle arrived home at 9:00 p.m., Melba went straight to bed but Norm broke his bedtime routine to stay up with what he saw as a hurt young lady. He invited Chantelle to have a seat on the house sofa, before Norm took to his reading chair across from her. She took a seat on the edge of the sofa, ready to listen, and Norm started the talk. "Chantelle, I don't profess to understand your world, but I think I understand that, for simple folk who have had to conform, when a beautiful young lady like you starts speaking a language radical to them, you can be quite a threat. I hope I am a Christian, if that does not offend you."

Chantelle bent forward toward Norm and folded her hands above her knees. She gave him an endearing smile. "Thank you for rescuing me a second time, Norm, and no, I don't think you could offend me."

Norm nodded an acknowledging smile. "Well, bless you, Chantelle... My limited experience has rather taught me that folks, even bad ones, are much more simplistic than you suppose. Some down here would condemn you for having vain expectations in wanting to know too much."

Chantelle backed off a bit. "I am curious, Norm, yes," and then she eased forward to hear Norm's response. "But many here are not, Chantelle. Call it fear, but folks in these parts want to worship nothing more than what is accepted as the way it is. When you come down here out of the North, speaking with an accent and using words in a way they have never heard before, offering them an alternative to the only way they've ever known, you can spook them."

Chantelle put her folded hands forward as if in a plea. "They want no choice in life, Norm?" and he leaned back in his big chair. "Not in what they worship, Chantelle. Nothing could frighten them more than to replace their religion with enough freedom to decide what is good and evil, using only their consciences and having no fixed image for their god. They would find that freedom too much to bear and would quickly reject what our leaders down here say is the work of the devil. People would then rush back to what they saw as tried and true, and the Sathers of the world would be only too ready to answer their questions and solve their problems."

Chantelle nudged forward more. "They want such slavery, Norm?" and he too bent forward with his eyes on hers. "Chantelle, I don't believe people are much different anywhere, and one thing that I have witnessed over and over again is the conflict that comes from anyone questioning authority. If I am alarmed by what is transpiring today in my beloved America, it is the backlash against free thinking. The religious right that dominated for 20 years was thought to be falling apart, but some are now taking over a Tea Party that was originally libertarian."

Chantelle sank back in the sofa opposite Norm and gave a long look at the floor before her eyes finally came back again, to see the wisdom of his. "I think I hear you, Norm, thank you. You remind me of my father."

Monday July 13 2009

Next morning, Melba and Norm bid farewell to Chantelle and insisted on paying for her help. Norm had also secured for Chantelle a temporary nursing job in Alabama's Mobile hospital, to replace a nurse who was on maternity leave. Chantelle would be able to eat and sleep in the hospital.

From the start at the Mobile hospital, Chantelle's nursing work proved exceptional but it raised jealousy among her peers. She also had the moves put on her at the end of day one by a Doctor Christopher Proud III, who in the hospital hallway outside her bedroom, proposed a date.

Chantelle tried a gracious decline but Proud then lowered his forehead at the young, new nurse who had not addressed him as "Doctor," but he recovered enough to raise his eyebrows and afford a sly grin. "May I help you in any way?"

Chantelle repeated her "No, thank you," this time more firmly than before.

Proud reared back and sucked in a breath that was pronounced enough to make his chest expand and his nostrils flare. "You arrive without a credential check, are given room and board in one of Alabama's finest medical facilities, and refuse the help of Christopher Proud the third?"

Chantelle held her ground. "Or the first or second," and Proud stood frozen in a pause, before shaking his head to the floor and offering in a huff, "People are right." He then pivoted on one of his heels and whisked away.

During the following work week, a veteran nurse and former schoolmate of Norm helped counter some of the jealousies acted out against Chantelle, and the same nurse helped facilitate Chantelle's speaking in the hospital's auditorium, on the Sunday at week's end. Patients and caregivers came, but so too did Ralph Sather.

Sunday July 19 2009

In deference to the small audience present, Chantelle opted to stand aside the podium, with the mic off. She began in a firm voice:

"I have learned this week that last year in 2008, people here in Mobile legally wagered the same portion of their income that they spent on food and drink in restaurants. And while an additional fifth of that income was gambled illegally, the main factor in Alabama's current gambling boom has been the rise in state-run lotteries."

Groans were heard among some of the fundraisers present, including Doctor Proud, but Sather remained quiet in his seat, looking content to let Chantelle speak on. "Ten years ago, several states faced a fiscal squeeze but wanted to avoid unpopular tax increases, and so created lotteries. But research shows that lotteries attract people with little money, and advertise a fast chance to become a millionaire, with odds poor even by bookie standards – state lotteries pay out only 50% of their dollars versus Vegas's 85%.

No new murmurs arose and the audience looked somewhat stunned. Chantelle continued: "Few of us medical people have stopped to evaluate the health costs of gambling – increased street crime, substance abuse, family break up, impoverished children. Fewer still have assessed the psychological effect of a game that promotes winning and not fair play, luck and not skill, greed and not responsibility. Politicians also seem prey to the trap of something-for-nothing, seeing lotteries as a panacea for many a problem, without the political risk of taxes. Gambling is thus a surplus tax for the poor and a loophole for the rich."

Chantelle went on for another 10 minutes but seemed to misread the degree to which she was antagonizing certain members of her audience. Sather did not. One more day was all the hospital would allow her to work. Chantelle then decided to venture west along the Gulf of Mexico, to a city she had heard about in Texas.

Monday July 20 2009

After my spending a July weekend in a Toronto too hot to do much, I grew increasingly anxious to reach my beloved Chantelle, and so at the end of the following workday, in the cool of her basement apartment, I tried yet again to reach Chantelle via Hardy.

Dearest Chantelle,

Israel is declaring that there has been a marked decline in terrorist bombings, since its Gaza operation renewed Israel's deterrent capacity. But there had been no terrorist attacks for five full years, not even during Israel's ravaging of Gaza in 2008 - 2009. As for the West Bank, 80% of it was already controlled by the Israeli army. Indeed, Hamas only launched its suicide bombings – long since halted – after an Israeli physician murdered 29 Muslims at prayer in a mosque, while wounding dozens of others.

Failure to apply to Palestine the preached American values of rule by the people and freedom of speech make for much of the anti-Americanism in Arab lands, and regardless of what Obama may come up with in terms of negotiations for a Palestinian state, Israel has an iron-fisted say, since it occupies the territories in question. The Palestinian West Bank for Israel is also the ancient Judea and Samaria, and there are hundreds of thousands of Israelis already settled there.

If Obama ever tries to negotiate an Israeli-Palestinian peace deal, with the starting point being the 1967 borders, regardless of what he pledges in support of Israel, including stopping Iran from going nuclear, the wrath of the U.S. Jewish lobby will come down on him. A half-century ago, Eisenhower said his forces had saved the remnants of the Jewish people for a new life in the reborn land of Israel, and today, despite there being 400 million people in the Arab world and eight million in Israel, the defense of Israel is nothing short of a religious obligation among American evangelical Christians.

As for the newly conservative Canada, it will remain only a medium power but Canada is also one of the G8 countries that have so far led the post-war world; so, now that the Canadian government has a policy of supporting whatever Israel's right wing wants, one can kiss goodbye any further Middle East peace talks that include a Palestine of any substance or with headquarters in East Jerusalem. Canada will punch above its weight and ensure that the G8 does not allow such a Palestine to happen, all in line with the Israeli long-term objective of taking 100% of Jerusalem and seeing the Palestinians cleansed from biblical Israel.

Israel does not want a two-state solution, but Israel will not allow itself to become a single bi-national state either, because it is the deemed homeland for the Jewish people via a Jewish majority. Democracy is only a pretense. Israelis moreover, both left and right, do not see Palestinians ever being granted citizenship or having equal voting rights within a single state. As for the Arab Israelis, an increasingly trendy way of referring to them is as "the 1948 Palestinians."

Within Israel, a current rabbinical edict on posters declares that Arab students are cruel vipers that seek to seduce Jewish girls and turn them into handmaidens. The edict adds that Israel should be Jewish and that the Arabs have 22 other countries to go to. The head of an ultra-Orthodox party has also described both Arab citizens and human rights groups as dangerous to the state.

Israel now is introducing a bill requiring new non-Jewish citizens to pledge an oath of loyalty to a "Jewish and democratic" state, and the government is trying to equate any dissent or advocacy for a two-state solution with disloyalty. And in deference to Israel's right-wing Likud and the country's Russian-born constituents, Israel is also politicizing judges and tabling laws that cripple any foreign aid judged unfriendly, as well as laws criminalizing critical journalism and non-Jewish dissent. Yes, there are cries of unfairness coming from a few Jews in Israel – the prime minister's wife herself added her voice to the debate on the nature of the Jewish state, objecting to a cabinet decision to deport 400 migrant workers' children – but protests from the Jewish conscience are often now mocked as cries from God's fools.

The Israeli government has a mandate for Arab East Jerusalem, not just from the right wing but also from a broad swath of Jews, who live in both Israel and beyond, as has the Israeli government for generations. It talks a two-state solution but does the opposite.

Israel is annexing Arab East Jerusalem and sees Obama as helpless before a looming Republican House majority, with its pro-Israeli alignment. The two-state solution does not truly exist and Israel soon will build 2,000 new settlements in Arab East Jerusalem, with the ring of settlements cutting it off from the rest of the Palestinian West Bank. This is the Arab East Jerusalem, where Palestine wants to have its headquarters for a future homeland.

Israel wants to break away from the "inevitable endgame" of a Palestinian state and focus instead on Israel's security needs, talking of preposterous interim borders that would become permanent by being truth on the ground. Israel is also trying to enlighten Obama that even if Israel did capitulate on a Palestinian nation, that 'grand concession' would only attenuate the Iranian threat, rather than make it disappear. Israel is also trying to up the ante by getting the U.S. to veto any UN Security Council resolutions against Israel, as well as provide the country with advanced aircraft and early warning systems.

Israeli tactics are intended to drive negotiations into the ground, while keeping the appearance of maintaining flexibility, thereby presenting the Palestinian Authority's Mr. Abbas as the spoiler. The Israelis did this trick with Arafat who, contrary to Western belief, tried in earnest for a peace deal.

If Hamas ever allies with say, a reborn Egypt instead of the pariah-cast Iran, Israel will renew efforts to cast Hamas as bent on destroying Israel, when all Hamas is really calling for is a return of the occupied land and a long-term truce. Yet Israel will continue to show no interest in confronting Hamas on the issue of Israel's right to exist, since it knows Hamas would say, "Yes, but with 1967 borders," leaving that as the starting point for negotiations, which Israel does not want. It wants instead the status quo, under which Israeli settlements continue to expand.

For Palestinians still negotiating for a state beside Israel, many fear their state would be too fragmented to be a reality but the reality is much worse – Israel wants Gaza gone, and the West Bank scenario is just a longer play-out before the Arabs leave. For years, Palestinians have tried by peaceful means to wrest back farm fields and olive groves lost when a concrete barrier was erected to separate their community from a settlement of ultra-Orthodox Israelis. And beyond that microcosm, another 60% of the West Bank is controlled by Israelis, with Palestinian farmers increasingly forced to demolish their homes.

Meanwhile, in those expanding areas of Israeli occupation, young Jewish settlers, known as "hilltop youths," harass Palestinians and burn mosques and related sacred things, with an impunity that stems from Israeli soldiers being mandated only to protect Jewish settlers and not arrest Israelis. The hilltop youths ironically plan to attack the soldiers' facilities and threaten that if the youths meet resistance, they will take out their supposed 'revenge' on innocent and helpless Palestinians.

Time will show that if the Palestinian negotiators concede all of the Jewish settlements in Arab East Jerusalem, a traditional Palestinian claim, that if they concede the sacred since 1948 right of return for expelled Palestinians, that if they continue to side with Israel in further attacks on Hamas in Gaza, and if they recognize Israel as a Jewish state, something not demanded by Israel in the 1979 peace treaty with Egypt or the 1994 one with Jordan, the Palestinian negotiators will remain betrayed by Israel and be utterly defeated at every turn.

While 70% of Israel officially believes that it should accept Palestinian statehood if the UN were ever to pass it, much of Israel, and not just the conservatives, have been brainwashed into regarding the UN as a theater of the absurd. If the Palestinians thus do try approaching the UN for recognition, one can count on Israel to up its annexation of the West Bank with Jewish settlers, to make any such UN recognition moot. If, moreover, the Palestinians try the UN route – their only alternative to futile talks with Israel – Israel will claim that the Palestinians don't want peace talks and will pressure the U.S. to cut off aid to the Palestinians or any approving UN body. Such Israeli pressure is already happening in the ravaged Gaza, after Hamas tried to audit suspicious sources of

American aid. Simultaneously, Israel is keeping up its censoring of any Hamas communications to the outside world, from Hamas theaters or otherwise.

Israel's ultra-right 1% runs the country and again officially, does not want to return "yet" to the negotiating table. But over half a million Israelis now live in what is designated as the future Palestinian state, and at the current rate of annexation, the "facts on the ground" will render a two-state solution impossible, with any direct talks between the unequal parties inevitably failing.

God bless them – one barely heard set of liberal Jewish voices is advocating to let Palestinian statehood proceed in tiny steps. Contrast that with the settlers, one of whom was recently killed in a car accident, and afterward the settlers were carrying signs in red paint, with words of revenge. The settlers managed to pressure Israeli police into declaring the accident a murder by the Palestinians, and now the settlers are bent on more of their "justified" killings.

Without ever accepting an independent state of Palestine, Israel's interim policy is to make life barely bearable in the West Bank, while hell in cut-off Gaza. When Hamas in Gaza does inevitably join with the more moderate Fatah, Hamas will thus be implicitly recognizing Israel's right to exist as well as any agreements that the PLO's ruling Fatah has already made with Israel. Such recognition should theoretically please Israel, but one can count on Israel to concoct a new excuse as to why such a merger is a catastrophe for world peace.

As for the Arabs as a whole, they have lived for half a century under repressive regimes buttressed by the U.S. to meet the demands of Israel and oil. Saudi Arabia is allied with Egypt, the United Arab Emirates and Jordan in a pro-U.S. clique, which supports policies supporting Israel and keeping Iran in check.

Israel also wants the U.S. to force the Arab states to take common cause against Iranian nuclear ambitions. Israeli intelligence knows that Iran supports Hamas in Gaza, and Israel wants potential revolts in Iran to model what could happen throughout the region. At the same time, the Israeli ally, Sunni Muslim Saudi Arabia, is in a power struggle with

Shia Muslim Iran over which of the two oil producers will control the non-Israeli Middle East.

If, as may come to pass, a mass revolution against oppression does take place across the Arab world, how the West treats and interprets such a rejuvenation will reveal much about Western attitudes, especially since many of the Arab countries currently have repressive authoritarian regimes allied with Israel and kept in place by the West. Western countries thus remain hesitant to acknowledge the full implications of a free and self-determined Arab people, with concomitant power to shape their national policies. The West also fears that any new Arab democracy might allow Islamists to be democratically voted in.

What is also not highlighted is that in the ring of Arab puppet-despots that encircle Israel, vulnerability to revolution may turn out to be a function of unemployment, as well as the economic repression of Shia Muslims by puppet Sunni states. The U.S. since 9/11 has bankrolled the military in the Arab world at the expense of jobs for young people, and while many are university educated, 40% earn less than $2 a day, with the jobless rate for young Arabs standing at 25%, Morocco at 37% and Yemen 40% versus a world average of 14%.

One thing to watch would be the different standards that the West came to apply to Arab rights in the Middle East. It is one thing for the West to call, say, a Libyan leader a madman but what about Yemen and Bahrain? Yemen, once a place of free and fair elections, is kept mute by both military support from the U.S. and billions in financing from Sunni Saudi Arabia. Yemen's Shia majority aspires to social equality, yet is suppressed by a Sunni dynasty supported by that Saudi Arabia. As for Bahrain, it is home base to the U.S. Fifth Fleet and is next door to Sunni Saudi Arabia, with that country remaining a strategic piece of real estate not only for oil but also as the wealthiest opponent of Shia Iran. Thus in Bahrain, the American ally Saudi Arabia will undoubtedly send in troops to crush any pro-democracy uprising, all with the West's passive support.

In good ol' Egypt, youths are aware that the 1979 peace deal between Israel and Egypt was made between leaders, not peoples, and Iran's leader *is popular in Egypt for defying the West. If Egypt's President Mubarak gets deposed and held for criminal investigations, the army that benefits from being a U.S. puppet might have mixed feelings, and Saudi Arabia, which considers Mubarak an ally in the campaign against Iran's regional influence, might cut off its billions of investment in Egypt. One thing seems certain – if Mubarak ever goes on trial for his alleged atrocities, it will teach other Arab governments such as Libya or Syria to repress their protest movements or else face a similar fate.*

Those currently autocratic Arab governments cry the predictable defense that the only alternative to their existence is Islamic fundamentalism, and Israel counts on so-called moderate Arab states – Egypt, Jordan and Saudi Arabia – to line up against Iran. In Egypt's case, the U.S. has provided more dollars and defense equipment than to any other country, other than Israel. The U.S. army thus controls the Egyptian army, and when Israel attacked Gaza, Egypt acted as an Israeli ally.

Egypt is thus seen by many Arabs as an Uncle Tom cowing to Israel, and Egypt's role as mediator with the Palestinians is seen in the same way, since Israel's blockade of the Gaza strip works only so long as Egypt plays along. The U.S.-controlled Egyptian army in turn controls Egypt; so, regardless of what happens on the streets of Cairo, the army may do whatever it can to ensure that Egypt does not get an anti-Israeli Islamist ruler and that Israeli warships continue to be able to cruise through the Suez.

It was the Egypt of 1923 that, to Britain's chagrin, became a democracy and gave the Waft or Delegation Party a landslide. Democracy then prevailed until the years leading up to World War II.

If Egypt ever does rebel against its rigged elections and puppets like Mubarak, it will be interesting to see what role women play in the protests. It's a safe bet that George Bush did not wrack his brains out over the oppression of women in Arab countries before 9/11.

The emergence of an assertive Sunni-Arab Egypt would undermine a Shiite-Persian Iran's wishes to be the vanguard of a Muslim Middle East, where Shiites overall are also a minority. And notwithstanding what we

in the West see via cyberspace – 95% being hearsay – Iran has zealous
supporters among its lower classes, and Iran did experience a true
revolution in the late 1970s, with authentic popular support, versus the
counterparts in Libya, Syria and Iraq, decades earlier, being military
coups.

In Islamic countries across North Africa and the Middle East, where
there have been elections in recent years, Islamist parties have increased
in size – Algeria in 1991, Turkey in the years following and then
Lebanon, Iraq, Jordan and the Palestinian territories. It is also worth
noting that in Egypt, 95% believe Islam should play a significant role in
the country's politics – the majority has come to appreciate, as shown by
Turkey, that secular democracy can dovetail with Islam.

U.S.-funded groups, however, describing themselves as human rights
advocates, are already hard at work in Arab countries such as Egypt,
trying to ensure that the Muslim Brotherhood does not get any measure
of power. The prospect of an Egypt with an Islamist majority alarms both
Israel and its puppet Saudi Arabia, not to mention Israel's other Uncle
Tom Palestinian Authority, with its fears of a buoyed-up rival Hamas. As
for that lauded Turkish model of Islamic government, Israeli puppets like
Canada associate Turkey with the genocide of 1.5 million Armenians
during World War I.

The Muslim Brotherhood remains an Islamic party outlawed in
Egypt and is an American nightmare because it could fill a void, as did
Hamas with its democratic win in Gaza and Hezbollah in Lebanon,
with its new sway there. The Muslim Brotherhood created what is called
Islamism, a religious adaptation to modernity, while still maintaining
sharia law in the state, much as does Israel with its Hebrew guidelines
and the U.S. with its bedrock of Judeo-Christianity.

Critics of the Muslim Brotherhood say that if it ever gained power in
Egypt, it would impose modest dress or hair covering on other women,
ban alcohol and prevent public displays of affection. Wouldn't it thus be
a surprise if the Muslim Brotherhood did nothing of the sort, and sent a
number of females to the Egyptian legislature? The Muslim Brotherhood
in Turkey has a pro-European approach and has also cooperated with the

West in advancing women's rights. The Muslim Brotherhood has
hospitals and clinics, offers scholarships for students, controls professional
organizations for doctors and lawyers, and provides food, shelter and
medical aid in times of disaster. The Muslim Brotherhood also acted
faster than the Egyptian government, when an earthquake struck Cairo
in 1992. Thus the experience of a slightly Islamist elected government
like Turkey, with a secular army keeping watch in the wings, may yet be
a model for Egypt.

Much of the Western press says the Muslim Brotherhood is an
ancestor, not only of Hamas but also of al-Qaeda, but when movements
like the Muslim Brotherhood are repressed in, say, Egypt for 60 years,
the frustrated adherents can switch to violent means – all jihadist
movements, including al-Qaeda, were born in response to such
frustration, and one can draw a direct line between the suffocating of
the Muslim Brotherhood and 9/11.

It is notable on the Muslim Brotherhood website that any future
referendum on the future of South Sudan looks quite different from its
portrayal in the West. On the Muslim site, the referendum is said to be
part of a century-old plot to close the Islamic gateway into Africa and
break up all other Arab countries into feeble statelets. If the Sudan does
break up, it will be the first case of secession from a modern Arab state.

Back in the U.S., Islamic terrorism is on the decline and is often
reported by other Muslims, yet two-thirds of conservative Republicans
and Tea Party supporters believe that the Islamic religion is more likely
than any others to encourage violence. The Western press also remains
baffled by the best-friends relationship between Libya's Gadhafi and
Nelson Mandela. Gadhafi has tried, perhaps quixotically, to initiate an
African Union, not unlike that of Europe, and has done much to help
out Black African countries with peacekeeping missions, humanitarian
aid and infrastructure.

The U.S. picked up Gadhafi in 2003 when he cried "uncle" to the
West and negotiated through Jewish-American officials to have the West's
trade embargo lifted. Libya was accordingly forced to shut down its
Palestinian training camps, and Libyan intelligence was compelled to

deliver documents revealing the whereabouts of Islamic terrorist camps around the world. Libya was then elevated to chair the UN Commission on Human Rights and in 2007, the Washington Post said Libya could become the first Arab country to change peacefully into a stable, non-autocratic state.

Libya has been a magnet for everyone in Africa and is a place where one can make money, if he plays along. It has also been peaceful and free from petty crime, albeit perhaps because of harsh deterrence, and one Canadian company is set to make a bundle building a new prison. Were Gadhafi to disappear, gone would be one of the few countries challenging China's mounting influence in Africa.

It has become popular in recent years to talk about Washington's failure to prevent genocide in the 20th century, and the U.S. has yet to join the International Criminal Court. But a doctrine of R2P or "responsibility to protect" was endorsed by the UN in 2005, giving rise to an age of humanitarian imperialism, where all Western wars became ones of 'noble altruism.' Neo-conservatives, now modeling themselves after the Iraq War architect Wolfowitz, will be gung-ho to intervene in, say, Libya. Given as well the strong Western belief that force is an acceptable tool of policy, many liberals who opposed the Iraq war will advocate such intervening, their being convinced of their own moral rightness. Count also on the West to play the genocide card in order to get UN sanction, and then watch the intervention objective change to, say, ousting Gadhafi, after a genocide charge has entrenched a Western presence.

If the West did switch from respecting a sovereign state such as Libya to painting it as an abomination, some like Sarkozy might condemn Libya's government for defending itself, so that other Arab leaders would not try to defend their regimes in the same way. The West could also demand, via the UN, a Libyan ceasefire and even if Gadhafi respected it, the West could then use some moral excuse like Gadhafi attacking civilians, despite the reality that those civilians would have tanks just like Gadhafi loyalists and be committing the same kind of atrocities within the theater of a civil war.

If the hypothetical Libyan rebels did in fact not respect the laws of armed conflict and the international Human Rights Watch expressed concern, one could be sure that no one in the West would in any measure take heed. And if Gadhafi were to be labeled a war criminal, such labeling could be used to justify NATO bombing after the fact, and he would have to fight to the end, unlike say a Saudi-protected dictator. One can also be sure that the West would sex up the story, probably in the form of Arab rape, to spark Christian fundamentalist outrage. Such stories are outrageous to Western ears and there is often a suspicious consistency about them.

As the ouster of Gadhafi came to reveal itself as the Western resolve, the West could then bomb Gadhafi, with thousands of civilians dying and millions displaced. Gadhafi could then in theory at least file a war crimes suit but fat chance for any success – he is not liked in the Arab world for his support of Persian Iran in its 1980s war with Iraq.

Egyptian leader Abdel Nasser once told Gadhafi that he was the future for the Arab revolution, yet if Arab countries do experience an awakening, Gadhafi would in any event be silenced – he expelled Libya's Jewish community after the 1967 Arab-Israeli war, and is thus a pariah in the Western press. The West also has huge financial investments in Libya, and Gadhafi has already said that he wants companies operating there to share their revenue. He has even suggested that landlords be stripped of their property rights. Gadhafi may have managed to hold warring tribes at bay but he has also proposed a single state for Israelis and Palestinians, a proposal totally unacceptable to Jewish Israel.

Obama may see beyond involvement of the U.S. in another regional civil war and so it would be interesting to see what, say, France's Sarkozy does and whether his NATO allies agree. Sarkozy is already known to want a common European defense onside with Israel but France might hesitate if Germany abstained. It would also be interesting to see if the Eurozone kept its internal borders open or became divided, shutting off potential Arab refugees, country by country. As for the new Israeli puppet, Canada, it could be at the forefront of any mission.

Watch the money-flow, since the West might seize Gadhafi's international bank accounts and transfer funds to any rebels. As it could do with any oil production that the rebels would seize.

Syria is another country that the West has tried to isolate. The Bush administration charged Syria with sending jihadists to Iraq and with having close relations with energy-source Iran, relaying Iranian arms to Hezbollah in Lebanon, all such moves ostensibly to foment terror against Israel. Syria's Assad regime is supported in the main by the Syrian people, but Syria remains the critical linchpin that connects Iran to Hezbollah in Lebanon and Syria provides a haven for militant Palestinian groups including Hamas. The decline of the current Baathist regime in Syria would be a severe blow to Iran, Hamas and Hezbollah, all Israel's bête noires.

While many in the West, in addition to Sunni Saudi Arabia, would therefore like to get at Shiite Iran through Syria, the West could find itself with no distinct Syrian region ostensibly to protect, let alone a rebel army that could benefit from air support – Syria is a loose connection of conflicting ethnicities, including its government-protected Christians, in contrast to, say, the persecuted Christian minority of post-Bush Iraq. Syria is thus not unlike the former Yugoslavia, with turmoil always at the ready, to be stirred up anywhere.

Given such Syrian complexity, the West might call for a war to be waged via propaganda. Actual physical attacks against the Syrian government could then be twisted to show how many deaths were happening in the country, with the implication being they were happening in the main to protesters. Were Syria then to claim that rebels were causing much of the damage, the Western press could dismiss such claims as Syrian propaganda, while Western states incited the opposition and supplied it with arms.

Washington could also adopt the age-old ruse of the Syrian regime's killing of civilians, while supporting the sham with unverified footage of people killed on either side. Spies with cell phones and ingestible cameras could be stationed on balconies and buildings everywhere, and then mischievous tweets and cell phone photos could be maneuvered over borders, for the pictures to be later "Photoshopped," and editorial information added to the filmed material.

What the West would not see, and what would be mocked again as the Syrian regime's official position, would be photographs of saboteurs, some wearing Jewish yarmulkes, or members of heavily armed gangs in revolt against that government. The Syrian rebels could also headquarter outside the country in Turkey and then, with Western urging, refuse to negotiate with the government, vowing that the only option would be to topple the regime by armed resistance, so that Syrian leader Assad had no choice but to retaliate in kind.

The non-democratic country of Sunni Saudi Arabia could also make known its paradoxical displeasure with Syrian leader Assad's failure to be receptive to demands for democracy. The Assad dynasty are members of the Alawite religion, which constitutes only 12% of the population of the country; the majority Sunni Muslims, accounting for 75% of the population, resent the minority-based Assads.

Most Syrian soldiers are also Sunnis, not members of the Alawite sect, and any break-off in Syrian ranks would have the ultimate goal of kicking Shia Muslim Iran out of the Arab League and letting it be dominated by Sunni Saudi Arabia, key ally of Israel. The irony is that, since Wolfowitz and his puppet Bush crushed the regime of Iraq's Saddam Hussein, that country's majority Shiites have taken a commanding voice, to the rage of indigenous Sunnis.

Famine is another popular propaganda tool in the West. Somalia is an area where drought and crop failure can often mean hunger lurks close by, and if, God forbid, food shortages were to occur, count on the West to say that the situation would be worsened by Islamic radicals questioning Western politicization of any aid – where the West has intervened in the case of famine, any resentment by Muslims pointing out that they are already there, has been painted by the Western press as ugly Islamicism, allowing thousands to starve for political reasons.

Such propaganda could become a harsh reality, despite Human Rights Watch documenting that those Islamic insurgents are far from being the only sources of abuse in the area. Muslim clinics, furthermore, *offering free health care or distributing huge food rations to starving parts of Africa, have been painted by the Western press as currying favor with the masses, in alleged attempts to gain Muslim power. One favorite weapon of the Western press is candid photos showing emaciated children, with the voice-over, "No famine has ever taken place in history within a functioning democracy." We in the West are urged to conquer politics and give foreign aid but rarely do we hear from the beleaguered people themselves, when they say they don't need Western interference.*

While the Western press loves to heighten sexual inequalities in the Muslim world, there is little awareness allowed of secular Israelis protesting "honor attacks" by Orthodox Jewish Haredim on young Israeli girls for dressing immodestly. The Orthodox have spat on the young girls and have loudly labeled them "whores" and "Nazis." The Haredim are also trying to remove images of women from billboards and to enforce gender segregation on public transport, and in shops and medical centers, while banning women soldiers from singing and dancing at army events.

We in the West should come to understand that many of the fantasies of the Middle East and surrounding areas are what we create. Thus in the case of Libya, if the West decides that Gadhafi heads the bad guys and is a tyrant who must go, Western intelligence will focus on the "how" and not the "why."

As for that long-time elusive Osama bin Laden, if the U.S. does find him and of course silence him, will the Western press tie in his killing with those possible Arab uprisings and ignore the fact that he stands for such uprisings himself? Osama bin Laden has always been clear that his two main targets for social upheaval are the Sunni countries of Egypt and Saudi Arabia – he talks of corrupt dictatorships like Saudi Arabia, propped up by the U.S. for cheap oil and the Saudi alliance with Israel. Saudi Arabia should be banned from the Olympics for not allowing women competitors as was Afghanistan, but since 9/11, Saudi enemy Osama bin Laden has come to symbolize Islam for much of the American population. In Pakistan, meanwhile, military authorities fear that if the United States someday finds bin Laden inside that country, the U.S. will highlight the need to rid Pakistan of its nuclear weapons.

In that very Pakistan, movie shops regularly display copies of 9/11 conspiracy films, and many Pakistanis believe that the attacks on the Twin Towers were schemed by Zionists to give the U.S. a pretext for war in the region. Pakistan has been labeled "dangerous" by the West and already the U.S. is sending unmanned drones into Pakistan, with 40 countries, including Canada, additionally investing in drone technology to root out Muslim radicals.

If an Arab revolution were ever to reach the border of Israel, the country would no doubt voice the old saw that Israel's very existence is threatened and use whatever means necessary to snuff out the protesters. Unless of course, those protesters came to include the Jewish Israeli have-nots, who were trying to expose the exploitation of them by the tycoon haves. In any event, a key information source for the entire Middle East is still the International Affairs Center in Israel, and the Center is now escalating fears that Islamists will try taking over the entire area as well as North Africa, if Israeli-friendly states fall.

Water is another matter. The Middle East's 1967 war was prompted in part by Jordan's proposal to divert the Jordan River, and water remains a divisive issue between Israel and its neighbors. Israel extracts two-thirds of the upper Jordan and leaves the West Bank with only a trickle and a mountain aquifer, the access to which Israel controls. In 2004, the average Israeli had a daily allowance of 290 liters of domestic water versus the Palestinian average of 70.

Also lingering is the issue of nuclear weapons. Israel has refused to sign the Nuclear Non-Proliferation Treaty and steers clear of any security summits, for fear the issue of the country's having a nuclear arsenal is raised. From 200 to 300 nuclear weapons are under Israel's control, making Israel more powerful than all of the Arab and Muslim countries combined.

Israel sees its nuclear image as the ultimate self-protection but refuses to discuss the issue and resists all attempts to reveal the extent to which it has developed nuclear weapons. Israel does not even acknowledge that it has them and absolutely refuses to join any efforts to make the Middle East a nuclear-weapons-free zone. Instead, Israel will keep open the

Samson Option of bringing the pillars down on itself, as well as its enemies, rather than risk its demise alone; thus, even if Iran does disarm, Israel will then say that Iran cannot be trusted and still refuse to do so.

As things stand, Israeli public opinion is being ratcheted up to attack Iran's nuclear facilities, with 40% of the country favoring such a strike. The Israeli intelligence Mossad has already teamed up with renegade Iranian militant groups to execute spot attacks. Israel and the U.S. are also continuing subversive operations in Iran, assassinating key scientists, generating explosions in Iranian nuclear facilities and throwing computer worms into the Iranian works, to sabotage Iran's nuclear development. Israel is even said to be behind staged counter-attacks against Israeli outposts, while blaming Iran, in order to prep its own people and us in the West. The International Atomic Energy Agency that monitors Iran's nuclear development is now said by Russia and others to be a propaganda tool of the West.

Perhaps not surprisingly, Israel is voicing indignation at Iran's treatment of its country's Jews, despite their being relatively well treated there. The Iranians recognize, respect and protect three religions other than Islam – Judaism, Christianity and Zoroastrianism. The Iranian government allows these religions to have services and run religious institutions. Jews are also free to leave Iran to go anywhere, with the exception of Israel.

How many in the West know such realities? Already, Israel and the U.S. right wing are hinting that, just as Jimmy Carter will go down in history as the president who lost Iran, Obama, whom one-quarter of Americans think is Muslim, will be remembered as the president who "lost" Lebanon, Turkey and other moderates, and during whose tenure America's alliances in the Middle East crumbled.

It is a sad truth that if despots anywhere can assure their respective countries a measure of wealth and stability, those countries' peoples are inclined to overlook their liberty – in a laboratory setting, participants leave unstructured groups for the order of an authoritarian regime that punishes cheaters. Successful rulers also remember that ideology conquers all and that rulers need to build accordant temples, whether those temples are secular or otherwise. In Israel's case, for those Jewish people – men – the rabbi stands at the ready to punish when necessary, including banishment, but with the caveat that the banished man's wife is to keep his accounting books current. Buying real estate on the moon is popular in Israel.

In Muslim puppet countries, the social sciences tend to be neglected but the social sciences are as critical to success as are any applied sciences to the extraction of oil or the feeding of people. Without the social sciences, questions are not asked as to where those states are going. Social clubs are lacking in Muslim countries, and other than at the mosque, the common people of, say, Libya, cannot congregate in clubs, pubs or coffee houses to argue the issues of the day.

It may take decades for a Middle East equilibrium to emerge – free elections have produced, after all, Hezbollah in Lebanon and Hamas in Gaza, after the U.S. pressured Israel into letting Hamas run. But vilifying Islamists as terrorists and refusing to deal with even elected ones won't work. Obama wants to reach out but the Israeli lobby won't let him and that lobby owns the Republican Congress. American priorities will continue to be oil, Israel and access to military bases, and though the junior Bush's mother asked him how it felt to be the first Jewish president, Obama has also firmly declared that America's special relationship with Israel is founded on shared values and deeply interwoven connections. Beyond the epic proportions of the Israeli lobby in the United States, there are 50 million Christian fundamentalists who relentlessly storm-troop for Israel on multiple fronts; thus, no matter how desperate remains the lot of Palestinians, polls show that Americans feel a greater sympathy for Israel.

I feel the maligned Obama may still have an opening, and it is one he created in his first presidential visit to Cairo. Arabs remember that President Obama came to seek a new beginning between the United States and Muslims around the world, a new beginning based on respect and mutual interest.

A revolution is predictably a time of enormous release, and that release comes to the world through images. Revolutions thus survive and

thrive on image and perception, as shaped by a select few. All but lost is
what the English Revolution of the 1640s shared with the French
Revolution of the 1790s, as well as the Russian one during World War I
– that none led to stable democratic governments. Few democracies, on
the other hand, have come about without violent eruption, and the short
list includes your Canada.

The first modern revolution, in England around 1640, occurred
when the executive strength of the king was all but quashed and
Cromwell's bloody republic followed with its figurehead monarchs. But
after that Cromwellian revolution, the power brokers wanted routine
from their government, while they themselves could remain to be free-
wheeling. In a not unlike manner, the American Revolution effectively
extended the life of slavery.

In engendering respect, perhaps we should look to a war-loser for
some objectivity and perhaps that war-loser should be Japan, where
atomic-bomb literature was suppressed until the end of the American
occupation in 1952. The Japanese, regardless of their secularism, seem to
understand from their Buddhist roots the impermanence of all things, as
well as the cleansing process needed in our fallacious and de-cultured
world.

History, Chantelle, now seems to me not a series of isolated moral
lessons but instead a collection of clashing ideas, boggling the inquisitive
mind as much as setting it straight. The U.S. is now trying to censor
the Twitterverse, to quash Taliban-and-the-like communications, and
the newly conservative Canada is trying to allow police the ability to
spy on every move of an Internet user. Both countries, by accident or
not, may turn the Internet into an all-you-can-sue buffet for media
lawyers. Meanwhile in Israel, the Silicon Valley between Tel Aviv and
Jerusalem is evolving to meet the requirements of the country's high-tech
military, executing such tactics as Photoshopping cell phone pictures or
recognition of faces from digital photos.

When I think now, Chantelle, about the history of humanity and my
Jewish heritage, one of the things giving me solace and hope is the fact
that, beyond the odd deceiver or mischief-maker among us Jews, there

have been contributors like Spinoza. He was a rabble-rouser in the best
Jewish sense of the word, and he caused us to reflect on what it means to
expose hypocrisies and rejuvenate our roots.

We need such prophets again, and instead of a Talmud or Zionism to
guide us, we need a Hillel, along with his successors Jesus and brother
James. We need a passionate humanism, in the name of both a true
history and us Jews. Israel will survive and thrive as it should, but we
Jews need to take it upon ourselves to grow beyond our early notions of
god and recognize new truths, with those truths being a beacon for us
and the world.

In the meantime, that early god has to mature, along with the god
within each of us. But the god-damned Orthodox do not like us
supposedly non-religious Jews being regarded in Israel as Jews, and like
their ancestors, those Orthodox spend their days praying for the arrival of
their Messiah. Then, as they so judge, they will be able to create a Jewish
state, according to the Torah and Talmud law. Until then, if those
damned Orthos get too close to us non-Orthodox at a food counter, their
rabbis frown – one knows he is in Israel when the arguments start.

Israel's ultra-Orthodox Haredi political parties function as
kingmakers in coalitions and have managed to get men-only sidewalks
in certain neighborhoods. Most Haredi men don't work but their families
have double the birth rate of other Israelis, and the ultra-Orthodox
portion of the Israeli population is soon to surge beyond its current 10%.

To increase even more the Haredim influence, the Orthodox are
volunteering for elite combat units, and they now constitute 20% of
senior and 50% of junior ranks. Many of those volunteers live in West
Bank settlements and have studied life in religious academies led by
charismatic hard-line rabbis, whom they view as their ultimate leaders.

To be any Israeli is to be a soldier in a perpetual war, with many an
Israeli dressed at the ready, while not questioning his or her governance
by some demi-god. Some of those Israelis, so drabbed, have the chutzpah
to say America did not enter World War II to help the Jews, alleging that
the U.S. had already known about Auschwitz and had done nothing to
stop the Nazi activities there, before the 1941 American war-entry. Those

same Israelis add that the U.S. entered only after being attacked by the Japanese at Pearl Harbor, followed by Germany declaring war on the United States four days later.

Because of the Holocaust, may Israelis think anti-Semites lurk around every corner, and Israelis remain snoopy of foreigners. Israeli men rarely look at women and vice versa, since the presence in Israel of the Orthodox flattens the atmosphere, and people are rude in their walk-and-talk. Kibbutzim stay encircled in barbed wire, and vicious-looking dogs are chained every several yards along those wires.

The Israeli people, in great part, revere symbols of hate like Menachem Begin, who in turn likened warmonger Vladimir Jacobtinsky to Moses, Aristotle, Maimonides and Leonardo da Vinci. And at the heart of all this aberration of Judaism is the Western Wall, where men have a wonderful time wailing on one side, while Israeli women are forced to the other.

The Arabs in Israel do all the unskilled labor, being street cleaners, gutter sweepers, garbage collectors and construction workers, and an Arab worker in Jewish Jerusalem knows enough to keep his eyes straight ahead. Like the Palestinians, the Arab Israelis are afraid to talk to the Jews.

The "Palestinian Question" now sounds uncomfortably like the "Jewish Question" of pre-war Europe. The Palestinians do appreciate that six million Jews were killed by Hitler, but many Palestinians also believe that there will never be a Palestinian state, because it would be too dangerous for Israel – like the Arab Israelis, the Palestinians have more children and they would thus threaten the biblical purity of an ultimate Eretz Yisra'el.

The "terrorist word" is a calumny fabricated by Western media, to deprive Arabs of their right to action. But a Palestinian youth is not necessarily a terrorist, until he is arbitrarily arrested and beaten by Israeli soldiers, who equate terrorism with being Palestinian. Like their Arab Israeli counterparts, Palestinians after dark are stopped, checked and beaten in their own neighborhoods, and 99% of those young Arabs have been imprisoned. Fewer than 5% of Israelis sympathize with the

Palestinians and the rest don't want to acknowledge in Israel that the Palestinians even exist – in the new trans-Samarian highway connecting the West Bank settlements to the Mediterranean, a Jewish Israeli can travel the length and breadth of it, without ever encountering a Palestinian society.

Yet in Jerusalem's Monument of Peace, sitting next to the wall of the Old City, there stands engraved in stone, in both Hebrew and Arabic, the words of Isaiah 2:4: "They shall beat their swords into plowshares, and their spears into pruning-hooks. Nation shall not lift up sword against nation, neither shall they learn war anymore."

Perhaps it is not a new god the Israelis need but the old one they once had.

All my love forever, Chantelle,

Arthur

Thursday July 23 2009

Chantelle was not long in setting up at the University of Texas in Austin, and many in the audience were eager to hear the young counter-evangelist:

"Thank you for letting me speak today. Since before the time of Jesus, the wild card in any game of war has been religious conflict between a chosen people and those others who are damned, and again in the 21st century, planet Earth is in a state of religious disequilibrium. Rome is on the march and the pope's orthodoxy dovetails well with a Vatican strategy of going after new growth among conservative Anglicans and others in the sub-Sahara. But within those emerging markets, Christian evangelists are now competing head-on with Rome in going after the most vulnerable.

"Christianity still commands a leading 33% share of market in the sub-Sahara but the number two Islam brand is now at 20% and is vying to take over the number-one position by the middle of the century. Pentecostalism, nevertheless, is a small but rapid-growth brand of Christian fundamentalism, and at half a billion followers, is also threatening Rome's market share. In any event, four-fifths of the planet by the year 2050 will revolve around these major brands."

The college's staff and students remained attentive in their auditorium seats and Chantelle charged on. "All three marketing leaders are evolving global strategies to meet changes in consumer attitudes, as populations among the target groups increase after the recession in wealth and concomitant knowledge. But factors of low income and related awareness still remain great determinants, and the greater the ignorance, the greater will still be the draw toward orthodoxy or fundamentalism.

"One exception remains the United States, which today is the only major country that is both wealthy and religious. A full 40% of Americans believe that human beings were created by god within the last 7,000 or so years, and only 15% acknowledge that human beings evolved through natural selection. By comparison, only 15% of Canadians believe the last-7,000-years story, and 60% accept the reality of natural selection.

"Research shows however that American religiosity can be as shallow as it is broad, and many American religions remain open to penetration via media advertising or point-of-sale merchandising. The American evangelical movement is well schooled in business, if not in theology, and the threats of globalization are making people in the target group clamor for quick fixes."

A few boos arose but soon they were drowned out by some strong, responsive clapping and Chantelle gave a thank you before continuing. "Key Christian marketers recognize the strength of having a common enemy, and are choosing to focus on negative campaigns, such as the ones against the Muslim *salafist*, a tiny Muslim sub-group that demands a return to Islam's original state under founder Muhammad. But the Muslim brand, like the Christian, is also adapting to global secular values, including humanistic concerns for the status of women and the environment.

"Meanwhile, in the mature-growth religious sectors, Rome is leaving them be and evangelists are moving in, presenting themselves as mainstream in accordance with market demand. As for Western secularists, it was not long ago that the West had its own icons of collective faith, and church spires still grace many European cities.

"Perhaps it is our Western emancipation from tradition that has brought some longing for a stable past, making Muslim minarets and head scarves threatening, since they remind us of our own breakaway. It is worth noting that a new anti-Muslim populism is also finding support among leftists who have lost much of their revolutionary faith – many leftists, like Marx, came from religious backgrounds, before turning to revolution."

What again followed Chantelle's speaking was some academically polite applause, and she held her ground. "Wars, I fear, will continue, particularly in areas of the planet where religious fanaticism is the strongest. One main hope – dialogue – remains a long shot. Will Israel, for example, allow the U.S. to have any meaningful dialogue with Iran, after the Iranian president alleged it was Zionists who instigated the 2003 invasion of Iraq, in concert with weapons manufacturers? The number one reason for invading Iraq, Iran claims, was to entrench a strategic flanker between Iran and Syria. Israel countered that, after the Holocaust, horrible new forces had arisen to annihilate Israel, and went on to say that the civilized world had only faint protest."

The audience mumbled, before again hushing to hear more of Chantelle. "The end times are being planned by the West for Iran's theocracy, and its young and restless are being penetrated via social media. Yet Iran is the largest Shia-majority country in the world, and its dissidents may simply be living up to the Shiite Muslims' most cherished tradition – challenging the government's monopoly on power. The Grand Ayatollah wants all Iranian governments to tolerate differing points of view and Iran is arguably the only democracy in the Middle East."

After several gasps, the college audience again went silent and Chantelle continued: "The heavyweight contra to Iran is Sunni Saudi Arabia, but the Shiite Iranians view the Sunni Arabs as despotic colonizers, who demean a rich and nuanced Persian civilization using religious dogma. Sunni Saudi Arabia is one of the most repressive Muslim countries, and Saudi journalists critical of Islam can be anathematized. In extending its position abroad, Saudi money recently tried to establish in Britain an Islamic mission for – note the priority – *social order*.

"Throughout the entire Middle East, the majority Sunni treatment of the minority Shiites has historically been less than generous. Such subjugation has been exemplified by Iraq's repression of Shiites under Saddam Hussein and Saudi Arabia's severe restrictions on Shia places of worship, education and identity. By comparison, Syria's rulers protect the country's minorities, and if the ruling al-Assad were ever to fall, the overthrow would bring about Sunni domination, with its predictable intolerance of minorities, including among others, Christians, Druze, Alawites and Kurds. The 15 million Alawites in neighboring Turkey would no doubt empathize with their threatened brethren in Syria and set off an Alawite grouping of refugee camps in Turkey. As for the minority Shiites, God help them – ever since Muhammad's death, Muslims have been fighting over the right to succeed.

"Soon, however, three million Muslims from all over the world will engage in the *hajj* or pilgrimage to the Saudi city of Mecca, birthplace of Muhammad. We in the West often hear about the pilgrimage only in terms of crowds and stampedes but Harvard research shows that participation in such gatherings increases Islamic practices like prayer and fasting, while decreasing certain cultural practices, such as keeping objects to maintain one's dowry. Research also shows that the same *hajj* increases belief in equality and harmony among ethnic groups and Islamic sects, and leads to more favorable attitudes toward women, including greater acceptance of female education and employment. *Hajjes* also generate an increased belief in peace, and in equality and harmony among adherents of different religions. Perhaps the transformation of Malcolm X during the 1964 *hajj* was not an isolated incident."

The mumbling became more audible but again the college audience returned to a disciplined quiet. "After looking at North America's mega-churches, I confess a prejudice that I have, my feeling that spending time with co-religionists would lead to more insular beliefs and attitudes. Yet the Harvard results suggest otherwise. Other studies suggest that models of social interaction based on a co-operative setting can be used to promote favorable feelings toward other groups. I have to ask, therefore, if the *hajj* model could not be applied to secular societies, to increase tolerance."

The audience held silent and Chantelle remained steady. "Recently, Iran set up talks to foster Shiite-Sunni unity but in short order, six Iranian leaders were murdered. The U.S. was perhaps not involved, because it openly states it will take years for Iran to produce a nuclear weapon, and the U.S. lacks any proof there is an active Iranian weapons program. Even Israeli experts currently label Iran only a "threshold country," technically able to produce a nuclear weapon but abstaining from doing so at present. A former Israeli intelligence director also rejected the apocalyptic language being used in some parts to claim that Iran will nuke Israel, his saying it is not possible, because Israel has not only defensive capabilities but also a variety of offensive ones.

"Blame for the recent attack on Iran has thus been placed on good old Britain – Iran was to begin, the following day, the process of negotiating a nuclear compromise with the West. Israel's prime minister is soon to view some new German-built submarines, believed capable of delivering nuclear missiles.

"Talks with the Iranian regime may dishearten its enemies but such engagement is a lesser evil than not talking with Iran. Voices formerly for such engagement are now opposing such talks, but I respectfully suggest they are misguided in saying that Twitter espionage can deliver us from so-called evil in Iran, or the supposed Muslim Brotherhood threat in Egypt. Only decent people on both sides can help, through a better understanding. Direct one-on-one dialogue seems the only hope, for not only peace but truth."

Sunday July 26 2009

Chantelle earned enough money from her Austin speech to drive back east, several hundred miles to Pensacola, Florida, where she had heard there was work. But to her shock, Chantelle was confronted there by Terry Hardy, who offered to whisk her off to a safe hotel, where she could reside alone and prepare notes for future talks.

Chantelle wanted no part of Hardy but he was adamant that he would not interfere and said he had taken to heart her final words with him, his trying to have a more balanced attitude toward conservative Jewish people. Hardy added that he was busy working in Miami and suggested to Chantelle that she could repay him in a week or so, after she had found work. Chantelle was not entirely comfortable in believing of his transformation but the hotel scenario seemed reasonable enough for the moment and Chantelle presumed she would soon earn enough money to pay for it herself. Thus with some trepidation, Chantelle accepted the short-term deal.

Soon, however, Chantelle found that her speeches had gone before her, and her next three days spent looking for work in healthcare, an area always in need of help, brought nothing. Yet as Hardy had suspected, Chantelle was also writing in her room, and he grabbed the chance to facilitate her speaking in the hotel on the afternoon of the following Sunday.

The audience was small but the setup professional and included, to Chantelle's surprise, an armed security guard. Among the people present, a number revealed themselves later to be concerned with Chantelle's former speeches as well as her very presence in the hotel, but perhaps in willful ignorance of this reality, she began:

"Health care costs in the United States will soon reach a staggering 17% of gross national product, the highest in the world and higher than any first-world country with socialized medicine, but over 40% of Americans still have no access to medical care. The pay cut-off for Medicaid is fractious, and those people over the monetary hairline work for employers that provide no coverage, with the employees too poor to insure themselves. If the employees get sick, they go bankrupt, or their unpaid bills are shifted to the bills of those who are covered by insurance, and the clandestine transfer raises costs. More frequently, the sick and poor get no medical help, and over 300,000 of the country's uninsured get turned away each year from hospital emergency units.

"I am Canadian and have been told that our country's system would not be appropriate for the United States, because here the individual is king. No one, I am told, wants to pay higher taxes to bail out someone else, but I confess I do not believe that Americans feel that way. Yes, the free enterprise healthcare system here generates high-tech equipment and cutting-edge medicine, but the system also generates a patchwork of private insurance claims that cost millions to administer. Patients and doctors have to perform gymnastics to reconcile what is covered and what is not, in a system that gives better healthcare to those whose funds provide more coverage. This fee-for-service system also entices doctors to treat ill patients in the most cosmetically high-tech, high-cost way, yet many above-board hospitals in this free-enterprise system border on bankruptcy.

"My American friends, Canadians are healthier, have a lower infant mortality rate, suffer 20% less heart disease and live two years longer."

Chantelle's speech soon concluded and was followed by some faint applause, but two questioning men dressed in their Sunday best were shortly out front in the lobby, talking with the hotel manager. Apparently, a few other men had during the week been harassing Chantelle at the pool, and some of the people of Pensacola had concluded that a jobless Chantelle must have been funding her lavish life through prostitution. The hotel asked her to leave and took Terry Hardy's credit card for payment, not wanting to hear of Chantelle's wish to repay the bill at a later date.

Friday July 31 2009

Chantelle drove across Florida's Panhandle in search of a job and found two days' work in a Tallahassee emergency unit, but the city would not tolerate any speaking engagement on grounds of security, and Chantelle then made her way south, figuring she could find work in the elderly tourist area. She came to a stop in the Gulf Coast city of Clearwater and there got an off-season room in the old Grey Moss Inn. During the following days, Chantelle did much to care for the resident seniors but also got an earful of complaints about some new Church of Scientology across the road.

Chantelle soon secured a permit to speak at week's end on a green mound atop a small hill next to the causeway leading to Clearwater Beach. Her talk was to be at a time of day when many seniors would be headed off to their favorite restaurants for their early-bird suppers.

On that late Friday afternoon, the gathering looked to be mostly retirees when Chantelle began. "Crime, violent crime, stains America. How can the world's richest country tolerate a murder rate that is four times that of Europe and three times that of Canada?

"Jacksonville, Florida, has a population equal to Canada's Edmonton but has five times the murders. Houston has a population similar to that of Montreal but has six times the murders. Washington, D.C., is the same size as Canada's Calgary but has nine times the murders. And my Toronto's population is almost that of Chicago but Chicago has 10 times the murders."

A token applause followed and Chantelle gave an accepting bow before she continued. "Thanks in part to a gargantuan gun lobby, possession of hand guns here is a contagion that afflicts the body politic and is a public health emergency, striking down multiple thousands of Americans every year. Guns are conceived, designed, manufactured, marketed and sold to hurt or kill.

"It is child's play in Florida to get a gun. Any adult who passes a simple test is permitted to carry a concealed weapon at work or play, and women can have a Derringer strapped to a garter holster or have a purse with a device that allows the gun to be fired without removing it. In Arizona, any law-abiding person over the age of 11 is allowed to carry a concealed handgun almost anywhere, including the state legislature, school grounds and even drinking establishments, if the person is of legal age.

"About 60% of the United States' 20,000 annual murders involve guns, with four-fifths being from handguns. The number of children killed by guns also continues to jump, and given the fact that most murders are not premeditated, the reality that a potential murderer has a gun makes death almost a certainty."

Some of the elderly audience began moving off as if in need of something more entertaining but Chantelle pressed on. "In formulating crime prevention policies, America appears to worry most about killing the bad guys, and maybe it is responding to the perceptions of bulk voters, whose TV viewing is focused on crime, loathing and the nailing of nogoodniks. Many of television's top-rated shows engender fear, and that fear resonates almost everywhere I have been in the United States."

More of the audience moved to leave, but a few new people began arriving to take their place, greeting other retirees they knew. Chantelle continued: "The fear, post-9/11, is not so much of serial killers, criminals, gangs or thieves but of terrorists. Yet of U.S. murders, post-9/11, only 33 or one in 1,000 has been due to terrorism. Still, in the world of perceptions, TV do-gooders are led by regular guys who echo the Sergeant Friday of a half century ago, and are appalled by the awfulness of the creeping world. Random killings are portrayed as part of a master Islamic plan to study the response time of authorities, and we see a car bomb explosion and how badly people have suffered, with the direct threat to the American family, and finally the good guy rescuing the family. Then comes the search for the Arab terrorist gang, and the good guy goes through a New York subway tunnel or the like, shouting words that are defacing to the swarthy-faced coward."

More of the audience moved to depart but Chantelle looked to be on a roll. "TV producers say these shows are grounded in a reality that is much worse, and they refer to the car bombings on American news channels. In fact, across the duration of each week, an American on average watches 150 acts of violence and 15 murders, while U.S. children see 25 acts of violence per viewing hour, skewed to them as a target group."

Only a few audience members remained, some perhaps being Canadians who had heard of Chantelle, and on that lazy day in Gulf Coast Florida, she did not let up. "There seems little consultation with European countries, many of which have done exhaustive studies on both the prevention of crime and rehabilitation of those found guilty. International studies also show that the American mandatory minimum sentences often lead juries to set criminals free.

"The United States also now stands almost alone among first-world countries in keeping capital punishment…" but before Chantelle could continue, there came a small round of applause, along with a cheer from one woman. Chantelle tried to hold composed and she resumed: "Capital punishment represents societal revenge and thus contributes to the evil. Capital punishment is state-sanctioned murder, where the victim knows in advance the time, place and killers.

"Almost all other counties have banned the execution of minors but the United States leaves them in jail until they become old enough for execution, and the U.S. did not halt capital punishment for the mentally handicapped until this 21st century. Up to the year 1964, 500 people in the U.S. were state-put-to-death for rape, and the death penalty is still in place for 34 federal offenses, though not a single criminological study has ever proven that the penalty deters."

Chantelle may have felt some encouragement from the silence in the audience, and she pressed on: "People are seduced by law-and-order talk but crime rates are not affected by how many people go to jail, only a state's deficit is, as California horribly knows. New York City's crime rate has dropped dramatically over the past 20 years, with no mass incarceration, but in the rest of the United States, since Nixon's war on drugs of the early 1970s, the incarceration rate has multiplied eight-fold, and 25% of American prisoners are serving time for drugs. A century ago, the American incarceration rate was the same as that of Canada but now it is four times as high, and while Canada is mocked as a bleeding heart, its imprisonment laws are some of the toughest in the world.

"It has been proven time and again that what does lower crime rates are strategically focused policing, thought-out parole evaluations, rehabilitation systems, anti-poverty initiatives, mental-health centers, retraining and education in general, including, yes, better fathering. Whereas, more imprisonment means more trained criminals. The tough-on-crime sentiment cannot be justified logically but it is easy to feel, and one reason for that rage is that crime victimizes people and is done so uncontrollably. The media then taps into that feeling and sensationalizes it.

"But before we try appealing to people who allow their anger to be misdirected – hanging was a boom industry during the Great Depression – we should note that even in my Canada, the Truth in Sentencing Act, passed last year, will cost an extra $10 billion over the next five years, due to lengthened sentences. And despite a declining crime rate and a need for governments to cut costs, a newly conservative Canada is going the opposite way of the world and is creating jails for more people, especially youths, to go to prison."

As the time on that Friday afternoon drew toward supper, some people in the audience were scowling a look of disapproval, and one man at the front was waving his hand dismissively to the ground. Suddenly, however, Chantelle's speech was cut short by the arrival of state police. Without a word, they handcuffed her, and before a shocked audience, escorted Chantelle away.

The real work of former sponsor Terry Hardy had come undone in Miami during that summer of 2009 – he had been abducting babies from prominent Jewish families and holding them for ransom – but Hardy had contrived a story in an attempt to get a sweetheart deal, placing blame on an innocent Chantelle. He had shown the police her notes that I, Arthur Franklin, had left on the property of a Toronto hospital, and Hardy had also shown police my recent letters. Terry Hardy had produced a trail of paperwork that pointed to Chantelle, including credit card bills showing his paying for a posh hotel in Pensacola and his allegedly secret meeting with her.

Florida police probed Chantelle's relationship with Terry Hardy and she acknowledged receipt of funds but when police told her of Hardy's confession of baby-snatching, a horrified Chantelle went stark white, and the police video camera caught her head turning down. Perhaps Chantelle was pondering how she, a doctor who had saved so many babies at Women's

College Hospital, could have for a full year not questioned her being financed by a baby-kidnapper. After a minute's silence, Chantelle nodded her head in acknowledgment of the horror, and the police took her nod as tacit admittance of her involvement with Hardy.

Sunday August 2 2009

Word of Chantelle's arrest soon reached Canada from the Clearwater onlookers, and the Canadian media immersed itself in the issue. I wanted desperately to be at Chantelle's side but discovered from the news that my letters had been seized and were being used against her – a Toronto lawyer and fellow AA member advised me that if I tried to go through customs at the airport, I would be detained. I was effectively barred from entering my own country.

Chantelle could do little in her pre-trial cell. All written communications were seized, and she was allowed no sun or space, nor any place to bathe. Food was given three times per day in accordance with state law, and those three were the only times her cell door opened.

One exception was a surprise visit from the Reverend Ralph Sather who used the pretense of pastoral help to secure entrance. It was on day two that Sather came, and as he entered, he obsequiously bowed his head to a seated Chantelle, before he stretched out his arms to her in surprising supplication. "Miss Fouriere! I must know!"

Sather fell to his knees on the cell floor. "And surely you know, Doctor Fouriere." Chantelle fell back in silence onto her little metal chair, and looked dumbfounded. He ranted on. "I have sinned and you know that."

Chantelle lifted a little on her metal seat as if she sensed what the man was feeling. Chantelle tried to console. "There is, Mr. Sather, no sin that God cannot forgive," and he gave a quick stare to the floor before, still on his knees, Sather straightened up as if an electric charge had run right through his body. "Yes, God will forgive me! I have dedicated my life to religion. I am devoted. God must know that. And with devotion comes immortality!"

Suddenly, though, the Reverend Sather looked troubled again. From his kneeling position, he folded again his hands as if in plea. "But how, Doctor, do I secure, for sure, God's forgiveness?"

Sather lowered his head to Chantelle as if expecting to be blessed. She looked at the top of his greasy hair and said calmly, "Love, Mr. Sather, and above all, don't lie to yourself."

557

Sather looked up at the jailed Chantelle with perhaps a touch of condemnation. "But look where that got you, Miss Fouriere!"

Chantelle responded as if his last comment was of no consequence, "As you move forward in love, Mr. Sather, your confidence in God will grow and you will become increasingly free. What is hell, Mr. Sather, if it is not suffering from being unable to love?"

Sather then lifted his head as if he was experiencing an epiphany. He stretched out his arms to the cell ceiling. "I'm saved!"

But when Sather did so, he did not notice that a pen fell out of his pocket. As Chantelle bent forward to pick it up, Sather shot to a standing position and called for the guard to release him.

Monday August 3 2009

On day three, Chantelle had a second visitor, and as the cell door clanked open she began a smile of greeting. But once the armed guard visitor was inside, he grabbed her hair, kicked Chantelle in the knee and slammed her body down onto the cold floor. She grimaced and tears began forming in her eyes, as if Chantelle sensed what was about to happen. The guard then yanked down her prison pants, rammed apart her long legs and raped her, while not for a moment looking at her face.

Once finished, the guard leapt back up and charged back through the iron opening, clanking the door shut. He shouted his conquest to the prison hallway but another guard scoffed and told him of Chantelle's reportedly having AIDS. That second guard added that she had been living with some New York freaks and had screwed someone in Chicago, after just meeting him in a downtown park.

The rapist's face went blank and his shouts of conquest fell away to whimpers.

On day four, Chantelle was sitting chilled on the little chair at the rear of her cell, trying from time to time to lift her thighs off the chair's cold metal. She was crumpled up like a child who had been beaten, with arms clutched around her knees for warmth and her face bent down. A shaft of light was piercing through the door's peep window as in days past, but this time the light was hitting the top of her hair, and the streak seemed the only life in an otherwise dying room.

Someone's eye peered through the peephole and then two more, before baritone voices murmured outside the cell door. Then came another clank and the icy sound of steel hitting steel as the thick lock broke open and the door hauled back. Suddenly, in the opening stood the figure of another male, silhouetted against the light. Chantelle's chills turned to shivers and she began to tremble in dread.

Chantelle could not decipher the silhouette against the glaring white behind, but the form was too short to be the rapist and too thin to be Sather. The person in the silhouette then spoke in the most humble of tones, "Chantelle?" and her eyes, head and shoulders lifted. "Daddy?"

Pantel made his way into the cell, before he fell down on his knees in front of Chantelle. He put his arms around his daughter's trembling body and squeezed her harder and harder, until Chantelle's trembling finally stopped. Tears formed in her eyes, but unlike those of the day before, Chantelle was looking through her tears into the eyes of Pantel. "Daddy, I thank God with all I can, for bringing you here now. Never have I needed you more."

Pantel and his daughter stayed locked in a loving hug, until he finally reared back to look at her. "Arthur would have joined me but they won't let him into the country, after his letters to you."

Chantelle looked perplexed by the comment about letters but she was more interested in another question. "Arthur! You have seen Arthur?"

Pantel still had his arms around Chantelle. "He and I are very close now, but from a distance."

For a second or more, Chantelle said nothing before she spouted out, "How is he?" and Pantel allowed himself a warming smile. "Arthur is okay.

When not working at Knox College, he helps other people with their alcohol problems."

Chantelle's head shot up and her eyes opened wide. "Alcohol?" and Pantel managed a slight beam. "Arthur and I are both in AA. He tells me he's going to write a book." Chantelle perked up more, and for a moment almost forgot that she had been raped the previous day. "Do you know about what?" and Pantel smiled, with what little joy he could impart to his beloved daughter. "About you, what you do and now he does, Chantelle."

Chantelle held firm in her dad's arms, and she tilted her head downward toward the floor. "Arthur was a fine man," but Pantel came back fast. "Is, Chantelle. You're talking about my best friend. Arthur quotes you in saying he is doing all he can. You choose better than me."

Chantelle went slightly back to look at her dad. "Mother?" and he gave a simple shrug. "Lives with some guy up in Midland. Roxanne lives there too. Only recently, did I hear they knew of your trial."

Chantelle felt strength coming from the little man who was her father, but she gave him a look of concern. "You are alone, Daddy?" and he smiled while offering again a slight shrug, "Not really. I have 30 school-bus kids every day and I have Arthur's letters."

Chantelle's head then fell deep into her father's chest. "Oh, Daddy, I'm scared," and Pantel tightened his fatherly embrace. "Chantelle, I never knew love until you grew into my life. You have taught me a world I did not know and I stand proud of the human race because of you."

They stayed locked in an embrace and Chantelle asked, "Daddy, are these men going to kill me?" and Pantel tightened his squeeze. "They can't, Chantelle. Your love is too strong. It helps keep me and Arthur going. You will be with us always."

Friday October 30 2009

I had been sober for almost a year and knew my falling off would be of no help to anybody; so, early in August, I got myself back on Ativan to hang on and get some needed sleep. I knew there would be withdrawal but my physician and I agreed that I had little option, at least over the short term, and perhaps even over the rest of 2009, but we hoped at some point, I could taper off if things went well for Chantelle.

But by that August of 2009, my faith in America was almost non-existent and my feelings for Florida rekindled memory of the AIDS story from a year earlier. America's early hopes of a Messiah in Obama were fading, and there was an unresolved anger rising up, with a right-wing backlash in many parts of my underemployed country. To my worried mind, Florida was the hottest spot.

The North American weather stayed hot through August and into early autumn when events unfolded to send Chantelle to trial for kidnapping. Evangelist Ralph Sather was set to testify against her and Chantelle's half-sister Roxanne furnished evidence that Chantelle had been a disgruntled, illegitimate child. Mother Camille also confirmed that Chantelle had been given everything a child could ask for, despite having a derelict father, and that her mother had slaved away to support both daughters, including an unappreciative Chantelle. Mother Camille then went on to write that Chantelle had been irreverent toward school, churches and all institutions "...within sight of her dark and glistening eyes."

U.S. police beyond the borders of Florida corroborated Chantelle's use of "inappropriate words" during her speeches as evidence of her endorsing such language for American families. Doctor Christopher Proud III provided evidence of Chantelle's public derision of American values, and Chantelle's notes were furnished as evidence of her seditious attacks on Christianity.

The prosecution nevertheless opted to coach both mother Camille and Christopher Proud into softening their written pieces to make them more legally acceptable, after Chantelle's defense lawyer displayed his eagerness to rip apart Terry Hardy's arguments in the pending court case. But Hardy was soon found dead in his cell on October 30 and had been hanged by a sheet.

It was not clear from the bed sheet and its positioning whether he had actually hanged himself or had been strangled beforehand, but in any event, in the official order of things, Hardy's death was ruled a suicide.

Hardy's gang members were eager to testify under state assurances of lesser sentences, and they claimed Chantelle would, after her speeches, wander off with strangers from her audience. They also talked of her wild ventures with AIDS-plagued homosexuals in San Francisco and spoke of her avoiding speaking in the country's capital, out of fear of indictment. This testimony, like that of mother Camille and Christopher Proud, had to be toned down before the pending trial but it all somehow made its way into the Florida press, where it was picked up in Canada.

Sources of power in Florida swept aside what they considered complicating factors and moved, with the help of Christian fundamentalists, to have capital punishment be the only retribution. Due to the heinousness of Chantelle's crimes as well as a continued American controversy over the death-needle's swiftness, some fundamentalists pushed for the tried-and-true method of the electric chair. Chantelle once told me that sociologists sometimes say that god is the same as society, and in places where religions have strong roots, culture and religion are more or less the same.

I could not stop thinking that my letters were going to help kill Chantelle, and try as I might, with a mile swim at Hart House and a milligram of Ativan at night, I was sleeping less and less, with the thought ever building of vodka caressing my chest. Finally, after hearing nothing for months but bad news about the lady I loved, on the Friday evening of October 30, when I heard of Hardy's death, I doubled the Ativan. I nonetheless awoke in the wee hours of Saturday but then went to the medicine cabinet and doubled the dosage again.

The November trial was over before the end of the month and Chantelle made no appeal. Sather and his supporters spearheaded a greater public to push the government to execute Chantelle, and local politicians reacted promptly, believing their fiat representative of the people's will. Greater governments in the United States and the newly conservative Canada were also pressured by a coalition of elements not to interfere in ridding the world of such a hate figure.

Before November's end, Chantelle was to be escorted into the execution chamber, and her head and legs shaved for the placement of electrodes. Beside the execution chamber and behind a glass wall sat two rows of observers, who were, in the main, state apparatchiks, but at the end of the front row sat Pantel. All eyes were turned to the front glass, which lent a full view of the execution chamber.

The door to Chantelle's anteroom swung open and she did exactly what her father had asked – she fastened her eyes on his and did not let them veer from his loving gaze. But Chantelle was then shoved sideways and put into the electric chair, six feet back from the glass wall.

Thick leather was used to strap together Chantelle's lower legs above her ankles and another strap was used to lock her lower arms, with yet another to contain her upper arms. A wider strap was then wrapped around each thigh and another to buckle her around the middle.

A restraining strap was then attached across her chin, snapping her head back against the chair, and a cap was placed over her shaved head. Saline-soaked electrodes were then pasted to Chantelle's body, one to her right calf and one to her head-cap, with each electrode then wing-nutted securely into a big black cord coming up from under the execution room floor.

Within the chamber stood a third man who had attached and secured nothing – the warden. He asked Chantelle if she had any last words and when she said "No," the warden asked her if she would like a prayer administered, but Chantelle replied she had already said one.

Different bodies absorb different levels of electricity, and Chantelle's womanhood suggested that she would require only 1,900 volts to be killed. Thus at 1:07 p.m. the voltage was shot through Chantelle's body and she shook violently. At some fraction of a second thereafter, Chantelle defecated and the feces stayed stuck between her and the chair.

Four seconds later, the voltage was eased down to 1,000, to begin the customary five-minute cool-down, but to Pantel's horror and the apparatchiks' dismay, Chantelle was still alive. The voltage was then cranked up again and again, until flames burst from her legs and head. Finally, after 14 full minutes, Chantelle's body was dead and burnt. The death chamber was clouded in smoke and stinking of scorched flesh.

Saturday October 31 2009

I awoke at noon after the nightmare and raced to Chantelle's laptop to ensure she was still alive. I learned her trial was to commence Monday, November 9, and my AA lawyer managed to track down Pantel. He had been given money by Melba and Norm to stay with Chantelle, the couple having gone to Florida shortly after Chantelle's arrest.

That night, I went to a Halloween AA meeting. Some of the attendees were dressed in elaborate costumes and I could not help thinking about the role theater plays in much of our lives.

Wednesday November 4 2009

The news that followed in the days thereafter killed any hope I had, as well as any sense I had of American justice. Were it not for my fellow AA members and a lot more Ativan, I doubt I could have stayed sober or even alive throughout the rest of that 2009. Chantelle was found shot and killed, presumably by the guard who had raped her, but he also was found dead, ostensibly from suicide. An inquiry followed and speculation ran wild as to who the real murderers were, including those of Hardy, but the official inquiry determined that the guard had acted alone.

Thursday November 5 2009

Melba and Norm arranged a Florida hearse for Chantelle's body to be shipped back on an Air Canada plane carrying Pantel to Toronto's main Pearson airport. Retired fireman Norm had been adroit enough to ask Pantel's permission to check Chantelle's belongings, and Norm had found an Ontario driver's license indicating that her critical body parts were all to go to hospitals in the event of a sudden death.

The plane was met by Chantelle's boss Doctor Abrams and me, and after my sharing a long embrace with Pantel, I asked him how he was doing. Pantel gave me an answer that perhaps only an alcoholic, long sober, could give. "Arthur, in the rust of time, I may change speeds, but I have changed speeds before and must now carry on, honoring the life Chantelle has given me. I will keep driving the school bus and with any luck, may someday join her."

My thoughts then turned to my beloved Chantelle and her living on forever in my mind, while her body lived on in others. It was the 923rd day that I had known Chantelle, if I had ever known her at all. By day 1,000, January 21st, 2010, birth date of my great-grandfather Arthur Franklin, buried in Toronto's Mount Pleasant Cemetery, I would have finally weaned myself off Ativan and begun writing from my diary, this story.

Friday November 6 2009

The University of Toronto's little Hart House chapel was full for the funeral. Doctor Abrams, nurses and doctors from Women's College Hospital were there. Northwestern Memorial's Doctors Flem, Martin English and Charles Marty attended. Thérèse Roberge, former Penetang librarian and English teacher to Chantelle, joined Pantel and me.

Saturday November 7 2009

Chantelle's old Volvo 544 was shipped back from Florida, and Pantel and I used it to follow the hearse up to Penetanguishene. Doctor Abrams had secured permission from Penetang's Hospital for the Criminally Insane for Chantelle to be buried there. Doctor Abrams rode in the hearse for the 100-mile trip.

In the hospital's green space for dead inmates, who had lived with no loved ones, Pantel and I slid Chantelle's body off a reusable Jewish slab, into a hole that was to be her grave. That day in November was seven-and-a-bit weeks before what would have been Chantelle's 28th birthday.

In some time to come, Chantelle's body would, we hoped, feed insects, worms and plants, and they in turn would form compost, eventually producing fauna. Then in the years that followed, there would possibly even be a tree.

It was a bright day in Penetanguishene, cold but almost cloudless. Pantel and I threw some earth onto the body of Chantelle, and after Doctor Abrams and the funeral director departed, I was left free with Chantelle and her father. I posed to him a question. "Pantel, did Chantelle leave behind anything, before Florida murdered her?" He lifted his eyebrows. "Not much, but she did hand me a piece of her underclothes she had written on, using a pen that Mr. Sather had dropped in her cell. Chantelle had written the note, in the hope that Sather would return but he did not. I have had it here in my pocket."

I will not comment, dear reader, on my feelings as I read that note in the clear cold of Penetanguishene, next to the Great Lake's Georgian Bay. I will instead let Chantelle's words speak for themselves:

Please, Mr. Sather, feel free to appreciate that all of us are responsible at all times to all others. If we grasp that freedom, heaven is here for us now.

Inner peace, I feel, is found not in me-first thinking but in social togetherness. If we restrict what we love, we come to obsess over those things chosen, and our love comes only from what other people have done for us, and not from what we have done for them.

To help people understand a broader love, sometimes we need to set an example, in order to help them out of their pits of self-oneness, even if others condemn us as crazy. When we see self-centered creatures down in their pits of Hell on Earth, we should try to help them out and learn to love God unconditionally.

They will then, I pray, begin to recognize their place in nature, stop lowering themselves to conquer it and begin to experience a daily joy in a life that makes up for all their old emotionally blackmailed fantasies of heaven. They can swallow their pride, see life's impermanency and accept their mortality, while learning to love one another for the sake of love alone. And such very awareness of the temporality of life will help fire up unending love, dissipating selfish dreams of eternal bliss beyond the grave.

Acknowledgements

The author is grateful to the Toronto Reference Library and the University of Toronto Robarts Library for their exhaustive assistance, David Sobelman for structural counsel, Douglas Hopp for thorough and meticulous reviewing, Matt Shaw for erudite story editing, Dana Snell for tight copy editing, Nina Callaghan for precise proofreading, Christopher Doda for final eyeing, Hudson Leavens for sensitive photography, Michael Callaghan for skillful book design and mapmaking, Bridgemark for reliable backup filing, Anne Calverley for energetic example and Glenn Davis for balance and stability.

The foreword was prepared by Douglas H. Hopp, DVM, DipCompMed, CD, MMW. Dr. Hopp is a consultant in experimental medicine and surgery, and a former research clinician in a number of prominent schools of medicine and teaching hospitals in the United States and Canada, including The Johns Hopkins University School of Medicine, Toronto Mount Sinai Hospital and the Toronto Hospital for Sick Children. At present, Dr. Hopp is coordinating a publication on bio-transmission, linking the fields of evolutionary biology, neurobiology, genetics, sexology, anatomy and behavioral psychophysiology.

Alan J Cooper
May, 2013